Modern
Stories in
English

8/01

Modern Stories in English

Edited by

W. H. New

and

H. J. Rosengarten

University of British Columbia

Thomas Y. Crowell Company
New York
Established 1834

Library of Congress Cataloging in Publication Data

New, William H comp.
  Modern stories in English.

  Includes bibliographies.
  1. Short stories, English. I. Rosengarten, H. J., joint comp. II. Title.
PZ1.N389Mo   [PR1309.S5]   823'.01   74–28447
ISBN 0–690–00765–5

Thomas Y. Crowell Company
666 Fifth Avenue
New York, New York 10019

Typography by Karin Batten and Elliot Kreloff

Manufactured in the United States of America

Table of Contents

Introduction 1

Chinua Achebe **Civil Peace** 7

John Barth **Title** 13

Donald Barthelme **Report** 21

Clark Blaise **Eyes** 26

Morley Callaghan **Two Fishermen** 32

George Clutesi **Ko-ishin-mit and the Shadow People** 40

William Faulkner **Dry September** 46

F. Scott Fitzgerald **Winter Dreams** 57

E. M. Forster **The Road from Colonus** 77

Janet Frame **The Mythmaker's Office** 88

Dave Godfrey **Two Smiths** 93

Nadine Gordimer **No Place Like** 100

Graham Greene **Brother** 108

Ernest Hemingway **Hills Like White Elephants** 115

Hugh Hood **The Dog Explosion** 120

Ted Hughes **Sunday** 128

Shirley Jackson **The Tooth** 139

Dan Jacobson **Fresh Fields** 154

James Joyce **The Boarding House** 166

Margaret Laurence **The Merchant of Heaven** 173

D. H. Lawrence **The Horse Dealer's Daughter** 194

Doris Lessing **Our Friend Judith** 209

Malcolm Lowry **Strange Comfort Afforded the Profession** 225

James Alan McPherson **Gold Coast** 238

Bernard Malamud **Black Is My Favorite Color** 257

Katherine Mansfield **The Doll's House** 266

Alice Munro **Thanks for the Ride** 273

V. S. Naipaul **My Aunt Gold Teeth**   285

Alden Nowlan **Miracle at Indian River**   293

Joyce Carol Oates **In the Region of Ice**   300

Hal Porter **First Love**   316

Katherine Anne Porter **He**   327

Sinclair Ross **Cornet at Night**   336

Muriel Spark **Come Along, Marjorie**   351

Audrey Thomas **If One Green Bottle ...**   362

John Updike **Giving Blood**   371

Kurt Vonnegut, Jr. **Report on the Barnhouse Effect**   382

Eric Walrond **Drought**   394

Patrick White **Willy-Wagtails by Moonlight**   404

Rudy Wiebe **Where Is the Voice Coming From?**   415

Chronological Table of Contents

E. M. Forster **The Road from Colonus** (from *The Celestial Omnibus*, 1911)   77

James Joyce **The Boarding House** (from *Dubliners*, 1914)   166

D. H. Lawrence **The Horse Dealer's Daughter** (from *England, My England*, 1922)   194

Katherine Mansfield **The Doll's House** (from *The Dove's Nest*, 1923)   266

F. Scott Fitzgerald **Winter Dreams** (from *All the Sad Young Men*, 1926)   57

Eric Walrond **Drought** (from *Tropic Death*, 1926)   394

Ernest Hemingway **Hills Like White Elephants** (from *Men Without Women*, 1927)   115

Katherine Anne Porter **He** (from *Flowering Judas*, 1930/1935)   327

William Faulkner **Dry September** (from *These Thirteen*, 1931)   46

Graham Greene **Brother** (from *The Basement Room and other stories*, 1935)   108

Morley Callaghan **Two Fishermen** (from *Now that April's Here and other stories*, 1936)   32

Sinclair Ross **Cornet at Night** (1939; from *The Lamp at Noon and other stories*, 1968)   336

Shirley Jackson **The Tooth** (from *The Lottery and other stories*, 1949)   139

Kurt Vonnegut, Jr. **Report on the Barnhouse Effect** (from *Colliers*, 1950)   382

Muriel Spark **Come Along, Marjorie** (from *The Go-Away
Bird and other stories*, 1958)   351

Malcolm Lowry **Strange Comfort Afforded by the
Profession** (from *Hear Us O Lord From Heaven Thy
Dwelling-Place*, 1961)   225

Janet Frame **The Mythmaker's Office** (from *Snowman
Snowman*, 1962)   88

Margaret Laurence **The Merchant of Heaven** (from *The
Tomorrow-Tamer and other stories*, 1963)   173

Bernard Malamud **Black Is My Favorite Color** (from
Idiots First, 1963)   257

Doris Lessing **Our Friend Judith** (from *A Man and
Two Women*, 1963)   209

Dan Jacobson **Fresh Fields** (from *Beggar My Neighbour*,
1964)   154

Patrick White **Willy-Wagtails by Moonlight** (from *The
Burnt Ones*, 1964)   404

Hal Porter **First Love** (from *The Cats of Venice*, 1965)   316

John Updike **Giving Blood** (from *The Music School*, 1966)   371

Audrey Thomas **If One Green Bottle ...** (from *Ten
Green Bottles*, 1967)   362

Ted Hughes **Sunday** (from *Wodwo*, 1967)   128

V. S. Naipaul **My Aunt Gold Teeth** (from *A Flag on the
Island*, 1967)   285

George Clutesi **Ko-ishin-mit and the Shadow People** (from
Son of Raven Son of Deer, 1967)   40

Dave Godfrey **Two Smiths** (from *Death Goes Better with Coca-Cola*, 1967) 93

Donald Barthelme **Report** (from *Unspeakable Practices, Unnatural Acts*, 1968) 21

Alden Nowlan **Miracle at Indian River** (from *Miracle at Indian River*, 1968) 293

Alice Munro **Thanks for the Ride** (from *Dance of the Happy Shades*, 1968) 273

John Barth **Title** (from *Lost in the Funhouse*, 1968) 13

James Alan McPherson **Gold Coast** (from *Hue and Cry*, 1969) 238

Joyce Carol Oates **In the Region of Ice** (from *The Wheel of Love*, 1970) 300

Rudy Wiebe **Where Is the Voice Coming From?** (from *Fourteen Stories High*, 1971) 415

Nadine Gordimer **No Place Like** (from *Livingstone's Companions*, 1972) 100

Chinua Achebe **Civil Peace** (from *Girls at War and other stories*, 1972) 7

Hugh Hood **The Dog Explosion** (from *The Fruit Man, The Meat Man & the Manager*, 1972) 120

Clark Blaise **Eyes** (from *A North American Education*, 1973) 26

Thematic Table of Contents

Childhood, Initiation, and Growth

Clutesi **Ko-ishin-mit and the Shadow People**   40

Godfrey **Two Smiths**   93

Hughes **Sunday**   128

Jacobson **Fresh Fields**   154

Lawrence **The Horse Dealer's Daughter**   194

Mansfield **The Doll's House**   266

Munro **Thanks for the Ride**   273

Naipaul **My Aunt Gold Teeth**   285

Oates **In the Region of Ice**   300

H. Porter **First Love**   316

K. Porter **He**   327

Ross **Cornet at Night**   336

Love, Marriage, and the Roles of Men and Women

Fitzgerald **Winter Dreams**   57

Gordimer **No Place Like**   100

Hemingway **Hills Like White Elephants**   115

Joyce **The Boarding House**   166

Lawrence **The Horse Dealer's Daughter**   194

Lessing **Our Friend Judith**   209

McPherson **Gold Coast**   238

Malamud **Black Is My Favorite Color**   257

Munro **Thanks for the Ride**   273

Naipual **My Aunt Gold Teeth**   285

Nowlan **Miracle at Indian River**   293

H. Porter **First Love**   316

Thomas **If One Green Bottle ...**   362

Updike **Giving Blood**   371

White **Willy-Wagtails by Moonlight**   404

Identity and Alienation

Barthelme **Report**   21

Blaise **Eyes**   26

Clutesi **Ko-ishin-mit and the Shadow People**   40

Forster **The Road from Colonus**   77

Godfrey **Two Smiths**   93

Gordimer **No Place Like**   100

Hemingway **Hills Like White Elephants**   115

Jackson **The Tooth**   139

Jacobson **Fresh Fields**   154

Laurence **The Merchant of Heaven**   173

Lowry **Strange Comfort Afforded by the Profession**   225

McPherson **Gold Coast**   238

Malamud **Black Is My Favorite Color**   257

Spark **Come Along, Marjorie**   351

Thomas **If One Green Bottle ...**   362

Death

Callaghan **Two Fishermen**   32

Faulkner **Dry September**   46

Frame **The Mythmaker's Office**   88

Greene **Brother**   108

Hughes **Sunday**   128

Naipaul **My Aunt Gold Teeth**   285

Walrond **Drought**   394

Nature, Towns and Cities

Callaghan **Two Fishermen**   32

Clutesi **Ko-ishin-mit and the Shadow People**   40

Faulkner **Dry September**   46

Godfrey **Two Smiths**   93

Hood **The Dog Explosion**   120

Hughes **Sunday**   128

Jackson **The Tooth**   139

Joyce **The Boarding House**   166

Laurence **The Merchant of Heaven**   173

Lawrence **The Horse Dealer's Daughter**   194

Munro **Thanks for the Ride**   273

Nowlan **Miracle at Indian River**   293

Ross **Cornet at Night**   336

Walrond **Drought**   394

White **Willy-Wagtails by Moonlight**   404

Social Conflict: Race, War, Class, and Civil Unrest

Achebe **Civil Peace**   7

Barthelme **Report**   21

xiv Thematic Table of Contents

Callaghan **Two Fishermen**	32
Frame **The Mythmaker's Office**	88
Faulkner **Dry September**	46
Godfrey **Two Smiths**	93
Gordimer **No Place Like**	100
Greene **Brother**	108
Joyce **The Boarding House**	166
Laurence **The Merchant of Heaven**	173
Lessing **Our Friend Judith**	209
McPherson **Gold Coast**	238
Malamud **Black Is My Favorite Color**	257
Mansfield **The Doll's House**	266
Vonnegut **Report on the Barnhouse Effect**	382
Walrond **Drought**	394
White **Willy-Wagtails by Moonlight**	404
Wiebe **Where is the Voice Coming From?**	415

Religious and Moral Values

Achebe **Civil Peace**	7
Barthelme **Report**	21
Callaghan **Two Fisherman**	32
Clutesi **Ko-ishin-mit and the Shadow People**	40
Fitzgerald **Winter Dreams**	57
Forster **The Road from Colonus**	77
Godfrey **Two Smiths**	93
Greene **Brother**	108
Jacobson **Fresh Fields**	154
Joyce **The Boarding House**	166

Laurence **The Merchant of Heaven**   173

McPherson **Gold Coast**   238

Naipaul **My Aunt Gold Teeth**   285

Nowlan **Miracle at Indian River**   293

Oates **In the Region of Ice**   300

*K. Porter **He**   327

Spark **Come Along, Marjorie**   351

Art and Reality

Barth **Title**   13

*Barthelme **Report**   21

*Jackson **The Tooth**   139

Jacobson **Fresh Fields**   154

*Lessing **Our Friend Judith**   209

Lowry **Strange Comfort Afforded by the Profession**   225

Ross **Cornet at Night**   336

Vonnegut **Report on the Barnhouse Effect**   382

White **Willy-Wagtails by Moonlight**   404

Wiebe **Where is the Voice Coming From?**   415

Modern
Stories in
English

Introduction

Good stories move us, entertain us, and arrest our minds. Their style delights, and their characters command our involvement. These are among the reasons why the short story, in the form of fables, fairy tales, and moral "exempla," has long been a part of narrative tradition. They also explain why, in its modern forms, the short story continues to appeal.

Since the nineteenth century, when American writers like Edgar Allan Poe and Nathaniel Hawthorne took the current features of prose fiction and molded them into unified models of narrative suspense and psychological drama, American writers have always been among the short story's foremost practitioners. But no one nation or culture, no one style or subject, has a monopoly on literary endeavor; and the twentieth century gave rise to a rich variety of points of view that has led to the continuing vigor of the short-story form.

The stories in this collection reflect that variety. They display diverse views and styles; they are representative of the century's main artistic developments; they also come from many cultures—mostly from the United States, Britain, and Canada, but also from Ireland, Africa, the South Pacific, and the Caribbean. They have in common the English language. To make that assertion, however, is to cover a wealth of specific differences, for in the relationship between language and culture, something happens that gives each story its particular form. An author's use of images (black, white; north, south; city, town) relates to his particular observation of human experience as well as to his vision of human potential. Idioms and dialects vary. Setting, too, serves to differentiate: Joyce's Dublin and Faulkner's South, like Naipaul's Trinidad and Achebe's Nigeria, are specific locales—"fictional," of course, but "true"—and the worlds of the Irish Catholic and the Trinidad Hindu are no more interchangeable than are the social patterns of the American and the Nigerian. Comparing their stories provides an opportunity to reveal those ethnic differences; at the same time it can bring about an understanding of the impact of cultural identity and a delight in the linguistic dexterity to which it has given rise.

The new awareness that such comparisons bring also underlines the common humanity of the experiences which the writers observe. If by its very nature, presenting a fragment of life, the short story reflects the essential assumptions of a writer in a given society, it inevitably draws upon shared human experiences—love, hate, work, war, worry, birth, death, and dreams. Whatever the details that enliven and give concrete form to an experience, the artist who uses them is responding with as much sensitivity as he can to the

1

humanity of individuals and the predicaments of mankind. Themes recur from society to society, therefore; and the function of the Thematic Table of Contents in this anthology is to guide readers to those point of comparison. The number of stories about prejudice, growing up, and the relations between men and women testifies to the common experiences of everyday life around the world. But the roles of men and women vary from society to society; attitudes to communal and individual values differ; and generation conflict in a culture that reveres tradition will obviously carry different overtones from those it would carry in a society committed to newness and change.

Though there is a danger, then, of making facile connections, twentieth-century technology, bringing us within reach of each other, has made some similarities apparent, so that stories about political or racial oppression (e.g., Greene's "Brother," Malamud's "Black Is My Favorite Color"), or about the advantages and disadvantages of modern scientific progress (Hood's "The Dog Explosion," Barthelme's "Report"), can awaken comparable responses in readers with widely varying backgrounds. Developments in transportation and communication, moreover, have allowed readier access to all parts of the world and a more immediate sharing of knowledge about contemporary occurrences everywhere. Many modern short stories therefore reflect the impact of issues which might once have been considered "regional" but now have an international significance. The Vietnamese war, for example, had a powerful effect outside the United States and Southeast Asia, as Dave Godfrey shows in his story "Two Smiths," which explores the moral significance of the decision by American draft dodgers to emigrate to Canada.

But though art is international both in its themes and in the fact that readers anywhere can respond to the essential human experiences to which it gives form, an author's society does affect the terms by which he will express his response to such issues, and even his method of expression. National literatures around the world which had been founded on English patterns and traditions moved away from them because new experiences, new landscapes, and new cultural affiliations led to new words and new ways of using them.

Walt Whitman's mid-nineteenth-century efforts to articulate a new language for the United States mirrored that "new" nation's large, expansionist, democratic, colloquial terms. The American stories in the book—from Hemingway and Fitzgerald to Updike and Barthelme—convey the characteristic sounds of the language that consequently evolved. Australia and New Zealand, faced with social origins and expectations different from those of American settlers, and with flora and fauna radically different from those in Europe, also had to create new tongues. Hal Porter's iconoclastic class consciousness and Katherine Mansfield's egalitarian individualism are characteristic of much Australian and New Zealand writing, and find voice in their stories "First Love" and "The Doll's House." Canadians, faced with a North American environment that is similar in many respects to that of Americans, determinedly celebrated their differences from both British and American patterns, developing in the process a lively rhetoric of regional identities that can be seen in the work of Sinclair Ross and Alice Munro, among others. Both of these writers (Ross in "Cornet at Night," about a Prairie boy's break from farm routine, and Munro in "Thanks for the Ride," about adolescent initiation and decay in a small Western Ontario town) acutely perceive the sounds and sights of a particular locale and reveal how their characters' lives and landscapes are inextricably intertwined. In Africa and the Caribbean, where storytelling was so much more profoundly an oral folk art, the tensions of modern life have been couched in a characteristically more "oral" form. Achebe and Naipaul both rely extensively on dialogue and contrasting rhythms. Achebe's "Civil Peace" points to the collapse of community solidarity during the Nigerian civil war; Naipaul's "My Aunt Gold Teeth" asserts the values of a tradition in which the narrator cannot participate but which he continues to admire.

If in the stories from England, from Forster to Hughes, there persists a sense of the traditions and the classed society that created an imperial culture, we find in all the other modern English-language literatures both a celebration of a new society and a sense of exile from tradition. Such an awareness of exile has taken various forms in the twentieth century: from Katherine Mansfield's rejection of the New Zealand provinciality and somewhat wistful memory of the innocence of a colonial childhood, or Hemingway's search in Paris for the *mots justes* with which to express the urbanity and violence of modern American life, to V. S. Naipaul's double alienation from both his Indian cultural heritage and his Trinidad upbringing. Whole societies, as well as individuals, can experience such alienation. The Indian writer George Clutesi observes, for example, that Indians and Eskimos are dispossessed without even moving from their homeland. As Eric Walrond's "Drought" serves to demonstrate, the various literatures of the West Indies respond insistently to a social history of deracination and slavery. Writers from ethnic minorities (Bernard Malamud, James Alan McPherson, Clark Blaise), using or responding to the language of the "majority" culture around them, live with an isolation of a related kind. And there is another alienation—intellectual and artistic, such as we find detailed in Rudy Wiebe's "Where is the Voice Coming From?"— suffered by a member of one culture who tries not only to understand another but also to give ordered utterance to his limited knowledge of it. All these experiences give rise to particular responses to the human condition: sometimes bitter and despairing, sometimes angry or ironic or affirmative, but always interesting and always alive. That range of tone—from the reflective sadness of Scott Fitzgerald and the barely controlled hysteria of Nadine Gordimer to the sardonic wit of Lowry, Barth, and Hood—again indicates the modern short story's flexibility.

Although most of the stories in this collection reflect their authors' sense of cultural tension, such a concern more often appears as an undertone than as a dominant theme. The writers included here have interests ranging from the neuroses attached to religion or education (Spark's "Come Along, Marjorie" and Oates's "In the Region of Ice") to love in its many guises (Lessing's "Our Friend Judith" and White's "Willy-Wagtails by Moonlight"). They are concerned with the emotional impact of birth, death, and the various results of initiation (Thomas' "If One Green Bottle ..." and Walrond's "Drought"). A single general topic can sustain a range of particular emotions.

The writer's role as a critic of his society's values is strongly in evidence here, too. In "The Boarding House," James Joyce draws a sober picture of the double standards and petty hypocrisies which govern our relations in public and private, while Donald Barthelme's grim humor in "Report" depicts a dehumanized society whose ingenuity is directed toward refining its methods of destroying life. And several of the stories take as their subject the very process of story making. The plot of Dan Jacobson's "Fresh Fields," for example, hinges on the ability of a writer to be an "original" voice, on the differences between a writer's ideas and his manner of expressing them. And John Barth's "Title" confronts abruptly and idiosyncratically, by its own structure, the problems of narrative communication.

Conscious of the privacy from which originality emerges and of the problem of giving literary form to real life, the writer is faced with the difficulty of finding the right language in which to couch the experience he wants to convey. The Indian critic Balachandra Rajan, in his essay "Identity and Nationality," makes a distinction between "the process of creative self-realization" ("the essential business of the artist") and "the establishing of a collective myth or image" which may enter into his art but which should not circumscribe it. If language is both the artist's "friend and enemy," and the artist himself is less willing than many people "to surrender the uniqueness of his personal vision to the received formulae of communication," however, he is still not simply a maker but a maker of meaning; and no act of definition can be enduringly valid for him unless it is also an act of communication, the re-establishing of his identity with others, the rendering of an individual vision without corruption, into a public language.

But each author's manner of asserting that independent voice depends largely on his concept of his function as artist. Chinua Achebe, responding directly to the position the tale teller had in traditional African society, as the voice of social pattern and guide of moral behavior, writes of the overt function of "The Novelist as Teacher":

The writer cannot expect to be excused from the task of re-education and regeneration that must be done. . . . I for one would not wish to be excused. I would be quite satisfied if my novels ... did no more than teach my readers that their past—with all its imperfections—was not one long night of savagery from which the first Europeans acting on God's behalf delivered them.

That his writing is not limited to a national audience indicates that his position is not irreconcilable with Rajan's, but his affirmation of a distinctive local function for art suggests also that the "regionalism" of a work might be a useful guide to a given society's "folk soul."

Myth provides another approach to such identities, and comparing George Clutesi's retelling of Pacific Coast Indian myth with Janet Frame's "The Mythmaker's Office" allows us to distinguish clearly between the kind of myth which—either as fact or as symbolic reality—articulates directly a culture's moral tradition, and the kind which works as a conscious literary device to sound "archetypes," to arouse in the reader a recognition of that which even in an age of change is spiritually true and eternal. Both kinds can be didactic; both can take the form of fable or allegory. Clutesi's "Ko-ishin-mit and the Shadow People" comes from a tradition in which such tales were designed (in the author's own words) "to teach the young the many wonders of nature; the importance of all living things, no matter how small and insignificant." Frame's story more clearly works as a socially critical fable for modern man. It abjures the techniques of "realism," where logical motivations are established for characters' actions, in order to explore the fanciful. Yet in so doing it attacks the structures of contemporary bureaucracies and celebrates the freedom of the mind. To compare these works with Forster's "The Road from Colonus" and Vonnegut's "Report on the Barnhouse Effect" is to probe further the willingness of the human mind to understand reality through the filter of fictional invention.

Myth, moral fable, social realism, psychological revelation—the structural modes available to the writer of short stories are as varied as the subjects at his disposal; and the genre's potential has been expanded by twentieth-century experiments in fiction, by the greater freedom won for prose by the daring of writers like Joyce and Lawrence, and by the ongoing inventiveness of writers like Barth and Wiebe. The variety of styles in this collection—for example, Hemingway's deceptive simplicity, Shirley Jackson's surrealism, Audrey Thomas' stream-of-consciousness—reflects the many different ways in which the writers represented here have celebrated the strength and flexibility of their common language: a language which has given form to a wide range of individual visions and separately realized worlds.

Chinua Achebe

(b. 1930)

Born in Ogidi, Nigeria, and educated at Umuahia, Ibadan, and London, Chinua Achebe has become established not only as an editor and publisher, and as his country's most important English-language fiction writer, but also as one of the most respected literary voices in contemporary Africa. He has written verse, books for juveniles, two books of short stories, and four novels, of which the first three won particularly enthusiastic reviews. *Things Fall Apart* (1958), *No Longer at Ease* (1961), and *Arrow of God* (1964) render different aspects of the conflict between European and African civilizations. The powerlessness of the traditional culture to remain intact in the face of European enslavement and colonization, the inability of a modern young African to reconcile his family attachments with his sense of independence and his observation of political corruption, the incapacity of both the lay African society and the European colonial bureaucracy to understand the function and identity of a traditional priest: these are Achebe's topics. His aim is openly political and didactic. In "The Novelist as Teacher," he asserts: "Here, then, is an adequate revolution for me to espouse—to help my society regain its belief in itself and put away the complexes of the years of denigration and self-denigration." In so doing he fulfills one of the traditional roles of the writer in African society: to educate the young to an appreciation of the moral truths of their own culture. His method, too, derives from traditional techniques; he relies on simple narrative structures and on the functional patterns of Igbo proverbs. "As long as one people sit on another and are deaf to their cry," he writes, "so long will understanding elude all of us."

"Civil Peace" is the concluding story of *Girls at War and Other Stories* (1972), a volume which reflects the civil war that disrupted Nigerian life in the late 1960s. Though the fatalistic ironies that permeate the story are not untouched by humour, the work is fundamentally serious and reveals Achebe's continuing account of his deeply held commitment to freedom. In exploring its nature, in attempting both to communicate to a national audience and to reach across cultural and racial boundaries, he shows himself to be an acute and humane observer of human behavior.

For further reading

Chinua Achebe, "The Novelist as Teacher," in *Commonwealth Literature*, ed. John Press (London: Heinemann, 1965), pp. 201–205.
David Carroll, *Chinua Achebe* (New York: Twayne, 1970).
G. D. Killam, *The Novels of Chinua Achebe* (London: Heinemann, 1969).
Margaret Laurence, *Long Drums and Cannons* (London: Macmillan, 1968).

Civil Peace

Jonathan Iwegbu counted himself extra-ordinarily lucky. "Happy survival!" meant so much more to him than just a current fashion of greeting old friends in the first hazy days of peace. It went deep to his heart. He had come out of the war with five inestimable blessings—his head, his wife Maria's head and the heads of three out of their four children. As a bonus he also had his old bicycle—a miracle too but naturally not to be compared to the safety of five human heads.

The bicycle had a little history of its own. One day at the height of the war it was commandeered "for urgent military action." Hard as its loss would have been to him he would still have let it go without a thought had he not had some doubts about the genuineness of the officer. It wasn't his disreputable rags, nor the toes peeping out of one blue and one brown canvas shoes, nor yet the two stars of his rank done obviously in a hurry in biro, that troubled Jonathan; many good and heroic soldiers looked the same or worse. It was rather a certain lack of grip and firmness in his manner. So Jonathan, suspecting he might be amenable to influence, rummaged in his raffia bag and produced the two pounds with which he had been going to buy firewood which his wife, Maria, retailed to camp officials for extra stock-fish and corn meal, and got his bicycle back. That night he buried it in the little clearing in the bush where the dead of the camp, including his own youngest son, were buried. When he dug it up again a year later after the surrender all it needed was a little palm-oil greasing. "Nothing puzzles God," he said in wonder.

He put it to immediate use as a taxi and accumulated a small pile of Biafran money ferrying camp officials and their families across the four-mile stretch to the nearest tarred road. His standard charge per trip was six pounds and those who had the money were only glad to be rid of some of it in this way. At the end of a fortnight he had made a small fortune of one hundred and fifteen pounds.

Then he made the journey to Enugu and found another miracle waiting for him. It was unbelievable. He rubbed his eyes and looked again and it was still standing there before him. But, needless to say, even that monumental blessing must be accounted also totally inferior to the five heads in the family. This newest miracle was his little house in Ogui Overside. Indeed nothing puzzles God! Only two houses away a huge concrete edifice some wealthy contractor had put up just before the war was a mountain of rubble. And here was Jonathan's little zinc house of no regrets built with mud blocks quite intact! Of course the doors and windows were missing and five sheets off the roof. But what was that? And anyhow he had returned to Enugu early enough to pick up bits of old zinc and wood and soggy sheets of cardboard lying around the neighbourhood before thousands more came out of their forest holes looking for the same things. He got a destitute carpenter with one old hammer, a blunt plane and a few bent and rusty nails in his tool bag to turn this assortment of wood, paper and metal into door and window shutters for five Nigerian shillings or fifty Biafran pounds. He paid the pounds, and moved in with his overjoyed family carrying five heads on their shoulders.

His children picked mangoes near the military cemetery and sold them to soliders' wives for a few pennies—real pennies this time—and his wife started making breakfast akara balls for neighbours in a hurry to start life again. With his family earnings he took his bicycle to the villages around and brought fresh palm-wine which he mixed generously in his rooms with the water which had recently started running again in the public tap down the road, and opened up a bar for soldiers and other lucky people with good money.

At first he went daily, then every other day and finally once a week, to the offices of the Coal Corporation where he used to be a miner, to find out what was what. The only thing he did find out in the end was that that little house of his was even a greater blessing then he had thought. Some of his fellow ex-miners who had nowhere to return at the end of the day's waiting just slept outside the doors of the offices and cooked what meal they could scrounge together in Bournvita tins. As the weeks lengthened and still nobody could say what was what Jonathan discontinued his weekly visits altogether and faced his palm-wine bar.

But nothing puzzles God. Came the day of the windfall when after five days of endless scuffles in queues and counter-queues in the sun outside the Treasury he had twenty pounds counted into his palms as ex-gratia award for the rebel money he had turned in. It was like Christmas for him and for many others like him when the payments began. They called it (since few could manage its proper official name) *egg-rasher.*

As soon as the pound notes were placed in his palm Jonathan simply closed it tight over them and buried fist and money inside his trouser pocket. He had to be extra careful because he had seen a man a couple of days earlier collapse into near-madness in an instant before that oceanic crowd because no sooner had he got his twenty pounds than some heartless ruffian picked it off him. Though it was not right that a man in such an extremity of agony should be blamed yet many in the queues that day were able to remark quietly on the victim's carelessness, especially after he pulled out the innards of his pocket and revealed a hole in it big enough to pass a thief's head. But of course he had insisted that the money had been in the other pocket, pulling it out to show its comparative wholeness. So one had to be careful.

Jonathan soon transferred the money to his left hand and pocket so as to leave his right free for shaking hands should the need arise, though by fixing his gaze at such an elevation as to miss all approaching human faces he made sure that the need did not arise, until he got home.

He was normally a heavy sleeper but that night he heard all the neighbourhood noises die down one after another. Even the night watchman who knocked the hour on some metal somewhere in the distance had fallen silent after knocking one o'clock. That must have been the last thought in Jonathan's mind before he was finally carried away himself. He couldn't have been gone for long, though, when he was violently awakened again.

"Who is knocking?" whispered his wife lying beside him on the floor.

"I don't know," he whispered back breathlessly.

The second time the knocking came it was so loud and imperious that the rickety old door could have fallen down.

"Who is knocking?" he asked then, his voice parched and trembling.

"Na* tief-man and him people," came the cool reply. "Make you hopen de door." This was followed by the heaviest knocking of all.

Maria was the first to raise the alarm, then he followed and all their children.

"Police-o! Thieves-o! Neighbours-o! Police-o! We are lost! We are dead! Neighbours, are you asleep? Wake up! Police-o!"

This went on for a long time and then stopped suddenly. Perhaps they had scared the thief away. There was total silence. But only for a short while.

"You done finish?" asked the voice outside. "Make we help you small. Oya, everybody!"

"Police-o! Tief-man-o! Neighbours-o! we done loss-o! Police-o! ..."

There were at least five other voices besides the leader's.

Jonathan and his family were now completely paralysed by terror. Maria and the children sobbed inaudibly like lost souls. Jonathan groaned continuously.

The silence that followed the thieves' alarm vibrated horribly. Jonathan all but begged their leader to speak again and be done with it.

"My frien," said he at long last, "we don try our best for call dem but I tink say dem all done sleep-o ... So wetin we go do now? Sometaim you wan call soja? Or you wan make we call dem for you? Soja better pass police. No be so?"

*Na = it is.

"Na so!" replied his men. Jonathan thought he heard even more voices now than before and groaned heavily. His legs were sagging under him and his throat felt like sand-paper.

"My frien, why you no de talk again. I de ask you say you wan make we call soja?"

"No."

"Awrighto. Now make we talk business. We no be bad tief. We no like for make trouble. Trouble done finish. War done finish and all the katakata wey de for inside. No Civil War again. This time na Civil Peace. No be so?"

"Na so!" answered the horrible chorus.

"What do you want from me? I am a poor man. Everything I had went with this war. Why do you come to me? You know people who have money. We ..."

"Awright! We know you say no get plenty money. But we sef no get even anini. So derefore make you open dis window and give us one hundred pound and we go commot. Orderwise we de come for inside now to show you guitar-boy like dis ..."

A volley of automatic fire rang through the sky. Maria and the children began to weep aloud again.

"Ah, missisi de cry again. No need for dat. We done talk say we na good tief. We just take our small money and go nwayorly. No molest. Abi we de molest?"

"At all!" sang the chorus.

"My friends," began Jonathan hoarsely. "I hear what you say and I thank you. If I had one hundred pounds ..."

"Lookia my frien, no be play we come play for your house. If we make mistake and step for inside you no go like am-o. So derefore ..."

"To God who made me; if you come inside and find one hundred pounds, take it and shoot me and shoot my wife and children. I swear to God. The only money I have in this life is this twenty-pounds *egg-rasher* they gave me today ..."

"OK. Time de go. Make you open dis window and bring the twenty pound. We go manage am like dat."

There were now loud murmurs of dissent among the chorus: "Na lie de man de lie; e get plenty money ... Make we go inside and search properly well ... Wetin be twenty pound? ..."

"Shurrup!" rang the leader's voice like a lone shot in the sky and silenced the murmuring at once. "Are you dere? Bring the money quick!"

"I am coming," said Jonathan fumbling in the darkness with the key of the small wooden box he kept by his side on the mat.

At the first sign of light as neighbours and others assembled to commiserate with him he was already strapping his five-gallon demijohn to his bicycle carrier and his wife, sweating in the open fire, was turning over akara balls in a wide clay bowl of boiling oil. In the corner his eldest son was rinsing out dregs of yesterday's palm wine from old beer bottles.

"I count it as nothing," he told his sympathizers, his eyes on the rope he was tying. "What is *egg-rasher?* Did I depend on it last week? Or is it greater than other things that went with the war? I say, let *egg-rasher* perish in the flames! Let it go where everything else has gone. Nothing puzzles God."

John Barth

(b. 1930)

John Barth, born and raised in Cambridge, Maryland, was educated at the Juilliard School of Music and Johns Hopkins University. After a period of teaching at Pennsylvania State University, he moved to the State University of New York at Buffalo, and then to Johns Hopkins, where he is a professor of English. His first novel, *The Floating Opera* (1956), though composed in relatively conventional form, raised questions about existence, identity, and artifice which have occupied him in all his subsequent writings. In *The End of the Road* (1958) and *The Sot-Weed Factor* (1960), through a bizarre mixture of allegory, parody, and Rabelaisian comedy, Barth began to turn his back on formal realism as being inadequate to convey his vision; in his view the way to deal "with the discrepancy between art and the Real Thing is to *affirm* the artificial element in art (you can't get rid of it anyhow), and make the artifice part of your point instead of working for higher and higher fi with a lot of literary woofers and tweeters." Barth's rejection of literary convention does not mean that his work has become incomprehensibly fragmentary or obscure; commenting on the novel *Giles Goat-Boy* (1966), a reviewer described his style as "the most literate, controlled prose since Joyce."

Disturbed by "the arbitrariness of physical facts," Barth challenges conventional notions of reality, history, and human personality, in literary forms which themselves come under scrutiny. "Title" is one of several fictions in Barth's collection *Lost in the Funhouse: Fiction for print, tape, live voice* (1968), which deal with the relationship between word and meaning, between story and storyteller. In an "Author's Note," Barth comments: " 'Title' makes somewhat separate but equally valid senses in several media: print, monophonic recorded authorial voice, stereophonic ditto in dialogue with itself, live authorial voice, live ditto in dialogue with monophonic ditto aforementioned, and live ditto interlocutory with stereophonic et cetera, my own preference; it's been 'done' in all six."

For Further Reading

John Enck, "John Barth: An Interview," *Wisconsin Studies in Contemporary Literature*, 6 (Winter–Spring 1965), 3–14.

Edgar H. Knapp, "Found in the Barthhouse: Novelist as Savior," *Modern Fiction Studies*, 14 (Winter 1968–1969), 446–451.

Gerhard Joseph, *John Barth* (Minneapolis: University of Minneapolis Press, 1970).

Title

Beginning: in the middle, past the middle, nearer three-quarters done, waiting for the end. Consider how dreadful so far: passionlessness, abstraction, pro, dis. And it will get worse. Can we possibly continue?

Plot and theme: notions vitiated by this hour of the world but as yet not successfully succeeded. Conflict, complication, no climax. The worst is to come. Everything leads to nothing: future tense; past tense; present tense. Perfect. The final question is, Can nothing be made meaningful? Isn't that the final question? If not, the end is at hand. Literally, as it were. Can't stand any more of this.

I think she comes. The story of our life. This the final test. Try to fill the blank. Only hope is to fill the blank. Efface what can't be faced or else fill the blank. With words or more words, otherwise I'll fill in the blank with this noun here in my prepositional object. Yes, she already said that. And I think. What now. Everything's been said already, over and over; I'm as sick of this as you are; there's nothing to say. Say nothing.

What's new? Nothing.

Conventional startling opener. Sorry if I'm interrupting the Progress of Literature, she said, in a tone that adjective clause suggesting good-humored irony but in fact defensively and imperfectly masking a taunt. The conflict is established though as yet unclear in detail. Standard conflict. Let's skip particulars. What do you want from me? What'll the story be this time? Same old story. Just thought I'd see if you were still around. Before. What? Quit right here. Too late. Can't we start over? What's past is past. On the contrary, what's forever past is eternally present. The future? Blank. All this is just fill in. Hang on.

Still around. In what sense? Among the gerundive. What is that supposed to mean? Did you think I meant to fill in the blank? Why should I? On the other hand, why not? What makes you think I wouldn't fill in the blank instead? Some conversation this is. Do you want to go on, or shall we end it right now? Suspense. I don't care for this either. It'll be over soon enough in any case. But it gets worse and worse. Whatever happens, the ending will be deadly. At least let's have just one real conversation. Dialogue or monologue? What has it been from the first? Don't ask me. What is there to say at this late date? Let me think; I'm trying to think. Same old story. Or. Or? Silence.

· This isn't so bad. Silence. There are worse things. Name three. This, that, the other. Some choices. Who said there was a choice?

Let's try again. That's what I've been doing; I've been thinking while you've been blank. Story of Our Life. However, this may be the final complication. The ending may be violent. That's been said before. Who cares? Let the end be blank; anything's better than this.

It didn't used to be so bad. It used to be less difficult. Even enjoyable. For whom? Both of us. To do what? Complicate the conflict. I am weary of this. What, then? To complete this sentence, if I may bring up a sore subject. That never used to be a problem. Now it's impossible; we just can't manage it. You can't fill in the blank; I can't fill in the blank. Or won't. Is this what we're going to talk about, our obscene verbal problem? It'll be our last conversation. Why talk at all? Are you paying attention? I dare you to quit now! Never dare a desperate person. On with it, calmly, one sentence after another, like a recidivist. A what? A common noun. Or another common noun. Hold tight. Or a chronic forger, let's say; committed to the pen for life. Which is to say, death. The point, for pity's sake! Not yet. Forge on.

We're more than halfway through, as I remarked at the outset: youthful vigor, innocent exposition, positive rising action—all that is behind us. How sophisticated we are today. I'll ignore her, he vowed, and went on. In this dehuman, exhausted, ultimate adjective hour, when every humane value has become untenable, and not only love, decency, and beauty but even compassion and intelligibility are no more than one or two subjective complements to complete the sentence. ...

This is a story? It's a story, he replied equably, or will be if the author can finish it. Without interruption I suppose you mean? she broke in. I can't finish anything; that is my final word. Yet it's these interruptions that make it a story. Escalate the conflict further. Please let me start over.

Once upon a time you were satisfied with incidental felicities and niceties of technique: the unexpected image, the refreshingly accurate word-choice, the memorable simile that yields deeper and subtler significances upon reflection, like a memorable simile. Somebody please stop me. Or arresting dialogue, so to speak. For example?

Why do you suppose it is, she asked, long participial phrase of the breathless variety characteristic of dialogue attributions in nineteenth-century fiction, that literate people such as we talk like characters in a story? Even supplying the dialogue-tags, she added with wry disgust. Don't put words in her mouth. The same old story, an old-fashioned one at that. Even if I should fill in the blank with my idle pen? Nothing new about that, to make a fact out of a figure. At least it's good for something. Every story is penned in red ink, to make a figure out of a fact. This whole idea is insane.

And might therefore be got away with.

No turning back now, we've gone too far. Everything's finished. Name eight. Story, novel, literature, art, humanism, humanity, the self itself. Wait: the story's not finished. And you and I, Howard? whispered Martha, her sarcasm belied by a hesitant alarm in her glance, flickering at it were despite herself to the blank instrument in his hand. Belied indeed; put that thing away! And what does flickering modify? A person who can't verb adverb ought at least to speak correctly.

A tense moment in the evolution of the story. Do you know, declared the narrator, one has no idea, especially nowadays, how close the end may be, nor will one necessarily be aware of it when it occurs. Who can say how near this universe has come to mere cessation? Or take two people, in a story of the sort it once was possible to tell. Love affairs, literary genres, third item in exemplary series, fourth—everything blossoms and decays, does it not, from the primitive and classical through the mannered and baroque to the abstract, stylized, dehumanized, unintelligible, blank. And you and I, Rosemary? Edward. Snapped! Patience. The narrator gathers that his audience no longer cherishes him. And conversely. But little does he know of the common noun concealed for months in her you name it, under her eyelet chemise. This is a slip. The point is the same. And she fetches it out nightly as I dream, I think. That's no slip. And she regards it and sighs, a quantum grimlier each night it may be. Is this supposed to be amusing? The world might end before this sentence, or merely someone's life. And/or someone else's. I speak metaphorically. Is the sentence ended? Very nearly. No telling how long a sentence will be until one reaches the stop It sounds as if somebody intends to fill in the blank. What *is* all this nonsense about?

It may not be nonsense. Anyhow it will presently be over. As the narrator was saying, things have been kaput for some time, and while we may be pardoned our great reluctance to acknowledge it, the fact is that the bloody century for example is nearing the three-quarter mark, and the characters in this little tale, for example, are similarly past their prime, as is the drama. About played out. Then God damn it let's ring the curtain. Wait wait. We're left with the following three possibilities, at least in theory. Horseshit. Hold onto yourself, it's too soon to fill in the blank. I hope this will be a short story.

Shorter than it seems. It seems endless. Be thankful it's not a novel. The novel is predicate adjective, as is the innocent anecdote of by-gone days when life made a degree of sense and subject joined to complement by copula. No longer are these things the case, as you have doubtless remarked. There was I believe some mention of possibilities, three in number. The first is rejuvenation: having become an exhausted parody of itself, perhaps a form—Of what? Of anything

—may rise neoprimitively from its own ashes. A tiresome prospect. The second, more appealing I'm sure but scarcely likely at this advanced date, is that moribund what-have-yous will be supplanted by vigorous new: the demise of the novel and short story, he went on to declare, needn't be the end of narrative art, nor need the dissolution of a used-up blank fill in the blank. The end of one road might be the beginning of another. Much good that'll do me. And you may not find the revolution as bloodless as you think, either. Shall we try it? Never dare a person who is fed up to the ears.

The final possibility is a temporary expedient, to be sure, the self-styled narrator of this so-called story went on to admit, ignoring the hostile impatience of his audience, but what is not, and every sentence completed is a step closer to the end. That is to say, every day gained is a day gone. Matter of viewpoint, I suppose. Go on. I am. Whether anyone's paying attention or not. The final possibility is to turn ultimacy, exhaustion, paralyzing self-consciousness and the adjective weight of accumulated history. . . . Go on. Go on. To turn ultimacy against itself to make something new and valid, the essence whereof would be the impossibility of making something new. What a nauseating notion. And pray how does it bear upon the analogy uppermost in everyone's mind? We've gotten this far, haven't we? Look how far we've come together. Can't we keep on to the end? I think not. Even another sentence is too many. Only if one believes the end to be a long way off; actually it might come at any moment; I'm surprised it hasn't before now. Nothing does when it's expected to.

Silence. There's a fourth possibility, I suppose. Silence. General anesthesia. Self-extinction. Silence.

Historicity and self-awareness, he asseverated, while ineluctable and even greatly to be prized, are always fatal to innocence and spontaneity. Perhaps adjective period Whether in a people, an art, a love affair, on a fourth term added not impossibly to make the third less than ultimate. In the name of suffering humanity cease this harangue. It's over. And the story? Is there a plot here? What's all this leading up to?

No climax. There's the story. Finished? Not quite. Story of our lives. The last word in fiction, in fact. I chose the first-person narrative viewpoint in order to reflect interest from the peculiarities of the technique (such as the normally unbearable self-consciousness, the abstration, and the blank) to the nature and situation of the narrator and his companion, despite the obvious possibility that the narrator and his companion might be mistaken for the narrator and his companion. Occupational hazard. The technique is advanced, as you see, but the situation of the characters is conventionally dramatic. That being the case, may one of them, or one who may be taken for one of them, make a longish speech in the old-fashioned manner, charged with obsolete emotion? Of course.

I begin calmly, though my voice may rise as I go along. Sometimes it seems as if things could instantly be altogether different and more admirable. The times be damned, one still wants a man vigorous, confident, bold, resourceful, adjective, and adjective. One still wants a woman spirited, spacious of heart, loyal, gentle, adjective, adjective. That man and that woman are as possible as the ones in this miserable story, and a good deal realer. It's as if they live in some room of our house that we can't find the door to, though it's so close we can hear echoes of their voices. Experience has made them wise instead of bitter; knowledge has mellowed instead of souring them; in their forties and fifties, even in their sixties, they're gayer and stronger and more authentic than they were in their twenties; for the twenty-year-olds they have only affectionate sympathy. So? Why aren't the couple in this story that man and woman, so easy to imagine? God, but I am surfeited with clever irony! Ill of sickness! Parallel phrase to wrap up series! This last-resort idea, it's dead in the womb, excuse the figure. A false pregnancy, excuse the figure. God damn me though if that's entirely my fault. Acknowledge your complicity. As you see, I'm trying to do something about the present mess; hence this story. Adjective in the noun! Don't lose your composure. You tell me it's self-defeating to talk about it instead of just up and doing it; but to acknowledge what I'm doing while I'm doing it is exactly the point. Self-defeat implies a victor, and who do you suppose it is, if not blank? That's the only victory left. Right? Forward! Eyes open.

No. The only way to get out of a mirror-maze is to close your eyes and hold out your hands. And be carried away by a valiant metaphor, I suppose, like a simile.

There's only one direction to go in. Ugh. We must make something out of nothing. Impossible. Mystics do. Not only turn contradiction into paradox, but *employ* it, to go on living and working. Don't bet on it. I'm betting my cliché on it, yours too. What is that supposed to mean? On with the refutation; every denial is another breath, every word brings us closer to the end.

Very well: to write this allegedly ultimate story is a form of artistic fill in the blank, or an artistic form of same, if you like. I don't. What I mean is, same idea in other terms. The storyteller's alternatives, as far as I can see, are a series of last words, like an aging actress making one farewell appearance after another, or actual blank. And I mean literally fill in the blank. Is this a test? But the former is contemptible in itself, and the latter will certainly become so when the rest of the world shrugs its shoulders and goes on about its business. Just as people would do if adverbial clause of obvious analogical nature. The fact is, the narrator has narrated himself into a corner, a state of affairs more tsk-tsk than boo-hoo, and because his position is absurd he calls the world absurd. That some writers lack lead in their pencils does not make writing obsolete. At this point they were both smiling despite themselves. At this point they were both flashing hatred despite themselves. Every woman has a blade concealed in the neighborhood of her garters. So disarm her, so to speak, don't geld yourself. At this point they were both despite themselves. Have we come to the point at last? Not quite. Where there's life there's hope.

There's no hope. This isn't working. But the alternative is to supply an alternative. That's no alternative. Unless I make it one. Just try; quit talking about it, quit talking, quit! Never dare a desperate man. Or woman. That's the one thing that can drive even the first part of a conventional metaphor to the second part of same. Talk, talk, talk. Yes yes, go on, I believe literature's not likely ever to manage abstraction successfully, like sculpture for example, is that a fact, what a time to bring up that subject, anticlimax, that's the point, do set forth the exquisite reason. Well, because wood and iron have a native appeal and first-order reality, whereas words are artificial to begin with, invented specifically to represent. Go on, please go on. I'm going. Don't you dare. Well, well, weld iron rods into abstract patterns, say, and you've still got real iron, but arrange words into abstract patterns and you've got nonsense. Nonsense is right. For example. On, God damn it; take linear plot, take resolution of conflict, take third direct object, all that business, they may very well be obsolete notions, indeed they are, no doubt untenable at this late date, no doubt at all, but in fact we still lead our lives by clock and calendar, for example, and though the seasons recur our mortal human time does not; we grow old and tired, we think of how things used to be or might have been and how they are now, and in fact, and in fact we get exasperated and desperate and out of expedients and out of words.

Go on. Impossible. I'm going, too late now, one more step and we're done, you and I. Suspense. The fact is, you're driving me to it, the fact is that people still lead lives, mean and bleak and brief as they are, briefer than you think, and people have characters and motives that we divine more or less inaccurately from their appearance, speech, behavior, and the rest, you aren't listening, go on then, what do you think I'm doing, people still fall in love, and out, yes, in and out, and out and in, and they please each other, and hurt each other, isn't that the truth, and they do these things in more or less conventionally dramatic fashion, unfashionable or not, go on, I'm going, and what goes on between them is still not only the most interesting but the most important thing in the bloody murderous world, pardon the adjectives. And that my dear is what writers have got to find ways to write about in this adjective adjective hour of the ditto ditto same noun as above, or their, that is to say our, accursed self-consciousness will lead them, that is to say us, to here it comes, say it straight out, I'm going to, say it in plain English for once, that's what I'm leading up to, me and my bloody anticlimactic noun, we're pushing each other to fill in the blank.

Goodbye. Is it over? Can't you read between the lines? One more step. Goodbye suspense goodbye.

Blank.

Oh God comma I abhor self-consciousness. I despise what we have come to; I loathe our loathesome loathing, our place our time our situation, our loathesome art, this ditto necessary story. The blank of our lives. It's about over. Let the *dénouement* be soon and unexpected, painless if possible, quick at least, above all soon. Now now! How in the world will it ever

Donald Barthelme

(b. 1931)

Born in Philadelphia, Donald Barthelme received his education in Texas. After graduating from the University of Houston, he worked for a time as a museum director,
and also as an editor of *Location,* a journal concerned with art and literature; and his
interest in the visual arts, including the cinema, is reflected in all his writing. The
title of his first collection of short stories, *Come Back, Dr. Caligari* (1964), alludes to
an early German film, which employed expressionistic and surrealistic techniques;
and Barthelme's extraordinary mixture and manipulation of styles at times seems to
approximate more closely film than traditional literary modes. The rejection of literary convention, as a means of conveying the writer's sense of absurdity or meaning-
lessness in life, is itself a convention which Barthelme inherits from Rabelais, Sterne,
and James Joyce; but his more immediate literary antecedents are Edgar Allan Poe
and Franz Kafka. Like them, he conveys a sense of a purposeless evil underlying the
surface of our lives; his stories are amusing and yet macabre, turning sense into
non-sense, and disturbing our notions of reality. In his novel *Snow White* (1967), and
his collection of stories entitled *City Life* (1971), he moves still further away from
conventional methods of narration, sometimes combining typographical devices and
pictures with his text, to create a dizzying series of surreal images. "Report" from
Unspeakable Practices, Unnatural Acts (1968), is not experimental in terms of technique; but by his adaptation and imitation of scientific jargon, Barthelme projects a
bizarre picture of man's potential for self-destruction, in an age when technology
seems to have deprived him of the capacity for natural feeling.

For further reading

John Ditsky, "The Man on the Quaker Oats Box: Characteristics of Recent Experimen-
tal Fiction," *Georgia Review,* 26 (Fall 1972), 297–313.
Francis Gillen, "Donald Barthelme's City: A Guide," *Twentieth Century Literature,* 18
(January–October 1972), 37–44.
Mark L. Krupnick, "Notes from the Funhouse," *Modern Occasions,* 1 (Fall 1970),
108–112.

Report

Our group is against the war. But the war goes on. I was sent to
Cleveland to talk to the engineers. The engineers were meeting in
Cleveland. I was supposed to persuade them not to do what they are
going to do. I took United's 4:45 from LaGuardia arriving in Cleveland at 6:13. Cleveland is dark blue at that hour. I went directly to

the motel, where the engineers were meeting. Hundreds of engineers attended the Cleveland meeting. I noticed many fractures among the engineers, bandages, traction. I noticed what appeared to be fracture of the carpal scaphoid in six examples. I noticed numerous fractures of the humeral shaft, of the os calcis, of the pelvic girdle. I noticed a high incidence of clay-shoveller's fracture. I could not account for these fractures. The engineers were making calculations, taking measurements, sketching on the blackboard, drinking beer, throwing bread, buttonholing employers, hurling glasses into the fireplace. They were friendly.

They were friendly. They were full of love and information. The chief engineer wore shades. Patella in Monk's traction, clamshell fracture by the look of it. He was standing in a slum of beer bottles and microphone cable. "Have some of this chicken à la Isambard Kingdom Brunel the Great Ingineer," he said. "And declare who you are and what we can do for you. What is your line, distinguished guest?"

"Software," I said. "In every sense. I am here representing a small group of interested parties. We are interested in your thing, which seems to be functioning. In the midst of so much dysfunction, function is interesting. Other people's things don't seem to be working. The State Department's thing doesn't seem to be working. The U.N.'s thing doesn't seem to be working. The democratic left's thing doesn't seem to be working. Buddha's thing—"

"Ask us anything about our thing, which seems to be working," the chief engineer said. "We will open our hearts and heads to you, Software Man, because we want to be understood and loved by the great lay public, and have our marvels appreciated by that public, for which we daily unsung produce tons of new marvels each more life-enhancing than the last. Ask us anything. Do you want to know about evaporated thin-film metallurgy? Monolithic and hybrid integrated-circuit processes? The algebra of inequalities? Optimization theory? Complex high-speed micro-miniature closed and open loop systems? Fixed variable mathematical cost searches? Epitaxial deposition of semi-conductor materials? Gross interfaced space gropes? We also have specialists in the cuckoo-flower, the doctorfish, and the dumdum bullet as these relate to aspects of today's expanding technology, and they do in the damnedest ways."

I spoke to him then about the war. I said the same things people always say when they speak against the war. I said that the war was wrong. I said that large countries should not burn down small countries. I said that the government had made a series of errors. I said that these errors once small and forgivable were now immense and unforgivable. I said that the government was attempting to conceal its original errors under layers of new errors. I said that the government was sick with error, giddy with it. I said that ten thousand of our soldiers had already been killed in pursuit of the government's errors. I said that tens of thousands of the enemy's soldiers and civilians had been killed because of various errors, ours and theirs. I said that we are responsible for errors made in our name. I said that the government should not be allowed to make additional errors.

"Yes, yes," the chief engineer said, "there is doubtless much truth in what you say, but we can't possibly *lose* the war, can we? And stopping is losing, isn't it? The war regarded as a process, stopping regarded as an abort? We don't know *how* to lose a war. That skill is not among our skills. Our array smashes their array, that is what we know. That is the process. That is what is.

"But let's not have any more of this dispiriting downbeat counterproductive talk. I have a few new marvels here I'd like to discuss with you just briefly. A few new marvels that are just about ready to be gaped at by the admiring layman. Consider for instance the area of realtime online computer-controlled wish evaporation. Wish evaporation is going to be crucial in meeting the rising expectations of the world's peoples, which are as you know rising entirely too fast."

I noticed then distributed about the room a great many transverse fractures of the ulna. "The development of the pseudo-ruminant stomach for underdeveloped peoples," he went on, "is one of our interesting things you should be interested in. With the pseudo-ruminant stomach they can chew cuds, that is to say, eat grass. Blue is the most popular color worldwide and for that reason we are working with certain strains of your native Kentucky *Poa pratensis,* or bluegrass, as the staple input for the p/r stomach cycle, which would also give a shot in the arm to our balance-of-payments thing don't you know. ...." I noticed about me then a great number of metatarsal fractures in banjo splints. "The kangaroo initiative ... eight hundred thousand harvested last year ... highest percentage of edible protein of any herbivore yet studied. ...."

"Have new kangaroos been planted?"

The engineer looked at me.

"I intuit your hatred and jealousy of our thing," he said. "The ineffectual always hate our thing and speak of it as anti-human, which is not at all a meaningful way to speak of our thing. Nothing mechanical is alien to me," he said (amber spots making bursts of light in his shades), "because I am human, in a sense, and if I think it up, then 'it' is human too, whatever 'it' may be. Let me tell you, Software Man, we have been damned forbearing in the matter of this little war you declare yourself to be interested in. Function is the cry, and our thing is functioning like crazy. There are things we could do that we have not done. Steps we could take that we have not taken. These steps are, regarded in a certain light, the light of our enlightened self-interest, quite justifiable steps. We could, of course, get irritated. We could, of course, *lose patience.*

"We could, of course, release thousands upon thousands of self-powered crawling-along-the-ground lengths of titanium wire eighteen inches long with a diameter of .0005 centimetres (that is to say, invisible) which, scenting an enemy, climb up his trouser leg and wrap themselves around his neck. We have developed those. They are within our capabilities. We could, of course, release in the arena of the upper air our new improved pufferfish toxin which precipitates an identity crisis. No special technical problems there. That is almost laughably easy. We could, of course, place up to two million maggots in their rice within twenty-four hours. The maggots are ready, massed in secret staging areas in Alabama. We have hypodermic darts capable of piebalding the enemy's pigmentation. We have rots, blights, and rusts capable of attacking his alphabet. Those are dandies. We have a hut-shrinking chemical which penetrates the fibres of the bamboo, causing it, the hut, to strangle its occupants. This operates only after 10 P.M., when people are sleeping. Their mathematics are at the mercy of a suppurating surd we have invented. We have a family of fishes trained to attack their fishes. We have the deadly testicle-destroying telegram. The cable companies are cooperating. We have a green substance that, well, I'd rather not talk about. We have a secret word that, if pronounced, produces multiple fractures in all living things in an area the size of four football fields."

"That's why—"

"Yes. Some damned fool couldn't keep his mouth shut. The point is that the whole structure of enemy life is within our power to *rend, vitiate, devour,* and *crush.* But that's not the interesting thing."

"You recount these possibilities with uncommon relish."

"Yes I realize that there is too much relish here. But *you* must realize that these capabilities represent in and of themselves highly technical and complex and interesting problems and hurdles on which our boys have expended many thousands of hours of hard work and brilliance. And that the effects are often grossly exaggerated by irresponsible victims. And that the whole thing represents a fantastic series of triumphs for the multi-disciplined problem-solving team concept."

"I appreciate that."

"We *could* unleash all this technology at once. You can imagine what would happen then. But that's not the interesting thing."

"What is the interesting thing?"

"The interesting thing is that we have *a moral sense.* It is on punched cards, perhaps the most advanced and sensitive moral sense the world has ever known."

"Because it is on punched cards?"

"It considers all considerations in endless and subtle detail," he said. "It even quibbles. With this great new moral tool, how can we go wrong? I confidently predict that, although we *could* employ all this splendid new weaponry I've been telling you about, *we're not going to do it.*"

"We're not going to do it?"

I took United's 5:44 from Cleveland arriving at Newark at 7:19. New Jersey is bright pink at that hour. Living things move about the surface of New Jersey at that hour molesting each other only in traditional ways. I made my report to the group. I stressed the friendliness of the engineers. I said, It's all right. I said, We have a moral sense. I said, *We're not going to do it.* They didn't believe me.

Clark Blaise

(b. 1940)

Associated, along with Hugh Hood and John Metcalf, with the Montreal Story-Tellers group, Clark Blaise moved to Canada after several years of residence in the United States. Born to Canadian parents in Fargo, North Dakota, he lived as a child on the urban American east coast and in the rural South, and was educated in Ohio and Iowa. His work reflects that mobility, asserts his French heritage and his American up-bringing, and focuses on the problems of alienation that in various ways beset modern man. His widely praised short story collection *A North American Education* (1973), expresses even by its title the continental range of his background; and the stories themselves, cast as personal narratives, draw readers into an intensely immediate world. The second-person narrative technique of "Eyes" enforces such a reaction, and the story's somber tone—the watchfulness it suggests—skillfully links method with meaning. But the immediacy rises from the author's intention as well.

In an essay on the short story form—"To Begin, To Begin," the title a quotation from Donald Barthelme—Blaise asserts that theme is of secondary importance to the writer who is undergoing the process of writing a story. Narrative climax and the elegant contrivance of resolution, however important, are also of less moment than the mysteries of genesis. A good story, he says, is made by its first sentence and by the embellishments which the first paragraph gives it. The first sentence must imply its own opposite—"a good sensuous description of May sets up the possibility of a May disaster"; it must start the story neither too late nor too soon; it must disrupt and reorder the reader's sense of how things are; and it must have a rhythm all its own. The moment plot appears, in "the simple terrifying adverb: *Then,*" the characters start to realize the implications of the initial mysteries; such a moment "is the cracking of the perfect, smug egg of possibility." But what preceded it is what allowed it; in the beginning is the identity that the story seems later to acquire or reveal. And in realizing and appreciating that identity, readers engage themselves with the artist in the creation of the story's own truths.

For further reading

Margaret Atwood, *Survival* (Toronto: Anansi, 1972), pp. 145–159.
Clark Blaise, "To Begin, To Begin," in *The Narrative Voice*, ed. John Metcalf (Toronto: McGraw-Hill Ryerson, 1972), pp. 22–26.

Eyes

You jump into this business of a new country cautiously. First you choose a place where English is spoken, with doctors and bus lines at hand, and a supermarket in a *centre d'achats* not too far away. You

26

ease yourself into the city, approaching by car or bus down a single artery, aiming yourself along the boulevard that begins small and tree-lined in your suburb but broadens into the canyoned aorta of the city five miles beyond. And by that first winter when you know the routes and bridges, the standard congestions reported from the helicopter on your favorite radio station, you start to think of moving. What's the good of a place like this when two of your neighbors have come from Texas and the French paper you've dutifully subscribed to arrives by mail two days late? These French are all around you, behind the counters at the shopping center, in a house or two on your block; why isn't your little boy learning French at least? Where's the nearest *maternelle?** Four miles away.

In the spring you move. You find an apartment on a small side street where dogs outnumber children and the row houses resemble London's, divided equally between the rundown and remodeled. Your neighbors are the young personalities of French television who live on delivered chicken, or the old pensioners who shuffle down the summer sidewalks in pajamas and slippers in a state of endless recuperation. Your neighbors pay sixty a month for rent, or three hundred; you pay two-fifty for a two-bedroom flat where the walls have been replastered and new fixtures hung. The bugs *d'antan* remain, as well as the hulks of cars abandoned in the fire alley behind, where downtown drunks sleep in the summer night.

Then comes the night in early October when your child is coughing badly, and you sit with him in the darkened nursery, calm in the bubbling of a cold-steam vaporizer while your wife mends a dress in the room next door. And from the dark, silently, as you peer into the ill-lit fire alley, he comes. You cannot believe it at first, that a rheumy, pasty-faced Irishman in slate-gray jacket and rubber-soled shoes has come purposely to *your* small parking space, that he has been here before and he is not drunk (not now, at least, but you know him as a panhandler on the main boulevard a block away), that he brings with him a crate that he sets on end under your bedroom window and raises himself to your window ledge and hangs there nose-high at a pencil of light from the ill-fitting blinds. And there you are, straining with him from the uncurtained nursery, watching the man watching your wife, praying silently that she is sleeping under the blanket. The man is almost smiling, a leprechaun's face that sees what you cannot. You are about to lift the window and shout, but your wheezing child lies just under you; and what of your wife in the room next door? You could, perhaps, throw open the window and leap to the ground, tackle the man before he runs and

*Maternelle = nursery school.

smash his face into the bricks, beat him senseless then call the cops
... Or better, find the camera, afix the flash, rap once at the window
and shoot when he turns. Do nothing and let him suffer. *He is at your
mercy,* no one will ever again be so helpless—but what can you do?
You know, somehow, he'll escape. If you hurt him, he can hurt you
worse, later, viciously. He's been a regular at your window, he's
watched the two of you when you prided yourself on being young
and alone and masters of the city. He knows your child and the park
he plays in, your wife and where she shops. He's a native of the
place, a man who knows the city and maybe a dozen such windows,
who knows the fire escapes and alleys and roofs, knows the habits
of the city's heedless young.

And briefly you remember yourself, an adolescent in another
country slithering through the mosquito-ridden grassy fields behind a housing development, peering into those houses where new-
lyweds had not yet put up drapes, how you could spend five hours
in a motionless crouch for a myopic glimpse of a slender arm reaching from the dark to douse a light. Then you hear what the man
cannot; the creaking of your bed in the far bedroom, the steps of your
wife on her way to the bathroom, and you see her as you never have
before: blond and tall and rangily built, a north-Europe princess
from a constitutional monarchy, sensuous mouth and prominent
teeth, pale, tennis-ball breasts cupped in her hands as she stands in
the bathroom's light.

"How's Kit?" she asks. "I'd give him a kiss except that there's no
blind in there," and she dashes back to bed, nude, and the man
bounces twice on the window ledge.

"You coming?"

You find yourself creeping from the nursery, turning left at the
hall and then running to the kitchen telephone; you dial the police,
then hang up. How will you prepare your wife, not for what is
happening, but for what has already taken place?

"It's stuffy in here," you shout back, "I think I'll open the window
a bit." You take your time, you stand before the blind blocking his
view if he's still looking, then bravely you part the curtains. He is
gone, the crate remains upright. "Do we have any masking tape?"
you ask, lifting the window a crack.

And now you know the city a little better. A place where millions
come each summer to take pictures and walk around must have its
voyeurs too. And that place in all great cities where rich and poor
co-exist is especially hard on the people in-between. It's health
you've been seeking, not just beauty; a tough urban health that will
save you money in the bargain, and when you hear of a place twice
as large at half the rent, in a part of town free of Texans, English, and

French, free of young actors and stewardesses who deposit their garbage in pizza boxes, you move again.

It is, for you, a city of Greeks. In the summer you move you attend a movie at the corner cinema. The posters advertise a war movie, in Greek, but the uniforms are unfamiliar. Both sides wear mustaches, both sides handle machine guns, both leave older women behind dressed in black. From the posters outside there is a promise of sex; blond women in slips, dark-eyed peasant girls. There will be rubble, executions against a wall. You can follow the story from the stills alone: mustached boy goes to war, embraces dark-eyed village girl. Black-draped mother and admiring young brother stand behind. Young soldier, mustache fuller, embraces blond prostitute on a tangled bed. Enter soldiers, boy hides under sheets. Final shot, back in village. Mother in black; dark-eyed village girl in black. Young brother marching to the front.

You go in, pay your ninety cents, pay a nickel in the lobby for a wedge of *halvah*-like sweets. You understand nothing, you resent their laughter and you even resent the picture they're running. Now you know the Greek for "Coming Attractions," for this is a gangster movie at least thirty years old. The eternal Mediterranean gangster movie set in Athens instead of Naples or Marseilles, with smaller cars and narrower roads, uglier women and more sinister killers. After an hour the movie flatters you. No one knows you're not a Greek, that you don't belong in this theater, or even this city. That, like the Greeks, you're hanging on.

Outside the theater the evening is warm and the wide sidewalks are clogged with Greeks who nod as you come out. Like the Ramblas in Barcelona, with children out past midnight and families walking back and forth for a long city block, the men filling the coffeehouses, the women left outside, chatting. Not a blond head on the sidewalk, not a blond head for miles. Greek music pours from the coffeehouses, flies stumble on the pastry, whole families munch their *torsades molles** as they walk. Dry goods are sold at midnight from the sidewalk, like New York fifty years ago. You're wandering happily, glad that you moved, you've rediscovered the innocence of starting over.

Then you come upon a scene directly from Spain. A slim blond girl in a floral top and white pleated skirt, tinted glasses, smoking, with bad skin, ignores a persistent young Greek in a shiny Salonika suit. "Whatsamatta?" he demands, slapping a ten-dollar bill on his open palm. And without looking back at him she drifts closer to the curb and a car makes a sudden squealing turn and lurches to a stop

torsades molles = soft, twisted rolls.

on the cross street. Three men are inside, the back door opens and not a word is exchanged as she steps inside. How? What refinement of gesture did we immigrants miss? You turn to the Greek boy in sympathy, you know just how he feels, but he's already heading across the street, shouting something to his friends outside a barbecue stand. You have a pocketful of bills and a Mediterranean soul, and money this evening means a woman, and blond means whore and you would spend it all on another blond with open pores; all this a block from your wife and tenement. And you hurry home.

Months later you know the place. You trust the Greeks in their stores, you fear their tempers at home. Eight bathrooms adjoin a central shaft, you hear the beatings of your son's friends, the thud of fist on bone after the slaps. Your child knows no French, but he plays cricket with Greeks and Jamaicans out in the alley behind Pascal's hardware. He brings home the oily tires from the Esso station, plays in the boxes behind the appliance store. You watch from a greasy back window, at last satisfied. None of his friends is like him, like you. He is becoming Greek, becoming Jamaican, becoming a part of this strange new land. His hair is nearly white; you can spot him a block away.

On Wednesdays the butcher quarters his meat. Calves arrive by refrigerator truck, still intact but for their split-open bellies and sawed-off hooves. The older of the three brothers skins the carcass with a small thin knife that seems all blade. A knife he could shave with. The hide rolls back in a continuous flap, the knife never pops the membrane over the fat.

Another brother serves. Like yours, his French is adequate. *"Twa lif* d'hamburger,"* you request, still watching the operation on the rickety sawhorse. Who could resist? It's a Levantine treat, the calf's stumpy legs high in the air, the hide draped over the edge and now in the sawdust, growing longer by the second.

The store is filling. The ladies shop on Wednesday, especially the old widows in black overcoats and scarves, shoes and stockings. Yellow, mangled fingernails. Wednesdays attract them with boxes in the window, and they call to the butcher as they enter, the brother answers, and the women dip their fingers in the boxes. The radio is loud overhead, music from the Greek station.

"Une et soixante, m'sieur. Du bacon, jambon?"

And you think, taking a few lamb chops but not their saltless bacon, how pleased you are to manage so well. It is a Byzantine moment with blood and widows and sides of dripping beef, contentment in a snowy slum at five below.

---

*Twa lif = trois livres (3 pounds).

The older brother, having finished the skinning, straightens, curses, and puts away the tiny knife. A brother comes forward to pull the hide away, a perfect beginning for a gameroom rug. Then, bending low at the rear of the glistening carcass, the legs spread high and stubby, the butcher digs in his hands, ripping hard where the scrotum is, and pulls on what seems to be a strand of rubber, until it snaps. He puts a single glistening prize in his mouth, pulls again and offers the other to his brother, and they suck.

The butcher is singing now, drying his lips and wiping his chin, and still he's chewing. The old black-draped widows with the parchment faces are also chewing. On leaving, you check the boxes in the window. Staring out are the heads of pigs and lambs, some with the eyes lifted out and a red socket exposed. A few are loose and the box is slowly dissolving from the blood, and the ice beneath.

The women have gathered around the body; little pieces are offered to them from the head and entrails. The pigs' heads are pink, perhaps they've been boiled, and hairless. The eyes are strangely blue. You remove your gloves and touch the skin, you brush against the grainy ear. How the eye attracts you! How you would like to lift one out, press its smoothness against your tongue, then crush it in your mouth. And you cannot. Already your finger is numb and the head, it seems, has shifted under you. And the eye, in panic, grows white as your finger approaches. You would take that last half inch but for the certainty, in this world you have made for yourself, that the eye would blink and your neighbors would turn upon you.

Morley Callaghan

(b. 1903)

Morley Callaghan, author of ten novels, many stories, and an important memoir of Paris in the 1920s, *That Summer in Paris* (1963), enjoyed a reputation outside Canada before he became a national literary figure. One of Ernest Hemingway's co-workers on the Toronto *Star*, he published in Ezra Pound's avant-garde magazine *exile*, as well as in *Transition, Scribner's, The New Yorker*, and other journals. A gathering of his work appeared in 1959 under the title *Morley Callaghan's Stories*. Yet from the 1930s until Edmund Wilson rediscovered him in 1960—"a writer whose work may be mentioned without absurdity in association with Chekhov's and Turgenev's"—he was virtually unknown. With English critics responding warmly to his work in the 1970s, his fortunes again altered; throughout, however, Callaghan himself remained fiercely committed to a sense of artistic independence.

Born in Toronto in 1903 and (though he has never practiced law) the recipient of an Osgoode Hall law degree in 1928, he has won several Canadian literary prizes. Yet his style and literary intention were shaped less by the cultural milieu in Toronto than by what he refers to as his own "North American" consciousness; Hemingway, Scott Fitzgerald, and particularly Sherwood Anderson were his guides. He worked at paring from his style any words that might draw attention away from his protagonists; he was concerned with focusing on moral dilemmas and with presenting clearly the forces that (for the people involved) turn ordinary events in ordinary lives into momentous drama. The result can more easily be termed parable than naturalism. If his stories are realistic, they are so only within their own terms; at their best they have the power of truth without the interference of petty detail, and the credibility that accompanies intense conviction. The impact of "Two Fishermen" derives from the tension between deeply held moral convictions and the placid surface style. Where the story leads is into a contemplation of the ways in which abstract principles —justice, for example—take real and imperfect forms, and so rake the lives of the people for whom they still have meaning.

For further reading

Morley Callaghan, "An Ocean Away," *TLS* (June 4, 1964), 493.
Fraser Sutherland, *The Style of Innocence* (Toronto: Clarke, Irwin, 1972).
Edmund Wilson, *O Canada* (New York: Farrar, Straus & Giroux, 1965).

Two Fishermen

The only reporter on the town paper, the *Examiner,* was Michael Foster, a tall, long-legged, eager young fellow, who wanted to go to the city some day and work on an important newspaper.

The morning he went into Bagley's Hotel, he wasn't at all sure of himself. He went over to the desk and whispered to the proprietor, Ted Bagley, "Did he come here, Mr. Bagley?"

Bagley said slowly, "Two men came here from this morning's train. They're registered." He put his spatulate forefinger on the open book and said, "Two men. One of them's a drummer. This one here, T. Woodley. I know because he was through this way last year and just a minute ago he walked across the road to Molson's hardward store. The other one ... here's his name, K. Smith."

"Who's K. Smith?" Michael asked.

"I don't know. A mild, harmless-looking little guy."

"Did he look like the hangman, Mr. Bagley?"

"I couldn't say that, seeing as I never saw one. He was awfully polite and asked where he could get a boat so he could go fishing on the lake this evening, so I said likely down at Smollet's place by the power-house."

"Well, thanks. I guess if he was the hangman, he'd go over to the jail first," Michael said.

He went along the street, past the Baptist church to the old jail with the high brick fence around it. Two tall maple trees, with branches drooping low over the sidewalk, shaded one of the walls from the morning sunlight. Last night, behind those walls, three carpenters, working by lamplight, had nailed the timbers for the scaffold. In the morning, young Thomas Delaney, who had grown up in the town, was being hanged: he had killed old Mathew Rhinehart whom he had caught molesting his wife when she had been berry-picking in the hills behind the town. There had been a struggle and Thomas Delaney had taken a bad beating before he had killed Rhinehart. Last night a crowd had gathered on the sidewalk by the lamp-post, and while moths and smaller insects swarmed around the high blue carbon light, the crowd had thrown sticks and bottles and small stones at the out-of-town workmen in the jail yard. Billy Hilton, the town constable, had stood under the light with his head down, pretending not to notice anything. Thomas Delaney was only three years older than Michael Foster.

Michael went straight to the jail office, where Henry Steadman, the sheriff, a squat, heavy man, was sitting on the desk idly wetting his long moustaches with his tongue. "Hello, Michael, what do you want?" he asked.

"Hello, Mr. Steadman, the *Examiner* would like to know if the hangman arrived yet."

"Why ask me?"

"I thought he'd come here to test the gallows. Won't he?"

"My, you're a smart young fellow, Michael, think of that."

"Is he in there now, Mr. Steadman?"

"Don't ask me. I'm saying nothing. Say, Michael, do you think there's going to be trouble? You ought to know. Does anybody seem sore at me? I can't do nothing. You can see that."

"I don't think anybody blames you, Mr. Steadman. Look here, can't I see the hangman? Is his name K. Smith?"

"What does it matter to you, Michael? Be a sport, go on away and don't bother us any more."

"All right, Mr. Steadman," Michael said very competently, "just leave it to me."

Early that evening, when the sun was setting, Michael Foster walked south of the town on the dusty road leading to the power-house and Smollet's fishing pier. He knew that if Mr. K. Smith wanted to get a boat he would go down to the pier. Fine powdered road dust whitened Michael's shoes. Ahead of him he saw the pow-er-plant, square and low, and the smooth lake water. Behind him the sun was hanging over the blue hills beyond the town and shining brilliantly on square patches of farm land. The air around the power-house smelt of steam.

Out of the jutting, tumbledown pier of rock and logs, Michael saw a little fellow without a hat, sitting down with his knees hunched up to his chin, a very small man with little gray baby curls on the back of his neck, who stared steadily far out over the water. In his hand he was holding a stick with a heavy fishing-line twined around it and a gleaming copper spoon bait, the hooks brightened with bits of feathers such as they used in the neighbourhood when trolling for lake trout. Apprehensively Michael walked out over the rocks to-ward the stranger and called, "Were you thinking of going fishing, mister?" Standing up, the man smiled. He had a large head, tapering down to a small chin, a birdlike neck and a very wistful smile. Puckering his mouth up, he said shyly to Michael, "Did you intend to go fishing?"

"That's what I came down here for. I was going to get a boat back at the boat-house there. How would you like if we went together?"

"I'd like it first rate," the shy little man said eagerly. "We could take turns rowing. Does that appeal to you?"

"Fine. Fine. You wait here and I'll go back to Smollet's place and ask for a row-boat and I'll row around here and get you."

"Thanks. Thanks very much," the mild little man said as he began to untie his line. He seemed very enthusiastic.

When Michael brought the boat around to the end of the old pier and invited the stranger to make himself comfortable so he could handle the line, the stranger protested comically that he ought to be allowed to row.

Pulling strongly at the oars, Michael was soon out in the deep
water and the little man was letting his line out slowly. In one
furtive glance, he had noticed that the man's hair, gray at the temples, was inclined to curl to his ears. The line was out full length.
It was twisted around the little man's forefinger, which he let drag
in the water. And then Michael looked full at him and smiled because he thought he seemed so meek and quizzical. "He's a nice little
guy," Michael assured himself and he said, "I work on the town
paper, the *Examiner.*"

"Is it a good paper? Do you like the work?"

"Yes. But it's nothing like a first-class city paper and I don't expect
to be working on it long. I want to get a reporter's job on a city paper.
My name's Michael Foster."

"Mine's Smith. Just call me Smitty."

"I was wondering if you'd been over to the jail yet."

Up to this time the little man had been smiling with the charming
ease of a small boy who finds himself free, but now he became
furtive and disappointed. Hesitating, he said, "Yes, I was over there
first thing this morning."

"Oh, I just knew you'd go there," Michael said. They were a bit
afraid of each other. By this time they were far out on the water
which had a mill-pond smoothness. The town seemed to get smaller,
with white houses in rows and streets forming geometric patterns,
just as the blue hills behind the town seemed to get larger at sundown.

Finally Michael said, "Do you know this Thomas Delaney that's
dying in the morning?" He knew his voice was slow and resent-
ful.

"No. I don't know anything about him. I never read about them.
Aren't there any fish at all in this old lake? I'd like to catch some
fish," he said rapidly. "I told my wife I'd bring her home some fish."
Glancing at Michael, he was appealing, without speaking, that they
should do nothing to spoil an evening's fishing.

The little man began to talk eagerly about fishing as he pulled out
a small flask from his hip pocket. "Scotch," he said, chuckling with
delight. "Here, take a swig." Michael drank from the flask and passed
it back. Tilting his head back and saying, "Here's to you, Michael,"
the little man took a long pull at the flask. "The only time I take a
drink," he said still chuckling, "is when I go on a fishing trip by
myself. I usually go by myself," he added apologetically as if he
wanted the young fellow to see how much he appreciated his company.

They had gone far out on the water but they had caught nothing.
It began to get dark. "No fish tonight, I guess, Smitty," Michael said.

"It's a crying shame," Smitty said. "I looked forward to coming up here when I found out the place was on the lake. I wanted to get some fishing in. I promised my wife I'd bring her back some fish. She'd often like to go fishing with me, but of course, she can't because she can't travel around from place to place like I do. Whenever I get a call to go some place, I always look at the map to see if it's by a lake or on a river, then I take my lines and hooks along."

"If you took another job, you and your wife could probably go fishing together," Michael suggested.

"I don't know about that. We sometimes go fishing together anyway." He looked away, waiting for Michael to be repelled and insist that he ought to give up the job. And he wasn't ashamed as he looked down at the water, but he knew that Michael thought he ought to be ashamed. "Somebody's got to do my job. There's got to be a hangman," he said.

"I just meant that if it was such disagreeable work, Smitty."

The little man did not answer for a long time. Michael rowed steadily with sweeping, tireless strokes. Huddled at the end of the boat, Smitty suddenly looked up with a kind of melancholy hopelessness and said midly, "The job hasn't been so disagreeable."

"Good God, man, you don't mean you like it?"

"Oh, no," he said, to be obliging, as if he knew what Michael expected him to say. "I mean you get used to it, that's all." But he looked down again at the water, knowing he ought to be ashamed of himself.

"Have you got any children?"

"I sure have. Five. The oldest boy is fourteen. It's funny, but they're all a lot bigger and taller than I am. Isn't that funny?"

They started a conversation about fishing rivers that ran into the lake farther north. They felt friendly again. The little man, who had an extraordinary gift for story-telling, made many quaint faces, puckered up his lips, screwed up his eyes and moved around restlessly as if he wanted to get up in the boat and stride around for the sake of more expression. Again he brought out the whiskey flask and Michael stopped rowing. Grinning, they toasted each other and said together, "Happy days." The boat remained motionless on the placid water. Far out, the sun's last rays gleamed on the water-line. And then it got dark and they could only see the town lights. It was time to turn around and pull for the shore. The little man tried to take the oars from Michael, who shook his head resolutely and insisted that he would prefer to have his friend catch a fish on the way back to the shore.

"It's too late now, and we may have scared all the fish away," Smitty laughed happily. "But we're having a grand time, aren't we?"

When they reached the old pier by the power-house, it was full night and they hadn't caught a single fish. As the boat bumped against the rocks Michael said, "You can get out here. I'll take the boat around to Smollet's."

"Won't you be coming my way?"

"Not just now. I'll probably talk with Smollet a while."

The little man got out of the boat and stood on the pier looking down at Michael. "I was thinking dawn would be the best time to catch some fish," he said. "At about five o'clock. I'll have an hour and a half to spare anyway. How would you like that?" He was speaking with so much eagerness that Michael found himself saying, "I could try. But if I'm not here at dawn, you go on without me."

"All right. I'll walk back to the hotel now."

"Good night, Smitty."

"Good night, Michael. We had a fine neighbourly time, didn't we?"

As Michael rowed the boat around to the boat-house, he hoped that Smitty wouldn't realize he didn't want to be seen walking back to town with him. And later, when he was going slowly along the dusty road in the dark and hearing all the crickets chirping in the ditches, he couldn't figure out why he felt so ashamed of himself.

At seven o'clock next morning Thomas Delaney was hanged in the town jail yard. There was hardly a breeze on that leaden gray morning and there were no small whitecaps out over the lake. It would have been a fine morning for fishing. Michael went down to the jail, for he thought it his duty as a newspaperman to have all the facts, but he was afraid he might get sick. He hardly spoke to all the men and women who were crowded under the maple trees by the jail wall. Everybody he knew was staring at the wall and muttering angrily. Two of Thomas Delaney's brothers, big, strapping fellows with bearded faces, were there on the sidewalk. Three automobiles were at the front of the jail.

Michael, the town newspaperman, was admitted into the courtyard by old Willie Mathews, one of the guards, who said that two newspapermen from the city were at the gallows on the other side of the building. "I guess you can go around there, too, if you want to," Mathews said, as he sat down slowly on the step. White-faced, and afraid, Michael sat down on the step with Mathews and they waited and said nothing.

At last the old fellow said, "Those people outside there are pretty sore, ain't they?"

"They're pretty sullen, all right. I saw two of Delaney's brothers there."

"I wish they'd go," Mathews said. "I don't want to see anything. I didn't even look at Delaney. I don't want to hear anything. I'm sick." He put his head back against the wall and closed his eyes.

The old fellow and Michael sat close together till a small procession came around the corner from the other side of the yard. First came Mr. Steadman, the sheriff, with his head down as though he were crying, then Dr. Parker, the physician, then two hard-looking young newspapermen from the city, walking with their hats on the backs of their heads, and behind them came the little hangman, erect, stepping out with military precision and carrying himself with a strange cocky dignity. He was dressed in a long black cutaway coat with gray striped trousers, a gates-ajar collar and a narrow red tie, as if he alone felt the formal importance of the occasion. He walked with brusque precision till he saw Michael, who was standing up, staring at him with his mouth open.

The little hangman grinned and as soon as the procession reached the doorstep, he shook hands with Michael. They were all looking at Michael. As though his work were over now, the hangman said eagerly to Michael, "I thought I'd see you here. You didn't get down to the pier at dawn?"

"No. I couldn't make it." "That was tough, Michael. I looked for you," he said. "But never mind. I've got something for you." As they all went into the jail, Dr. Parker glanced angrily at Michael, then turned his back on him. In the office, where the doctor prepared to sign a certificate, Smitty was bending down over his fishing-basket which was in the corner. Then he pulled out two good-sized salmon-bellied trout, folded in a newspaper, and said, "I was saving these for you, Michael. I got four in an hour's fishing." Then he said, "I'll talk about that later, if you'll wait. We'll be busy here, and I've got to change my clothes."

Michael went out to the street with Dr. Parker and the two city newspapermen. Under his arm he was carrying the fish, folded in the newspaper. Outside, at the jail door, Michael thought that the doctor and the two newpapermen were standing a little apart from him. Then the small crowd, with their clothes all dust-soiled from the road, surged forward, and the doctor said to them, "You might as well go home, boys. It's all over."

"Where's old Steadman?" somebody demanded. "We'll wait for the hangman," somebody else shouted.

The doctor walked away by himself. For a while Michael stood beside the two city newspapermen, and tried to look as nonchalant as they were looking, but he lost confidence in them when he smelled whiskey. They only talked to each other. Then they mingled with the crowd, and Michael stood alone. At last he could stand there no longer looking at all those people he knew so well, so he, too, moved out and joined the crowd.

When the sheriff came out with the hangman and two of the

guards, they got half-way down to one of the automobiles before someone threw an old boot. Steadman ducked into one of the cars, as the boot hit him on the shoulder, and the two guards followed him. Those in the car must have thought at first that the hangman was with them for the car suddenly shot forward, leaving him alone on the sidewalk. The crowd threw small rocks and sticks, hooting at him as the automobile backed up slowly towards him. One small stone hit him on the head. Blood trickled from the side of his head as he looked around helplessly at all the angry people. He had the same expression on his face, Michael thought, as he had had last night when he had seemed ashamed and had looked down steadily at the water. Only now, he looked around wildly, looking for someone to help him as the crowd kept pelting him. Farther and farther Michael backed into the crowd and all the time he felt dreadfully ashamed as though he were betraying Smitty, who last night had had such a good neighbourly time with him. "It's different now, it's different," he kept thinking, as he held the fish in the newspaper tight under his arm. Smitty started to run toward the automobile, but James Mortimer, a big fisherman, shot out his foot and tripped him and sent him sprawling on his face.

Mortimer, the big fisherman, looking for something to throw, said to Michael, "Sock him, sock him."

Michael shook his head and felt sick.

"What's the matter with you, Michael?"

"Nothing. I got nothing against him."

The big fisherman started pounding his fists up and down in the air. "He just doesn't mean anything to me at all," Michael said quickly. The fisherman, bending down, kicked a small rock loose from the road bed and heaved it at the hangman. Then he said, "What are you holding there, Michael, what's under your arm? Fish. Pitch them at him. Here, give them to me." Still in a fury, he snatched the fish, and threw them one at a time at the little man just as he was getting up from the road. The fish fell in the thick dust in front of him, sending up a little cloud. Smitty seemed to stare at the fish on the road mouth hanging open, then he didn't even look at the crowd. That expression on Smitty's face as he saw the fish on the road made Michael hot with shame and he tried to get out of the crowd.

Smitty had his hands over his head, to shield his face as the crowd pelted him, yelling, "Sock the little rat. Throw the runt in the lake." The sheriff pulled him into the automobile. The car shot forward in a cloud of dust.

George Clutesi

(b. 1906)

A member of the Tse-Shaht band of the Pacific coast, George Clutesi is one of Canada's foremost Indian artists. A painter as well as a writer, he has shown his work internationally; a forty-foot mural, designed for the world fair Expo 67, is now on display at Montreal's permanent "Man and His World" exhibition, and his own designs illustrate *Son of Raven Son of Deer* (1967), from which "Ko-ishin-mit and the Shadow People" is taken. Contact with the "European" bureaucracies of the Canadian government—particularly in regard to Indian affairs—led Clutesi to become a teacher of native culture, confident that it had significant meaning for both Indians and whites.

"Ko-ishin-mit and the Shadow People," like all folktales, emerges directly from a specific culture; though it can often be related to parallel stories from other cultures, it reflects its own society's structure, beliefs, superstitions, and values, and draws its particular language, its metaphors and analogies, from the local landscape. Primarily an oral art, the folktale generally served a moral purpose and functioned as the didactic medium through which traditional values were handed from generation to generation. In his introduction to *Son of Raven Son of Deer,* Clutesi notes that it was "Nan-is," the grandparent, who told such tales to his "ka-coots" (grandchildren), and that this pattern of behavior not only gave the aged a respected position within society but also gave the young a sense of security. He criticizes such tales as "Henny Penny" and "Little Jack Horner," both for their implicit violence and for the gap between the child behavior that society expects and approves, and the models hallowed by the stories themselves. The Indian stories, by contrast, assert the closeness between man and nature, focus on the interpenetration between mythic stories and moral truths, and give expression (in Clutesi's own words) to the "imaginative, romantic and resourceful" capacities of the Indian mind.

For further reading

J. W. Chalmers, "When You Tell a Story," *Canadian Author and Bookman* (Fall 1971), 5.

Ko-ishin-mit and the Shadow People

"Finders keepers—losers weepers."
Most of you, no doubt, have heard this old saying. To the non-Indian way of life it means that if anyone finds anything it is his to keep, while the one who has lost it may as well cry because it is lost to

him, even though someone may have found it. This did not apply to the Indian way of life.

Ko-ishin-mit, the Son of Raven, was a very selfish and greedy person. He was always longing to own other people's possessions and coveted everything that was not his. Oh, he was greedy!

One fine day, early in the spring of the year, when the sun was shining and smiling with warmth, Ko-ishin-mit overheard a group of menfolk talking about a strange place where you could see everything you could think of lying about, with never a person in sight.

"What kind of things? Where is this place? How far is it from here?" Ko-ishin-mit demanded in a high state of excitement. He was hoppping up and down and his voice became croaky as he kept asking where to find the place.

The menfolk ignored his frantic questions and the speaker, a grey-haired, wizened old man, kept on with his story.

"There are canoes," he told, "big ones and small ones, paddles, fishing gear, tools, all sorts of play things and food galore. Oh, there is lots and lots of food, and the food is always fresh, even though no one is ever seen in the place."

Ko-ishin-mit became more and more excited and his voice was raspy as he screamed, "Who owns all these things? Where? How can I find them?"

The storyteller continued with his tale. "It is said that this strange place is on a little isle around the point and across the bay. The secret is that one must get there by sundown, and one must leave before sunup. It is said, too, that the first person who finds this place may keep everything."

Ko-ishin-mit ran all the way home. "I must find this strange place first," he kept repeating to himself. "I must find the place first. I must. I must."

He flitted into his little house, and because he was out of breath he rasped and croaked, "Pash-hook, Pash-hook, Pash-hook, nah, my dear, get ready quickly. We are going out. Make some lunch. We may be gone all night," he croaked.

Pash-hook, the Daughter of Dsim-do the squirrel, scurried about. She did not need to be coaxed for she was always a fast and frisky little person. She never questioned her husband's wishes. Whatever her husband said had always been good enough for her and she was always eager to please him. So she hurried and she hurried.

Ko-ishin-mit grew more and more excited as he flitted here and hopped there inside his little house. He got out two paddles. He hopped down to the beach and pulled and tugged at his canoe until he had it to the water, a feat he had never before done alone.

Flitting back to the house he pressed and coaxed his little wife.

"Hurry, hurry! Pash-hook, hurry! We must get there first. Hurry before we are too late. We must get there first. Oh, let us be first," he kept repeating, mostly to himself.

The sun was setting when they paddled into the bay of the little isle around the point. It was a beautiful little isle with small clumpy spreading spruce trees growing from mossy green hills. The little bay was ringed with white sandy beaches. The tide was out and the green sea-grass danced and waved at them to come ashore and rest awhile. This is what Pash-hook imagined as she eased her paddling and glided their little canoe towards the glistening beach. Pash-hook was the dreamer.

"Paddle harder! Paddle harder!" Ko-ishin-mit commanded his little wife.

Straight for the beach they glided. Ko-ishin-mit flitted out onto the wet sand. "Pull the canoe up," he ordered as he hopped up the beach, looking about to see if there was anyone else there ahead of him. He could see long rows of beautiful canoes, big and small, pulled up well above the high-water mark. They all had pretty canoe mats covering them from the heat of the day and the cool of the night. There was no one in sight. Ko-ishin-mit was hopping up the beach. He did not wait to help his small wife with their canoe.

"I got here first!" he rasped as he hopped and flitted up to the neat row of houses on the grassy knoll that lay just below the spreading and clumpy spruce trees.

"I got here first!" the greedy Ko-ishin-mit croaked as he flitted swiftly to the biggest of the great houses. The huge door was shut and he pushed it open and hopped inside. He did not look back to see if his little wife Pash-hook was following. "I got here first," he chanted. Ko-ishin-mit, Son of Raven, was very, very greedy.

No one was to be seen. There was not a sound to be heard other than, "I got here first." Ko-ishin-mit's beady little black eyes grew even smaller in his greed to grab, grab, grab. "All is mine! All is mine!" his voice rasped out as he croaked, the way ravens do when they espy food.

"The whole village is mine. I got here first," he reasoned to himself. He hopped around the earthen floor of the great room. Big cedar boxes lined the walls. Ko-ishin-mit's greedy instinct told him that they would be full of dried and smoked food-stuffs. Indeed he did find smoked salmon, cured meats, oils, preserved fish eggs, dried herring roe, cured qwanis (camus bulbs), and dried berries.

"Everything, everything! All is mine. All is mine," he croaked as he flitted and hopped about opening boxes of oil, dried bulbs and fish-heads. Everything he saw he wanted. He wanted it all. His own drool spilled out of his mouth. He was very greedy.

Presently Pash-hook came into the great house. For the first time in her life she was not hurrying to do her husband's bidding. She did not scurry one little bit. Instead of helping her husband to carry out all the things and food-stuff down to their little canoe on the sandy beach, she slowly approached a small pile of embers that were still glowing on the centre hearth. There was no flame. The embers glowed warmly and invitingly. Pash-hook sat down and began to warm herself. She spread out her tiny hands. The embers still glowed warmly.

Ko-ishin-mit was so excited and so busy carrying out the food-stuff that he, for the first time in their married lives, forgot to make his wife do all the work.

"I shall never be hungry again. I shall never be hungry again," he kept repeating.

He worked hard packing, packing, packing, all he could lift and move down the long sloping beach. The tide was out and their little canoe was far down from the great houses. Pash-hook sat by the embers warming herself while Ko-ishin-mit worked at loading the canoe. At last the canoe was filled. It was so full there was hardly any room left for himself or for Pash-hook.

"One more trip. One more trip." How greedy Ko-ishin-mit was! He decided to put the last load where his wife would sit. He hopped up the high sloping beach and flitted into the now nearly empty cedar box and decided again he would put the very last load where Pash-hook would sit.

All of a sudden he remembered her. Pash-hook was still sitting by the fire warming herself at the embers.

"Come Pash-hook! Hurry! We must come back as fast as we can. We must take all. We must take all. We must come back before daylight returns. Hurry, hurry, Pash-hook!"

But Pash-hook still sat without moving, before the embers of the fire. Ko-ishin-mit lost his temper. He hopped to his wife's side demanding in his raspy voice, "What's the matter with you, woman? You have never disobeyed me like this before. Get up at once. We must go."

Pash-hook did not move. She did not speak. She did not look up at her husband.

Ko-ishin-mit was alarmed. He became very frightened.

"Get up, get up!" he croaked. In anger he grabbed Pash-hook by the shoulders and tried to pull her up. The harder he pulled the heavier she became. He could not budge the small little person. She felt like a rooted stone. Ko-ishin-mit was now trembling with fear. He hop-flitted out and down to his canoe and pushed and heaved trying to move it out to deeper water, but the harder he pulled and heaved the heavier the little canoe became.

"Something is wrong. Something is terribly wrong," he told himself. He tried to shout but only a weak croak came out. He flitted back to the great house and hopped inside. Pash-hook still sat by the embers of the fire.

Ko-ishin-mit noticed she was trying very hard to tell him something. He very gingerly approached her and bent his head towards her moving lips. Brave, gallant Pash-hook tried with all her might.

"There are strange people holding me down. I can't move," she whispered, almost out of breath. "Put back all you took," she entreated her husband.

Ko-ishin-mit flitted back to his canoe and once more tried to push it out into the stream. It would not move. He tried pulling it farther up onto the beach. It moved with hardly any effort at all. Trembling, Ko-ishin-mit grabbed the topmost bale and hauled it back to the great house. He worked very hard toting all the boxes and bales back to where he found them. When the last article had been returned to its own cedar box then only did Pash-hook stir.

"Heahh," she breathed, "I'm free," and shook herself and stood up. Her husband led her out and down the long, long beach to their canoe.

Pash-hook hopped in as her now very meek husband pushed the canoe into the stream. They both paddled with all their might and main until they were at a safe distance from the strange, strange place. When they at last stopped to rest Pash-hook spoke her first words since leaving the great house.

"Heahh, I'm free," she repeated. "There are people up there in the great house with the earthern floors. I'm sure of it. I felt hands, heavy hands, upon my shoulders holding me down. I'm certain that one of them sat on me because I felt so crushed down from above. I was very frightened. I couldn't speak. I couldn't tell you."

Ko-ishin-mit looked at his wife with great love. "Choo, choo, choo, all right, all right, Pash-hook my mate. Don't be afraid any more. We shall never go to that isle again."

It is said that all things belong to someone. The old people say it is not wise to keep anything you find.

Around the point and across the bay
There is an Isle with clumpy spruce
That stands on mossy knolls
Green with salal.

The beaches are covered with sea-shells white
When the tide runs out sea-grasses wave and beckon you in.
The shadow people live there, it is said—
Shadow people one cannot see until the sun is up
To cast their shadows on the sands of sea-shells white.

William Faulkner

(1897–1962)

The main body of Faulkner's fiction stands as a memorial to the American South, the old South of rich plantation owners and poor white trash, of slavery and sudden violence: a region not without its glories, but suffering a progressive decay from within. Faulkner was born in Oxford, Mississippi, into a family whose roots reached back into the old South; and out of this background grew the fictional city of Jefferson in Yoknapatawpha County, the history of which forms the principal subject of Faulkner's work. After service in the Canadian Flying Corps during World War I and a period at the University of Mississippi, he turned to literature as a profession, publishing his first novel, *Soldiers' Pay*, in 1926. With *Sartoris* (1929), he began his re-creation and exploration of the South, which was to continue in such works as *The Sound and the Fury* (1929), *As I Lay Dying* (1930), *Light in August* (1932), *Absalom, Absalom!* (1936), and *Go Down, Moses* (1942). In these and other works, Faulkner chronicles the fortunes of the Sartorises and the Snopeses, the Compsons and the McCaslins, characters who recur throughout his writings, sometimes at the center, at other times at the periphery of the action; and although the novels and stories do not form a continuous series, they are linked by common themes and preoccupations: the breakdown of social traditions, the strengths and weaknesses of the old southern code, the strained and often bloody relations between black and white in the aftermath of slavery. "Dry September," from Faulkner's first collection of stories, *These Thirteen* (1931), is a powerful evocation of the frustration, bigotry, and passion pervading a society in which old fears and hatreds die hard.

Faulkner's achievement extends beyond the dramatic creation of a southern myth, however; in the moral problems and the racial tensions of his imaginary community in Mississippi, he has imaged sources of guilt and conflict which beset our larger society. In his address upon receiving the Nobel prize for literature in 1950, Faulkner spoke of the role of the artist in terms applicable to himself, exhorting young writers to depict "the old verities and truths of the heart, the old universal truths lacking which any story is ephemeral and doomed—love and honor and pity and pride and compassion and sacrifice."

For further reading

Malcolm Cowley, "William Faulkner's Legend of the South," *Sewanee Review,* 53 (1945), 343–361.

Jean Stein, "The Art of Fiction XII: William Faulkner," *Paris Review,* 12 (Spring 1956), 28–52.

J. B. Vickery, "Ritual and Theme in Faulkner's 'Dry September,'" *Arizona Quarterly,* 18 (Spring 1962), 5–14

Dry September

Through the bloody September twilight, aftermath of sixty-two rainless days, it had gone like a fire in dry grass—the rumor, the story, whatever it was. Something about Miss Minnie Cooper and a Negro. Attacked, insulted, frightened: none of them, gathered in the barber shop on that Saturday evening where the ceiling fan stirred, without freshening it, the vitiated air, sending back upon them, in recurrent surges of stale pomade and lotion, their own stale breath and odors, knew exactly what had happened.

"Except it wasn't Will Mayes," a barber said. He was a man of middle age; a thin, sand-colored man with a mild face, who was shaving a client. "I know Will Mayes. He's a good nigger. And I know Miss Minnie Cooper, too."

"What do you know about her?" a second barber said.

"Who is she?" the client said. "A young girl?"

"No," the barber said. "She's about forty, I reckon. She aint married. That's why I dont believe—"

"Believe, hell!" a hulking youth in a sweat-stained silk shirt said. "Wont you take a white woman's word before a nigger's?"

"I dont believe Will Mayes did it," the barber said. "I know Will Mayes."

"Maybe you know who did it, then. Maybe you already got him out of town, you damn niggerlover."

"I dont believe anybody did anything. I dont believe anything happened. I leave it to you fellows if them ladies that get old without getting married dont have notions that a man cant—"

"Then you are a hell of a white man," the client said. He moved under the cloth. The youth had sprung to his feet.

"You dont?" he said. "Do you accuse a white woman of lying?"

The barber held the razor poised above the half-risen client. He did not look around.

"It's this durn weather," another said. "It's enough to make a man do anything. Even to her."

Nobody laughed. The barber said in his mild, stubborn tone: "I aint accusing nobody of nothing. I just know and you fellows know how a woman that never—"

"You damn niggerlover!" the youth said.

"Shut up, Butch," another said. "We'll get the facts in plenty of time to act."

"Who is? Who's getting them?" the youth said. "Facts, hell! I—"

"You're a fine white man," the client said. "Aint you?" In his frothy beard he looked like a desert rat in moving pictures. "You can tell them, Jack," he said to the youth. "If there aint any white men in this town, you can count on me, even if I aint only a drummer and a stranger."

"That's right, boys," the barber said. "Find out the truth first. I know Will Mayes."

"Well, by God!" the youth shouted. "To think that a white man in this town—"

"Shut up, Butch," the second speaker said. "We got plenty of time."

The client sat up. He looked at the speaker. "Do you claim that anything excuses a nigger attacking a white woman? Do you mean to tell me you are a white man and you'll stand for it? You better go back North where you came from. The South dont want your kind here."

"North what?" the second said. "I was born and raised in this town."

"Well, by God!" the youth said. He looked about with a strained, baffled gaze, as if he was trying to remember what it was he wanted to say or to do. He drew his sleeve across his sweating face. "Damn if I'm going to let a white woman—"

"You tell them, Jack," the drummer said. "By God, if they—"

The screen door crashed open. A man stood in the floor, his feet apart and his heavy-set body poised easily. His white shirt was open at the throat; he wore a felt hat. His hot, bold glance swept the group. His name was McLendon. He had commanded troops at the front in France and had been decorated for valor.

"Well," he said, "are you going to sit there and let a black son rape a white woman on the streets of Jefferson?"

Butch sprang up again. The silk of his shirt clung flat to his heavy shoulders. At each armpit was a dark halfmoon. "That's what I been telling them! That's what I—"

"Did it really happen?" a third said. "This aint the first man scare she ever had, like Hawkshaw says. Wasn't there something about a man on the kitchen roof, watching her undress, about a year ago?"

"What?" the client said. "What's that?" The barber had been slowly forcing him back into the chair; he arrested himself reclining, his head lifted, the barber still pressing him down.

McLendon whirled on the third speaker. "Happen? What the hell difference does it make? Are you going to let the black sons get away with it until one really does it?"

"That's what I'm telling them!" Butch shouted. He cursed, long and steady, pointless.

"Here, here," a fourth said. "Not so loud. Dont talk so loud."

"Sure," McLendon said; "no talking necessary at all. I've done my talking. Who's with me?" He poised on the balls of his feet, roving his gaze.

The barber held the drummer's face down, the razor poised. "Find out the facts first, boys. I know Willy Mayes. It wasn't him. Let's get the sheriff and do this thing right."

McLendon whirled upon him his furious, rigid face. The barber did not look away. They looked like men of different races. The other barbers had ceased also above their prone clients. "You mean to tell me," McLendon said, "that you'd take a nigger's word before a white woman's? Why, you damn niggerloving—"

The third speaker rose and grasped McLendon's arm; he too had been a soldier. "Now, now. Let's figure this thing out. Who knows anything about what really happened?"

"Figure out hell!" McLendon jerked his arm free. "All that're with me get up from there. The ones that aint—" He roved his gaze, dragging his sleeve across his face.

Three men rose. The drummer in the chair sat up. "Here," he said, jerking at the cloth about his neck; "get this rag off me. I'm with him. I dont live here, but by God, if our mothers and wives and sisters—" He smeared the cloth over his face and flung it to the floor. McLendon stood in the floor and cursed the others. Another rose and moved toward him. The remainder sat uncomfortable, not looking at one another, then one by one they rose and joined him.

The barber picked the cloth from the floor. He began to fold it neatly. "Boys, dont do that. Will Mayes never done it. I know."

"Come on," McLendon said. He whirled. From his hip pocket protruded the butt of a heavy automatic pistol. They went out. The screen door crashed behind them reverberant in the dead air.

The barber wiped the razor carefully and swiftly, and put it away, and ran to the rear, and took his hat from the wall. "I'll be back as soon as I can," he said to the other barbers. "I cant let—" He went out, running. The two other barbers followed him to the door and caught it on the rebound, leaning out and looking up the street after him. The air was flat and dead. It had a metallic taste at the base of the tongue.

"What can he do?" the first said. The second one was saying "Jees Christ, Jees Christ" under his breath. "I'd just as lief be Will Mayes as Hawk, if he gets McLendon riled."

"Jees Christ, Jees Christ," the second whispered.

"You reckon he really done it to her?" the first said.

II

She was thirty-eight or thirty-nine. She lived in a small frame house with her invalid mother and a thin, sallow, unflagging aunt, where each morning between ten and eleven she would appear on the porch in a lace-trimmed boudoir cap, to sit swinging in the porch swing until noon. After dinner she lay down for a while, until the afternoon began to cool. Then, in one of the three or four new voile dresses which she had each summer, she would go downtown to spend the afternoon in the stores with the other ladies, where they would handle the goods and haggle over the prices in cold, immediate voices, without any intention of buying.

She was of comfortable people—not the best in Jefferson, but good people enough—and she was still on the slender side of ordinary-looking, with a bright, faintly haggard manner and dress. When she was young she had had a slender nervous body and a sort of hard vivacity which had enabled her for a time to ride upon the crest of the town's social life as exemplified by the high school party and church social period of her contemporaries while still children enough to be unclassconscious.

She was the last to realize that she was losing ground; that those among whom she had been a little brighter and louder flame than any other were beginning to learn the pleasure of snobbery—male —and retaliation—female. That was when her face began to wear that bright, haggard look. She still carried it to parties on shadowy porticoes and summer lawns, like a mask or a flag, with that bafflement of furious repudiation of truth in her eyes. One evening at a party she heard a boy and two girls, all schoolmates, talking. She never accepted another invitation.

She watched the girls with whom she had grown up as they married and got homes and children, but no man ever called on her steadily until the children of the other girls had been calling her "aunty" for several years, the while their mothers told them in bright voices about how popular Aunt Minnie had been as a girl. Then the town began to see her driving on Sunday afternoons with the cashier in the bank. He was a widower of about forty—a high-colored man, smelling always faintly of the barber shop or of whisky. He owned the first automobile in town, a red runabout; Minnie had the first motoring bonnet and veil the town ever saw. Then the town began to say: "Poor Minnie." "But she is old enough to take care of herself," others said. That was when she began to ask her old schoolmates that their children call her "cousin" instead of "aunty."

It was twelve years now since she had been relegated into adultery by public opinion, and eight years since the cashier had gone to a Memphis bank, returning for one day each Christmas, which he spent at an annual bachelors' party at a hunting club on the river. From behind their curtains the neighbors would see the party pass, and during the over-the-way Christmas day visiting they would tell her about him, about how well he looked, and how they heard that he was prospering in the city, watching with bright, secret eyes her haggard, bright face. Usually by that hour there would be the scent of whisky on her breath. It was supplied her by a youth, a clerk at the soda fountain: "Sure; I buy it for the old gal. I reckon she's entitled to a little fun."

Her mother kept to her room altogether now; the gaunt aunt ran the house. Against that background Minnie's bright dresses, her idle and empty days, had a quality of furious unreality. She went out in the evenings only with women now, neighbors, to the moving pictures. Each afternoon she dressed in one of the new dresses and went downtown alone, where her young "cousins" were already strolling in the late afternoons with their delicate, silken heads and thin, awkward arms and conscious hips, clinging to one another or shrieking and giggling with paired boys in the soda fountain when she passed and went on along the serried store fronts, in the doors of which the sitting and lounging men did not even follow her with their eyes any more.

III

The barber went swiftly up the street where the sparse lights, insect-swirled, glared in rigid and violent suspension in the lifeless air. The day had died in a pall of dust; above the darkened square, shrouded by the spent dust, the sky was as clear as the inside of a brass bell. Below the east was a rumor of the twice-waxed moon.

When he overtook them McLendon and three others were getting into a car parked in an alley. McLendon stooped his thick head, peering out beneath the top. "Changed your mind, did you?" he said. "Damn good thing; by God, tomorrow when this town hears about how you talked tonight—"

"Now, now," the other ex-soldier said. "Hawkshaw's all right. Come on, Hawk; jump in."

"Will Mayes never done it, boys," the barber said. "If anybody done it. Why, you all know well as I do there aint any town where they got better niggers than us. And you know how a lady will kind of think things about men when there aint any reason to, and Miss Minnie anyway—"

"Sure, sure," the soldier said. "We're just going to talk to him a little; that's all."

"Talk hell!" Butch said. "When we're through with the—"

"Shut up, for God's sake!" the soldier said. "Do you want everybody in town—"

"Tell them, by God!" McLendon said. "Tell every one of the sons that'll let a white woman—"

"Let's go; let's go: here's the other car." The second car slid squealing out of a cloud of dust at the alley mouth. McLendon started his car and took the lead. Dust lay like a fog in the street. The street lights hung nimbused as in water. They drove out of town.

A rutted lane turned at right angles. Dust hung above it too, and above all the land. The dark bulk of the ice plant, where the Negro Mayes was night watchman, rose against the sky. "Better stop here, hadn't we?" the soldier said. McLendon did not reply. He hurled the car up and slammed to a stop, the headlights glaring on the blank wall.

"Listen here, boys," the barber said; "if he's here, dont that prove he never done it? Dont it? If it was him, he would run. Dont you see he would?" The second car came up and stopped. McLendon got down; Butch sprang down beside him. "Listen, boys," the barber said.

"Cut the lights off!" McLendon said. The breathless dark rushed down. There was no sound in it save their lungs as they sought air in the parched dust in which for two months they had lived; then the diminishing crunch of McLendon's and Butch's feet, and a moment later McLendon's voice:

"Will! ... Will!"

Below the east the wan hemorrhage of the moon increased. It heaved above the ridge, silvering the air, the dust, so that they seemed to breathe, live, in a bowl of molten lead. There was no sound of nightbird nor insect, no sound save their breathing and a faint ticking of contracting metal about the cars. Where their bodies touched one another they seemed to sweat dryly, for no more moisture came. "Christ!" a voice said; "let's get out of here."

But they didn't move until vague noises began to grow out of the darkness ahead; then they got out and waited tensely in the breathless dark. There was another sound: a blow, a hissing expulsion of breath and McLendon cursing in undertone. They stood a moment longer, then they ran forward. They ran in a stumbling clump, as though they were fleeing something. "Kill him, kill the son," a voice whispered. McLendon flung them back.

"Not here," he said. "Get him into the car." "Kill him, kill the black son!" the voice murmured. They dragged the Negro to the car. The barber had waited beside the car. He could feel himself sweating and he knew he was going to be sick at the stomach.

"What is it, captains?" the Negro said. "I aint done nothing. 'Fore God, Mr John." Someone produced handcuffs. They worked busily about the Negro as though he were a post, quiet, intent, getting in one another's way. He submitted to the handcuffs, looking swiftly and constantly from dim face to dim face. "Who's here, captains?" he said, leaning to peer into the faces until they could feel his breath and smell his sweaty reek. He spoke a name or two. "What you all say I done, Mr John?"

McLendon jerked the car door open. "Get in!" he said.

The Negro did not move. "What you all going to do with me, Mr John? I aint done nothing. White folks, captains, I aint done nothing: I swear 'fore God." He called another name.

"Get in!" McLendon said. He struck the Negro. The others expelled their breath in a dry hissing and struck him with random blows and he whirled and cursed them, and swept his manacled hands across their faces and slashed the barber upon the mouth, and the barber struck him also. "Get him in there," McLendon said. They pushed at him. He ceased struggling and got in and sat quietly as the others took their places. He sat between the barber and the soldier, drawing his limbs in so as not to touch them, his eyes going swiftly and constantly from face to face. Butch clung to the running board. The car moved on. The barber nursed his mouth with his handkerchief.

"What's the matter, Hawk?" the soldier said.

"Nothing," the barber said. They regained the highroad and turned away from town. The second car dropped back out of the dust. They went on, gaining speed; the final fringe of houses dropped behind.

"Goddamn, he stinks!" the soldier said.

"We'll fix that," the drummer in front beside McLendon said. On the running board Butch cursed into the hot rush of air. The barber leaned suddenly forward and touched McLendon's arm.

"Let me out, John," he said.

"Jump out, niggerlover," McLendon said without turning his head. He drove swiftly. Behind them the sourceless lights of the second car glared in the dust. Presently McLendon turned into a narrow road. It was rutted with disuse. It led back to an abandoned brick kiln—a series of reddish mounds and weed- and vine-choked vats without bottom. It had been used for pasture once, until one day the owner missed one of his mules. Although he prodded carefully in the vats with a long pole, he could not even find the bottom of them.

"John," the barber said.

"Jump out, then," McLendon said, hurling the car along the ruts. Beside the barber the Negro spoke:

"Mr Henry."

The barber sat forward. The narrow tunnel of the road rushed up and past. Their motion was like an extinct furnace blast: cooler, but utterly dead. The car bounded from rut to rut.

"Mr Henry," the Negro said.

The barber began to tug furiously at the door. "Look out, there!" the soldier said, but the barber had already kicked the door open and swung onto the running board. The soldier leaned across the Negro and grasped at him, but he had already jumped. The car went on without checking speed.

The impetus hurled him crashing through dust-sheathed weeds, into the ditch. Dust puffed about him, and in a thin, vicious crackling of sapless stems he lay choking and retching until the second car passed and died away. Then he rose and limped on until he reached the highroad and turned toward town, brushing at his clothes with his hands. The moon was higher, riding high and clear of the dust at last, and after a while the town began to glare beneath the dust. He went on, limping. Presently he heard cars and the glow of them grew in the dust behind him and he left the road and crouched again in the weeds until they passed. McLendon's car came last now. There were four people in it and Butch was not on the running board.

They went on; the dust swallowed them; the glare and the sound died away. The dust of them hung for a while, but soon the eternal dust absorbed it again. The barber climbed back onto the road and limped on toward town.

IV

As she dressed for supper on that Saturday evening, her own flesh felt like fever. Her hands trembled among the hooks and eyes, and her eyes had a feverish look, and her hair swirled crisp and crackling under the comb. While she was still dressing the friends called for her and sat while she donned her sheerest underthings and stockings and a new voile dress. "Do you feel strong enough to go out?" they said, their eyes bright too, with a dark glitter. "When you have had time to get over the shock, you must tell us what happened. What he said and did; everything."

In the leafed darkness, as they walked toward the square, she began to breathe deeply, something like a swimmer preparing to dive, until she ceased trembling, the four of them walking slowly because of the terrible heat and out of solicitude for her. But as they neared the square she began to tremble again, walking with her head up, her hands clenched at her sides, their voices about her murmurous, also with that feverish, glittering quality of their eyes.

They entered the square, she in the center of the group, fragile in her fresh dress. She was trembling worse. She walked slower and slower, as children eat ice cream, her head up and her eyes bright in the haggard banner of her face, passing the hotel and the coatless drummers in chairs along the curb looking around at her: "That's the one: see? The one in pink in the middle." "Is that her? What did they do with the nigger? Did they—?" "Sure. He's all right." "All right, is he?" "Sure. He went on a little trip." Then the drug store, where even the young men lounging in the doorway tipped their hats and followed with their eyes the motion of her hips and legs when she passed.

They went on, passing the lifted hats of the gentlemen, the suddenly ceased voices, deferent, protective. "Do you see?" the friends said. Their voices sounded like long, hovering sighs of hissing exultation. "There's not a Negro on the square. Not one."

They reached the picture show. It was like a miniature fairyland with its lighted lobby and colored lithographs of life caught in its terrible and beautiful mutations. Her lips began to tingle. In the dark, when the picture began, it would be all right; she could hold back the laughing so it would not waste away so fast and so soon. So she hurried on before the turning faces, the undertones of low astonishment, and they took their accustomed places where she could see the aisle against the silver glare and the young men and girls coming in two and two against it.

The lights flicked away; the screen glowed silver, and soon life began to unfold, beautiful and passionate and sad, while still the young men and girls entered, scented and sibilant in the half dark, their paired backs in silhouette delicate and sleek, their slim, quick bodies awkward, divinely young, while beyond them the silver dream accumulated, inevitably on and on. She began to laugh. In trying to suppress it, it made more noise than ever; heads began to turn. Still laughing, her friends raised her and led her out, and she stood at the curb, laughing on a high, sustained note, until the taxi came up and they helped her in.

They removed the pink voile and the sheer underthings and the stockings, and put her to bed, and cracked ice for her temples, and sent for the doctor. He was hard to locate, so they ministered to her with hushed ejaculations, renewing the ice and fanning her. While the ice was fresh and cold she stopped laughing and lay still for a time, moaning only a little. But soon the laughing welled again and her voice rose screaming.

"Shhhhhhhhhhh! Shhhhhhhhhhhhhh!" they said, freshening the icepack, smoothing her hair, examining it for gray; "poor girl!" Then to one another: "Do you suppose anything really happened?" their eyes darkly aglitter, secret and passionate. "Shhhhhhhhhh! Poor girl! Poor Minnie!"

V

It was midnight when McLendon drove up to his neat new house. It was trim and fresh as a birdcage and almost as small, with its clean, green-and-white paint. He locked the car and mounted the porch and entered. His wife rose from a chair beside the reading lamp. McLendon stopped in the floor and stared at her until she looked down.

"Look at that clock," he said, lifting his arm, pointing. She stood before him, her face lowered, a magazine in her hands. Her face was pale, strained, and weary-looking. "Haven't I told you about sitting up like this, waiting to see when I come in?"

"John," she said. She laid the magazine down. Poised on the balls of his feet, he glared at her with his hot eyes, his sweating face.

"Didn't I tell you?" He went toward her. She looked up then. He caught her shoulder. She stood passive, looking at him.

"Dont, John. I couldn't sleep . . . The heat; something. Please, John. You're hurting me."

"Didn't I tell you?" He released her and half struck, half flung her across the chair, and she lay there and watched him quietly as he left the room.

He went on through the house, ripping off his shirt, and on the dark, screened porch at the rear he stood and mopped his head and shoulders with the shirt and flung it away. He took the pistol from his hip and laid it on the table beside the bed, and sat on the bed and removed his shoes, and rose and slipped his trousers off. He was sweating again already, and he stooped and hunted furiously for the shirt. At last he found it and wiped his body again, and, with his body pressed against the dusty screen, he stood panting. There was no movement, no sound, not even an insect. The dark world seemed to lie stricken beneath the cold moon and the lidless stars.

F. Scott Fitzgerald

(1896–1940)

America during the 1920s, the era of the Jazz Age, had its prophet and historian in Francis Scott Key Fitzgerald, whose writing conveys his mixed feelings of attraction and repulsion for a society dizzied by material success and devoted to a search for pleasure. Fitzgerald was always fascinated by the rich, by their confidence and careless grace; and it was partly this which drove him to seek social rather than academic success at Princeton, which he attended from 1913 to 1917. When America entered the war in 1917, he joined the army as a lieutenant; and while in training camp he produced the manuscript of his first novel, published in 1920 as *This Side of Paradise*. The financial success of this work made it possible for him to marry Zelda Sayre, the reckless and unconventional daughter of a respectable Alabama judge; but despite the romantic promise of its beginnings, their relationship was a stormy one, culminating in Zelda's insanity and their gradual separation in the 1930s. Spurred on by his early success, as well as by his constant need of money, Fitzgerald began writing for popular periodicals, and many of his best stories were gathered in such collections as *Flappers and Philosophers* (1921) and *Tales of the Jazz Age* (1922). *The Great Gatsby,* perhaps his finest work, appeared in 1925; in it, he captured the extraordinary flavor of a time when dreams were grounded in deception, when fulfillment led only to excess, when the noble possibilities inherent in wealth attracted vulgarity and brutality. Fitzgerald's later novels, *Tender Is the Night* (1934) and the incomplete *The Last Tycoon* (1941), show a maturing of his powers, but lack the imaginative conviction and concentration of *Gatsby*.

Most of his work reflects a sober awareness of man's capacity for illusion; and it is appropriate that he should have spent some years writing film scripts in Hollywood. In his own life he behaved like the heroes of some of his stories, enjoying the luxuries of the good life, traveling, partying; yet like the age he portrayed, he suffered a slump, a state of "emotional bankruptcy" (a phrase of his own) from which he never wholly recovered. Like Dexter Green in "Winter Dreams" (*All the Sad Young Men,* 1926), he found life less romantically satisfying than it had seemed when he was young. In "The Crack-Up," an autobiographical essay published in 1935, Fitzgerald commented despondently: "the natural state of the sentient adult is a qualified unhappiness. I think also that in an adult the desire to be finer in grain than you are . . . only adds to this unhappiness in the end—that end that comes to our youth and hope."

For further reading

Malcolm Cowley, "F. Scott Fitzgerald: The Romance of Money," *Western Review,* 17 (Summer 1953), 245–255.
Arthur Mizener, *The Far Side of Paradise* (Boston: Houghton Mifflin, 1951).
Edmund Wilson, ed., *The Crack-Up* (New York: New Directions, 1942).

Winter Dreams

Some of the caddies were poor as sin and lived in one-room houses with a neurasthenic cow in the front yard, but Dexter Green's father owned the second best grocery-store in Black Bear—the best one was "The Hub," patronized by the wealthy people from Sherry Island— and Dexter caddied only for pocket-money.

In the fall when the days became crisp and gray, and the long Minnesota winter shut down like the white lid of a box, Dexter's skis moved over the snow that hid the fairways of the golf course. At these times the country gave him a feeling of profound melancholy —it offended him that the links should lie in enforced fallowness, haunted by ragged sparrows for the long season. It was dreary, too, that on the tees where the gay colors fluttered in summer there were now only the desolate sand-boxes knee-deep in crusted ice. When he crossed the hills the wind blew cold as misery, and if the sun was out he tramped with his eyes squinted up against the hard dimensionless glare.

In April the winter ceased abruptly. The snow ran down into Black Bear Lake scarcely tarrying for the early golfers to brave the season with red and black balls. Without elation, without an interval of moist glory, the cold was gone.

Dexter knew that there was something dismal about this Northern spring, just as he knew there was something gorgeous about the fall. Fall made him clinch his hands and tremble and repeat idiotic sentences to himself, and make brisk abrupt gestures of command to imaginary audiences and armies. October filled him with hope which November raised to a sort of ecstatic triumph, and in this mood the fleeting brilliant impressions of the summer at Sherry Island were ready grist to his mill. He became a golf champion and defeated Mr. T. A. Hedrick in a marvellous match played a hundred times over the fairways of his imagination, a match each detail of which he changed about untiringly—sometimes he won with almost laughable ease, sometimes he came up magnificently from behind. Again, stepping from a Pierce-Arrow automobile, like Mr. Mortimer Jones, he strolled frigidly into the lounge of the Sherry Island Golf Club—or perhaps, surrounded by an admiring crowd, he gave an exhibition of fancy diving from the spring-board of the club raft. ... Among those who watched him in open-mouthed wonder was Mr. Mortimer Jones.

And one day it came to pass that Mr. Jones—himself and not his ghost—came up to Dexter with tears in his eyes and said that Dexter was the — — best caddy in the club, and wouldn't he decide not to quit if Mr. Jones made it worth his while, because every other — — caddy in the club lost one ball a hole for him—regularly — —

"No, sir," said Dexter decisively, "I don't want to caddy any more." Then, after a pause: "I'm too old."

"You're not more than fourteen. Why the devil did you decide just this morning that you wanted to quit? You promised that next week you'd go over to the State tournament with me."

"I decided I was too old."

Dexter handed in his "A Class" badge, collected what money was due him from the caddy master, and walked home to Black Bear Village.

"The best — — caddy I ever saw," shouted Mr. Mortimer Jones over a drink that afternoon. "Never lost a ball! Willing! Intelligent! Quiet! Honest! Grateful!"

The little girl who had done this was eleven—beautifully ugly as little girls are apt to be who are destined after a few years to be inexpressibly lovely and bring no end of misery to a great number of men. The spark, however, was perceptible. There was a general ungodliness in the way her lips twisted down at the corners when she smiled, and in the—Heaven help us!—in the almost passionate quality of her eyes. Vitality is born in such women. It was utterly in evidence now, shining through her thin frame in a sort of glow.

She had come eagerly out on to the course at nine o'clock with a white linen nurse and five small new golf-clubs in a white canvas bag which the nurse was carrying. When Dexter first saw her she was standing by the caddy house, rather ill at ease and trying to conceal the fact by engaging her nurse in an obviously unnatural conversation graced by startling and irrelevant grimaces from herself.

"Well, it's certainly a nice day, Hilda," Dexter heard her say. She drew down the corners of her mouth, smiled, and glanced furtively around, her eyes in transit falling for an instant on Dexter.

Then to the nurse:

"Well, I guess there aren't very many people out here this morning, are there?"

The smile again—radiant, blatantly artificial—convincing.

"I don't know what we're supposed to do now," said the nurse, looking nowhere in particular.

"Oh, that's all right. I'll fix it up."

Dexter stood perfectly still, his mouth slightly ajar. He knew that if he moved forward a step his stare would be in her line of vision —if he moved backward he would lose his full view of her face. For a moment he had not realized how young she was. Now he remembered having seen her several times the year before—in bloomers.

Suddenly, involuntarily, he laughed, a short abrupt laugh—then, startled by himself, he turned and began to walk quickly away.

"Boy!"

Dexter stopped.

"Boy— —"

Beyond question he was addressed. Not only that, but he was treated to that absurd smile, that preposterous smile—the memory of which at least a dozen men were to carry into middle age.

"Boy, do you know where the golf teacher is?"

"He's giving a lesson."

"Well, do you know where the caddy-master is?"

"He isn't here yet this morning."

"Oh." For a moment this baffled her. She stood alternately on her right and left foot.

"We'd like to get a caddy," said the nurse. "Mrs. Mortimer Jones sent us out to play golf, and we don't know how without we get a caddy."

Here she was stopped by an ominous glance from Miss Jones, followed immediately by the smile.

"There aren't any caddies here except me," said Dexter to the nurse, "and I got to stay here in charge until the caddy-master gets here."

"Oh."

Miss Jones and her retinue now withdrew, and at a proper distance from Dexter became involved in a heated conversation, which was concluded by Miss Jones taking one of the clubs and hitting it on the ground with violence. For further emphasis she raised it again and was about to bring it down smartly upon the nurse's bosom, when the nurse seized the club and twisted it from her hands.

"You damn little mean old *thing!*" cried Miss Jones wildly.

Another argument ensued. Realizing that the elements of comedy were implied in the scene, Dexter several times began to laugh, but each time restrained the laugh before it reached audibility. He could not resist the monstrous conviction that the little girl was justified in beating the nurse.

The situation was resolved by the fortuitous appearance of the caddy-master, who was appealed to immediately by the nurse.

"Miss Jones is to have a little caddy, and this one says he can't go."

"Mr. McKenna said I was to wait here till you came," said Dexter quickly.

"Well, he's here now." Miss Jones smiled cheerfully at the caddy-master. Then she dropped her bag and set off at a haughty mince toward the first tee.

"Well?" The caddy-master turned to Dexter. "What you standing there like a dummy for? Go pick up the young lady's clubs."

"I don't think I'll go out to-day, " said Dexter.

"You don't— —"

"I think I'll quit."

The enormity of his decision frightened him. He was a favorite caddy, and the thirty dollars a month he earned through the summer were not be be made elsewhere around the lake. But he had received a strong emotional shock, and his perturbation required a violent and immediate outlet.

It is not so simple as that, either. As so frequently would be the case in the future, Dexter was unconsciously dictated to by his winter dreams.

II

Now, of course, the quality and the seasonability of these winter dreams varied, but the stuff of them remained. They persuaded Dexter several years later to pass up a business course at the State university—his father, prospering now, would have paid his way—for the precarious advantage of attending an older and more famous university in the East, where he was bothered by his scanty funds. But do not get the impression, because his winter dreams happened to be concerned at first with musings on the rich, that there was anything merely snobbish in the boy. He wanted not association with glittering things and glittering people—he wanted the glittering things themselves. Often he reached out for the best without knowing why he wanted it—and sometimes he ran up against the mysterious denials and prohibitions in which life indulges. It is with one of those denials and not with his career as a whole that this story deals.

He made money. It was rather amazing. After college he went to the city from which Black Bear Lake draws its wealthy patrons. When he was only twenty-three and had been there not quite two years, there were already people who liked to say: "Now *there's* a boy—" All about him rich men's sons were peddling bonds precariously, or investing patrimonies precariously, or plodding through the two dozen volumes of the "George Washington Commercial Course," but Dexter borrowed a thousand dollars on his college degree and his confident mouth, and bought a partnership in a laundry.

It was a small laundry when he went into it, but Dexter made a specialty of learning how the English washed fine woolen golf-stockings without shrinking them, and within a year he was catering to the trade that wore knickerbockers. Men were insisting that their Shetland hose and sweaters go to his laundry, just as they had insisted on a caddy who could find golf-balls. A little later he was doing their wives' lingerie as well—and running five branches in different parts of the city. Before he was twenty-seven he owned the largest string of laundries in his section of the country. It was then that he sold out and went to New York. But the part of his story that concerns us goes back to the days when he was making his first big success.

When he was twenty-three Mr. Hart—one of the gray-haired men who like to say "Now there's a boy"—gave him a guest card to the Sherry Island Golf Club for a week-end. So he signed his name one day on the register, and that afternoon played golf in a foursome with Mr. Hart and Mr. Sandwood and Mr. T. A. Hedrick. He did not consider it necessary to remark that he had once carried Mr. Hart's bag over this same links, and that he knew every trap and gully with his eyes shut—but he found himself glancing at the four caddies who trailed them, trying to catch a gleam or gesture that would remind him of himself, that would lessen the gap which lay between his present and his past.

It was a curious day, slashed abruptly with fleeting, familiar impressions. One minute he had the sense of being a trespasser—in the next he was impressed by the tremendous superiority he felt toward Mr. T. A. Hedrick, who was a bore and not even a good golfer any more.

Then, because of a ball Mr. Hart lost near the fifteenth green, an enormous thing happened. While they were searching the stiff grasses of the rough there was a clear call of "Fore!" from behind a hill in their rear. And as they all turned abruptly from their search a bright new ball sliced abruptly over the hill and caught Mr. T. A. Hedrick in the abdomen.

"By Gad!" cried Mr. T. A. Hedrick, "they ought to put some of these crazy women off the course. It's getting to be outrageous."

A head and a voice came up together over the hill:

"Do you mind if we go through?"

"You hit me in the stomach!" declared Mr. Hedrick wildly.

"Did I?" The girl approached the group of men. "I'm sorry. I yelled 'Fore!' "

Her glance fell casually on each of the men—then scanned the fairway for her ball.

"Did I bounce into the rough?"

It was impossible to determine whether this question was ingenuous or malicious. In a moment, however, she left no doubt, for as her partner came up over the hill she called cheerfully:

"Here I am! I'd have gone on the green except that I hit something."

As she took her stance for a short mashie shot, Dexter looked at her closely. She wore a blue gingham dress, rimmed at throat and shoulders with a white edging that accentuated her tan. The quality of exaggeration, of thinness, which had made her passionate eyes and

down-turning mouth absurd at eleven, was gone now. She was ar-
restingly beautiful. The color in her checks was centered like the
color in a picture—it was not a "high" color, but a sort of fluctuating
and feverish warmth, so shaded that it seemed at any moment it
would recede and disappear. This color and the mobility of her
mouth gave a continual impression of flux, of intense life, of passionate vitality—balanced only partially by the sad luxury of her eyes.

She swung her mashie impatiently and without interest, pitching
the ball into a sand-pit on the other side of the green. With a quick,
insincere smile and a careless "Thank you!" she went on after it.

"That Judy Jones!" remarked Mr. Hedrick on the next tee, as they
waited—some moments—for her to play on ahead. "All she needs is
to be turned up and spanked for six months and then to be married
off to an old-fashioned cavalry captain."

"My God, she's good-looking!" said Mr. Sandwood, who was just
over thirty.

"Good-looking!" cried Mr. Hedrick contemptuously. "She always
looks as if she wanted to be kissed! Turning those big cow-eyes on
every calf in town!"

It was doubtful if Mr. Hedrick intended a reference to the maternal instinct.

"She'd play pretty good golf if she'd try," said Mr. Sandwood.

"She has no form," said Mr. Hedrick solemnly.

"She has a nice figure," said Mr. Sandwood.

"Better thank the Lord she doesn't drive a swifter ball," said Mr.
Hart, winking at Dexter.

Later in the afternoon the sun went down with a riotous swirl of
gold and varying blues and scarlets, and left the dry, rustling night
of Western summer. Dexter watched from the veranda of the Golf
Club, watched the even overlap of the waters in the little wind,
silver molasses under the harvest-moon. Then the moon held a
finger to her lips and the lake became a clear pool, pale and quiet.
Dexter put on his bathing-suit and swam out to the farthest raft,
where he stretched dripping on the wet canvas of the springboard.

There was a fish jumping and a star shining and the lights around
the lake were gleaming. Over on a dark peninsula a piano was playing the songs of last summer and of summers before that—songs
from "Chin-Chin" and "The Count of Luxemburg" and "The Chocolate Soldier"—and because the sound of a piano over a stretch of
water had always seemed beautiful to Dexter he lay perfectly quiet
and listened.

The tune the piano was playing at that moment had been gay and
new five years before when Dexter was a sophomore at college. They
had played it at a prom once when he could not afford the luxury

of proms, and he had stood outside the gymnasium and listened. The sound of the tune precipitated in him a sort of ecstasy and it was with that ecstasy he viewed what happened to him now. It was a mood of intense appreciation, a sense that, for once, he was magnificently attuned to life and that everything about him was radiating a brightness and a glamour he might never know again.

A low, pale oblong detached itself suddenly from the darkness of the Island, spitting forth the reverberated sound of a racing motor-boat. Two white streamers of cleft water rolled themselves out behind it and almost immediately the boat was beside him, drowning out the hot tinkle of the piano in the drone of its spray. Dexter raising himself on his arms was aware of a figure standing at the wheel, of two dark eyes regarding him over the lengthening space of water—then the boat had gone by and was sweeping in an immense and purposeless circle of spray round and round in the middle of the lake. With equal eccentricity one of the circles flattened out and headed back toward the raft.

"Who's that?" she called, shutting off her motor. She was so near now that Dexter could see her bathing-suit, which consisted apparently of pink rompers.

The nose of the boat bumped the raft, and as the latter tilted rakishly he was precipitated toward her. With different degrees of interest they recognized each other.

"Aren't you one of those men we played through this afternoon?" she demanded.

He was.

"Well, do you know how to drive a motor-boat? Because if you do I wish you'd drive this one so I can ride on the surf-board behind. My name is Judy Jones"—she favored him with an absurd smirk—rather, what tried to be a smirk, for, twist her mouth as she might, it was not grotesque, it was merely beautiful—"and I live in a house over there on the Island, and in that house there is a man waiting for me. When he drove up at the door I drove out of the dock because he says I'm his ideal."

There was a fish jumping and a star shining and the lights around the lake were gleaming. Dexter sat beside Judy Jones and she explained how her boat was driven. Then she was in the water, swimming to the floating surf-board with a sinuous crawl. Watching her was without effort to the eye, watching a branch waving or a sea-gull flying. Her arms, burned to butternut, moved sinuously among the dull platinum ripples, elbow appearing first, casting the forearm back with a cadence of falling water, then reaching out and down, stabbing a path ahead.

They moved out into the lake; turning, Dexter saw that she was kneeling on the low rear of the now uptilted surf-board.

"Go faster," she called, "fast as it'll go."

Obediently he jammed the lever forward and the white spray mounted at the bow. When he looked around again the girl was standing up on the rushing board, her arms spread wide, her eyes lifted toward the moon.

"It's awful cold," she shouted. "What's your name?"

He told her.

"Well, why don't you come to dinner to-morrow night?"

His heart turned over like the fly-wheel of the boat, and, for the second time, her casual whim gave a new direction to his life.

III

Next evening while he waited for her to come down-stairs, Dexter peopled the soft deep summer room and the sun-porch that opened from it with the men who had already loved Judy Jones. He knew the sort of men they were—the men who when he first went to college had entered from the great prep schools with graceful clothes and the deep tan of healthy summers. He had seen that, in one sense, he was better than these men. He was newer and stronger. Yet in acknowledging to himself that he wished his children to be like them he was admitting that he was but the rough, strong stuff from which they eternally sprang.

When the time had come for him to wear good clothes, he had known who were the best tailors in America, and the best tailors in America had made him the suit he wore this evening. He had acquired that particular reserve peculiar to his university, that set it off from other universities. He recognized the value to him of such a mannerism and he had adopted it; he knew that to be careless in dress and manner required more confidence than to be careful. But carelessness was for his children. His mother's name had been Krimplich. She was a Bohemian of the peasant class and she had talked broken English to the end of her days. Her son must keep to the set patterns.

At a little after seven Judy Jones came down-stairs. She wore a blue silk afternoon dress, and he was disappointed at first that she had not put on something more elaborate. This feeling was accentuated when, after a brief greeting, she went to the door of a butler's pantry and pushing it open called: "You can serve dinner, Martha." He had rather expected that a butler would announce dinner, that there would be a cocktail. Then he put these thoughts behind him as they sat down side by side on a lounge and looked at each other.

"Father and mother won't be here," she said thoughtfully.

He remembered the last time he had seen her father, and he was glad the parents were not to be here to-night—they might wonder who he was. He had been born in Keeble, a Minnesota village fifty miles farther north, and he always gave Keeble as his home instead of Black Bear Village. Country towns were well enough to come from if they weren't inconveniently in sight and used as footstools by fashionable lakes.

They talked of his university, which she had visited frequently during the past two years, and of the near-by city which supplied Sherry Island with its patrons, and whither Dexter would return next day to his prospering laundries.

During dinner she slipped into a moody depression which gave Dexter a feeling of uneasiness. Whatever petulance she uttered in her throaty voice worried him. Whatever she smiled at—at him, at a chicken liver, at nothing—it disturbed him that her smile could have no root in mirth, or even in amusement. When the scarlet corners of her lips curved down, it was less a smile than an invitation to a kiss.

Then, after dinner, she led him out on the dark sun-porch and deliberately changed the atmosphere.

"Do you mind if I weep a little?" she said.

"I'm afraid I'm boring you," he responded quickly.

"You're not. I like you. But I've just had a terrible afternoon. There was a man I cared about, and this afternoon he told me out of a clear sky that he was poor as a churchmouse. He'd never even hinted it before. Does this sound horribly mundane?"

"Perhaps he was afraid to tell you."

"Suppose he was," she answered. "He didn't start right. You see, if I'd thought of him as poor—well, I've been mad about loads of poor men, and fully intended to marry them all. But in this case, I hadn't thought of him that way, and my interest in him wasn't strong enough to survive the shock. As if a girl calmly informed her fiancé that she was a widow. He might not object to widows, but— —

"Let's start right," she interrupted herself suddenly. "Who are you, anyhow?"

For a moment Dexter hesitated. Then:

"I'm nobody," he announced. "My career is largely a matter of futures."

"Are you poor?"

"No," he said frankly, "I'm probably making more money than any man my age in the Northwest. I know that's an obnoxious remark, but you advised me to start right."

There was a pause. Then she smiled and the corners of her mouth drooped and an almost imperceptible sway brought her closer to him, looking up into his eyes. A lump rose in Dexter's throat, and he waited breathless for the experiment, facing the unpredictable compound that would form mysteriously from the elements of their lips. Then he saw—she communicated her excitement to him, lavishly, deeply, with kisses that were not a promise but a fulfillment. They aroused in him not hunger demanding renewal but surfeit that would demand more surfeit ... kisses that were like charity, creating want by holding back nothing at all.

It did not take him many hours to decide that he had wanted Judy Jones ever since he was a proud, desirous little boy.

IV

It began like that—and continued, with varying shades of intensity, on such a note right up to the dénouement. Dexter surrendered a part of himself to the most direct and unprincipled personality with which he had ever come in contact. Whatever Judy wanted, she went after with the full pressure of her charm. There was no divergence of method, no jockeying for position or premeditation of effects —there was a very little mental side to any of her affairs. She simply made men conscious to the highest degree of her physical loveliness. Dexter had no desire to change her. Her deficiencies were knit up with a passionate energy that transcended and justified them.

When, as Judy's head lay against his shoulder that first night, she whispered, "I don't know what's the matter with me. Last night I thought I was in love with a man and to-night I think I'm in love with you— —" —it seemed to him a beautiful and romantic thing to say. It was the exquisite excitability that for the moment he controlled and owned. But a week later he was compelled to view this same quality in a different light. She took him in her roadster to a picnic supper, and after supper she disappeared, likewise in her roadster, with another man. Dexter became enormously upset and was scarcely able to be decently civil to the other people present. When she assured him that she had not kissed the other man, he knew she was lying—yet he was glad that she had taken the trouble to lie to him.

He was, as he found before the summer ended, one of a varying dozen who circulated about her. Each of them had at one time been favored above all others—about half of them still basked in the solace of occasional sentimental revivals. Whenever one showed signs of dropping out through long neglect, she granted him a brief honeyed hour, which encouraged him to tag along for a year or so longer. Judy made these forays upon the helpless and defeated without malice, indeed half unconscious that there was anything mischievous in what she did.

When a new man came to town every one dropped out—dates were automatically cancelled.

The helpless part of trying to do anything about it was that she did it all herself. She was not a girl who could be "won" in the kinetic sense—she was proof against cleverness, she was proof against charm; if any of these assailed her too strongly she would immediately resolve the affair to a physical basis, and under the magic of her physical splendor the strong as well as the brilliant played her game and not their own. She was entertained only by the gratification of her desires and by the direct exercise of her own charm. Perhaps from so much youthful love, so many youthful lovers, she had come, in self-defense, to nourish herself wholly from within.

Succeeding Dexter's first exhilaration came restlessness and dissatisfaction. The helpless ecstasy of losing himself in her was opiate rather than tonic. It was fortunate for his work during the winter that those moments of ecstasy came infrequently. Early in their acquaintance it had seemed for a while that there was a deep and spontaneous mutual attraction—that first August, for example—three days of long evenings on her dusky veranda, of strange wan kisses through the late afternoon, in shadowy alcoves or behind the protecting trellises of the garden arbors, of mornings when she was fresh as a dream and almost shy at meeting him in the clarity of the rising day. There was all the ecstasy of an engagement about it, sharpened by his realization that there was no engagement. It was during those three days that, for the first time, he had asked her to marry him. She said "maybe some day," she said "kiss me," she said "I'd like to marry you," she said "I love you"—she said—nothing.

The three days were interrupted by the arrival of a New York man who visited at her house for half September. To Dexter's agony, rumor engaged them. The man was the son of the president of a great trust company. But at the end of a month it was reported that Judy was yawning. At a dance one night she sat all evening in a motorboat with a local beau, while the New Yorker searched the club for her frantically. She told the local beau that she was bored with her visitor, and two days later he left. She was seen with him at the station, and it was reported that he looked very mournful indeed.

On this note the summer ended. Dexter was twenty-four, and he found himself increasingly in a position to do as he wished. He joined two clubs in the city and lived at one of them. Though he was by no means an integral part of the stag-lines at these clubs, he managed to be on hand at dances where Judy Jones was likely to appear. He could have gone out socially as much as he liked—he was an eligible young man, now, and popular with down-town fathers. His confessed devotion to Judy Jones had rather solidified his position. But he had no social aspirations and rather despised the dancing men who were always on tap for the Thursday or Saturday parties and who filled in at dinners with the younger married set. Already he was playing with the idea of going East to New York. He wanted to take Judy Jones with him. No disillusion as to the world in which she had grown up could cure his illusion as to her desirability.

Remember that—for only in the light of it can what he did for her be understood.

Eighteen months after he first met Judy Jones he became engaged to another girl. Her name was Irene Scheerer, and her father was one of the men who had always believed in Dexter. Irene was light-haired and sweet and honorable, and a little stout, and she had two suitors whom she pleasantly relinquished when Dexter formally asked her to marry him.

Summer, fall, winter, spring, another summer, another fall—so much he had given of his active life to the incorrigible lips of Judy Jones. She had treated him with interest, with encouragement, with malice, with indifference, with contempt. She had inflicted on him the innumerable little slights and indignities possible in such a case —as if in revenge for having ever cared for him at all. She had beckoned him and yawned at him and beckoned him again and he had responded often with bitterness and narrowed eyes. She had brought him ecstatic happiness and intolerable agony of spirit. She had caused him untold inconvenience and not a little trouble. She had insulted him, and she had ridden over him, and she had played his interest in her against his interest in his work—for fun. She had done everything to him except to criticise him—this she had not done—it seemed to him only because it might have sullied the utter indifference she manifested and sincerely felt toward him.

When autumn had come and gone again it occurred to him that he could not have Judy Jones. He had to beat this into his mind but he convinced himself at last. He lay awake at night for a while and argued it over. He told himself the trouble and the pain she had caused him, he enumerated her glaring deficiencies as a wife. Then he said to himself that he loved her, and after a while he fell asleep. For a week, lest he imagined her husky voice over the telephone or her eyes opposite him at lunch, he worked hard and late, and at night he went to his office and plotted out his years.

At the end of a week he went to a dance and cut in on her once. For almost the first time since they had met he did not ask her to sit out with him or tell her that she was lovely. It hurt him that she did not miss these things—that was all. He was not jealous when he saw that there was a new man to-night. He had been hardened against jealousy long before.

He stayed late at the dance. He sat for an hour with Irene Scheerer and talked about books and about music. He knew very little about either. But he was beginning to be master of his own time now, and he had a rather priggish notion that he—the young and already fabulously successful Dexter Green—should know more about such things.

That was in October, when he was twenty-five. In January, Dexter and Irene became engaged. It was to be announced in June, and they were to be married three months later.

The Minnesota winter prolonged itself interminably, and it was almost May when the winds came soft and the snow ran down into Black Bear Lake at last. For the first time in over a year Dexter was enjoying a certain tranquillity of spirit. Judy Jones had been in Florida, and afterward in Hot Springs, and somewhere she had been engaged, and somewhere she had broken it off. At first, when Dexter had definitely given her up, it had made him sad that people still linked them together and asked for news of her, but when he began to be placed at dinner next to Irene Scheerer people didn't ask him about her any more—they told him about her. He ceased to be an authority on her.

May at last. Dexter walked the streets at night when the darkness was damp as rain, wondering that so soon, with so little done, so much of ecstasy had gone from him. May one year back had been marked by Judy's poignant, unforgivable, yet forgiven turbulence— it had been one of those rare times when he fancied she had grown to care for him. That old penny's worth of happiness he had spent for this bushel of content. He knew that Irene would be no more than a curtain spread behind him, a hand moving among gleaming tea-cups, a voice calling to children . . . fire and loveliness were gone, the magic of nights and the wonder of the varying hours and seasons . . . slender lips, down-turning, dropping to his lips and bearing him up into a heaven of eyes. . . . The thing was deep in him. He was too strong and alive for it to die lightly.

In the middle of May when the weather balanced for a few days on the thin bridge that led to deep summer he turned in one night at Irene's house. Their engagement was to be announced in a week now—no one would be surprised at it. And to-night they would sit together on the lounge at the University Club and look on for an hour at the dancers. It gave him a sense of solidity to go with her —she was so sturdily popular, so intensely "great."

He mounted the steps of the brownstone house and stepped inside. "Irene," he called.

Mrs. Scheerer came out of the living-room to meet him.

"Dexter," she said, "Irene's gone up-stairs with a splitting head-ache. She wanted to go with you but I made her go to bed."

"Nothing serious, I— —"

"Oh, no. She's going to play golf with you in the morning. You can spare her for just one night, can't you Dexter?"

Her smile was kind. She and Dexter liked each other. In the living-room he talked for a moment before he said good-night.

Returning to the University Club, where he had rooms, he stood in the doorway for a moment and watched the dancers. He leaned against the door-post, nodded at a man or two—yawned.

"Hello, darling."

The familiar voice at his elbow startled him. Judy Jones had left a man and crossed the room to him—Judy Jones, a slender enamelled doll in cloth of gold: gold in a band at her head, gold in two slipper points at her dress's hem. The fragile glow of her face seemed to blossom as she smiled at him. A breeze of warmth and light blew through the room. His hands in the pockets of his dinner-jacket tightened spasmodically. He was filled with a sudden excitement.

"When did you get back?" he asked casually.

"Come here and I'll tell you about it."

She turned and he followed her. She had been away—he could have wept at the wonder of her return. She had passed through enchanted streets, doing things that were like provocative music. All mysterious happenings, all fresh and quickening hopes, had gone away with her, come back with her now.

She turned in the doorway.

"Have you a car here? If you haven't, I have."

"I have a coupé."

In then, with a rustle of golden cloth. He slammed the door. Into so many cars she had stepped—like this—like that—her back against the leather, so—her elbow resting on the door—waiting. She would have been soiled long since had there been anything to soil her—except herself—but this was her own self outpouring.

With an effort he forced himself to start the car and back into the street. This was nothing, he must remember. She had done this before, and he had put her behind him, as he would have crossed a bad account from his books.

He drove slowly down-town and, affecting abstraction, traversed the deserted streets of the business section, peopled here and there where a movie was giving out its crowd or where consumptive or pugilistic youth lounged in front of pool halls. The clink of glasses and the slap of hands on the bars issued from saloons, cloisters of glazed glass and dirty yellow light.

She was watching him closely and the silence was embarrassing, yet in this crisis he could find no casual word with which to profane the hour. At a convenient turning he began to zigzag back toward the University Club.

"Have you missed me?" she asked suddenly.

"Everybody missed you."

He wondered if she knew of Irene Scheerer. She had been back only a day—her absence had been almost contemporaneous with his engagement.

"What a remark!" Judy laughed sadly—without sadness. She looked at him searchingly. He became absorbed in the dashboard.

"You're handsomer than you used to be," she said thoughtfully. "Dexter, you have the most rememberable eyes."

He could have laughed at this, but he did not laugh. It was the sort of thing that was said to sophomores. Yet it stabbed at him.

"I'm awfully tired of everything, darling." She called every one darling, endowing the endearment with careless, individual camaraderie. "I wish you'd marry me."

The directness of this confused him. He should have told her now that he was going to marry another girl, but he could not tell her. He could as easily have sworn that he had never loved her.

"I think we'd get along," she continued, on the same note, "unless probably you've forgotten me and fallen in love with another girl."

Her confidence was obviously enormous. She had said, in effect, that she found such a thing impossible to believe, that if it were true he had merely committed a childish indiscretion—and probably to show off. She would forgive him, because it was not a matter of any moment but rather something to be brushed aside lightly.

"Of course you could never love anybody but me," she continued, "I like the way you love me. Oh, Dexter, have you forgotten last year?"

"No, I haven't forgotten."

"Neither have I!"

Was she sincerely moved—or was she carried along by the wave of her own acting?

"I wish we could be like that again," she said, and he forced himself to answer:

"I don't think we can."

"I suppose not. . . . I hear you're giving Irene Scheerer a violent rush."

There was not the faintest emphasis on the name, yet Dexter was suddenly ashamed.

"Oh, take me home," cried Judy suddenly; "I don't want to go back to that idiotic dance—with those children."

Then, as he turned up the street that led to the residence district, Judy began to cry quietly to herself. He had never seen her cry before.

The dark street lightened, the dwellings of the rich loomed up around them, he stopped his coupé in front of the great white bulk of the Mortimer Joneses' house, somnolent, gorgeous, drenched with the splendor of the damp moonlight. Its solidity startled him. The strong walls, the steel of the girders, the breadth and beam and pomp of it were there only to bring out the contrast with the young beauty beside him. It was sturdy to accentuate her slightness—as if to show what a breeze could be generated by a butterfly's wing.

He sat perfectly quiet, his nerves in wild clamor, afraid that if he moved he would find her irresistibly in his arms. Two tears had rolled down her wet face and trembled on her upper lip.

"I'm more beautiful than anybody else," she said brokenly, "why can't I be happy?" Her moist eyes tore at his stability—her mouth turned slowly downward with an exquisite sadness: "I'd like to marry you if you'll have me, Dexter. I suppose you think I'm not worth having, but I'll be so beautiful for you, Dexter."

A million phrases of anger, pride, passion, hatred, tenderness fought on his lips. Then a perfect wave of emotion washed over him, carrying off with it a sediment of wisdom, of convention, of doubt, of honor. This was his girl who was speaking, his own, his beautiful, his pride.

"Won't you come in?" He heard her draw in her breath sharply. Waiting.

"All right," his voice was trembling, "I'll come in."

V

It was strange that neither when it was over nor a long time afterward did he regret that night. Looking at it from the perspective of ten years, the fact that Judy's flare for him endured just one month seemed of little importance. Nor did it matter that by his yielding he subjected himself to a deeper agony in the end and gave serious hurt to Irene Scheerer and to Irene's parents, who had befriended him. There was nothing sufficiently pictorial about Irene's grief to stamp itself on his mind.

Dexter was at bottom hard-minded. The attitude of the city on his action was of no importance to him, not because he was going to leave the city, but because any outside attitude on the situation seemed superficial. He was completely indifferent to popular opinion. Nor, when he had seen that it was no use, that he did not possess in himself the power to move fundamentally or to hold Judy Jones, did he bear any malice toward her. He loved her, and he would love her until the day he was too old for loving—but he could not have her. So he tasted the deep pain that is reserved only for the strong, just as he had tasted for a little while the deep happiness.

Even the ultimate falsity of the grounds upon which Judy terminated the engagement that she did not want to "take him away" from Irene—Judy, who had wanted nothing else—did not revolt him. He was beyond any revulsion or any amusement.

He went East in February with the intention of selling out his laundries and settling in New York—but the war came to America in March and changed his plans. He returned to the West, handed over the management of the business to his partner, and went into the first officers' training-camp in late April. He was one of those young thousands who greeted the war with a certain amount of relief, welcoming the liberation from webs of tangled emotion.

VI

This story is not his biography, remember, although things creep into it which have nothing to do with those dreams he had when he was young. We are almost done with them and with him now. There is only one more incident to be related here, and it happens seven years farther on.

It took place in New York, where he had done well—so well that there were no barriers too high for him. He was thirty-two years old, and, except for one flying trip immediately after the war, he had not been West in seven years. A man named Devlin from Detroit came into his office to see him in a business way, and then and there this incident occurred, and closed out, so to speak, this particular side of his life.

"So you're from the Middle West," said the man Devlin with careless curiosity. "That's funny—I thought men like you were probably born and raised on Wall Street. You know—wife of one of my best friends in Detroit came from your city. I was an usher at the wedding."

Dexter waited with no apprehension of what was coming.

"Judy Simms," said Devlin with no particular interest; "Judy Jones she was once."

"Yes, I knew her." A dull impatience spread over him. He had heard, of course, that she was married—perhaps deliberately he had heard no more.

"Awfully nice girl," brooded Devlin meaninglessly, "I'm sort of sorry for her."

"Why?" Something in Dexter was alert, receptive, at once.

"Oh, Lud Simms has gone to pieces in a way. I don't mean he ill-uses her, but he drinks and runs around— —"

"Doesn't she run around?"

"No. Stays at home with her kids."

"Oh."

"She's a little too old for him," said Devlin.

"Too old!" cried Dexter. "Why, man, she's only twenty-seven."

He was possessed with a wild notion of rushing out into the streets and taking a train to Detroit. He rose to his feet spasmodically.

"I guess you're busy," Devlin apologized quickly. "I didn't realize — —"

"No, I'm not busy," said Dexter, steadying his voice. "I'm not busy at all. Not busy at all. Did you say she was—twenty-seven? No, I said she was twenty-seven."

"Yes, you did," agreed Devlin dryly.

"Go on, then. Go on."

"What do you mean?"

"About Judy Jones."

Devlin looked at him helplessly.

"Well, that's—I told you all there is to it. He treats her like the devil. Oh, they're not going to get divorced or anything. When he's particularly outrageous she forgives him. In fact, I'm inclined to think she loves him. She was a pretty girl when she first came to Detroit."

A pretty girl! The phrase struck Dexter as ludicrous.

"Isn't she—a pretty girl, any more?"

"Oh, she's all right."

"Look here," said Dexter, sitting down suddenly. "I don't understand. You say she was a 'pretty girl' and now you say she's 'all right.' I don't understand what you mean—Judy Jones wasn't a pretty girl, at all. She was a great beauty. Why, I knew her, I knew her. She was — —"

Devlin laughed pleasantly.

"I'm not trying to start a row," he said. "I think Judy's a nice girl and I like her. I can't understand how a man like Lud Simms could fall madly in love with her, but he did." Then he added: "Most of the women like her."

Dexter looked closely at Devlin, thinking widly that there must be a reason for this, some insensitivity in the man or some private malice.

"Lots of women fade just like *that*," Devlin snapped his fingers. "You must have seen it happen. Perhaps I've forgotten how pretty she was at her wedding. I've seen her so much since then, you see. She has nice eyes."

A sort of dullness settled down upon Dexter. For the first time in his life he felt like getting very drunk. He knew that he was laughing loudly at something Devlin had said, but he did not know what it was or why it was funny. When, in a few minutes, Devlin went he lay down on his lounge and looked out the window at the New York sky-line into which the sun was sinking in dull lovely shades of pink and gold.

He had thought that having nothing else to lose he was invulnerable at last—but he knew that he had just lost something more, as surely as if he had married Judy Jones and seen her fade away before his eyes.

The dream was gone. Something had been taken from him. In a sort of panic he pushed the palms of his hands into his eyes and tried to bring up a picture of the waters lapping on Sherry Island and the moonlit veranda, and gingham on the golf-links and the dry sun and the gold color of her neck's soft down. And her mouth damp to his kisses and her eyes plaintive with melancholy and her freshness like new fine linen in the morning. Why, these things were no longer in the world! They had existed and they existed no longer.

For the first time in years the tears were streaming down his face. But they were for himself now. He did not care about mouth and eyes and moving hands. He wanted to care, and he could not care. For he had gone away and he could never go back any more. The gates were closed, the sun was gone down, and there was no beauty but the gray beauty of steel that withstands all time. Even the grief he could have borne was left behind in the country of illusion, of youth, of the richness of life, where his winter dreams had flourished.

"Long ago," he said, "long ago, there was something in me, but now that thing is gone. Now that thing is gone, that thing is gone. I cannot cry. I cannot care. That thing will come back no more."

E. M. Forster

(1879–1970)

Edward Morgan Forster was born in London, into a family connected with the group of wealthy Evangelicals known as the Clapham Sect. His upbringing and education (Tonbridge School and King's College, Cambridge) were solidly middle class; yet despite this background, Forster turned a critical and satirical eye on the snobbery and superficiality of English society. After leaving Cambridge in 1901, he took a journey through Italy and Greece, and in the Mediterranean temperament he perceived qualities of passion and responsiveness very different from the coldness and reserve of the English character. In his novels *Where Angels Fear to Tread* (1905), *The Longest Journey* (1907), and *Howards End* (1910), he exposes middle-class illusions, and sets the deadening force of social convention against the liberating power of feeling, a conflict enacted on both the spiritual and the sexual level. This opposition between social pressures and individual feeling is often expressed as a clash between the rational faculties and the imagination, and it takes on a broader significance in *A Passage to India* (1924), in which two cultures meet but do not merge: the Englishman and the Indian are symbolically parted at the end of that novel, as if to emphasize how the Western mind has lost touch with the deeper springs of intuitive awareness and the sources of natural harmony.

These concerns also find expression in Forster's short stories, collected in *The Celestial Omnibus* (1911) and *The Eternal Moment* (1928), where he gives freer rein to allegorical and mythical tendencies. In "The Road from Colonus" (*The Celestial Omnibus*), Forster juxtaposes the shallowness of contemporary English values with the spirit of life in an ancient land. The title alludes to the story of Oedipus, who, old and blind, was transfigured by his experience in the sacred grove at Colonus, and enabled to meet his death with pride and dignity.

For further reading

E. M. Forster, *Aspects of the Novel* (London: Edward Arnold, 1927; reprinted by Penguin Books, 1962).

F. P. W. McDowell, "Forster's 'Natural Supernaturalism': The Tales," *Modern Fiction Studies,* 7 (1961), 271–283.

Lionel Trilling, *E. M. Forster,* 2d ed. (New York: New Directions, 1964).

The Road from Colonus

I

For no very intelligible reason, Mr Lucas had hurried ahead of his party. He was perhaps reaching the age at which independence becomes valuable, because it is so soon to be lost. Tired of attention and consideration, he liked breaking away from the younger members, to ride by himself, and to dismount unassisted. Perhaps he also relished that more subtle pleasure of being kept waiting for lunch, and of telling the others on their arrival that it was of no consequence.

So, with childish impatience, he battered the animal's sides with his heels, and made the muleteer bang it with a thick stick and prick it with a sharp one, and jolted down the hill sides through clumps of flowering shrubs and stretches of anemones and asphodel, till he heard the sound of running water, and came in sight of the group of plane trees where they were to have their meal.

Even in England those trees would have been remarkable, so huge were they, so interlaced, so magnificently clothed in quivering green. And here in Greece they were unique, the one cool spot in that hard brilliant landscape, already scorched by the heat of an April sun. In their midst was hidden a tiny Khan or country inn, a frail mud building with a broad wooden balcony in which sat an old woman spinning, while a small brown pig, eating orange peel, stood beside her. On the wet earth below squatted two children, playing some primaeval game with their fingers; and their mother, none too clean either, was messing with some rice inside. As Mrs Forman would have said, it was all very Greek, and the fastidious Mr Lucas felt thankful that they were bringing their own food with them, and should eat it in the open air.

Still, he was glad to be there—the muleteer had helped him off— and glad that Mrs Forman was not there to forestall his opinions— glad even that he should not see Ethel for quite half an hour. Ethel was his youngest daughter, still unmarried. She was unselfish and affectionate, and it was generally understood that she was to devote her life to her father, and be the comfort of his old age. Mrs Forman always referred to her as Antigone, and Mr Lucas tried to settle down to the role of Oedipus, which seemed the only one that public opinion allowed him.

He had this in common with Oedipus, that he was growing old. Even to himself it had become obvious. He had lost interest in other people's affairs, and seldom attended when they spoke to him. He was fond of talking himself but often forgot what he was going to say, and even when he succeeded, it seldom seemed worth the effort. His phrases and gestures had become stiff and set, his anecdotes, once so successful, fell flat, his silence was as meaningless as his speech. Yet he had led a healthy, active life, had worked steadily, made money, educated his children. There was nothing and no one to blame: he was simply growing old.

At the present moment, here he was in Greece, and one of the dreams of his life was realized. Forty years ago he had caught the fever of Hellenism, and all his life he had felt that could he but visit that land, he would not have lived in vain. But Athens had been dusty, Delphi wet, Thermopylae flat, and he had listened with amazement and cynicism to the rapturous exclamations of his companions. Greece was like England: it was a man who was growing old, and it made no difference whether that man looked at the Thames or the Eurotas. It was his last hope of contradicting that logic of experience, and it was failing.

Yet Greece had done something for him, though he did not know it. It had made him discontented, and there are stirrings of life in discontent. He knew that he was not the victim of continual ill-luck. Something great was wrong, and he was pitted against no mediocre or accidental enemy. For the last month a strange desire had possessed him to die fighting.

"Greece is the land for young people," he said to himself as he stood under the plane trees, "but I will enter into it, I will possess it. Leaves shall be green again, water shall be sweet, the sky shall be blue. They were so forty years ago, and I will win them back. I do mind being old, and I will pretend no longer."

He took two steps forward, and immediately cold waters were gurgling over his ankle.

"Where does the water come from?" he asked himself. "I do not even know that." He remembered that all the hill sides were dry; yet here the road was suddenly covered with flowing streams.

He stopped still in amazement, saying: "Water out of a tree—out of a hollow tree? I never saw nor thought of that before."

For the enormous plane that leant towards the Khan was hollow —it had been burnt out for charcoal—and from its living trunk there gushed an impetuous spring, coating the bark with fern and moss, and flowing over the mule track to create fertile meadows beyond. The simple country folk had paid to beauty and mystery such tribute as they could, for in the rind of the tree a shrine was cut, holding a lamp and a little picture of the Virgin, inheritor of the Naiad's and Dryad's joint abode.

"I never saw anything so marvellous before," said Mr Lucas. "I could even step inside the trunk and see where the water comes from."

For a moment he hesitated to violate the shrine. Then he remembered with a smile his own thought—"the place shall be mine; I will enter it and possess it"—and leapt almost aggressively on to a stone within.

The water pressed up steadily and noiselessly from the hollow roots and hidden crevices of the plane, forming a wonderful amber pool ere it spilt over the lip of bark on to the earth outside. Mr Lucas tasted it and it was sweet, and when he looked up the black funnel of the trunk he saw sky which was blue, and some leaves which were green; and he remembered, without smiling, another of his thoughts.

Others had been before him—indeed he had a curious sense of companionship. Little votive offerings to the presiding Power were fastened on to the bark—tiny arms and legs and eyes in tin, grotesque models of the brain or the heart—all tokens of some recovery of strength or wisdom or love. There was no such thing as the solitude of nature, for the sorrows and joys of humanity had pressed even into the bosom of a tree. He spread out his arms and steadied himself against the soft charred wood, and then slowly leant back, till his body was resting on the trunk behind. His eyes closed, and he had the strange feeling of one who is moving, yet at peace—the feeling of the swimmer, who, after long struggling with chopping seas, finds that after all the tide will sweep him to his goal.

So he lay motionless, conscious only of the stream below his feet, and that all things were a stream, in which he was moving.

He was aroused at last by a shock—the shock of an arrival perhaps, for when he opened his eyes, something unimagined, indefinable, had passed over all things, and made them intelligible and good.

There was meaning in the stoop of the old woman over her work, and in the quick motions of the little pig, and in her diminishing globe of wool. A young man came singing over the streams on a mule, and there was beauty in his pose and sincerity in his greeting. The sun made no accidental patterns upon the spreading roots of the trees, and there was intention in the nodding clumps of asphodel, and in the music of the water. To Mr Lucas, who, in a brief space of time, had discovered not only Greece, but England and all the world and life, there seemed nothing ludicrous in the desire to hang within the tree another votive offering—a little model of an entire man.

"Why, here's papa, playing at being Merlin."

All unnoticed they had arrived—Ethel, Mrs Forman, Mr Graham, and the English-speaking dragoman. Mr Lucas peered out at them suspiciously. They had suddenly become unfamiliar, and all that they did seemed strained and coarse.

"Allow me to give you a hand," said Mr Graham, a young man who was always polite to his elders.

Mr Lucas felt annoyed. "Thank you, I can manage perfectly well by myself," he replied. His foot slipped as he stepped out of the tree, and went into the spring.

"Oh papa, my papa!" said Ethel, "what are you doing? Thank goodness I have got a change for you on the mule."

She tended him carefully, giving him clean socks and dry boots, and then sat him down on the rug beside the lunch basket, while she went with the others to explore the grove.

They came back in ecstasies, in which Mr Lucas tried to join. But he found them intolerable. Their enthusiasm was superficial, commonplace, and spasmodic. They had no perception of the coherent beauty that was flowering around them. He tried at least to explain his feelings, and what he said was:

"I am altogether pleased with the appearance of this place. It impresses me very favourably. The trees are fine, remarkably fine for Greece, and there is something very poetic in the spring of clear running water. The people too seem kindly and civil. It is decidedly an attractive place."

Mrs Forman upbraided him for his tepid praise.

"Oh, it is a place in a thousand!" she cried, "I could live and die here! I really would stop if I had not to be back at Athens! It reminds me of the Colonus of Sophocles."

"Well, *I* must stop," said Ethel. "I positively must."

"Yes, do! You and your father! Antigone and Oedipus. Of course you must stop at Colonus!"

Mr Lucas was almost breathless with excitement. When he stood within the tree, he had believed that his happiness would be independent of locality. But these few minutes' conversation had undeceived him. He no longer trusted himself to journey through the world, for old thoughts, old wearinesses might be waiting to rejoin him as soon as he left the shade of the planes, and the music of the virgin water. To sleep in the Khan with the gracious, kind-eyed country people, to watch the bats flit about within the globe of shade, and see the moon turn the golden patterns into silver—one such night would place him beyond relapse, and confirm him for ever in the kingdom he had regained. But all his lips could say was: "I should be willing to put in a night here."

"You mean a week, papa! It would be sacrilege to put in less."

"A week then, a week," said his lips, irritated at being corrected, while his heart was leaping with joy. All through lunch he spoke to them no more, but watched the place he should know so well, and the people who would so soon be his companions and friends. The inmates of the Khan only consisted of an old woman, a middle-aged woman, a young man and two children, and to none of them had he spoken, yet he loved them as he loved everything that moved or breathed or existed beneath the benedictory shade of the planes.

"En route!" said the shrill voice of Mrs Forman. "Ethel! Mr. Graham! The best of things must end."

"To-night," thought Mr Lucas, "they will light the little lamp by the shrine. And when we all sit together on the balcony, perhaps they will tell me which offerings they put up."

"I beg your pardon, Mr Lucas," said Graham, "but they want to fold up the rug you are sitting on."

Mr Lucas got up, saying to himself: "Ethel shall go to bed first, and then I will try to tell them about my offering too—for it is a thing I must do. I think they will understand if I am left with them alone."

Ethel touched him on the cheek. "Papa! I've called you three times. All the mules are here."

"Mules? What mules?"

"Our mules. We're all waiting. Oh, Mr Graham, do help my father on."

"I don't know what you're talking about, Ethel."

"My dearest papa, we must start. You know we have to get to Olympia to-night."

Mr Lucas in pompous, confident tones replied: "I always did wish, Ethel, that you had a better head for plans. You know perfectly well that we are putting in a week here. It is your own suggestion."

Ethel was startled into impoliteness. "What a perfectly ridiculous idea. You must have known I was joking. Of course I meant I wished we could."

"Ah! if we could only do what we wished!" sighed Mrs Forman, already seated on her mule.

"Surely," Ethel continued in calmer tones, "you didn't think I meant it."

"Most certainly I did. I have made all my plans on the supposition that we are stopping here, and it will be extremely inconvenient, indeed, impossible for me to start."

He delivered this remark with an air of great conviction, and Mrs Forman and Mr Graham had to turn away to hide their smiles.

"I am sorry I spoke so carelessly; it was wrong of me. But, you know, we can't break up our party, and even one night here would make us miss the boat at Patras."

Mrs Forman, in an aside, called Mr Graham's attention to the excellent way in which Ethel managed her father.

"I don't mind about the Patras boat. You said that we should stop here, and we are stopping."

It seemed as if the inhabitants of the Khan had divined in some mysterious way that the altercation touched them. The old woman stopped her spinning, while the young man and the two children stood behind Mr Lucas, as if supporting him.

Neither arguments nor entreaties moved him. He said little, but he was absolutely determined, because for the first time he saw his daily life aright. What need had he to return to England? Who would miss him? His friends were dead or cold. Ethel loved him in a way, but, as was right, she had other interests. His other children he seldom saw. He had only one other relative, his sister Julia, whom he both feared and hated. It was no effort to struggle. He would be a fool as well as a coward if he stirred from the place which brought him happiness and peace.

At last Ethel, to humour him, and not disinclined to air her modern Greek, went into the Khan with the astonished dragoman to look at the rooms. The woman inside received them with loud welcomes, and the young man, when no one was looking, began to lead Mr Lucas' mule to the stable.

"Drop it, you brigand!" shouted Graham, who always declared that foreigners could understand English if they chose. He was right, for the man obeyed, and they all stood waiting for Ethel's return.

She emerged at last, with close-gathered skirts, followed by the dragoman bearing the little pig, which he had bought at a bargain.

"My dear papa, I will do all I can for you, but stop in that Khan —no."

"Are there—fleas?" asked Mrs Forman.

Ethel intimated that "fleas" was not the word.

"Well, I am afraid that settles it," said Mrs Forman, "I know how particular Mr Lucas is."

"It does not settle it," said Mr Lucas. "Ethel, you go on. I do not want you. I don't know why I ever consulted you. I shall stop here alone."

"That is absolute nonsense," said Ethel, losing her temper. "How can you be left alone at your age? How would you get your meals or your bath? All your letters are waiting for you at Patras. You'll miss the boat. That means missing the London operas, and upsetting all your engagements for the month. And as if you could travel by yourself!"

"They might knife you," was Mr Graham's contribution.

The Greeks said nothing; but whenever Mr Lucas looked their way, they beckoned him towards the Khan. The children would even have drawn him by the coat, and the old woman on the balcony stopped her almost completed spinning, and fixed him with mysterious appealing eyes. As he fought, the issue assumed gigantic proportions, and he believed that he was not merely stopping because he had regained youth or seen beauty or found happiness, but because in that place and with those people a supreme event was awaiting him which would transfigure the face of the world. The moment was so tremendous that he abandoned words and arguments as useless, and rested on the strength of his mighty unrevealed allies: silent men, murmuring water, and whispering trees. For the whole place called with one voice, articulate to him, and his garrulous opponents became every minute more meaningless and absurd. Soon they would be tired and go chattering away into the sun, leaving him to the cool grove and the moonlight and the destiny he foresaw.

Mrs Forman and the dragoman had indeed already started, amid the piercing screams of the little pig, and the struggle might have gone on indefinitely if Ethel had not called in Mr Graham.

"Can you help me?" she whispered. "He is absolutely unmanageable."

"I'm no good at arguing—but if I could help you in any other way —" and he looked down complacently at his well-made figure.

Ethel hesitated. Then she said: "Help me in any way you can. After all, it is for his good that we do it."

"Then have his mule led up behind him."

So when Mr Lucas thought he had gained the day, he suddenly felt himself lifted off the ground, and sat sideways on the saddle, and at the same time the mule started off at a trot. He said nothing, for he had nothing to say, and even his face showed little emotion as he felt the shade pass and heard the sound of the water cease. Mr Graham was running at his side, hat in hand, apologizing.

"I know I had no business to do it, and I do beg your pardon awfully. But I do hope that some day you too will feel that I was— damn!"

A stone had caught him in the middle of the back. It was thrown by the little boy, who was pursuing them along the mule track. He was followed by his sister, also throwing stones.

Ethel screamed to the dragoman, who was some way ahead with Mrs Forman, but before he could rejoin them, another adversary appeared. It was the young Greek, who had cut them off in front, and now dashed down at Mr Lucas' bridle. Fortunately Graham was an expert boxer, and it did not take him a moment to beat down the youth's feeble defence, and to send him sprawling with a bleeding mouth into the asphodel. By this time the dragoman had arrived, the children, alarmed at the fate of their brother, had desisted, and the rescue party, if such it is to be considered, retired in disorder to the trees.

"Little devils!" said Graham, laughing with triumph. "That's the modern Greek all over. Your father meant money if he stopped, and they consider we were taking it out of their pocket."

"Oh, they are terrible—simple savages! I don't know how I shall ever thank you. You've saved my father."

"I only hope you didn't think me brutal."

"No," replied Ethel with a little sigh. "I admire strength."

Meanwhile the cavalcade reformed, and Mr Lucas, who, as Mrs Forman said, bore his disappointment wonderfully well, was put comfortably on to his mule. They hurried up the opposite hillside, fearful of another attack, and it was not until they had left the eventful place far behind that Ethel found an opportunity to speak to her father and ask his pardon for the way she had treated him.

"You seemed so different, dear father, and you quite frightened me. Now I feel that you are your old self again."

He did not answer, and she concluded that he was not unnaturally offended at her behaviour.

By one of those curious tricks of mountain scenery, the place they had left an hour before suddenly reappeared far below them. The Khan was hidden under the green dome, but in the open there still stood three figures, and through the pure air rose up a faint cry of defiance or farewell.

Mr Lucas stopped irresolutely, and let the reins fall from his hand.

"Come, father dear," said Ethel gently.

He obeyed, and in another moment a spur of the hill hid the dangerous scene for ever.

II

It was breakfast time, but the gas was alight, owing to the fog. Mr Lucas was in the middle of an account of a bad night he had spent. Ethel, who was to be married in a few weeks, had her arms on the table, listening.

"First the door bell rang, then you came back from the theatre. Then the dog started, and after the dog the cat. And at three in the morning a young hooligan passed by singing. Oh yes: then there was the water gurgling in the pipe above my head."

"I think that was only the bath water running away," said Ethel, looking rather worn.

"Well, there's nothing I dislike more than running water. It's perfectly impossible to sleep in the house. I shall give it up. I shall give notice next quarter. I shall tell the landlord plainly, 'The reason I am giving up the house is this: it is perfectly impossible to sleep in it.' If he says—says—well, what has he got to say?"

"Some more toast, father?"

"Thank you, my dear." He took it, and there was an interval of peace.

But he soon recommenced. "I'm not going to submit to the practising next door as tamely as they think. I wrote and told them so—didn't I?"

"Yes," said Ethel, who had taken care that the letter should not reach. "I have seen the governess, and she has promised to arrange it differently. And Aunt Julia hates noise. It will sure to be all right."

Her aunt, being the only unattached member of the family, was coming to keep house for her father when she left him. The reference was not a happy one, and Mr Lucas commenced a series of half articulate sighs, which was only stopped by the arrival of the post.

"Oh, what a parcel!" cried Ethel. "For me! What can it be! Greek stamps. This is most exciting!"

It proved to be some asphodel bulbs, sent by Mrs Forman from Athens for planting in the conservatory.

"Doesn't it bring it all back! You remember the asphodels, father. And all wrapped up in Greek newspapers. I wonder if I can read them still. I used to be able to, you know."

She rattled on, hoping to conceal the laughter of the children next door—a favourite source of querulousness at breakfast time.

"Listen to me! 'A rural disaster.' Oh, I've hit on something sad. But never mind. 'Last Tuesday at Plataniste, in the province of Messenia, a shocking tragedy occurred. A large tree'—aren't I getting on well? —'blew down in the night and'—wait a minute—oh, dear! 'crushed to death the five occupants of the little Khan there, who had apparently been sitting in the balcony. The bodies of Maria Rhomaides, the aged proprietress, and of her daughter, aged forty-six, were easily recognizable, whereas that of her grandson'—oh, the rest is really too horrid; I wish I had never tried it, and what's more I feel to have heard the name Plataniste before. We didn't stop there, did we, in the spring?"

"We had lunch," said Mr Lucas, with a faint expression of trouble on his vacant face. "Perhaps it was where the dragoman bought the pig."

"Of course," said Ethel in a nervous voice. "Where the dragoman bought the little pig. How terrible!"

"Very terrible!" said her father, whose attention was wandering to the noisy children next door. Ethel suddenly started to her feet with genuine interest.

"Good gracious!" she exclaimed. "This is an old paper. It happened not lately but in April—the night of Tuesday the eighteenth—and we—we must have been there in the afternoon."

"So we were," said Mr Lucas. She put her hand to her heart, scarcely able to speak.

"Father, dear father, I must say it: you wanted to stop there. All those people, those poor half savage people, tried to keep you, and they're dead. The whole place, it says, is in ruins, and even the stream has changed its course. Father, dear, if it had not been for me, and if Arthur had not helped me, you must have been killed."

Mr Lucas waved his hand irritably. "It is not a bit of good speaking to the governess, I shall write to the landlord and say, 'The reason I am giving up the house is this: the dog barks, the children next door are intolerable, and I cannot stand the noise of running water.'"

Ethel did not check his babbling. She was aghast at the narrowness of the escape, and for a long time kept silence. At last she said: "Such a marvellous deliverance does make one believe in Providence."

Mr Lucas, who was still composing his letter to the landlord, did not reply.

Janet Frame

(b. 1924)

Born in Dunedin, New Zealand, Janet Frame was educated to be a teacher, but now writes full time. Her country's leading contemporary writer, she is the author of a volume of verse, a book of children's stories, nine novels, and three books of short stories. The most successful of the novels are *Owls Do Cry* (1957); *The Edge of the Alphabet* (1962); *The Rainbirds* (1968), which appeared in the United States in 1969 as *Yellow Flowers in the Antipodean Room; Intensive Care* (1970); and *Daughter Buffalo* (1972). They evoke tormented territory, a world where the mind's restless dreaming leads always into nightmares of vision, danger, apocalypse, and isolation. yet it is a world into which the author insists people must venture. To stay in what she calls the "safety zones"—the world of rules and boundaries and "sane" social conventions—is to dull one's senses and to deprive one's mind of the creative insights of which it is capable. To taste the dispossessions of nightmare, by contrast, is to educate oneself to apocalyptic change and to train one's eyes to adapt to survival in the strange geographies "at the edge of the alphabet." For an artist the problem is particularly acute. To be subject to arbitrary conventions of syntax and style is to have one's vision contained. Yet Frame acknowledges that she must still communicate. Her methods of breaking through such boundaries involve her in anagrammatic Joycean punning and in telling stories within stories; she relies on the formidable power of images and employs as an elliptical approach to truth the deceptive simplicities of fabular form.

The subtitle of *Snowman Snowman* (1963), the collection from which "The Mythmaker's Office" is taken, is "Fables and Fantasies," which gives some indication of the story's character. Its language is straightforward, its tone is wry, its social moral is clear. And over it is cast a sense of the fantastic, the bizarre, which has the effect of making us realize (perhaps with discomfort) how strange and incredible are many of the everyday patterns of life which people blindly accept. Frame's intent is not to reform society, but merely to illuminate the mind's eyes of the people within it; she urges an openness toward change because only change is vital, and an acceptance of time and mortality because they are implicitly part of the process of living.

For further reading

P. Evans, *An Inward Sun* (Wellington: Price Milburn, 1971).
Janet Frame, "Beginnings," *Landfall,* 19 (March 1965), 40–47.

The Mythmaker's Office

"The sun," they said, "is unmentionable. You must never refer to it."
But that ruse did not work. People referred to the sun, wrote

poems about it, suffered under it, lying beneath the chariot wheels, and their eyes were pierced by the sapphire needles jabbing in the groove of light. The sun lolled in the sky. The sun twitched like an extra nerve in the mind. And the sunflowers turned their heads, watching the ceremony, like patient ladies at a tennis match.

So that ruse did not work.

But the people in charge persisted, especially the Minister of Mythmaking who sat all day in his empty office beating his head with a gold-mounted stick in order to send up a cloud of ideas from underneath his wall-to-wall carpet of skin. Alas, when the ideas flew up they arrived like motes in other people's eyes and the Minister of Mythmaking as an habitually polite occupier of his ceiling-to-floor glass ministry did not care to remove ideas from the eyes of other people.

Instead, he went outside and threw colored stones against the Office of Mythmaking.

"What are you doing, my good chap?" the Prime Minister asked, on his way to a conference.

"Playing fictional fives," the Minister of Mythmaking replied, after searching for an explanation.

"You would be better occupied," the Prime Minister told him, "in performing the correct duties of your office."

Dazed, shoulders drooping with care, the Minister of Mythmaking returned to his office where once again he sat alone, staring at the big empty room and seeing his face four times in the glass walls. Once more he took his gold-mounted stick and, beating his head, he sent up another cloud of ideas which had a stored musty smell for they had been swept under the carpet years ago and had never been removed or disturbed until now. One idea pierced the Minister in the eye.

"Ah," he said. "Death, Death is unmentionable. Surely that will please all concerned. Death is obscene, unpublishable. We must ban all reference to it, delete the death notices from the newspapers, make it an indecent offense to be seen congregating at funerals, drive Death underground.

"Yes," the Minister of Mythmaking said to himself. "This will surely please the public, the majority, and prove the ultimate value of Democracy. All will co-operate in the denial of Death." Accordingly he drafted an appropriate bill which passed swiftly with averted eyes through the House of Parliament and joined its forbears in the worm-eaten paper territories in paneled rooms.

Death notices disappeared from the newspapers. Periodical raids were carried out by the police upon undertakers' premises and crematoria to ensure that no indecent activities were in progress. Death became relegated to a Resistance Movement, a Black Market, and furtive shovelings on the outskirts of the city.

For people did not stop dying. Although it was now against the law, obscene, subversive, Death remained an intense part of the lives of every inhabitant of the kingdom. In the pubs and clubs after work the citizens gathered to exchange stories which began, "Do you know the one about ...?" and which were punctuated with whispered references to Death, the Dead, Cemeteries, Mortuaries. Often you could hear smothered laughter and observe expressions of shame and guilt as ribaldry placed its fear-releasing hand simultaneously upon Death and Conscience. At other times arguments broke out, fights began, the police were called in, and the next day people were summoned to court on charges relating to indecent behavior and language, with the witness for the prosecution exclaiming, "He openly uttered the word ... the word ... well I shall write it upon a piece of paper and show it to the learned judge...." And when the judge read the words "Death," "the dead" upon the paper his expression would become severe; he would pronounce the need for a heavy penalty, citizens must learn to behave as normal citizens, and not flout the laws of common decency by referring to Death and the practices of burial. ...

In books the offending five-letter word was no longer written in full; letters other than the first and last were replaced by dots or a dash. When one writer boldly used the word Death several times, and gave detailed descriptions of the ceremonies attending death and burial, there followed such an outcry that his publishers were prosecuted for issuing an indecent work.

But the prosecutors did not win their case, for witnesses convinced the jury that the references to death and its ceremonies were of unusual beauty and power, and should be read by all citizens.

"In the end," a witness reminded the court, "each one of us is involved in dying, and though we are forbidden by law to acknowledge this, surely it is necessary for us to learn the facts of death and burial?"

"What!" the public in court said. "And corrupt the rising generation!" You should have seen the letters to the paper after the court's decision was made known!

The book in question sold many millions of copies; its relevant passages were marked and thumbed; but people placed it on their bookshelves with its title facing the wall.

Soon, however, the outcry and publicity which attended the case were forgotten and the city of the kingdom reverted to its former habits of secrecy. People died in secret, were buried in secret. At one

time there was a wave of righteous public anger (which is a dangerous form of anger) against the existence of buildings such as hospitals which in some ways cater to the indecencies of death and are
thus an insult to the pure-minded. So effective had been the work of
the Mythmaker's Office that the presence of a hospital, its evil sug-
gestiveness, made one close one's eyes in disgust. Many of the buildings were deliberately burned to the ground, during occasions of
night-long uninhibited feasting and revelry where people rejoiced,
naked, dancing, making love while the Watch Committee, also
naked, but with pencils and notebooks, maintained their vigilance
by recording instances of behavior which stated or implied reference to the indecencies of Death.

People found dying in a public place were buried in secrecy and
shame. Furtive obscene songs were sung about road accidents, im-
modesties such as influenza, bronchitis, and the gross facts of the
sickroom. Doctors, in spite of their vowed alliance with living,
became unmentionable evils, and were forced to advertise in glass
cabinets outside tobacconist's and night clubs in the seedier districts
of the kingdom.

The avoidance of Death, like the avoidance of all inevitability,
overflowed into the surrounding areas of living, like a river laying
waste the land which it had formerly nourished and made fertile.

The denial of Death became also a denial of life and growth.

"Well," said the Prime Minister surrounded by last week's
wrapped, sliced, crumbling policies, "Well," he said proudly to the
Minister of Mythmaking, "you have accomplished your purpose.
You have done good work. You may either retire on a substantial
pension or take a holiday in the South of France, at the kingdom's
expense. We have abolished Death. We are now immortal. Prepare
the country for thousands of years of green happiness."

And leaning forward he took a bite of a new policy which had just
been delivered to him. It was warm and doughy, with bubbles of air
inside to give it lightness.

"New policies, eaten quickly, are indigestible," the Minister of
Mythmaking advised, wishing to be of service before he retired to
the South of France.

The Prime Minister frowned. "I have remedies," he said coldly.
Then he smiled. "Thousands of years of green happiness!"

Yet by the end of that year the whole kingdom except for one man
and one woman had committed suicide. Death, birth, life had been
abolished. People arrived from the moon, rubbing their hands with
glee and sucking lozenges which were laid in rows, in tins, and
dusted with sugar.

In a hollow upon dead grass and dead leaves the one human couple left alive on earth said, Let's make Death."

And the invalid sun opened in the sky, erupting its contagious boils of light, pouring down the golden matter upon the waste places of the earth.

Dave Godfrey

(b. 1938)

Born in Winnipeg, Dave Godfrey was educated in Canada and the United States and later taught in Toronto, where he established three independent publishing houses: Anansi, New Press, and Press Porcépic. Between 1963 and 1965 he lived in Ghana and taught at Adisadel College, Cape Coast. His intense response to the traditional cultures and current politics of African society focused for him an interest to which his fiction later gave voice. A number of the stories of *Death Goes Better with Coca-Cola* (1967), and the whole of his prize-winning novel *The New Ancestors* (1970), are set in Africa, and they probe two recurring themes: the multiple significance of myth and history to the human imagination, and the colonizing impact that one culture can have on another.

With political events of the 1960s as his main subject in "Two Smiths," he keeps his eye on myth and history together, invoking archetype to his own artistic ends. His radical national stance is supported by a conservative assertion of moral independence and communal pattern. In an interview with Donald Cameron, he explains his belief that aggressive low-synergy societies like the United States will always overrun high-synergy states. Such a belief derives from Konrad Lorenz's *On Aggression*, from which Godfrey takes the epigraph for *Death Goes Better with Coca-Cola*. It reads in part: "To kill a culture, it is often sufficient to bring it into contact with another. . . ." Whether his subject is the effect of the great powers on Africa, or the power of the white man over American slave society, or the effect of the United States on Canada, he analyzes the cultural contact with passion and intelligence. The complex result is sometimes witty, sometimes angry, sometimes chillingly objective.

The epigraph to "Two Smiths" is the *Po* hexagram ("Splitting Apart") from the *I Ching*.

For further reading

Donald Cameron, *Conversations with Canadian Novelists,* vol. 2 (Toronto: Macmillan, 1973), pp. 34–47.

Graeme Gibson, *Eleven Canadian Novelists* (Toronto: Anansi, 1973), pp. 155–179.

Margaret Laurence, "Des voix ancestrales prophetisant . . .," *Ellipse* (Sherbrooke, P. Q.), 4 (Summer 1970), 71–80; trans. in *Mysterious East* (Fredericton, N. B.), December book supplement (1970), 6–10.

Two Smiths

Po

 Splitting apart. It does not further one to go anywhere. Learn to bestow. The earth is docility; the earth is devotion. Remain quiet. When those who rule do not bestow, the mountain must

weaken on the earth, must tumble. The fruit must rot. Look, the leg of the bed is split. Slander destroys the loyal. Look, the bed is split at the edge. No comrades. Extreme caution. Adjust or flee. Now you must look: the bed is split up to the skin. Even wisdom is of no use: the roof shatters.

A shoal of fishes marks the change. Were the queen's ladies as senseless as we thought? There is fruit still uneaten. Do not despair; your carriage will arrive; the house of the inferior man will be split apart by its own evil. Learn to bestow: the earth remains devotion, the earth remains docility. Share your house so that it may remain yours.

May. Spring is late to come. Slush and the streets full of shivering lushes near the Spadina LCBO.* The boy standing in front of me eager to talk, hair as long as that of Charles Dickens at nineteen, a gold circle in one ear; impetuous to talk, a bright orange and green sailor jersey striped boldly above his Levi Strauss blue jeans, blue-eyed; determined to tell me how it is with him, why he clipped out on the reserves, where he smoked across the border, his smile twisted in a billy-jo, mountain boy way; gurgling out how it was with him when he got to enjoying his brother's enjoyment of killing people way over there in Asia and how it was when he knew he just had to get out, to cut out, because he could see how easy it would be for him to start enjoying the same killing. He, Jimmy Randall Smith.

Sure. January. Full winter may never come. Rhett Smith is beside me in the midwest, lifting an old twelve gauge out of his flower-painted Chevy. His young man's clipped beard is gone.

"Have to have the car repainted now," I say.

Rhett doesn't answer. His face is tight in the cold, near winter wind. Something else is bothering him. Something else is keeping him from talking, from replying to my jest about his repainted Chevy. So that I talk, uncharacteristically. Once we have climbed over the fence and are into the corn fields, completely stripped down now, completely ready for winter. He waves at the thin-faced girl with peroxide hair who sits in the Chevy and looks discontented, as though the heat may be suddenly and mysteriously turned off while we are hunting.

"A funny old bird is all that I'm sure is left," I say. "I've almost given him a name. I've seen him three or four times in the whole

---

*Spadina LCBO = branch of the Liquor Control Board of Ontario on Spadina Street, Toronto.

year. He's got one singular habit that keeps him alive. He flies
straight up."

I look at Rhett Smith. I am not amusing him. He's back in the
south, or he's back in the county seat, or in the state's capital, in a
courtroom under pressure. He is unable to relax, as I can now in the
cleared corn field, looking for that one old bird with the singular
habit.

"Shouldn't hunt him down," I say, "but you know how it is, sometimes you reach a certain intensity about getting something done.
I've got my freezer stocked. He's probably tough, probably full of old
lead."

"Put some lead near him myself, one time, doing it the local way:
without dogs, just lots of men in a line. We came through the fields
six at a time. Twice we peppered away at that old bird. It's a well-
analyzed way of hunting, the way you do it here. The birds go up,
they go along, or they go away; it doesn't really matter. There's
always two or three men who can get an angle on him. Sometimes
more if he flies the wrong way."

"This bird seemed to know there was something else. Went up like
a partridge into a pine tree. Went up thirty or forty feet. Everybody
had a shot at him, more or less. Good business for the hardware store
—that was about all. We all shot into one another's shot. It's just not
something you're used to. You're used to a long, quick lean flight.
You're used to aiming ahead. A transcendental bird, I guess. A romantic out of place in the pragmatic west."

Rhett Smith is not looking at me.

"They put a lot of pressure on you, I guess." I say.

"Wasn't bad," he says. "Wasn't bad at all. I admit I made a mistake."

I know him, Rhett Smith. In the modern way I know details, facts,
histories. Who he stayed with when he went down south for freedom. What kind of beer he drank with the people he stayed with,
the Haydts. What Mr. Haydt did for a living. But I couldn't have
predicted that he was going to peak out at this stage. Anger and a
desire for action were building up inside of him, that was obvious.
And some desire for fame or attention. Then he just threw in the
whole sponge. Took a dive or got smart. Realized that he was being
led astray by forces inimicable to the American way of life. The way
you describe him now doesn't matter, the way you describe him is
forever relative. I know details about his beard. I know what precise
moment of awareness triggered all the actions of the past three
years. The thing, the moment, and all that. Somewhere inside the
rented farmhouse it sits in a file.

Now, the corn is soggy with the damp that comes when a real cold
delays. A rustle. Down the field, a long shot, the old cock is running

through the stubble. Smith listens to it, as though it were a distant crow, something distant and bleak. Into the scrub weed along the fence, the wild marijuana? Or a right turn and across the furrows and back up distant stubble?

"Funny all that wild pot up here, so far from Mexico," I say. "We had a good crop this year, but you have to get it at the right time."

"I was never one for that," he replies. There is something Baptisty about him, small town Methodist, and I wonder why I am wasting this unusual hunting time with him.

It was newspaper reports of a girl being raped in New York which set him going. A lot of people saw it from an office building, stood up, and went to the windows to watch. But nobody did a thing. Apathy, that got to him. Religious disgust welled up in him. Apathy is one of his key words. Lack of compassion. That's what he didn't want to suffer from when he came of age. The apathy that the newspapers and magazines chronicled for him during the 60's. Oil millionaires and rat-infested slums. He was going to do something and he went down to Mississippi.

Where the police beat him up but didn't shoot him. He thought that if he had been Jewish they might have, but he was a boy of German extraction from Iowa. He came back with a lot of stories to tell and decided to go on a hunger strike. He sat in bars and apartments with the young radicals and poets who listened to his stories. He told them how young Haydt's car had been shot up by the police as they drove home late one evening. "Car's getting a bad case of rust there boys," one policeman said. "Better be careful it doesn't spread." Laughing a little. "That been like that long?" the other policeman said about the shattered windshield. "Ought not to drive around like that. Might have to ticket you. You boys better take better care of that car; bet it ain't even paid for yet."

He told all his new stories and enjoyed the response and trimmed his beard a little more neatly and then in the winter went out with three other friends and sat in front of the Federal Post Office with only a tent and sleeping bags and they promised not to eat until they had raised five thousand dollars for people who had been deprived of shelter and amenities during the troubles in the south.

And raised quite a good proportion of the five thousand dollars, although two of his friends quit and Rhett caught the third one eating candy bars one night and would have asked even that one to acknowledge defeat except that he didn't want to have to go through it all alone.

Then when spring came he painted his car with flowers and became more interested in the war and eventually burnt his draft card. He was the second person in the whole country to do that.

Events swirled about him. A washing machine millionaire, third-generation, offered him financial support.

Now, he explains to me very seriously where the wild marijuana came from.

"During the war, the second war, they tried to grow hemp in the state because there was a shortage of rope and they felt that anything would grow here. But it didn't do too well for that purpose. It spread all over the place, but nobody cared. The war was over by then and nobody was interested in drugs. Now they're beginning to worry."

We come down to the corner and the bird hasn't gone up. I kick along through the weeds, but nothing happens.

Repetition. The thin thread of reality. Suddenly the cock goes high, still the colours of the sun and the fall in this dull season lingering beyond reason. The bird goes high enough so that Rhett comes out of his lethargy and gets his gun up and bangs off a shot and I am glad enough at that sudden action to forego my careful watching for the moment when the bird must level off, when it gets beyond even its unlearned height.

"Perhaps he's inherited it," I say. "It's a whole new breed to make things hard on us killers."

A glimmer of a smile.

I have been up to the small town which bred Rhett. His father runs a shoe repair shop which also stocks boots and tennis sneakers and slippers. In the front window is a sign which states that one can pay his American Legion dues here. I have been up to the town school from which Rhett graduated and talked to the teacher he says helped spark him towards this life of action.

"Most of the people here are kinda anti-Rhett," she said, with just the smallest of nervous smiles as though I might be weird enough not to understand what was implied, what all Americans would understand was implied. "If not, you just don't say anything. When Rhett wanted to speak on civil rights here in the school last fall, before any of this worse trouble came, there were some who felt he should be let to talk, but those who didn't had a point and what could you answer? We're a public supported school; we have to walk a middle path. Otherwise you get yourself too involved. My husband didn't want me to come at all to talk to you. I told him what you wanted to know about, about Rhett, and, well, we own a rent house over in Cedar Rapids and we're renting it to Negroes now, but that's our first real contact. I do quite a bit with the Negro in American History of the twentieth century and I was glad to see that this year the English people were reading *Raisin in the Sun* in that magazine they work out of, *Cavalcade.* One of the younger teachers asked me about it, there's a conservative minister or two in town who could stir up trouble if it were handled wrong, but—of course English's different than history—but I told her to handle it just as people. The play was about people in a slum, she said, so I said to her just have them judge it as a family living in a slum and what they would do if they were in similar condition."

Such is inspiration.

The bird has flown east and landed again in the stubble. We walk slowly up back towards the farmhouse. A light snow is falling. When we reach the fence around the old orchard which surrounds the house, Rhett relaxes and unloads his gun, but I am still alert, the phrases of the woman teacher in his small town still running through my mind. Repetition. I kick through the weeds, walking towards the far fence, and the old cock goes up thirty yards ahead of me. I down him very quickly, before he can do his spiral act.

I offer the tail feather to the blond girl who has been waiting unhappily in the Chevy, but she refuses it. I know that she suspects me as one of those people who led Rhett astray, and we are awkward, so I let them leave and turn to clean the old bird. His left eye has been shot out.

Don Silverbuck phones while I am still plucking wing feathers. He is very excited. He has been following all of Rhett's activities, planning to write another *In Cold Blood* as soon as Rhett is jailed. That is why our house is full of files.

"I'll be home in about two hours," he hollers into the phone. "You should have seen that trial yesterday, you wouldn't have believed it. Clarence Darrow all over again. What a phrase. Rhett was late and he said: 'I'm sorry, judge, we took a wrong turn on the way to the courtroom.' How's that for a title? Sell a million. I've been checking a few things. I don't know how they got to him; he just crumpled. But there's going to be a big protest meeting and all the poets are going to read."

"He told me he got off."

"Suspended sentence. It's a different thing. Christ, what I'm learning about law. They should have let him off completely, that's our point, Or he should have gone to jail. I don't know, something's happened to him. Drugs maybe, I wouldn't put it past them. The FBI were out in force. He's going straight. Did you get anything out of him? We're having real signs printed for the protest."

"No, Don. We just hunted. I'm going to get ready to leave. As soon as they start bombing Hanoi I'm going to leave."

"What? We've got to finish this. It'll make us both rich. We'd never do that anyhow. Bomb Hanoi, you must be out of your mind. Even the generals aren't suggesting that. Christ, we've got to finish this. All the hard work's done; we've got all the details in the bag."

"I shot the old bird today," I say. "Somebody shot his left eye out a long time ago, that was all. That was why he kept going high. That was all."

"Look, you've got to stay. Write a poem, you could do it, and come to the protest. It's all going to be recorded and we'll get some of it on the AP wire. That old woman, you remember, the one we talked to who leaned on the lockers in the hall as though she was going to make them and said please don't repeat any of this, she was there today and she didn't say a damn thing. Just Rhett was a good student, and Rhett went a little astray, but Rhett was going to be okay now."

"I don't know, Don. All you guys are like flies or ants somehow. One of these days somebody's going to lift the swatter and that'll be it. I'll see you at supper."

May. This mountain boy, Frank Randall Smith, walks up a wide and dirty street in my city. He's never heard of Pratt. He doesn't know who donated this street to the city and where the farmhouses used to be, before the high rises, before the grand houses. But he is intent on talking to me, talking about how he got to enjoy his brother's enjoyment of killing, especially one story where the squad had taken three prisoners and nobody wanted to kill them so they dressed the three of them up in uniforms of their own dead buddies, American uniforms, and then let them go a little until the Cong shot the hell out of them. That pleased him to a frightening extent and he is desperate to tell me about it, desperate, while I take him in and buy him a hamburger and some chips and a coke and tell him where he can get a bed for a few nights while he settles into his new life.

Nadine Gordimer

(b. 1923)

A native of Springs, Transvaal, educated in South Africa, and still a resident of that country, Nadine Gordimer focuses almost exclusively in her work on the impact of South Africa on the individual consciousness. Though she has been a visiting lecturer at several American universities (Harvard, Princeton, Northwestern, Michigan, Columbia), and has lived for short periods in England, the world outside South Africa enters her fictional world only through the experience of exiles, émigrés, and foreign travelers. Yet the appeal of her work is not diminished by that restriction in locale. She is not a polemical writer, even though she does respond morally to such questions as justice and apartheid in her country. Writing should not, she observes in an interview with Alan Ross, be put at the service of a cause, although a cause may itself become the topic of a story. "I write about ... private selves," she adds; but these, "even in the most private situations, ... are what they are because ... lives are regulated and ... mores formed by the political situation. You see, in South Africa, society *is* the political situation. To paraphrase, one might say ..., politics is character."

This relationship between society and individual behavior is one which she has variously probed in five novels and six volumes of short stories published between 1949 and 1971. *A World of Strangers* (1958), for example, examines the inability of a young Englishman to reconcile his attraction to South Africa with his rejection of the racial divisions he finds there. *The Late Bourgeois World* (1966) presents the paralysis of will that affects one level of white society in the country—a world in which a clock ticking "afraid, alive, afraid, alive ..." renders the moral tension in a single terse image. "No Place Like," which originally appeared in *The Southern Review* and then was collected in *Livingstone's Companions* (1971), demonstrates the same talent for trenchant observation. Details of setting and style—the fragmentary phrases, the tone, the repetitiousness, and the point of view—all contribute to the story's effect. Momentary experiences are made into arenas where the mind can discover or fail to discover significant meaning in life, and ideas about human behavior and human potential are distilled into precise images and exactly rendered scenes.

For further reading

Thomas H. Gullason, "The Short Story: an Underrated Art," *Studies in Short Fiction*, 2 (Fall 1964), 13–31.

Ezekiel Mphahlele, *The African Image* (London: Faber, 1962).

Alan Ross, "A Writer in South Africa: Nadine Gordimer," *London Magazine*, 5 (May 1965), 21–28.

No Place Like

The relief of being down, out, and on the ground after hours in the plane was brought up short for them by the airport building: dirty,

full of up-ended chairs like a closed restaurant. *Transit? Transit?*
Some of them started off on a stairway but were shooed back exasper-
atedly in a language they didn't understand. The African heat in the
place had been cooped up for days and nights; somebody tried to
open one of the windows but again there were remonstrations from
the uniformed man and the girl in her white gloves and leopard-skin
pillbox hat. The windows were sealed, anyway, for the air-conditioning that wasn't working; the offender shrugged. The spokesman
that every group of travellers produces made himself responsible for
a complaint; at the same time some of those sheep who can't resist
a hole in a fence had found a glass door unlocked on the far side of
the transit lounge—they were leaking to an open passage-way: grass,
bougainvillea trained like standard roses, a road glimpsed there! But
the uniformed man raced to round them up and a cleaner trailing his
broom was summoned to bolt the door.

The woman in beige trousers had come very slowly across the
tarmac, putting her feet down on this particular earth once more,
and she was walking even more slowly round the dirty hall. Her
coat dragged from the crook of her elbow, her shoulder was weighed
by the strap of a bag that wouldn't zip over a package of duty-free
European liquor, her bright silk shirt opened dark mouths of wet
when she lifted her arms. Fellow-glances of indignance or the sea-
soned superiority of a sense of humour found no answer in her. As
her pace brought her into the path of the black cleaner, the two faces
matched perfect indifference: his, for whom the distance from which
these people came had no existence because he had been nowhere
outside the two miles he walked from his village to the airport; hers,
for whom the distance had no existence because she had been everywhere and arrived back.

Another black man, struggling into a white jacket as he unlocked
wooden shutters, opened the bar, and the businessmen with their
hard-top briefcases moved over to the row of stools. Men who had
got talking to unattached women—not much promise in that now;
the last leg of the journey was ahead—carried them glasses of gaudy
synthetic fruit juice. The Consul who had wanted to buy her a drink
with dinner on the plane had found himself a girl in red boots with
a small daughter in identical red boots. The child waddled away and
flirtation took the form of the two of them hurrying after to scoop
it up, laughing. There was a patient queue of ladies in cardigans
waiting to get into the lavatories. She passed—once, twice, three
times in her slow rounds—a woman who was stitching petit-point.
The third time she made out that the subject was a spaniel dog with
orange-and-black-streaked ears. Beside the needlewoman was a husband of a species as easily identifiable as the breed of dog—an American, because of the length of bootlace, slotted through some emblem

or badge, worn in place of a tie. He sighed and his wife looked up over her glasses as if he had made a threatening move.

The woman in the beige trousers got rid of her chit for Light Refreshment in an ashtray but she had still the plastic card that was her authority to board the plane again. She tried to put it in the pocket of the coat but she couldn't reach, so she had to hold the card in her teeth while she unharnessed herself from the shoulder-bag and the coat. She wedged the card into the bag beside the liquor packages, leaving it to protrude a little so that it would be easy to produce when the time came. But it slipped down inside the bag and she had to unpack the whole thing—the hairbrush full of her own hair, dead, shed; yesterday's newspaper from a foreign town; the book whose jacket tore on the bag's zip as it came out; wads of pink paper handkerchiefs, gloves for a cold climate, the quota of duty-free cigarettes, the Swiss pocket-knife that you couldn't buy back home, the wallet of travel documents. There at the bottom was the shiny card. Without it, you couldn't board the plane again. With it, you were committed to go on to the end of the journey, just as the passport bearing your name committed you to a certain identity and place. It was one of the nervous tics of travel to feel for the reassurance of that shiny card. She had wandered to the revolving stand of paperbacks and came back to make sure where she had put the card: yes, it was there. It was not a bit of paper; shiny plastic, you couldn't tear it up—indestructible, it looked, of course they use them over and over again. *Tropic of Capricorn, Kamasutra, Something of Value.* The stand revolved and brought round the same books, yet one turned it again in case there should be a book that had escaped notice, a book you'd been wanting to read all your life. If one were to find such a thing, here and now, on this last stage, this last stop ... She felt strong hope, the excitation of weariness and tedium perhaps. They came round—*Something of Value, Kamasutra, Tropic of Capricorn.*

She went to the seat where she had left her things and loaded up again, the coat, the shoulder-bag bearing down. Somebody had fallen asleep, mouth open, bottom fly-button undone, an Austrian hat with plaited cord and feather cutting into his damp brow. How long had they been in this place? What time was it where she had left? (Some airports had a whole series of clockfaces showing what time it was everywhere.) Was it still yesterday, there? —Or tomorrow. And where she was going? She thought, I shall find out when I get there.

A pair of curio vendors had unpacked their wares in a corner. People stood about in a final agony of indecision: What would he do with a thing like that? Will she appreciate it, I mean? A woman repeated as she must have done in bazaars and shops and marketplaces all over the world, I've seen them for half the price. . . . But this was the last stop of all, the last chance *to take back something.* How else stake a claim? The last place of all the other places of the world.

Bone bracelets lay in a collapsed spiral of overlapping circles. Elephant hair ones fell into the pattern of the Olympic symbol. There were the ivory paper-knives and the little pictures of palm trees, huts and dancers on black paper. The vendor, squatting in the posture that derives from the necessity of the legless beggar to sit that way and has become as much a mark of the street professional, in such towns as the one that must be somewhere behind the airport, as the hard-top briefcase was of the international businessman drinking beer at the bar, importuned her with the obligation to buy. To refuse was to upset the ordination of roles. He was there to sell "ivory" bracelets and "African" art; they—these people shut up for him in the building—had been brought there to buy. He had a right to be angry. But she shook her head, she shook her head, while he tried out his few words of German and French (*bon marché, billig*) as if it could only be a matter of finding the right cue to get her to play the part assigned to her. He seemed to threaten, in his own tongue, finally, his head in its white skullcap hunched between jutting knees. But she was looking again at the glass case full of tropical butterflies under the President's picture. The picture was vivid, and new; a general successful in coup only months ago, in full dress uniform, splendid as the dark one among the Magi. The butterflies, relic of some colonial conservationist society, were beginning to fall away from their pins in grey crumbs and gauzy fragments. But there was one big as a bat and brilliantly emblazoned as the general: something in the soil and air, in whatever existed out there —whatever "out there" there was—that caused nature and culture to imitate each other . . . ?

If it were possible to take a great butterfly. Not take back; just take. But she had the Swiss knife and the bottles, of course. The plastic card. It would see her onto the plane once more. Once the plastic card was handed over, nowhere to go but across the tarmac and up the stairway into the belly of the plane, no turning back past the air hostess in her leopard-skin pillbox, past the barrier. It wasn't allowed; against regulations. The plastic card would send her to the plane, the plane would arrive at the end of the journey, the Swiss knife would be handed over for a kiss, the bottles would be exchanged for an embrace—she was shaking her head at the curio vendor (he had actually got up from his knees and come after her, waving his pictures), *no thanks, no thanks.* But he wouldn't give up and she had to move away, to walk up and down once more in the hot, enclosed course dictated by people's feet, the up-ended chairs and tables, the little shored-up piles of hand-luggage. The Consul was swinging the child in red boots by its hands, in an arc. It was half-whimpering, half-laughing, yelling to be let down, but the larger version of the same model, the mother, was laughing in a way to make her small breasts shake for the Consul, and to convey to everyone how marvellous such a distinguished man was with children.

There was a gritty crackle and then the announcement in careful, African-accented English, of the departure of the flight. A kind of concerted shuffle went up like a sigh: at last! The red-booted mother was telling her child it was silly to cry, the Consul was gathering their things together, the woman was winding the orange thread for her needlework rapidly round a spool, the sleepers woke and the beer-drinkers threw the last of their foreign small change on the bar counter. No queue outside the Ladies' now and the woman in the beige trousers knew there was plenty of time before the second call. She went in and, once more, unharnessed herself among the crumpled paper towels and spilt powder. She tipped all the liquid soap containers in turn until she found one that wasn't empty; she washed her hands thoroughly in hot and then cold water and put her wet palms on the back of her neck, under her hair. She went to one of the row of mirrors and looked at what she saw there a moment, and then took out from under the liquor bottles, the Swiss knife and the documents, the hairbrush. It was full of hair; a web of dead hairs that bound the bristles together so that they could not go through a head of live hair. She raked her fingers slowly through the bristles and was aware of a young Indian woman at the next mirror, moving quickly and efficiently about an elaborate toilet. The Indian back-combed the black, smooth hair cut in Western style to hang on her shoulders, painted her eyes, shook her ringed hands dry rather than use the paper towels, sprayed French perfume while she extended her neck, repleated the green and silver sari that left bare a small roll of lavender-grey flesh between waist and *choli*.

This is the final call for all passengers.

The hair from the brush was no-colour, matted and coated with fluff. Twisted round the forefinger (like the orange thread for the spaniel's ears) it became a fibrous funnel, dusty and obscene. She didn't want the Indian girl to be confronted with it and hid it in her palm while she went over to the dustbin. But the Indian girl saw only herself, watching her reflection appraisingly as she turned and swept out.

The brush went easily through the living hair, now. Again and again, until it was quite smooth and fell, as if it had a memory, as if it were cloth that had been folded and ironed a certain way, along the lines in which it had been arranged by professional hands in another hemisphere. A latecomer rushed into one of the lavatories, sounded the flush and hurried out, plastic card in hand.

The woman in the beige trousers had put on lipstick and run a nail-file under her nails. Her bag was neatly packed. She dropped a coin in the saucer set out, like an offering for some humble household god, for the absent attendant. The African voice was urging all passengers to proceed immediately through Gate B. The voice had some difficulty with *l*'s, pronouncing them more like *r*'s; a pleasant, reasoning voice, asking only for everyone to present the boarding pass, avoid delay, come quietly.

She went into one of the lavatories marked "Western-type toilet" that bolted automatically as the door shut, a patent device ensuring privacy; there was no penny to pay. She had the coat and bag with her and arranged them, the coat folded and balanced on the bag, on the cleanest part of the floor. She thought what she remembered thinking so many times before: not much time, I'll have to hurry. That was what the plastic card was for—surety for not being left behind, never. She had it stuck in the neck of the shirt now, in the absence of a convenient pocket; it felt cool and wafer-stiff as she put it there but had quickly taken on the warmth of her body. Some tidy soul determined to keep up Western-type standards had closed the lid and she sat down as if on a bench—the heat and the weight of the paraphernalia she had been carrying about were suddenly exhausting. She thought she would smoke a cigarette; there was no time for that. But the need for a cigarette hollowed out a deep sigh within her and she got the pack carefully out of the pocket of her coat without disturbing the arrangement on the floor. All passengers delaying the departure of the flight were urged to proceed immediately through Gate B. Some of the words were lost over the echoing intercommunication system and at times the only thing that could be made out was the repetition, Gate B, a vital fact from which all grammatical contexts could fall away without rendering the message unintelligible. Gate B. If you remembered, if you knew Gate B, the key to mastery of the whole procedure remained intact with you. Gate B was the converse of the open sesame; it would keep you, passing safely through it, in the known, familiar, and inescapable, safe from caves of treasure and shadow. *Immediately. Gate B. Gate B.*

She could sense from the different quality of the atmosphere outside the door, and the doors beyond it, that the hall was emptying now. They were trailing, humping along under their burdens—the petit-point, the child in red boots—to the gate where the girl in the leopard-skin pillbox collected their shiny cards.

She took hers out. She looked around the cell as one looks around for a place to set down a vase of flowers or a note that mustn't blow away. It would not flush down the outlet; plastic doesn't disintegrate in water. As she had idly noticed before, it wouldn't easily tear up. She was not at all agitated; she was simply looking for somewhere to dispose of it, now. She heard the voice (was there a shade of hurt embarrassment in the rolling *r*-shaped *l*'s) appealing to the passenger who was holding up flight so-and-so to please . . . She noticed for the first time that there was actually a tiny window, with the sort of pane that tilts outwards from the bottom, just above the cistern. She stood on the seat-lid and tried to see out, just managing to post the shiny card like a letter through the slot.

Gate B, the voice offered, *Gate B.* But to pass through Gate B you had to have a card, without a card Gate B had no place in the procedure. She could not manage to see anything at all, straining precariously from up there, through the tiny window; there was no knowing at all where the card had fallen. But as she half-jumped, half-clambered down again, for a second the changed angle of her vision brought into sight something like a head—the top of a huge untidy palm tree, up in the sky, rearing perhaps between buildings or above shacks and muddy or dusty streets where there were donkeys, bicycles and barefoot people. She saw it only for that second but it was so very clear, she saw even that it was an old palm tree, the fronds rasping and sharpening against each other. And there was a crow—she was sure she had seen the black flap of a resident crow.

She sat down again. The cigarette had made a brown aureole round itself on the cistern. In the corner what she had thought was a date-pit was a dead cockroach. She flicked the dead cigarette butt at it. Heel-taps clattered into the outer room, an African voice said, Who is there? Please, are you there? She did not hold her breath or try to keep particularly still. There was no one there. All the lavatory doors were rattled in turn. There was a high-strung pause, as if the owner of the heels didn't know what to do next. Then the heels rang away again and the door of the Ladies' swung to with the heavy sound of fanned air.

There were bursts of commotion without, reaching her muffledly where she sat. The calm grew longer. Soon the intermittent commotion would cease; the jets must be breathing fire by now, the belts fastened and the cigarettes extinguished, although the air-conditioning wouldn't be working properly yet, on the ground, and they would be patiently sweating. They couldn't wait forever, when they were so nearly there. The plane would be beginning to trundle like a huge perambulator, it would be turning, winking, shuddering in summoned power.

Take off. It was perfectly still and quiet in the cell. She thought of the great butterfly; of the general with his beautiful markings of braid and medals. Take off.

So that was the sort of place it was: crows in old dusty palm trees, crows picking the carrion in open gutters, legless beggars threatening in an unknown tongue. Not Gate B, but some other gate. Suppose she were to climb out that window, would they ask her for her papers and put her in some other cell, at the general's pleasure? The general had no reason to trust anybody who did not take Gate B. No sound at all, now. The lavatories were given over to their own internal rumblings; the cistern gulped now and then. She was quite sure, at last, that flight so-and-so had followed its course; was gone. She lit another cigarette. She did not think at all about what to do next, not at all; if she had been inclined to think that, she would not have been sitting wherever it was she was. The butterfly, no doubt, was extinct and the general would dislike strangers; the explanations (everything has an explanation) would formulate themselves, in her absence, when the plane reached its destination. The duty-free liquor could be poured down the lavatory, but there remained the problem of the Swiss pocket-knife. And yet—through the forbidden doorway: grass, bougainvillea trained like standard roses, a road glimpsed there!

Graham Greene

(b. 1904)

In a writing career spread over forty years (his first novel, *The Man Within,* appeared in 1929), Graham Greene has published over thirty volumes of fiction, essays, plays, and poetry, and written a number of film scripts, including the screenplays of some of his own novels. He has been a journalist, film critic, intelligence officer (in Africa from 1941 to 1943), and an indefatigable traveler. His fictional writings reflect the breadth of his experience, and may be divided into three main groups: adventure stories, which Greene calls "entertainments," usually about spies or criminals, books such as *A Gun for Sale* (1936) or *The Third Man* (1950); "political" thrillers dramatizing ideological conflicts, as *England Made Me* (1935) or *The Quiet American* (1955); and "Catholic" novels which reflect Greene's preoccupation with sin, damnation, and the struggle between good and evil (Greene became a convert to Catholicism in 1926). The works in the last-named group (e.g., *Brighton Rock,* 1938, *The Power and the Glory,* 1940), are primarily concerned with the spiritual state of their protagonists, but they also make use of the conventions of the thriller: pursuit, betrayal, capture, violent death (sometimes self-inflicted). Even in his "entertainments," Greene is an essentially serious writer, always exploring questions of conduct and belief. The world of Greeneland—a world stretching from Brighton to Saigon, from Vienna to Haiti—is populated by priests and murderers, gangsters and revolutionaries, who live on the fringe of society, outcasts or rebels, whose spiritual and moral crises epitomize the modern search for values in an anarchic world.

"Brother" (1935; in *Collected Stories,* 1973) presents one of Greene's favorite themes, that of trust and betrayal. It deals with the political agitation of a restless Europe in the 1930s, and reflects his sympathy for leftist causes. Greene has always rejected comfortable orthodoxies in favor of a questioning spirit; he believes that the task of the storyteller is "to act as the devil's advocate, to elicit sympathy and a measure of understanding for those who lie outside the boundaries of State approval."

For further reading

Robert O. Evans, ed., *Graham Greene: Some Critical Considerations* (Lexington: University of Kentucky Press, 1963).

David Lodge, *Graham Greene* (New York: Columbia University Press, 1966).

Martin Shuttleworth and Simon Raven, "The Art of Fiction: III. Graham Greene," *Paris Review,* 1 (Autumn 1953), 24–41.

Brother

The Communists were the first to appear. They walked quickly, a group of about a dozen, up the boulevard which runs from Combat to Ménilmontant; a young man and a girl lagged a little way behind because the man's leg was hurt and the girl was helping him along. They looked impatient, harassed, hopeless, as if they were trying to catch a train which they knew already in their hearts they were too late to catch.

The proprietor of the café saw them coming when they were still a long way off; the lamps at that time were still alight (it was later that the bullets broke the bulbs and dropped darkness all over that quarter of Paris), and the group showed up plainly in the wide barren boulevard. Since sunset only one customer had entered the café, and very soon after sunset firing could be heard from the direction of Combat; the Métro station had closed hours ago. And yet something obstinate and undefeatable in the proprietor's character prevented him from putting up the shutters; it might have been avarice; he could not himself have told what it was as he pressed his broad yellow forehead against the glass and stared this way and that, up the boulevard and down the boulevard.

But when he saw the group and their air of hurry he began immediately to close his café. First he went and warned his only customer, who was practising billiard shots, walking round and round the table, frowning and stroking a thin moustache between shots, a little green in the face under the low diffused lights.

"The Reds are coming," the proprietor said, "you'd better be off. I'm putting up the shutters."

"Don't interrupt. They won't harm me," the customer said. "This is a tricky shot. Red's in baulk. Off the cushion. Screw on spot." He shot his ball straight into a pocket.

"I knew you couldn't do anything with that," the proprietor said, nodding his bald head. "You might just as well go home. Give me a hand with the shutters first. I've sent my wife away." The customer turned on him maliciously, rattling the cue between his fingers. "It was your talking that spoilt the shot. You've cause to be frightened, I dare say. But I'm a poor man. I'm safe. I'm not going to stir." He went across to his coat and took out a dry cigar. "Bring me a bock." He walked round the table on his toes and the balls clicked and the proprietor padded back into the bar, elderly and irritated. He did not fetch the beer but began to close the shutters; every move he made was slow and clumsy. Long before he had finished the group of Communists was outside.

He stopped what he was doing and watched them with furtive dislike. He was afraid that the rattle of the shutters would attract their attention. If I am very quiet and still, he thought, they may go on, and he remembered with malicious pleasure the police barricade across the Place de la République. That will finish them. In the meanwhile I must be very quiet, very still, and he felt a kind of warm satisfaction at the idea that worldly wisdom dictated the very attitude most suited to his nature. So he stared through the edge of a shutter, yellow, plump, cautious, hearing the billiard balls crackle in the other room, seeing the young man come limping up the pavement on the girl's arm, watching them stand and stare with dubious faces up the boulevard towards Combat.

But when they came into the café he was already behind the bar, smiling and bowing and missing nothing, noticing how they had divided forces, how six of them had begun to run back the way they had come.

The young man sat down in a dark corner above the cellar stairs and the others stood round the door waiting for something to happen. It gave the proprietor an odd feeling that they should stand there in his café not asking for a drink, knowing what to expect, when he, the owner, knew nothing, understood nothing. At last the girl said "Cognac," leaving the others and coming to the bar, but when he had poured it out for her, very careful to give a fair and not a generous measure, she simply took it to the man sitting in the dark and held it to his mouth.

"Three francs," the proprietor said. She took the glass and sipped a little and turned it so that the man's lips might touch the same spot. Then she knelt down and rested her forehead against the man's forehead and so they stayed.

"Three francs," the proprietor said, but he could not make his voice bold. The man was no longer visible in his corner, only the girl's back, thin and shabby in a black cotton frock, as she knelt, leaning forward to find the man's face. The proprietor was daunted by the four men at the door, by the knowledge that they were Reds who had no respect for private property, who would drink his wine and go away without paying, who would rape his women (but there was only his wife, and she was not there), who would rob his bank, who would murder him as soon as look at him. So with fear in his heart he gave up the three francs as lost rather than attract any more attention.

Then the worst that he contemplated happened.

One of the men at the door came up to the bar and told him to pour out four glasses of cognac. "Yes, yes," the proprietor said, fumbling with the cork, praying secretly to the Virgin to send an angel, to send the police, to send the Gardes Mobiles, now, immediately, before the cork came out, "that will be twelve francs."

"Oh, no, " the man said, "we are all comrades here. Share and share alike. Listen," he said, with earnest mockery, leaning across the bar, "all we have is yours just as much as it's ours, comrade," and stepping back a pace he presented himself to the proprietor, so that he might take his choice of stringy tie, of threadbare trousers, of starved features. "And it follows from that, comrade, that all you have is ours. So four cognacs. Share and share alike."

"Of course," the proprietor said, "I was only joking." Then he stood with bottle poised, and the four glasses tingled upon the counter. "A machine-gun," he said, "up by Combat," and smiled to see how for the moment the men forgot their brandy as they fidgeted near the door. Very soon now, he thought, and I shall be quit of them.

"A machine-gun," the Red said incredulously, "they're using machine-guns?"

"Well," the proprietor said, encouraged by this sign that the Gardes Mobiles were not very far away, "you can't pretend that you aren't armed yourselves." He leant across the bar in a way that was almost paternal. "After all, you know, your ideas—they wouldn't do in France. Free love."

"Who's talking of free love?" the Red said.

The proprietor shrugged and smiled and nodded at the corner. The girl knelt with her head on the man's shoulder, her back to the room. They were quite silent and the glass of brandy stood on the floor beside them. The girl's beret was pushed back on her head and one stocking was laddered and darned from knee to ankle.

"What, those two? They aren't lovers."

"I," the proprietor said, "with my bourgeois notions would have thought ... "

"He's her brother," the Red said.

The men came clustering round the bar and laughed at him, but softly as if a sleeper or a sick person were in the house. All the time they were listening for something. Between their shoulders the proprietor could look out across the boulevard; he could see the corner of the Faubourg du Temple.

"What are you waiting for?"

"For friends," the Red said. He made a gesture with open palm as if to say, You see, we share and share alike. We have no secrets.

Something moved at the corner of the Faubourg du Temple.

"Four more cognacs," the Red said.

"What about those two?" the proprietor asked.

"Leave them alone. They'll look after themselves. They're tired."

How tired they were. No walk up the boulevard from Ménilmontant could explain the tiredness. They seemed to have come farther and fared a great deal worse than their companions. They were more starved; they were infinitely more hopeless, sitting in their dark corner away from the friendly gossip, the amicable desperate voices which now confused the proprietor's brain, until for a moment he believed himself to be a host entertaining friends.

He laughed and made a broad joke directed at the two of them; but they made no sign of understanding. Perhaps they were to be pitied, cut off from the camaraderie round the counter; perhaps they were to be envied for their deeper comradeship. The proprietor thought for no reason at all of the bare grey trees of the Tuileries like a series of exclamation marks drawn against the winter sky. Puzzled, disintegrated, with all his bearings lost, he stared out through the door towards the Faubourg.

It was as if they had not seen each other for a long while and would soon again be saying good-bye. Hardly aware of what he was doing he filled the four glasses with brandy. They stretched out worn blunted fingers for them.

"Wait," he said. "I've got something better than this"; then paused, conscious of what was happening across the boulevard. The lamplight splashed down on blue steel helmets; the Gardes Mobiles were lining out across the entrace to the Faubourg, and a machine-gun pointed directly at the café windows.

So, the proprietor thought, my prayers are answered. Now I must do my part, not look, not warn them, save myself. Have they covered the side door? I will get the other bottle. Real Napoleon brandy. Share and share alike.

He felt a curious lack of triumph as he opened the trap of the bar and came out. He tried not to walk quickly back towards the billiard room. Nothing that he did must warn these men; he tried to spur himself with the thought that every slow casual step he took was a blow for France, for his café, for his savings. He had to step over the girl's feet to pass her; she was asleep. He noted the sharp shoulder blades thrusting through the cotton, and raised his eyes and met her brother's, filled with pain and despair.

He stopped. He found he could not pass without a word. It was as if he needed to explain something, as if he belonged to the wrong party. With false bonhomie he waved the corkscrew he carried in the other's face. "Another cognac, eh?"

"It's no good talking to them," the Red said. They're German. They don't understand a word."

"German?"

"That's what's wrong with his leg. A concentration camp."

The proprietor told himself that he must be quick, that he must put a door between him and them, that the end was very close, but he was bewildered by the hopelessness in the man's gaze. "What's he doing here?" Nobody answered him. It was as if his question were too foolish to need a reply. With his head sunk upon his breast the proprietor went past, and the girl slept on. He was like a stranger leaving a room where all the rest are friends. A German. They don't understand a word; and up, up through the heavy darkness of his mind, through the avarice and the dubious triumph, a few German words remembered from very old days climbed like spies into the light: a line from the *Lorelei* learnt at school, *Kamerad* with its war-time suggestion of fear and surrender, and oddly from nowhere the phrase *mein Bruder.* He opened the door of the billiard room and closed it behind him and softly turned the key.

"Spot in baulk," the customer explained and leant across the great green table, but while he took aim, wrinkling his narrow peevish eyes, the firing started. It came in two bursts with a rip of glass between. The girl cried out something, but it was not one of the words he knew. Then feet ran across the floor, the trap of the bar slammed. The proprietor sat back against the table and listened and listened for any further sound; but silence came in under the door and silence through the keyhole.

"The cloth. My God, the cloth," the customer said, and the proprietor looked down at his own hand which was working the corkscrew into the table.

"Will this absurdity ever end?" the customer said. "I shall go home."

"Wait," the proprietor said. "Wait." He was listening to voices and footsteps in the other room. These were voices he did not recognize. Then a car drove up and presently drove away again. Somebody rattled the handle of the door.

"Who is it?" the proprietor called.

"Who are you? Open that door."

"Ah," the customer said with relief, "the police. Where was I now? Spot in baulk." He began to chalk his cue. The proprietor opened the door. Yes, the Gardes Mobiles had arrived; he was safe again, though his windows were smashed. The Reds had vanished as if they had never been. He looked at the raised trap, at the smashed electric bulbs, at the broken bottle which dripped behind the bar. The café was full of men, and he remembered with odd relief that he had not had time to lock the side door.

"Are you the owner?" the officer asked. "A bock for each of these men and a cognac for myself. Be quick about it."

The proprietor calculated: "Nine francs fifty," and watched closely with bent head the coins rattle down upon the counter.

"You see," the officer said with significance, "we pay." He nodded towards the side door. "Those others: did they pay?"

No, the proprietor admitted, they had not paid, but as he counted the coins and slipped them into the till, he caught himself silently repeating the officer's order—"A bock for each of these men." Those others, he thought, one's got to say that for them, they weren't mean about the drink. It was four cognacs with them. But, of course, they did not pay. "And my windows," he complained aloud with sudden asperity, "what about my windows?"

"Never you mind," the officer said, "the government will pay. You have only to send in your bill. Hurry up now with my cognac. I have no time for gossip."

"You can see for yourself," the proprietor said, "how the bottles have been broken. Who will pay for that?"

"Everything will be paid for," the officer said.

"And now I must go to the cellar to fetch more."

He was angry at the reiteration of the word pay. They enter my café, he thought, they smash my windows, they order me about and think that all is well if they pay, pay, pay. It occurred to him that these men were intruders.

"Step to it," the officer said and turned and rebuked one of the men who had leant his rifle against the bar.

At the top of the cellar stairs the proprietor stopped. They were in darkness, but by the light from the bar he could just make out a body half-way down. He began to tremble violently, and it was some seconds before he could strike a match. The young German lay head downwards, and the blood from his head had dropped on to the step below. His eyes were open and stared back at the proprietor with the old despairing expression of life. The proprietor would not believe that he was dead. "Kamerad," he said bending down, while the match singed his fingers and went out, trying to recall some phrase in German, but he could only remember, as he bent lower still, "mein Bruder." Then suddenly he turned and ran up the steps, waved the match-box in the officer's face, and called out in a low hysterical voice to him and his men and to the customer stooping under the low green shade, "Cochons. Cochons."

"What was that? What was that?" the officer exclaimed. "Did you say that he was your brother? It's impossible," and he frowned incredulously at the proprietor and rattled the coins in his pocket.

Ernest Hemingway

(1899–1961)

Perhaps the most widely read and influential writer of his generation, Ernest Hemingway embodied the vigor, the restlessness, and the despair of the twentieth century, in his life as well as his writings. The son of a physician, he was born in Oak Park, near Chicago, and spent his boyhood in Illinois and Michigan. After leaving school in 1917 and working briefly as a reporter for the *Kansas City Star,* he joined the Red Cross, and drove an ambulance on the Italian front until he was wounded. After the war, he became a reporter for the Toronto *Star,* in company with Morley Callaghan. Then Hemingway began to produce the series of novels and stories in which he drew the sense of waste and sterility that marked the postwar period, and which had led his friend Gertrude Stein to remark, "You are all a lost generation." *In Our Time* appeared in 1924, followed by *The Sun Also Rises* (1926), and *Men Without Women* (1927); in these works Hemingway revealed an originality of plot and a striking economy of style which quickly established him as a major writer. *A Farewell to Arms* (1929) was inspired by Hemingway's war experiences in Italy; and *For Whom the Bell Tolls* (1940) grew out of the period he spent in Spain in 1937 during the Spanish Civil War. Between 1941 and 1945 he was a war correspondent in Europe and the Far East. His last major work was *The Old Man and the Sea* (1952), which brought him a Pulitzer Prize in 1953; and in 1954 he was awarded the Nobel Prize for literature. In his last years Hemingway suffered periods of illness and depression; and while in Idaho in July 1961 he committed suicide with a shotgun.

Hemingway's life was filled with action and adventure; and his preoccupation with the physical aspect of existence, particularly its violence, is reflected in most of his writing. Whether his subject is the horror of war, or the struggle between man and nature, Hemingway draws a picture of a world where the only certainties are pain, deprivation, or death. Whatever their hopes or ideals may have been, his characters learn that life is a futile ordeal; to counter this, they must develop a protective shell of toughness, or endure their fate with numb resignation. Even in "Hills Like White Elephants" (from *Men Without Women*), a story far removed from the brutalities of war or the bullring, there is an undercurrent of emotional violence. The dialogue is terse and laconic; but Hemingway's spare style conveys hidden tensions with admirable understatement, hinting at the sterility and breakdown of a whole way of life.

For further reading

Leo Gurko, *Ernest Hemingway and the Pursuit of Heroism* (New York: T. Y. Crowell, 1968).

Eusebio L. Rodrigues, " 'Hills Like White Elephants': An Analysis," *Literary Criterion,* 5 (1962), 105–109.

Philip Young, *Ernest Hemingway* (New York: Holt, Rinehart and Winston, 1952).

Hills Like White Elephants

The hills across the valley of the Ebro were long and white. On this side there was no shade and no trees and the station was between two lines of rails in the sun. Close against the side of the station there was the warm shadow of the building and a curtain, made of strings of bamboo beads, hung across the open door into the bar, to keep out flies. The American and the girl with him sat at a table in the shade, outside the building. It was very hot and the express from Barcelona would come in forty minutes. It stopped at this junction for two minutes and went on to Madrid.

"What should we drink?" the girl asked. She had taken off her hat and put it on the table.

"It's pretty hot," the man said.

"Let's drink beer."

"Dos cervezas," the man said into the curtain.

"Big ones?" a woman asked from the doorway.

"Yes. Two big ones."

The woman brought two glasses of beer and two felt pads. She put the felt pads and the beer glasses on the table and looked at the man and the girl. The girl was looking off at the line of hills. They were white in the sun and the country was brown and dry.

"They look like white elephants," she said.

"I've never seen one," the man drank his beer.

"No, you wouldn't have."

"I might have," the man said. "Just because you say I wouldn't have doesn't prove anything."

The girl looked at the bead curtain. "They've painted something on it," she said. "What does it say?"

"Anis del Toro. It's a drink."

"Could we try it?"

The man called "Listen" through the curtain. The woman came out from the bar.

"Four reales."

"We want two Anis del Toro."

"With water?"

"Do you want it with water?"

"I don't know," the girl said. "Is it good with water?"

"It's all right."

"You want them with water?" asked the woman.

"Yes, with water."

"It tastes like licorice," the girl said and put the glass down.

"That's the way with everything."

"Yes," said the girl. "Everything tastes of licorice. Especially all the things you've waited so long for, like absinthe."

"Oh, cut it out."

"You started it," the girl said. "I was being amused. I was having a fine time."

"Well, let's try and have a fine time."

"All right. I was trying. I said the mountains looked like white elephants. Wasn't that bright?"

"That was bright."

"I wanted to try this new drink. That's all we do, isn't it—look at things and try new drinks?"

"I guess so."

The girl looked across at the hills.

"They're lovely hills," she said. "They don't really look like white elephants. I just meant the coloring of their skin through the trees."

"Should we have another drink?"

"All right."

The warm wind blew the bead curtain against the table.

"The beer's nice and cool," the man said.

"It's lovely," the girl said.

"It's really an awfully simple operation, Jig," the man said. "It's not really an operation at all."

The girl looked at the ground the table legs rested on.

"I know you wouldn't mind it, Jig. It's really not anything. It's just to let the air in."

The girl did not say anything.

"I'll go with you and I'll stay with you all the time. They just let the air in and then it's all perfectly natural."

"Then what will we do afterward?"

"We'll be fine afterward. Just like we were before."

"What makes you think so?"

"That's the only thing that bothers us. It's the only thing that's made us unhappy."

The girl looked at the bead curtain, put her hand out and took hold of two of the strings of beads.

"And you think then we'll be all right and be happy."

"I know we will. You don't have to be afraid. I've known lots of people that have done it."

"So have I," said the girl. "And afterward they were all so happy."

"Well," the man said, "if you don't want to you don't have to. I wouldn't have you do it if you didn't want to. But I know it's perfectly simple."

"And you really want to?"

"I think it's the best thing to do. But I don't want you to do it if you don't really want to."

"And if I do it you'll be happy and things will be like they were and you'll love me?"

"I love you now. You know I love you."

"I know. But if I do it, then it will be nice again if I say things are like white elephants, and you'll like it?"

"I'll love it. I love it now but I just can't think about it. You know how I get when I worry."

"If I do it you won't ever worry?"

"I won't worry about that because it's perfectly simple."

"Then I'll do it. Because I don't care about me."

"What do you mean?"

"I don't care about me."

"Well, I care about you."

"Oh, yes. But I don't care about me. And I'll do it and then everything will be fine."

"I don't want you to do it if you feel that way."

The girl stood up and walked to the end of the station. Across, on the other side, were fields of grain and trees along the banks of the Ebro. Far away, beyond the river, were mountains. The shadow of a cloud moved across the field of grain and she saw the river through the trees.

"And we could have all this," she said. "And we could have everything and every day we make it more impossible."

"What did you say?"

"I said we could have everything."

"We can have everything."

"No, we can't."

"We can have the whole world."

"No, we can't."

"We can go everywhere."

"No, we can't. It isn't ours any more."

"It's ours."

"No, it isn't. And once they take it away, you never get it back."

"But they haven't taken it away." ·

"We'll wait and see."

"Come on back in the shade," he said. "You mustn't feel that way."

"I don't feel any way," the girl said. "I just know things."

"I don't want you to do anything that you don't want to do—"

"Nor that isn't good for me," she said. "I know. Could we have another beer?"

"All right. But you've got to realize—"

"I realize," the girl said. "Can't we maybe stop talking?"

They sat down at the table and the girl looked across at the hills on the dry side of the valley and the man looked at her and at the table.

"You've got to realize," he said, "that I don't want you to do it if you don't want to. I'm perfectly willing to go through with it if it means anything to you."

"Doesn't it mean anything to you? We could get along."

"Of course it does. But I don't want anybody but you. I don't want any one else. And I know it's perfectly simple."

"Yes, you know it's perfectly simple."

"It's all right for you to say that, but I do know it."

"Would you do something for me now?"

"I'd do anything for you."

"Would you please please please please please please please stop talking?"

He did not say anything but looked at the bags against the wall of the station. There were labels on them from all the hotels where they had spent nights.

"But I don't want you to," he said. "I don't care anything about it."

"I'll scream," the girl said.

The woman came out through the curtains with two glasses of beer and put them down on the damp felt pads. "The train comes in five minutes," she said.

"What did she say?" asked the girl.

"That the train is coming in five minutes."

The girl smiled brightly at the woman, to thank her.

"I'd better take the bags over to the other side of the station," the man said. She smiled at him.

"All right. Then come back and we'll finish the beer."

He picked up the two heavy bags and carried them around the station to the other tracks. He looked up the tracks but could not see the train. Coming back, he walked through the barroom, where people waiting for the train were drinking. He drank an Anis at the bar and looked at the people. They were all waiting reasonably for the train. He went out through the bead curtain. She was sitting at the table and smiled at him.

"Do you feel better?" he asked.

"I feel fine," she said. "There's nothing wrong with me. I feel fine."

Hugh Hood

(b. 1928)

"I think," said Hugh Hood in an interview, "rituals and liturgies are artistic forms of group behavior, the means by which we try to preserve the culture, and acting the values of the culture over and over again, keep asserting that we want to stay together for this reason, keep asserting that the ocean won't conquer us, or that famine won't conquer us and so on." A practicing Catholic, whose examination of the function of religion in life has led him, as it did Morley Callaghan, to contemplate the relation between innocence and pride, Hood posits that human assertions are man's only defence against the chaos of the universe. Of these, religion is one of the most complex in form and function and one of the most necessary for human survival. It represents man's appreciation of the transcendental in everyday reality, and, as a corollary, it allows Hood to reject theories of the unconscious as explanations of the irrational and visionary in human experience.

Novels like *White Figure, White Ground* (1964) and *A Game of Touch* (1970) and his three volumes of short stories express this perspective in different ways. His characteristic setting is the province of Quebec, where he now lives—born in Toronto, he teaches at l'université de Montréal—and one of his collections, a unified work called *Around the Mountain: Scenes from Montreal Life* (1967), has been his most critically successful book. But other novels have employed American and African settings, and his landscapes, sharply perceived, often take on (in Hood's own words) a Fellini-like "super-realism." Sometimes his works end up as fantasies, and sometimes (as in "The Dog Explosion," from *The Fruit Man, The Meat Man & The Manager,* 1972) the fantasy catches satirically at the absurdities of modern institutions. Science, advertising, faddishness, the media, and social-reform groups all prove targets for Hood's wit, but the satire is gentle and sympathetic; it does not stridently call for reform. Fads are themselves rituals of a kind, after all, and are therefore attempts to act out a culture's values.

For further reading

Dennis Duffy, "The Novels of Hugh Hood," *Canadian Literature,* 47 (Winter 1971), 10–25.

Victoria G. Hale, "An Interview with Hugh Hood," *WLWE,* 11, no. 1 (April 1972), 35–41.

Hugh Hood, *The Governor's Bridge Is Closed* (Ottawa: Oberon, 1973).

The Dog Explosion

For Raymond Fraser and Sharon Johnston

Not used to foreseeing consequences, a bit of a kidder, Tom Fuess sat quietly in his living-room, in a comfortable armchair in front of the fire. He thought of making mischief. His wife Connie had her legs curled up underneath her on the davenport; she was reading some book or other and looked absorbed in it. Tom looked at her thighs, then at the fireplace; the light reflected on her pantie-hose excited him. He shook out the evening paper, making plenty of noise so that Connie would look up. Then he folded the sheets back and squinted at the middle of page three, as if concentrating on the news. He spoke in a level voice:

Science Strikes at New Scare

Dogs to Cover Earth by Year 2000

Baltimore, Oct. 9, A.P. While North American and European foreign-aid programs strive to control man's threat to reproduce himself out of existence, via birth-control clinics in underdeveloped lands (see picture Page 4), an unforeseen new peril strikes at efforts to limit food-consuming populations, said Doctor Bentley French, famed animal ecologist and head of the Johns Hopkins Institute for Canine Reproduction Research, today at the second annual international conference on dog population.

"Unless steps to correct an unmistakable statistical trend are taken immediately," said Doctor French, "the balance of world food supply is gravely in danger of irreparable shock. Worse still, if present dog birth-rates are maintained, and the extension of normal canine life-expectancies continues, a drastic over-population problem will confront us in the mid-seventies."

"Congress must act immediately to appropriate funds and inaugurate programs for world dog-population surveillance. By the year 1980 these trends will be irreversible, and the dog explosion will amount to nothing less than Armageddon."

"According to latest figures obtained from all quarters of the scientific community," said Doctor French emphatically, "unless we in the free world move at once, the entire habitable living-space of the globe will be covered with dogs' bodies to a depth exceeding three feet, by the year 2000."

"Samoyedes are the worst for some reason," concluded the Johns Hopkins spokesman."

"Hmmmnn," said Tom, ostensibly to himself, "here's another item, like kind of a continuing dialogue."

Samoyede Owners Rebut French

A.S.P.C.A. "Deeply Involved" Says Prexy

"Hmmmmnn ... rejection of any measure to extirpate man's best friend ... dog's inalienable right to multiply his kind ... pariah dogs on Indian sub-continent ... give a dog a bad name ... science no ultimate authority ... Samoyede breeders press counter-charges against Afghans and Pomeranians."

He glanced up at Connie, who was now staring at him with electrified attention. "I'll be a son of a bitch," he said, "I always thought dogs were some kind of sacred cow."

"You!" said his wife.

"No, no."

"You made that up. You did, Tom."

"Not at all."

"Read it again."

He repeated what he had said, making slight changes in the word-ing. Connie got up off the davenport and came around behind his chair. "Show me where it says that," she commanded.

"Got it right here," he said, "let's see. 'Nudie shows ruled accept-able to general public.' 'Jacqueline Onassis fells cameraman with karate chop.' I tell you, it's here somewhere."

"Balls," said his wife, and he dropped the paper and started to laugh helplessly. "The dog explosion, Christ, can't you just see it?"

Connie began to get a malicious gleam in her eye. "See what?"

"It's a natural, that's all. If I went up to the university and said something about this casually to, oh, let's say, three people, it would galvanize the intellectual community. I'm willing to bet you the Montreal *Star* would have a full-page story on it within a month, anyway six weeks."

"There isn't a word of truth in it, is there?"

"Not an atom. It just came to me. Imagine the possible implica-tions. Serious men in lab coats hunched over our four-legged friends in the small hours, seeking a way to implant anti-ovulatory capsules in the thigh at birth."

"And trying to figure out how to keep them from scratching?"

"Now you've got it. Programs of public education in the Bombay and Calcutta metropolitan areas, with pictures and easy-to-under-stand diagrams because, naturally, dogs can't read."

"But they sure can screw."

"You bet they can, the little buggers. Doggy diaphragms. Research into whether or not contraceptives have undesirable side-effects. High incidence of migraine among Pekingese on the pill."

"Do owners who forget the daily dose unconsciously desire their pet's pregnancy?" asked Connie.

"Or their own," said Tom. "Then there's the darker side of the program: mass neurosis, the threat to individual dog living space, the resentments of dogs in the have-not nations."

"Now you're letting your imagination run away with you."

"Well maybe, just a bit. If there's anything I can't stand, though, it's discrimination on the basis of race, colour or breed."

Connie said, "It's a good thing you don't talk to anybody but me this way. You could stir up a lot of animosity."

"All the same ..." he said.

"You mustn't."

"It's worth a try."

"Don't say I encouraged you."

"Certainly not."

A day or two later, Tom started to circulate this rumour among faculty members chosen apparently at random: a junior lecturer known for his radicalism and espousal of all humanitarian causes; two men from the computer centre he bumped into at the coffee machines.

"It doesn't seem possible," one of them said.

"I don't know ... I don't know," said the other, looking upset. "Remember, they laughed at Malthus. Where did you hear this?" he asked Tom.

"I read it somewhere, I think in the *Star*."

"It's possible all right. It's all a question of the curve of progression. I never thought of it before, but you do see a hell of a lot of dogs around."

"Sure do," said Tom, finishing his coffee. He watched the two information theorists walk away agitatedly, and felt pleased with himself. The next person he inoculated was an elderly department chairman, close to retirement, a kindly man unwilling to think ill of anybody and therefore very receptive to fantasy.

"Have you heard about this dog business, sir?"

Professor Joyce gave a start. "I don't want to hear any scandal, Fuess," he said.

Tom told him his tale.

"The poor creatures, surely something can be done for them," said Professor Joyce.

"Well, you see sir, the whole problem is in the communications breakdown."

"Of course, of course."

"It's a question of getting across to them, don't you see?"

"Perfectly."

"I understand that a number of linguistics departments are trying to evolve a code for dog language." When he said this a flicker of doubt crossed Professor Joyce's face, and he went on hastily, giving the story colour, "You know, like the work they've been doing with dolphins. Apparently dolphins have a consistent system of verbal signals on regular wave-lengths, with logical structures. Now if they could only break down the language of dogs in the same way. . . ."

"I don't think there's any consistency in a dog's utterances," said the professor. "I should think the right way to tackle the problem would be to help them to retrain their impulses, I mean to begin with. Get right at the heart of the matter and alleviate misery. I don't like to think of any sentient creature suffering the pangs of hunger."

"Maybe some dogs would sooner reproduce than eat," said Tom.

"There is that," said Professor Joyce. "Tell me, do you know of any program of public education?" He fumbled around in his attaché case, and to Tom's amazement produced his cheque book.

"I don't think the public has been alerted, sir."

"Pity," said the old department chairman, letting his cheque book flap open and looking vaguely around him, "a great pity."

Tom went home and announced his results to Connie, who was already beginning to chicken out on the experiment. "You better not mess around with Joyce," she said. "For one, he's too nice, and for two, he has an awful conscience."

"That's why I picked him out."

"Do you think he'll remember that it was you?"

"I'll deny it."

"You'd better let it drop."

He really meant to take her advice, and make no further references to the dog explosion for some time, except now and then to drop the phrase into conversation as though it were one of the recognized social problems of our time, like the generation gap or the mono-lithic nature of the power structure. He mentioned it in a couple of classes and noticed that the students nodded wisely, as though they were wholly *au courant* dogwise. This reaction seemed promising to him, and he idled through his lectures and his daily routine, waiting for feedback.

A month later he met Professor Joyce in the cafeteria, and they had lunch together, from time to eyeing one another with misgivings. Over dessert the professor broke a silence of some minutes by clear-ing his throat twice, then saying, "This dog affair is snowballing, eh?"

Tom ate two spoonfuls of caramel pudding without answering.

"The dogs, the dogs," said Joyce.

"What?" said Tom.

"You know. C.A.N.I.N.E. *Committee Against Native Instincts and Natural Energies.*"

Tom almost choked, but managed to preserve his composure. "I don't understand you," he said.

"I'm a founding member," said Professor Joyce. "I don't like the name too much. I mean generally I'm in favour of nature and energy. Lifetime of studies in Nietzsche, you know. All that. Still, they were the only words that would fit the letters, and I suppose they stick in your mind. Good advertising."

"But what is it?"

"C.A.N.I.N.E.?"

"Yes."

"It's the official relief agency to combat dog overpopulation, for this area to start with. But we hope to extend our activities internationally. We plan to get in touch with that fellow in Baltimore, what's his name? Baldwin French?"

"Who?"

"Baldwin French, isn't that it?"

"The big dog man at Hopkins?" said Tom, hoping to mislead. "French doesn't sound quite right to me. Might be Francis."

"You've heard of him then," said the professor with relief.

"Somebody said something to me about him, when was it, might have been a month ago."

"It wasn't you who mentioned the problem to me?"

"Me, sir? No, I've never mentioned it to a soul." In case this should seem heartless, he added, "I've thought about it quite a lot, naturally. You might say it's been constantly on my mind."

Professor Joyce looked sad. "I was certain it was you, Fuess. Must have been somebody else. Sorry. Pressure of work, you know, and then I have all these committees and my work with C.A.N.I.N.E. It may have been somebody in the biology department."

Tom got away as soon as he could, which was not too soon because the professor insisted on giving him a full rundown on animal population.

"I don't know where he got all those figures," he said to Connie that evening. "Do you suppose he was kidding me?"

"I don't like to think about it. That's exactly how these things get started," she said. She did a lot of grumbling while washing the dishes and hurried off to bed an hour earlier than usual on the pretext of a sick headache, leaving Tom to wander around downstairs. He knew that she liked old Joyce and thought that perhaps he had exceeded certain unspoken limits. He might say something about what he had done next time he saw the professor, but decided that he wouldn't go looking for him. It would be better if they just came across each other accidentally.

The old guy might look like a bumbler on the brink of senile decay, but he had terrific energy and a well-known reluctance to let anything drop, once he'd taken it up out of humanitarian impulse. Tom considered this out of line; he couldn't see why anybody had to make a Federal case out of a mere prank. After all, what he had done was harmless sport, in no way destructive, and it seemed to him kind of a shame that he would now have to embarrass himself with such a confession. Maybe nothing would come of the affair; better wait and see. Meanwhile there was Connie to placate. She upbraided him continually for his frivolity.

"A joke is one thing and malice is something else."

"Malice?"

"You've got a nasty habit of speaking out of both sides of your mouth at once."

"White man speak with forked tongue," said Tom thoughtlessly.

"Oh, cut it out!"

"Sorry."

He came home one afternoon to find her staring morosely at the paper, and when he asked what was the matter she pointed out a tiny box on page sixty-four, next to the comics:

C.A.N.I.N.E.

All contributions gratefully accepted
Star. Box 261b. Montreal

"That's nothing," he said, but all the same he was worried. He kept seeing Professor Joyce away down at the end of a corridor or turning into somebody's office, arm-in-arm with men from the computer center. The old man would wave to him cheerily, mouthing good news at him from a distance, his pockets bulging with papers. It got so that when Tom saw dogs making love in alleys or pissing against posts, digging in garbage cans or just walking along on the end of a leash, he would snarl mentally, sometimes even mumbling curses under his breath.

Around Hallowe'en Tom and Connie were sitting in the playroom watching TV late at night when the station breaks are surrounded by commercials. The movie on the CBC station was lousy, so they switched to the NBC outlet in Burlington just as the Carson show went away for a break and a string of half-minute spots came on. They drowsed through Uncle Ben's Converted Rice, Northern New England Light and Power, and Albert's Restaurant-Hotel on the Northway, just outside of Glen's Falls. Then they came sharply awake when the familiar face of one of the great movie stars of the forties hove in view on the screen.

"Hi there, I'm X.Y.Z. (famous movie star of the forties)," he said. "Say, do you know that over seventy percent of the world's dogs kennel-up hungry every night?"

"Christ," said Tom.

The star continued. "When your Rover or Prince or Spot beds down on his warm blanket in your kitchen, do you ever stop to think about his millions of cousins in Asia and Africa and Latin America who sleep in ditches and swamps, who go hungry because they have no master to feed them, who breed irresponsibly because they just don't know any better? Are you and your neighbours aware that unless the unplanned reproduction of world dog population is brought under control now—NOT TOMORROW—NOW—that human and animal food supplies will be inadequate in five years, and at mass famine level by 1980? More dogs are alive today than in the entire previous history of the world. Ninety-five percent of all dogs ever born are alive now and the numbers are increasing hourly. Help us to avoid the crisis of the dog explosion! Write today for the free pamphlet, *From Pillar to Post,* and send your contributions to C.A.N.I.N.E., Box 500, Washington, D.C. Remember, only you can help avert disaster. Don't forget. That's C.A.N.I.N.E., Committee Against Native Instincts and Natural Energies. Post Office Box 500, Washington, D.C."

The station's call letters came on the screen; then Johnny Carson reappeared, but Tom switched the set off. He and Connie looked at each other silently for a while. Finally she said, "You must never, never admit that you had anything to do with this."

Tom said, "Half a minute on the network. Can you imagine what that cost? They've got it institutionalized now—somebody has a letter-drop in Washington and he just sits there opening envelopes with cheques in them. There's no way to stop it."

"That's right," said Mrs. Fuess.

After that whenever they saw one of that series of public-service announcements they would huddle close together as if for mutual protection, giving themselves up to apprehension and dismay.

Ted Hughes
(b. 1930)

Ted Hughes is known primarily as a poet, whose writing focuses largely on the physical aspects of nature and reflects the stark and rugged quality of the Yorkshire moors where he grew up. After serving in the Royal Air Force, he completed his education at Cambridge University, and in 1956 married the American poet Sylvia Plath (d. 1963). In his first collection of poems, *The Hawk in the Rain* (1957), and again in *Lupercal* (1960), Hughes gives powerful expression to a dual vision: he celebrates the vibrancy and vivid sensuousness of life in all its forms, but is equally conscious of nature's menace and latent violence. His imagination seems preoccupied with images of strife, with the perpetual conflict between hunter and hunted, and with the primitive brutality of which man is no less capable than the animals. Even his writings for children, such as the story *The Iron Man* (1968), present baleful monsters which loom out of the night. Creatures of prey—hawks, pikes, foxes, jaguars—move darkly through his pages; and he pursues the theme of a natural universe wracked by bloody violence in his collection of poems entitled *Crow* (1970).

"Sunday" is taken from *Wodwo* (1967), a collection of poems, stories, and a play, which, according to an Author's Note, "are intended to be read together, as parts of a single work." "Wodwo," a word in the Middle English poem *Sir Gawayne and the Green Knight,* means wild satyr or troll of the forest; and Hughes's book confronts the reader with harsh images of dark and inarticulate forces lurking in and around man, like the monsters lying in wait for Sir Gawayne. In "Sunday" man himself is the agent of predatory violence, sloughing off his humanity and descending to the level of a rat, in a pagan and ritualistic combat which both fascinates and repels.

For further reading

John Ferns, "Over the Same Ground: Ted Hughes, *Wodwo,"Far Point,* 1 (1968), 66–70.
C. J. Rawson, "Ted Hughes: A Reappraisal," *Essays in Criticism,* 15 (1965), 77–94.
Keith Sagar, *Ted Hughes* (Harlow, Essex: Longmans, 1972).

Sunday

Michael marched off to chapel beside his sister, rapping his Sunday shoes down on to the pavement to fetch the brisk, stinging echo off housewalls, wearing the detestable blue blazer with its meaningless badge as a uniform loaded with honours and privilege. In chapel he sat erect, arms folded, instead of curling down on to his spine like a prawn and sinking his chin between his collar-bones as under the

steady pressure of a great hand, which was his usual attitude of
worship. He sang the hymns and during the prayers thought exult-
antly of Top Wharf Pub, trying to remember what time those places
opened.

All this zest, however, was no match for the sermon. The minister's voice soared among the beams, tireless, as if he were still re-
hearsing, and after ten minutes these organ-like modulations began
to work Michael into a torment of impatience. The nerve-ends all
over his body prickled and swarmed. He almost had to sink to his
knees. Thoughts of shouting, "Oh, well!"—one enormous sigh, or
simply running out of chapel, brought a fine sweat on to his temples.
Finally he closed his eyes and began to imagine a wolf galloping
through snow-filled, moonlit forest. Without fail this image was the
first thing in his mind whenever he shut his eyes on these situations
of constraint, in school, in waiting-rooms, with visitors. The wolf
urged itself with all its strength through a land empty of everything
but trees and snow. After a while he drifted to vaguer things, a few
moments of freedom before his impatience jerked him back to see
how the sermon was doing. It was still soaring. He closed his eyes
and the wolf was there again.

By the time the doors opened, letting light stream in, he felt
stupefied. He edged out with the crowd. Then the eleven-o'clock
Sunday sky struck him. He had forgotten it was so early in the day.
But with the light and the outside world his mind returned in a
rush. Leaving his sister deep in the chapel, buried in a pink and blue
bouquet of her friends, and evading the minister who, having pro-
cessed his congregation generally within, had darted round the side
of the chapel to the porch and was now setting his personal seal, a
crushing smile and a soft, supporting handclasp, on each member of
the flock as they stumbled out, Michael took the three broad steps
at a leap and dodged down the crowded path among the graves, like
a person with an important dispatch.

But he was no sooner out through the gate than the stitches of his
shoes seemed suddenly to tighten, and his damped hair tightened on
his scalp. He slowed to a walk.

To the farthest skyline it was Sunday. The valley walls, throughout the week wet, hanging, uncomfortable woods and mud-hole
farms, were today neat, remote, and irreproachably pretty, postcard
pretty. The blue sky, the sparklingly smokeless Sunday air, had
disinfected them. Picnickers and chapel-hikers were already up
there, sprinkled like confetti along the steep lanes and paths, creeping imperceptibly upward towards the brown line of the moors.
Spotless, harmless, church-going slopes! Life, over the whole countryside, was suspended for the day.

Below him the town glittered in the clear air and sunlight. Throughout the week it resembled from this point a volcanic pit, bottomless in places, a jagged fissure into a sulphurous underworld, the smoke dragging off the chimneys of the mills and houserows like a tearing fleece. Now it lay as under shallow, slightly warm, clear water, with still streets and bright yards.

There was even something Sundayish about the pavements, something untouchably proper, though nothing had gone over them since grubby Saturday except more feet and darkness.

Superior to all this for once, and quite enjoying it again now he was on his way, Michael went down the hill into the town with strides that jammed his toes into the ends of his shoes. He turned into the Memorial Gardens, past prams, rockeries, forbidden grass, trees with labels, and over the ornamental canal bridge to the bowling greens that lay on the level between canal and river.

His father was there, on the farthest green, with two familiar figures—Harry Rutley, the pork butcher, and Mr Stinson, a tall, sooty, lean man who held his head as if he were blind and spoke rarely, and then only as if phrasing his most private thoughts to himself. A man Michael preferred not to look at. Michael sat on a park bench behind their jack and tried to make himself obvious.

The paths were full of people. Last night this had been a parade of couples, foursomes, gangs and lonely ones—the electricity gathered off looms, sewing-machines and shop counters since Monday milling round the circuit and discharging up the sidepaths among the shrubbery in giggling darkness and shrieks. But now it was families, an after-chapel procession of rustlings and murmurings, lacy bosoms, tight blue pinstripe suits and daisy-chains of children. Soon Michael was worn out, willing the bowls against their bias or against the crown of the green or to roll one foot farther and into the trough or to collide and fall in halves. He could see the Wesleyan Church clock at quarter past eleven and stared at it for what seemed like five minutes, convinced it had stopped.

He stood up as the three men came over to study the pattern of the bowls.

"Are we going now, Dad?"

"Just a minute, lad. Come and have a game."

That meant at least another game whether he played or not. Another quarter of an hour! And to go and get out a pair of bowls was as good as agreeing to stay there playing till one.

"We might miss him."

His father laughed. Only just remembering his promise, thought Michael.

"He'll not be there till well on. We shan't miss him."

His father kicked his bowls together and Harry Rutley slewed the rubber mat into position.

"But will he be there sure?"

Sunday dinner was closer every minute. Then it was sleepy Sunday afternoon. Then Aunt-infested Sunday tea. His father laughed again.

"Billy Red'll be coming down today, won't he, Harry?"

Harry Rutley, pale, slow, round, weighed his jack. He had lost the tip of an ear at the Dardanelles and carried a fragment of his fifth rib on the end of his watch-chain. Now he narrowed his eyes, choosing a particular blade of grass on the far corner of the green.

"Billy Red? Every Sunday. Twelve on the dot." He dipped his body to the underswing of his arm and came upright as the jack curled away across the green. "I don't know how he does it."

The jack had come to rest two feet from the far corner. There followed four more games. They played back to Michael, then across to the far right, then a short one down to the far left, then back to the near right. At last the green was too full, with nine or ten games interweaving and shouts of "feet" every other minute and bowls bocking together in mid-green.

At quarter to twelve on the clock—Michael now sullen with the punishment he had undergone and the certainty that his day had been played away—the three men came off the green, put away their bowls, and turned down on to the canal bank towpath.

The valley became narrower and its sides steeper. Road, river and canal made their way as best they could, with only a twenty-yard strip of wasteland—a tangle of rank weeds, elderberry bushes and rubble, bleached debris of floods—separating river and canal. Along the far side of the river squeezed the road, rumbling from Monday to Saturday with swaying lorry-loads of cotton and wool and cloth. The valley wall on that side, draped with a network of stone-walled fields and precariously-clinging farms and woods, came down sheer out of the sky into the backyards of a crouched stone row of weavers' cottages whose front doorsteps were almost part of the road. The river ran noisily over pebbles. On the strip of land between river and canal stood Top Wharf Pub—its buildings tucked in under the bank of the canal so that the towpath ran level with the back bedroom windows. On this side the valley wall, with overshadowing woods, dived straight into the black, motionless canal as if it must be a mile deep. The water was quite shallow, however, with its collapsed banks and accumulation of mud, so shallow that in some places the rushes grew right across. For years it had brought nothing to Top Wharf Pub but a black greasy damp and rats.

They turned down off the towpath into the wide, cobbled yard in front of the pub.

"You sit here. Now what would you like to drink?"

Michael sat on the cracked, weather-scrubbed bench in the yard under the bar-room window and asked for ginger beer.

"And see if he's come yet. And see if they have any rats ready."

He had begun to notice the heat and now leaned back against the wall to get the last slice of shade under the eaves. But in no time the sun had moved out over the yard. The valley sides funnelled its rays down as into a trap, dazzling the quartz-points of the worn cobbles, burning the colour off everything. The flies were going wild, swirling in the air, darting and basking on the cobbles—big, green-glossed bluebottles that leapt on to his hand when he laid it along the hot bench.

In twos and threes men came over the hog-backed bridge leading from the road into the yard, or down off the towpath. Correct, leisurely and a little dazed from morning service, or in overalls that were torn and whitened from obscure Sabbath labours, all disappeared through the door. The hubbub inside thickened. Michael strained to catch some mention of Billy Red.

At last his father brought him his ginger beer and informed him that Billy Red had not arrived yet but everybody was expecting him and he shouldn't be long. They had some nice rats ready.

In spite of the heat, Michael suddenly did not feel like drinking. His whole body seemed to have become frailer and slightly faint, as with hunger. When he sipped, the liquid trickled with a cold, tasteless weight into his disinterested stomach.

He left the glass on the bench and went to the Gents. Afterwards he walked stealthily round the yard, looking in at the old stables and coach-house, the stony cave silences. Dust, cobwebs, rat droppings. Old timbers, old wheels, old harness. Barrels, and rusty stoves. He listened for rats. Walking back across the blinding, humming yard he smelt roast beef and heard the clattering of the pub kitchen and saw through the open window fat arms working over a stove. The whole world was at routine Sunday dinner. The potatoes were already steaming, people sitting about killing time and getting impatient and wishing that something would fall out of the blue and knowing that nothing would. The idea stifled him, he didn't want to think of it. He went quickly back to the bench and sat down, his heart beating as if he had run.

A car nosed over the little bridge and stopped at the far side of the yard, evidently not sure whether it was permitted to enter the yard at all. Out of it stepped a well-to-do young man and a young woman. The young man unbuttoned his pale tweed jacket, thrust his hands into his trouser pockets and came sauntering towards the pub door, the girl on her high heels following beside him, patting her hair and looking round at the scenery as if she had just come up out of a dark pit. They stood at the door for a moment, improvising their final decisions about what she would drink, whether this was the right place, and whether she ought to come in. He was sure it was the right place, this was where they did it all right, and he motioned her to sit on the end of the bench beside Michael. Michael moved accommodatingly to the other end. She ignored him, however, and perched on the last ten inches of the bench, arrayed her wide-skirted, summery, blue-flowered frock over her knees, and busied herself with her mirror. The flies whirled around, inspecting this new thing of scents.

Suddenly there came a shout from the doorway of the pub, long drawn words: "Here comes the man."

Immediately several crowded to the doorway, glasses in their hands.

"Here he comes."

"The Red Killer!"

"Poor little beggar. He looks as if he lives on rat meat."

"Draw him a half, Gab."

Over the bridge and into the yard shambled a five-foot, ragged figure. Scarecrowish, tawny to colourless, exhausted, this was Billy Red, the rat-catcher. As a sideline he kept hens, and he had something of the raw, flea-bitten look of a red hen, with his small, sunken features and gingery hair. From the look of his clothes you would think he slept on the hen-house floor, under the roosts. One hand in his pocket, his back at a half-bend, he drifted aimlessly to a stop. Then, to show that after all he had only come for a sit in the sun, he sat down beside Michael with a long sigh.

"It's a grand day," he announced. His voice was not strong—lungless, a shaky wisp, full of hen-fluff and dust.

Michael peered closely and secretly at this wrinkled, neglected fifty-year-old face shrunk on its small skull. Among the four-day stubble and enlarged pores and deep folds it was hard to make out anything, but there were one or two marks that might have been old rat bites. He had a little withered mouth and kept moving the lips about as if he couldn't get them comfortable. After a sigh he would pause a minute, leaning forward, one elbow on his knees, then sigh again, changing his position, the other elbow now on the other knee, like a man too weary to rest.

"Here you are, Billy."

A hand held a half-pint high at the pub door like a sign and with startling readiness Billy leapt to his feet and disappeared into the pub, gathering the half-pint on the way and saying:

"I've done a daft bloody thing. I've come down all this way wi'out brass."

There was an obliging roar of laughter and Michael found himself looking at the girl's powdered profile. She was staring down at her neatly-covered toe as it twisted this way and that, presenting all its polished surfaces.

Things began to sound livelier inside—sharp, loud remarks kicking up bursts of laughter and showering exclamations. The young man came out, composed, serious, and handed the girl a long-stemmed clear glass with a cherry in it. He sat down between her and Michael, splaying his knees as he did so and lunging his face forward to meet his streamingly raised pint—one smooth, expert motion.

"He's in there now," he said, wiping his mouth. "They're getting him ready."

The girl gazed into his face, tilting her glass till the cherry bobbed against her pursed red lips, opening her eyes wide.

Michael looked past her to the doorway. A new figure had appeared. He supposed this must be the landlord, Gab—an aproned hemisphere and round, red greasy face that screwed itself up to survey the opposite hillside.

"Right," called the landlord. "I'll get 'em." Away he went, wiping his hands on his apron, then letting them swing wide of his girth like penguin flippers, towards the coach-house. Now everybody came out of the pub and Michael stood up, surprised to see how many had been crowded in there. They were shouting and laughing, pausing to browse their pints, circulating into scattered groups. Michael went over and stood beside his father who was one of an agitated four. He had to ask twice before he could make himself heard. Even to himself his voice sounded thinner than usual, empty, as if at bottom it wanted nothing so much as to dive into his stomach and hide there in absolute silence, letting events go their own way.

"How many is he going to do?"

"I think they've got two." His father half turned down towards him. "It's usually two or three."

Nobody took any notice of Billy Red who was standing a little apart, his hands hanging down from the slight stoop that seemed more or less permanent with him, smiling absently at the noisy, hearty groups. He brightened and straightened as the last man out of the pub came across, balancing a brimming pint glass. Michael watched. The moment the pint touched those shrivelled lips the pale little eye set with a sudden strangled intentness. His long, skinny, unshaven throat writhed and the beer shrank away in the glass. In two or three seconds he lowered the glass empty, wiped his mouth on his sleeve and looked around. Then as nobody stepped forward to offer him a fill-up he set the glass down to the cobbles and stood drying his hands on his jacket.

Michael's gaze shifted slightly, and he saw the girl. He recognized his own thoughts in her look of mesmerized incredulity. At her side the young man was watching too, but shrewdly, between steady drinks.

The sun seemed to have come to a stop directly above. Two or three men had taken their jackets off, with irrelevant, noisy clowning, a few sparring feints. Somebody suggested they all go and stand in the canal and Billy Red do his piece under water, and another laughed so hard at this that the beer came spurting from his nostrils. High up on the opposite slope Michael could see a line of Sunday walkers, moving slowly across the dazed grey of the fields. Their coats would be over their shoulders, their ties in their pockets, their shoes agony, the girls asking to be pushed—but if they stood quite still they would feel a breeze. In the cobbled yard the heat had begun to dance.

"Here we are."

The landlord waddled into the middle of the yard holding up an oblong wire cage. He set it down with a clash on the cobbles.

"Two of the best."

Everybody crowded round. Michael squeezed to the front and crouched down beside the cage. There was a pause of admiration. Hunched in opposite corners of the cage, their heads low and drawn in and their backs pressed to the wires so that the glossy black-tipped hairs bristled out, were two big brown rats. They sat quiet. A long pinkish-grey tail, thick at the root as his thumb, coiled out by Michael's foot. He touched the hairy tip of it gently with his forefinger.

"Watch out, lad!"

The rat snatched its tail in, leapt across the cage with a crash and gripping one of the zinc bars behind its curved yellow teeth, shook till the cage rattled. The other rat left its corner and began gliding to and fro along one side—a continuous low fluidity, sniffing up and down the bars. Then both rats stopped and sat up on their hind-legs, like persons coming out of a trance, suddenly recognizing people. Their noses quivered as they directed their set, grey-chinned, inquisitive expressions at one face after another.

The landlord had been loosening the nooses in the end of two long pieces of dirty string. He lifted the cage again.

"Catch a tail, Walt."

The group pressed closer. A hand came out and roamed in readiness under the high-held cage floor. The rats moved uneasily. The landlord gave the cage a shake and the rats crashed. A long tail swung down between the wires. The hand grabbed and pulled.

"Hold it."

The landlord slipped the noose over the tail, down to the very butt, and pulled it tight. The caught rat, not quite convinced before but now understanding the whole situation, doubled round like a thing without bones, and bit and shook the bars and forced its nose out between them to get at the string that held its buttocks tight to the cage side.

"Just you hold that string, Walt. So's it can't get away when we open up."

Now the landlord lifted the cage again, while Walt held his string tight. The other rat, watching the operation on its companion, had bunched up in a corner, sitting on its tail.

"Clever little beggar. You know what I'm after, don't you?"

The landlord gave the cage a shake, but the rat clung on, its pink feet gripping the wires of the cage floor like hands. He shook the cage violently.

"Move, you stubborn little beggar," demanded the landlord. He went on shaking the cage with sharp, jerking movements.

Then the rat startled everybody. Squeezing still farther into its corner, it opened its mouth wide and began to scream—a harsh, ripping, wavering scream travelling out over the yard like some thin, metallic, dazzling substance that decomposed instantly. As one scream died the rat started another, its mouth wide. Michael had never thought a rat could make so much noise. As it went on at full intensity, his stomach began to twist and flex like a thick muscle. For a moment he was so worried by these sensations that he stopped looking at the rat. The landlord kept on shaking the cage and the scream shook in the air, but the rat clung on, still sitting on its tail.

"Give him a poke, Gab, stubborn little beggar!"

The landlord held the cage still, reached into his top pocket and produced a pencil. At this moment, Michael saw the girl, extricating herself from the press, pushing out backwards. The ring of rapt faces and still legs closed again. The rat was hurtling round the cage, still screaming, leaping over the other, attacking the wires first at this side then at that. All at once it crouched in a corner, silent. A hand came out and grabbed the loop of tail. The other noose was there ready. The landlord set the cage down.

Now the circle relaxed and everyone looked down at the two rats flattened on the cage bottom, their tails waving foolishly outside the wires.

"Well then, Billy," said the landlord. "How are they?"

Billy Red nodded and grinned.

"Them's grand," he said. "Grand." His little rustling voice made Michael want to cough.

"Right. Stand back."

Everybody backed obediently, leaving the cage, Walt with his foot on one taut string and the landlord with his foot on the other in the middle of an arena six or seven yards across. Michael saw the young man on the far side, his glass still half full in his hand. The girl was nowhere to be seen.

Billy Red peeled his coat off, exposing an old shirt, army issue, most of the left arm missing. He pulled his trousers up under his belt, spat on his hands, and took up a position which placed the cage door a couple of paces or so from his left side and slightly in front of him. He bent forward a little more than usual, his arms hanging like a wary wrestler's, his eye fixed on the cage.

"Eye like a bloody sparrow-hawk," somebody murmured.

There was a silence. The landlord waited, kneeling now beside the cage. Nothing disturbed the dramatic moment but the distant, brainless church bells.

"This one first, Walt," said the landlord. "Ready, Billy?"

He pushed down the lever that raised the cage door and let his rat have its full five- or six-yard length of string. He had the end looped round his hand. Walt kept his rat on a tight string.

Everybody watched intently. The freed rat pulled its tail in delicately and sniffed at the noose round it, ignoring the wide-open door. Then the landlord reached to tap the cage and in a flash the rat vanished.

Michael lost sight of it. But he saw Billy Red spin half round and drop smack down on his hands and knees on the cobbles.

"He's got it!"

Billy Red's face was compressed in a snarl and as he snapped his head from side to side the dark, elongated body of the rat whipped around his neck. He had it by the shoulders. Michael's eyes fixed like cameras.

A dozen shakes, and Billy Red stopped, his head lowered. The rat hanging from his mouth was bunching and relaxing, bunching and relaxing. He waited. Everyone waited. Then the rat spasmed, fighting with all its paws, and Billy shook again wildly, the rat's tail flying like a lash. This time when he stopped the body hung down limply. The piece of string, still attached to the tail, trailed away across the cobbles.

Gently Billy took the rat from his mouth and laid it down. He stood up, spat a couple of times, and began to wipe his mouth, smiling shamefacedly. Everybody breathed out—an exclamation of marvelling disgust and admiration, and loud above the rest:

"Pint now, Billy?"

The landlord walked back into the pub and most of the audience followed him to refresh their glasses. Billy Red stood separate, still wiping his mouth with a scrap of snuff-coloured cloth.

Michael went over and bent to look at the dead rat. Its shoulders were wet-black with saliva, and the fur bitten. It lay on its left side, slightly curved, its feet folded, its eyes still round and bright in their alert, inquisitive expression. He touched its long, springy whiskers. A little drip of blood was puddling under its nose on the cobble-stones. As he watched, a bluebottle alighted on its tail and sprang off again, then suddenly reappeared on its nose, inspecting the blood.

He walked over to the cage. Walt was standing there talking, his foot on the taut string. This rat crouched against the wires as if they afforded some protection. It made no sign of noticing Michael as he bent low over it. Its black beads stared outward fixedly, its hot brown flanks going in and out. There was a sparkle on its fur, and as he looked more closely, thinking it must be perspiration, he became aware of the heat again.

He stood up, a dull pain in his head. He put his hand to his scalp and pressed the scorch down into his skull, but that didn't seem to connect with the dull, thick pain.

"I'm off now, Dad," he called.

"Already? Aren't you going to see this other one?"

"I think I'll go." He set off across the yard.

"Finish your drink," his father called after him.

He saw his glass almost full on the end of the white bench but walked past it and round the end of the pub and up on to the tow-path. The sycamore trees across the canal arched over black damp shade and the still water. High up, the valley slopes were silvered now, frizzled with the noon brightness. The earthen tow-path was like stone. Fifty yards along he passed the girl in the blue-flowered frock sauntering back towards the pub, pulling at the heads of the tall bank grasses.

"Have they finished yet?" she asked.

Michael shook his head. He found himself unable to speak. With all his strength he began to run.

Shirley Jackson

(1919–1965)

A native of California, Shirley Jackson was educated at Syracuse University, New York, and was married to the critic Stanley Edgar Hyman. As she indicates in her amusing fictionalized memoirs *Life Among the Savages* (1953) and *Raising Demons* (1957), she led a warm and happy domestic life; but her writing reveals a much darker side, an awareness of cruelty and madness and alienation. Her best stories are those concerned with the mysterious and the macabre, but she was not simply a writer of ghost stories or Gothic tales; she firmly believed that "the genesis of any fictional work has to be human experience"; and in her own work she sought "to make stories out of things that happen, things like moving, and kittens, and Christmas concerts at the grade school, and broken bicycles." It is her power to make the ordinary seem chilling, to turn mundane reality into nightmare, that gives her fiction such impact. Like Mrs. Spencer in "The Tooth" (from *The Lottery,* 1949), Jackson's protagonists are confronted by bus drivers or shop assistants, not by ghosts or monsters; but they suffer a distortion or disturbance of vision, and the ordinary world suddenly takes on a hostile and menacing aspect. The horrors perceived by Shirley Jackson are sometimes "real" in the sense of being external to her characters; but often they are projections of inner disturbance, of a personality in the process of breaking down and no longer able to cope with external pressures.

For further reading

Shirley Jackson, "Experience and Fiction," in *Come Along with Me: Part of a Novel, Sixteen Stories and Three Lectures,* ed. Stanley Edgar Hyman (New York: Viking, 1968), pp. 195–204.

The Tooth

The bus was waiting, panting heavily at the curb in front of the small bus station, its great blue-and-silver bulk glittering in the moonlight. There were only a few people interested in the bus, and at that time of night no one passing on the sidewalk: the one movie theatre in town had finished its show and closed its doors an hour before, and all the movie patrons had been to the drugstore for ice cream and gone on home; now the drugstore was closed and dark, another silent doorway in the long midnight street. The only town lights were the street lights, the lights in the all-night lunchstand across the street, and the one remaining counter lamp in the bus station where the girl sat in the ticket office with her hat and coat on, only waiting for the New York bus to leave before she went home to bed.

Standing on the sidewalk next to the open door of the bus, Clara Spencer held her husband's arm nervously. "I feel so funny," she said.

"Are you all right?" he asked. "Do you think I ought to go with you?"

"No, of course not," she said. "I'll be all right." It was hard for her to talk because of her swollen jaw; she kept a handkerchief pressed to her face and held hard to her husband. "Are you sure *you*'ll be all right?" she asked. "I'll be back tomorrow night at the latest. Or else I'll call."

"Everything will be fine," he said heartily. "By tomorrow noon it'll all be gone. Tell the dentist if there's anything wrong I can come right down."

"I feel so funny" she said. "Light-headed, and sort of dizzy."

"That's because of the dope," he said. "All that codeine, and the whisky, and nothing to eat all day."

She giggled nervously. "I couldn't comb my hair, my hand shook so. I'm glad it's dark."

"Try to sleep in the bus," he said. "Did you take a sleeping pill?"

"Yes," she said. They were waiting for the bus driver to finish his cup of coffee in the lunchstand; they could see him through the glass window, sitting at the counter, taking his time. "I feel so *funny,*" she said.

"You know, Clara," he made his voice very weighty, as though if he spoke more seriously his words would carry more conviction and be therefore more comforting, "you know, I'm glad you're going down to New York to have Zimmerman take care of this. I'd never forgive myself if it turned out to be something serious and I let you go to this butcher up here."

"It's just a *toothache,*" Clara said uneasily, "nothing very serious about a *toothache.*"

"You can't tell," he said. "It might be abscessed or something; I'm sure he'll have to pull it."

"Don't even talk like that," she said, and shivered.

"Well, it looks pretty bad," he said soberly, as before. "Your face so swollen, and all. Don't you worry."

"I'm not worrying," she said. "I just feel as if I were all tooth. Nothing else."

The bus driver got up from the stool and walked over to pay his check. Clara moved toward the bus, and her husband said, "Take your time, you've got plenty of time."

"I just feel funny," Clara said.

"Listen," her husband said, "that tooth's been bothering you off and on for years; at least six or seven times since I've known you you've had trouble with that tooth. It's about time something was done. You had a toothache on our honeymoon," he finished accusingly.

"Did I?" Clara said. "You know," she went on, and laughed, "I was in such a hurry I didn't dress properly. I have on old stockings and I just dumped everything into my good pocketbook."

"Are you sure you have enough money?" he said.

"Almost twenty-five dollars," Clara said. "I'll be home tomorrow."

"Wire if you need more," he said. The bus driver appeared in the doorway of the lunchroom. "Don't worry," he said.

"Listen," Clara said suddenly, "are you *sure* you'll be all right? Mrs. Lang will be over in the morning in time to make breakfast, and Johnny doesn't need to go to school if things are too mixed up."

"I know," he said.

"Mrs. Lang," she said, checking on her fingers. "I called Mrs. Lang, I left the grocery order on the kitchen table, you can have the cold tongue for lunch and in case I don't get back Mrs. Lang will give you dinner. The cleaner ought to come about four o'clock, I won't be back so give him your brown suit and it doesn't matter if you forget but be sure to empty the pockets."

"Wire if you need more money," he said. "Or call. I'll stay home tomorrow so you can call at home."

"Mrs. Lang will take care of the baby," she said.

"Or you can wire," he said.

The bus driver came across the street and stood by the entrance to the bus.

"Okay?" the bus driver said.

"Good-bye," Clara said to her husband.

"You'll feel all right tomorrow," her husband said. "It's only a toothache."

"I'm fine," Clara said. "Don't you worry." She got on the bus and then stopped, with the bus driver waiting behind her. "Milkman," she said to her husband. "Leave a note telling him we want eggs."

"I will," her husband said. "Good-bye."

"Good-bye," Clara said. She moved on into the bus and behind her the driver swung into his seat. The bus was nearly empty and she went far back and sat down at the window outside which her husband waited. "Good-bye," she said to him through the glass, "take care of yourself."

"Good-bye," he said, waving violently.

The bus stirred, groaned, and pulled itself forward. Clara turned her head to wave good-bye once more and then lay back against the heavy soft seat. Good Lord, she thought, what a thing to do! Outside, the familiar street slipped past, strange and dark and seen, unexpectedly, from the unique station of a person leaving town, going away on a bus. It isn't as though it's the first time I've ever been to New York, Clara thought indignantly, it's the whisky and the codeine and the sleeping pill and the toothache. She checked hastily to see if her codeine tablets were in her pocketbook; they had been standing, along with the aspirin and a glass of water, on the diningroom sideboard, but somewhere in the lunatic flight from her home she must have picked them up, because they were in her pocketbook now, along with the twenty-odd dollars and her compact and comb and lipstick. She could tell from the feel of the lipstick that she had brought the old, nearly finished one, not the new one that was a darker shade and had cost two-fifty. There was a run in her stocking and a hole in the toe that she never noticed at home wearing her old comfortable shoes, but which was now suddenly and disagreeably apparent inside her best walking shoes. Well, she thought, I can buy new stockings in New York tomorrow, after the tooth is fixed, after everything's all right. She put her tongue cautiously on the tooth and was rewarded with a split-second crash of pain.

The bus stopped at a red light and the driver got out of his seat and came back toward her. "Forgot to get your ticket before," he said.

"I guess I was a little rushed at the last minute," she said. She found the ticket in her coat pocket and gave it to him. "When do we get to New York?" she asked.

"Five-fifteen," he said. "Plenty of time for breakfast. One-way ticket?"

"I'm coming back by train," she said, without seeing why she had to tell him, except that it was late at night and people isolated together in some strange prison like a bus had to be more friendly and communicative than at other times.

"Me, I'm coming back by bus," he said, and they both laughed, she painfully because of her swollen face. When he went back to his seat far away at the front of the bus she lay back peacefully against the seat. She could feel the sleeping pill pulling at her; the throb of the toothache was distant now, and mingled with the movement of the bus, a steady beat like her heartbeat which she could hear louder and louder, going on through the night. She put her head back and her feet up, discreetly covered with her skirt, and fell asleep without saying good-bye to the town.

She opened her eyes once and they were moving almost silently through the darkness. Her tooth was pulsing steadily and she turned her cheek against the cool back of the seat in weary resignation. There was a thin line of lights along the ceiling of the bus and no other light. Far ahead of her in the bus she could see the other people sitting; the driver, so far away as to be only a tiny figure at the end of a telescope, was straight at the wheel, seemingly awake. She fell back into her fantastic sleep.

She woke up later because the bus had stopped, the end of that silent motion through the darkness so positive a shock that it woke her stunned, and it was a minute before the ache began again. People were moving along the aisle of the bus and the driver, turning around, said, "Fifteen minutes." She got up and followed everyone else out, all but her eyes still asleep, her feet moving without awareness. They were stopped beside an all-night restaurant, lonely and lighted on the vacant road. Inside, it was warm and busy and full of people. She saw a seat at the end of the counter and sat down, not aware that she had fallen asleep again when someone sat down next to her and touched her arm. When she looked around foggily he said, "Traveling far?"

"Yes," she said.

He was wearing a blue suit and he looked tall; she could not focus her eyes to see any more.

"You want coffee?" he asked.

She nodded and he pointed to the counter in front of her where a cup of coffee sat steaming.

"Drink it quickly," he said.

She sipped at it delicately; she may have put her face down and tasted it without lifting the cup. The strange man was talking.

"Even farther than Samarkand," he was saying, "and the waves ringing on the shore like bells."

"Okay, folks," the bus driver said, and she gulped quickly at the coffee, drank enough to get her back into the bus.

When she sat down in her seat again the strange man sat down beside her. It was so dark in the bus that the lights from the restaurant were unbearably glaring and she closed her eyes. When her eyes were shut, before she fell asleep, she was closed in alone with the toothache.

"The flutes play all night," the strange man said, "and the stars are as big as the moon and the moon is as big as a lake."

As the bus started up again they slipped back into the darkness and only the thin thread of lights along the ceiling of the bus held them together, brought the back of the bus where she sat along with the front of the bus where the driver sat and the people sitting there so far away from her. The lights tied them together and the strange man next to her was saying, "Nothing to do all day but lie under the trees."

Inside the bus, traveling on, she was nothing; she was passing the trees and the occasional sleeping houses, and she was in the bus but she was between here and there, joined tenuously to the bus driver by a thread of lights, being carried along without effort of her own.

"My name is Jim," the strange man said.

She was so deeply asleep that she stirred uneasily without knowledge, her forehead against the window, the darkness moving along beside her.

Then again that numbing shock, and, driven awake, she said, frightened, "What's happened?"

"It's all right," the strange man—Jim—said immediately. "Come along."

She followed him out of the bus, into the same restaurant, seemingly, but when she started to sit down at the same seat at the end of the counter he took her hand and led her to a table. "Go and wash your face," he said. "Come back here afterward."

She went into the ladies' room and there was a girl standing there powdering her nose. Without turning around the girl said, "Costs a nickel. Leave the door fixed so's the next one won't have to pay."

The door was wedged so it would not close, with half a match folder in the lock. She left it the same way and went back to the table where Jim was sitting.

"What do you want?" she said, and he pointed to another cup of coffee and a sandwich. "Go ahead," he said.

While she was eating her sandwich she heard his voice, musical and soft, "And while we were sailing past the island we heard a voice calling us. . . . "

Back in the bus Jim said, "Put your head on my shoulder now, and go to sleep."

"I'm all right," she said.

"No," Jim said. "Before, your head was rattling against the window."

Once more she slept, and once more the bus stopped and she woke frightened, and Jim brought her again to a restaurant and more coffee. Her tooth came alive then, and with one hand pressing her cheek she searched through the pockets of her coat and then through her pocketbook until she found the little bottle of codeine pills and she took two while Jim watched her.

She was finishing her coffee when she heard the sound of the bus motor and she started up suddenly, hurrying, and with Jim holding her arm she fled back into the dark shelter of her seat. The bus was moving forward when she realized that she had left her bottle of codeine pills sitting on the table in the restaurant and now she was at the mercy of her tooth. For a minute she stared back at the lights of the restaurant through the bus window and then she put her head on Jim's shoulder and he was saying as she fell asleep, "The sand is so white it looks like snow, but it's hot, even at night it's hot under your feet."

Then they stopped for the last time, and Jim brought her out of the bus and they stood for a minute in New York together. A woman passing them in the station said to the man following her with suitcases, "We're just on time, it's five-fifteen."

"I'm going to the dentist," she said to Jim.

"I know," he said. "I'll watch out for you."

He went away, although she did not see him go. She thought to watch for his blue suit going through the door, but there was nothing.

I ought to have thanked him, she thought stupidly, and went slowly into the station restaurant, where she ordered coffee again. The counter man looked at her with the worn sympathy of one who has spent a long night watching people get off and on buses.

"Sleepy?" he asked.

"Yes," she said.

She discovered after a while that the bus station joined Pennsylvania Terminal and she was able to get into the main waiting-room and find a seat on one of the benches by the time she fell asleep again.

Then someone shook her rudely by the shoulder and said, "What train you taking, lady, it's nearly seven." She sat up and saw her pocketbook on her lap, her feet neatly crossed, a clock glaring into her face. She said, "Thank you," and got up and walked blindly past the benches and got on to the escalator. Someone got on immediately behind her and touched her arm; she turned and it was Jim. "The grass is so green and so soft," he said, smiling, " and the water of the river is so cool."

She stared at him tiredly. When the escalator reached the top she stepped off and started to walk to the street she saw ahead. Jim came along beside her and his voice went on, "The sky is bluer than anything you've ever seen, and the songs. . . . "

She stepped quickly away from him and thought that people were looking at her as they passed. She stood on the corner waiting for the light to change and Jim came swiftly up to her and then away. "Look," he said as he passed, and he held out a handful of pearls.

Across the street there was a restaurant, just opening. She went in and sat down at a table, and a waitress was standing beside her frowning. "You was asleep," the waitress said accusingly.

"I'm very sorry," she said. It was morning. "Poached eggs and coffee, please."

It was a quarter to eight when she left the restaurant, and she thought, if I take a bus, and go straight downtown now, I can sit in the drugstore across the street from the dentist's office and have more coffee until about eight-thirty and then go into the dentist's when it opens and he can take me first.

The buses were beginning to fill up; she got into the first bus that came along and could not find a seat. She wanted to go to Twenty-third Street, and got a seat just as they were passing Twenty-sixth Street; when she woke she was so far downtown that it took her nearly half-an-hour to find a bus and get back to Twenty-third.

At the corner of Twenty-third Street, while she was waiting for the light to change, she was caught up in a crowd of people, and when they crossed the street and separated to go different directions someone fell into step beside her. For a minute she walked on without looking up, staring resentfully at the sidewalk, her tooth burning her, and then she looked up, but there was no blue suit among the people pressing by on either side.

When she turned into the office building where her dentist was, it was still very early morning. The doorman in the office building was freshly shaven and his hair was combed; he held the door open briskly, as at five o'clock he would be sluggish, his hair faintly out of place. She went in through the door with a feeling of achievement; she had come successfully from one place to another, and this was the end of her journey and her objective.

The clean white nurse sat at the desk in the office; her eyes took in the swollen cheek, the tired shoulders, and she said, "You poor thing, you look worn out."

"I have a toothache." The nurse half-smiled, as though she were still waiting for the day when someone would come in and say, "My feet hurt." She stood up into the professional sunlight. "Come right in," she said. "We won't make you wait."

There was sunlight on the headrest of the dentist's chair, on the round white table, on the drill bending its smooth chromium head. The dentist smiled with the same tolerance as the nurse; perhaps all human ailments were contained in the teeth, and he could fix them if people would only come to him in time. The nurse said smoothly, "I'll get her file, doctor. We thought we'd better bring her right in."

She felt, while they were taking an X-ray, that there was nothing in her head to stop the malicious eye of the camera, as though the camera would look through her and photograph the nails in the wall next to her, or the dentist's cuff buttons, or the small thin bones of the dentist's instruments; the dentist said, "Extraction," regretfully to the nurse, and the nurse said, "Yes, doctor, I'll call them right away."

Her tooth, which had brought her here unerringly, seemed now the only part of her to have any identity. It seemed to have had its picture taken without her; it was the important creature which must be recorded and examined and gratified; she was only its unwilling vehicle, and only as such was she of interest to the dentist and the nurse, only as the bearer of her tooth was she worth their immediate and practiced attention. The dentist handed her a slip of paper with the picture of a full set of teeth drawn on it; her living tooth was checked with a black mark, and across the top of the paper was written "Lower molar; extraction."

"Take this slip," the dentist said, "and go right up to the address on this card; it's a surgeon dentist. They'll take care of you there."

"What will they do?" she said. Not the question she wanted to ask, not: What about me? or, How far down do the roots go?

"They'll take that tooth out," the dentist said testily, turning away. "Should have been done years ago."

I've stayed too long, she thought, he's tired of my tooth. She got up out of the dentist chair and said, "Thank you. Good-bye."

"Good-bye," the dentist said. At the last minute he smiled at her, showing her his full white teeth, all in perfect control.

"Are you all right? Does it bother you too much?" the nurse asked. "I'm all right."

"I can give you some codeine tablets," the nurse said. "We'd rather you didn't take anything right now, of course, but I think I could let you have them if the tooth is really bad."

"No," she said, remembering her little bottle of codeine pills on the table of a restaurant between here and there. "No, it doesn't bother me too much."

"Well," the nurse said, "good luck."

She went down the stairs and out past the doorman; in the fifteen minutes she had been upstairs he had lost a little of his pristine morningness, and his bow was just a fraction smaller than before.

"Taxi?" he asked, and, remembering the bus down to Twenty-third Street, she said, "Yes."

Just as the doorman came back from the curb, bowing to the taxi he seemed to believe he had invented, she thought a hand waved to her from the crowd across the street.

She read the address on the card the dentist had given her and repeated it carefully to the taxi driver. With the card and the little slip of paper with "Lower molar" written on it and her tooth identified so clearly, she sat without moving, her hands still around the papers, her eyes almost closed. She thought she must have been asleep again when the taxi stopped suddenly, and the driver, reaching around to open the door, said, "Here we are, lady." He looked at her curiously.

"I'm going to have a tooth pulled," she said.

"Jesus," the taxi driver said. She paid him and he said, "Good luck," as he slammed the door.

This was a strange building, the entrance flanked by medical signs carved in stone; the doorman here was faintly professional, as though he were competent to prescribe if she did not care to go any farther. She went past him, going straight ahead until an elevator opened its door to her. In the elevator she showed the elevator man the card and he said, "Seventh floor."

She had to back up in the elevator for a nurse to wheel in an old lady in a wheel chair. The old lady was calm and restful, sitting there in the elevator with a rug over her knees; she said, "Nice day" to the elevator operator and he said, "Good to see the sun," and then the old lady lay back in her chair and the nurse straightened the rug around her knees and said, "Now we're not going to worry," and the old lady said irritably, "Who's worrying?"

They got out at the fourth floor. The elevator went on up and then the operator said, "Seven," and the elevator stopped and the door opened.

"Straight down the hall and to your left," the operator said.

There were closed doors on either side of the hall. Some of them said "DDS," some of them said "Clinic," some of them said "X-Ray." One of them, looking wholesome and friendly and somehow most comprehensible, said "Ladies." Then she turned to the left and found a door with the name on the card and she opened it and went in. There was a nurse sitting behind a glass window, almost as in a bank, and potted palms in tubs in the corners of the waiting room, and new magazines and comfortable chairs. The nurse behind the glass window said, "Yes?" as though you had overdrawn your account with the dentist and were two teeth in arrears.

She handed her slip of paper through the glass window and the nurse looked at it and said, "Lower molar, yes. They called about you. Will you come right in, please? Through the door to your left."

Into the vault? she almost said, and then silently opened the door and went in. Another nurse was waiting, and she smiled and turned, expecting to be followed, with no visible doubt about her right to lead.

There was another X-ray, and the nurse told another nurse: "Lower molar," and the other nurse said, "Come this way, please."

There were labyrinths and passages, seeming to lead into the heart of the office building, and she was put, finally, in a cubicle where there was a couch with a pillow and a washbasin and a chair.

"Wait here," the nurse said. "Relax if you can."

"I'll probably go to sleep," she said.

"Fine," the nurse said. "You won't have to wait long."

She waited, probably for over an hour, although she spent the time half-sleeping, waking only when someone passed the door; occasionally the nurse looked in and smiled, once she said, "Won't have to wait much longer." Then, suddenly, the nurse was back, no longer smiling, no longer the good hostess, but efficient and hurried. "Come along," she said, and moved purposefully out of the little room into the hallways again.

Then, quickly, more quickly than she was able to see, she was sitting in the chair and there was a towel around her head and a towel under her chin and the nurse was leaning a hand on her shoulder.

"Will it hurt?" she asked.

"No," the nurse said, smiling. "You know it won't hurt, don't you?"

"Yes," she said.

The dentist came in and smiled down on her from over her head. "Well," he said.

"Will it hurt?" she said.

"Now," he said cheerfully, "we couldn't stay in business if we hurt people." All the time he talked he was busying himself with metal hidden under a towel, and great machinery being wheeled in almost silently behind her. "We couldn't stay in business at all," he said. "All you've got to worry about is telling us all your secrets while you're asleep. Want to watch out for that, you know. Lower molar?" he said to the nurse.

"Lower molar, doctor," she said.

Then they put the metal-tasting rubber mask over her face and the dentist said, "You know," two or three times absent-mindedly while she could still see him over the mask. The nurse said "Relax your hands, dear," and after a long time she felt her fingers relaxing.

First of all, things get so far away, she thought, remember this. And remember the metallic sound and taste of all of it. And the outrage.

And then the whirling music, the ringing confusedly loud music that went on and on, around and around, and she was running as fast as she could down a long horribly clear hallway with doors on both sides and at the end of the hallway was Jim, holding out his hands and laughing, and calling something she could never hear because of the loud music, and she was running and then she said, "I'm not afraid," and someone from the door next to her took her arm and pulled her through and the world widened alarmingly until it would never stop and then it stopped with the head of the dentist looking down at her and the window dropped into place in front of her and the nurse was holding her arm.

"Why did you pull me back?" she said, and her mouth was full of blood. "I wanted to go on."

"I didn't pull you," the nurse said, but the dentist said, "She's not out of it yet."

She began to cry without moving and felt the tears rolling down her face and the nurse wiped them off with a towel. There was no blood anywhere around except in her mouth; everything was as clean as before. The dentist was gone, suddenly, and the nurse put out her arm and helped her out of the chair. "Did I talk?" she asked suddenly, anxiously. "Did I say anything?"

"You said, 'I'm not afraid,' " the nurse said soothingly. "Just as you were coming out of it."

"No," she said, stopping to pull at the arm around her. "Did I *say* anything. Did I say where he is?"

"You didn't say *anything*," the nurse said. "The doctor was only teasing you."

"Where's my tooth?" she asked suddenly, and the nurse laughed and said, "All gone. Never bother you again."

She was back in the cubicle, and she lay down on the couch and cried, and the nurse brought her whisky in a paper cup and set it on the edge of the washbasin.

"God has given me blood to drink," she said to the nurse, and the nurse said, "Don't rinse your mouth or it won't clot."

After a long time the nurse came back and said to her from the doorway, smiling, "I see you're awake again."

"Why?" she said.

"You've been asleep," the nurse said. "I didn't want to wake you."

She sat up; she was dizzy and it seemed that she had been in the cubicle all her life.

"Do you want to come along now?" the nurse said, all kindness again. She held out the same arm, strong enough to guide any wavering footstep; this time they went back through the long corridor to where the nurse sat behind the bank window.

"All through?" this nurse said brightly. "Sit down a minute, then." She indicated a chair next to the glass window, and turned away to write busily. "Do not rinse your mouth for two hours," she said, without turning around. "Take a laxative tonight, take two aspirin if there is any pain. If there is much pain or excessive bleeding, notify this office at once. All right?" she said, and smiled brightly again.

There was a new little slip of paper; this one said, "Extraction," and underneath, "Do not rinse mouth. Take mild laxative. Two aspirin for pain. If pain is excessive or any hemorrhage occurs, notify office."

"Good-bye," the nurse said pleasantly.

"Good-bye," she said.

With the little slip of paper in her hand, she went out through the glass door and, still almost asleep, turned the corner and started down the hall. When she opened her eyes a little and saw that it was a long hall with doorways on either side, she stopped and then saw the door marked "Ladies" and went in. Inside there was a vast room with windows and wicker chairs and glaring white tiles and glittering silver faucets; there were four or five women around the washbasins, combing their hair, putting on lipstick. She went directly to the nearest of the three washbasins, took a paper towel, dropped her pocketbook and the little slip of paper on the floor next to her, and fumbled with the faucets, soaking the towel until it was dripping. Then she slapped it against her face violently. Her eyes cleared and she felt fresher, so she soaked the paper again and rubbed her face with it. She felt out blindly for another paper towel, and the woman next to her handed her one, with a laugh she could hear, although she could not see for the water in her eyes. She heard one of the women say, "Where we going for lunch?" and another one say, "Just downstairs, prob'ly. Old fool says I gotta be back in half-an-hour."

Then she realized that at the washbasin she was in the way of the women in a hurry so she dried her face quickly. It was when she stepped a little aside to let someone else get to the basin and stood up and glanced into the mirror that she realized with a slight stinging shock that she had no idea which face was hers.

She looked into the mirror as though into a group of strangers, all staring at her or around her; no one was familiar in the group, no one smiled at her or looked at her with recognition; you'd think my own face would know me, she thought, with a queer numbness in her throat. There was a creamy chinless face with bright blonde hair, and a sharp-looking face under a red veiled hat, and a colorless anxious face with brown hair pulled straight back, and a square rosy face under a square haircut, and two or three more faces pushing close to the mirror, moving, regarding themselves. Perhaps it's not a mirror, she thought, maybe it's a window and I'm looking straight through at women washing on the other side. But there were women combing their hair and consulting the mirror; the group was on her side, and she thought, I hope I'm not the blonde, and lifted her hand and put it on her cheek.

She was the pale anxious one with the hair pulled back and when she realized it she was indignant and moved hurriedly back through the crowd of women, thinking, It isn't fair, why don't I have any color in my face? There were some pretty faces there, why didn't I take one of those? I didn't have time, she told herself sullenly, they didn't give me time to think, I could have had one of the nice faces, even the blonde would be better.

She backed up and sat down in one of the wicker chairs. It's mean, she was thinking. She put her hand up and felt her hair; it was loosened after her sleep but that was definitely the way she wore it, pulled straight back all around and fastened at the back of her neck with a wide tight barrette. Like a schoolgirl, she thought, only—remembering the pale face in the mirror—only I'm older than that. She unfastened the barrette with difficulty and brought it around where she could look at it. Her hair fell softly around her face; it was warm and reached to her shoulders. The barrette was silver; engraved on it was the name, "Clara."

"Clara," she said aloud. *"Clara?"* Two of the women leaving the room smiled back at her over their shoulders; almost all the women were leaving now, correctly combed and lipsticked, hurrying out talking together. In the space of a second, like birds leaving a tree, they all were gone and she sat alone in the room. She dropped the barrette into the ashstand next to her chair; the ashstand was deep and metal, and the barrette made a satisfactory clang falling down. Her hair down on her shoulders, she opened her pocketbook, and began to take things out, setting them on her lap as she did so. Handkerchief, plain, white, uninitialled. Compact, square and brown tortoiseshell plastic, with a powder compartment and a rouge compartment; the rouge compartment had obviously never been used, although the powder cake was half-gone. That's why I'm so pale, she thought, and set the compact down. Lipstick, a rose shade, almost finished. A comb, an opened package of cigarettes and a package of matches, a change purse, and a wallet. The change purse was red imitation leather with a zipper across the top; she opened it and dumped the money out into her hand. Nickels, dimes, pennies, a quarter. Ninety-seven cents. Can't go far on that, she thought, and opened the brown leather wallet; there was money in it but she looked first for papers and found nothing. The only thing in the wallet was money. She counted it; there were nineteen dollars. I can go a little farther on *that,* she thought.

There was nothing else in the pocketbook. No keys—shouldn't I have keys? she wondered—no papers, no address book, no identification. The pocketbook itself was imitation leather, light grey, and she looked down and discovered that she was wearing a dark grey flannel suit and a salmon pink blouse with a ruffle around the neck. Her shoes were black and stout with moderate heels and they had laces, one of which was untied. She was wearing beige stockings and there was a ragged tear in the right knee and a great ragged run going down her leg and ending in a hole in the toe which she could feel inside her shoe. She was wearing a pin on the lapel of her suit which, when she turned it around to look at it, was a blue plastic letter C. She took the pin off and dropped it into the ashstand, and it made a sort of clatter at the bottom, with a metallic clang when it landed on the barrette. Her hands were small, with stubby fingers and no nail polish; she wore a thin gold wedding ring on her left hand and no other jewelry.

Sitting alone in the ladies' room in the wicker chair, she thought, The least I can do is get rid of these stockings. Since no one was around she took off her shoes and stripped away the stockings with a feeling of relief when her toe was released from the hole. Hide them, she thought: the paper towel wastebacket. When she stood up she got a better sight of herself in the mirror; it was worse than she had thought: the grey suit bagged in the seat, her legs were bony, and her shoulders sagged. I look fifty, she thought; and then, consulting the face, but I can't be more than thirty. He hair hung down untidily around the pale face and with sudden anger she fumbled in the pocketbook and found the lipstick; she drew an emphatic rosy mouth on the pale face, realizing as she did so that she was not very expert at it, and with the red mouth the face looking at her seemed somehow better to her, so she opened the compact and put on pink cheeks with the rouge. The cheeks were uneven and patent, and the red mouth glaring, but at least the face was no longer pale and anxious.

She put the stockings into the wastebasket and went barelegged out into the hall again, and purposefully to the elevator. The elevator operator said, "Down?" when he saw her and she stepped in and the elevator carried her silently downstairs. She went back past the grave professional doorman and out into the street where people were passing, and she stood in front of the building and waited. After a few minutes Jim came out of a crowd of people passing and came over to her and took her hand.

Somewhere between here and there was her bottle of codeine pills, upstairs on the floor of the ladies' room she had left a little slip of paper headed "Extraction"; seven floors below, oblivious of the people who stepped sharply along the sidewalk, not noticing their occasional curious glances, her hand in Jim's and her hair down on her shoulders, she ran barefoot through hot sand.

Dan Jacobson

(b. 1929)

Born and educated in Johannesburg, South Africa, though now living in England, Dan Jacobson has written seven novels and several volumes of short stories. They have earned him much critical praise in England, and a growing readership in the United States, where he has twice (at Stanford and Syracuse universities) been a visiting professor and fellow in creative writing. Not an innovative stylist, he has preferred to work within the realistic mode, where he handles language with a deftness and assuredness that give his best works their characteristic voice. Jacobson's response to the present is honed by his knowledge of history, and his experience of human behavior is informed by his sensitivity to his cultural background. There is nothing naive or superficial about his appreciation of life, and his quiet assertion of ordinary virtues derives in part from his sensitivity to the plight of cultural minorities. A Jew in South Africa, he was pressured both by his feeling for the political difficulties facing Jews in Europe and by his observation of the inequities suffered by black South Africans. But in his work he strives to render that consciousness rather than to propagandize. "The novelist," he observes in "Why Read Novels?" an essay in *Time of Arrival* (1963), "must be capable of understanding the attractions of ideology, if only because so many men live by ideology; but, as a novelist, he knows that any political or moral abstraction has its real life and importance solely within the individual men who are affected by it." The exploration and illumination of that individuality takes him into the moral preoccupations of his writings.

"Fresh Fields," which appeared in his 1964 collection *Beggar My Neighbour*, provides a clear sense of Jacobson's concern for asserting an individuality that is consistent with moral action. Questioning the nature of plagiarism and probing the limitations that might be imposed by regional roots, he sketches a careful picture of an exiled artist's dilemma. Exile ought not, he observes in another essay in *Time of Arrival*, to stultify one's creative powers; and he asks: "Is there any novelist today who writes with a firm sense of who his audience will be and what they will find familiar or unfamiliar in his work? ... Under the assault of specialized knowledge of all kinds is there any of us who does not feel both intellectually disinherited and set free?"

For further reading

Midge Decter, "Novelist of South Africa," *Commentary*, 25 (1958), 539–544, reprinted in *The Liberated Woman and Other Essays* (New York: Coward-McCann, 1971).

Fresh Fields

When I was a student there was one living South African writer whom I, like most of my friends with literary inclinations or ambitions, greatly admired. That writer was Frederick Traill, poet, essayist, and novelist. To us it seemed that Traill, almost alone in the twentieth century, had shown that it was possible for a man to make poetry out of the forlorn, undramatic landscapes of our country; out of its ragged *dorps;** out of its brash little cities that pushed their buildings towards a sky too high above them; out of its multitudes of people who shared with one another no prides and no hopes. And because Traill had done it, we felt that with luck, with devotion, we might manage to do the same. Like Traill, we might be able to give a voice to what had previously been dumb, dignity to what previously had been without association or depth; in our less elevated moods, we could hope simply that like Traill we would be able to have our books published in London, and have them discussed in the literary reviews.

Traill was for us, therefore, not only a poet, he was a portent or a promise. It was taken for granted among us that Traill should live in England, whence all our books came; his exile, indeed, was part of the exhortatory significance of his career. And in England, too, Traill had remained aloof from the political and artistic furores of his time. He had issued no polemics; he had not voiced his opinions of Britain's foreign policies; he had lived in obscurity throughout the war. The little that we knew of him in South Africa was that he lived in the country, well away from London, that he had always shunned publicity, and that he was known to few people.

All of this, I found out when I first came to England a few years after the war, was true. Everybody had heard of him; nobody knew where he lived; many people thought he was dead, for it was a very long time since he had published his last volume of verse. For me the revelation of that first visit to England can be described by saying that in England I saw, wherever I looked, the word made flesh —made brick, too; made colour; made light; made trunk and leaf. But in the midst of this sudden solidification or enfleshment of almost everything I had ever read, Traill remained no more than a name to me. All around me was the country that others had described and celebrated; the one man who had uttered the words for my own distant country remained unknown. Whatever gossip I could pick up about him, I treasured eagerly; but there was very little of it. I heard that he was married; that he was childless; that his wife was ailing. And that was about all. Eventually, when I met a director of the firm which had published Traill's books—Parkman was the man's name, Arnold Parkman—I blurted out to him the admiration I felt for Traill, and my sense of frustration that there seemed no chance of meeting him. The publisher replied, "You should write to

---

**Dorps* = rural towns.

him. I'm sure he'll be pleased to hear from you." He must have seen
that I was taken aback by the simplicity of the suggestion, because
he added, "Frederick's really a very friendly man, you know. I wish
he wrote more, that's all."

"So do I," I said.

But I made no promise to write to Traill. Like many people of my
generation (I suspect) I wished to lead some kind of "literary life"
without in any way appearing to do so. The thought of writing, as
an aspirant author, to a great name—and Traill's name was a great
one to me—made me feel embarrassed, pushful, and, worst of all,
unfashionable. That kind of thing, I felt, might have been all very
well twenty or thirty years before; but in post-war, comfort-clutch-
ing, cigarette-grabbing, shabby, soiled Britain—no, it just wouldn't
do. All the same, when the publisher told me that Traill lived in
South Devon, and gave me the name of the village in which he lived,
I made a careful note of it. I felt I had a proprietary interest in South
Devon; my girlfriend's parents lived there, and I had visited them,
and had travelled about a little in the area.

I didn't remember seeing the name of the village, Colne, on any
map or signboard; but when I next visited my future in-laws, I took
out a large-scale map and found the village on it without any difficulty. And one fine day (the day was really fine: in mid-summer,
cloudless and hot) I set out on a cross-country bus-trip to Colne. The
trip promised to be a long one, involving two or three changes, and
I did not know what I would do when I got there; I did not even know
the name of the house in which Traill lived. But I set out on the trip
as though it was something I had always intended to do, and without
any doubt that I should succeed in seeing him.

Colne was pleasant without being picturesque. It had a stubby
little church with a tower, hidden behind trees, it had a village store
and a whitewashed pub with a bench and table in front of it, it had
a police station, a village hall and a war memorial. The road did not
run straight through the village, but turned, spread itself between
the pub and the store, and then swung upwards again, towards
Dartmoor. For miles the road had been climbing, and from Colne one
looked back and saw fields, hedges and woodlands tilted against one
another, or sweeping smoothly over the curves of hills, or lying in
sunken valleys. Above them all, on the far side of Colne, was the
bald, high brow of the moor, its nakedness made more emphatic by
the rich, close signs of cultivation evident everywhere else. Below
Colne, the land had been measured and measured again, parcelled
into little lots, divided a hundredfold by the hedges which met at
corners, ran at angles from one another, lost themselves in the woodlands, emerged at angles beyond. But for the purplish shade of the

moor, there was greenness everywhere—so many shades of green, from the palest yellow-green of the stubble where the first fields had been cut, to the darkness of the hedges, which you would have thought to be black, had they not been green also.

Most of the houses in Colne seemed to advertise Devonshire Cream Teas, but I went to the pub where I was offered a plate of biscuits with some cheese. I took the food and a lager, and went outside to eat my meal in the sun. The little open space in front of the pub was almost at the edge of the village, not its centre, and I looked out directly on a hedge, the road, a field, an open barn. There were few people about. I saw the village store being closed for the lunch-hour; some workmen who had been bending over a tractor in the barn nearby went into the public bar; a moustached old man with a military bearing and a hard red skin went into the saloon bar. Several carloads of tourists passed along the main road, on their way to the moor; several other cars came in the other direction, from the moor, with bunches of heather stuck into their radiator grilles. Three packed coaches went up in a convoy: I had heard the complaint of their engines, in the quiet of the afternoon, from miles away.

And then I saw Frederick Traill walking towards me. Though he had rarely been photographed, I knew it was him immediately. He was tall, he was bent, bald, and old. I felt a pang to see how old he was; the photographs, my own image of him, had prepared me to meet a younger man. He walked by me, with a glance down at the table, through his small steel-rimmed glasses. I was sure that I was betraying some kind of confusion; I was embarrassed by the crumbs on the table. But he walked on without a second glance, and I turned to see him go into the pub, bending his head at the door. His tweed jacket was peaked over the back of his neck; it hung loosely, wide over his hips.

I finished my food in a hurry; I did not want to be caught with it still in my hands when he came out. But I need not have worried, or hurried. The minutes passed; the workmen came out and went back to their tractor; a car carrying two men and two women stopped a few yards from me, and they all went noisily into the bar. I could have followed them, but I sat where I was: I felt that I would rather approach Traill where no curious or affable barman could overhear us, no stranger could stare. As I sat there I rehearsed how I was going to introduce myself to him; what I was going to say to him. Vainly, foolishly, I even permitted myself the fantasy that he might have heard of me, might have read something I had written, though I had so far published only a couple of stories in the most obscure and ill-printed of little magazines.

In fact, when I approached him as he came out of the pub, he shook his head almost as soon as I opened my mouth. "Mr Traill?" I had said, and he stood there, shaking his head, looking at me and over me at the same time, his glasses low on his small nose.

"You aren't Frederick Traill?" I felt foolish, and small—literally small, because he was much taller than I, and had the advantage of the step as well.

Still he shook his head. But he said, "Yes, I am Frederick Traill."

I was relieved to hear him speak, and not only because he had acknowledged his identity. He kept his mouth half-closed as he spoke, but his accent was unmistakable: it was my own. "I thought you must be," I said. "I recognized you from your photographs."

He looked suspiciously at me; then moved forward, as if to come down the step. I took a pace back. "I hoped I might see you," I said. "I heard from Arnold Parkman that you lived in Colne. I'm staying near High Coombe for a few weeks. I'm from South Africa originally."

I caught a glance from his small, pale blue eyes. "You are? What part of South Africa?"

"Lyndhurst."

For the first time he smiled faintly. "I know Lyndhurst. I used to visit an uncle of mine there, when I was a boy."

"You wrote *Open Mine* about it."

"Yes, I did," he said, without much apparent interest in what he was saying; without surprise that I should have known the poem. He stepped down and began walking away; I hung behind, at a loss. I might have let him go, without another word, if I hadn't thought to myself, *That man there is Frederick Traill.* I saw his bald head, and beyond it the Devon countryside; and I felt that if I let him go the encounter would seem no more than a childish dream of my own.

How I was to wish later that I had let him go! But I did not. I called out, "Mr Traill."

He stopped and turned to me. "Yes."

"I wanted to talk to you," I said. "Your work meant so much to me, when I was in South Africa. And—and to lots of people I knew. I'd be so glad if I could—if you would let me—"

"I don't give interviews," he said bluntly.

The oddity of the remark did not strike me at the time: how many people could there have been who had made the pilgrimage to Colne in order to interview him for the press? "I don't belong to any newspaper," I replied.

"No?"

"No, it's just that I've read your work."

He seemed to consider for a moment what I had said, and then asked hesitatingly, "What did you want to ask me about?"

"Everything."

Again he smiled faintly, as if from a distance. "Well, as long as you don't expect me to answer everything. . . ." The gesture of his shoulders was an invitation to me to join him, which I eagerly did. Together, we walked up through the village; then we turned from the main road and went up a stony little lane. There were a couple of small houses on the lane, but we passed these, and came to a wooden gate, set at the right angle between a brick wall on one side and a stone wall on the other. The stone wall ran on with the lane, until trees hid it from sight. "This is the back-entrance to the house," Traill explained, as he led me through the gate, and closed it behind us. "The lane goes right round to the front." Then he said, "My vegetable-garden; I spend a lot of time on it." The vegetable-garden was big and obviously kept up with great care. The house itself was an old rambling double-storey cottage with a slate roof and walls half-clad with slate. The house leaned, it bulged, it opened out unexpectedly at doors and little windows; it straightened itself at a chimney that ran all the way down one wall. We walked around the house, past a walled flower-garden; in front of the house there was a meadow, as green and sunken as any pond, with a gravelled drive running to one side of it. The entrance to the drive was hidden behind a bank of trees. Beyond those trees, at a distance of many miles, the single pale curve of a hill filled the horizon.

It was a lovely, ripe, worked-over place. We sat down in deck-chairs on a little lawn in front of the house, and talked casually, for a little while, about the weather and the view. But eventually the conversation turned to Traill's work. I told him of the admiration I felt for it; I told him something of what I and my friends had felt his career to be for us; I said how sorry I was that he had not written anything for so long. And while I talked I kept looking at him, taking in, for memory's sake, his long, slack figure, with his legs crossed at the ankles and his hands clasped behind his head; his bespectacled, small-featured face, with its clusters of wrinkles at the sides of his mouth and eyes. His head was almost entirely bald, and his scalp was faintly freckled. I could see that he was pleased by what I was saying, but I felt that he was saddened by it too, and eventually I fell silent, though there was much which I hadn't yet said to him and though I was disappointed that I had not drawn him out to speak more.

But he said nothing about his work; instead he asked me about mine. He asked me what I had done, where I had published; he questioned me about themes and settings. He had read nothing of my work, but his questions were all kindly, and he spoke to me as I had hardly dared to hope he would: as a professional speaking to an apprentice to the same trade or craft. His voice was deep; his manner of speech was lazy; still he spoke through a half-closed mouth. I was all the more suprised, therefore, when, without changing his position or opening his mouth wider, yet speaking with great vehemence, he said suddenly, "Go home!"

For a moment I thought he was simply dismissing me, and I got up, confused and taken aback. Again he said, "Go home!" and added a moment later, with one hand waving me back into my chair. "Don't do what I did! Go home!"

I sat down again, and stared at him. "Can't you understand what I mean?" he said, in response to that stare. "You'll do nothing if you stay here. It's your only chance, I tell you. Go home. Get out of this place."

He leaned forward and said bitterly, "I don't want to tell you how many years it is since I've published anything. And that's why I tell you to go back to South Africa. I know, I know," he said, waving off an interruption with one hand, though I had not spoken, "I know you'll tell me that South Africa's provincial, and dull—except for the politics, and who wants that kind of excitement?—and there's nobody to talk to. And here there's everything—books, and people, and everything you've ever read about. Elm trees," he said sardonically, and pointed to the trees at the bottom of the meadow—"and meadows," he added, "and villages like Colne. It's wonderful, you can't imagine anything better. You can't imagine ever tearing yourself away from it. But can't you see that as you live in it, year after year, all the time your own country is getting further and further away from you? And then what do you do?" He slumped back in his chair and put his hands behind his head again. "I can tell you," he said. "You sit here, looking at the elm trees and the meadow. You work in the garden; you go for a drink at lunch-time; you go to the market-town once a week, and sit in the cinema there. They've got three, you know, in Mardle, three cinemas! And you try to work; and there's nothing there for you to work on, because you've left it all behind."

We were both silent, though I could see that he had not yet finished what he had to say. And soon he did go on. "I tell you," he said, "when I came here I had my store with me, and I began unpacking it, and the more I unpacked the more there seemed to be. I felt free and happy, ready to work for a lifetime. All around me was this —all this—just what I had hankered for, out there in the veld. Until one day I found that there was no more work for me to do, the store was finished. And then what was I to do? Where was I? What did

I have left? Nothing—nothing that I felt was really my own. So now I'm dumb. Dumb, that's all."

This time he had finished, and still there was nothing I could say. At last, not so much because I was curious and wished to draw him out, but simply because I felt sorry for him, I asked, "Why didn't you go home? You could have, all these years."

He looked at me oddly. Then he said, "My wife isn't well. She hasn't been well for many years. I suppose you could call her bed-ridden, though it's a word she hates to hear."

"I am sorry."

He said nothing to this; and shortly afterwards I got up from my chair; I had to be going back to the village, to catch my bus.

"You must be off?" Traill asked.

"Yes, I'm afraid so. It really has been a privilege meeting you, Mr Traill. And I do appreciate the way you've given your time to me."

"Oh—time! I've got lots of time."

He saw me off as far as the back gate; right at the end, as we said good-bye and shook hands, he seemed reluctant to let me go. "All this you understand," he said, "is my wife's." He did not gesture, but I knew him to be referring to the house and the grounds. He stood with his eyes half-closed, and the sunlight glinted off the top of his head. "She loves this place. So do I really. It was quite impossible for me to leave. How could I?" Then he grasped my hand again, and said firmly, "Go home, while you can. Don't make the mistake I made. Go home!"

He turned and went through the gate; I stood for a moment in the shadowed lane, with the sunlight streaming above me and falling in bright patches on the grass of the bank on the other side. There was no sound but that of his footsteps, beyond the stone wall. I did not like to think of what he was going back to; of what he lived with. Yet the place was beautiful.

The place was beautiful, England was beautiful: rich, various, ancient, crowded, elaborate. But I was much dispirited, as I rode away from Colne in the bus that evening. The warnings and advice Traill had given to me echoed all the fears I had felt about coming to England, even before Traill had spoken to me of his life. And that life, and the work it had produced, we had conceived to be our models! Give up England, or give up writing, Traill had seemed to say to me; and I wanted to do neither.

I was much surprised, and flattered, when I received a letter from Frederick Traill a few weeks later. It had been addressed to me at one of the magazines which I had mentioned to Traill as having pub-lished a story of mine. In the letter Traill asked me to send on to him, if I would, something of my work, published or unpublished, as he would really be most interested to see it. The day on which I received the letter I made up a parcel of carbon copies of stories and other pieces, most of which had been going from magazine to magazine for months, and posted the parcel to him, with a letter in which I thanked him for the interest he was showing in my work, and again for his kindness to me when we had met.

I began waiting for a reply almost immediately. One week passed, a second, a third. Two months after I had sent the manuscripts away I was still waiting for a reply. Four months later, when I thought about it at all, my impatience had given way to a sense of injury which I tried to convince myself was unwarranted. Six months later I was horrified to read a long narrative poem by Traill which was unmistakably a reworking of one of the unpublished stories I had sent him.

Traill's poem was published in one of the leading literary monthlies. Delighted to see Traill's name on the cover, I had bought a copy of the magazine at a tube-station. I read the poem sitting on one of the benches on the platform. The train for which I had been waiting came in and went out, and still I sat there—hotly, shamefully embarrassed, as though I had been the one who had committed the offence. I had no doubt that the offence was gross; but I did not in the least know what I could do about it. How could I write to him, the man whom I had so much admired and had wanted to emulate, accusing him of having stolen my plot, my character, my setting? And there was no doubt that he had done so, none at all; there could be no question here of "unconscious reminiscence." As I sat on that station bench I cursed myself for my curiosity in going to see Traill; I damned myself for ever wanting to have anything to do with writers or writing. And within the general flush of shame I felt resentment and anger, too. The crook! The phoney! With his cottage in the country and his bald head and his sick wife and his advice. His advice! I went home and drafted twenty letters to Traill, but I tore them all up. Shame was stronger than anger. I just couldn't say to him what he had done, let alone tell him what I felt about it.

Not only could I not write to Traill; I could not tell anyone else about it either. The sense of shame I felt held me back; and so too did my feeling that no one would believe me. It enraged me to think that Traill had relied on the strength of his position as against mine, and on the very shamefulness of what he had done, to secure my silence. I couldn't smile at what had happened (after all, it had happened to *me*!) nor, though I tried, could I find much comfort in the lofty thought that it was better to be cribbed from than to crib.

When in the "Forthcoming Features" panel in the same magazine I saw shortly afterwards an announcement of another long poem by Frederick Traill, I went back to my pile of manuscripts and chose one among them as the most likely for Traill to have stolen from this time. I was not wrong. The poem appeared—a long poem in dialogue. Again, it had my characters, my setting, even a scrap or two of my dialogue. I felt strangely proud of having made the correct guess, when I read the poem; and then I knew that it hadn't been a guess at all: I had chosen correctly because I knew Traill's work so intimately.

Mockingly, winkingly, the idea suddenly presented itself to me of writing a story with the deliberate intention of suiting it to Traill's purposes, and of sending it on to him, challenging him to make the same use of it as he had made of the others. The idea came as if it were no more than a joke; but that night, all night, I was working on the joke. And the next evening I had finished the story. Like the others, it was set in South Africa. I typed it out the day after, and before I could get cold feet I put it in an envelope and posted it off to Traill, together with a note saying that I was pleased to see that my stories had stimulated him into writing once again, and I hoped he would find the story I was sending him equally profitable. It was a sly little note, really, all innuendo, like the submission to him of the story itself, but I didn't feel ashamed of it. To tell the truth, now that I had approached Traill, even in this way, I felt a lessening of shame about the whole series of events; for the first time I began to think of them as comical, looked at in a certain aspect.

Then I prepared to wait for Traill's response, which I fully expected to read, in due course, in the pages of one of the literary magazines. What I did not expect was that I should answer a ring on the door one afternoon, shortly after I had come back from the school at which I was then teaching, and find Traill waiting shyly for me on the porch. He was wearing a fawn raincoat and a hat with its brim turned down at the front and the back; he looked ill-at-ease and more rustic, in Swiss Cottage, than I had remembered him as being in Devon. "I hoped I'd find you in," he said awkwardly. "How are you?"

I stared at him. In my imagination he had become a monster of hypocrisy and unscrupulousness; but he stood before me simply as a rather slow and soft-spoken old man, with a small tired, bespectacled face. "Won't you come in?" I asked; and then, while he hesitated, I remembered what my room looked like. "Actually," I said, "I was just on my way down to have a cup of tea somewhere. Won't you join me?"

"With pleasure."

We went to a tearoom which has since disappeared; it is now a bamboo-decorated coffee-bar. But then it was still sombre, Edwardian and mahogany-coloured. The panelled walls and the massive chairs and tables were agleam with polish; the waitresses wore long black multi-buttoned dresses and little green caps on their heads; an open fire burned in a grate. The food, inevitably, was execrable. Traill was hungry, as it turned out, and had to eat a meat pie which was a little paler outside, and a little darker inside, than the sauce in which it lay. I just had tea. While he ate Traill told me that he very rarely came up to London; it was difficult to leave his wife as they had to get a woman to live in the house while he was away; in any case he did not much care for London. But he had had to come up to attend to various business matters, and he had thought that it would be a good opportunity to look me up.

Was he going to make his confession now? As I waited, I was wondering how I was going to respond to it? Coldly? Angrily? Or pityingly? But Traill gave me no opportunity to adopt any predetermined attitude. He said in a firm, guiltless voice. "Those stories of yours, they're pretty ghostly, derivative stuff, aren't they? The last one you sent me is by no means the worst, in that way. And you do know," he went on, "who they're derived from, don't you?"

His blue eyes were severe in expression, and they stared directly at me. "It gave me a strange feeling, at first, to meet my own ghosts like that," he said. "It was very disturbing; I didn't like it. When I read the stories I felt ... how can I describe it to you? ... that was where I'd been, yes; there was where I had come from. But none of it was clear, none of it was right, those ghosts had never really lived. And then the more I read the clearer it became to me what the ghosts were trying to say. I understood them. I knew them," he said, "even if you didn't."

"So you took them—" I interrupted.

"Yes," he admitted calmly. "And surely you can see that I made a better job of them than you did. My poems are better poems than your stories are stories, if you see what I mean."

"But even if that's true—!"

"You mean, I still had no right to take your ideas? I thought that's what you'd say. And I sympathize with you, believe me. I'd sympathize even more if you hadn't told me what you did about my work, and what it meant to you. And if I hadn't been able to see it for myself, in the work. Your ideas? Your ideas?" he repeated with scorn; and then, as if collecting himself, "All the same, I'm most grateful to you. Those manuscripts of yours have stimulated me, in all sorts of ways, they've set me going again. I'm tremendously grateful."

He fell silent abruptly, leaving me struggling for breath, for relief, for release. When I finally brought out my reply it surprised me almost as much as it did Traill. "Then you can have the lot," I said. "And you're welcome to them. I don't want any of them. I don't want to be like you. I don't want to go home." Suddenly I discarded a burden I had been carrying for too long, and all sorts of scruples, hesitations and anxieties fell away with it. "I'll take my chance right here, where I am. It's my only hope. If I don't strike out now, I'm sunk. And if I am to be sunk," I said, "I'd rather it happened now, than when I'm at your age. You can have what you've already got, and you can have all the stuff that's still in my room. It's all yours, if you want it. Take it, take the lot."

"I will," Traill said simply, after a long silence.

So we parted amicably enough, outside the house in which I boarded, Traill with his arms full of the files I had thrust enthusiastically upon him. "Good luck," I said; I had difficulty in restraining myself from clapping him on the back. There went my youth, I thought, looking at the bundle in Traill's arms; but I felt younger and more hopeful than I had for many months, than I had since coming to England.

I still feel that I did the right thing. The only trouble is that Traill has just published a new and very successful volume of poems; whereas I still live on hope, just on hope.

James Joyce

(1882–1941)

Born in Dublin, the city which figures so largely in all his writing, James Joyce was educated at two Jesuit schools, and at University College, Dublin. He early showed himself to be a rebel against tradition, rejecting his Catholic background and leaving Ireland soon after his graduation in 1902. With his lifelong companion Nora Barnacle, whom he eventually married in 1931, Joyce spent most of his life in self-imposed exile in various parts of Europe, supporting himself first by teaching, and then with the help of wealthy patrons. Though his writing career spanned forty years, Joyce published relatively little; his major works being *Dubliners* (1914), *A Portrait of the Artist as a Young Man* (1916), *Ulysses* (1922), and *Finnegan's Wake* (1939). Despite this limited output, Joyce's experiments in language and technique had an enormous influence, even in his own lifetime. But his work was also controversial: *Ulysses* was charged with obscenity on its first appearance, and banned in both England and America.

Dubliners, too, was regarded as a daring book, and Joyce fought for many years over its publication. Though it was completed initially in 1905, the publisher objected to some parts of the book (for example, to the use of the word "bloody" in several stories), and feared that publication would lead to a prosecution for indecency. Joyce fought to retain his stories intact, because, as he wrote to the publisher concerned (Grant Richards), "I believe that in composing my chapter of moral history in exactly the way I have composed it I have taken the first step towards the spiritual liberation of my country."

In "The Boarding House," as in the other stories in *Dubliners*, Joyce presents an episode in the life of his native city, turning a pitiless light on its follies and frailties. Within an astonishingly small compass, he creates a vivid sense of the seedy gentility of such establishments as that run by Mrs. Mooney; and he conveys too the moral duplicity practiced by mother and daughter on their helpless victim, a man made only too vulnerable by his own sense of decency. The tone of the story is drily comic; but its effect is not far removed from "the odour of ashpits and old weeds and offal" which Joyce said hung around his stories.

For further reading

Richard Ellmann, *James Joyce* (New York: Oxford University Press, 1959).
Hugh Kenner, *Dublin's Joyce* (Bloomington: Indiana University Press, 1956).
Bruce A. Rosenberg, "The Crucifixion in 'The Boarding House,'" *Studies in Short Fiction*, 5 (1967), 44–53.

The Boarding House

Mrs Mooney was a butcher's daughter. She was a woman who was quite able to keep things to herself: a determined woman. She had married her father's foreman, and opened a butcher's shop near Spring Gardens. But as soon as his father-in-law was dead Mr Mooney began to go to the devil. He drank, plundered the till, ran headlong into debt. It was no use making him take the pledge: he was sure to break out again a few days after. By fighting his wife in the presence of customers and by buying bad meat he ruined his business. One night he went for his wife with the cleaver, and she had to sleep in a neighbour's house.

After that they lived apart. She went to the priest and got a separation from him, with care of the children. She would give him neither money nor food nor house-room; and so he was obliged to enlist himself as a sheriff's man. He was a shabby stooped little drunkard with a white face and a white moustache and white eyebrows, pencilled above his little eyes, which were pink-veined and raw; and all day long he sat in the bailiff's room, waiting to be put on a job. Mrs Mooney, who had taken what remained of her money out of the butcher business and set up a boarding house in Hardwicke Street, was a big imposing woman. Her house had a floating population made up of tourists from Liverpool and the Isle of Man and, occasionally, *artistes* from the music halls. Its resident population was made up of clerks from the city. She governed the house cunningly and firmly, knew when to give credit, when to be stern and when to let things pass. All the resident young men spoke of her as *The Madam.*

Mrs Mooney's young men paid fifteen shillings a week for board and lodgings (beer or stout at dinner excluded). They shared in common tastes and occupations and for this reason they were very chummy with one another. They discussed with one another the chances of favourites and outsiders. Jack Mooney, the Madam's son, who was clerk to a commission agent in Fleet Street, had the reputation of being a hard case. He was fond of using soldiers' obscenities: usually he came home in the small hours. When he met his friends he had always a good one to tell them, and he was always sure to be on to a good thing—that is to say, a likely horse or a likely *artiste.* He was also handy with the mits and sang comic songs. On Sunday nights there would often be a reunion in Mrs Mooney's front drawing-room. The music-hall *artistes* would oblige; and Sheridan played waltzes and polkas and vamped accompaniments. Polly Mooney, the Madam's daughter, would also sing. She sang:

I'm a ... naughty girl
You needn't sham:
You know I am.

Polly was a slim girl of nineteen; she had light soft hair and a small full mouth. Her eyes, which were grey with a shade of green through them, had a habit of glancing upwards when she spoke with anyone, which made her look like a little perverse madonna. Mrs Mooney had first sent her daughter to be a typist in a corn-factor's office, but as a disreputable sheriff's man used to come every other day to the office, asking to be allowed to say a word to his daughter, she had taken her daughter home again and set her to do housework. As Polly was very lively, the intention was to give her the run of the young men. Besides, young men like to feel that there is a young woman not very far away. Polly, of course, flirted with the young men, but Mrs Mooney, who was a shrewd judge, knew that the young men were only passing the time away: none of them meant business. Things went on so for a long time, and Mrs Mooney began to think of sending Polly back to typewriting, when she noticed that something was going on between Polly and one of the young men. She watched the pair and kept her own counsel.

Polly knew that she was being watched, but still her mother's persistent silence could not be misunderstood. There had been no open complicity between mother and daughter, no open understanding, but though people in the house began to talk of the affair, still Mrs Mooney did not intervene. Polly began to grow a little strange in her manner, and the young man was evidently perturbed. At last, when she judged it to be the right moment, Mrs Mooney intervened. She dealt with moral problems as a cleaver deals with meat: and in this case she had made up her mind.

It was a bright Sunday morning of early summer, promising heat, but with a fresh breeze blowing. All the windows of the boarding house were open and the lace curtains ballooned gently towards the street beneath the raised sashes. The belfry of George's Church sent out constant peals, and worshippers, singly or in groups, traversed the little circus before the church, revealing their purpose by their self-contained demeanour no less than by the little volumes in their gloved hands. Breakfast was over in the boarding house, and the table of the breakfast-room was covered with plates on which lay yellow streaks of eggs with morsels of bacon-fat and bacon-rind. Mrs Mooney sat in the straw arm-chair and watched the servant Mary remove the breakfast things. She made Mary collect the crusts and pieces of broken bread to help to make Tuesday's bread-pudding. When the table was cleared, the broken bread collected, the sugar and butter safe under lock and key, she began to reconstruct the interview which she had had the night before with Polly. Things were as she had suspected: she had been frank in her questions and Polly had been frank in her answers. Both had been somewhat awkward, of course. She had been made awkward by her not wishing to receive the news in too cavalier a fashion or to seem to have con-

nived, and Polly had been made awkward not merely because allu-
sions of that kind always made her awkward, but also because she
did not wish it to be thought that in her wise innocence she had
divined the intention behind her mother's tolerance.

Mrs Mooney glanced instinctively at the little gilt clock on the
mantelpiece as soon as she had become aware through her reverie
that the bells of George's Church had stopped ringing. It was seventeen minutes past eleven: she would have lots of time to have the
matter out with Mr Doran and then catch short twelve at Marl-
borough Street. She was sure she would win. To begin with, she had
all the weight of social opinion on her side: she was an outraged
mother. She had allowed him to live beneath her roof, assuming that
he was a man of honour, and he had simply abused her hospitality.
He was thirty-four or thirty-five years of age, so that youth could not
be pleaded as his excuse; nor could ignorance be his excuse, since he
was a man who had seen something of the world. He had simply
taken advantage of Polly's youth and inexperience: that was evident.
The question was: What reparation would he make?

There must be reparation made in such a case. It is all very well
for the man: he can go his ways as if nothing had happened, having
had his moment of pleasure, but the girl has to bear the brunt. Some
mothers would be content to patch up such an affair for a sum of
money: she had known cases of it. But she would not do so. For her
only one reparation could make up for the loss of her daughter's
honour: marriage.

She counted all her cards again before sending Mary up to Mr
Doran's room to say that she wished to speak with him. She felt sure
she would win. He was a serious young man, not rakish or loud-
voiced like the others. If it had been Mr Sheridan or Mr Meade or
Bantam Lyons, her task would have been much harder. She did not
think he would face publicity. All the lodgers in the house knew
something of the affair; details had been invented by some. Besides,
he had been employed for thirteen years in a great Catholic wine-
merchant's office, and publicity would mean for him, perhaps, the
loss of his job. Whereas if he agreed all might be well. She knew he
had a good screw for one thing, and she suspected he had a bit of stuff
put by.

Nearly the half-hour! She stood up and surveyed herself in the
pier-glass. The decisive expression of her great florid face satisfied
her, and she thought of some mothers she knew who could not get
their daughters off their hands.

Mr Doran was very anxious indeed this Sunday morning. He had
made two attempts to shave, but his hand had been so unsteady that
he had been obliged to desist. Three days' reddish beard fringed his

jaws, and every two or three minutes a mist gathered on his glasses so that he had to take them off and polish them with his pocket-handkerchief. The recollection of his confession of the night before was a cause of acute pain to him; the priest had drawn out every ridiculous detail of the affair, and in the end had so magnified his sin that he was almost thankful at being afforded a loophole of reparation. The harm was done. What could he do now but marry her or run away? He could not brazen it out. The affair would be sure to be talked of, and his employer would be certain to hear of it. Dublin is such a small city: everyone knows everyone else's business. He felt his heart leap warmly in his throat as he heard in his excited imagination old Mr Leonard calling out in his rasping voice: "Send Mr Doran here, please."

All his long years of service gone for nothing! All his industry and diligence thrown away! As a young man he had sown his wild oats, of course; he had boasted of his free-thinking and denied the existence of God to his companions in public-houses. But that was all passed and done with . . . nearly. He still bought a copy of *Reynolds Newspaper* every week, but he attended to his religious duties, and for nine-tenths of the year lived a regular life. He had money enough to settle down on; it was not that. But the family would look down on her. First of all there was her disreputable father, and then her mother's boarding house was beginning to get a certain fame. He had a notion that he was being had. He could imagine his friends talking of the affair and laughing. She *was* a little vulgar; sometimes she said "I seen" and "If I had've known." But what would grammar matter if he really loved her? He could not make up his mind whether to like her or despise her for what she had done. Of course he had done it too. His instinct urged him to remain free, not to marry. Once you are married you are done for, it said.

While he was sitting helplessly on the side of the bed in shirt and trousers, she tapped lightly at his door and entered. She told him all, that she had made a clean breast of it to her mother and that her mother would speak with him that morning. She cried and threw her arms round his neck, saying:

"O Bob! Bob! What am I to do? What am I to do at all?"

She would put an end to herself, she said.

He comforted her feebly, telling her not to cry, that it would be all right, never fear. He felt against his shirt the agitation of her bosom.

It was not altogether his fault that it had happened. He remembered well, with the curious patient memory of the celibate, the first casual caresses her dress, her breath, her fingers had given him.

Then late one night as he was undressing for bed she had tapped at his door, timidly. She wanted to relight her candle at his, for hers had been blown out by a gust. It was her bath night. She wore a loose open combing-jacket of printed flannel. Her white instep shone in the opening of her furry slippers and the blood glowed warmly behind her perfumed skin. From her hands and wrists too as she lit and steadied her candle a faint perfume arose.

On nights when he came in very late it was she who warmed up his dinner. He scarcely knew what he was eating, feeling her beside him alone, at night, in the sleeping house. And her thoughtfulness! If the night was anyway cold or wet or windy there was sure to be a little tumbler of punch ready for him. Perhaps they could be happy together . . .

They used to go upstairs together on tiptoe, each with a candle, and on the third landing exchange reluctant good nights. They used to kiss. He remembered well her eyes, the touch of her hand and his delirium . . .

But delirium passes. He echoed her phrase, applying it to himself: *"What am I to do?"* The instinct of the celibate warned him to hold back. But the sin was there; even his sense of honour told him that reparation must be made for such a sin.

While he was sitting with her on the side of the bed Mary came to the door and said that the missus wanted to see him in the parlour. He stood up to put on his coat and waistcoat, more helpless than ever. When he was dressed he went over to her to comfort her. It would be all right, never fear. He left her crying on the bed and moaning softly: *"O my God!"*

Going down the stairs his glasses became so dimmed with moisture that he had to take them off and polish them. He longed to ascend through the roof and fly away to another country where he would never hear again of his trouble, and yet a force pushed him downstairs step by step. The implacable faces of his employer and of the Madam stared upon his discomfiture. On the last flight of stairs he passed Jack Mooney, who was coming up from the pantry nursing two bottles of *Bass.* They saluted coldly; and the lover's eyes rested for a second or two on a thick bulldog face and a pair of thick short arms. When he reached the foot of the staircase he glanced up and saw Jack regarding him from the door of the return-room.

Suddenly he remembered the night when one of the music-hall *artistes,* a little blond Londoner, had made a rather free allusion to Polly. The reunion had been almost broken up on account of Jack's violence. Everyone tried to quiet him. The music-hall *artiste,* a little paler than usual, kept smiling and saying that there was no harm meant; but Jack kept shouting at him that if any fellow tried that sort

of a game on with his sister he'd bloody well put his teeth down his
throat: so he would.

Polly sat for a little time on the side of the bed, crying. Then she
dried her eyes and went over to the looking-glass. She dipped the end
of the towel in the water-jug and refreshed her eyes with the cool
water. She looked at herself in profile and readjusted a hairpin above
her ear. Then she went back to the bed again and sat at the foot. She
regarded the pillows for a long time, and the sight of them awakened
in her mind secret, amiable memories. She rested the nape of her
neck against the cool iron bedrail and fell into a reverie. There was
no longer any perturbation visible on her face.

She waited on patiently, almost cheerfully, without alarm, her
memories gradually giving place to hopes and visions of the future.
Her hopes and visions were so intricate that she no longer saw the
white pillows on which her gaze was fixed, or remembered that she
was waiting for anything.

At last she heard her mother calling. She started to her feet and
ran to the banisters.

"Polly! Polly!"

"Yes, mamma?"

"Come down, dear. Mr Doran wants to speak to you."

Then she remembered what she had been waiting for.

Margaret Laurence
(b. 1926)

"The Merch Heaven"

In several of her novels and stories, Margaret Wemyss Laurence has transformed her Manitoba birthplace—a town called Neepawa (Cree for "land of plenty")—into a town called Manawaka. *The Stone Angel* (1964), *A Jest of God* (1966) (upon which the film *Rachel Rachel* was based), and *A Bird in the House* (1970) are all set in this rural landscape. Ukrainians and Scots and others have all emigrated there to start a new life, and though generations pass, pride and folly and other traits of human individuality continue to interfere with their happiness. Laurence is extraordinarily sensitive to that individuality and also respectful of it, however much she may disagree with particular points of view. It is a frame of mind that gives her both insight into the lives of the women around whom these stories revolve and perspective toward them. Her characters are by turns bound by convention, in search of freedom, constrained by weakness, and aroused by anger, love, and pride; above all, they are separate human beings, alive and warm, needing and demanding a recognition of their distinctive selves.

Sympathy toward that need for self-expression found another outlet for Margaret Laurence in her African stories. From 1950 to 1952 she lived in Somaliland, and from 1952 to 1957 in Ghana. Out of that experience came several books, including *The Tomorrow-Tamer* (1963), the collection of stories and tales in which "The Merchant of Heaven" appears. They focus on some of the realities of modern Africa: the enthusiasms and ideals that accompanied independence, the conflicts between traditional and European ways of life, and the problems with expatriates. The task of making these subjects appear to be realistic segments from actual life is one of rigorous selection. "I don't think of the form as something imposed upon a novel," she wrote to Clara Thomas, "but as its bone, the skeleton which makes it possible for the flesh to move and be revealed as itself."

For further reading

Henry Kreisel, "The African Stories of Margaret Laurence," *Canadian Forum*, 41 (Spring 1961), 8–10.

Margaret Laurence, "Ten Years' Sentences," *Canadian Literature*, 41 (Summer 1969), 10–16.

W. H. New, "Equatorial Zones and Polar Opposites," in *Articulating West* (Toronto: New Press, 1972), pp. 216–233.

Clara Thomas, *Margaret Laurence* (Toronto: McClelland & Stewart, 1969).

The Merchant of Heaven

Across the tarmac the black-and-orange dragon lizards skitter, occasionally pausing to raise their wrinkled necks and stare with ancient saurian eyes on a world no longer theirs. In the painted light of mid-day, the heat shimmers like molten glass. No shade anywhere. You sweat like a pig, and inside the waiting-room you nearly stifle. The African labourers, trundling baggage or bits of air-freight, work stripped to the waist, their torsos sleek and shining. The airport officials in their white drill uniforms are damp and crumpled as gulls newly emerged from the egg.

In this purgatorially hot and exposed steam bath, I awaited with some trepidation the arrival of Amory Lemon, proselytizer for a mission known as the Angel of Philadelphia.

Above the buildings flew the three-striped flag—red, yellow and green—with the black star of Africa in its centre. I wondered if the evangelist would notice it or know what it signified. Very likely not. Brother Lemon was not coming here to study political developments. He was coming—as traders once went to Babylon—for the souls of men.

I had never seen him before, but I knew him at once, simply because he looked so different from the others who came off the plane—ordinary English people, weary and bored after the long trip, their still-tanned skins indicating that this was not their first tour in the tropics. Brother Lemon's skin was very white and smooth— it reminded me of those sea pebbles which as a child I used to think were the eyeballs of the drowned. He was unusually tall; he walked in a stately and yet brisk fashion, with controlled excitement. I realized that this must be a great moment for him. The apostle landing at Cyprus or Thessalonica, the light of future battles already kindling in his eyes, and replete with faith as a fresh-gorged mosquito is with blood.

"Mr. Lemon? I'm Will Kettridge—the architect. We've corresponded—"

He looked at me with piercing sincerity from those astonishing turquoise eyes of his.

"Yes, of course," he said, grasping me by the hand. "I'm very pleased to make your acquaintance. It surely was nice of you to meet me. The name's Lee-*mon*. Brother Lee-*mon*. Accent on the last syllable. I really appreciate your kindness, Mr. Kettridge."

I felt miserably at a disadvantage. For one thing, I was wearing khaki trousers which badly needed pressing, whereas Brother Lemon was clad in a dove-grey suit of a miraculously immaculate material. For another, when a person interprets your selfish motive as pure altruism, what can you tactfully say?

"Fine," I said. "Let's collect your gear."

Brother Lemon's gear consisted of three large wardrobe suitcases, a pair of water skis, a box which from its label and size appeared to contain a gross of cameras but turned out to contain only a Rolleiflex and a cine-camera complete with projector and editing equipment, a carton of an anti-malarial drug so new that we in this infested region had not yet heard of it, and finally, a lovely little pigskin case which enfolded a water-purifier. Brother Lemon unlocked the case and took out a silvery mechanism. His face glowed with a boyish fascination.

"See? It works like a syringe. You just press this thing, and the water is sucked up here. Then you squirt it out again, and there you are. Absolutely guaranteed one hundred per cent pure. Not a single bacteria. You can even drink swamp water."

I was amused and rather touched. He seemed so frankly hopeful of adventure. I was almost sorry that this was not the Africa of Livingstone or Burton.

"Wonderful," I said. "The water is quite safe here, though. All properly filtered and chlorinated."

"You can't be too careful," Brother Lemon said. "I couldn't afford to get sick—I'll be the only representative of our mission, for a while at least."

He drew in a deep breath of the hot salty tar-stinking air.

"I've waited six years for this day, Mr. Kettridge," he said. "Six years of prayer and preparation."

"I hope the country comes up to your expectations, then."

He looked at me in surprise.

"Oh, it will," he said with perfect equanimity. "Our mission, you know, is based on the Revelation of St. John the Divine. We believe there is a special message for us in the words given by the Spirit to the Angel of the Church in Philadelphia——"

"A different Philadelphia, surely."

His smile was confident, even pitying.

"These things do not happen by accident, Mr. Kettridge. When Andrew McFetters had his vision, back in 1924, it was revealed that the ancient Church would be reborn in our city of the same name, and would take the divine word to unbelievers in seven different parts of the world."

Around his head his fair hair sprouted and shone like some fantastic marigold halo in a medieval painting.

"I believe my mission has been foretold," he said with stunning simplicity. "I estimate I'll have a thousand souls within six months."

Suddenly I saw Brother Lemon as a kind of soul-purifier, sucking in the septic souls and spewing them back one hundred per cent pure.

That evening I told Danso of my vague uneasiness. He laughed, as I had known he would.

"Please remember you are an Englishman, Will," he said. "Englishmen should not have visions. It is not suitable. Leave that to Brother Lemon and me. Evangelists and Africans always get on well —did you know? It is because we are both so mystical. Did you settle anything?"

"Yes, I'm getting the design work. He says he doesn't want contemporary for the church, but he's willing to consider it for his house."

"What did he say about money?" Danso asked. "That's what I'm interested in."

"His precise words were—"the Angel of Philadelphia Mission isn't going to do this thing on the cheap.'"

Danso was short and slim, but he made up for it in mercurial energy. Now he crouched tigerish by the chaise-longue, and began feinting with clenched fists like a bantamweight—which, as a matter of fact, he used to be, before a scholarship to an English university and an interest in painting combined to change the course of his life.

"Hey, come on, you Brother Lemon!" he cried. "That's it, man! You got it and I want it—very easy, very simple. Bless you, Brother Lemon, benedictions on your name, my dear citric sibling."

"I have been wondering," I said, "how you planned to profit from Brother Lemon's presence."

"Murals, of course."

"Oh, Danso, don't be an idiot. He'd never——"

"All right, all right, man. Pictures, then. A nice oil. Everybody wants holy pictures in a church, see?"

"He'll bring them from Philadelphia," I said. "Four-tone prints, done on glossy paper."

Danso groaned. "Do you really think he'll do that, Will?"

"Maybe not," I said encouragingly. "You could try."

"Listen—how about this? St. Augustine, bishop of hippos."

"Hippo, you fool. A place."

"I know that," Danso said witheringly. "But, hell, who wants to look at some fly-speckled North African town, all mudbrick and camel dung? Brother Lemon wants colour, action, you know what I mean. St. Augustine is on the river bank, see, the Congo or maybe the Niger. Bush all around. Ferns thick as a woman's hair. Palms— great big feathery palms. But very stiff, very stylized—Rousseau stuff—like this——"

His brown arms twined upward, became the tree trunks, and his thick fingers the palm fans, precise, sharp in the sun.

"And in the river—real blue and green river, man, all sky and scum—in that river is the congregation, only they're hippos, see— enormous fat ones, all bulging eyes, and they're singing 'Hallelujah'

like the angels themselves, while old St. Augustine leads them to
paradise——"

"Go ahead—paint it," I began, "and we'll——"

I stopped. My smile withdrew as I looked at Danso.

"Whatsamatter?" he said. "Don't you think the good man will buy
it?"

In his eyes there was an inexpressible loathing.

"Danso! How can you——? You haven't even met him yet."

The carven face remained ebony, remained black granite.

"I have known this pedlar of magic all my life, Will. My mother
always took me along to prayer meetings, when I was small."

The mask slackened into laughter, but it was not the usual laughter.

"Maybe he thinks we are short of ju-ju," Danso remarked. "Maybe
he thinks we need a few more devils to exorcise."

When I first met Brother Lemon, I had seen him as he must have
seen himself, an apostle. Now I could almost see him with Danso's
bitter eyes—as sorcerer.

I undertook to show Brother Lemon around the city. He was impressed by the profusion and cheapness of tropical fruit; delightedly
he purchased baskets of oranges, pineapples, paw-paw. He loaded
himself down with the trinkets of Africa—python-skin wallets,
carved elephants, miniature *dono* drums.

On our second trip, however, he began to notice other things. A
boy with suppurating yaws covering nearly as much of his body as
did his shreds of clothing. A loin-clothed labourer carrying a head-
load so heavy that his flimsy legs buckled and bent. A trader woman
minding a roadside stall on which her living was spread—half a
dozen boxes of cube sugar and a handful of pink plastic combs. A girl
child squatting modestly in the filth-flowing gutter. A grinning
penny-pleading gamin with a belly outpuffed by navel hernia. A
young woman, pregnant and carrying another infant on her back,
her placid eyes growing all at once proud and hating as we passed
comfortably by. An old Muslim beggar who howled and shouted
*sura** from the Qoran, and then, silent, looked and looked with the
unclouded innocent eyes of lunacy. Brother Lemon nodded absently
as I dutifully pointed out the new Post Office, the library, the Law
Courts, the Bank.

We reached shanty town, where the mud and wattle huts crowded
each other like fish in a net, where plantains were always frying on
a thousand smoky charcoal burners, where the rhythm of life was

Sura = a chapter from the Koran.

forever that of the women's lifted and lowered wooden pestles as the cassava was pounded into meal, where the crimson portulaca and the children swarmed over the hard soil and survived somehow, at what loss of individual blossom or brat one could only guess.

"It's a crime," Brother Lemon said, "that people should have to live like this."

He made the mistake all kindly people make. He began to give money to children and beggars—sixpences, shillings—thinking it would help. He overpaid for everything he bought. He distributed largesse.

"These people are poor, real poor, Mr. Kettridge," he said seriously, "and the way I figure it—if I'm able through the Angel of Philadelphia Mission to ease their lives, then it's my duty to do so."

"Perhaps," I said. "But the shilling or two won't last long, and then what? You're not prepared to take them all on as permanent dependants, are you?"

He gazed at me blankly. I guess he thought I was stony-hearted. He soon came to be surrounded by beggars wherever he went. They swamped him; their appalling voices followed him down any street. Fingerless hands reached out; half-limbs hurried at his approach. He couldn't cope with it, of course. Who could? Finally, he began to turn away, as ultimately we all turn, frightened and repelled by the outrageous pain and need.

Brother Lemon was no different from any stranger casting his tiny shillings into the wishful well of good intentions, and seeing them disappear without so much as a splash or tinkle. But unlike the rest of us, he at least could console himself.

"Salvation is like the loaves and fishes," he said. "There's enough for all, for every person in this world. None needs to go empty away."

He could hardly wait to open his mission. He frequently visited my office, in order to discuss the building plans. He wanted me to hurry with them, so construction could begin the minute his landsite was allocated. I knew there was no hurry—he'd be lucky if he got the land within six months—but he was so keen that I hated to discourage him.

He did not care for the hotel, where the bottles and glasses clinked merrily the night through, disturbing his sombre slumbers. I helped him find a house. It was a toy-size structure on the outskirts of the city. It had once (perhaps in another century) been whitewashed, but now it was ashen. Brother Lemon immediately had it painted azure. When I remonstrated with him—why spend money on a rented bungalow?—he gave me an odd glance.

"I grew up on the farm," he said. "We never did get around to painting that house."

He overpaid the workmen and was distressed when he discovered one of them had stolen a gallon of paint. The painters, quite simply, regarded Brother Lemon's funds as inexhaustible. But he did not understand and it made him unhappy. This was the first of a myriad annoyances.

A decomposing lizard was found in his plumbing. The wiring was faulty and his lights winked with persistent malice. The first cook he hired turned out to have both forged references and gonorrhoea.

Most of his life, I imagine, Brother Lemon had been fighting petty battles in preparation for the great one. And now he found even this battle petty. As he recounted his innumerable domestic difficulties, I could almost see the silken banners turn to grey. He looked for dragons to slay, and found cockroaches in his store-cupboard. Jacob-like, he came to wrestle for the Angel's blessing, and instead was bent double with cramps in his bowels from eating unwashed salad greens.

I was never tempted to laugh. Brother Lemon's faith was of a quality that defied ridicule. He would have preferred his trials to be on a grander scale, but he accepted them with humility. One thing he could not accept, however, was the attitude of his servants. Perhaps he had expected to find an African Barnabas, but he was disappointed. His cook was a decent enough chap, but he helped himself to tea and sugar.

"I pay Kwaku half again as much as the going wage—you told me so yourself. And now he does this."

"So would you," I said, "in his place."

"That's where you're wrong," Brother Lemon contradicted, so sharply that I never tried that approach again.

"All these things are keeping me from my work," he went on plaintively. "That's the worst of it. I've been in the country three weeks tomorrow, and I haven't begun services yet. What's the home congregation going to think of me?"

Then he knotted his big hands in sudden and private anguish.

"No——" he said slowly. "I shouldn't say that. It shouldn't matter to me. The question is—what is the Almighty going to think?"

"I expect He's learned to be patient," I ventured.

But Brother Lemon hadn't even heard. He wore the fixed expression of a man beholding a vision.

"That's it," he said finally. "Now I see why I've been feeling so let down and miserable. It's because I've been putting off the work of my mission. I had to look around—oh yes, see the sights, buy souvenirs.

Even my worry about the servants, and the people who live so poor and all. I let these things distract me from my true work."

He stood up, there in his doll's house, an alabaster giant.

"My business," he said, "is with the salvation of their immortal souls. That, and that alone. It's the greatest kindness I can do these people."

After that day, he was busy as a nesting bird. I met him one morning in the Post Office, where he was collecting packages of Bibles. He shook my hand in that casually formal way of his.

"I reckon to start services within a week," he said. "I've rented an empty lot, temporarily, and I'm having a shelter put up."

"You certainly haven't wasted any time recently."

"There isn't any time to waste," Brother Lemon's bell voice tolled. "Later may be too late."

"You can't carry all that lot very far," I said. "Can I give you a lift?"

"That's very friendly of you, Mr. Kettridge, but I'm happy to say I've got my new car at last. Like to see it?"

Outside, a dozen street urchins rushed up, and Brother Lemon allowed several of them to carry his parcels on their heads. We reached the appointed place, and the little boys, tattered and dusty as fallen leaves, lively as clickety-winged cockroaches, began to caper and jabber.

"Mastah—I beg you—you go dash me!"

A "dash" of a few pennies was certainly in order. But Brother Lemon gave them five shillings apiece. They fled before he could change his mind. I couldn't help commenting wryly on the sum, but his eyes never wavered.

"You have to get known somehow," Brother Lemon said. "Lots of churches advertise nowadays."

He rode off, then, in his new two-toned orchid Buick.

Brother Lemon must have been lonely. He knew no other Europeans, and one evening he dropped in, uninvited, to my house.

"I've never explained our teaching to you, Mr. Kettridge," he said, fixing me with his blue-polished eyes. "I don't know, mind you, what your views on religion are, or how you look at salvation——"

He was so pathetically eager to preach that I told him to go ahead. He plunged into his spiel like the proverbial hart into cooling streams. He spoke of the seven golden candlesticks, which were the seven churches of Asia, and the seven stars—the seven angels of the churches. The seven lamps of fire, the heavenly book sealed with seven seals, the seven-horned Lamb which stood as it had been slain.

I had not read Revelation in years, but its weird splendour came back to me as I listened to him. Man, however, is many-eyed as the beasts around that jewelled throne. Brother Lemon did not regard the Apocalypse as poetry.

"We have positive proof," he cried, "that the Devil—he who bears the mark of the beast—shall be loosed out of his prison and shall go out to deceive the nations."

This event, he estimated, was less than half a century away. Hence the urgency of his mission, for the seven churches were to be reborn in strategic spots throughout the world, and their faithful would spearhead the final attack against the forces of evil. Every soul saved now would swell that angelic army; every soul unsaved would find the gates of heaven eternally barred. His face was tense and ecstatic. Around his head shone the terrible nimbus of his radiant hair.

"Whosoever is not found written in the book of life will be cast into the lake of fire and brimstone, and will be tormented day and night for ever and ever. But the believers will dwell in the new Jerusalem, where the walls are of jasper and topaz and amethyst, and the city is of pure gold."

I could not find one word to say. I was thinking of Danso. Danso as a little boy, in the evangel's meeting place, listening to the same sermon while the old gods of his own people still trampled through the night forests of his mind. The shadow spirits of stone and tree, the hungry gods of lagoon and grove, the fetish hidden in its hut of straw, the dark soul-hunter Sasabonsam—to these were added the dragon, the serpent, the mark of the beast, the lake of fire and the anguish of the damned. What had Danso dreamed about, those years ago, when he slept?

"I am not a particularly religious man," I said abruptly.

"Well, okay," he said regretfully. "Only—I like you, Mr. Kettridge, and I'd like to see you saved."

Later that evening Danso arrived. I had tried to keep him from meeting Brother Lemon. I felt somehow I had to protect each from the other.

Danso was dressed in his old khaki trousers and a black mammy-cloth shirt patterned with yellow diamonds. He was all harlequin tonight. He dervished into the room, swirled a bow in the direction of Brother Lemon, whose mouth had dropped open, then spun around and presented me with a pile of canvases.

Danso knew it was not fashionable, but he painted people. A globe-hipped market mammy stooped while her friends loaded a brass tray full of tomatoes onto her head. A Hausa trader, encased in his long embroidered robe, looked haughtily on while boys floated stick boats down a gutter. A line of little girls in their yellow mission-school dresses walked lightfoot back from the well, with buckets on their heads.

A hundred years from now, when the markets and shanties have been supplanted by hygienic skyscrapers, when the gutters no longer reek, when pidgin English has grown from a patois into a sedate language boasting grammar texts and patriotic poems, then Africans will look nostalgically at Danso's pictures of the old teeming days, and will probably pay fabulous prices. At the moment, however, Danso could not afford to marry, and were it not for his kindly but conservative uncles, who groaned and complained and handed over a pound here, ten shillings there, he would not have been able to paint, either.

I liked the pictures. I held one of them up for Brother Lemon to see.

"Oh yes, a market scene," he said vaguely. "Say, that reminds me, Mr. Kettridge. Would you like me to bring over my colour slides some evening? I've taken six rolls of film so far, and I haven't had one failure."

Danso, slit-eyed and lethal, coiled himself up like a spitting cobra.

"Colour slides, eh?" he hissed softly. "Very fine—who wants paintings if you can have the real thing? But one trouble—you can't use them in your church. Every church needs pictures. Does it look like a church, with no pictures? Of course not. Just a cheap meeting place, that's all. Real religious pictures. What do you say, Mr. Lemon?"

I did not know whether he hoped to sell a painting, or whether the whole thing was one of his elaborate farces. I don't believe he knew, either.

Brother Lemon's expression stiffened. "Are you a Christian, Mr. Danso?"

Immediately, Danso's demeanour altered. His muscular grace was transformed into the seeming self-effacement of a spiritual grace. Even the vivid viper markings of his mammy-cloth shirt appeared to fade into something quiet as mouse fur or monk's robe.

"Of course," he said with dignity. "I am several times a Christian. I have been baptised into the Methodist, Baptist and Roman Catholic churches, and one or two others whose names I forget."

He laughed at Brother Lemon's rigid face.

"Easy, man—I didn't mean it. I am only once a Christian—that's better, eh? Even then, I may be the wrong kind. So many, and each says his is the only one. The Akan church was simpler."

"Beg pardon?"

"The Akan church—African." Danso snapped his fingers. "Didn't you know we had a very fine religion here before ever a whiteman came?"

"Idolatry, paganism," Brother Lemon said. "I don't call that a religion."

Danso had asked for it, admittedly, but now he was no longer able to hold around himself the cloak of usual mockery.

"You are thinking of fetish," he said curtly. "But that is not all. There is plenty more. Invisible, intangible—real proper gods. If we'd been left alone, our gods would have grown, as yours did, into One. It was happening already—we needed only a prophet. But now our prophet will never come. Sad, eh?"

And he laughed. I could see he was furious at himself for having spoken. Danso was a chameleon who felt it was self-betrayal to show his own hues. He told me once he sympathized with the old African belief that it was dangerous to tell a stranger all your name, as it gave him power over you.

Brother Lemon pumped the bellows of his preacher voice.

"Paganism in any form is an abomination! I'm surprised at you, a Christian, defending it. In the words of Jeremiah—'Pour out thy fury upon the heathen!' "

"You pour it out, man," Danso said with studied languor. "You got lots to spare."

He began leafing through the Bible that was Brother Lemon's invariable companion, and suddenly he leapt to his feet.

"Here you are!" he cried. "For a painting. The throne of heaven, with all the elders in white, and the many-eyed beasts saying 'Holy, Holy'—what about it?"

He was perfectly serious. One might logically assume that he had given up any thought of a religious picture, but not so. The apocalyptic vision had caught his imagination, and he frowned in concentration, as though he were already planning the arrangement of figures and the colours he would use.

Brother Lemon looked flustered. Then he snickered. I was unprepared, and the ugly little sound startled me.

"You?" he said. "To paint the throne of heaven?"

Danso snapped the book shut. His face was volcanic rock, hard and dark, seeming to bear the marks of the violence that formed it. Then he picked up his pictures and walked out of the house.

"Well, I must say there was no need for him to go and fly off the handle like that," Brother Lemon said indignantly. "What's wrong with him, anyway?"

He was not being facetious. He really didn't know.

"Mr. Lemon," I asked at last, "don't you ever—not even for an instant—have any doubts?"

"What do you mean, doubts?" His eyes were genuinely puzzled.

"Don't you ever wonder if salvation is—well—yours to dole out?"

"No," he replied slowly. "I don't have any doubts about my religion, Mr. Kettridge. Why, without my religion, I'd be nothing."

I wondered how many drab years he must have lived, years like unpainted houses, before he set out to find his golden candlesticks and jewelled throne in far places.

By the time Danso and I got around to visiting the Angel of Philadelphia Mission, Brother Lemon had made considerable headway. The temporary meeting place was a large open framework of poles, roofed with sun-whitened palm boughs. Rough benches had been set up inside, and at the front was Brother Lemon's pulpit, a mahogany box draped with delphinium-coloured velvet. A wide silken banner proclaimed "Ye Shall Be Saved."

At the back of the hall, a long table was being guarded by muscular white-robed converts armed with gilt staves. I fancied it must be some sort of communion set-up, but Danso, after a word with one of the men, enlightened me. Those who remained for the entire service would receive free a glass of orange squash and a piece of *kenkey*.*

Danso and I stationed ourselves unobtrusively at the back, and watched the crowd pour in. Mainly women, they were. Market woman and fishwife, quail-plump and bawdy, sweet-oiled flesh gleaming brownly, gaudy as melons in trade cloth and headscarf. Young women with sleeping children strapped to their backs by the cover cloth. Old women whose unsmiling eyes had witnessed heaven knows how much death and who now were left with nothing to share their huts and hearts. Silent as sandcrabs, frightened and fascinated, women who sidled in, making themselves slight and unknown, as though apologizing for their presence on earth. Crones and destitutes, shrunken skins scarcely covering their insistent bones, dried dugs hanging loose and shrivelled.

Seven boys, splendidly uniformed in white and scarlet, turbanned in gold, fidgeted and tittered their way into the hall, each one carrying his fife or drum. Danso began to laugh.

"Did you wonder how he trained a band so quickly, Will? They're all from other churches. I'll bet that cost him a good few shillings. He said he wasn't going to do things on the cheap."

I was glad Danso was amused. He had been sullen and tense all evening, and had changed his mind a dozen times about coming.

The band began to whistle and boom. The women's voices shrilled in hymn. Slowly, regally, his bright hair gleaming like every crown in Christendom, Brother Lemon entered his temple. Over his orlon suit he wore a garment that resembled an academic gown, except that his was a resplendent peacock-blue, embroidered with stars,

---

*Kenkey = a Ghanaian food made of fermented cornmeal.

seven in number. He was followed by seven mites or sprites, somebody's offspring, each carrying a large brass candlestick complete
with lighted taper. These were placed at intervals across the platform, and each attendant stood wide-eyed behind his charge, like
small bedazzled genii.

Brother Lemon raised both arms. Silence. He began to speak, pausing from time to time in order that his two interpreters might trans-
late into Ga and Twi. Although most of his listeners could not
understand the words of Brother Lemon himself, they could scarcely
fail to perceive his compulsive fire.

In the flickering flarelight of torches and tapers, the smoky light
of the sweat-stinking dark, Brother Lemon seemed to stretch tall as
a shadow, tall as the pale horseman at night when children cry in
their sleep.

Beside me, Danso sat quietly, never stirring. His face was blank
and his eyes were shuttered.

The sun would become black as sackcloth of hair, and the moon
would become as blood. In Brother Lemon's voice the seven trumpets sounded, and the fire and hail were cast upon earth. The bitter
star fell upon the fountains of waters; the locusts of hell emerged
with wings like the sound of chariots. And for the unbelieving and
idolatrous—plague and flagellation and sorrow.

The women moaned and chanted. The evening was hot and dank,
and the wind from the sea did not reach here.

"Do you think they really do believe, though?" I whispered to
Danso.

"If you repeat something often enough, someone will believe you.
The same people go to the fetish priest, this man's brother."

But I looked at Brother Lemon's face. "He believes what he says."

"A wizard always believes in his own powers," Danso said.

Now Brother Lemon's voice softened. The thunders and trumpets
of impending doom died, and there was hope. He told them how
they could join the ranks of saints and angels, how the serpent could
be quelled for evermore. He told them of the New Jerusalem, with
its walls of crysolyte and beryl and jacinth, with its twelve gates
each of a single pearl. The women shouted and swayed. Tears like
the rains of spring moistened their parched and praising faces. I felt
uneasy, but I did not know why.

"My people," Danso remarked, "drink dreams like palm wine."

"What is the harm in that?"

"Oh, nothing. But if you dream too long, nothing else matters.
Listen—he is telling them that life on earth doesn't matter. So the
guinea worm stays in the flesh. The children still fall into the pit
latrines and die with excrement in their mouths. And women sit for

all eternity, breaking building-stones with hammers for two shillings a day."

Brother Lemon was calling them up to the front. Come up, come up, all ye who would be saved. In front of the golden candlesticks of brass the women jostled and shoved, hands outstretched. Half in a trance, a woman walked stiffly to the evangel's throne, her voice keening and beseeching. She fell, forehead in the red dust.

"Look at that one," I said with open curiosity. "See?"

Danso did not reply. I glanced at him. He sat with his head bowed, and his hands were slowly clenching and unclenching, as though cheated of some throat.

We walked back silently through the humming streets.

"My mother," Danso said suddenly, "will not see a doctor. She has a lot of pain. So what can I do?"

"What's the matter with her?"

"A malignant growth. She believes everything will be all right in a very short time. Everything will be solved. A few months, maybe, a year at most——"

"I don't see——"

Danso looked at me.

"She was the woman who fell down," he said, "who fell down there at his feet."

Danso's deep-set eyes were fathomless and dark as sea; life could drown there.

The next morning Brother Lemon phoned and asked me to accompany him to the African market-place. He seemed disturbed, so I agreed, although without enthusiasm.

"Where are the ju-ju stalls?" he enquired, when we arrived.

"Whatever for?"

"I've heard a very bad thing," he said grimly, "and I want to see if it's true."

So I led him past the stalls piled with green peppers and tomatoes and groundnuts, past the tailors whirring on their treadle sewing machines, past trader women in wide hats of woven rushes, and babies creeping like lost toads through the centipede-legged crowd. In we went, into the recesses of a labyrinthian shelter, always shadowed and cool, where the stalls carried the fetish priests' stock-in-trade, the raw materials of magic. Dried roots, parrot beak, snail shell, chunks of sulphur and bluestone, cowrie shells and strings of bells.

Brother Lemon's face was strained, skin stretched luminous over sharp bones. I only realized then how thin he had grown. He searched and searched, and finally he found what he had hoped not to find. At a little stall in a corner, the sort of place you would never find again once you were outside the maze, a young girl sat. She was selling crudely carved wooden figures, male and female, of the type used to kill by sorcery. I liked the look of the girl. She wasn't more than seventeen, and her eyes were almond and daylight. She was laughing, although she sold death. I half expected Brother Lemon to speak to her, but he did not. He turned away.

"All right," he said. "We can go now."

"You know her?"

"She joined my congregation," he said heavily. "Last week, she came up to the front and was saved. Or so I thought."

"This is her livelihood, after all," I said inadequately. "Anyway, they can't all be a complete success."

"I wonder how many are," Brother Lemon said. "I wonder if any are."

I almost told him of one real success he had had. How could I? The night before I could see only Danso's point of view, yet now, looking at the evangelist's face, I came close to betraying Danso. But I stopped myself in time. And the thought of last night's performance made me suddenly angry.

"What do you expect?" I burst out. "Even Paul nearly got torn to pieces by the the Ephesians defending their goddess. And who knows—maybe Diana was better for them than Jehovah. She was theirs, anyway."

Brother Lemon gazed at me as though he could hardly believe I had spoken the words. A thought of the design contract flitted through my mind, but when you've gone so far, you can't go back.

"How do you think they interpret your golden candlesticks and gates of pearl?" I went on. "The ones who go because they've tried everywhere else? As ju-ju, Mr. Lemon, just a new kind of ju-ju. That's all."

All at once I was sorrier than I could possibly say. Why the devil had I spoken? He couldn't comprehend, and if he ever did, he would be finished and done for.

"That's—not true——" he stammered. "That's—why, that's an awful thing to say."

And it was. It was.

This city had assimilated many gods. A priest of whatever faith would not have had to stay here very long in order to realize that the competition was stiff. I heard indirectly that Brother Lemon's conversions, after the initial success of novelty, were tailing off. The Homowo festival was absorbing the energies of the Ga people as they paid homage to the ancient gods of the coast. A touring faith-healer from Rhodesia was drawing large crowds. The Baptists staged a parade. The Roman Catholics celebrated a saint's day, and the Methodists parried with a picnic. A new god arrived from the northern deserts and its priests were claiming for it marvellous powers in overcoming sterility. The oratory of a visiting *imam** from Nigeria was boosting the local strength of Islam. Allah has ninety-nine names, say the Muslims. But in this city, He must have had nine hundred and ninety-nine, at the very least. I remembered Brother Lemon's brave estimate—a thousand souls within six months. He was really having to scrabble for them now.

I drove over to the meeting place one evening to take some building plans. The service was over, and I found Brother Lemon, still in his blue and starred robe, frantically looking for one of his pseudo-golden candlesticks which had disappeared. He was enraged, positive that someone had stolen it.

"Those candlesticks were specially made for my mission, and each member of the home congregation contributed towards them. It's certainly going to look bad if I have to write back and tell them one's missing——"

But the candlestick had not been stolen. Brother Lemon came into my office the following day to tell me. He stumbled over the words as though they were a matter of personal shame to him.

"It was one of my converts. He—borrowed it. He told me his wife was barren. He said he wanted the candlestick so he could touch her belly with it. He said he'd tried plenty of other—fetishes, but none had worked. So he thought this one might work."

He avoided my eyes.

"I guess you were right," he said.

"You shouldn't take it so hard," I said awkwardly. "After all, you can't expect miracles."

He looked at me, bewildered.

His discoveries were by no means at an end. The most notable of all occurred the night I went over to his bungalow for dinner and found him standing bleak and fearful under the flame tree, surrounded by half a dozen shouting and gesticulating ancients who shivered with years and anger. Gaunt as pariah dogs, bleached tatters fluttering like wind-worn prayer flags, a delegation of mendicants—come to wring from the next world the certain mercy they had not found in this?

"What's going on?" I asked.

Brother Lemon looked unaccountably relieved to see me.

"There seems to have been some misunderstanding," he said. "Maybe you can make sense of what they say."

*_Imam_ = Muslim priest.

The old men turned milky eyes to me, and I realized with a start that every last one of them was blind. Their leader spoke pidgin.

"Dis man"—waving in Brother Lemon's direction—"he say, meka we come heah, he go find we some shade place, he go dash me plenty plenty chop, he mek all t'ing fine too much, he mek we eye come strong. We wait long time, den he say 'go, you.' We no savvy dis palavah. I beg you, mastah, you tell him we wait long time."

"I never promised anything," Brother Lemon said helplessly. "They must be crazy."

Screeched protestations from the throng. They pressed around him, groping and grotesque beside his ivory height and his eyes. The tale emerged, bit by bit. Somehow, they had received the impression that the evangelist intended to throw a feast for them, at which, in the traditional African manner, a sheep would be throat-slit and sacrificed, then roasted and eaten. Palm wine would flow freely. Brother Lemon, furthermore, would restore the use of their eyes.

Brother Lemon's voice was unsteady.

"How could they? How could they think——"

"Who's your Ga interpreter?" I asked.

Brother Lemon looked startled.

"Oh no. He wouldn't say things I hadn't said. He's young, but he's a good boy. It's not just a job to him, you know. He's really interested. He'd never——"

"All the same, I think it would be wise to send for him."

The interpreter seemed all right, although perhaps not in quite the way Brother Lemon meant. This was his first job, and he was performing it with all possible enthusiasm. But his English vocabulary and his knowledge of fundamentalist doctrine were both strictly limited. He had not put words into Brother Lemon's mouth. He had only translated them in his own way, and the listening beggars had completed the transformation of text by hearing what they wanted to hear.

In a welter of words in two tongues, the interpreter and Brother Lemon sorted out the mess. The ancients still clung to him, though, claw hands plucking at his suit. He pulled away from them, almost in desperation, and finally they left. They did not know why they were being sent away, but they were not really surprised, for hope to them must always have been suspect. Brother Lemon did not see old men trailing eyeless out of his compound and back to the begging streets. I think he saw something quite different—a procession of souls, all of whom would have to be saved again.

The text that caused the confusion was from chapter seven of Revelation. "They shall hunger no more, neither thirst any more; neither shall the sun light on them, nor any heat. For the Lamb which is in the midst of the throne shall feed them, and shall lead them unto living fountains of waters, and God shall wipe away all tears from their eyes."

I thought I would not see Brother Lemon for a while, but a few days later he was at my office once more. Danso was in the back, working out some colour schemes for a new school I was doing, and I hoped he would not come into the main office. Brother Lemon came right to the point.

"The municipal authorities have given me my building site, Mr. Kettridge."

"Good. That's fine."

"No, it's not fine," Brother Lemon said. "That's just what it's not."

"What's the matter? Where is it?"

"Right in the middle of shantytown."

"Well?"

"It's all right for the mission, perhaps, but they won't give me a separate site for my house."

"I wasn't aware that you wanted a separate site."

"I didn't think there would be any need for one," he said. "I certainly didn't imagine they'd put me there. You know what that place is like."

He made a gesture of appeal.

"It isn't that I mind Africans, Mr. Kettridge. Honest to goodness, it isn't that at all. But shantytown—the people live so close together, and it smells so bad, and at night the drums and that lewd dancing they do, and the idolatry. I can't—I don't want to be reminded every minute——"

He broke off and we were silent. Then he sighed.

"They'd always be asking," he said, "for things I can't give. It's not my business, anyway. It's not up to me. I won't be kept from my work."

I made no comment. The turquoise eyes once more glowed with proselytizing zeal. He towered; his voice cymballed forth.

"Maybe you think I was discouraged recently. Well, I was. But I'm not going to let it get me down. I tell you straight, Mr. Kettridge, I intend to salvage those souls, as many as I can, if I have to give my very life to do it."

And seeing his resilient radiance, I could well believe it. But I drew him back to the matter at hand.

"It would be a lot easier if you accepted this site, Mr. Lemon. Do you think, perhaps, a wall——"

"I can't," he said. "I—I'm sorry, but I just can't. I thought if you'd speak to the authorities. You're an Englishman——"

I told him I had no influence in high places. I explained gently that
this country was no longer a colony. But Brother Lemon only
regarded me mournfully, as though he thought I had betrayed
him.

When he had gone, I turned and there was Danso, lean as a leopard,
draped in the doorway.

"Yes," he said, "I heard. At least he's a step further than the slavers.
They didn't admit we had souls."

"It's not that simple, Danso——"

"I didn't say it was simple," Danso corrected. "It must be quite a
procedure—to tear the soul out of a living body, and throw the
inconvenient flesh away like fruit rind."

"He doesn't want to live in that area," I tried ineffectually to explain, "because in some way the people there are a threat to him, to
everything he is——"

"Good," Danso said. "That makes it even."

I saw neither Danso nor Brother Lemon for several weeks. The
plans for the mission were still in abeyance, and for the moment I
almost forgot about them. Then one evening Danso ambled in, carrying a large wrapped canvas.

"What's this?" I asked.

He grinned. "My church picture. The one I have done for Brother
Lemon."

I reached out, but Danso pulled it away.

"No, Will. I want Brother Lemon to be here. You ask him to come
over."

"Not without seeing the picture," I said. "How do I know what
monstrosity you've painted?"

"No—I swear it—you don't need to worry."

I was not entirely convinced, but I phoned Brother Lemon. Somewhat reluctantly he agreed, and within twenty minutes we heard
the Buick scrunching on the gravel drive.

He looked worn out. His unsuccessful haggling with the municipal authorities seemed to have exhausted him. He had been briefly
ill with malaria despite his up-to-date preventive drugs. I couldn't
help remembering how he had looked that first morning at the
airport, confidently stepping onto the alien soil of his chosen Thessalonica, to take up his ordained role.

"Here you are, Mr. Lemon," Danso said. "I painted a whole lot of
stars and candlesticks and other junk in the first version, then I
threw it away and did this one instead."

He unwrapped the painting and set it up against a wall. It was a
picture of the Nazarene. Danso had not portrayed any emaciated

mauve-veined ever sorrowful Jesus. This man had the body of a
fisherman or a carpenter. He was well built. He had strong wrists
and arms. His eyes were capable of laughter. Danso had shown Him
with a group of beggars, sore-fouled, their mouths twisted in perpetual leers of pain.

Danso was looking at me questioningly.

"It's the best you've done yet," I said.

He nodded and turned to Brother Lemon. The evangelist's eyes
were fixed on the picture. He did not seem able to look away. For a
moment I thought he had caught the essential feeling of the thing,
but then he blinked and withdrew his gaze. His tall frame sagged
as though he had been struck and—yes—hurt. The old gods he could
fight. He could grapple with and overcome every obstacle, even his
own pity. But this was a threat he had never anticipated. He spoke
in a low voice.

"Do many—do all of you—see Him like that?"

He didn't wait for an answer. He did not look at Danso or myself
as he left the house. We heard the orchid Buick pull away.

Danso and I did not talk much. We drank beer and looked at the
picture.

"I have to tell you one thing, Danso," I said at last. "The fact that
you've shown Him as an African doesn't seem so very important one
way or another."

Danso set down his glass and ran one finger lightly over the painting.

"Perhaps not," he admitted reluctantly. "But could anyone be
shown as everything? How to get past the paint, Will?"

"I don't know."

Danso laughed and began slouching out to the kitchen to get another beer.

"We will invent new colours, man," he cried. "But for this we may
need a little time."

I was paid for the work I had done, but the mission was never
built. Brother Lemon did not obtain another site, and in a few
months, his health—as they say—broke down. He returned whence
he had come, and I have not heard anything about the Angel of
Philadelphia Mission from that day to this.

Somewhere, perhaps, he is still preaching, heaven and hell pouring from his apocalyptic eyes, and around his head that aureole, hair
the colour of light. Whenever Danso mentions him, however, it is
always as the magician, the pedlar who bought souls cheap, and sold
dear his cabbalistic word. But I can no longer think of Brother
Lemon as either Paul or Elymas, apostle or sorcerer.

I bought Danso's picture. Sometimes, when I am able to see through black and white, until they merge and cease to be separate or apart, I look at those damaged creatures clustering so despairingly hopeful around the Son of Man, and it seems to me that Brother Lemon, after all, is one of them.

David Herbert Lawrence

(1885–1930)

The son of a coal miner in Nottingham, Lawrence was brought up in a household very similar to that depicted in his novel *Sons and Lovers* (1913), in which the father's coarse sensuality struggled against the mother's finer sensibilities. With his mother's encouragement, Lawrence developed his literary abilities; and after a spell as a teacher in Croydon, near London, he made writing his full-time profession, producing a great many essays, poems, and short stories. His work, particularly his novels, often aroused controversy because of his frank treatment of sexual relations; two of his novels, *The Rainbow* (1915) and *Lady Chatterley's Lover* (1928), were declared obscene and banned in England for many years. Disgusted by the response of the press and public, Lawrence left England with his German wife in 1919, and traveled in various parts of the world for a number of years, chiefly in the United States and Mexico.

In much of his writing, Lawrence examined the tension between man in society, hemmed in by conventions and "responsibilities," and man as a feeling creature, part of a larger universe of instinctive response. "The Horse Dealer's Daughter" dramatizes this conflict through the relationship of Dr. Ferguson with Mabel Pervin. Initially, both are creatures of habit and convention, cut off from true feeling and turned in upon themselves. Once relieved of their social roles, they respond to each other with almost brutal urgency, in a manner reflecting Lawrence's antiromantic ideas about love and sexual awareness. "Accept the sexual, physical being of yourself," he wrote, "and of every other creature. Don't be afraid of the physical functions. . . . Conquer the fear of sex, and restore the natural flow" ("The State of Funk").

For further reading

Donald Junkins, "D. H. Lawrence's 'The Horse-Dealer's Daughter,'" *Studies in Short Fiction,* 6 (1969), 210–212.

D. H. Lawrence, *Fantasia of the Unconscious and Psychoanalysis and the Unconscious* (Melbourne: Heinemann, 1961).

Harry T. Moore, *The Intelligent Heart: The Story of D. H. Lawrence* (New York: Farrar, Straus & Giroux, 1954).

Mark Spilka, *The Love Ethic of D. H. Lawrence* (Bloomington: Indiana University Press, 1955).

The Horse Dealer's Daughter

"Well, Mabel, and what are you going to do with yourself?" asked Joe, with foolish flippancy. He felt quite safe himself. Without listening for an answer, he turned aside, worked a grain of tobacco to the tip of his tongue, and spat it out. He did not care about anything, since he felt safe himself.

The three brothers and the sister sat round the desolate breakfast table, attempting some sort of desultory consultation. The morning's post had given the final tap to the family fortune, and all was over. The dreary dining-room itself, with its heavy mahogany furniture, looked as if it were waiting to be done away with.

But the consultation amounted to nothing. There was a strange air of ineffectuality about the three men, as they sprawled at table, smoking and reflecting vaguely on their own condition. The girl was alone, a rather short, sullen-looking young woman of twenty-seven. She did not share the same life as her brothers. She would have been good-looking, save for the impressive fixity of her face, "bulldog," as her brothers called it.

There was a confused tramping of horses' feet outside. The three men all sprawled round in their chairs to watch. Beyond the dark holly bushes that separated the strip of lawn from the high-road, they could see a cavalcade of shire horses swinging out of their own yard, being taken for exercise. This was the last time. These were the last horses that would go through their hands. The young men watched with critical, callous look. They were all frightened at the collapse of their lives, and the sense of disaster in which they were involved left them no inner freedom.

Yet they were three fine, well-set fellows enough. Joe, the eldest, was a man of thirty-three, broad and handsome in a hot, flushed way. His face was red, he twisted his black moustache over a thick finger, his eyes were shallow and restless. He had a sensual way of uncovering his teeth when he laughed, and his bearing was stupid. Now he watched the horses with a glazed look of helplessness in his eyes, a certain stupor of downfall.

The great draught-horses swung past. They were tied head to tail, four of them, and they heaved along to where a lane branched off from the high-road, planting their great hoofs floutingly in the fine black mud, swinging their great rounded haunches sumptuously, and trotting a few sudden steps as they were led into the lane, round the corner. Every movement showed a massive, slumbrous strength, and a stupidity which held them in subjection. The groom at the head looked back, jerking the leading rope. And the cavalcade moved out of sight up the lane, the tail of the last horse, bobbed up tight and stiff, held out taut from the swinging great haunches as they rocked behind the hedges in a motion-like sleep.

Joe watched with glazed hopeless eyes. The horses were almost like his own body to him. He felt he was done for now. Luckily he was engaged to a woman as old as himself, and therefore her father, who was steward of a neighbouring estate, would provide him with a job. He would marry and go into harness. His life was over, he would be a subject animal now.

He turned uneasily aside, the retreating steps of the horses echoing in his ears. Then, with foolish restlessness, he reached for the scraps of bacon-rind from the plates, and making a faint whistling sound, flung them to the terrier that lay against the fender. He watched the dog swallow them, and waited till the creature looked into his eyes. Then a faint grin came on his face, and in a high, foolish voice he said:

"You won't get much more bacon, shall you, you little b——?"

The dog faintly and dismally wagged its tail, then lowered its haunches, circled round, and lay down again.

There was another helpless silence at the table. Joe sprawled uneasily in his seat, not willing to go till the family conclave was dissolved. Fred Henry, the second brother, was erect, clean-limbed, alert. He had watched the passing of the horses with more *sang-froid*. If he was an animal, like Joe, he was an animal which controls, not one which is controlled. He was master of any horse, and he carried himself with a well-tempered air of mastery. But he was not master of the situations of life. He pushed his coarse brown moustache upwards, off his lip, and glanced irritably at his sister, who sat impassive and inscrutable.

"You'll go and stop with Lucy for a bit, shan't you?" he asked. The girl did not answer.

"I don't see what else you can do," persisted Fred Henry.

"Go as a skivvy,"* Joe interpolated laconically.

The girl did not move a muscle.

"If I was her, I should go in for training for a nurse," said Malcolm, the youngest of them all. He was the baby of the family, a young man of twenty-two, with a fresh, jaunty *museau*.†

But Mabel did not take any notice of him. They had talked at her and round her for so many years, that she hardly heard them at all.

The marble clock on the mantelpiece softly chimed the half-hour, the dog rose uneasily from the hearthrug and looked at the party at the breakfast table. But still they sat on in ineffectual conclave.

"Oh, all right," said Joe suddenly, apropos of nothing. "I'll get a move on."

He pushed back his chair, straddled his knees with a downward jerk, to get them free, in horsey fashion, and went to the fire. Still he did not go out of the room; he was curious to know what the

---

*Skivvy = cleaning woman.
†Museau = snout, face.

others would do or say. He began to charge his pipe, looking down at the dog and saying in a high, affected voice:

"Going wi' me? Going wi' me are ter?* Tha'rt goin' further than tha counts on just now, dost hear?"

The dog faintly wagged its tail, the man stuck out his jaw and covered his pipe with his hands, and puffed intently, losing himself in the tobacco, looking down all the while at the dog with an absent brown eye. The dog looked up at him in mournful distrust. Joe stood with his knees stuck out, in real horsey fashion.

"Have you had a letter from Lucy?" Fred Henry asked of his sister.

"Last week," came the neutral reply.

"And what does she say?"

There was no answer.

"Does she *ask* you to go and stop there?" persisted Fred Henry.

"She says I can if I like."

"Well, then, you'd better. Tell her you'll come on Monday."

This was received in silence.

"That's what you'll do then, is it?" said Fred Henry, in some exasperation.

But she made no answer. There was a silence of futility and irritation in the room. Malcolm grinned fatuously.

"You'll have to make up your mind between now and next Wednesday," said Joe loudly, "or else find yourself lodgings on the kerbstone."

The face of the young woman darkened, but she sat on immutable.

"Here's Jack Fergusson!" exclaimed Malcolm, who was looking aimlessly out of the window.

"Where?" exclaimed Joe, loudly.

"Just gone past."

"Coming in?"

Malcolm craned his neck to see the gate.

"Yes," he said.

There was a silence. Mabel sat on like one condemned, at the head of the table. Then a whistle was heard from the kitchen. The dog got up and barked sharply. Joe opened the door and shouted:

"Come on."

After a moment a young man entered. He was muffled up in overcoat and a purple woollen scarf, and his tweed cap, which he did not remove, was pulled down on his head. He was of medium height, his face was rather long and pale, his eyes looked tired.

"Hello, Jack! Well, Jack!" exclaimed Malcolm and Joe. Fred Henry merely said, "Jack."

*Are ter = are you.

"What's doing?" asked the newcomer, evidently addressing Fred Henry.

"Same. We've got to be out by Wednesday. Got a cold?"

"I have—got it bad, too."

"Why don't you stop in?"

"*Me* stop in? When I can't stand on my legs, perhaps I shall have a chance." The young man spoke huskily. He had a slight Scotch accent.

"It's a knock-out, isn't it," said Joe, boisterously, "if a doctor goes round croaking with a cold. Looks bad for the patients, doesn't it?"

The young doctor looked at him slowly.

"Anything the matter with *you,* then?" he asked sarcastically.

"Not as I know of. Damn your eyes, I hope not. Why?"

"I thought you were very concerned about the patients, wondered if you might be one yourself."

"Damn it, no, I've never been patient to no flaming doctor, and hope I never shall be," returned Joe.

At this point Mabel rose from the table, and they all seemed to become aware of her existence. She began putting the dishes together. The young doctor looked at her, but did not address her. He had not greeted her. She went out of the room with the tray, her face impassive and unchanged.

"When are you off then, all of you?" asked the doctor.

"I'm catching the eleven-forty," replied Malcolm. "Are you goin' down wi' th' trap, Joe?"

"Yes, I've told you I'm goind down wi' th' trap, haven't I?"

"We'd better be getting her in then. So long, Jack, if I don't see you before I go," said Malcolm, shaking hands.

He went out, followed by Joe, who seemed to have his tail between his legs.

"Well, this is the devil's own," exclaimed the doctor, when he was left alone with Fred Henry. "Going before Wednesday, are you?"

"That's the orders," replied the other.

"Where, to Northampton?"

"That's it."

"The devil!" exclaimed Fergusson, with quiet chagrin.

And there was silence between the two.

"All settled up, are you?" asked Fergusson.

"About."

There was another pause.

"Well, I shall miss yer, Freddy, boy," said the young doctor.

"And I shall miss thee, Jack," returned the other.

"Miss you like hell," mused the doctor.

Fred Henry turned aside. There was nothing to say. Mabel came in again, to finish clearing the table.

"What are *you* going to do, then, Miss Pervin?" asked Fergusson. "Going to your sister's, are you?"

Mabel looked at him with her steady, dangerous eyes, that always made him uncomfortable, unsettling his superficial ease.

"No," she said.

"Well, what in the name of fortune *are* you going to do? Say what you mean to do," cried Fred Henry, with futile intensity.

But she only averted her head, and continued her work. She folded the white table-cloth, and put on the chenille cloth.

"The sulkiest bitch that ever trod!" muttered her brother.

But she finished her task with perfectly impassive face, the young doctor watching her interestedly all the while. Then she went out.

Fred Henry stared after her, clenching his lips, his blue eyes fixing in sharp antagonism, as he made a grimace of sour exasperation.

"You could bray her into bits, and that's all you'd get out of her," he said, in a small, narrowed tone.

The doctor smiled faintly.

"What's she *going* to do, then?" he asked.

"Strike me if *I* know!" returned the other.

There was a pause. Then the doctor stirred.

"I'll be seeing you to-night, shall I?" he said to his friend.

"Ay—where's it to be? Are we going over to Jessdale?"

"I don't know. I've got such a cold on me. I'll come round to the 'Moon and Stars', anyway."

"Let Lizzie and May miss their night for once, eh?"

"That's it—if I feel as I do now."

"All's one—"

The two young men went through the passage and down to the back door together. The house was large, but it was servantless now, and desolate. At the back was a small bricked house-yard, and beyond that a big square, gravelled fine and red, and having stables on two sides. Sloping, dank, winter-dark fields stretched away on the open sides.

But the stables were empty. Joseph Pervin, the father of the family, had been a man of no education, who had become a fairly large horse dealer. The stables had been full of horses, there was a great turmoil and come-and-go of horses and of dealers and grooms. Then the kitchen was full of servants. But of late things had declined. The old man had married a second time, to retrieve his fortunes. Now he was dead and everything was gone to the dogs, there was nothing but debt and threatening.

For months, Mabel had been servantless in the big house, keeping the home together in penury for her ineffectual brothers. She had kept house for ten years. But previously it was with unstinted means. Then, however brutal and coarse everything was, the sense of money had kept her proud, confident. The men might be foul-mouthed, the women in the kitchen might have bad reputations, her brothers might have illegitimate children. But so long as there was money, the girl felt herself established, and brutally proud, reserved.

No company came to the house, save dealers and coarse men. Mabel had no associates of her own sex, after her sister went away. But she did not mind. She went regularly to church, she attended to her father. And she lived in the memory of her mother, who had died when she was fourteen, and whom she had loved. She had loved her father, too, in a different way, depending upon him, and feeling secure in him, until at the age of fifty-four he married again. And then she had set hard against him. Now he had died and left them all hopelessly in debt.

She had suffered badly during the period of poverty. Nothing, however, could shake the curious sullen, animal pride that dominated each member of the family. Now, for Mabel, the end had come. Still she would not cast about her. She would follow her own way just the same. She would always hold the keys of her own situation. Mindless and persistent, she endured from day to day. Why should she think? Why should she answer anybody? It was enough that this was the end, and there was no way out. She need not pass any more darkly along the main street of the small town, avoiding every eye. She need not demean herself any more, going into the shops and buying the cheapest food. This was at an end. She thought of nobody, not even of herself. Mindless and persistent, she seemed in a sort of ecstasy to be coming nearer to her fulfilment, her own glorification, approaching her dead mother, who was glorified.

In the afternoon she took a little bag, with shears and sponge and a small scrubbing brush, and went out. It was a grey, wintry day, with saddened, dark green fields and an atmosphere blackened by the smoke of foundries not far off. She went quickly, darkly along the causeway, heeding nobody, through the town to the churchyard.

There she always felt secure, as if no one could see her, although as a matter of fact she was exposed to the stare of every one who passed along under the churchyard wall. Nevertheless, once under the shadow of the great looming church, among the graves, she felt immune from the world, reserved within the thick churchyard wall as in another country.

Carefully she clipped the grass from the grave, and arranged the pinky white, small chrysanthemums in the tin cross. When this was done, she took an empty jar from a neighbouring grave, brought water, and carefully, most scrupulously sponged the marble headstone and the coping-stone.

It gave her sincere satisfaction to do this. She felt in immediate contact with the world of her mother. She took minute pains, went through the park in a state bordering on pure happiness, as if in performing this task she came into a subtle, intimate connection with her mother. For the life she followed here in the world was far less real than the world of death she inherited from her mother.

The doctor's house was just by the church. Fergusson, being a mere hired assistant, was slave to the country-side. As he hurried now to attend to the outpatients in the surgery, glancing across the graveyard with his quick eye, he saw the girl at her task at the grave. She seemed so intent and remote, it was like looking into another world. Some mystical element was touched in him. He slowed down as he walked, watching her as if spell-bound.

She lifted her eyes, feeling him looking. Their eyes met. And each looked away again at once, each feeling, in some way, found out by the other. He lifted his cap and passed on down the road. There remained distinct in his consciousness, like a vision, the memory of her face, lifted from the tombstone in the churchyard, and looking at him with slow, large, portentous eyes. It *was* portentous, her face. It seemed to mesmerize him. There was a heavy power in her eyes which laid hold of his whole being, as if he had drunk some powerful drug. He had been feeling weak and done before. Now the life came back into him, he felt delivered from his own fretted, daily self.

He finished his duties at the surgery as quickly as might be, hastily filling up the bottles of the waiting people with cheap drugs. Then, in perpetual haste, he set off again to visit several cases in another part of his round, before teatime. At all times he preferred to walk if he could, but particularly when he was not well. He fancied the motion restored him.

The afternoon was falling. It was grey, deadened, and wintry, with a slow, moist, heavy coldness sinking in and deadening all the faculties. But why should he think or notice? He hastily climbed the hill and turned across the dark green fields, following the black cinder-track. In the distance, across a shallow dip in the country, the small town was clustered like smouldering ash, a tower, a spire, a heap of low, raw, extinct houses. And on the nearest fringe of the town, sloping into the dip, was Oldmeadow, the Pervins' house. He could see the stables and the outbuildings distinctly, as they lay towards him on the slope. Well, he would not go there many more times! Another resource would be lost to him, another place gone: the only company he cared for in the alien, ugly little town he was losing. Nothing but work, drudgery, constant hastening from dwelling to dwelling among the colliers and the iron-workers. It wore him out, but at the same time he had a craving for it. It was a stimulant to him to be in the homes of the working people, moving, as it were, through the innermost body of their life. His nerves were excited and gratified. He could come so near, into the very lives of the rough, inarticulate, powerfully emotional men and women. He grumbled, he said he hated the hellish hole. But as a matter of fact it excited him, the contact with the rough, strongly-feeling people was a stimulant applied direct to his nerves.

Below Oldmeadow, in the green, shallow, soddened hollow of fields, lay a square, deep pond. Roving across the landscape, the doctor's quick eye detected a figure in black passing through the gate of the field, down towards the pond. He looked again. It would be Mabel Pervin. His mind suddenly became alive and attentive.

Why was she going down there? He pulled up on the path on the slope above, and stood staring. He could just make sure of the small black figure moving in the hollow of the failing day. He seemed to see her in the midst of such obscurity, that he was like a clairvoyant, seeing rather with the mind's eye than with ordinary sight. Yet he could see her positively enough, whilst he kept his eye attentive. He felt, if he looked away from her, in the thick, ugly falling dusk, he would lose her altogether.

He followed her minutely as she moved, direct and intent, like something transmitted rather than stirring in voluntary activity, straight down the field towards the pond. There she stood on the bank for a moment. She never raised her head. Then she waded slowly into the water.

He stood motionless as the small black figure walked slowly and deliberately towards the centre of the pond, very slowly, gradually moving deeper into the motionless water, and still moving forward as the water got up to her breast. Then he could see her no more in the dusk of the dead afternoon.

"There!" he exclaimed. "Would you believe it?"

And he hastened straight down, running over the wet, soddened fields, pushing through the hedges, down into the depression of callous wintry obscurity. It took him several minutes to come to the pond. He stood on the bank, breathing heavily. He could see nothing. His eyes seemed to penetrate the dead water. Yes, perhaps that was the dark shadow of her black clothing beneath the surface of the water.

He slowly ventured into the pond. The bottom was deep, soft clay, he sank in, and the water clasped dead cold round his legs. As he stirred he could smell the cold, rotten clay that fouled up into the water. It was objectionable in his lungs. Still, repelled and yet not heeding, he moved deeper into the pond. The cold water rose over his thighs, over his loins, upon his abdomen. The lower part of his body was all sunk in the hideous cold element. And the bottom was so deeply soft and uncertain, he was afraid of pitching with his mouth underneath. He could not swim, and was afraid.

He crouched a little, spreading his hands under the water and moving them round, trying to feel for her. The dead cold pond swayed upon his chest. He moved again, a little deeper, and again, with his hands underneath, he felt all around under the water. And he touched her clothing. But it evaded his fingers. He made a desperate effort to grasp it.

And so doing he lost his balance and went under, horribly, suffocating in the foul earthy water, struggling madly for a few moments. At last, after what seemed an eternity, he got his footing, rose again into the air and looked around. He gasped, and knew he was in the world. Then he looked at the water. She had risen near him. He grasped her clothing, and drawing her nearer, turned to take his way to land again.

He went very slowly, carefully, absorbed in the slow progress. He rose higher, climbing out of the pond. The water was now only about his legs; he was thankful, full of relief to be out of the clutches of the pond. He lifted her and staggered on to the bank, out of the horror of wet, grey clay.

He laid her down on the bank. She was quite unconscious and running with water. He made the water come from her mouth, he worked to restore her. He did not have to work very long before he could feel the breathing begin again in her; she was breathing naturally. He worked a little longer. He could feel her live beneath his hands; she was coming back. He wiped her face, wrapped her in his overcoat, looked round into the dim, dark grey world, then lifted her and staggered down the bank and across the fields.

It seemed an unthinkably long way, and his burden so heavy he felt he would never get to the house. But at last he was in the stable-yard, and then in the house-yard. He opened the door and went into the house. In the kitchen he laid her down on the hearth-rug, and called. The house was empty. But the fire was burning in the grate.

Then again he kneeled to attend to her. She was breathing regularly, her eyes were wide open and as if conscious, but there seemed something missing in her look. She was conscious in herself, but unconscious of her surroundings.

He ran upstairs, took blankets from a bed, and put them before the fire to warm. Then he removed her saturated, earthy-smelling clothing, rubbed her dry with a towel, and wrapped her naked in the blankets. Then he went into the dining-room, to look for spirits.

There was a little whisky. He drank a gulp himself, and put some into her mouth.

The effect was instantaneous. She looked full into his face, as if she had been seeing him for some time, and yet had only just become conscious of him.

"Dr. Fergusson?" she said.

"What?" he answered.

He was divesting himself of his coat, intending to find some dry clothing upstairs. He could not bear the smell of the dead, clayey water, and he was mortally afraid for his own health.

"What did I do?" she asked.

"Walked into the pond," he replied. He had begun to shudder like one sick, and could hardly attend to her. Her eyes remained full on him, he seemed to be going dark in his mind, looking back at her helplessly. The shuddering became quieter in him, his life came back to him, dark and unknowing, but strong again.

"Was I out of my mind?" she asked, while her eyes were fixed on him all the time.

"Maybe, for the moment," he replied. He felt quiet, because his strength had come back. The strange fretful strain had left him.

"Am I out of my mind now?" she asked.

"Are you?" he reflected a moment. "No," he answered truthfully, "I don't see that you are." He turned his face aside. He was afraid now, because he felt dazed, and felt dimly that her power was stronger than his, in this issue. And she continued to look at him fixedly all the time. "Can you tell me where I shall find some dry things to put on?" he asked.

"Did you dive into the pond for me?" she asked.

"No," he answered. "I walked in. But I went in overhead as well."

There was silence for a moment. He hesitated. He very much wanted to go upstairs to get into dry clothing. But there was another desire in him. And she seemed to hold him. His will seemed to have gone to sleep, and left him, standing there slack before her. But he felt warm inside himself. He did not shudder at all, though his clothes were sodden on him.

"Why did you?" she asked.

"Because I didn't want you to do such a foolish thing," he said.

"It wasn't foolish," she said, still gazing at him as she lay on the floor, with a sofa cushion under her head. "It was the right thing to do. *I* knew best, then."

"I'll go and shift these wet things," he said. But still he had not the power to move out of her presence, until she sent him. It was as if she had the life of his body in her hands, and he could not extricate himself. Or perhaps he did not want to.

Suddenly she sat up. Then she became aware of her own immediate condition. She felt the blankets about her, she knew her own limbs. For a moment it seemed as if her reason were going. She looked round, with wild eye, as if seeking something. He stood still with fear. She saw her clothing lying scattered.

"Who undressed me?" she asked, her eyes resting full and inevitable on his face.

"I did," he replied, "to bring you round."

For some moments she sat and gazed at him awfully, her lips parted.

"Do you love me, then?" she asked.

He only stood and stared at her, fascinated. His soul seemed to melt.

She shuffled forward on her knees, and put her arms round him, round his legs, as he stood there, pressing her breasts against his knees and thighs, clutching him with strange, convulsive certainty, pressing his thighs against her, drawing him to her face, her throat, as she looked up at him with flaring, humble eyes of transfiguration, triumphant in first possession.

"You love me," she murmured, in strange transport, yearning and triumphant and confident. "You love me. I know you love me, I know."

And she was passionately kissing his knees, through the wet clothing, passionately and indiscriminately kissing his knees, his legs, as if unaware of everything.

He looked down at the tangled wet hair, the wild, bare, animal shoulders. He was amazed, bewildered, and afraid. He had never thought of loving her. He had never wanted to love her. When he rescued her and restored her, he was a doctor, and she was a patient. He had had no single personal thought of her. Nay, this introduction of the personal element was very distasteful to him, a violation of his professional honour. It was horrible to have her there embracing his knees. It was horrible. He revolted from it, violently. And yet— and yet—he had not the power to break away.

She looked at him again, with the same supplication of powerful love, and that same transcendent, frightening light of triumph. In view of the delicate flame which seemed to come from her face like a light, he was powerless. And yet he had never intended to love her. He had never intended. And something stubborn in him could not give way.

"You love me," she repeated, in a murmur of deep, rhapsodic assurance. "You love me."

Her hands were drawing him, drawing him down to her. He was afraid, even a little horrified. For he had, really, no intention of loving her. Yet her hands were drawing him towards her. He put out his hand quickly to steady himself, and grasped her bare shoulder. A flame seemed to burn the hand that grasped her soft shoulder. He had no intention of loving her: his whole will was against his yielding. It was horrible. And yet wonderful was the touch of her shoulders, beautiful the shining of her face. Was she perhaps mad? He had a horror of yielding to her. Yet something in him ached also.

He had been staring away at the door, away from her. But his hand remained on her shoulder. She had gone suddenly very still. He looked down at her. Her eyes were now wide with fear, with doubt, the light was dying from her face, a shadow of terrible greyness was returning. He could not bear the touch of her eyes' question upon him, and the look of death behind the question.

With an inward groan he gave way, and let his heart yield towards her. A sudden gentle smile came on his face. And her eyes, which never left his face, slowly, slowly filled with tears. He watched the strange water rise in her eyes, like some slow fountain coming up. And his heart seemed to burn and melt away in his breast.

He could not bear to look at her any more. He dropped on his knees and caught her head with his arms and pressed her face against his throat. She was very still. His heart, which seemed to have broken, was burning with a kind of agony in his breast. And he felt her slow, hot tears wetting his throat. But he could not move.

He felt the hot tears wet his neck and the hollows of his neck, and he remained motionless, suspended through one of man's eternities. Only now it had become indispensable to him to have her face pressed close to him; he could never let her go again. He could never let her head go away from the close clutch of his arm. He wanted to remain like that for ever, with his heart hurting him in a pain that was also life to him. Without knowing, he was looking down on her damp, soft brown hair.

Then, as it were suddenly, he smelt the horrid stagnant smell of that water. And at the same moment she drew away from him and looked at him. Her eyes were wistful and unfathomable. He was afraid of them, and he fell to kissing her, not knowing what he was doing. He wanted her eyes not to have that terrible, wistful, unfathomable look.

When she turned her face to him again, a faint delicate flush was glowing, and there was again dawning that terrible shining of joy in her eyes, which really terrified him, and yet which he now wanted to see, because he feared the look of doubt still more.

"You love me?" she said, rather faltering.

"Yes." The word cost him a painful effort. Not because it wasn't true. But because it was too newly true, the *saying* seemed to tear open again his newly-torn heart. And he hardly wanted it to be true, even now.

She lifted her face to him, and he bent forward and kissed her on the mouth, gently, with the one kiss that is an eternal pledge. And as he kissed her his heart strained again in his breast. He never intended to love her. But now it was over. He had crossed over the gulf to her, and all that he had left behind had shrivelled and become void.

After the kiss, her eyes again slowly filled with tears. She sat still, away from him, with her face drooped aside, and her hands folded in her lap. The tears fell very slowly. There was complete silence. He too sat there motionless and silent on the hearthrug. The strange pain of his heart that was broken seemed to consume him. That he should love her? That his was love! That he should be ripped open in this way! Him, a doctor! How they would all jeer if they knew! It was agony to him to think they might know.

In the curious naked pain of the thought he looked again to her. She was sitting there drooped into a muse. He saw a tear fall, and his heart flared hot. He saw for the first time that one of her shoulders was quite uncovered, one arm bare, he could see one of her small breasts; dimly, because it had become almost dark in the room.

"Why are you crying?" he asked, in an altered voice.

She looked up at him, and behind her tears the consciousness of her situation for the first time brought a dark look of shame to her eyes.

"I'm not crying, really," she said, watching him, half frightened.

He reached his hand, and softly closed it on her bare arm.

"I love you! I love you!" he said in a soft, low vibrating voice, unlike himself.

She shrank, and dropped her head. The soft, penetrating grip of his hand on her arm distressed her. She looked up at him.

"I want to go," she said. "I want to go and get you some dry things."

"Why?" he said. "I'm all right."

"But I want to go," she said. "And I want you to change your things."

He released her arm, and she wrapped herself in the blanket, looking at him rather frightened. And still she did not rise.

"Kiss me," she said wistfully.

He kissed her, but briefly, half in anger.

Then, after a second, she rose nervously, all mixed up in the blanket. He watched her in her confusion, as she tried to extricate herself and wrap herself up so that she could walk. He watched her relentlessly, as she knew. And as she went, the blanket trailing, and as he saw a glimpse of her feet and her white leg, he tried to remember her as she was when he had wrapped her in the blanket. But then he didn't want to remember, because she had been nothing to him then, and his nature revolted from remembering her as she was when she was nothing to him.

A tumbling, muffled noise from within the dark house startled him. Then he heard her voice:—"There are clothes." He rose and went to the foot of the stairs, and gathered up the garments she had thrown down. Then he came back to the fire, to rub himself down and dress. He grinned at his own appearance when he had finished.

The fire was sinking, so he put on coal. The house was now quite dark, save for the light of a street-lamp that shone in faintly from beyond the holly trees. He lit the gas with matches he found on the mantelpiece. Then he emptied the pockets of his own clothes, and threw all his wet things in a heap into the scullery. After which he gathered up her sodden clothes, gently, and put them in a separate heap on the copper-top in the scullery.

It was six o'clock on the clock. His own watch had stopped. He ought to go back to the surgery. He waited, and still she did not come down. So he went to the foot of the stairs and called:

"I shall have to go."

Almost immediately he heard her coming down. She had on her best dress of black voile, and her hair was tidy, but still damp. She looked at him—and in spite of herself, smiled.

"I don't like you in those clothes," she said.

"Do I look a sight?" he answered.

They were shy of one another.

"I'll make you some tea," she said.

"No, I must go."

"Must you?" And she looked at him again with the wide, strained, doubtful eyes. And again, from the pain of his breast, he knew how he loved her. He went and bent to kiss her, gently, passionately, with his heart's painful kiss.

"And my hair smells so horrible," she murmured in distraction. "And I'm so awful, I'm so awful! Oh, no, I'm too awful." And she broke into bitter, heart-broken sobbing. "You can't want to love me, I'm horrible."

"Don't be silly, don't be silly," he said, trying to comfort her, kissing her, holding her in his arms. "I want you, I want to marry you, we're going to be married, quickly, quickly—tomorrow if I can."

But she only sobbed terribly, and cried:

"I feel awful. I feel awful. I feel I'm horrible to you."

"No, I want you, I want you," was all he answered, blindly, with that terrible intonation which frightened her almost more than her horror lest he should *not* want her.

Doris Lessing

(b. 1919)

Born in Kermanshah, Persia, Doris Lessing (née Tayler) was the elder child of a banker who gave up his job for idealistic reasons and in 1925 took his family to farm in Rhodesia. It was there, despite crop failures and other farm misfortunes that affected her family, and after two unsuccessful marriages, that she stayed until 1949. With the manuscript of her first novel, *The Grass Is Singing,* she then went to England, where it was published the following year. Like her *African Stories* (1964), it expresses a deep sense of injustice, of opposition toward the racism that has resulted so often from the European and American presences in Africa. It was that outrage, together with her observations of social inequalities (particularly those which affected the English working class), which led her to communism in 1942. But throughout her work there persists a tension between the collective good and the individual conscience. In the *New Statesman* in 1956, she wrote: "A large number of my friends are locked out of countries and unable to return; locked into countries and unable to get out; have been deported, prohibited and banned." In context she is referring to Africa, but the phrase also makes a kind of symbolic gesture; her characters, too, are locked into or out of experience and must locate the world that can be their own. The five novels about Martha Quest, for example—the *Children of Violence* cycle—portray the growing political, marital, intellectual, and emotional freedom of a woman who is taken to typify her generation. "Our Friend Judith," from *A Man and Two Women* (1963) focuses on some of the particular difficulties of being an independent woman in the modern world—on the double standards, petty interferences, and social pressures that disrupt her life—and in so doing it tries to distinguish between frustration and enlightenment. *The Golden Notebook* (1962) probes a similar distinction, revealing the many simultaneous impulses that direct and bedevil a writer's consciousness. The apocalyptic political visions of *The Four-Gated City* (1969) and *Briefing for a Descent into Hell* (1971) emerge from that sense of division, of commitment at once to a world of social reality and a world of private sensibility. But in rendering them both, Doris Lessing has managed to transform both social history and personal experience into art.

For further reading

Dorothy Brewster, *Doris Lessing* (New York: Twayne, 1969).
Doris Lessing, *Going Home* (London: Michael Joseph, 1957).
Roy Newquist, "Interview with Doris Lessing," in *Counterpoint* (New York: Rand McNally, 1964), pp. 413–424.

Our Friend Judith

I stopped inviting Judith to meet people when a Canadian woman remarked, with the satisfied fervour of one who has at last pinned a label on a rare specimen: "She is, of course, one of your typical English spinsters."

This was a few weeks after an American sociologist, having elicited from Judith the facts that she was forty-ish, unmarried, and living alone, had inquired of me: "I suppose she has given up?" "Given up what?" I asked; and the subsequent discussion was unrewarding.

Judith did not easily come to parties. She would come after pressure, not so much—one felt—to do one a favour, but in order to correct what she believed to be a defect in her character. "I really ought to enjoy meeting new people more than I do," she said once. We reverted to an earlier pattern of our friendship: odd evenings together, an occasional visit to the cinema, or she would telephone to say: "I'm on my way past you to the British Museum. Would you care for a cup of coffee with me? I have twenty minutes to spare."

It is characteristic of Judith that the word spinster, used of her, provoked fascinated speculation about other people. There are my aunts, for instance: aged seventy-odd, both unmarried, one an ex-missionary from China, one a retired matron of a famous London hospital. These two old ladies live together under the shadow of the Cathedral in a country town. They devote much time to the Church, to good causes, to letter writing with friends all over the world, to the grandchildren and the great-grand-children of relatives. It would be a mistake, however, on entering a house in which nothing has been moved for fifty years, to diagnose a condition of fossilized late-Victorian integrity. They read every book reviewed in the *Observer* or *The Times,* so that I recently got a letter from Aunt Rose inquiring whether I did not think that the author of *On the Road* was not perhaps?—exaggerating his difficulties. They know a good deal about music, and write letters of encouragement to young composers they feel are being neglected—"You must understand that anything new and original takes time to be understood." Well-informed and critical Tories, they are as likely to dispatch telegrams of protest to the Home Secretary as letters of support. These ladies, my aunts Emily and Rose, are surely what is meant by the phrase *English spinster.* And yet, once the connection had been pointed out, there is no doubt that Judith and they are spiritual cousins, if not sisters. Therefore it follows that one's pitying admiration for women who have supported manless and uncomforted lives needs a certain modification?

One will, of course, never know; and I feel now that it is entirely my fault that I shall never know. I had been Judith's friend for upwards of five years before the incident occurred which I involuntarily thought of—stupidly enough—as "the first time Judith's mask slipped."

A mutual friend, Betty, had been given a cast-off Dior dress. She was too short for it. Also she said: "It's not a dress for a married woman with three children and a talent for cooking. I don't know why not, but it isn't." Judith was the right build. Therefore one evening the three of us met by appointment in Judith's bedroom, with the dress. Neither Betty nor I were surprised at the renewed discovery that Judith was beautiful. We had both too often caught each other, and ourselves, in moments of envy when Judith's calm and severe face, her undemonstratively perfect body, succeeded in making everyone else in a room or a street look cheap.

Judith is tall, small-breasted, slender. Her light brown hair is parted in the centre and cut straight around her neck. A high straight forehead, straight nose, a full grave mouth are a setting for her eyes, which are green, large and prominent. Her lids are very white, fringed with gold, and moulded close over the eyeball, so that in profile she has the look of a staring gilded mask. The dress was of dark green glistening stuff, cut straight, with a sort of loose tunic. It opened simply at the throat. In it Judith could of course evoke nothing but classical images. Diana, perhaps, back from the hunt, in a relaxed moment? A rather intellectual wood nymph who had opted for an afternoon in the British Museum reading-room? Something like that. Neither Betty nor I said a word, since Judith was examining herself in a long mirror, and must know she looked magnificent.

Slowly she drew off the dress and laid it aside. Slowly she put on the old cord skirt and woollen blouse she had taken off. She must have surprised a resigned glance between us, for she then remarked, with the smallest of mocking smiles: "One surely ought to stay in character, wouldn't you say?" She added, reading the words out of some invisible book, written not by her, since it was a very vulgar book, but perhaps by one of us: "It does everything *for* me, I must admit."

"After seeing you in it," Betty cried out, defying her, "I can't bear for anyone else to have it. I shall simply put it away." Judith shrugged, rather irritated. In the shapeless skirt and blouse, and without make-up, she stood smiling at us, a woman at whom forty-nine out of fifty people would not look twice.

A second revelatory incident occurred soon after. Betty telephoned me to say that Judith had a kitten. Did I know that Judith adored cats? "No, but of course she would," I said.

Betty lived in the same street as Judith and saw more of her than I did. I was kept posted about the growth and habits of the cat and

its effect on Judith's life. She remarked, for instance, that she felt it
was good for her to have a tie and some responsibility. But no sooner
was the cat out of kittenhood than all the neighbours complained.
It was a tomcat, ungelded, and making every night hideous. Finally
the landlord said that either the cat or Judith must go, unless she was
prepared to have the cat "fixed." Judith wore herself out trying to
find some person, anywhere in Britain, who would be prepared to
take the cat. This person would, however, have to sign a written
statement not to have the cat "fixed." When Judith took the cat to the
vet to be killed, Betty told me she cried for twenty-four hours.

"She didn't think of compromising? After all, perhaps the cat
might have preferred to live, if given the choice?"

"Is it likely I'd have the nerve to say anything so sloppy to Judith?
It's the nature of a male cat to rampage lustfully about, and therefore
it would be morally wrong for Judith to have the cat fixed, simply
to suit her own convenience."

"She said that?"

"She wouldn't have to *say* it, surely?"

A third incident was when she allowed a visiting young American, living in Paris, the friend of a friend and scarcely known to her,
to use her flat while she visited her parents over Christmas. The
young man and his friends lived it up for ten days of alcohol and sex
and marijuana, and when Judith came back it took a week to get the
place clean again and the furniture mended. She telephoned twice
to Paris, the first time to say that he was a disgusting young thug
and if he knew what was good for him he would keep out of her way
in the future; the second time to apologize for losing her temper. "I
had a choice either to let someone use my flat, or to leave it empty.
But having chosen that you should have it, it was clearly an unwar-
rantable infringement of your liberty to make any conditions at all.
I do most sincerely ask your pardon." The moral aspects of the matter
having been made clear, she was irritated rather than not to receive
letters of apology from him—fulsome, embarrassed, but above all,
baffled.

It was the note of curiosity in the letters—he even suggested
coming over to get to know her better—that irritated her most.
"What do you suppose he means?" she said to me. "He lived in my
flat for ten days. One would have thought that should be enough,
wouldn't you?"

The facts about Judith, then, are all in the open, unconcealed, and
plain to anyone who cares to study them; or, as it became plain she
feels—to anyone with the intelligence to interpret them.

She has lived for the last twenty years in a small two-roomed flat
high over a busy West London street. The flat is shabby and badly

heated. The furniture is old, was never anything but ugly, is now frankly rickety and fraying. She has an income of £200 a year from a dead uncle. She lives on this and what she earns from her poetry, and from lecturing on poetry to night classes and extra-mural University classes.

She does not smoke or drink, and eats very little, from preference, not self-discipline.

She studied poetry and biology at Oxford, with distinction.

She is a Castlewell. That is, she is a member of one of the academic upper-middle-class families, which have been producing for centuries a steady supply of brilliant but sound men and women who are the backbone of the arts and sciences in Britain. She is on cool good terms with her family who respect her and leave her alone.

She goes on long walking tours, by herself, in such places as Exmoor or West Scotland.

Every three or four years she publishes a volume of poems.

The walls of her flat are completely lined with books. They are scientific, classical and historical; there is a great deal of poetry and some drama. There is not one novel. When Judith says: "Of course I don't read novels," this does not mean that novels have no place, or a small place, in literature; or that people should not read novels; but that it must be obvious that she can't be expected to read novels.

I had been visiting her flat for years before I noticed two long shelves of books, under a window, each shelf filled with the works of a single writer. The two writers are not, to put it at the mildest, the kind one would associate with Judith. They are mild, reminiscent, vague and whimsical. Typical English *belles-lettres*, in fact, and by definition abhorrent to her. Not one of the books in the two shelves has been read; some of the pages are still uncut. Yet each book is inscribed or dedicated to her: gratefully, admiringly, sentimentally and, more than once, amorously. In short, it is open to anyone who cares to examine these two shelves, and to work out dates, to conclude that Judith from the age of fifteen to twenty-five had been the beloved young companion of one elderly literary gentleman, and from twenty-five to thirty-five, the inspiration of another.

During all that time she had produced her own poetry, and the sort of poetry, it is quite safe to deduce, not at all likely to be admired by her two admirers. Her poems are always cool and intellectual; that is their form, which is contradicted or supported by a gravely sensuous texture. They are poems to read often; one has to, to understand them.

I did not ask Judith a direct question about these two eminent but rather fusty lovers. Not because she would not have answered, or because she would have found the question impertinent, but because such questions are clearly unnecessary. Having those two shelves of books where they are, and books she could not conceivably care for, for their own sake, is publicly giving credit where credit is due. I can imagine her thinking the thing over, and deciding it was only fair, or perhaps honest, to place the books there; and this despite the fact that she would not care at all for the same attention to be paid to her. There is something almost contemptuous in it. For she certainly despises people who feel they need attention.

For instance, more than once a new emerging wave of "modern" young poets have discovered her as the only "modern" poet among their despised and well-credited elders. This is because, since she began writing at fifteen, her poems have been full of scientific, mechanical and chemical imagery. This is how she thinks, or feels.

More than once has a young poet hastened to her flat, to claim her as an ally, only to find her totally and by instinct unmoved by words like modern, new, contemporary. He has been outraged and wounded by her principle, so deeply rooted as to be unconscious, and to need no expression but a contemptuous shrug of the shoulders, that publicity seeking or to want critical attention is despicable. It goes without saying that there is perhaps one critic in the world she has any time for. He has sulked off, leaving her on her shelf, which she takes it for granted is her proper place, to be read by an appreciative minority.

Meanwhile she gives her lectures, walks alone through London, writes her poems, and is seen sometimes at a concert or a play with a middle-aged professor of Greek who has a wife and two children.

Betty and I speculated about this Professor, with such remarks as: Surely she must sometimes be lonely? Hasn't she ever wanted to marry? What about that awful moment when one comes in from somewhere at night to an empty flat?

It happened recently that Betty's husband was on a business trip, her children visiting, and she was unable to stand the empty house. She asked Judith for a refuge until her own home filled again.

Afterwards Betty rang me up to report:

"Four of the five nights Professor Adams came in about ten or so."

"Was Judith embarrassed?"

"Would you expect her to be?"

"Well if not embarrassed at least conscious there was a situation?"

"No, not at all. But I must say I don't think he's good enough for her. He can't possibly understand her. He calls her Judy."

"Good God."

"Yes. But I was wondering. Suppose the other two called her Judy
—"little Judy"—imagine it! Isn't it awful! But it does rather throw
a light on Judith?"

"It's rather touching."

"I suppose it's touching. But *I* was embarrassed—oh, not because
of the situation. Because of how she was, with him. 'Judy, is there
another cup of tea in that pot?' And she, rather daughterly and
demure, pouring him one."

"Well yes, I can see how you felt."

"Three of the nights he went to her bedroom with her—very
casual about it, because she was being. But he was not there in the
mornings. So I asked her. You know how it is when you ask her a
question. As if you've been having long conversations on that very
subject for years and years, and she is merely continuing where you
left off last. So when she says something surprising, one feels such
a fool to be surprised?"

"Yes. And then?"

"I asked her if she was sorry not to have children. She said yes, but
one couldn't have everything."

"One can't have everything, she said?"

"Quite clearly feeling she *has* nearly everything. She said she
thought it was a pity, because she would have brought up children
very well."

"When you come to think of it, she would, too."

"I asked about marriage, but she said on the whole the rôle of a
mistress suited her better."

"She used the word mistress?"

"You must admit it's the accurate word."

"I suppose so."

"And then she said that while she liked intimacy and sex and
everything, she enjoyed waking up in the morning alone and *her
own person.*"

"Yes, *of course.*"

"Of course. But now she's bothered because the Professor would
like to marry her. Or he feels he ought. At least, he's getting all
guilty and obsessive about it. She says she doesn't see the point of
divorce, and anyway, surely it would be very hard on his poor old
wife after all these years particularly after bringing up two children
so satisfactorily. She talks about his wife as if she's a kind of nice old
charwoman, and it wouldn't be *fair* to sack her, you know. Anyway.
What with one thing and another Judith's going off to Italy soon in
order *to collect herself.*"

"But how's she going to pay for it?"

"Luckily the Third Programme's commissioning her to do some arty programmes. They offered her a choice of The Cid—El Thid, you know—and the Borgias. Well, the Borghese, then. And Judith settled for the Borgias."

"The Borgias," I said, "*Judith*?"

Yes quite. I said that too, in that tone of voice. She saw my point. She says the epic is right up her street, whereas the Renaissance has never been on her wavelength. Obviously it couldn't be, all the magnificence and cruelty and *dirt.* But of course chivalry and a high moral code and all those idiotically noble goings-on are right on her wavelength."

"Is the money the same?"

"Yes. But is it likely Judith would let money decide? No, she said that one should always choose something new, that isn't up one's street. Well, because it's better for her character, and so on, to get herself unsettled by the Renaissance. She didn't say *that,* of course."

"Of course not."

Judith went to Florence; and for some months postcards informed us tersely of her doings. Then Betty decided she must go by herself for a holiday. She had been appalled by the discovery that if her husband was away for a night she couldn't sleep; and when he went to Australia for three weeks, she stopped living until he came back. She had discussed this with him, and he had agreed that, if she really felt the situation to be serious, he would dispatch her by air, to Italy, in order to recover her self-respect. As she put it.

I got this letter from her: "It's no use, I'm coming home. I might have known. Better face it, once you're really married you're not fit for man nor beast. And if you remember what I used to be like! *Well!* I moped around Milan. I sun-bathed in Venice, then I thought my tan was surely worth something, so I was on the point of starting an affair with another lonely soul, but I lost heart, and went to Florence to see Judith. She wasn't there. She'd gone to the Italian Riviera. I had nothing better to do, so I followed her. When I saw the place I wanted to laugh, it's so much not Judith, you know, all those palms and umbrellas and gaiety at all costs and ever such an ornamental blue sea. Judith is in an enormous stone room up on the hillside above the sea, with grape-vines all over the place. You should see her, she's got beautiful. It seems for the last fifteen years she's been going to Soho every Saturday morning to buy food at an Italian shop. I must have looked surprised, because she explained she liked Soho. I suppose because all that dreary vice and nudes and prostitutes and everything prove how right she is to be as she is? She told the people in the shop she was going to Italy, and the signora said what a coincidence, she was going back to Italy too, and she did hope an old friend like Miss Castlewell would visit her there. Judith said to me: "I felt lacking, when she used the word friend. Our relations have always been formal. Can you understand it?" she said to me. "For fifteen years," I said to her. She said: "I think I must feel it's a kind of imposition, don't you know, expecting people to feel friendship for one." *Well.* I said: "You ought to understand it, because you're like that yourself." "Am I?" she said. "Well, think about it," I said. But I could see she didn't want to think about it. Anyway, she's here, and I've spent a week with her. The widow Maria Rineiri inherited her mother's house, so she came home, from Soho. On the ground floor is a tatty little Rosticcheria patronized by the neighbours. They are all working people. This isn't tourist country, up on the hill. The widow lives above the shop with her little boy, a nasty little brat of about ten. Say what you like, the English are the only people who know how to bring up children, I don't care if that's insular. Judith's room is at the back, with a balcony. Underneath her room is the barber's shop, and the barber is Luigi Rineiri, the widow's younger brother. Yes, I was keeping him until the last. He is about forty, tall dark handsome, a great *bull,* but rather a sweet fatherly bull. He has cut Judith's hair and made it lighter. Now it looks like a sort of gold helmet. Judith is all brown. The widow Rineiri has made her a white dress and a green dress. They fit, for a change. When Judith walks down the street to the lower town, all the Italian males take one look at the golden girl and melt in their own oil like ice-cream. Judith takes all this in her stride. She sort of acknowledges the homage. Then she strolls into the sea and vanishes into the foam. She swims five miles every day. *Naturally.* I haven't asked Judith whether she has collected herself, because you can see she hasn't. The widow Rineiri is match-making. When I noticed this I wanted to laugh, but luckily I didn't, because Judith asked me, really wanting to know, Can you see me married to an Italian barber? (Not being snobbish, but stating the position, so to speak.) "Well yes," I said, "you're the only woman I know who I can see married to an Italian barber." Because it wouldn't matter who she married, she'd always be her *own person.* "At any rate, for a time," I said. At which she said, asperously: "You can use phrases like for a time in England but not in Italy." Did you ever see England, at least London, as the home of licence, liberty and free love? No, neither did I, but of course she's right. Married to Luigi it would be the family, the neighbours, the church and the bambini. All the same she's thinking about it, believe it or not. Here she's quite different, all relaxed and free. She's melting in the attention she gets. The widow mothers her and makes her coffee all the time, and listens to a lot of good advice about how to bring up that nasty brat of hers. Unluckily she doesn't take it.

Luigi is crazy for her. At mealtimes she goes to the trattoria in the upper square and all the workmen treat her like a goddess. Well, a film-star then. I said to her, you're mad to come home. For one thing her rent is ten bob a week, and you eat pasta and drink red wine till you bust for about one and sixpence. No, she said, it would be nothing but self-indulgence to stay. Why? I said. She said, she's got nothing to stay for. (Ho ho!) And besides, she's done her research on the Borghese, though so far she can't see her way to an honest presentation of the facts. What made these people tick? she wants to know. And so she's only staying because of the cat. I forgot to mention the cat. This is a town of cats. The Italians here love their cats. I wanted to feed a stray cat at the table, but the waiter said no; and after lunch, all the waiters came with trays crammed with left-over food and stray cats came from everywhere to eat. And at dark when the tourists go in to feed and the beach is empty—you know how empty and forlorn a beach is at dusk?—well, cats appear from everywhere. The beach seems to move, then you see it's cats. They go stalking along the thin inch of grey water at the edge of the sea, shaking their paws crossly at each step, snatching at the dead little fish, and throwing them with their mouths up on to the dry sand. Then they scamper after them. You've never seen such a snarling and fighting. At dawn when the fishing-boats come in to the empty beach, the cats are there in dozens. The fishermen throw them bits of fish. The cats snarl and fight over it. Judith gets up early and goes down to watch. Sometimes Luigi goes too, being tolerant. Because what he really likes is to join the evening promenade with Judith on his arm around and around the square of the upper town. Showing her off. Can you *see* Judith? But she does it. Being tolerant. But she smiles and enjoys the attention she gets, there's no doubt of it.

"She has a cat in her room. It's a kitten really, but it's pregnant. Judith says she can't leave until the kittens are born. The cat is too young to have kittens. Imagine Judith. She sits on her bed in that great stone room, with her bare feet on the stone floor and watches the cat, and tries to work out why a healthy uninhibited Italian cat always fed on the best from the Rosticcheria should be neurotic. Because it is. When it sees Judith watching it gets nervous and starts licking at the roots of its tail. But Judith goes on watching, and says about Italy that the reason why the English love the Italians is because the Italians make the English feel superior. They have no discipline. And that's a despicable reason for one nation to love another. Then she talks about Luigi and says he has no sense of guilt, but a sense of sin; whereas she has no sense of sin but she has guilt. I haven't asked her if this has been an insuperable barrier, because judging from how she looks, it hasn't. She says she would rather

have a sense of sin, because sin can be atoned for, and if she understood sin, perhaps she would be more at home with the Renaissance.
Luigi is very healthy, she says, and not neurotic. He is a Catholic,
of course. He doesn't mind that she's an atheist. His mother has
explained to him that the English are all pagans, but good people at
heart. I suppose he thinks a few smart sessions with the local priest
would set Judith on the right path for good and all. Meanwhile, the
cat walks nervously around the room, stopping to lick, and when it
can't stand Judith watching it another second, it rolls over on the
floor, with its paws tucked up, and rolls up its eyes, and Judith
scratches its lumpy pregnant stomach and tells it to relax. It makes
me nervous to see her, it's not like her, I don't know why. Then Luigi
shouts from the barber's shop, then he comes up and stands at the
door laughing, and Judith laughs, and the widow says: Children
enjoy yourselves. And off they go, walking down to the town eating
ice-cream. The cat follows them. It won't let Judith out of its sight,
like a dog. When she swims miles out to sea, the cat hides under a
beach-hut until she comes back. Then she carries it back up the hill,
because that nasty little boy chases it. *Well.* I'm coming home tomorrow, thank God, to my dear old Billy, I was mad to ever leave
him. There is something about Judith and Italy that has upset me,
I don't know what. The point is, what on earth can Judith and Luigi
talk about? Nothing. How can they? And, of course, it doesn't matter. So I turn out to be a prude as well. See you next week."

It was my turn for a dose of the sun, so I didn't see Betty. On my
way back from Rome I stopped off in Judith's resort and walked up
through narrow streets to the upper town, where, in the square with
the vine-covered trattoria at the corner, was a house with Rosticcheria written in black print on a cracked wooden board over a low
door. There was a door-curtain of red beads, and flies settled on the
beads. I opened the beads with my hands and looked in to a small
dark room with a stone counter. Loops of salami hung from metal
hooks. A glass bell covered some plates of cooked meats. There were
flies on the salami and on the glass bell. A few tins on the wooden
shelves, a couple of pale loaves, some wine-casks and an open case
of sticky pale green grapes covered with fruit flies, seemed to be the
only stock. A single wooden table with two chairs stood in a corner,
and two workmen sat there, eating lumps of sausage and bread.
Through another bead curtain at the back came a short, smoothly fat,
slender limbed woman with greying hair. I asked for Miss Castlewell, and her face changed. She said in an offended, offhand way:
"Miss Castlewell left last week." She took a white cloth from under
the counter, and flicked at the flies on the glass bell. "I'm a friend of
hers," I said, and she said "Si," and put her hands, palm down, on the
counter and looked at me, expressionless. The workmen got up,

gulped down the last of their wine, nodded and went. She ciao'd them; and looked back at me. Then, since I didn't go, she called "Luigi!" A shout came from the back room, there was a rattle of beads, and in came first a wiry sharp-faced boy, and then Luigi. He was tall, heavy shouldered, and his black rough hair was like a cap, pulled low over his brows. He looked good-natured, but at the moment, uneasy. His sister said something, and he stood beside her, an ally, and confirmed: "Miss Castlewell went away." I was on the point of giving up, when through the bead curtain that screened off a dazzling light eased a thin, tabby cat. It was ugly and it walked uncomfortably, with its back quarters bunched up. The child suddenly let out a 'Sssss' through his teeth, and the cat froze. Luigi said something sharp to the child, and something encouraging to the cat, which sat down, looked straight in front of it, then began frantically licking at its flanks. "Miss Castlewell was offended with us," said Mrs Rineiri suddenly, and with dignity. "She left early one morning. We did not expect her to go." I said: "Perhaps she had to go home and finish some work."

Mrs Rineiri shrugged, then sighed. Then she exchanged a hard look with her brother. Clearly the subject had been discussed, and closed for ever.

"I've known Judith a long time," I said, trying to find the right note. "She's a remarkable woman. She's a poet." But there was no response to this at all. Meanwhile the child, with a fixed bared-teeth grin, was staring at the cat, narrowing his eyes. Suddenly he let out another "Ssssssss," and added a short, high yelp. The cat shot backwards, hit the wall, tried desperately to claw its way up the wall, came to its senses and again sat down and began its urgent, undirected licking at its fur. This time Luigi cuffed the child, who yelped in earnest, and then ran out into the street past the cat. Now that the way was clear the cat shot across the floor, up on to the counter, and bounded past Luigi's shoulder and straight through the bead curtain into the barber's shop, where it landed with a thud.

"Judith was sorry when she left us," said Mrs Rineiri uncertainly. "She was crying."

"I'm sure she was."

"And so," said Mrs Rineiri, with finality, laying her hands down again, and looking past me at the bead curtain. That was the end. Luigi nodded brusquely at me, and went into the back. I said goodbye to Mrs Rineiri and walked back to the lower town. In the square I saw the child, sitting on the running-board of a lorry parked outside the trattoria, drawing in the dust with his bare toes, and directing in front of him a blank, unhappy stare.

I had to go through Florence, so I went to the address Judith had been at. No, Miss Castlewell had not been back. Her papers and books were still here. Would I take them back with me to England? I made a great parcel and brought them back to England.

I telephoned Judith and she said she had already written for the papers to be sent, but it was kind of me to bring them. There had seemed to be no point, she said, in returning to Florence.

"Shall I bring them over?"

"I would be very grateful, of course."

Judith's flat was chilly, and she wore a bunchy sage-green woollen dress. Her hair was still a soft gold helmet, but she looked pale and rather pinched. She stood with her back to a single bar of electric fire —lit because I demanded it—with her legs apart and her arms folded. She contemplated me.

"I went to the Rineiris' house."

"Oh. Did you?"

"They seemed to miss you."

She said nothing.

"I saw the cat too."

"Oh. Oh, I suppose you and Betty discussed it?" This was with a small unfriendly smile.

"Well, Judith, you must see we were likely to?"

She gave this her consideration and said: "I don't understand why people discuss other people. Oh—I'm not criticizing you. But I don't see why you are so interested. I don't understand human behaviour and I'm not particularly interested."

"I think you should write to the Rineiris."

"I wrote and thanked them, of course."

"I don't mean that."

"You and Betty have worked it out?"

"Yes, we talked about it. We thought we should talk to you, so you should write to the Rineiris."

"Why?"

"For one thing, they are both very fond of you."

"Fond," she said smiling.

"Judith, I've never in my life felt such an atmosphere of being let down."

Judith considered this. "When something happens that shows one there is really a complete gulf in understanding, what is there to say?"

"It could scarcely have been a complete gulf in understanding. I suppose you are going to say we are being interfering?"

Judith showed distaste. "That is a very stupid word. And it's a stupid idea. No one can interfere with me if I don't let them. No, it's that I don't understand people. I don't understand why you or Betty should care. Or why the Rineiris should, for that matter," she added with the small tight smile.

"Judith!"

"If you've behaved stupidly, there's no point in going on. You put an end to it."

"What happened? Was it the cat?"

"Yes, I suppose so. But it's not important." She looked at me, saw my ironical face, and said: "The cat was too young to have kittens. That is all there was to it."

"Have it your way. But that is obviously not all there is to it."

"What upsets me is that I don't understand at all why I was so upset then."

"What happened? Or don't you want to talk about it?"

"I don't give a damn whether I talk about it or not. You really do say the most extraordinary things, you and Betty. If you want to know, I'll tell you, what does it matter?"

"I would like to know, of course."

"*Of course!*" she said. "In your place I wouldn't care. Well, I think the essence of the thing was that I must have had the wrong attitude to that cat. Cats are supposed to be independent. They are supposed to go off by themselves to have their kittens. This one didn't. It was climbing up on to my bed all one night and crying for attention. I don't like cats on my bed. In the morning I saw she was in pain. I stayed with her all that day. Then Luigi—he's the brother, you know."

"Yes."

"Did Betty mention him? Luigi came up to say it was time I went for a swim. He said the cat should look after itself. I blame myself very much. That's what happens when you submerge yourself in somebody else."

Her look at me was now defiant; and her body showed both defensiveness and aggression. "Yes. It's true. I've always been afraid of it. And in the last few weeks I've behaved badly. It's because I let it happen."

"Well, go on."

"I left the cat and swam. It was late, so it was only for a few minutes. When I came out of the sea the cat had followed me and had had a kitten on the beach. That little beast Michele—the son, you know?—Well, he always teased the poor thing, and now he had frightened her off the kitten. It was dead, though. He held it up by the tail and waved it at me as I came out of the sea. I told him to bury it. He scooped two inches of sand away and pushed the kitten in— on the beach, where people are all day. So I buried it properly. He had run off. He was chasing the poor cat. She was terrified and running up the town. I ran too. I caught Michele and I was so angry I hit him. I don't believe in hitting children. I've been feeling beastly about it ever since."

"You were angry."

"It's no excuse. I would never have believed myself capable of hitting a child. I hit him very hard. He went off, crying. The poor cat had got under a big lorry parked in the square. Then she screamed. And then a most remarkable thing happened. She screamed just once, and all at once cats just materialized. One minute there was just one cat, lying under a lorry, and the next, dozens of cats. They sat in a big circle around the lorry, all quite still, and watched my poor cat."

"Rather moving," I said.

"Why?"

"There is no evidence one way or the other," I said in inverted commas, "that the cats were there out of concern for a friend in trouble."

"No," she said energetically. "There isn't. It might have been curiosity. Or anything. How do we know? However, I crawled under the lorry. There were two paws sticking out of the cat's back end. The kitten was the wrong way round. It was stuck. I held the cat down with one hand and I pulled the kitten out with the other." She held out her long white hands. They were still covered with fading scars and scratches. "She bit and yelled, but the kitten was alive. She left the kitten and crawled across the square into the house. Then all the cats got up and walked away. It was the most extraordinary thing I've ever seen. They vanished again. One minute they were all there, and then they had vanished. I went after the cat, with the kitten. Poor little thing, it was covered with dust—being wet, don't you know. The cat was on my bed. There was another kitten coming, but it got stuck too. So when she screamed and screamed I just pulled it out. The kittens began to suck. One kitten was very big. It was a nice fat black kitten. It must have hurt her. But she suddenly bit out—snapped, don't you know, like a reflex action, at the back of the kitten's head. It died, just like that. Extraordinary, isn't it?" she said, blinking hard, her lips quivering. "She was its mother, but she killed it. Then she ran off the bed and went downstairs into the shop under the counter. I called to Luigi. You know, he's Mrs Rineiri's brother."

"Yes, I know."

"He said, she was too young, and she was badly frightened and very hurt. He took the alive kitten to her but she got up and walked away. She didn't want it. Then Luigi told me not to look. But I followed him. He held the kitten by the tail and he banged it against the wall twice. Then he dropped it into the rubbish heap. He moved aside some rubbish with his toe, and put the kitten here and pushed rubbish over it. Then Luigi said the cat should be destroyed. He said she was badly hurt and it would always hurt her to have kittens."

"He hasn't destroyed her. She's still alive. But it looks to me as if he were right."

"Yes, I expect he was."

"What upset you—that he killed the kitten?"

"Oh no, I expect the cat would if he hadn't. But that isn't the point, is it?"

"What is the point?"

"I don't think I really know." She had been speaking breathlessly, and fast. Now she said slowly: "It's not a question of right or wrong is it? Why should it be? It's a question of what one is. That night Luigi wanted to go promenading with me. For him, that was *that*. Something had to be done, and he'd done it. But I felt ill. He was very nice to me. He's a very good person," she said, defiantly.

"Yes, he looks it."

"That night I couldn't sleep. I was blaming myself. I should never have left the cat to go swimming. Well, and then I decided to leave the next day. And I did. And that's all. The whole thing was a mistake, from start to finish."

"Going to Italy at all?"

"Oh, to go for a holiday would have been all right."

"You've done all that work for nothing? You mean you aren't going to make use of all that research?"

"No. It was a mistake."

"Why don't you leave it a few weeks and see how things are then?"

"Why?"

"You might feel differently about it."

"What an extraordinary thing to say. Why should I? Oh, you mean, time passing, healing wounds—that sort of thing? What an extraordinary idea. It's always seemed to me an extraordinary idea. No, right from the beginning I've felt ill at ease with the whole business, not myself at all."

"Rather irrationally, I should have said."

Judith considered this, very seriously. She frowned while she thought it over. Then she said: "But if one cannot rely on what one feels, what can one rely on?"

"On what one thinks, I should have expected you to say."

"Should you? Why? Really, you people are all very strange. I don't understand you." She turned off the electric fire, and her face closed up. She smiled, friendly and distant and said: "I don't really see any point at all in discussing it."

Malcolm Lowry

(1909–1957)

Malcolm Lowry's life constantly metamorphosed into his books. Events from his orthodox Methodist childhood in England, from his public school and Cambridge experiences, and from his later travels through Europe, in the Orient, and in North America all entered his novels and short stories. There they took on a portentous character and became part of the author's elaborate quest for spiritual meaning. About his work as a whole (for it was all intended to connect into a cycle called "The Voyage that Never Ends"), Lowry wrote that it was more the journey of an unconscious than that of a man. To this end, his narrators continually shift identity—Wilderness in "Strange Comfort Afforded by the Profession" is an American professor, for example, while in other stories he is a Canadian novelist—and they discover within themselves a capacity both for the torments of hell and for the joys of heaven. The balance is all, and much of Lowry's writing attempts to work its way from emotional imbalance back to intellectual and psychic harmony. His best-known novel, *Under the Volcano* (1947)—a complex story about tragic love, political intrigue in Mexico, alcoholic hallucination, isolation in the modern world, and cabbalistic disharmony—demonstrates the depth of the abyss Lowry could fathom. The interrelated stories of *Hear Us O Lord from Heaven Thy Dwelling-Place* (1961), by contrast, with their subtle blend of terror and comic wit, trace the difficult route back to Paradise.

If "Paradise" had any concrete form for Lowry, he found it in Dollarton, on the west coast of Canada, where he lived and wrote for fourteen years. This is the framing landscape for *Hear Us O Lord*—a harmony between man and nature most beautifully realized in the final section of that book, a novella called "The Forest Path to the Spring". Against it the American and Mediterranean landscapes of "Strange Comfort" must be balanced. In the process of translation from one state to another, his characters undergo intense psychological distress, which Lowry probed with a wry humor and an unrelenting seriousness.

For further reading

Douglas Day, *Malcolm Lowry* (New York: Oxford University Press, 1973).
William H. New, *Malcolm Lowry* (Toronto: McClelland & Stewart, 1971).
George Woodcock, ed., *Malcolm Lowry: the man and his work* (Vancouver: University of British Columbia, 1971).

Strange Comfort Afforded by the Profession

Sigbjørn Wilderness, an American writer in Rome on a Guggenheim Fellowship, paused on the steps above the flower stall and wrote, glancing from time to time at the house before him, in a black notebook:

Il poeta inglese Giovanni Keats mente maravigliosa quanto precoce mori in questa casa il 24 Febraio 1821 nel ventiseesimo anno dell' eta sua.

Here, in a sudden access of nervousness, glancing now not only at the house, but behind him at the church of Trinita dei Monti, at the woman in the flower stall, the Romans drifting up and down the steps, or passing in the Piazza di Spagna below (for though it was several years after the war he was afraid of being taken for a spy), he drew, as well as he was able, the lyre, similar to the one on the poet's tomb, that appeared on the house between the Italian and its translation:

Then he added swiftly the words below the lyre:

The young English poet, John Keats, died in this house on the 24th of February 1821, aged 26.

This accomplished, he put the notebook and pencil back in his pocket, glanced around him again with a heavier, more penetrating look—that in fact was informed by such a malaise he saw nothing at all but which was intended to say "I have a perfect right to do this," or "If you saw me do that, very well then, I *am* some sort of detective, perhaps even some kind of a painter"—descended the remaining steps, looked around wildly once more, and entered, with a sigh of relief like a man going to bed, the comforting darkness of Keats's house.

Here, having climbed the narrow staircase, he was almost instantly confronted by a legend in a glass case which said:

Remnants of aromatic gums used by Trelawny when cremating the body of Shelley.

And these words, for his notebook with which he was already rearmed felt ratified in this place, he also copied down, though he failed to comment on the gums themselves, which largely escaped his notice, as indeed did the house itself—there had been those stairs, there was a balcony, it was dark, there were many pictures, and these glass cases, it was a bit like a library—in which he saw no books of his—these made about the sum of Sigbjørn's unrecorded perceptions. From the aromatic gums he moved to the enshrined marriage license of the same poet, and Sigbjørn transcribed this document too, writing rapidly as his eyes became more used to the dim light:

Percy Bysshe Shelley of the Parish of Saint Mildred, Bread Street, London, Widower, *and* Mary Wollstonecraft Godwin *of* the City of Bath, Spinster, a minor, *were married in this* Church *by* Licence *with Consent of* William Godwin her father *this* Thirtieth *Day of December in the year one thousand eight hundred and sixteen.* By me Mr. Heydon, Curate. This marriage was solemnized between us.

PERCY BYSSHE SHELLEY
MARY WOLLSTONECRAFT GODWIN

In the presence of:
WILLIAM GODWIN
M. J. GODWIN.

Beneath this Sigbjørn added mysteriously:

Nemesis. Marriage of drowned Phoenician sailor. A bit odd here at all. Sad—feel swine to look at such things.

Then he passed on quickly—not so quickly he hadn't time to wonder with a remote twinge why, if there was no reason for any of his own books to be there on the shelves above him, the presence was justified of *In Memoriam, All Quiet on the Western Front, Green Light,* and the *Field Book of Western Birds*—to another glass case in which appeared a framed and unfinished letter, evidently from Severn, Keats's friend, which Sigbjørn copied down as before:

My dear Sir:
Keats has changed somewhat for the worse—at least his mind has much—very much—yet the blood has ceased to come, his digestion is better and but for a cough he must be improving, that is as respects his body—but the fatal prospect of consumption hangs before his mind yet—and turns everything to despair and wretchedness —he will not hear a word about living—nay, I seem to lose his confidence by trying to give him this hope [the following lines had been crossed out by Severn but Sigbjorn ruthlessly wrote them down just the same: *for his knowledge of internal anatomy enables him to judge of any change accurately and largely adds to his torture*], he will not think his future prospect favorable—he says the continued stretch of his imagination has already killed him and were he to recover he would not write another line —he will not hear of his good friends in England except for what they have done— and this is another load—but of their high hopes of him—his certain success—his experience—he will not hear a word—then the want of some kind of hope to feed his vivacious imagination—

The letter having broken off here, Sigbjørn, notebook in hand, tiptoed lingeringly to another glass case where, another letter from Severn appearing, he wrote:

My dear Brown—He is gone—he died with the most perfect ease—he seemed to go to sleep. On the 23rd at half past four the approaches of death came on. "Severn—lift me up for I am dying—I shall die easy—don't be frightened, I thank God it has come." I lifted him upon my arms and the phlegm seemed boiling in his throat. This increased until 11 at night when he gradually sank into death so quiet I still thought he slept—But I cannot say more now. I am broken down beyond my strength. I cannot be left alone. I have not slept for nine days—the days since. On Saturday a gentleman came to cast his hand and foot. On Thursday the body was opened. The lungs were completely gone. The doctors would not—

Much moved, Sigbjørn reread this as it now appeared in his note-book, then added beneath it:

On Saturday a gentleman come to cast his hand and foot—that is the most sinister line to me. Who is this gentlemen?

Once outside Keats's house Wilderness did not pause nor look to left or right, not even at the American Express, until he had reached a bar which he entered, however, without stopping to copy down its name. He felt he had progressed in one movement, in one stride, from Keats's house to this bar, partly just because he had wished to avoid signing his own name in the visitor's book. Sigbjørn Wilderness! The very sound of his name was like a bell-buoy—or more euphoniously a light-ship—broken adrift, and washing in from the Atlantic on a reef. Yet how he hated to write it down (loved to see it in print?)—though like so much else with him it had little reality unless he did. Without hesitating to ask himself why, if he was so disturbed by it, he did not choose another name under which to write, such as his second name which was Henry, or his mother's, which was Sanderson-Smith, he selected the most isolated booth he could find in the bar, that was itself an underground grotto, and drank two grappas in quick succession. Over his third he began to experience some of the emotions one might have expected him to undergo in Keats's house. He felt fully the surprise which had barely affected him that some of Shelley's relics were to be found there, if a fact no more astonishing than that Shelley—whose skull moreover had narrowly escaped appropriation by Byron as a drinking goblet, and whose heart, snatched out of the flames by Trelawny, he seemed to recollect from Proust, was interred in England—should have been buried in Rome at all (where the bit of Ariel's song inscribed on his gravestone might have anyway prepared one for the rich and strange), and he was touched by the chivalry of those Italians who, during the war, it was said, had preserved, at considerable risk to themselves, the contents of that house from the Germans. Moreover he now thought he began to see the house itself more clearly, though no doubt not as it was, and he produced his notebook again with the object of adding to the notes already taken these impressions that came to him in retrospect.

"Mamertine Prison," he read . . . He'd opened it at the wrong place, at some observations made yesterday upon a visit to the historic dungeon, but being gloomily entertained by what he saw, he read on as he did so feeling the clammy confined horror of that underground cell, or other underground cell, not, he suspected, really sensed at the time, rise heavily about him.

MAMERTINE PRISON [ran the heading]
  The lower is the true prison
of Mamertine, the state prison of ancient Rome.
  The lower cell called Tullianus is probably the most ancient building in Rome. The prison was used to imprison malefactors and enemies of the State. In the lower cell is seen the well where according to tradition St. Peter miraculously made a spring to baptise the gaolers Processus and Martinianus. Victims: politicians. Pontius, King of the Sanniti. Died 290 B.C. Giurgurath (Jugurtha), Aristobulus, Vercingetorix.—The Holy Martyrs, Peter and Paul. Apostles imprisoned in the reign of Nero.—Processus, Abondius, *and many others unknown* were:
>   decapitato
>   suppliziato (suffocated)
>   strangolato
>   morto per fame.
  Vercingetorix, the King of the Gauls, was certainly strangolato 49 B.C. and Jugurtha, King of Numidia, dead by starvation 104 B.C.

The lower is the true prison—why had he underlined that? Sigbjørn wondered. He ordered another grappa and, while awaiting it, turned back to his notebook where, beneath his remarks on the Mamertine prison, and added as he now recalled in the dungeon itself, this memorandum met his eyes:

Find Gogol's house—where wrote part of Dead Souls—1838. Where died Vielgorsky? "They do not heed me, nor see me, nor listen to me," wrote Gogol. "What have I done to them? Why do they torture me? What do they want of poor me? What can I give them? I have nothing. My strength is gone. I cannot endure all this." Suppliziato. Strangolato. In wonderful-horrible book of Nabokov's when Gogol was dying —he says—"you could feel his spine through his stomach." Leeches dangling from nose: "Lift them up, keep them away . . . " Henrik Ibsen, Thomas Mann, ditto brother: Buddenbrooks and Pippo Spano. A—where lived? became sunburned? Perhaps happy here. Prosper Merimée and Schiller. Suppliziato. Fitzgerald in Forum. Eliot in Colosseum?

And underneath this was written enigmatically:

And many others.

And beneath this:

Perhaps Maxim Gorky too. This is funny. Encounter between Volga Boatman and saintly Fisherman.

What was funny? While Sigbjørn, turning over his pages toward Keats's house again, was wondering what he had meant, beyond the fact that Gorky, like most of those other distinguished individuals, had at one time lived in Rome, if not in the Mamertine prison—though with another part of his mind he knew perfectly well—he realized that the peculiar stichometry of his observations, jotted down as if he imagined he were writing a species of poem, had caused him prematurely to finish the notebook:

On Saturday a gentleman came to cast his hand and foot—that is the most sinister line to me—who is this gentleman?

With these words his notebook concluded.

That didn't mean there was no more space, for his notebooks, he reflected avuncularly, just like his candles, tended to consume themselves at both ends; yes, as he thought, there was some writing at the beginning. Reversing this, for it was upside down, he smiled and forgot about looking for space, since he immediately recognized these notes as having been taken in America two years ago upon a visit to Richmond, Virginia, a pleasant time for him. So, amused, he composed himself to read, delighted also, in an Italian bar, to be thus transported back to the South. He had made nothing of these notes, hadn't even known they were there, and it was not always easy accurately to visualize the scenes they conjured up:

The wonderful slanting square in Richmond and the tragic silhouette of interlaced leafless trees.
On a wall: *dirty stinking Degenerate Bobs was here from Boston, North End, Mass. Warp son of a bitch.*

Sigbjørn chuckled. Now he clearly remembered the biting winter day in Richmond, the dramatic courthouse in the precipitous park, the long climb up to it, and the caustic attestation to solidarity with the North in the (white) men's wash room. Smiling he read on:

In Poe's shrine, strange preserved news clipping: CAPACITY CROWD HEARS TRIBUTE TO POE'S WORKS. *University student, who ended life, buried at Wytherville.*

Yes, yes, and this he remembered too, in Poe's house, or one of Poe's houses, the one with the great dark wing of shadow on it at sunset, where the dear old lady who kept it, who'd showed him the news clipping, had said to him in a whisper: "So you see, *we* think these stories of his drinking can't *all* be true." He continued:

Opposite Craig house, where Poe's Helen lived, these words upon façade, windows, stoop of the place from which E. A. P.—if I am right—must have watched the lady with the agate lamp: Headache—A. B. C.—Neuralgia: LIC-OFF-PREM—enjoy Pepsi —Drink Royal Crown Cola—Dr. Swell's Root Beer—"Furnish room for rent": did Poe really live here? Must have, could only have spotted Psyche from the regions which are Lic-Off-Prem.—Better than no Lic at all though. Bet Poe does not still live in Lic-Off-Prem. Else might account for "Furnish room for rent"?
    Mem: Consult Talking Horse Friday.
    —Give me Liberty or give me death [Sigbjørn now read]. In churchyard, with Patrick Henry's grave; a notice: No smoking within ten feet of the church; then:
    Outside Robert E. Lee's house:
    Please pull the bell
    To make it ring.
    —Inside Valentine Museum, with Poe's relics—

Sigbjørn paused. Now he remembered that winter day still more clearly. Robert E. Lee's house was of course far below the courthouse, remote from Patrick Henry and the Craig house and the other Poe shrine, and it would have been a good step hence to the Valentine Museum, even had not Richmond, a city whose Hellenic character was not confined to its architecture, but would have been recognized in its gradients by a Greek mountain goat, been grouped about streets so steep it was painful to think of Poe toiling up them. Sigbjørn's notes were in the wrong order, and it must have been morning then, and not sunset as it was in the other house with the old lady, when he went to the Valentine Museum. He saw Lee's house again, and a faint feeling of the beauty of the whole frostbound city outside came to his mind, then a picture of a Confederate white house, near a gigantic redbrick factory chimney, with far below a glimpse of an old cobbled street, and a lone figure crossing a waste, as between three centuries, from the house toward the railway tracks and this chimney, which belonged to the Bone Dry Fertilizer Company. But in the sequence of his notes "Please pull the bell, to make it ring," on Lee's house, had seemed to provide a certain musical effect of solemnity, yet ushering him instead into the Poe museum which Sigbjørn now in memory re-entered.

Inside Valentine Museum, with Poe's relics [he read once more]
Please
Do not smoke
Do not run
Do not touch walls or exhibits
Observation of these rules will insure your own and others' enjoyment of the museum.

—Blue silk coat and waistcoat, gift of the Misses Boykin, that belonged to one of George Washington's dentists.

Sigbjorn closed his eyes, in his mind Shelley's crematory gums and the gift of the Misses Boykin struggling for a moment helplessly, then he returned to the words that followed. They were Poe's own, and formed part of some letters once presumably written in anguished and private desperation, but which were now to be perused at leisure by anyone whose enjoyment of them would be "insured" so long as they neither smoked nor ran nor touched the glass case in which, like the gums (on the other side of the world), they were preserved. He read:

Excerpt from a letter by Poe—after having been dismissed from West Point—to his foster father. Feb. 21, 1831.
"It will however be the last time I ever trouble any human being—I feel I am on a sick bed from which I shall never get up."

Sigbjørn calculated with a pang that Poe must have written these words almost seven years to the day after Keats's death, then, that far from never having got up from his sick bed, he had risen from it to change, thanks to Baudelaire, the whole course of European literature, yes, and not merely to trouble, but to frighten the wits out of several generations of human beings with such choice pieces as "King Pest," "The Pit and the Pendulum," and "A Descent into the Maelstrom," not to speak of the effect produced by the compendious and prophetic *Eureka*.

My *ear* has been too shocking for any description—I am wearing away every day, even if my last sickness had not completed it.

Sigbjørn finished his grappa and ordered another. The sensation produced by reading these notes was really very curious. First, he was conscious of himself reading them here in this Roman bar, then of himself in the Valentine Museum in Richmond, Virginia, reading the letters through the glass case and copying fragments from these down, then of poor Poe sitting blackly somewhere writing them. Beyond this was the vision of Poe's foster father likewise reading some of these letters, for all he knew unheedingly, yet solemnly putting them away for what turned out to be posterity, these letters which, whatever they might not be, were certainly—he thought again—intended to be private. But were they indeed? Even here at this extremity Poe must have felt that he was transcribing the story that was E. A. Poe, at this very moment of what he conceived to be his greatest need, his final—however consciously engineered—disgrace, felt a certain reluctance, perhaps, to send what he wrote, as if he were thinking: Damn it, I could use some of that, it may not be so hot, but it is at least too good to waste on my foster father. Some of Keats's own published letters were not different. And yet it was almost bizarre how, among these glass cases, in these museums, to what extent one revolved about, was hemmed in by, this cinereous evidence of anguish. Where was Poe's astrolabe, Keats's tankard of claret, Shelley's "Useful Knots for the Yachtsman"? It was true that Shelley himself might not have been aware of the aromatic gums, but even that beautiful and irrelevant circumstantiality that was the gift of the Misses Boykin seemed not without its suggestion of suffering, at least for George Washington.

Baltimore, April 12, 1833.

I am perishing—absolutely perishing for want of aid. And yet I am not idle—nor have I committed any offence against society which would render me deserving of so hard a fate. For God's sake pity me and save me from destruction.

E. A. Poe

Oh, God, thought Sigbjørn. But Poe had held out another sixteen years. He had died in Baltimore at the age of forty, Sigbjørn himself was nine behind on that game so far, and—with luck—should win easily. Perhaps if Poe had held out a little longer—perhaps if Keats —he turned over the pages of his notebook rapidly, only to be confronted by the letter from Severn:

My dear Sir:

Keats has changed somewhat for the worse—at least his mind has much—very much—yet the blood has ceased to come ... but the fatal prospect hangs ... *for his knowledge of internal anatomy ... largely adds to his torture.*

Suppliziato, strangolato, he thought ... *The lower is the true prison. And many others.* Nor have I committed any offense against society. Not much you hadn't, brother. Society might pay you the highest honors, even to putting your relics in the company of the waistcoat belonging to George Washington's dentist, but in its heart it cried:—*dirty stinking Degenerate Bobs was here from Boston, North End, Mass. Warp son of a bitch!* ... "On Saturday a gentleman came to cast his hand and foot ... " Had anybody done that, Sigbjørn wondered, tasting his new grappa, and suddenly cognizant of his diminishing Guggenheim, compared, that was, Keats and Poe?—But compare in what sense, Keats, with what, in what sense, with Poe? What was it he wanted to compare? Not the aesthetic of the two poets, nor the breakdown of *Hyperion,* in relation to Poe's conception of the short poem, nor yet the philosophic ambition of the one, with the philosophic achievement of the other. Or could that more properly be discerned as negative capability, as opposed to negative achievement? Or did he merely wish to relate their melancholias? potations? hangovers? Their sheer guts—which commentators so obligingly forgot!—character, in a high sense of that word, the sense in which Conrad sometimes understood it, for were they not in their souls like hapless shipmasters, determined to drive their leaky commands full of valuable treasure at all costs, somehow, into port, and always against time, yet through all but interminable tempest, typhoons that so rarely abated? Or merely what seemed funereally analogous within the mutuality of their shrines? Or he could even speculate, starting with Baudelaire again, upon what the French movie director Epstein who had made *La Chute de la Maison Usher* in a way that would have delighted Poe himself, might have done with *The Eve of St. Agnes: And they are gone!* ... "For God's sake pity me and save me from destruction!"

Ah ha, now he thought he had it: did not the preservation of such relics betoken—beyond the filing cabinet of the malicious foster father who wanted to catch one out—less an obscure revenge for the poet's nonconformity, than for his magical monopoly, his possession of words? On the one hand he could write his translunar "Ulalume," his enchanted "To a Nightingale" (which might account for the *Field Book of Western Birds*), on the other was capable of saying, simply, "I am perishing ... For God's sake pity me ... " You see, after all, he's just like folks ... What's this? ... Conversely, there might appear almost a tragic condescension in remarks such as Flaubert's often quoted "Ils sont dans le vrai" perpetuated by Kafka—Kaf— and others, and addressed to child-bearing rosy-cheeked and jolly humanity at large. Condescension, nay, inverse self-approval, something downright unnecessary. And Flaub—Why should they be dans le vrai any more than the artist was dans le vrai? All people and poets are much the same but some poets are more the same than others, as George Orwell might have said. George Or— And yet, what modern poet would be caught dead (though they'd do their best to catch him all right) with his "For Christ's sake send aid," unrepossessed, unincinerated, to be put in a glass case? It was a truism to say that poets not only were, but looked like folks these days. Far from ostensible nonconformists, as the daily papers, the very writers themselves—more shame to them—took every opportunity triumphantly to point out, they dressed like, and as often as not were bank clerks, or, marvelous paradox, engaged in advertising. It was true. He, Sigbjørn, dressed like a bank clerk himself—how else should he have courage to go into a bank? It was questionable whether poets especially, in uttermost private, any longer allowed themselves to say things like "For God's sake pity me!" Yes, they had become more like folks even than folks. And the despair in the glass case, all private correspondence carefully destroyed, yet destined to become ten thousand times more public than ever, viewed through the great glass case of art, was now transmuted into hieroglyphics, masterly compressions, obscurities to be deciphered by experts— yes, and poets—like Sigbjørn Wilderness. Wil—

And many others. Probably there was a good idea somewhere, lurking among these arrant self-contradictions; pity could not keep him from using it, nor a certain sense of horror that he felt all over again that these mummified and naked cries of agony should lie thus exposed to human view in permanent incorruption, as if embalmed evermore in their separate eternal funeral parlors: separate, yet not separate, for was it not as if Poe's cry from Baltimore, in a mysterious manner, in the manner that the octet of a sonnet, say, is answered by its sestet, had already been answered, seven years before, by Keats's cry from Rome; so that according to the special reality of Sigbjørn's notebook at least, Poe's own death appeared like something extraformal, almost extraprofessional, an afterthought. Yet inerrably it was part of the same poem, the same story. "And yet the fatal prospect hangs ... " "Severn, lift me up, for I am dying." "Lift them up, keep them away." Dr. Swell's Root Beer.

Good idea or not, there was no more room to implement his thoughts within this notebook (the notes on Poe and Richmond ran, through Fredericksburg, into his remarks upon Rome, the Mamertine Prison, and Keats's house, and vice versa), so Sigbjørn brought out another one from his trousers pocket.

This was a bigger notebook altogether, its paper stiffer and stronger, showing it dated from before the war, and he had brought it from America at the last minute, fearing that such might be hard to come by abroad.

In those days he had almost given up taking notes: every new notebook bought represented an impulse, soon to be overlaid, to write afresh; as a consequence he had accumulated a number of notebooks like this one at home, yet which were almost empty, which he had never taken with him on his more recent travels since the war, else a given trip would have seemed to start off with a destructive stoop, from the past, in its soul: this one had looked an exception so he'd packed it.

Just the same, he saw, it was not innocent of writing: several pages at the beginning were covered with his handwriting, so shaky and hysterical of appearance, that Sigbjørn had to put on his spectacles to read it. Seattle, he made out. July? 1939. Seattle! Sigbjørn swallowed some grappa hastily. Lo, death hath reared himself a throne in a strange city lying alone far down within the dim west, where the good and the bad and the best and the rest, have gone to their eternal worst! The lower is the true Seattle ... Sigbjørn felt he could be excused for not fully appreciating Seattle, its mountain graces, in those days. For these were not notes he had found but the draft of a letter, written in the notebook because it was that type of letter possible for him to write only in a bar. A bar? Well, one might have called it a bar. For in those days, in Seattle, in the state of Washington, they still did not sell hard liquor in bars—as, for that matter, to this day they did not, in Richmond, in the state of Virginia—which was half the gruesome and pointless point of his having been in the state of Washington. LIC-OFF-PREM, he thought. No, no, go not to Virginia Dare ... Neither twist Pepso—tight-rooted!—for its poisonous bane. The letter dated—no question of his recognition of it, though whether he'd made another version and posted it he had forgotten—from absolutely the lowest ebb of those low tides of his life, a time marked by the baleful circumstance that the small legacy on which he then lived had been suddenly put in charge of a Los Angeles lawyer, to whom this letter indeed was written, his family, who considered him incompetent, having refused to have anything further to do with him, as, in effect, did the lawyer, who had sent him to a religious-minded family of Buchmanite* tendencies in Seattle on the understanding he be entrusted with not more than 25¢ a day.

Dear Mr. Van Bosch:

It is, psychologically, apart from anything else, of extreme urgency that I leave Seattle and come to Los Angeles to see you. I fear a complete mental collapse else. I have cooperated far beyond what I thought was the best of my ability here in the matter of liquor and I have also tried to work hard, so far, alas, without selling anything. I cannot say either that my ways have been as circumscribed exactly as I thought they would be by the Mackorkindales, who at least have seen my point of view on some matters, and if they pray for guidance on the very few occasions when they do see fit to exceed the stipulated 25¢ a day, they are at least sympathetic with my wishes to return. This may be because the elder Mackorkindale is literally and physically worn out following me through Seattle, or because you have failed to supply sufficient means for my board, but this is certainly as far as the sympathy goes. In short, they sympathize, but cannot honestly agree; nor will they advise you I should return. And in anything that applies to my writing—and this I find almost the hardest to bear—I am met with the opinion that I "should put all that behind me." If they merely claimed to be abetting yourself or my parents in this it would be understandable, but this judgment is presented to me independently, somewhat blasphemously in my view—though without question they believe it—as coming directly from God, who stoops daily from on high to inform the Mackorkindales, if not in so many words, that as a serious writer I am lousy. Scenting some hidden truth

---

*Buchmanite = moral rearmament.

about this, things being what they are, I would find it discouraging enough if it stopped there, and were not beyond that the hope held out, miraculously congruent also with that of my parents and yourself, that I could instead turn myself into a successful writer of advertisements. Since I cannot but feel, I repeat, and feel respectfully, that they are sincere in their beliefs, all I can say is that in this daily rapprochement with their Almighty in Seattle I hope some prayer that has slipped in by mistake to let the dreadful man for heaven's sake return to Los Angeles may eventually be answered. For I find it impossible to describe my spiritual isolation in this place, nor the gloom into which I have sunk. I enjoyed of course the seaside—the Mackorkindales doubtless reported to you that the Group were having a small rally in Bellingham (I wish you could go to Bellingham one day)—but I have completely exhausted any therapeutic value in my stay. God knows I ought to know, I shall never recover in this place, isolated as I am from Primrose who, whatever you may say, I want with all my heart to make my wife. It was with the greatest of anguish that I discovered that her letters to me were being opened, finally, even having to hear lectures on her moral character by those who had read these letters, which I had thus been prevented from replying to, causing such pain to her as I cannot think of. This separation from her would be an unendurable agony, without anything else, but as things stand I can only say I would be better off in a prison, in the worst dungeon that could be imagined, than to be incarcerated in this damnable place with the highest suicide rate in the Union. Literally I am dying in this macabre hole and I appeal to you to send me, out of the money that is after all mine, enough that I may return. Surely I am not the only writer, there have been others in history whose ways have been misconstrued and who have failed . . . who have won through . . . success . . . publicans and sinners . . . I have no intention——

Sigbjørn broke off reading, and resisting an impulse to tear the letter out of the notebook, for that would loosen the pages, began meticulously to cross it out, line by line.

And now this was half done he began to be sorry. For now, damn it, he wouldn't be able to use it. Even when he'd written it he must have thought it a bit too good for poor old Van Bosch, though one admitted that wasn't saying much. Wherever or however he could have used it. And yet, what if they had found this letter—whoever "they" were—and put it, glass-encased, in a museum among *his* relics? Not much—Still, you never knew!—Well, they wouldn't do it now. Anyhow, perhaps he would remember enough of it . . . "I am dying, absolutely perishing." "What have I done to them?" "My dear Sir." "The worst dungeon." And many others: and *dirty stinking Degenerate Bobs was here from Boston, North End, Mass. Warp son —!*

Sigbjørn finished his fifth unregenerate grappa and suddenly gave a loud laugh, a laugh which, as if it had realized itself it should become something more respectable, turned immediately into a prolonged—though on the whole relatively pleasurable—fit of coughing. . . .

James Alan McPherson

(b. 1943)

A native of Savannah, Georgia, James Alan McPherson attended all-black schools in Atlanta and Baltimore, then graduated from Harvard Law School in 1968. He has taught at Iowa State University, worked as a journalist in Roxbury, Massachusetts, and in 1969 became a contributing editor to the *Atlantic*. His stories reflect the dilemma confronting the black intellectual in America: on the one hand attracted by much that white society has to offer, on the other embittered by that society's racist record. Though his writings lack the fiery bitterness of a Cleaver or a Baldwin, McPherson is alive to the bigotry and injustice which vitiate American life, and which nullify the attempts of those seeking, like the narrator of "Gold Coast" (from *Hue and Cry*, 1969), to ignore or overcome racial barriers. But McPherson is not a revolutionary; his politics are the politics of feeling, and his concerns are for people rather than slogans. Even the bigoted old Irish janitor in "Gold Coast," a bitter wreck of a man, is drawn with sympathy and respect for his suffering. An earlier version of this story, lacking the final sections, first appeared in the *Atlantic* for November 1968, and won an Atlantic Award as the best short story of the year.

For further reading

Herbert Hill, ed., *Anger, and Beyond: The Negro Writer in the United States* (New York: Harper & Row, 1966).

C. W. E. Bigsby, ed., *The Black American Writer: Volume I: Fiction* (Deland, Fla.: Everett/Edwards, 1969).

Gold Coast

That spring, when I had a great deal of potential and no money at all, I took a job as a janitor. That was when I was still very young and spent money very freely, and when, almost every night, I drifted off to sleep lulled by sweet anticipation of that time when my potential would suddenly be realized and there would be capsule biographies of my life on dust jackets of many books, all proclaiming: " ... He knew life on many levels. From shoeshine boy, free-lance waiter, 3rd cook, janitor, he rose to ... " I had never been a janitor before and I did not really have to be one and that is why I did it. But now, much later, I think it might have been because it is possible to be a janitor without really becoming one, and at parties or at mixers when asked what it was I did for a living, it was pretty

238

good to hook my thumbs in my vest pockets and say comfortably: "Why, I am an apprentice janitor." The hippies would think it degenerate and really dig me and it made me feel good that people in Philosophy and Law and Business would feel uncomfortable trying to make me feel better about my station while wondering how the hell I had managed to crash the party.

"What's an apprentice janitor?" they would ask.

"I haven't got my card yet," I would reply. "Right now I'm just taking lessons. There's lots of complicated stuff you have to learn before you get your card and your own building."

"What kind of stuff?"

"Human nature, for one thing. *Race* nature, for another."

"Why race?"

"Because," I would say in a low voice looking around lest someone else should overhear, "you have to be able to spot Jews and Negroes who are passing."

"That's terrible," would surely be said then with a hint of indignation.

"It's an art," I would add masterfully.

After a good pause I would invariably be asked: "But you're a Negro yourself, how can you keep your own people out?"

At which point I would look terribly disappointed and say: "*I* don't keep them out. But if they get in it's my job to make their stay just as miserable as possible. Things are changing."

Now the speaker would just look at me in disbelief.

"It's Janitorial Objectivity," I would say to finish the thing as the speaker began to edge away. "Don't hate me," I would call after him to his considerable embarrassment. "Somebody has to do it."

It was an old building near Harvard Square. Conrad Aiken had once lived there and in the days of the Gold Coast, before Harvard built its great Houses, it had been a very fine haven for the rich; but that was a world ago, and this building was one of the few monuments of that era which had survived. The lobby had a high ceiling with thick redwood beams and it was replete with marble floor, fancy ironwork, and an old-fashioned house telephone that no longer worked. Each apartment had a small fireplace, and even the large bathtubs and chain toilets, when I was having my touch of nature, made me wonder what prominent personage of the past had worn away all the newness. And, being there, I felt a certain affinity toward the rich.

It was a funny building; because the people who lived there made it old. Conveniently placed as it was between the Houses and Harvard Yard, I expected to find it occupied by a company of hippies, hopeful working girls, and assorted graduate students. Instead, there were a majority of old maids, dowagers, asexual middle-aged men, homosexual young men, a few married couples and a teacher. No one was shacking up there, and walking through the quiet halls in the early evening, I sometimes had the urge to knock on a door and expose myself just to hear someone breathe hard for once.

It was a Cambridge spring: down by the Charles happy students were making love while sad-eyed middle-aged men watched them from the bridge. It was a time of activity: Law students were busy sublimating, Business School people were making records of the money they would make, the Harvard Houses were clearing out, and in the Square bearded pot-pushers were setting up their restaurant tables in anticipation of the Summer School faithfuls. There was a change of season in the air, and to comply with its urgings, James Sullivan, the old superintendent, passed his three beaten garbage cans on to me with the charge that I should take up his daily rounds of the six floors, and with unflinching humility, gather whatever scraps the old-maid tenants had refused to husband.

I then became very rich, with my own apartment, a sensitive girl, a stereo, two speakers, one tattered chair, one fork, a job, and the urge to acquire. Having all this and youth besides made me pity Sullivan: he had been in that building thirty years and had its whole history recorded in the little folds of his mind, as his own life was recorded in the wrinkles of his face. All he had to show for his time there was a berserk dog, a wife almost as mad as the dog, three cats, bursitis, acute myopia, and a drinking problem. He was well over seventy and could hardly walk, and his weekly check of twenty-two dollars from the company that managed the building would not support anything. So, out of compromise, he was retired to superintendent of my labor.

My first day as a janitor, while I skillfully lugged my three overflowing cans of garbage out of the building, he sat on his bench in the lobby, faded and old and smoking in patched, loose blue pants. He watched me. He was a chain smoker and I noticed right away that he very carefully dropped all of the ashes and butts on the floor and crushed them under his feet until there was a yellow and gray smear. Then he laboriously pushed the mess under the bench with his shoe, all the while eyeing me like a cat in silence as I hauled the many cans of muck out to the big disposal unit next to the building. When I had finished, he gave me two old plates to help stock my kitchen and his first piece of advice.

"Sit down, for Chrissake, and take a load off your feet," he told me.

I sat on the red bench next to him and accepted the wilted cigarette he offered me from the crushed package he kept in his sweater pocket.

"Now I'll tell you something to help you get along in the building." he said.

I listened attentively.

"If any of these sons-of-bitches ever ask you to do something extra, be sure to charge them for it."

I assured him that I absolutely would.

"If they can afford to live here, they can afford to pay. The bastards."

"Undoubtedly," I assured him again.

"And another thing," he added. "Don't let any of these girls shove any cat shit under your nose. That ain't your job. You tell them to put it in a bag and take it out themselves."

I reminded him that I knew very well my station in life, and that I was not about to haul cat shit or anything of that nature. He looked at me through his thick-lensed glasses. He looked like a cat himself. "That's right," he said at last. "And if they still try to sneak it in the trash be sure to make the bastards pay. They can afford it." He crushed his seventh butt on the floor and scattered the mess some more while he lit up another. "I never hauled out no cat shit in the thirty years I been here and you don't do it either."

"I'm going up to wash my hands," I said.

"Remember," he called after me, "don't take no shit from any of them."

I protested once more that, upon my life, I would never, never do it, not even for the prettiest girl in the building. Going up in the elevator, I felt comfortably resolved that I would never do it. There were no pretty girls in the building.

I never found out what he had done before he came there, but I do know that being a janitor in that building was as high as he ever got in life. He had watched two generations of the rich pass the building on their way to the Yard, and he had seen many governors ride white horses thirty times into that same Yard to send sons and daughters of the rich out into life to produce, to acquire, to procreate and to send back sons and daughters so that the cycle would continue. He had watched the cycle from when he had been able to haul the cans out for himself, and now he could not, and he was bitter.

He was Irish, of course, and he took pride in Irish accomplishments when he could have none of his own. He had known Frank O'Connor when that writer had been at Harvard. He told me on many occasions how O'Connor had stopped to talk every day on his way to the Yard. He had also known James Michael Curley, and his most colorful memory of the man was a long ago day when he and James Curley sat in a Boston bar and one of Curley's runners had come in and said: "Hey Jim, Sol Bernstein the Jew wants to see you."

And Curley, in his deep, memorial voice had said to James Sullivan: "Let us go forth and meet this Israelite Prince." These were his memories, and I would obediently put aside my garbage cans and laugh with him over the hundred or so colorful, insignificant little details which made up a whole lifetime of living in the basement of Harvard. And although they were of little value to me then, I knew that they were the reflections of a lifetime and the happiest moments he would ever have, being sold to me cheap, as youthful time is cheap, for as little time and interest as I wanted to spend. It was a buyer's market.

II

In those days I believed myself gifted with a boundless perception and attacked my daily garbage route with a gusto superenforced by the happy knowledge that behind each of the fifty or so doors in our building lived a story which could, if I chose to grace it with the magic of my pen, become immortal. I watched my tenants fanatically, noting their perversions, their visitors, and their eating habits. So intense was my search for material that I had to restrain myself from going through their refuse scrap by scrap; but at the topmost layers of muck, without too much hand-soiling in the process, I set my perceptions to work. By late June, however, I had discovered only enough to put together a skimpy, rather naïve Henry Miller novel. The most colorful discoveries being:

(1) The lady in #24 was an alumna of Paducah College.
(2) The couple in #55 made love at least five hundred times a week and the wife had not yet discovered the pill.
(3) The old lady in #36 was still having monthly inconvenience.
(4) The two fatsos in #56 consumed nightly an extraordinary amount of chili.
(5) The fat man in #54 had two dogs that were married to each other, but he was not married to anyone at all.
(6) The middle-aged single man in #63 threw out an awful lot of flowers.

Disturbed by the snail's progress I was making, I confessed my futility to James one day as he sat on his bench chain-smoking and smearing butts on my newly waxed lobby floor. "So you want to know about the tenants?" he said, his cat's eyes flickering over me.
I nodded.
"Well the first thing to notice is how many Jews there are."
"I haven't noticed many Jews," I said.
He eyed me in amazement.

"Well, a few," I said quickly to prevent my treasured perception from being dulled any further.

"A few, hell," he said. "There's more Jews here than anybody."

"How can you tell?"

He gave me that undecided look again. "Where do you think all that garbage comes from?" He nodded feebly toward my bulging cans. I looked just in time to prevent a stray noodle from slipping over the brim. "That's right," he continued. "Jews are the biggest eaters in the world. They eat the best too."

I confessed then that I was of the chicken-soup generation and believed that Jews ate only enough to muster strength for their daily trips to the bank.

"Not so!" he replied emphatically. "You never heard the expression: 'Let's get to the restaurant before the Jews get there'?"

I shook my head sadly.

"You don't know that in certain restaurants they take the free onions and pickles off the tables when they see Jews coming?"

I held my head down in shame over the bounteous heap.

He trudged over to my can and began to turn back the leaves of noodles and crumpled tissues from #47 with his hand. After a few seconds of digging he unmucked an empty paté can. "Look at that," he said triumphantly. "Gourmet stuff, no less."

"That's from #44," I said.

"What else?" he said all-knowingly. "In 1946 a Swedish girl moved in up there and took a Jewish girl for her roommate. Then the Swedish girl moved out and there's been a Jewish Dynasty up there ever since."

I recalled that #44 was occupied by a couple that threw out a good number of S. S. Pierce cans, Chivas Regal bottles, assorted broken records, and back issues of *Evergreen* and the *Realist*.

"You're right," I said.

"Of course," he replied as if there was never any doubt. "I can spot them anywhere, even when they think they're passing." He leaned closer and said in a you-and-me voice:

"But don't ever say aything bad about them in public, the Anti-Defamation League will get you."

Just then his wife screamed for him from the second floor, and the dog joined her and beat against the door. He got into the elevator painfully and said: "Don't ever talk about them in public. You don't know who they are and that Defamation League will take everything you got."

Sullivan did not really hate Jews. He was just bitter toward anyone better off than himself. He liked me because I seemed to like hauling garbage and because I listened to him and seemed to respect what he said and seemed to imply, by lingering on even when he repeated himself, that I was eager to take what wisdom he had for no other reason than that I needed it in order to get along.

He lived with his wife on the second floor and his apartment was very dirty because both of them were sick and old, and neither could move very well. His wife swept dirt out into the hall, and two hours after I had mopped and waxed their section of the floor, there was sure to be a layer of dirt, grease, and crushed-scattered tobacco from their door to the end of the hall. There was a smell of dogs and cats and age and death about their door, and I did not ever want to have to go in there for any reason because I feared something about it I cannot name.

Mrs. Sullivan, I found out, was from South Africa. She loved animals much more than people and there was a great deal of pain in her face. She kept little pans of meat posted at strategic points about the building, and I often came across her in the early morning or late at night throwing scraps out of the second-floor window to stray cats. Once, when James was about to throttle a stray mouse in their apartment, she had screamed at him to give the mouse a sporting chance. Whenever she attempted to walk she had to balance herself against a wall or a rail, and she hated the building because it confined her. She also hated James and most of the tenants. On the other hand, she loved the *Johnny Carson Show,* she loved to sit outside on the front steps (because she could get no further unassisted), and she loved to talk to anyone who would stop to listen. She never spoke coherently except when she was cursing James, and then she had a vocabulary like a sailor. She had great, shrill lungs, and her screams, accompanied by the rabid barks of the dog, could be heard all over the building. She was never really clean, her teeth were bad, and the first most pathetic thing in the world was to see her sitting on the steps in the morning watching the world pass, in a stained smock and a fresh summer blue hat she kept just to wear downstairs, with no place in the world to go. James told me, on the many occasions of her screaming, that she was mentally disturbed and could not control herself. The admirable thing about him was that he never lost his temper with her, no matter how rough her curses became and no matter who heard them. And the second most pathetic thing in the world was to see them slowly making their way in Harvard Square, he supporting her, through the hurrying crowds of mini-skirted summer girls, J-Pressed Ivy Leaguers, beatniks, and bused Japanese tourists, decked in cameras, who would take pictures of every inch of Harvard Square except them. Once, he told me, a hippie had brushed past them and called back over his shoulder: "Don't break any track records, Mr. and Mrs. Speedy Molasses."

Also on the second floor lived Miss O'Hara, a spinster who hated Sullivan as only an old maid can hate an old man. Across from her lived a very nice, gentle, celibate named Murphy who had once served with Montgomery in North Africa and who was now spending the rest of his life cleaning his little apartment and gossiping with Miss O'Hara. It was an Irish floor.

I never found out just why Miss O'Hara hated the Sullivans with such a passion. Perhaps it was because they were so unkempt and she was so superciliously clean. Perhaps it was because Miss O'Hara had a great deal of Irish pride and they were stereotyped Irish. Perhaps it was because she merely had no reason to like them. She was a fanatic about cleanliness and put out her little bit of garbage wrapped very neatly in yesterday's *Christian Science Monitor* and tied in a bow with a fresh piece of string. Collecting all those little neat packages, I would wonder where she got the string and imagined her at night picking meat-market locks with a hairpin and hobbling off with yards and yards of white cord concealed under the gray sweater she always wore. I could even imagine her back in her little apartment chuckling and rolling the cord into a great white ball by candlelight. Then she would stash it away in her breadbox. Miss O'Hara kept her door slightly open until late at night, and I suspected that she heard everything that went on in the building. I had the feeling that I should never dare to make love with gusto for fear that she would overhear and write down all my happy-time phrases, to be maliciously recounted to me if she were ever provoked.

She had been in the building longer than Sullivan, and I suppose that her greatest ambition in life was to outlive him and then attend his wake with a knitting ball and needles. She had been trying to get him fired for twenty-five years or so and did not know when to quit. On summer nights when I painfully mopped the second floor, she would offer me root beer, apples, or cupcakes while trying to pump me for evidence against him.

"He's just a filthy old man, Robert," she would declare in a little-old-lady whisper. "And don't think you have to clean up those dirty old butts of his. Just report him to the Company."

"Oh, I don't mind," I would tell her, gulping the root beer as fast as possible.

"Well, they're both a couple of lushes, if you ask me. They haven't been sober a day in twenty-five years."

"Well, she's sick too, you know."

"Ha!" She would throw up her hands in disgust. "She's only sick when he doesn't give her the booze."

I fought to keep down a burp. "How long have *you* been here?"

She motioned for me to step out of the hall and into her dark apartment. "Don't tell him,"—she nodded towards Sullivan's door—"but I've been here for thirty-four years." She waited for me to be taken aback. Then she added: "And it was a better building before those two lushes came."

She then offered me an apple, asked five times if the dog's barking bothered me, forced me to take a fudge brownie, said that the cats had wet the floor again last night, got me to dust the top of a large chest too high for her to reach, had me pick up the minute specks of dust which fell from my dustcloth, pressed another root beer on me, and then showed me her family album. As an afterthought, she had me take down a big old picture of her great-grandfather, also too high for her to reach, so that I could dust that too. Then together we picked up the dust from it which might have fallen to the floor. "He's really a filthy old man, Robert," she said in closing, "and don't be afraid to report him to the property manager any time you want."

I assured her that I would do it at the slightest provocation from Sullivan, finally accepted an apple but refused the money she offered, and escaped back to my mopping. Even then she watched me, smiling, from her half-opened door.

"Why does Miss O'Hara hate you?" I asked James once.

He lifted his cigaretted hand and let the long ash fall elegantly to the floor. "That old bitch has been an albatross around my neck ever since I got here," he said. "Don't trust her, Robert. It was her kind that sat around singing hymns and watching them burn saints in this state."

There was never an adequate answer to my question. And even though the dog was noisy and would surely kill someone if it ever got loose, no one could really dislike the old man because of it. The dog was all they had. In his garbage each night, for every wine bottle, there would be an equally empty can of dog food. Some nights he took the brute out for a long walk, when he could barely walk himself, and both of them had to be led back to the building.

III

In those days I had forgotten that I was first of all a black and I had a very lovely girl who was not first of all a black. We were both young and optimistic then, and she believed with me in my potential and liked me partly because of it; and I was happy because she belonged to me and not to the race, which made her special. It made me special too because I did not have to wear a beard or hate or be especially hip or ultra-Ivy Leaguish. I did not have to smoke pot or

supply her with it, or be for any other cause at all except myself. I
only had to be myself, which pleased me; and I only had to produce,
which pleased both of us. Like many of the artistically inclined rich,
she wanted to own in someone else what she could not own in
herself. But this I did not mind, and I forgave her for it because she
forgave me moods and the constant smell of garbage and a great deal
of latent hostility. She only minded James Sullivan and all the valuable time I was wasting listening to him rattle on and on. His conversations, she thought, were useless, repetitious, and promised nothing
of value to me. She was accustomed to the old-rich whose conversations meandered around a leitmotiv of how well off they were and
how much they would leave behind very soon. She was not at all
cold, but she had been taught how to tolerate the old-poor and perhaps toss them a greeting in passing. But nothing more.

Sullivan did not like her when I first introduced them because he
saw that she was not a hippie and could not be dismissed. It is in the
nature of things that liberal people will tolerate two interracial
hippies more than they will an intelligent, serious-minded mixed
couple. The former liaison is easy to dismiss as the dregs of both
races; but the latter poses a threat because there is no immediacy or
overpowering sensuality or "you-pick-my-fleas-I'll-pick-yours" apparent on the surface of things, and people, even the most publicly
liberal, cannot dismiss it so easily.

"That girl is Irish, isn't she?" he had asked one day in my apartment soon after I had introduced them.

"No," I said definitely.

"What's her name again?"

"Judy Smith," I said, which was not her name at all.

"Well, I can spot it," he said. "She's got Irish blood, all right."

"Everybody's got a little Irish blood," I told him.

He looked at me cattily and craftily from behind his thick lenses.
"Well, she's from a good family, I suppose."

"I suppose," I said.

He paused to let some ashes fall to the rug. "They say the Colonel's
Lady and Nelly O'Grady are sisters under the skin." Then he added:
"Rudyard Kipling."

"That's true," I said with equal innuendo, "that's why you have to
maintain a distinction by marrying the Colonel's Lady."

An understanding passed between us then, and we never spoke
more on the subject.

Almost every night the cats wet the second floor while Meg Sullivan watched the *Johnny Carson Show* and the dog howled and
clawed the door. During commercials Meg would curse James to get

out and stop dropping ashes on the floor or to take the dog out or
something else, totally unintelligible to those of us on the fourth,
fifth and sixth floors. Even after the *Carson Show* she would still
curse him to get out, until finally he would go down to the basement
and put away a bottle or two of wine. There was a steady stench of
cat functions in the basement, and with all the grease and dirt,
discarded trunks, beer bottles, chairs, old tools and the filthy sofa on
which he sometimes slept, seeing him there made me want to cry.
He drank the cheapest sherry, the wino kind, straight from the
bottle; and on many nights that summer at 2:00 A.M. my phone
would ring me out of bed.

"Rob? Jimmy Sullivan here. What are you doing?"

There was nothing suitable to say.

"Come on down to the basement for a drink."

"I have to be at work at eight-thirty," I would protest.

"Can't you have just one drink?" he would say pathetically.

I would carry down my own glass so that I would not have to
drink out of the bottle. Looking at him on the sofa, I could not be mad
because now I had many records for my stereo, a story that was
going well, a girl who believed in me and belonged to me and not
to the race, a new set of dishes, and a tomorrow morning with
younger people.

"I don't want to burden you unduly," he would always preface.

I would force myself not to look at my watch and say: "Of course
not."

"My Meg is not in the best health, you know," he would say,
handing the bottle to me.

"She's just old."

"The doctors say she should be in an institution."

"That's no place to be."

"I'm a sick man myself, Rob. I can't take much more. She's crazy."

"Anybody who loves animals can't be crazy."

He took another long draw from the bottle. "I won't live another
year. I'll be dead in a year."

"You don't know that."

He looked at me closely, without his glasses, so that I could see the
desperation in his eyes. "I just hope Meg goes before I do. I don't want
them to put her in an institution after I'm gone."

At 2:00 A.M. with the cat stench in my nose and a glass of bad
sherry standing still in my hand because I refused in my mind to
touch it, and when all my dreams of greatness were above him and
the basement and the building itself, I did not know what to say. The
only way I could keep from hating myself was to talk about the

AMA or the Medicare program or hippies. He was pure hell on all three. To him, the medical profession was "morally bankrupt," Medicare was a great farce which deprived oldsters like himself of their "rainy-day dollars," and hippies were "dropouts from the human race." He could rage on and on in perfect phrases about all three of his major dislikes, and I had the feeling that because the sentences were so well constructed and well turned, he might have memorized them from something he had read. But then he was extremely well read and it did not matter if he had borrowed a phrase or two from someone else. The ideas were still his own.

It would be 3:00 A.M. before I knew it, and then 3:30, and still he would go on. He hated politicians in general and liked to recount, at these times, his private catalogue of political observations. By the time he got around to Civil Rights it would be 4:00 A.M., and I could not feel sorry or responsible for him at that hour. I would begin to yawn and at first he would just ignore it. Then I would start to edge toward the door, and he would see that he could hold me no longer, not even by declaring that he wanted to be an honorary Negro because he loved the race so much.

"I hope I haven't burdened you unduly," he would say again.

"Of course not," I would say, because it was over then and I could leave him and the smell of the cats there and sometimes I would go out in the cool night and walk around the Yard and be thankful that I was only an assistant janitor, and a transient one at that. Walking in the early dawn and seeing the Summer School fellows sneak out of the girls' dormitories in the Yard gave me a good feeling, and I thought that tomorrow night it would be good to make love myself so that I could be busy when he called.

IV

"Why don't you tell that old man your job doesn't include baby-sitting with him?" Jean told me many times when she came over to visit during the day and found me sleeping.

I would look at her and think to myself about social forces and the pressures massing and poised, waiting to attack us. It was still July then. It was hot and I was working good. "He's just an old man," I said. "Who else would listen to him?"

"You're too soft. As long as you do your work you don't have to be bothered with him."

"He could be a story if I listened long enough."

"There are too many stories about old people."

"No," I said, thinking about us again, "there are just too many people who have no stories."

Sometimes he would come up and she would be there, but I would let him come in anyway, and he would stand in the room looking dirty and uncomfortable, offering some invented reason for having intruded. At these times something silent would pass between them, something I cannot name, which would reduce him to exactly what he was: an old man, come out of his basement to intrude where he was not wanted. But all the time this was being communicated, there would be a surface, friendly conversation between them. And after five minutes or so of being unwelcome, he would apologize for having come, drop a few ashes on the rug and back out the door. Downstairs we could hear his wife screaming.

We endured and aged and August was almost over. Inside the building the cats were still wetting, Meg was still screaming, the dog was getting madder, and Sullivan began to drink during the day. Outside it was hot and lush and green, and the summer girls were wearing shorter miniskirts and no panties and the middle-aged men down by the Charles were going wild on their bridge. Everyone was restless for change, for August is the month when undone summer things must be finished or regretted all through the winter.

V

Being imaginative people, Jean and I played a number of original games. One of them we called "Social Forces," the object of which was to see which side could break us first. We played it with the unknown nightriders who screamed obscenities from passing cars. And because that was her side I would look at her expectantly, but she would laugh and say: "No." We played it at parties with unaware blacks who attempted to enchant her with skillful dances and hip vocabulary, believing her to be community property. She would be polite and aloof, and much later, it then being my turn, she would look at me expectantly. And I would force a smile and say: "No." The last round was played while taking her home in a subway car, on a hot August night, when one side of the car was black and tense and hating and the other side was white and of the same mind. There was not enough room on either side for the two of us to sit and we would not separate; and so we stood, holding on to a steel post through all the stops, feeling all the eyes, between the two sides of the car and the two sides of the world. We aged. And, getting off finally at the stop which was no longer ours, we looked at each other, again expectantly, and there was nothing left to say.

I began to avoid the old man, would not answer the door when I knew it was he who was knocking, and waited until very late at night, when he could not possibly be awake, to haul the trash down.

I hated the building then; and I was really a janitor for the first time. I slept a lot and wrote very little. And I did not give a damn about Medicare, the AMA, the building, Meg or the crazy dog. I began to consider moving out.

In that same month, Miss O'Hara finally succeeded in badgering Murphy, the celibate Irishman, and a few other tenants into signing a complaint about the dog. No doubt Murphy signed because he was a nice fellow and women like Miss O'Hara had always dominated him. He did not really mind the dog: he did not really mind anything. She called him "Frank Dear," and I had the feeling that when he came to that place, fresh from Montgomery's Campaign, he must have had a will of his own; but she had drained it all away, year by year, so that now he would do anything just to be agreeable.

One day soon after the complaint, the Property Manager came around to tell Sullivan that the dog had to be taken away. Miss O'Hara told me the good news later, when she finally got around to my door.

"Well, that crazy dog is gone now, Robert. Those two are enough."

"Where is the dog?" I asked.

"I don't know, but Albert Rustin made them get him out. You should have seen the old drunk's face," she said. "That dirty useless old man."

"You should be at peace now," I said.

"Almost," was her reply. "The best thing would be to get rid of those two old boozers along with the dog."

I congratulated Miss O'Hara again and then went out. I knew that the old man would be drinking and would want to talk. I did not want to talk. But very late that evening he called on the telephone and caught me in.

"Rob?" he said. "James Sullivan here. Would you come down to my apartment like a good fellow? I want to ask you something important."

I had never been in his apartment before and did not want to go then. But I went down anyway.

They had three rooms, all grimy from corner to corner. There was a peculiar odor in that place I did not want to ever smell again, and his wife was dragging herself around the room talking in mumbles. When she saw me come in the door, she said: "I can't clean it up. I just can't. Look at that window. I can't reach it. I can't keep it clean." She threw up both her hands and held her head down and to the side. "The whole place is dirty and I can't clean it up."

"What do you want?" I said to Sullivan.

"Sit down." He motioned me to a kitchen chair. "Have you changed that bulb on the fifth floor?"

"It's done."

He was silent for a while, drinking from a bottle of sherry, and he offered me some and a dirty glass. "You're the first person who's been in here in years," he said. "We couldn't have company because of the dog."

Somewhere in my mind was a note that I should never go into his apartment. But the dog had not been the reason. "Well, he's gone now," I said, fingering the dirty glass of sherry.

He began to cry. "They took my dog away," he said. "It was all I had. How can they take a man's dog away from him?"

There was nothing I could say.

"I couldn't do nothing," he continued. After a while he added: "But I know who it was. It was that old bitch O'Hara. Don't ever trust her, Rob. She smiles in your face but it was her kind that laughed when they burned Joan of Arc in this state."

Seeing him there, crying and making me feel unmanly because I wanted to touch him or say something warm, also made me eager to be far away and running hard. "Everybody's got problems," I said. "I don't have a girl now."

He brightened immediately, and for a while he looked almost happy in his old cat's eyes. Then he staggered over to my chair and held out his hand. I did not touch it, and he finally pulled it back. "I know how you feel," he said. "I know just how you feel."

"Sure," I said.

"But you're a young man, you have a future. But not me. I'll be dead inside of a year."

Just then his wife dragged in to offer me a cigar. They were being hospitable and I forced myself to drink a little of the sherry.

"They took my dog away today," she mumbled. "That's all I had in the world, my dog."

I looked at the old man. He was drinking from the bottle.

VI

During the first week of September one of the middle-aged men down by the Charles got tired of looking and tried to take a necking girl away from her boyfriend. The police hauled him off to jail, and the girl pulled down her dress tearfully. A few days later another man exposed himself near the same spot. And that same week a dead body was found on the banks of the Charles.

The miniskirted brigade had moved out of the Yard and it was quiet and green and peaceful there. In our building another Jewish couple moved into #44. They did not eat gourmet stuff and, on occasion, threw out pork-and-beans cans. But I had lost interest in perception. I now had many records for my stereo, loads of S. S. Pierce stuff, and a small bottle of Chivas Regal which I never opened. I was working good again and did not miss other things as much; or at least I told myself that.

The old man was coming up steadily now, at least three times a day, and I had resigned myself to it. If I refused to let him in he would always come back later with a missing bulb on the fifth floor. We had taken to buying cases of beer together, and when he had finished his half, which was very frequently, he would come up to polish off mine. I began to enjoy talking about politics, the AMA, Medicare, and hippies, and listening to him recite from books he had read. I discovered that he was very well read in history, philosophy, literature and law. He was extraordinarily fond of saying: "I am really a cut above being a building superintendent. Circumstances made me what I am." And even though he was drunk and dirty and it was very late at night, I believed him and liked him anyway because having him there was much better than being alone. After he had gone I could sleep and I was not lonely in sleep; and it did not really matter how late I was at work the next morning, because when I really thought about it all, I discovered that nothing really matters except not being old and being alive and having potential to dream about, and not being alone.

Whenever I passed his wife on the steps she would say: "That no-good bastard let them take my dog away." And whenever her husband complained that he was sick she said. "That's good for him. He took my dog away."

Sullivan slept in the basement on the sofa almost every night because his wife would think about the dog after the *Carson Show* and blame him for letting it be taken away. He told her, and then me, that the dog was on a farm in New Hampshire; but that was unlikely because the dog had been near mad, and it did not appease her. It was nearing autumn and she was getting violent. Her screams could be heard for hours through the halls and I knew that beyond her quiet door Miss O'Hara was plotting again. Sullivan now had little cuts and bruises on his face and hands, and one day he said: "Meg is like an albatross around my neck. I wish she was dead. I'm sick myself and I can't take much more. She blames me for the dog and I couldn't help it."

"Why don't you take her out to see the dog?" I said.

"I couldn't help it Rob," he went on. "I'm old and I couldn't help it."

"You ought to just get her out of here for a while."

He looked at me, drunk as usual. "Where would we go? We can't even get past the Square."

There was nothing left to say.

"Honest to God, I couldn't help it," he said. He was not saying it to me.

That night I wrote a letter from a mythical New Hampshire farmer telling them that the dog was very fine and missed them a great deal because he kept trying to run off. I said that the children and all the other dogs liked him and that he was not vicious any more. I wrote that the open air was doing him a lot of good and added that they should feel absolutely free to come up to visit the dog at any time. That same night I gave him the letter.

One evening, some days later, I asked him about it.

"I tried to mail it, I really tried," he said.

"What happened?"

"I went down to the Square and looked for cars with New Hampshire license plates. But I never found anybody."

"That wasn't even necessary, was it?"

"It had to have a New Hampshire postmark. You don't know my Meg."

"Listen," I said. "I have a friend who goes up there. Give me the letter and I'll have him mail it."

He held his head down. "I'll tell you the truth. I carried that letter in my pocket so much it got ragged and dirty and I got tired of carrying it. I finally just tore it up."

Neither one of us said anything for a while.

"If I could have sent it off it would have helped some," he said at last. "I know it would have helped."

"Sure," I said.

"I wouldn't have to ask anybody if I had my strength."

"I know."

"If I had my strength I would have mailed it myself."

"I know," I said.

That night we both drank from his bottle of sherry and it did not matter at all that I did not provide my own glass.

VII

In late September the Cambridge police finally picked up the bearded pot-pusher in the Square. He had been in a restaurant all summer, at the same table, with the same customers flocking around him; but now that summer was over, they picked him up. The leaves were changing. In the early evening students passed the building and Meg, blue-hatted and waiting on the steps, carrying sofas and chairs and coffee tables to their suites in the Houses. Down by the Charles the middle-aged men were catching the last phases of sum-

mer sensuality before the grass grew cold and damp, and before the
young would be forced indoors to play. I wondered what those
hungry, spying men did in the winter or at night when it was too
dark to see. Perhaps, I thought, they just stood there and listened.

In our building Miss O'Hara was still listening. She had never
stopped. When Meg was outside on the steps it was very quiet and
I felt good that Miss O'Hara had to wait a long, long time before she
heard anything. The company gave the halls and ceilings a new coat
of paint, but it was still old in the building. James Sullivan got his
yearly two-week vacation and they went to the Boston Common for
six hours: two hours going, two hours sitting on the benches, and
two hours coming back. Then they both sat on the steps, watching,
and waiting.

At first I wanted to be kind because he was old and dying in a
special way and I was young and ambitious. But at night, in my
apartment, when I heard his dragging feet in the hall outside and
knew that he would be drunk and repetitious and imposing on my
privacy, I did not want to be kind any more. There were girls outside
and I knew that I could have one now because that desperate look
had finally gone somewhere deep inside. I was young and now I did
not want to be bothered.

"Did you read about the lousy twelve per cent Social Security
increase those bastards in Washington gave us?"

"No."

He would force himself past me, trying to block the door with my
body, and into the room. "When those old pricks tell me to count my
blessings, I tell them, 'You're not one of them.'" He would seat
himself at the table without meeting my eyes. "The cost of living's
gone up more than twelve per cent in the last six months."

"I know."

"What unmitigated bastards."

I would try to be busy with something on my desk.

"But the Texas Oil Barons got another depletion allowance."

"They can afford to bribe politicians," I would mumble.

"They tax away our rainy-day dollars and give us a lousy twelve
per cent."

"It's tough."

He would know that I did not want to hear any more and he would
know that he was making a burden of himself. It made me feel bad
that it was so obvious to him, but I could not help myself. It made
me feel bad that I disliked him more every time I heard a girl laugh
on the street far below my window. So I would nod occasionally and
say half-phrases and smile slightly at something witty he was saying for the third time. If I did not offer him a drink he would go

sooner and so I gave him Coke when he hinted at how dry he was. Then, when he had finally gone, saying, "I hope I haven't burdened you unduly," I went to bed and hated myself.

VIII

If I am a janitor it is either because I have to be a janitor or because I want to be a janitor. And if I do not have to do it, and if I no longer want to do it, the easiest thing in the world, for a young man, is to step up to something else. Any move away from it is a step up because there is no job more demeaning than that of a janitor. One day I made myself suddenly realize that the three dirty cans would never contain anything of value to me, unless, of course, I decided to gather material for Harold Robbins or freelance for the *Realist*. Neither alternative appealed to me.

Toward dawn one day, during the first part of October, I rented a U-Haul truck and took away two loads of things I had accumulated. The records I packed very carefully, and the stereo I placed on the front seat of the truck beside me. I slipped the Chivas Regal and a picture of Jean under some clothes in a trunk I will not open for a long time. And I left the rug on the floor because it was dirty and too large for my new apartment. I also left the two plates given to me by James Sullivan, for no reason at all. Sometimes I want to go back to get them, but I do not know how to ask for them or explain why I left them in the first place. But sometimes at night, when there is a sleeping girl beside me, I think that I cannot have them again because I am still young and do not want to go back into that building.

I saw him once in the Square walking along very slowly with two shopping bags, and they seemed very heavy. As I came up behind him I saw him put them down and exercise his arms while the crowd moved in two streams around him. I had an instant impulse to offer help and I was close enough to touch him before I stopped. I will never know why I stopped. And after a few seconds of standing behind him and knowing that he was not aware of anything at all except the two heavy bags waiting to be lifted after his arms were sufficiently rested, I moved back into the stream of people which passed on the left of him. I never looked back.

Bernard Malamud

(b. 1914)

Bernard Malamud is a leading figure among the many Jewish writers who have made a significant contribution to the literature of North America. He was born and raised in Brooklyn, received his education at the City College of New York and Columbia University, and taught English for nine years in New York high schools. After a period at Oregon State University, he moved to Bennington College, Vermont, in 1961. His first novel, *The Natural,* was published in 1952, and since then he has produced five more novels and three collections of short stories; he has won two National Book Awards, and received a Pulitzer Prize for his novel *The Fixer* (1966), which was made into a film in 1968.

Malamud's appeal lies in the universality of his Jewish heroes and their sufferings; in Jewish character and tradition, he finds apt metaphors for his vision of the plight of humanity. Much of his work deals with man's sense of guilt and his search for redemption—issues which have obvious significance for an America wracked by self-doubt, and yearning to recover its heroic self-image. Beset by uncertainty and bewilderment, Malamud's characters struggle toward some form of affirmation, trying to find a relationship with another human being which will give meaning to their own existence. For the most part, they fail; their search for fulfillment is frustrated by their own inadequacies, or else they are trapped within their social role, like Nat Lime in "Black Is My Favorite Color" (from *Idiots First,* 1963), and unable to escape inherited values and attitudes. Yet even as they fail, Malamud's characters achieve a sort of helpless nobility, a dignity which in itself is a kind of affirmation.

For further reading

Leslie A. Field and Joyce W. Field, eds., *Bernard Malamud and the Critics* (New York: New York University Press, 1970).

Charles A. Hoyt, "Bernard Malamud and the New Romanticism," in *Contemporary American Novelists,* ed. Harry T. Moore (Carbondale, Ill., Southern Illinois University Press, 1964), pp. 65–79.

Sidney Richman, *Bernard Malamud* (New York: Twayne, 1966).

Black Is My Favorite Color

Charity Sweetness sits in the toilet eating her two hardboiled eggs while I'm having my ham sandwich and coffee in the kitchen. That's how it goes only don't get the idea of ghettoes. If there's a ghetto I'm the one that's in it. She's my cleaning woman from Father Divine and comes in once a week to my small three-room apartment on my day off from the liquor store. "Peace," she says to me, "Father reached on down and took me right up in Heaven." She's a small person with a flat body, frizzy hair, and a quiet face that the light shines out of, and Mama had such eyes before she died. The first time Charity Sweetness came in to clean, a little more than a year and a half, I made the mistake to ask her to sit down at the kitchen table with me and eat her lunch. I was still feeling not so hot after Ornita left but I'm the kind of a man—Nat Lime, forty-four, a bachelor with a daily growing bald spot on the back of my head, and I could lose frankly fifteen pounds—who enjoys company so long as he has it. So she cooked up her two hardboiled eggs and sat down and took a small bite out of one of them. But after a minute she stopped chewing and she got up and carried the eggs in a cup in the bathroom, and since then she eats there. I said to her more than once, "Okay, Charity Sweetness, so have it your way, eat the eggs in the kitchen by yourself and I'll eat when you're done," but she smiles absent-minded, and eats in the toilet. It's my fate with colored people.

Although black is still my favorite color you wouldn't know it from my luck except in short quantities even though I do all right in the liquor store business in Harlem, on Eighth Avenue between 110th and 111th. I speak with respect. A large part of my life I've had dealings with Negro people, most on a business basis but sometimes for friendly reasons with genuine feeling on both sides. I'm drawn to them. At this time of my life I should have one or two good colored friends but the fault isn't necessarily mine. If they knew what was in my heart towards them, but how can you tell that to anybody nowadays? I've tried more than once but the language of the heart either is a dead language or else nobody understands it the way you speak it. Very few. What I'm saying is, personally for me there's only one human color and that's the color of blood. I like a black person if not because he's black, then because I'm white. It comes to the same thing. If I wasn't white my first choice would be black. I'm satisfied to be white because I have no other choice. Anyway, I got an eye for color. I appreciate. Who wants everybody to be the same? Maybe it's like some kind of a talent. Nat Lime might be a liquor dealer in Harlem, but once in the jungle in New Guinea in the Second War, I got the idea when I shot at a running Jap and missed him, that I had some kind of a talent, though maybe it's the kind where you have a marvelous idea now and then but in the end what do they come to? After all, it's a strange world.

Where Charity Sweetness eats her eggs makes me think about Buster Wilson when we were both boys in the Williamsburg section of Brooklyn. There was this long block of run-down dirty frame houses in the middle of a not-so-hot white neighborhood full of pushcarts. The Negro houses looked to me like they had been born and died there, dead not long after the beginning of the world. I lived on the next street. My father was a cutter with arthritis in both hands, big red knuckles and swollen fingers so he didn't cut, and my mother was the one who went to work. She sold paper bags from a second-hand pushcart in Ellery Street. We didn't starve but nobody ate chicken unless we were sick or the chicken was. This was my first acquaintance with a lot of black people and I used to poke around on their poor block. I think I thought, brother, if there can be like this, what can't there be? I mean I caught an early idea what life was about. Anyway I met Buster Wilson there. He used to play marbles by himself. I sat on the curb across the street, watching him shoot one marble lefty and the other one righty. The hand that won picked up the marbles. It wasn't so much of a game but he didn't ask me to come over. My idea was to be friendly, only he never encouraged, he discouraged. Why did I pick him out for a friend? Maybe because I had no others then, we were new in the neighborhood, from Manhattan. Also I liked his type. Buster did everything alone. He was a skinny kid and his brothers' clothes hung on him like worn-out potato sacks. He was a beanpole boy, about twelve, and I was then ten. His arms and legs were burnt out matchsticks. He always wore a brown wool sweater, one arm half unraveled, the other went down to the wrist. His long and narrow head had a white part cut straight in the short woolly hair, maybe with a ruler there, by his father, a barber but too drunk to stay a barber. In those days though I had little myself I was old enough to know who was better off, and the whole block of colored houses made me feel bad in the daylight. But I went there as much as I could because the street was full of life. In the night it looked different, it's hard to tell a cripple in the dark. Sometimes I was afraid to walk by the houses when they were dark and quiet. I was afraid there were people looking at me that I couldn't see. I liked it better when they had parties at night and everybody had a good time. The musicians played their banjos and saxophones and the houses shook with the music and laughing. The young girls, with their pretty dresses and ribbons in their hair, caught me in my throat when I saw them through the windows.

But with the parties came drinking and fights. Sundays were bad days after the Saturday night parties. I remember once that Buster's father, also long and loose, always wearing a dirty gray Homburg hat, chased another black man in the street with a half-inch chisel. The other one, maybe five feet high, lost his shoe and when they wrestled on the ground he was already bleeding through his suit, a thick red blood smearing the sidewalk. I was frightened by the blood and wanted to pour it back in the man who was bleeding from the chisel. On another time Buster's father was playing in a crap game with two big bouncy red dice, in the back of an alley between two middle houses. Then about six men started fist-fighting there, and they ran out of the alley and hit each other in the street. The neighbors, including children, came out and watched, everybody afraid but nobody moving to do anything. I saw the same thing near my store in Harlem, years later, a big crowd watching two men in the street, their breaths hanging in the air on a winter night, murdering each other with switch knives, but nobody moved to call a cop. I didn't either. Anyway, I was just a young kid but I still remember how the cops drove up in a police paddy wagon and broke up the fight by hitting everybody they could hit with big nightsticks. This was in the days before LaGuardia. Most of the fighters were knocked out cold, only one or two got away. Buster's father started to run back in his house but a cop ran after him and cracked him on his Homburg hat with a club, right on the front porch. Then the Negro men were lifted up by the cops, one at the arms and the other at the feet, and they heaved them in the paddy wagon. Buster's father hit the back of the wagon and fell, with his nose spouting very red blood, on top of three other men. I personally couldn't stand it, I was scared of the human race so I ran home, but I remember Buster watching without any expression in his eyes. I stole an extra fifteen cents from my mother's pocketbook and I ran back and asked Buster if he wanted to go the movies. I would pay. He said yes. This was the first time he talked to me.

So we went more than once to the movies. But we never got to be friends. Maybe because it was a one-way proposition—from me to him. Which includes my invitations to go with me, my (poor mother's) movie money, Hershey chocolate bars, watermelon slices, even my best Nick Carter and Merriwell books that I spent hours picking up in the junk shops, and that he never gave me back. Once he let me go in his house to get a match so we could smoke some butts we found, but it smelled so heavy, so impossible, I died till I got out of there. What I saw in the way of furniture I won't mention—the best was falling apart in pieces. Maybe we went to the movies all together five or six matinees that spring and in the summertime, but when the shows were over he usually walked home by himself.

"Why don't you wait for me, Buster?" I said. "We're both going in the same direction."

But he was walking ahead and didn't hear me. Anyway he didn't answer.

One day when I wasn't expecting it he hit me in the teeth. I felt like crying but not because of the pain. I spit blood and said, "What did you hit me for? What did I do to you?"

"Because you a Jew bastard. Take your Jew movies and your Jew candy and shove them up your Jew ass."

And he ran away.

I thought to myself how was I to know he didn't like the movies. When I was a man I thought, you can't force it.

Years later, in the prime of my life, I met Mrs. Ornita Harris. She was standing by herself under an open umbrella at the bus stop, crosstown 110th, and I picked up her green glove that she had dropped on the wet sidewalk. It was in the end of November. Before I could ask her was it hers, she grabbed the glove out of my hand, closed her umbrella, and stepped in the bus. I got on right after her.

I was annoyed so I said, "If you'll pardon me, Miss, there's no law that you have to say thanks, but at least don't make a criminal out of me."

"Well, I'm sorry," she said, "but I don't like white men trying to do me favors."

I tipped my hat and that was that. In ten minutes I got off the bus but she was already gone.

Who expected to see her again but I did. She came into my store about a week later for a bottle of scotch.

"I would offer you a discount," I told her, "but I know you don't like a certain kind of a favor and I'm not looking for a slap in the face."

Then she recognized me and got a little embarrassed.

"I'm sorry I misunderstood you that day."

"So mistakes happen."

The result was she took the discount. I gave her a dollar off.

She used to come in about every two weeks for a fifth of Haig and Haig. Sometimes I waited on her, sometimes my helpers, Jimmy or Mason, also colored, but I said to give the discount. They both looked at me but I had nothing to be ashamed. In the spring when she came in we used to talk once in a while. She was a slim woman, dark but not the most dark, about thirty years I would say, also well built, with a combination nice legs and a good-size bosom that I like. Her face was pretty, with big eyes and high cheek bones, but lips a little thick and nose a little broad. Sometimes she didn't feel like talking, she paid for the bottle, less discount, and walked out. Her eyes were tired and she didn't look to me like a happy woman.

I found out her husband was once a window cleaner on the big buildings, but one day his safety belt broke and he fell fifteen stories. After the funeral she got a job as a manicurist in a Times Square barber shop. I told her I was a bachelor and lived with my mother in a small three-room apartment on West Eighty-third near Broadway. My mother had cancer, and Ornita said she was very sorry.

One night in July we went out together. How that happened I'm still not so sure. I guess I asked her and she didn't say no. Where do you go out with a Negro woman? We went to the Village. We had a good dinner and walked in Washington Square Park. It was a hot night. Nobody was surprised when they saw us, nobody looked at us like we were against the law. If they looked maybe they saw my new lightweight suit that I bought yesterday and my shiny bald spot when we walked under a lamp, also how pretty she was for a man of my type. We went in a movie on West Eighth Street. I didn't want to go in but she said she had heard about the picture. We went in like strangers and we came out like strangers. I wondered what was in her mind and I thought to myself, whatever is in there it's not a certain white man that I know. All night long we went together like we were chained. After the movie she wouldn't let me take her back to Harlem. When I put her in a taxi she asked me, "Why did we bother?"

For the steak, I wanted to say. Instead I said, "You're worth the bother."

"Thanks anyway."

Kiddo, I thought to myself after the taxi left, you just found out what's what, now the best thing is forget her.

It's easy to say. In August we went out the second time. That was the night she wore a purple dress and I thought to myself, my God, what colors. Who paints that picture paints a masterpiece. Everybody looked at us but I had pleasure. That night when she took off her dress it was in a furnished room I had the sense to rent a few days before. With my sick mother, I couldn't ask her to come to my apartment, and she didn't want me to go home with her where she lived with her brother's family on West 115th near Lenox Avenue. Under her purple dress she wore a black slip, and when she took that off she had white underwear. When she took off the white underwear she was black again. But I know where the next white was, if you want to call it white. And that was the night I think I fell in love with her, the first time in my life though I have liked one or two nice girls I used to go with when I was a boy. It was a serious proposition. I'm the kind of a man when I think of love I'm thinking of marriage. I guess that's why I am a bachelor.

That same week I had a holdup in my place, two big men—both black—with revolvers. One got excited when I rang open the cash register so he could take the money and he hit me over the ear with his gun. I stayed in the hospital a couple of weeks. Otherwise I was insured. Ornita came to see me. She sat on a chair without talking much. Finally I saw she was uncomfortable so I suggested she ought to go home.

"I'm sorry it happened," she said.

"Don't talk like it's your fault."

When I got out of the hospital my mother was dead. She was a wonderful person. My father died when I was thirteen and all by herself she kept the family alive and together. I sat shive* for a week and remembered how she sold paper bags on her pushcart. I remembered her life and what she tried to teach me. Nathan, she said, if you ever forget you are a Jew a goy will remind you. Mama, I said, rest in peace on this subject. But if I do something you don't like, remember, on earth it's harder than where you are. Then when my week of mourning was finished, one night I said, "Ornita, let's get married. We're both honest people and if you love me like I love you it won't be such a bad time. If you don't like New York I'll sell out here and we'll move someplace else. Maybe to San Francisco where nobody knows us. I was there for a week in the Second War and I saw white and colored living together.

"Nat," she answered me, "I like you but I'd be afraid. My husband woulda killed me."

"Your husband is dead."

"Not in my memory."

"In that case I'll wait."

"Do you know what it'd be like—I mean the life we could expect?"

"Ornita," I said, "I'm the kind of a man, if he picks his own way of life he's satisfied."

"What about children? Were you looking forward to half-Jewish polka dots?"

"I was looking forward to children."

"I can't," she said.

Can't is can't. I saw she was afraid and the best thing was not to push. Sometimes when we met she was so nervous that whatever we did she couldn't enjoy it. At the same time I still thought I had a chance. We were together more and more. I got rid of my furnished room and she came to my apartment—I gave away Mama's bed and bought a new one. She stayed with me all day on Sundays. When she wasn't so nervous she was affectionate, and if I know what love is, I had it. We went out a couple of times a week, the same way— usually I met her in Times Square and sent her home in a taxi, but I talked more about marriage and she talked less against it. One night she told me she was still trying to convince herself but she was almost convinced. I took an inventory of my liquor stock so I could put the store up for sale.

*shive = mourning period.

Ornita knew what I was doing. One day she quit her job, the next she took it back. She also went away a week to visit her sister in Philadelphia for a little rest. She came back tired but said maybe. Maybe is maybe so I'll wait. The way she said it it was closer to yes. That was the winter two years ago. When she was in Philadelphia I called up a friend of mine from the Army, now a CPA, and told him I would appreciate an invitation for an evening. He knew why. His wife said yes right away. When Ornita came back we went there. The wife made a fine dinner. It wasn't a bad time and they told us to come again. Ornita had a few drinks. She looked relaxed, wonderful. Later, because of a twenty-four hour taxi strike I had to take her home on the subway. When we got to the 116th Street station she told me to stay on the train, and she would walk the couple of blocks to her house. I didn't like a woman walking alone on the streets at that time of the night. She said she never had any trouble but I insisted nothing doing. I said I would walk to her stoop with her and when she went upstairs I would go back to the subway.

On the way there, on 115th in the middle of the block before Lenox, we were stopped by three men—maybe they were boys. One had a black hat with a half-inch brim, one a green cloth hat, and the third wore a black leather cap. The green hat was wearing a short coat and the other two had long ones. It was under a street light but the leather cap snapped a six-inch switchblade open in the light.

"What you doin' with this white son of a bitch?" he said to Ornita.

"I'm minding my own business," she answered him, "and I wish you would too."

"Boys," I said, "we're all brothers. I'm a reliable merchant in the neighborhood. This young lady is my dear friend. We don't want any trouble. Please let us pass."

"You talk like a Jew landlord," said the green hat. "Fifty a week for a single room."

"No charge fo' the rats," said the half-inch brim.

"Believe me, I'm no landlord. My store is 'Nathan's Liquors' between Hundred Tenth and Eleventh. I also have two colored clerks, Mason and Jimmy, and they will tell you I pay good wages as well as I give discounts to certain customers."

"Shut your mouth, Jewboy," said the leather cap, and he moved the knife back and forth in front of my coat button. "No more black pussy for you."

"Speak with respect about this lady, please."

I got slapped on my mouth.

"That ain't no lady," said the long face in the half-inch brim, "that's black pussy. She deserve to have evvy bit of her hair shave off. How you like to have evvy bit of your hair shave off, black pussy?"

"Please leave me and this gentleman alone or I'm gonna scream long and loud. That's my house three doors down."

They slapped her. I never heard such a scream. Like her husband was falling fifteen stories.

I hit the one that slapped her and the next I knew I was laying in the gutter with a pain in my head. I thought, goodbye, Nat, they'll stab me for sure, but all they did was take my wallet and run in three different directions.

Ornita walked back with me to the subway and she wouldn't let me go home with her again.

"Just get home safely."

She looked terrible. Her face was gray and I still remembered her scream. It was a terrible winter night, very cold February, and it took me an hour and ten minutes to get home. I felt bad for leaving her but what could I do?

We had a date downtown the next night but she didn't show up, the first time.

In the morning I called her in her place of business.

"For God's sake, Ornita, if we got married and moved away we wouldn't have that kind of trouble that we had. We wouldn't come in that neighborhood any more."

"Yes, we would. I have family there and don't want to move anyplace else. The truth of it is I can't marry you, Nat. I got troubles enough of my own."

"I coulda sworn you love me."

"Maybe I do but I can't marry you."

"For God's sake, why?"

"I got enough trouble of my own."

I went that night in a cab to her brother's house to see her. He was a quiet man with a thin mustache. "She gone," he said, "left for a long visit to some close relatives in the South. She said to tell you she appreciate your intentions but didn't think it will work out."

"Thank you kindly," I said.

Don't ask me how I got home.

Once on Eighth Avenue, a couple of blocks from my store, I saw a blind man with a white cane tapping on the sidewalk. I figured we were going in the same direction so I took his arm.

"I can tell you're white," he said.

A heavy colored woman with a full shopping bag rushed after us.

"Never mind," she said, "I know where he live."

She pushed me with her shoulder and I hurt my leg on the fire hydrant.

That's how it is. I give my heart and they kick me in my teeth.

"Charity Sweetness—you hear me?—come out of that goddamn toilet!"

Katherine Mansfield

(1888–1923)

The third of five children of a prosperous New Zealand businessman who was later knighted for his financial services to his country, Katherine Mansfield—born Kathleen Beauchamp—bears some resemblance to the character "Kezia" in several of her stories. She grew up in rural Karori, near Wellington, and reportedly sought to break down the social barriers that stood between the Beauchamp children and the daughters of a local washerwoman whose name was McKelvey; the place and the names suggest an obvious source for the experience dramatized in "The Doll's House." Rejecting much of the provincialism she saw in New Zealand life, Mansfield left for England in 1903. After studying at Queen's College, London, where she met her lifelong friend "L. M." (Ida Baker), she went briefly back to New Zealand; but by 1908 she was again in England, living what was thought of as a bohemian life, and starting to write the deft vignettes with which she established her reputation.

Her stories, often compared with those of Chekhov, introduced into English a sharpness of detail and a spareness of style that were quite remarkable. She spurned elaborate plots and focused instead on the illuminating impact that single moments can have on the minds of individual human beings. She published in an innovative little magazine, *Rhythm,* which was edited by John Middleton Murry (whom she married in 1918), and her short stories were collected in several volumes. Of these, *Bliss* (1920), *The Garden Party* (1922), and the posthumous *The Doves' Nest* (1923) are the most important. In a contemporary review, the poet Walter de la Mare wrote of her work: "The pitch of mind is invariably emotional, the poise lyrical. None the less that mind is absolutely tranquil and attentive in its intellectual grasp of the matter in hand. And through all, Miss Mansfield's personality, whatever its disguises, haunts her work just as its customary inmate may haunt a vacant room, its *genius* a place." The personality was one which was both fed and desolated by isolation, one which was always reaching for freedom and an evanescent beauty and increasingly searching for order and harmony. It was perhaps that desire which sent her in vain to the Gurdjieff Institute in Paris for a cure for her tuberculosis in 1922; certainly it was the impulse behind her writing, and it gave her work its muted tones.

For further reading

Antony Alpers, *Katherine Mansfield* (London: Cape, 1954).

Ida Baker, *Katherine Mansfield: The Memories of L. M.* (London: Michael Joseph, 1971).

George S. Hubbell, "Katherine Mansfield and Kezia," *Sewanee Review,* 25 (1927), 325–335.

The Doll's House

When dear old Mrs. Hay went back to town after staying with the Burnells she sent the children a doll's house. It was so big that the carter and Pat carried it into the courtyard, and there it stayed, propped up on two wooden boxes beside the feed-room door. No harm could come to it; it was summer. And perhaps the smell of paint would have gone off by the time it had to be taken in. For, really, the smell of paint coming from that doll's house ("Sweet of old Mrs. Hay, of course; most sweet and generous!")—but the smell of paint was quite enough to make anyone seriously ill, in Aunt Beryl's opinion. Even before the sacking was taken off. And when it was. . . .

There stood the doll's house, a dark, oily, spinach green, picked out with bright yellow. Its two solid little chimneys, glued on to the roof, were painted red and white, and the door, gleaming with yellow varnish, was like a little slab of toffee. Four windows, real windows, were divided into panes by a broad streak of green. There was actually a tiny porch, too, painted yellow, with big lumps of congealed paint hanging along the edge.

But perfect, perfect little house! Who could possibly mind the smell. It was part of the joy, part of the newness.

"Open it quickly, someone!"

The hook at the side was stuck fast. Pat prised it open with his penknife, and the whole house front swung back, and—there you were, gazing at one and the same moment into the drawing-room and dining-room, the kitchen and two bedrooms. That is the way for a house to open! Why don't all houses open like that? How much more exciting than peering through the slit of a door into a mean little hall with a hat-stand and two umbrellas! That is—isn't it?— what you long to know about a house when you put your hand on the knocker. Perhaps it is the way God opens houses at the dead of night when He is taking a quiet turn with an angel. . . .

"Oh-oh!" The Burnell children sounded as though they were in despair. It was too marvellous; it was too much for them. They had never seen anything like it in their lives. All the rooms were papered. There were pictures on the walls, painted on the paper, with gold frames complete. Red carpet covered all the floors except the kitchen; red plush chairs in the drawing-room, green in the dining-room; tables, beds with real bedlcothes, a cradle, a stove, a dresser with tiny plates and one big jug. But what Kezia liked more than anything, what she liked frightfully, was the lamp. It stood in the middle of the dining-room table, an exquisite little amber lamp with a white globe. It was even filled all ready for lighting, though, of course, you couldn't light it. But there was something inside that looked like oil and moved when you shook it.

The father and mother dolls, who sprawled very still as though they had fainted in the drawing-room, and their two little children asleep upstairs, were really too big for the doll's house. They didn't look as though they belonged. But the lamp was perfect. It seemed to smile at Kezia, to say "I live here." The lamp was real.

The Burnell children could hardly walk to school fast enough the next morning. They burned to tell everybody, to describe, to—well —to boast about their doll's house before the schoolbell rang.

"I'm to tell," said Isabel, "because I'm the eldest. And you two can join in after. But I'm to tell first."

There was nothing to answer. Isabel was bossy, but she was always right, and Lottie and Kezia knew too well the powers that went with being eldest. They brushed through the thick buttercups at the road edge and said nothing.

"And I'm to choose who's to come and see it first. Mother said I might."

For it had been arranged that while the doll's house stood in the courtyard they might ask the girls at school, two at a time, to come and look. Not to stay to tea, of course, or to come traipsing through the house. But just to stand quietly in the courtyard while Isabel pointed out the beauties, and Lottie and Kezia looked pleased. . . .

But hurry as they might, by the time they had reached the tarred palings of the boys' playground the bell had begun to jangle. They only just had time to whip off their hats and fall into line before the roll was called. Never mind. Isabel tried to make up for it by looking very important and mysterious and by whispering behind her hand to the girls near her, "Got something to tell you at playtime."

Playtime came and Isabel was surrounded. The girls of her class nearly fought to put their arms round her, to walk away with her, to beam flatteringly, to be her special friend. She held quite a court under the huge pine trees at the side of the playground. Nudging, giggling together, the little girls pressed up close. And the only two who stayed outside the ring were the two who were always outside, the little Kelveys. They knew better than to come anywhere near the Burnells.

For the fact was, the school the Burnell children went to was not at all the kind of place their parents would have chosen if there had been any choice. But there was none. It was the only school for miles. And the consequence was all the children of the neighbourhood, the Judge's little girls, the doctor's daughters, the storekeeper's children, the milkman's, were forced to mix together. Not to speak of there being an equal number of rude, rough little boys as well. But the line had to be drawn somewhere. It was drawn at the Kelveys. Many of the children, including the Burnells, were not allowed even to speak to them. They walked past the Kelveys with their heads in the air, and as they set the fashion in all matters of behaviour, the Kelveys

were shunned by everybody. Even the teacher had a special voice
for them, and a special smile for the other children when Lil Kelvey
came up to her desk with a bunch of dreadfully common-looking
flowers.

They were the daughters of a spry, hard-working little washerwoman, who went about from house to house by the day. This was
awful enough. But where was Mr. Kelvey? Nobody knew for certain.
But everybody said he was in prison. So they were the daughters of
a washerwoman and a gaolbird. Very nice company for other people's children! And they looked it. Why Mrs. Kelvey made them so
conspicuous was hard to understand. The truth was they were
dressed in "bits" given to her by the people for whom she worked.
Lil, for instance, who was a stout, plain child, with big freckles, came
to school in a dress made from a green art-serge tablecloth of the
Burnells', with red plush sleeves from the Logans' curtains. Her hat,
perched on top of her high forehead, was a grown-up woman's hat,
once the property of Miss Lecky, the postmistress. It was turned up
at the back and trimmed with a large scarlet quill. What a little guy
she looked! It was impossible not to laugh. And her little sister, our
Else, wore a long white dress, rather like a nightgown, and a pair of
little boy's boots. But whatever our Else wore she would have looked
strange. She was a tiny wishbone of a child, with cropped hair and
enormous solemn eyes—a little white owl. Nobody had ever seen
her smile; she scarcely ever spoke. She went through life holding on
to Lil, with a piece of Lil's skirt screwed up in her hand. Where Lil
went, our Else followed. In the playground, on the road going to and
from school, there was Lil marching in front and our Else holding
on behind. Only when she wanted anything, or when she was out
of breath, our Else gave Lil a tug, a twitch, and Lil stopped and
turned around. The Kelveys never failed to understand each other.

Now they hovered at the edge; you couldn't stop them listening.
When the little girls turned round and sneered, Lil, as usual, gave
her silly, shamefaced smile, but our Else only looked.

And Isabel's voice, so very proud, went on telling. The carpet
made a great sensation, but so did the beds with real bedclothes, and
the stove with an over door.

When she finished Kezia broke in. "You've forgotten the lamp,
Isabel."

"Oh yes," said Isabel, "and there's a teeny little lamp, all made of
yellow glass, with a white globe that stands on the dining-room
table. You couldn't tell it from a real one."

"The lamp's best of all," cried Kezia. She thought Isabel wasn't
making half enough of the little lamp. But nobody paid any attention. Isabel was choosing the two who were to come back with them

that afternoon and see it. She chose Emmie Cole and Lena Logan. But when the others knew they were all to have a chance, they couldn't be nice enough to Isabel. One by one they put their arms round Isabel's waist and walked her off. They had something to whisper to her, a secret. "Isabel's *my* friend."

Only the little Kelveys moved away forgotten; there was nothing more for them to hear.

Days passed, and as more children saw the doll's house, the fame of it spread. It became the one subject, the rage. The one question was, "Have you seen Burnells' doll's house? Oh, ain't it lovely!" "Haven't you seen it? Oh, I say!"

Even the dinner hour was given up to talking about it. The little girls sat under the pines eating their thick mutton sandwiches and big slabs of johnny cake spread with butter. While always, as near as they could get, sat the Kelveys, our Else holding on to Lil, listening too, while they chewed their jam sandwiches out of a newspaper soaked with large red blobs.

"Mother," said Kezia, "can't I ask the Kelveys just once?"

"Certainly not, Kezia."

"But why not?"

"Run away, Kezia; you know quite well why not."

At last everybody had seen it except them. On that day the subject rather flagged. It was the dinner hour. The children stood together under the pine trees, and suddenly, as they looked at the Kelveys eating out of their paper, always by themselves, always listening, they wanted to be horrid to them. Emmie Cole started the whisper.

"Lil Kelvey's going to be a servant when she grows up."

"O-oh, how awful!" said Isabel Burnell, and she made eyes at Emmie.

Emmie swallowed in a very meaning way and nodded to Isabel as she'd seen her mother do on those occasions.

"It's true—it's true—it's true," she said.

Then Lena Logan's little eyes snapped. "Shall I ask her?" she whispered.

"Bet you don't," said Jessie May.

"Pooh, I'm not frightened," said Lena. Suddenly she gave a little squeal and danced in front of the other girls. "Watch! Watch me! Watch me now!" said Lena. And sliding, gliding, dragging one foot, giggling behind her hand, Lena went over to the Kelveys.

Lil looked up from her dinner. She wrapped the rest quickly away. Our Else stopped chewing. What was coming now?

"Is it true you're going to be a servant when you grow up, Lil Kelvey?" shrilled Lena.

Dead silence. But instead of answering, Lil only gave her silly, shamefaced smile. She didn't seem to mind the question at all. What a sell for Lena! The girls began to titter.

Lena couldn't stand that. She put her hands on her hips; she shot forward. "Yah, yer father's in prison!" she hissed spitefully.

This was such a marvellous thing to have said that the little girls rushed away in a body, deeply, deeply excited, wild with joy. Some-one found a long rope, and they began skipping. And never did they skip so high, run in and out so fast, or do such daring things as on that morning.

In the afternoon Pat called for the Burnell children with the buggy and they drove home. There were visitors. Isabel and Lottie, who liked visitors, went upstairs to change their pinafores. But Kezia thieved out at the back. Nobody was about; she began to swing on the big white gates of the courtyard. Presently, looking along the road, she saw two little dots. They grew bigger, they were coming towards her. Now she could see that one was in front and one close behind. Now she could see that they were the Kelveys. Kezia stopped swinging. She slipped off the gate as if she was going to run away. Then she hesitated. The Kelveys came nearer, and beside them walked their shadows, very long, stretching right across the road with their heads in the buttercups. Kezia clambered back on the gate; she had made up her mind; she swung out.

"Hullo," she said to the passing Kelveys.

They were so astounded that they stopped. Lil gave her silly smile. Our Else stared.

"You can come and see our doll's house if you want to," said Kezia, and she dragged one toe on the ground. But at that Lil turned red and shook her head quickly.

"Why not?" asked Kezia.

Lil gasped, then she said, "Your ma told our ma you wasn't to speak to us."

"Oh, well," said Kezia. She didn't know what to reply. "It doesn't matter. You can come and see our doll's house all the same. Come on. Nobody's looking."

But Lil shook her head still harder.

"Don't you want to?" asked Kezia.

Suddenly there was a twitch, a tug at Lil's skirt. She turned round. Our Else was looking at her with big, imploring eyes; she was frown-ing; she wanted to go. For a moment Lil looked at our Else very doubtfully. But then our Else twitched her skirt again. She started forward. Kezia led the way. Like two little stray cats they followed across the courtyard to where the doll's house stood.

"There it is," said Kezia.

There was a pause. Lil breathed loudly, almost snorted; our Else was still as stone.

"I'll open it for you," said Kezia kindly. She undid the hook and they looked inside.

"There's the drawing-room and the dining-room, and that's the—"

"Kezia!"

Oh, what a start they gave!

"Kezia!"

It was Aunt Beryl's voice. They turned round. At the back door stood Aunt Beryl, staring as if she couldn't believe what she saw.

"How dare you ask the little Kelveys into the courtyard!" said her cold, furious voice. "You know as well as I do, you're not allowed to talk to them. Run away, children, run away at once. And don't come back again," said Aunt Beryl. And she stepped into the yard and shooed them out as if they were chickens.

"Off you go immediately!" she called, cold and proud.

They did not need telling twice. Burning with shame, shrinking together, Lil huddling along like her mother, our Else dazed, somehow they crossed the big courtyard and squeezed through the white gate.

"Wicked, disobedient little girl!" said Aunt Beryl bitterly to Kezia, and she slammed the doll's house to.

The afternoon had been awful. A letter had come from Willie Brent, a terrifying, threatening letter, saying if she did not meet him that evening in Pulman's Bush, he'd come to the front door and ask the reason why! But now that she had frightened those little rats of Kelveys and given Kezia a good scolding, her heart felt lighter. That ghastly pressure was gone. She went back to the house humming.

When the Kelveys were well out of sight of Burnells', they sat down to rest on a big red drainpipe by the side of the road. Lil's cheeks were still burning; she took off the hat with the quill and held it on her knee. Dreamily they looked over the hay paddocks, past the creek, to the group of wattles where Logan's cows stood waiting to be milked. What were their thoughts?

Presently our Else nudged up close to her sister. But now she had forgotten the cross lady. She put out a finger and stroked her sister's quill; she smiled her rare smile.

"I seen the little lamp," she said softly.

Then both were silent once more.

Alice Munro

(b. 1931)

Alice Munro has relied on the small towns and rural landscapes of her native Western Ontario for the settings of her prose fiction. Starting to publish short stories in such journals as *Queen's Quarterly, Tamarack Review,* and *Canadian Forum* in the 1950s, she published no book until 1968, when a collection of fifteen stories appeared under the title *Dance of the Happy Shades* and immediately won critical acclaim. Like the novel which followed in 1971, *Lives of Girls and Women,* her stories explore tensions between the orderly and the uncontrollable in modern life, particularly as they affect women. The orderly manifests itself in conventions of various kinds: the moral and social structure of small-town society, the dimensions of family life, the roles accorded men and women by tradition and inertia.

Munro's dramatization of these social realities brings her characters up against the knowledge of the limits which such order imposes on them. They rebel, or they surrender, or they question their ability to escape themselves, to escape the identities which the conventions have inevitably helped create. When the father in one of her stories ("Boys and Girls"), for example, dismisses his daughter's intentional rebellion with the phrase "she's only a girl," he dismisses implicitly her capacities for intelligence and independent judgment; moreover, the girl has become so pressured by family expectations, that she acknowledges "maybe it was true." The characters in the sardonically titled "Thanks for the Ride" also are circumscribed by imposed stereotypes. Those who know what limits them do not delight in their knowledge; those who do not know are equally joyless, for their very lack of knowledge creates an emptiness in their lives. The story is one which gains its meaning not just from the characters' behavior, but also from the writer's control over setting and style; the language seems alive, and the unity of the whole gives evidence that the act of storytelling is both a fine art and a careful craft.

For further reading

Hallvard Dahlie, "Unconsummated Relationships: Isolation and Rejection in Alice Munro's Stories," *WLWE,* 11 (April 1972), 43–48.

Alice Munro, "The Colonel's Hash Resettled," in *The Narrative Voice,* ed. John Metcalf (Toronto: McGraw-Hill Ryerson, 1972), pp. 181–183.

Thanks for the Ride

My cousin George and I were sitting in a restaurant called Pop's Cafe, in a little town close to the Lake. It was getting dark in there, and they had not turned the lights on, but you could still read the signs plastered against the mirror between the fly-speckled and slightly yellowed cutouts of strawberry sundaes and tomato sandwiches.

"Don't ask for information," George read. "If we knew anything we wouldn't be here" and "If you've got nothing to do, you picked a hell of a good place to do it in." George always read everything out loud —posters, billboards, Burma-Shave signs, "Mission Creek. Population 1700. Gateway to the Bruce. We love our children."

I was wondering whose sense of humour provided us with the signs. I thought it would be the man behind the cash register. Pop? Chewing on a match, looking out at the street, not watching for anything except for somebody to trip over a crack in the sidewalk or have a blowout or make a fool of himself in some way that Pop, rooted behind the cash register, huge and cynical and incurious, was never likely to do. Maybe not even that; maybe just by walking up and down, driving up and down, going places, the rest of the world proved its absurdity. You see the judgment on the faces of people looking out of windows, sitting on front steps in some little towns; so deeply, deeply uncaring they are, as if they had sources of disillusionment which they would keep, with some satisfaction, in the dark.

There was only the one waitress, a pudgy girl who leaned over the counter and scraped at the polish on her fingernails. When she had flaked most of the polish off her thumbnail she put the thumb against her teeth and rubbed the nail back and forth absorbedly. We asked her what her name was and she didn't answer. Two or three minutes later the thumb came out of her mouth and she said, inspecting it: "That's for me to know and you to find out."

"All right," George said. "Okay if I call you Mickey?"

"I don't care."

"Because you remind me of Mickey Rooney," George said. "Hey, where's everybody go in this town? Where's everybody go?" Mickey had turned her back and begun to drain out the coffee. It looked as if she didn't mean to talk any more, so George got a little jumpy, as he did when he was threatened with having to be quiet or be by himself. "Hey, aren't there any girls in this town?" he said almost plaintively. "Aren't there any girls or dances or anything? We're strangers in town," he said. "Don't you want to help us out?"

"Dance hall down on the beach closed up Labour Day," Mickey said coldly.

"There any other dance halls?"

"There's a dance tonight out at Wilson's *school,*" Mickey said.

"That old-time? No, no, I don't go for the old-time. *All-a-man left* and that, used to have that down in the basement of the church.

Yeah, *ever'body swing*—I don't go for that. Inna basement of the *church,*" George said, obscurely angered. "You don't remember that," he said to me. "Too young."

I was just out of high-school at this time, and George had been working for three years in the Men's Shoes in a downtown department store, so there was that difference. But we had never bothered with each other back in the city. We were together now because we had met unexpectedly in a strange place and because I had a little money, while George was broke. Also I had my father's car, and George was in one of his periods between cars, which made him always a little touchy and dissatisfied. But he would have to rearrange these facts a bit, they made him uneasy. I could feel him manufacturing a sufficiency of good feeling, old-pal feeling, and dressing me up as Old Dick, good kid, real character—which did not matter one way or the other, though I did not think, looking at his tender blond piggish handsomeness, the nudity of his pink mouth, and the surprised, angry creases that frequent puzzlement was beginning to put into his forehead, that I would be able to work up an Old George.

I had driven up to the Lake to bring my mother home from a beach resort for women, a place where they had fruit juice and cottage cheese for reducing, and early-morning swims in the Lake, and some religion, apparently, for there was a little chapel attached. My aunt, George's mother, was staying there at the same time, and George arrived about an hour or so after I did, not to take his mother home, but to get some money out of her. He did not get along well with his father, and he did not make much money working in the shoe department, so he was very often broke. His mother said he could have a loan if he would stay over and go to church with her the next day. George said he would. Then George and I got away and drove half a mile along the lake to this little town neither of us had seen before, which George said would be full of bootleggers and girls.

It was a town of unpaved, wide, sandy streets and bare yards. Only the hardy things like red and yellow nasturtiums, or a lilac bush with brown curled leaves, grew out of that cracked earth. The houses were set wide apart, with their own pumps and sheds and privies out behind; most of them were built of wood and painted green or grey or yellow. The trees that grew there were big willows or poplars, their fine leaves greyed with the dust. There were no trees along the main street, but spaces of tall grass and dandelions and blowing thistles—open country between the store buildings. The town hall was surprisingly large, with a great bell in a tower, the red brick rather glaring in the midst of the town's walls of faded, pale-painted wood. The sign beside the door said that it was a memorial to the soldiers who had died in the First World War. We had a drink out of the fountain in front.

We drove up and down the main street for a while, with George saying: "What a dump! Jesus, what a dump!" and "Hey, look at that! Aw, not so good either." The people on the street went home to supper, the shadows of the store buildings lay solid across the street, and we went into Pop's.

"Hey," George said, "is there any other restaurant in this town? Did you see any other restaurant?"

"No," I said.

"Any other town I ever been," George said, "pigs hangin' out the windows, practically hangin' off the trees. Not here. Jesus! I guess it's late in the season," he said.

"You want to go to a show?"

The door opened. A girl came in, walked up and sat on a stool, with most of her skirt bunched up underneath her. She had a long somnolent face, no bust, frizzy hair; she was pale, almost ugly, but she had that inexplicable aura of sexuality. George brightened, though not a great deal. "Never mind," he said. "This'll do. This'll do in a pinch, eh? In a pinch."

He went to the end of the counter and sat down beside her and started to talk. In about five minutes they came back to me, the girl drinking a bottle of orange pop.

"This is Adelaide," George said. "Adelaide, Adeline—Sweet Adeline. I'm going to call her Sweet A, Sweet A."

Adelaide sucked at her straw, paying not much attention.

"She hasn't got a date," George said. "You haven't got a date have you, honey?"

Adelaide shook her head very slightly.

"Doesn't hear half what you say to her," George said. "Adelaide, Sweet A, have you got any friends? Have you got any nice, young little girl friend to go out with Dickie? You and me and her and Dickie?"

"Depends," said Adelaide. "Where do you want to go?"

"Anywhere you say. Go for a drive. Drive up to Owen Sound, maybe."

"You got a car?"

"Yeah, yeah, we got a car. C'mon, you must have some nice little friend for Dickie." He put his arm around this girl, spreading his fingers over her blouse. "C'mon out and I'll show you the car."

Adelaide said: "I know one girl might come. The guy she goes around with, he's engaged, and his girl came up and she's staying at his place up the beach, his mother and dad's place, and—"

"Well that is certainly int-er-esting," George said. "What's her name? Come on, let's go round and get her. You want to sit around drinking pop all night?"

"I'm finished," Adelaide said. "She might not come. I don't know."

"Why not? Her mother not let her out nights?"

"Oh, she can do what she likes," said Adelaide. "Only there's times she don't want to. I don't know."

We went out and got into the car, George and Adelaide in the back. On the main street about a block from the cafe we passed a thin, fair-haired girl in slacks and Adelaide cried: "Hey stop! That's her! That's Lois!"

I pulled in and George stuck his head out of the window, whistling. Adelaide yelled, and the girl came unhesitatingly, unhurriedly to the car. She smiled, rather coldly and politely, when Adelaide explained to her. All the time George kept saying: "Hurry up, come on, get in! We can talk in the car." The girl smiled, did not really look at any of us, and in a few moments, to my surprise, she opened the door and slid into the car.

"I don't have anything to do," she said. "My boy friend's away."

"That so?" said George, and I saw Adelaide, in the rear-vision mirror, make a cross warning face. Lois did not seem to have heard him.

"We better drive around to my house," she said. "I was just going down to get some Cokes, that's why I only have my slacks on. We better drive around to my house and I'll put on something else."

"Where are we going to go," she said, "so I know what to put on?"

I said: "Where do you want to go?"

"Okay, okay," George said. "First things first. We gotta get a bottle, then we'll decide. You know where to get one?" Adelaide and Lois both said yes, and then Lois said to me: "You can come in the house and wait while I change, if you want to." I glanced in the rear mirror and thought that there was probably some agreement she had with Adelaide.

Lois's house had an old couch on the porch and some rugs hanging down over the railing. She walked ahead of me across the yard. She had her long pale hair tied at the back of her neck; her skin was dustily freckled, but not tanned; even her eyes were light-coloured. She was cold and narrow and pale. There was derision, and also great gravity, about her mouth. I thought she was about my age or a little older.

She opened the front door and said in a clear, stilted voice: "I would like you to meet my family."

The little front room had linoleum on the floor and flowered paper curtains at the windows. There was a glossy chesterfield with a

Niagara Falls and a To Mother cushion on it, and there was a little
black stove with a screen around it for summer, and a big vase of
paper apple blossoms. A tall, frail woman came into the room drying
her hands on a dishtowel, which she flung into a chair. Her mouth
was full of blue-white china teeth, and long cords trembled in her
neck. I said how-do-you-do to her, embarrassed by Lois's announcement, so suddenly and purposefully conventional. I wondered if she
had any misconceptions about this date, engineered by George for
such specific purposes. I did not think so. Her face had no innocence
in it that I could see; it was knowledgeable, calm, and hostile. She
might have done it, then, to mock me, to make me into this caricature
of The Date, the boy who grins and shuffles in the front hall and
waits to be presented to the nice girl's family. But that was a little
far-fetched. Why should she want to embarrass me when she had
agreed to go out with me without even looking into my face? Why
should she care enough?

Lois's mother and I sat down on the chesterfield. She began to
make conversation, giving this the Date interpretation. I noticed the
smell in the house, the smell of stale small rooms, bedclothes, frying,
washing, and medicated ointments. And dirt, though it did not look
dirty. Lois's mother said: "That's a nice car you got out front. Is that
your car?"

"My father's."

"Isn't that lovely! Your father has such a nice car. I always think
it's lovely for people to have things. I've got no time for these people
that's just eaten up with malice 'n envy. I say it's lovely. I bet your
mother, every time she wants anything, she just goes down to the
store and buys it—new coat, bedspread, pots and pans. What does
you father do? Is he a lawyer or doctor or something like that?"

"He's a chartered accountant."

"Oh. That's in an office, is it?"

"Yes."

"My brother, Lois's uncle, he's in the office of the CPR in London.
He's quite high up there, I understand."

She began to tell me about how Lois's father had been killed in an
accident at the mill. I noticed an old woman, the grandmother probably, standing in the doorway of the room. She was not thin like the
others, but as soft and shapeless as a collapsed pudding, pale brown
spots melting together on her face and arms, bristles of hairs in the
moisture around her mouth. Some of the smell in the house seemed
to come from her. It was a smell of hidden decay, such as there is
when some obscure little animal has died under the verandah. The
smell, the slovenly, confiding voice—something about this life I had
not known, something about these people. I thought: my mother,

George's mother, they are innocent. Even George, George is innocent. But these others are born sly and sad and knowing.

I did not hear much about Lois's father except that his head was cut off.

"Clean off, imagine, and rolled on the floor! Couldn't open the coffin. It was June, the hot weather. And everybody in town just stripped their gardens, stripped them for the funeral. Stripped their spirea bushes and peenies and climbin' clemantis. I guess it was the worst accident ever took place in this town.

"Lois had a nice boy friend this summer," she said. "Used to take her out and sometimes stay here overnight when his folks weren't up at the cottage and he didn't feel like passin' his time there all alone. He'd bring the kids candy and even me he'd bring presents. That china elephant up there, you can plant flowers in it, he brought me that. He fixed the radio for me and I never had to take it into the shop. Do your folks have a summer cottage up here?"

I said no, and Lois came in, wearing a dress of yellow-green stuff —stiff and shiny like Christmas wrappings—high-heeled shoes, rhinestones, and a lot of dark powder over her freckles. Her mother was excited.

"You like that dress?" she said. "She went all the way to London and bought that dress, didn't get it anywhere round here!"

We had to pass by the old woman as we went out. She looked at us with sudden recognition, a steadying of her pale, jellied eyes. Her mouth trembled open, she stuck her face out at me.

"You can do what you like with my gran'daughter," she said in her old, strong voice, the rough voice of a country woman. "But you be careful. And you know what I mean!"

Lois's mother pushed the old woman behind her, smiling tightly, eyebrows lifted, skin straining over her temples. "Never mind," she mouthed at me, grimacing distractedly. "Never mind. Second child-hood." The smile stayed on her face; the skin pulled back from it. She seemed to be listening all the time to a perpetual din and racket in her head. She grabbed my hand as I followed Lois out. "Lois is a nice girl," she whispered. "You have a nice time, don't let her mope!" There was a quick, grotesque, and, I suppose, originally flirtatious, flickering of brows and lids. "Night!"

Lois walked stiffy ahead of me, rustling her papery skirt. I said: "Did you want to go to a dance or something?"

"No," she said. "I don't care."

"Well you got all dressed up—"

"I always get dressed up on Saturday night," Lois said, her voice floating back to me, low and scornful. Then she began to laugh, and I had a glimpse of her mother in her, that jaggedness and hysteria.

"Oh, my God!" she whispered. I knew she meant what had happened in the house, and I laughed too, not knowing what else to do. So we went back to the car laughing as if we were friends, but we were not.

We drove out of town to a farmhouse where a woman sold us a whiskey bottle full of muddy-looking liquor, something George and I had never had before. Adelaide had said that this woman would probably let us use her front room, but it turned out that she would not, and that was because of Lois. When the woman peered up at me from under the man's cap she had on her head and said to Lois, "Change's as good as a rest, eh?" Lois did not answer, kept a cold face. Then later the woman said that if we were so stuck-up tonight her front room wouldn't be good enough for us and we better go back to the bush. All the way back down the lane Adelaide kept saying: "Some people can't take a joke, can they? Yeah, stuck-up is right—" until I passed her the bottle to keep her quiet. I saw George did not mind, thinking this had taken her mind off driving to Owen Sound.

We parked at the end of the lane and sat in the car drinking. George and Adelaide drank more than we did. They did not talk, just reached for the bottle and passed it back. This stuff was different from anything I had tasted before; it was heavy and sickening in my stomach. There was no other effect, and I began to have the depressing feeling that I was not going to get drunk. Each time Lois handed the bottle back to me she said "Thank you" in a mannerly and subtly contemptuous way. I put my arm around her, not much wanting to. I was wondering what was the matter. This girl lay against my arm, scornful, acquiescent, angry, inarticulate and out-of-reach. I wanted to talk to her then more than to touch her, and that was out of the question; talk was not so little a thing to her as touching. Meanwhile I was aware that I should be beyond this, beyond the first stage and well into the second (for I had a knowledge, though it was not very comprehensive, of the orderly progression of stages, the ritual of back- and front-seat seduction). Almost I wished I was with Adelaide.

"Do you want to go for a walk?" I said.

"That's the first bright idea you've had all night," George told me from the back seat. "Don't hurry," he said as we got out. He and Adelaide were muffled and laughing together. "Don't hurry back!"

Lois and I walked along a wagon track close to the bush. The fields were moonlit, chilly and blowing. Now I felt vengeful, and I said softly, "I had quite a talk with your mother."

"I can imagine," said Lois.

"She told me about that guy you went out with last summer."

"This summer."

"It's last summer now. He was engaged or something, wasn't he?"

"Yes."

I was not going to let her go. "Did he like you better?" I said. "Was that it? Did he like you better?"

"No, I wouldn't say he liked me," Lois said. I thought, by some thickening of the sarcasm in her voice, that she was beginning to be drunk. "He liked Momma and the kids okay but he didn't like me. *Like me*," she said. "What's that?"

"Well, he went out with you—"

"He just went around with me for the summer. That's what those guys from up the beach always do. They come down here to the dances and get a girl to go around with. For the summer. They always do.

"How I know he didn't *like* me," she said, "he said I was always bitching. You have to act grateful to those guys, you know, or they say you're bitching."

I was a little startled at having loosed all this. I said: "Did you like him?"

"Oh, sure! I should, shouldn't I? I should just get down on my knees and thank him. That's what my mother does. He brings her a cheap old spotted elephant—"

"Was this guy the first?" I said.

"The first steady. Is that what you mean?"

It wasn't. "How old are you?"

She considered. "I'm almost seventeen. I can pass for eighteen or nineteen. I can pass in a beer parlour. I did once."

"What grade are you in at school?"

She looked at me, rather amazed. "Did you think I still went to school? I quit that two years ago. I've got a job at the glove-works in town."

"That must have been against the law. When you quit."

"Oh, you can get a permit if your father's dead or something."

"What do you do at the glove-works?" I said.

"Oh, I run a machine. It's like a sewing machine. I'll be getting on piecework soon. You make more money."

"Do you like it?"

"Oh, I wouldn't say I loved it. It's a job—you ask a lot of questions," she said.

"Do you mind?"

"I don't have to answer you," she said, her voice flat and small again. "Only if I like." She picked up her skirt and spread it out in her hands. "I've got burrs on my skirt," she said. She bent over, pulling them one by one, "I've got burrs on my dress," she said. "It's my good dress. Will they leave a mark? If I pull them all—slowly —I won't pull any threads."

"You shouldn't have worn that dress," I said. "What'd you wear that dress for?"

She shook the skirt, tossing a burr loose. "I don't know," she said. She held it out, the stiff, shining stuff, with faintly drunken satisfaction. "I wanted to show you guys!" she said, with a sudden small explosion of viciousness. The drunken, nose-thumbing, toe-twirling satisfaction could not now be mistaken as she stood there foolishly, tauntingly, with her skirt spread out. "I've got an imitation cashmere sweater at home. It cost me twelve dollars," she said. "I've got a fur coat I'm paying on, paying on for next winter. I've got a fur coat—"

"That's nice," I said. "I think it's lovely for people to have things."

She dropped the skirt and struck the flat of her hand on my face. This was a relief to me, to both of us. We felt a fight had been building in us all along. We faced each other as warily as we could, considering we were both a little drunk, she tensing to slap me again and I to grab her or slap her back. We would have it out, what we had against each other. But the moment of this keenness passed. We let out our breath; we had not moved in time. And the next moment, not bothering to shake off our enmity, nor thinking how the one thing could give way to the other, we kissed. It was the first time, for me, that a kiss was accomplished without premeditation, or hesitancy, or over-haste, or the usual vague ensuing disappointment. And laughing shakily against me, she began to talk again, going back to the earlier part of our conversation as if nothing had come between.

"Isn't it funny?" she said. "You know, all winter all the girls do is talk about last summer, talk and talk about those guys, and I bet you those guys have forgotten even what their names were—"

But I did not want to talk any more, having discovered another force in her that lay side by side with her hostility, that was, in fact, just as enveloping and impersonal. After a while I whispered: "Isn't there some place we can go?"

And she answered: "There's a barn in the next field."

She knew the countryside; she had been there before.

We drove back into town after midnight. George and Adelaide were asleep in the back seat. I did not think Lois was asleep, though she kept her eyes closed and did not say anything. I had read somewhere about *Omne animal,* and I was going to tell her, but then I thought she would not know Latin words and would think I was being—oh, pretentious and superior. Afterwards I wished that I had told her. She would have known what it meant.

Afterwards the lassitude of the body, and the cold; the separation. To brush away the bits of hay and tidy ourselves with heavy unconnected movements, to come out of the barn and find the moon gone down, but the flat stubble fields still there, and the poplar trees, and the stars. To find our same selves, chilled and shaken, who had gone that headlong journey and were here still. To go back to the car and find the others sprawled asleep. That is what it is: *triste. Triste est.*

That headlong journey. Was it like that because it was the first time, because I was a little, strangely drunk? No. It was because of Lois. There are some people who can go only a little way with the act of love, and some others who can go very far, who can make a greater surrender, like the mystics. And Lois, this mystic of love, sat now on the far side of the carseat, looking cold and rumpled, and utterly closed up in herself. All the things I wanted to say to her went clattering emptily through my head. *Come and see you again —Remember—Love—*I could not say any of these things. They would not seem even half-true across the space that had come between us. I thought: I will say something to her before the next tree, the next telephone pole. But I did not. I only drove faster, too fast, making the town come nearer.

The street lights bloomed out of the dark trees ahead; there were stirrings in the back seat.

"What time is it?" George said.

"Twenty past twelve."

"We musta finished that bottle. I don't feel so good. Oh, Christ, I don't feel so good. How do you feel?"

"Fine."

"Fine, eh? Feel like you finished your education tonight, eh? That how you feel? Is yours asleep? Mine is."

"I am not," said Adelaide drowsily. "Where's my belt? George—oh. Now where's my other shoe? It's early for Saturday night, isn't it? We could go and get something to eat."

"I don't feel like food," George said. "I gotta get some sleep. Gotta get up early tomorrow and go to church with my mother."

"Yeah, I know," said Adelaide, disbelieving, though not too ill-humoured. "You could've anyways bought me a hamburger!"

I had driven around to Lois's house. Lois did not open her eyes until the car stopped.

She sat still a moment, and then pressed her hands down over the skirt of her dress, flattening it out. She did not look at me. I moved to kiss her, but she seemed to draw slightly away, and I felt that there had after all been something fraudulent and theatrical about this final gesture. She was not like that.

George said to Adelaide: "Where do you live? You live near here?"

"Yeah. Half a block down."

"Okay. How be you get out here too? We gotta get home sometime tonight."

He kissed her and both the girls got out.

I started the car. We began to pull away, George settling down on the back seat to sleep. And then we heard the female voice calling after us, the loud, crude, female voice, abusive and forlorn:

"Thanks for the ride!"

It was not Adelaide calling; it was Lois.

V. S. Naipaul

(b. 1932)

A Trinidadian who emigrated to England in 1950, an Oxonian, a novelist, a reporter, and the winner of such prestigious awards as the Hawthornden and Booker Prizes, Vidiadhar Surajprasad Naipaul is a man of extraordinary talent and complex motivations. Profoundly influenced by both his Indian and West Indian heritages, he yet finds India and Trinidad to be constraining environments; and his travel books (*The Middle Passage,* 1962, and *An Area of Darkness,* 1964) shrewdly observe the details of life in the two societies and brood over his own sense of alienation from them. From one vantage point, such "exile" can be seen as a reflection of the Caribbean predicament: that of societies founded by exiles and historically uncertain of their allegiances and identities. From another, it reflects twentieth-century existential sensibilities and identities: the acute consciousness of being alive and alone, the laconic acceptance of the fugitive joys and persistent sadness of life, the alternately grim and wry rendering of a society that cannot locate or cannot believe in a sustaining code of values. Naipaul's characteristically tragicomic tone catches at exactly this ambivalence.

The most lighthearted of his works are early books—the sketches of *Miguel Street* (1959) and the novel *The Mystic Masseur* (1957). But the vein of dislocating irony that occurs even here grew larger with each succeeding work: *A House for Mr. Biswas* (1961), an inventive portrait of Trinidad domestic crises and individual pride; *A Flag on the Island* (1967), from which "My Aunt Gold Teeth" is taken; *The Mimic Men* (1967), about middle-class drive and human emptiness; *In a Free State* (1971), a collection of stories and journal entries that explores the dimensions of freedom in the mind and the modern world. Accompanying that intellectual development is an increasing stylistic skill. Naipaul's incisive portraits, his intelligent understanding of human behavior, and his powers of rendering intense awareness have made him one of the most significant of modern prose writers and the most accomplished to have yet emerged from the nations of the Caribbean.

For further reading

V. S. Naipaul, *The Overcrowded Barracoon and Other Articles* (London: Andre Deutsch, 1972).

V. S. Naipaul and Ian Hamilton, "Without a Place," *Times Literary Supplement,* August 30, 1971, pp. 897–898.

William Walsh, *A Manifold Voice* (London: Chatto & Windus, 1970), pp. 62–85.

My Aunt Gold Teeth

I never knew her real name and it is quite likely that she did have one, though I never heard her called anything but Gold Teeth. She did, indeed, have gold teeth. She had sixteen of them. She had married early and she had married well, and shortly after her marriage she exchanged her perfectly sound teeth for gold ones, to announce to the world that her husband was a man of substance.

Even without her gold teeth my aunt would have been noticeable. She was short, scarely five foot, and she was very fat. If you saw her in silhouette you would have found it difficult to know whether she was facing you or whether she was looking sideways.

She ate little and prayed much. Her family being Hindu, and her husband being a pundit, she, too, was an orthodox Hindu. Of Hinduism she knew little apart from the ceremonies and the taboos, and this was enough for her. Gold Teeth saw God as a Power, and religious ritual as a means of harnessing that Power for great practical good, her good.

I may have given the impression that Gold Teeth prayed because she wanted to be less fat. The fact was that Gold Teeth had no children and she was almost forty. It was her childlessness, not her fat, that oppressed her, and she prayed for the curse to be removed. She was willing to try any means—any ritual, any prayer—in order to trap and channel the supernatural Power.

And so it was that she began to indulge in surreptitious Christian practices.

She was living at the time in a country village called Cunupia, in County Caroni. Here the Canadian Mission had long waged war against the Indian heathen, and saved many. But Gold Teeth stood firm. The Minister of Cunupia expended his Presbyterian piety on her; so did the headmaster of the Mission school. But all in vain. At no time was Gold Teeth persuaded even to think about being converted. The idea horrified her. Her father had been in his day one of the best-known Hindu pundits, and even now her husband's fame as a pundit, as a man who could read and write Sanskrit, had spread far beyond Cunupia. She was in no doubt whatsoever the Hindus were the best people in the world, and that Hinduism was a superior religion. She was willing to select, modify and incorporate alien eccentricities into her worship; but to abjure her own faith—never!

Presbyterianism was not the only danger the good Hindu had to face in Cunupia. Besides, of course, the ever-present threat of open Muslim aggression, the Catholics were to be reckoned with. Their pamphlets were everywhere and it was hard to avoid them. In them Gold Teeth read of novenas and rosaries, of squads of saints and angels. These were things she understood and could even sympathize with, and they encouraged her to seek further. She read of the mysteries and the miracles, of penances and indulgences. Her scepticism sagged, and yielded to a quickening, if reluctant, enthusiasm.

One morning she took the train for the County town of Chaguanas, three miles, two stations and twenty minutes away. The Church of St Philip and St James in Chaguanas stands imposingly at the end of the Caroni Savannah Road, and although Gold Teeth knew Chaguanas well, all she knew of the church was that it had a clock, at which she had glanced on her way to the railway station nearby. She had hitherto been far more interested in the drab ochre-washed edifice opposite, which was the police station.

She carried herself into the churchyard, awed by her own temerity, feeling like an explorer in a land of cannibals. To her relief, the church was empty. It was not as terrifying as she had expected. In the gilt and images and the resplendent cloths she found much that reminded her of her Hindu temple. Her eyes caught a discreet sign: CANDLES TWO CENTS EACH. She undid the knot in the end of her veil, where she kept her money, took out three cents, popped them into the box, picked up a candle and muttered a prayer in Hindustani. A brief moment of elation gave way to a sense of guilt, and she was suddenly anxious to get away from the church as fast as her weight would let her.

She took a bus home, and hid the candle in her chest of drawers. She had half feared that her husband's Brahminical flair for clairvoyance would have uncovered the reason for her trip to Chaguanas. When after four days, which she spent in an ecstasy of prayer, her husband had mentioned nothing, Gold Teeth thought it safe to burn the candle. She burned it secretly at night, before her Hindu images, and sent up, as she thought, prayers of double efficacy.

Every day her religious schizophrenia grew, and presently she began wearing a crucifix. Neither her husband nor her neighbours knew she did so. The chain was lost in the billows of fat around her neck, and the crucifix was itself buried in the valley of her gargantuan breasts. Later she acquired two holy pictures, one of the Virgin Mary, the other of the crucifixion, and took care to conceal them from her husband. The prayers she offered to these Christian things filled her with new hope and buoyancy. She became an addict of Christianity.

Then her husband, Ramprasad, fell ill.

Ramprasad's sudden, unaccountable illness alarmed Gold Teeth. It was, she knew, no ordinary illness, and she knew, too, that her religious transgression was the cause. The District Medical Officer at Chaguanas said it was diabetes, but Gold Teeth knew better. To be on the safe side, though, she used the insulin he prescribed and, to be even safer, she consulted Ganesh Pundit, the masseur with mystic leanings, celebrated as a faith-healer.

Ganesh came all the way from Fuente Grove to Cunupia. He came in great humility, anxious to serve Gold Teeth's husband, for Gold Teeth's husband was a Brahmin among Brahmins, a *Panday,* a man who knew all five Vedas; while he, Ganesh, was a mere *Chaubay* and knew only four.

With spotless white *koortah,** his dhoti† cannily tied, and a tasselled green scarf as a concession to elegance, Ganesh exuded the confidence of the professional mystic. He looked at the sick man, observed his pallor, sniffed the air. "This man," he said, "is bewitched. Seven spirits are upon him."

He was telling Gold Teeth nothing she didn't know. She had known from the first that there were spirits in the affair, but she was glad that Ganesh had ascertained their number.

"But you mustn't worry," Ganesh added. "We will 'tie' the house —in spiritual bonds—and no spirit will be able to come in."

Then, without being asked, Gold Teeth brought out a blanket, folded it, placed it on the floor and invited Ganesh to sit on it. Next she brought him a brass jar of fresh water, a mango leaf and a plate full of burning charcoal.

"Bring me some ghee," Ganesh said, and after Gold Teeth had done so, he set to work. Muttering continuously in Hindustani he sprinkled the water from the brass jar around him with the mango leaf. Then he melted the ghee in the fire and the charcoal hissed so sharply that Gold Teeth could not make out his words. Presently he rose and said, "You must put some of the ash of this fire on your husband's forehead, but if he doesn't want you to do that, mix it with his food. You must keep the water in this jar and place it every night before your front door."

Gold teeth pulled her veil over her forehead.

Ganesh coughed. "That," he said, rearranging his scarf, "is all. There is nothing more I can do. God will do the rest."

He refused payment for his services. It was enough honour, he said, for a man as humble as he was to serve Pundit Ramprasad, and she, Gold Teeth, had been singled out by fate to be the spouse of such a worthy man. Gold Teeth received the impression that Ganesh spoke from a first-hand knowledge of fate and its designs, and her heart, buried deep down under inches of mortal, flabby flesh, sank a little.

"Baba," she said hesitantly, "revered Father, I have something to say to you." But she couldn't say anything more and Ganesh, seeing this, filled his eyes with charity and love.

"What is it, my child?"

Koortah = long shirt.
†*Dhoti* = loincoth.

"I have done a great wrong, Baba."

"What sort of wrong?" he asked, and his tone indicated that Gold Teeth could do no wrong.

"I have prayed to Christian things."

And to Gold Teeth's surprise, Ganesh chuckled benevolently. "And do you think God minds, daughter? There is only one God and different people pray to Him in different ways. It doesn't matter how you pray, but God is pleased if you pray at all."

"So it is not because of me that my husband has fallen ill?"

"No, to be sure, daughter."

In his professional capacity Ganesh was consulted by people of many faiths, and with the licence of the mystic he had exploited the commodiousness of Hinduism, and made room for all beliefs. In this way he had many clients, as he called them, many satisfied clients.

Henceforward Gold Teeth not only pasted Ramprasad's pale forehead with the sacred ash Ganesh had prescribed, but mixed substantial amounts with his food. Ramprasad's appetite, enormous even in sickness, diminished; and he shortly entered into a visible and alarming decline that mystified his wife.

She fed him more ash than before, and when it was exhausted and Ramprasad perilously macerated, she fell back on the Hindu wife's last resort. She took her husband home to her mother. That venerable lady, my grandmother, lived with us in Port-of-Spain.

Ramprasad was tall and skeletal, and his face was grey. The virile voice that had expounded a thousand theological points and recited a hundred *puranas**was now a wavering whisper. We cooped him up in a room called, oddly, "the pantry." It had never been used as a pantry and one can only assume that the architect had so designated it some forty years before. It was a tiny room. If you wished to enter the pantry you were compelled, as soon as you opened the door, to climb on to the bed: it fitted the room to a miracle. The lower half of the walls were concrete, the upper close lattice-work; there were no windows.

My grandmother had her doubts about the suitability of the room for a sick man. She was worried about the lattice-work. It let in air and light, and Ramprasad was not going to die from these things if she could help it. With cardboard, oil-cloth and canvas she made the lattice-work air-proof and light-proof.

And, sure enough, within a week Ramprasad's appetite returned, insatiable and insistent as before. My grandmother claimed all the credit for this, though Gold Teeth knew that the ash she had fed him had not been without effect. Then she realized with horror that she

Puranas = Hindu scriptures.

had ignored a very important thing. The house in Cunupia had been tied and no spirits could enter, but the house in the city had been given no such protection and any spirit could come and go as it chose. The problem was pressing.

Ganesh was out of the question. By giving his services free he had made it impossible for Gold Teeth to call him in again. But thinking in this way of Ganesh, she remembered his words: "It doesn't matter how you pray, but God is pleased if you pray at all."

Why not, then, bring Christianity into play again?

She didn't want to take any chances this time. She decided to tell Ramprasad.

He was propped up in bed, and eating. When Gold Teeth opened the door he stopped eating and blinked at the unwonted light. Gold Teeth, stepping into the doorway and filling it, shadowed the room once more and he went on eating. She placed the palms of her hands on the bed. It creaked.

"Man," she said.

Ramprasad continued to eat.

"Man," she said in English, "I thinking about going to the church to pray. You never know, and it better to be on the safe side. After all, the house ain't tied—"

"I don't want you to pray in no church," he whispered, in English too.

Gold Teeth did the only thing she could do. She began to cry.

Three days in succession she asked his permission to go to church, and his opposition weakened in the face of her tears. He was now, besides, too weak to oppose anything. Although his appetite had returned, he was still very ill and very weak, and every day his condition became worse.

On the fourth day he said to Gold Teeth, "Well, pray to Jesus and go to church, if it will put your mind at rest."

And Gold Teeth straight away set about putting her mind at rest. Every morning she took the trolley-bus to the Holy Rosary Church, to offer worship in her private way. Then she was emboldened to bring a crucifix and pictures of the Virgin and the Messiah into the house. We were all somewhat worried by this, but Gold Teeth's religious nature was well known to us; her husband was a learned pundit and when all was said and done this was an emergency, a matter of life and death. So we could do nothing but look on. Incense and camphor and ghee burned now before the likeness of Krishna and Shiva as well as Mary and Jesus. Gold Teeth revealed an appetite for prayer that equalled her husband's for food, and we marvelled at both, if only because neither prayer nor food seemed to be of any use to Ramprasad.

One evening, shortly after bell and gong and conch-shell had announced that Gold Teeth's official devotions were almost over, a sudden chorus of lamentation burst over the house, and I was summoned to the room reserved for prayer. "Come quickly, something dreadful has happened to your aunt."

The prayer-room, still heavy with fumes of incense, presented an extraordinary sight. Before the Hindu shrine, flat on her face, Gold Teeth lay prostrate, rigid as a sack of flour. I had only seen Gold Teeth standing or sitting, and the aspect of Gold Teeth prostrate, so novel and so grotesque, was disturbing.

My grandmother, an alarmist by nature, bent down and put her ear to the upper half of the body on the floor. "I don't seem to hear her heart," she said.

We were all somewhat terrified. We tried to lift Gold Teeth but she seemed as heavy as lead. Then, slowly, the body quivered. The flesh beneath the clothes rippled, then billowed, and the children in the room sharpened their shrieks. Instinctively we all stood back from the body and waited to see what was going to happen. Gold Teeth's hand began to pound the floor and at the same time she began to gurgle.

My grandmother had grasped the situation. "She's got the spirit," she said.

At the word "spirit," the children shrieked louder, and my grandmother slapped them into silence.

The gurgling resolved itself into words pronounced with a lingering ghastly quaver. "Hail Mary, Hare Ram," Gold Teeth said, "the snakes are after me. Everywhere snakes. Seven snakes. Rama! Rama! Full of grace. Seven spirits leaving Cunupia by the four-o'clock train for Port-of-Spain."

My grandmother and my mother listened eagerly, their faces lit up with pride. I was rather ashamed at the exhibition, and annoyed with Gold Teeth for putting me into a fright. I moved towards the door.

"Who is that going away? Who is the young *caffar*, the unbeliever?" the voice asked abruptly.

"Come back quickly, boy," my grandmother whispered. "Come back and ask her pardon."

I did as I was told.

"It is all right, son," Gold Teeth replied, "you don't know. You are young."

Then the spirit appeared to leave her. She wrenched herself up to a sitting position and wondered why we were all there. For the rest of that evening she behaved as if nothing had happened, and she pretended she didn't notice that everyone was looking at her and treating her with unusual respect.

"I have always said it, and I will say it again," my grandmother said, "that these Christians are very religious people. That is why I encouraged Gold Teeth to pray to Christian things."

Ramprasad died early next morning and we had the announcement on the radio after the local news at one o'clock. Ramprasad's death was the only one announced and so, although it came between commercials, it made some impression. We buried him that afternoon in Mucurapo Cemetery.

As soon as we got back my grandmother said, "I have always said it, and I will say it again: I don't like these Christian things. Ramprasad would have got better if only you, Gold Teeth, had listened to me and not gone running after these Christian things."

Gold Teeth sobbed her assent; and her body squabbered and shook as she confessed the whole story of her trafficking with Christianity. We listened in astonishment and shame. We didn't know that a good Hindu, and a member of our family, could sink so low. Gold Teeth beat her breast and pulled ineffectually at her long hair and begged to be forgiven. "It is all my fault," she cried. "My own fault, Ma. I fell in a moment of weakness. Then I just couldn't stop."

My grandmother's shame turned to pity. "It's all right, Gold Teeth. Perhaps it was this you needed to bring you back to your senses."

That evening Gold Teeth ritually destroyed every reminder of Christianity in the house.

"You have only yourself to blame," my grandmother said, "if you have no children now to look after you."

Alden Nowlan

(b. 1933)

Born and educated in Nova Scotia, Alden Nowlan moved in 1952 to the neighboring province of New Brunswick, where he became editor of the Hartland *Observer*. His Maritime roots go deep, and his insights into the stark details and laconic tempo of rural Maritime life derive from his sympathetic experience of it. Better known as a poet than as a short-story writer, he has produced only two volumes of prose: *Miracle at Indian River* (1968) and a novel that takes the form of loosely linked episodes in the shifting identity of the title character, *Various Persons Named Kevin O'Brien* (1973). Of his several volumes of poetry, *Bread, Wine and Salt* won the Governor-General's Award when it appeared in 1967, and a volume of selected poems, *Playing the Jesus Game*, was published in Trumansburg, New York, in 1970.

Nowlan's characters typically are constrained by their Calvinist Maritime heritage. Life is dour; authority is firm; and joy is not to be trusted. Yet they are not without humor, nor is the writer without a strong sense of irony as he views their predicament. The portrait of the Evangelical church in "Miracle at Indian River" neither ridicules nor condemns the naïveté it discloses. Relying as heavily as it does on the techniques of the anecdote, however, the story communicates its central joke with broad humor. The exaggeration of the tall tale is there, tempered by controlled understatement. The result is a witty satire of a whole way of life, which never loses sight of the realities in which it is founded, and never takes lightly the seriousness with which those realities affect individual human lives.

For further reading

Keath Fraser, "Notes on Alden Nowlan," *Canadian Literature*, 45 (Summer 1970), 41–51.

Alden Nowlan, "An Interview with Alden Nowlan," *Fiddlehead*, 81 (1969), 5–13.

Miracle at Indian River

This is the story of how mates were chosen for all the marriageable young men and women in the congregation of the Fire-Baptized Tabernacle of the Living God in Indian River, New Brunswick. It is a true story, more or less, and whether it is ridiculous or pathetic or even oddly beautiful depends a good deal on the mood you're in when you read it.

Indian River is one of those little places that don't really exist, except in the minds of their inhabitants. Passing through it as a stranger you might not even notice that it is there. Or if you did notice it, you'd think it was no different from thousands of other little backwoods communities in Canada and the United States. But you'd be wrong. Indian River, like every community large and small, has a character all its own.

The inhabitants of Indian River are pure Dutch, although they don't know it. Their ancestors settled in New Amsterdam more than three hundred years ago and migrated to New Brunswick after the American Revolution. But they've always been isolated, always intermarried, so that racially they're probably more purely Dutch than most of the Dutch in Holland, even though they've long ago forgotten the language and few of them could locate the Netherlands on a map.

The village contains a railway station which hasn't been used since 1965 when the CNR discontinued passenger service in that part of northwestern New Brunswick, a one-room school that was closed five years ago when the government began using buses to carry local children to the regional school in Cumberland Centre, a general store and two churches: St. Edward's Anglican, which used to be attended by the station agent, the teacher and the store-keeper, and the Fire-Baptized Tabernacle of the Living God, attended by practically everyone else in Indian River.

The tabernacle, formerly a barracks, was bought from the Department of National Defence and brought in on a flatcar. "Jesus Saves" is painted in big red letters over the door. A billboard beside the road warns drivers to prepare to meet their God. There is an evergreen forest to the north, a brook full of speckled trout to the west and, in the east, a pasture in which a dozen Holstein cattle and a team of Clydesdale horses graze together. The pastor, Rev. Horace Zwicker, his wife, Myrtle, and their five children live in a flat behind the pulpit.

Pastor Zwicker was born in Indian River and, before he was called of God to the ministry, was a door-to-door salesman of magazine subscriptions and patent medicines, chauffeur for a chiropractor, and accordionist in a hillbilly band that toured the Maritime Provinces and Maine.

Services are held in the tabernacle Wednesday night, Sunday morning and Sunday night. During the summer evangelists arrive, usually from Alabama, Georgia or Tennessee, and then there are services every night of the week. Almost every one of the evangelists has some sort of speciality, like painting a pastel portrait of Christ as he delivers his sermon or playing "The Old Rugged Cross" on an instrument made from empty whiskey bottles. Once there was a man with a long black beard and shoulder-length hair who claimed to have gone to school with Hitler; another time a professed ex-convict named Bent-Knee Benjamin preached in striped pajamas, a ball and chain fastened to his leg.

Fire-Baptized people worry a good deal about sin—mostly innocent little rural sins like smoking, drinking, watching television and going to the movies. Fire-Baptized women, of whom there are several thousands in northwestern New Brunswick, are easy to identify on the streets of towns like Woodstock and Fredericton because they don't use cosmetics and wear their hair in a sort of Oregon Trail bun at the backs of their necks. Fire-Baptized girls are made to dress somewhat the way Elizabeth dressed before she met Philip. There is a legend, invented presumably by Anglicans and Catholics, that Fire-Baptized girls are extraordinarily agreeable and inordinately passionate.

A few years ago there happened to be an unusually large number of unmarried young men and women in Indian River.

Pastor Zwicker frequently discussed this matter with his Lord.

"Lord," he said, "You know as well as I do that it isn't good to have a pack of hot young bucks and fancy-free young females running around loose. Like Paul says, those who don't marry are apt to burn, and when they've burned long enough they'll do just about anything to put the fire out. Now, tell me straight, Lord, what do You figure I should do about it?"

The Lord offered various suggestions and Pastor Zwicker tried them all.

He had long and prayerful conversations with each young man and woman. He told Harris Brandt, for example, that Rebecca Vaneyck was not only a sweet Christian girl, pure and obedient, she made the best blueberry pie of any cook her age in Connaught County. "Never cared much for blueberries myself, Pastor," Harris said. He told Rebecca that Harris was a stout Christian youth who wouldn't get drunk, except if he were sorely tempted of the devil on election day, and wouldn't beat her unless she really deserved it. And she replied: "But, Pastor, he has such bad teeth!"

His conversations with the others were equally fruitless. The Lord advised stronger methods.

"Look here, Brother," the pastor admonished young Francis Witt's father, "it's time that young fellow of yours settled down and got himself a wife. I was talking it over with the Lord just the other night. Now, as you're well aware, Brother, the Scriptures tell us that a son should be obedient to his father. So if I was you—"

"Need the boy," replied the father. "Couldn't run this place without him. Talked to the Lord about it myself. Wife did too. Lord said maybe Francis wouldn't ever get married. Might be an old bachelor like his Uncle Ike. Nothing wrong in that, Lord said."

Other parents made other excuses. If even one couple had responded favourably to his efforts, Pastor Zwicker might have decided that he was worrying himself and the Lord needlessly. But to be met everywhere by disinterest! It was unnatural. Was the devil turning his flock into a herd of Papist celibates?

He had talked once with an escapee from a nunnery in Ireland. A tunnel to the rectory. Lecherous old men, naked under their black nightgowns. Babies' bones in the walls.

His body trembled and his soul—although he did not know this and would have been horrified had he known—made the sign of the cross. What was there left for a man of God to do?

God moves in a mysterious way His wonders to perform. The following Sunday night the power of the Holy Ghost shook the tabernacle to its very foundations. The Day of Pentecost described in the Acts of the Apostles was reenacted with more fervour than ever before in Indian River.

Pastor Zwicker has summoned a guitarist from Houlton, Maine, and a fiddler from Fredericton. He himself played the accordion and his wife the Jew's harp. Old Sister Rossa was at the piano and little Billy Wagner was sent home to fetch his harmonica and mandolin.

There was music—music even as the pastor laid aside his accordion and preached, music and singing and, as the service progressed, a Jericho dance up and down the aisle.

Later, old men said it was the best sermon they had ever heard. "Brother Zwicker just opened his mouth and let the Lord fill it," they said.

His theme was the sins of the flesh. As near as Woodstock, as near as Fredericton, as near as Presque Isle, half-naked women with painted faces and scented bodies prowled the streets seeking whom they might devour. He had looked upon their naked thighs, observed the voluptuous movements of their rumps, had noted that their nipples were visible through their blouses. In King Square in Saint John he had stepped aside to allow a young lady to precede him onto a bus and had discovered to his horrified amazement that she was not wearing drawers. Saint John was another Babylon where before long men and women would be dancing together naked in the streets.

There was much more of the same kind of thing, interspersed, of course, with many quotations from the Bible, particularly from Genesis, Leviticus and Revelation. The Bible was almost the only book that Pastor Zwicker had ever read and he knew great stretches of it by heart.

"Praise the Lord!" the people shouted. "Hallelujah! Thank you, Jesus!"

Old Ike Witt stood on his chair and danced.

"Oh, diddly-doe-dum, diddly-dee-doe-dee," he sang. "Oh, too-row-lou-row-tiddly-lou-do-dee! Glory to Jesus! Diddly-day-dum! Glory to Jesus! Tiddly-lee-tum-tee!"

Matilda Rega threw herself on the floor, laughing and crying, yelling: "Oh, Jesus! Christ Almighty! Oh, sweet Jesus! God Almighty! Oh, Jesus!"

She began crawling down the aisle toward the altar.

The Jericho dancers leapt back and forth across her wriggling body:

We are marching to Zion!
Beautiful, beautiful Zion!
We are marching to Zion,
The beautiful City of God!

Kneeling before the altar, Timothy Fairvort whimpered and slapped his own face, first one cheek, then the other.

"I have sinned," he moaned.

SLAP!

"I have lusted in my heart."

SLAP!

"I will burn in hell if I am not saved."

SLAP!

"Oh, help me, Jesus."

SLAP!

The Jericho dancers sang:

Joy, Joy, Joy, There is joy in my heart!
Joy in my heart! Joy in my heart!
Joy, Joy, Joy, There is joy in my heart!
Joy in my heart TODAY!

It was as if the midway of the Fredericton Exhibition, Hank Snow and the Rainbow Ranch Boys, Oral Roberts, Billy Graham, a Salvation Army band, Lester Flatt and Earl Scruggs, Garner Ted Armstrong and a Tory leadership convention were somehow all rolled into one and compressed into the lobby of the Admiral Beatty Hotel in Saint John.

Then it happened.

Sister Zwicker began speaking in an unknown tongue.

"Elohim!" she yelled. "Elohim, angaro metalani negat! Gonolariski motono etalo bene! Wanga! Wanga! Angaro talans fo do easta analandanoro!"

"Listen!" roared the pastor. "Listen!"

The Jericho dancers sang:

When the saints go marching in!
When the saints go marching in!
How I long to be in that company
When the saints go marching in!

"Elohim!" screamed Myrtle Zwicker. "Wanga! Ortoro ortoro clana estanatoro! Wanga!"

"Listen!" bellowed the pastor. "Listen!"

Others took up the cry. At last the Jericho dancers returned to their seats, exhausted, sweat pouring down their hot, red faces. The music faded away. Old Ike Witt climbed down from his chair. Matilda Rega lay still, quietly sobbing, at the foot of the altar. Timothy Fairvort put his jacket over his head, like a criminal in a newspaper photograph. There was silence except for the voices of the pastor and his wife.

"The Lord is talking to us!" shouted the pastor, who had by now taken off his jacket and tie and unbuttoned his shirt to the waist. "Harken to the voice of the Lord!"

"Elohim!" cried his wife. "Naro talaro eganoto wanga! Tao laro matanotalero. Wanga!"

"It is Egyptian," the pastor explained. "The Lord is addressing us in the language of Pharaoh, the tongue that Joseph spoke when he was a prisoner in the land of Egypt."

"Egyptian," murmured the congregation. "Thank you, Jesus."

"Taro wanga sundaro—"

"The Lord is telling us that His heart is saddened."

"Metizo walla toro delandonaro—"

"His heart is saddened by the disobedience of His people."

"Crena wontano meta kleva sancta danco—"

"The disobedience and perversity of His young people is heavy upon His heart."

"Zalanto wanga—"

"For they have refused to marry and multiply and be fruitful and replenish the earth, as He has commanded them."

"Toronalanta wanga—"

"In His mercy He has chosen to give them one more chance to escape the just punishment for their disobedience."

"Praise His name! Thank you, Jesus!"

"Willo morto innitaro—"

"It is His will that His handmaiden, Rebecca Vaneyck, should become the bride of—"

"Altaro mintanaro—"

"Yes, yes, the bride of Harris Brandt. This is the will of the God of Abraham and of Isaac and of Jacob, for it was He who brought you out of the land of Egypt."

"Yes, yes," chanted the congregation. "It is the Lord's will. Let it be done. Hallelujah!"

Rebecca and Harris were led to the altar. They looked at one another with dazed, wondering faces. After a moment he reached out and took her hand.

Within half an hour, three other couples stood with them. The Lord had revealed His will. Puny mortals such as they had no say in the matter.

The Jericho dancers leapt and cavorted in thanksgiving. So did Ike Witt and Timothy Fairvort, whose face was still hidden by his jacket. He stumbled blindly around the tabernacle, knocking over chairs, singing behind his jacket:

When the roll is called up yonder!
When the roll is called up yonder!
When the roll is called up yonder!
When the roll is called up yonder,
I'll be there!

Pastor Zwicker fanned himself with a copy of *The Fire-Baptized Quarterly.* Next week there would be four marriages in his tabernacle. The Lord's will had been accomplished.

"Thank you, Jesus," he murmured.

Then he remembered Ike Witt and Matilda Rega, the old bachelor and the old maid. Could it be the Lord's will that they, too, should be joined together? He would discuss it with Myrtle. Perhaps next Sunday the Lord would reveal His thoughts about the matter.

Joyce Carol Oates

(b. 1938)

Joyce Carol Oates was born in New York, and educated at Syracuse University and the University of Wisconsin. She now lives in Canada, and teaches English at the University of Windsor. Her work has received wide critical acclaim, and brought her many awards, including a Guggenheim Fellowship in 1967 and an O. Henry Special Award for Continuing Achievement in 1970. She has written five novels and two volumes of poetry, and had two plays produced on the New York stage; in addition to these successes, her short stories have appeared in many journals and anthologies, and have been published in four collections, the latest of which is *Marriages and Infidelities* (1972).

In her preoccupation with violence, emotional disturbance, and familial conflict, Oates has been likened to William Faulkner; and there is undoubtedly a dark, sometimes melodramatic, quality to her writing which recalls the "Gothic" element in Faulkner's books. Her novel *Wonderland* (1971), for example, opens with the shotgun slaying of five people. Many of her characters are ordinary people who, confronted by the apparent senselessness of life, are driven to extremes by fear or frustration; or they are stunned, like Sister Irene in "In the Region of Ice" (*The Wheel of Love*, 1970), by an awareness of human helplessness and isolation. In an exchange of letters with the American writer Joe David Bellamy, Oates wrote: "I believe that the storm of emotion constitutes our human tragedy, if anything does. It's our constant battle with nature (Nature), trying to subdue chaos outside and inside ourselves, occasionally winning small victories, then being swept along by some cataclysmic event of our own making. I feel an enormous sympathy with people who've gone under, who haven't won even the smallest victories. . . . "

For further reading

J. D. Bellamy, "The Dark Lady of American Letters," *Atlantic Monthly*, 229 (February 1972), 63–67.

Joyce Carol Oates, "Building Tension in the Short Story," *Writer*, 79 (June 1966), 11–12; "Background and Foreground in Fiction," *Writer*, 80 (August 1967), 11–13.

Carolyn Walker, "Fear, Love, and Art in Oates' 'Plot,'" *Critique: Studies in Modern Fiction*, 15, i (1973), 59–70.

In the Region of Ice

Sister Irene was a tall, deft woman in her early thirties. What one could see of her face made a striking impression—serious, hard gray eyes, a long slender nose, a face waxen with thought. Seen at the right time, from the right angle, she was almost handsome. In her past teaching positions she had drawn a little upon the fact of her being young and brilliant and also a nun, but she was beginning to grow out of that.

This was a new university and an entirely new world. She had heard—of course it was true—that the Jesuit administration of this school had hired her at the last moment to save money and to head off the appointment of a man of dubious religious commitment. She had prayed for the necessary energy to get her through this first semester. She had no trouble with teaching itself; once she stood before a classroom she felt herself capable of anything. It was the world immediately outside the classroom that confused and alarmed her, though she let none of this show—the cynicism of her colleagues, the indifference of many of the students, and, above all, the looks she got that told her nothing much would be expected of her because she was a nun. This took energy, strength. At times she had the idea that she was on trial and that the excuses she made to herself about her discomfort were only the common excuses made by guilty people. But in front of a class she had no time to worry about herself or the conflicts in her mind. She became, once and for all, a figure existing only for the benefit of others, an instrument by which facts were communicated.

About two weeks after the semester began, Sister Irene noticed a new student in her class. He was slight and fair-haired, and his face was blank, but not blank by accident, blank on purpose, suppressed and restricted into a dumbness that looked hysterical. She was prepared for him before he raised his hand, and when she saw his arm jerk, as if he had at last lost control of it, she nodded to him without hesitation.

"Sister, how can this be reconciled with Shakespeare's vision in *Hamlet?* How can these opposing views be in the same mind?"

Students glanced at him, mildly surprised. He did not belong in the class, and this was mysterious, but his manner was urgent and blind.

"There is no need to reconcile opposing views," Sister Irene said, leaning forward against the podium. "In one play Shakespeare suggests one vision, in another play another; the plays are not simultaneous creations, and even if they were, we never demand a logical —"

"We must demand a logical consistency," the young man said. "The idea of education is itself predicated upon consistency, order, sanity—"

He had interrupted her, and she hardened her face against him—for his sake, not her own, since she did not really care. But he noticed nothing. "Please see me after class," she said.

After class the young man hurried up to her.

"Sister Irene, I hope you didn't mind my visiting today. I'd heard some things, interesting things," he said. He stared at her, and something in her face allowed him to smile. "I . . . could we talk in your office? Do you have time?"

They walked down to her office. Sister Irene sat at her desk, and the young man sat facing her; for a moment they were self-conscious and silent.

"Well, I suppose you know—I'm a Jew," he said.

Sister Irene stared at him. "Yes?" she said.

"What am I doing at a Catholic university, huh?" He grinned. "That's what you want to know."

She made a vague movement of her hand to show that she had no thoughts on this, nothing at all, but he seemed not to catch it. He was sitting on the edge of the straight-backed chair. She saw that he was young but did not really look young. There were harsh lines on either side of his mouth, as if he had misused that youthful mouth somehow. His skin was almost as pale as hers, his eyes were dark and not quite in focus. He looked at her and through her and around her, as his voice surrounded them both. His voice was a little shrill at times.

"Listen, I did the right thing today—visiting your class! God, what a lucky accident it was; some jerk mentioned you, said you were a good teacher—I thought, what a laugh! These people know about good teachers here? But yes, listen, yes, I'm not kidding—you are good. I mean that."

Sister Irene frowned. "I don't quite understand what all this means."

He smiled and waved aside her formality, as if he knew better. "Listen, I got my B.A. at Columbia, then I came back here to this crappy city. I mean, I did it on purpose, I wanted to come back. I wanted to. I have my reasons for doing things. I'm on a three-thousand-dollar fellowship," he said, and waited for that to impress her. "You know, I could have gone almost anywhere with that fellowship, and I came back home here—my home's in the city—and enrolled here. This was last year. This is my second year. I'm working on a thesis, I mean I was, my master's thesis—but the hell with that. What I want to ask you is this: Can I enroll in your class, is it too late? We have to get special permission if we're late."

Sister Irene felt something nudging her, some uneasiness in him that was pleading with her not to be offended by his abrupt, familiar manner. He seemed to be promising another self, a better self, as if his fair, childish, almost cherubic face were doing tricks to distract her from what his words said.

"Are you in English studies?" she asked.

"I was in history. Listen," he said, and his mouth did something odd, drawing itself down into a smile that made the lines about it deepen like knives, "listen, they kicked me out."

He sat back, watching her. He crossed his legs. He took out a package of cigarettes and offered her one. Sister Irene shook her head, staring at his hands. They were small and stubby and might have belonged to a ten-year-old, and the nails were a strange near-violet color. It took him awhile to extract a cigarette.

"Yeah, kicked me out. What do you think of that?"

"I don't understand."

"My master's thesis was coming along beautifully, and then this bastard—I mean, excuse me, this professor, I won't pollute your office with his name—he started making criticisms, he said some things were unacceptable, he—" The boy leaned forward and hunched his narrow shoulders in a parody of secrecy. "We had an argument. I told him some frank things, things only a broad-minded person could hear about himself. That takes courage, right? He didn't have it! He kicked me out of the master's program, so now I'm coming into English. Literature is greater than history; European history is one big pile of garbage. Sky-high. Filth and rotting corpses, right? Aristotle says that poetry is higher than history; he's right; in your class today I suddenly realized that this is my field, Shakespeare, only Shakespeare is—"

Sister Irene guessed that he was going to say that only Shakespeare was equal to him, and she caught the moment of recognition and hesitation, the half-raised arm, the keen, frowning forehead, the narrowed eyes; then he thought better of it and did not end the sentence. "The students in your class are mainly negligible, I can tell you that. You're new here, and I've been here a year—I would have finished my studies last year but my father got sick, he was hospitalized, I couldn't take exams and it was a mess—but I'll make it through English in one year or drop dead. I can do it, I can do anything. I'll take six courses at once—" He broke off, breathless. Sister Irene tried to smile. "All right then, it's settled? You'll let me in? Have I missed anything so far?"

He had no idea of the rudeness of his question. Sister Irene, feeling suddenly exhausted, said, "I'll give you a syllabus of the course."

"Fine! Wonderful!"

He got to his feet eagerly. He looked through the schedule, muttering to himself, making favorable noises. It struck Sister Irene that she was making a mistake to let him in. There were these moments when one had to make an intelligent decision.... But she was sympathetic with him, yes. She was sympathetic with something about him.

She found out his name the next day: Allen Weinstein.

After this she came to her Shakespeare class with a sense of excitement. It became clear to her at once that Weinstein was the most intelligent student in the class. Until he had enrolled, she had not understood what was lacking, a mind that could appreciate her own. Within a week his jagged, protean mind had alienated the other students, and though he sat in the center of the class, he seemed totally alone, encased by a miniature world of his own. When he spoke of the "frenetic humanism of the High Renaissance," Sister Irene dreaded the raised eyebrows and mocking smiles of the other students, who no longer bothered to look at Weinstein. She wanted to defend him, but she never did, because there was something rude and dismal about his knowledge; he used it like a weapon, talking passionately of Nietzsche and Goethe and Freud until Sister Irene would be forced to close discussion.

In meditation, alone, she often thought of him. When she tried to talk about him to a young nun, Sister Carlotta, everything sounded gross. "But no, he's an excellent student," she insisted. "I'm very grateful to have him in class. It's just that ... he thinks ideas are real." Sister Carlotta, who loved literature also, had been forced to teach grade-school arithmetic for the last four years. That might have been why she said, a little sharply, "You don't think ideas are real?"

Sister Irene acquiesced with a smile, but of course she did not think so: only reality is real.

When Weinstein did not show up for class on the day the first paper was due, Sister Irene's heart sank, and the sensation was somehow a familiar one. She began her lecture and kept waiting for the door to open and for him to hurry noisily back to his seat, grinning an apology toward her—but nothing happened.

If she had been deceived by him, she made herself think angrily, it was as a teacher and not as a woman. He had promised her nothing.

Weinstein appeared the next day near the steps of the liberal arts building. She heard someone running behind her, a breathless exclamation: "Sister Irene!" She turned and saw him, panting and grinning in embarrassment. He wore a dark-blue suit with a necktie, and he looked, despite his childish face, like a little old man; there was something oddly precarious and fragile about him. "Sister Irene, I owe you an apology, right?" He raised his eyebrows and smiled a sad, forlorn, yet irritatingly conspiratorial smile. "The first paper— not in on time, and I know what your rules are. . . . You won't accept late papers, I know—that's good discipline, I'll do that when I teach too. But, unavoidably, I was unable to come to school yesterday. There are many—many—" He gulped for breath, and Sister Irene had the startling sense of seeing the real Weinstein stare out at her, a terrified prisoner behind the confident voice. "There are many complications in family life. Perhaps you are unaware—I mean—"

She did not like him, but she felt this sympathy, something tug- ging and nagging at her the way her parents had competed for her love so many years before. They had been whining, weak people, and out of their wet need for affection, the girl she had been (her name was Yvonne) had emerged stronger than either of them, con- temptuous of tears because she had seen so many. But Weinstein was different; he was not simply weak—perhaps he was not weak at all —but his strength was confused and hysterical. She felt her custom- ary rigidity as a teacher begin to falter. "You may turn your paper in today if you have it," she said, frowning.

Weinstein's mouth jerked into an incredulous grin. "Wonderful! Marvelous!" he said. "You are very understanding, Sister Irene, I must say. I must say . . . I didn't expect, really . . . " He was fumbling in a shabby old briefcase for the paper. Sister Irene waited. She was prepared for another of his excuses, certain that he did not have the paper, when he suddenly straightened up and handed her some- thing. "Here! I took the liberty of writing thirty pages instead of just fifteen," he said. He was obviously quite excited; his cheeks were mottled pink and white. "You may disagree violently with my inter- pretation—I expect you to, in fact I'm counting on it—but let me warn you, I have the exact proof, right here in the play itself!" He was thumping at a book, his voice growing louder and shriller. Sister Irene, startled, wanted to put her hand over his mouth and soothe him.

"Look," he said breathlessly, "may I talk with you? I have a class now I hate, I loathe, I can't bear to sit through! Can I talk with you instead?"

Because she was nervous, she stared at the title page of the paper: " 'Erotic Melodies in *Romeo and Juliet*' by Allen Weinstein, Jr."

"All right?" he said. "Can we walk around here? Is it all right? I've been anxious to talk with you about some things you said in class."

She was reluctant, but he seemed not to notice. They walked slowly along the shaded campus paths. Weinstein did all the talking, of course, and Sister Irene recognized nothing in his cascade of words that she had mentioned in class. "The humanist must be committed to the totality of life," he said passionately. "This is the failing one finds everywhere in the academic world! I found it in New York and I found it here and I'm no ingénu, I don't go around with my mouth hanging open—I'm experienced, look, I've been to Europe, I've lived in Rome! I went everywhere in Europe except Germany, I don't talk about Germany . . . Sister Irene, think of the significant men in the last century, the men who've changed the world! Jews, right? Marx, Freud, Einstein! Not that I believe Marx, Marx is a madman . . . and Freud, no, my sympathies are with spiritual humanism. I believe that the Jewish race is the exclusive . . . the exclusive, what's the word, the exclusive means by which humanism will be extended. . . . Humanism begins by excluding the Jew, and now," he said with a high, suprised laugh, "the Jew will perfect it. After the Nazis, only the Jew is authorized to understand humanism, its limitations and its possibilities. So, I say that the humanist is committed to life in its totality and not just to his profession! The religious person is totally religious, he is his religion! What else? I recognize in you a humanist and a religious person—"

But he did not seem to be talking to her or even looking at her.

"Here, read this," he said. "I wrote it last night." It was a long free-verse poem, typed on a typewriter whose ribbon was worn out.

"There's this trouble with my father, a wonderful man, a lovely man, but his health—his strength is fading, do you see? What must it be to him to see his son growing up? I mean, I'm a man now, he's getting old, weak, his health is bad—it's hell, right? I sympathize with him. I'd do anything for him, I'd cut open my veins, anything for a father—right? That's why I wasn't in school yesterday," he said, and his voice dropped for the last sentence, as if he had been dragged back to earth by a fact.

Sister Irene tried to read the poem, then pretended to read it. A jumble of words dealing with "life" and "death" and "darkness" and "love." "What do you think?" Weinstein said nervously, trying to read it over her shoulder and crowding against her.

"It's very . . . passionate," Sister Irene said.

This was the right comment; he took the poem back from her in silence, his face flushed with excitement. "Here, at this school, I have few people to talk with. I haven't shown anyone else that poem." He looked at her with his dark, intense eyes, and Sister Irene felt them focus upon her. She was terrified at what he was trying to do—he was trying to force her into a human relationship.

"Thank you for your paper," she said, turning away.

When he came the next day, ten minutes late, he was haughty and disdainful. He had nothing to say and sat with his arms folded. Sister Irene took back with her to the convent a feeling of betrayal and confusion. She had been hurt. It was absurd, and yet—She spent too much time thinking about him, as if he were somehow a kind of crystallization of her own loneliness; but she had no right to think so much of him. She did not want to think of him or of her loneliness. But Weinstein did so much more than think of his predicament: he embodied it, he acted it out, and that was perhaps why he fascinated her. It was as if he were doing a dance for her, a dance of shame and agony and delight, and so long as he did it, she was safe. She felt embarrassment for him, but also anxiety; she wanted to protect him. When the dean of the graduate school questioned her about Weinstein's work, she insisted that he was an "excellent" student, though she knew the dean had not wanted to hear that.

She prayed for guidance, she spent hours on her devotions, she was closer to her vocation than she had been for some years. Life at the convent became tinged with unreality, a misty distortion that took its tone from the glowering skies of the city at night, identical smokestacks ranged against the clouds and giving to the sky the excrement of the populated and successful earth. This city was not her city, this world was not her world. She felt no pride in knowing this, it was a fact. The little convent was not like an island in the center of this noisy world, but rather a kind of hole or crevice the world did not bother with, something of no interest. The convent's rhythm of life had nothing to do with the world's rhythm, it did not violate or alarm it in any way. Sister Irene tried to draw together the fragments of her life and synthesize them somehow in her vocation as a nun: she was a nun, she was recognized as a nun and had given herself happily to that life, she had a name, a place, she had dedicated her superior intelligence to the Church, she worked without pay and without expecting gratitude, she had given up pride, she did not think of herself but only of her work and her vocation, she did not think of anything external to these, she saturated herself daily in the knowledge that she was involved in the mystery of Christianity.

A daily terror attended this knowledge, however, for she sensed herself being drawn by that student, that Jewish boy, into a relationship she was not ready for. She wanted to cry out in fear that she was being forced into the role of a Christian, and what did that mean? What could her studies tell her? What could the other nuns tell her? She was alone, no one could help; he was making her into a Christian, and to her that was a mystery, a thing of terror, something others slipped on the way they slipped on their clothes, casually and thoughtlessly, but to her a magnificent and terrifying wonder.

For days she carried Weinstein's paper, marked A, around with her; he did not come to class. One day she checked with the graduate office and was told that Weinstein had called in to say his father was ill and that he would not be able to attend classes for a while. "He's strange, I remember him," the secretary said. "He missed all his exams last spring and made a lot of trouble. He was in and out of here every day."

So there was no more of Weinstein for a while, and Sister Irene stopped expecting him to hurry into class. Then, one morning, she found a letter from him in her mailbox.

He had printed it in black ink, very carefully, as if he had not trusted handwriting. The return address was in bold letters that, like his voice, tried to grab onto her: Birchcrest Manor. Somewhere north of the city. "Dear Sister Irene," the block letters said, "I am doing well here and have time for reading and relaxing. The Manor is delightful. My doctor here is an excellent, intelligent man who has time for me, unlike my former doctor. If you have time, you might drop in on my father, who worries about me too much, I think, and explain to him what my condition is. He doesn't seem to understand. I feel about this new life the way that boy, what's his name, in *Measure for Measure,* feels about the prospects of a different life; you remember what he says to his sister when she visits him in prison, how he is looking forward to an escape into another world. Perhaps you could *explain* this to my father and he would stop worrying." The letter ended with the father's name and address, in letters that were just a little too big. Sister Irene, walking slowly down the corridor as she read the letter, felt her eyes cloud over with tears. She was cold with fear, it was something she had never experienced before. She knew what Weinstein was trying to tell her, and the desperation of his attempt made it all the more pathetic; he did not deserve this, why did God allow him to suffer so?

She read through Claudio's speech to his sister, in *Measure for Measure:*

Ay, but to die, and go we know not where;
To lie in cold obstruction and to rot;
This sensible warm motion to become
A kneaded clod; and the delighted spirit
To bathe in fiery floods, or to reside
In thrilling region of thick-ribbed ice,
To be imprison'd in the viewless winds
And blown with restless violence round about
The pendent world; or to be worse than worst
Of those that lawless and incertain thought
Imagines howling! 'Tis too horrible!
The weariest and most loathed worldly life

That age, ache, penury, and imprisonment
Can lay on nature is a paradise
To what we fear of death.

Sister Irene called the father's number that day. "Allen Weinstein residence, who may I say is calling?" a woman said, bored. "May I speak to Mr. Weinstein? It's urgent—about his son," Sister Irene said. There was a pause at the other end. "You want to talk to his mother, maybe?" the woman said. "His mother? Yes, his mother, then. Please. It's very important."

She talked with this strange, unsuspected woman, a disembodied voice that suggested absolutely no face, and insisted upon going over that afternoon. The woman was nervous, but Sister Irene, who was a university professor, after all, knew enough to hide her own nervousness. She kept waiting for the woman to say, "Yes, Allen has mentioned you ... " but nothing happened.

She persuaded Sister Carlotta to ride over with her. This urgency of hers was something they were all amazed by. They hadn't suspected that the set of her gray eyes could change to this blurred, distracted alarm, this sense of mission that seemed to have come to her from nowhere. Sister Irene drove across the city in the late afternoon traffic, with the high whining noises from residential streets where trees were being sawed down in pieces. She understood now the secret, sweet wildness that Christ must have felt, giving himself for man, dying for the billions of men who would never know of him and never understand the sacrifice. For the first time she approached the realization of that great act. In her troubled mind the city traffic was jumbled and yet oddly coherent, an image of the world that was always out of joint with what was happening in it, its inner history struggling with its external spectacle. This sacrifice of Christ's, so mysterious and legendary now, almost lost in time—it was that by which Christ transcended both God and man at one moment, more than man because of his fate to do what no other man could do, and more than God because no god could suffer as he did. She felt a flicker of something close to madness.

She drove nervously, uncertainly, afraid of missing the street and afraid of finding it too, for while one part of her rushed forward to confront these people who had betrayed their son, another part of her would have liked nothing so much as to be waiting as usual for the summons to dinner, safe in her room. ... When she found the street and turned onto it, she was in a state of breathless excitement. Here lawns were bright green and marred with only a few leaves, magically clean, and the houses were enormous and pompous, a mixture of styles: ranch houses, colonial houses, French country houses, white-bricked wonders with curving glass and clumps of birch trees somehow encircled by white concrete. Sister Irene stared as if she had blundered into another world. This was a kind of heaven, and she was too shabby for it.

The Weinstein's house was the strangest one of all: it looked like a small Alpine lodge, with an inverted-V-shaped front entrance. Sister Irene drove up the black-topped driveway and let the car slow to a stop; she told Sister Carlotta she would not be long.

At the door she was met by Weinstein's mother, a small, nervous woman with hands like her son's. "Come in, come in," the woman said. She had once been beautiful, that was clear, but now in missing beauty she was not handsome or even attractive but looked ruined and perplexed, the misshapen swelling of her white-blond professionally set hair like a cap lifting up from her surprised face. "He'll be right in. Allen?" she called, "our visitor is here." They went into the living room. There was a grand piano at one end and an organ at the other. In between were scatterings of brilliant modern furniture in conversational groups, and several puffed-up white rugs on the polished floor. Sister Irene could not stop shivering.

"Professor, it's so strange, but let me say when the phone rang I had a feeling—I had a feeling," the woman said, with damp eyes. Sister Irene sat, and the woman hovered about her. "Should I call you Professor? We don't . . . you know . . . we don't understand the technicalities that go with—Allen, my son, wanted to go here to the Catholic school; I told my husband why not? Why fight? It's the thing these days, they do anything they want for knowledge. And he had to come home, you know. He couldn't take care of himself in New York, that was the beginning of the trouble. . . . Should I call you Professor?"

"You can call me Sister Irene."

"Sister Irene?" the woman said, touching her throat in awe, as if something intimate and unexpected had happened.

Then Weinstein's father appeared, hurrying. He took long, impatient strides. Sister Irene stared at him and in that instant doubted everything—he was in his fifties, a tall, sharply handsome man, heavy but not fat, holding his shoulders back with what looked like an effort, but holding them back just the same. He wore a dark suit and his face was flushed, as if he had run a long distance.

"Now," he said, coming to Sister Irene and with a precise wave of his hand motioning his wife off, "now, let's straighten this out. A lot of confusion over that kid, eh?" He pulled a chair over, scraping it across a rug and pulling one corner over, so that its brown underside was exposed. "I came home early just for this, Libby phoned me. Sister, you got a letter from him, right?"

The wife looked at Sister Irene over her husband's head as if trying somehow to coach her, knowing that this man was so loud and impatient that no one could remember anything in his presence.

"A letter—yes—today—"

"He says what in it? You got the letter, eh? Can I see it?"

She gave it to him and wanted to explain, but he silenced her with a flick of his hand. He read through the letter so quickly that Sister Irene thought perhaps he was trying to impress her with his skill at reading. "So?" he said, raising his eyes, smiling, "so what is this? He's happy out there, he says. He doesn't communicate with us any more, but he writes to you and says he's happy—what's that? I mean, what the hell is that?"

"But he isn't happy. He wants to come home," Sister Irene said. It was so important that she make him understand that she could not trust her voice; goaded by this man, it might suddenly turn shrill, as his son's did. "Someone must read their letters before they're mailed, so he tried to tell me something by making an allusion to—"

"What?"

"—an allusion to a play, so that I would know. He may be thinking suicide, he must be very unhappy—"

She ran out of breath. Weinstein's mother had begun to cry, but the father was shaking his head jerkily back and forth. "Forgive me, Sister, but it's a lot of crap, he needs the hospital, he needs help— right? It costs me fifty a day out there, and they've got the best place in the state, I figure it's worth it. He needs help, that kid, what do I care if he's unhappy? He's unbalanced!" he said angrily. "You want us to get him out again? We argued with the judge for two hours to get him in, an acquaintance of mine. Look, he can't control himself —he was smashing things here, he was hysterical. They need help, lady, and you do something about it fast! You do something! We made up our minds to do something and we did it! This letter—what the hell is this letter? He never talked like that to us!"

"But he means the opposite of what he says—"

"Then he's crazy! I'm the first to admit it." He was perspiring, and his face had darkened. "I've got no pride left this late. He's a little bastard, you want to know? He calls me names, he's filthy, got a filthy mouth—that's being smart, huh? They give him a big scholarship for his filthy mouth? I went to college too, and I got out and knew something, and I for Christ's sake did something with it; my wife is an intelligent woman, a learned woman, would you guess she does book reviews for the little newspaper out here? Intelligent isn't crazy—crazy isn't intelligent. Maybe for you at the school he writes nice papers and gets an A, but out here, around the house, he can't control himself, and we got him committed!"

"But—"

"We're fixing him up, don't worry about it!" He turned to his wife. "Libby, get out of here, I mean it. I'm sorry, but get out of here, you're making a fool of yourself, go stand in the kitchen or something, you and the goddamn maid can cry on each other's shoulders. That one in the kitchen is nuts too, they're all nuts. Sister," he said, his voice lowering, "I thank you immensely for coming out here. This is wonderful, your interest in my son. And I see he admires you—that letter there. But what about that letter? If he did want to get out, which I don't admit—he was willing to be committed, in the end he said okay himself—if he wanted out I wouldn't do it. Why? So what if he wants to come back? The next day he wants something else, what then? He's a sick kid, and I'm the first to admit it."

Sister Irene felt that sickness spread to her. She stood. The room was so big it seemed it must be a public place; there had been nothing personal or private about their conversation. Weinstein's mother was standing by the fireplace, sobbing. The father jumped to his feet and wiped his forehead in a gesture that was meant to help Sister Irene on her way out. "God, what a day," he said, his eyes snatching at hers for understanding, "you know—one of those days all day long? Sister, I thank you a lot. There should be more people in the world who care about others, like you. I mean that."

On the way back to the convent, the man's words returned to her, and she could not get control of them; she could not even feel anger. She had been pressed down, forced back, what could she do? Weinstein might have been watching her somehow from a barred window, and he surely would have understood. The strange idea she had had on the way over, something about understanding Christ, came back to her now and sickened her. But the sickness was small. It could be contained.

About a month after her visit to his father, Weinstein himself showed up. He was dressed in a suit as before, even the necktie was the same. He came right into her office as if he had been pushed and could not stop.

"Sister," he said, and shook her hand. He must have seen fear in her because he smiled ironically. "Look, I'm released. I'm let out of the nut house. Can I sit down?"

He sat. Sister Irene was breathing quickly, as if in the presence of an enemy who does not know he is an enemy.

"So, they finally let me out. I heard what you did. You talked with him, that was all I wanted. You're the only one who gave a damn. Because you're a humanist and a religious person, you respect . . . the individual. Listen," he said, whispering, "it was hell out there! Hell Birchcrest Manor! All fixed up with fancy chairs and *Life* magazines lying around—and what do they do to you? They locked me up, they gave me shock treatments! Shock treatments, how do you like that, it's discredited by everybody now—they're crazy out there themselves, sadists. They locked me up, they gave me hypodermic shots, they didn't treat me like a human being! Do you know what that is," Weinstein demanded savagely, "not to be treated like a human being? They made me an animal—for fifty dollars a day! Dirty filthy swine! Now I'm an outpatient because I stopped swearing at them. I found somebody's bobby pin, and when I wanted to scream I pressed it under my fingernail and it stopped me—the screaming went inside and not out—so they gave me good reports, those sick bastards. Now I'm an outpatient and I can walk along the street and breathe in the same filthy exhaust from the buses like all you normal people! Christ," he said, and threw himself back against the chair.

Sister Irene stared at him. She wanted to take his hand, to make some gesture that would close the aching distance between them. "Mr. Weinstein—"

"Call me Allen!" he said sharply.

"I'm very sorry—I'm terribly sorry—"

"My own parents committed me, but of course they didn't know what it was like. It was hell," he said thickly, "and there isn't any hell except what other people do to you. The psychiatrist out there, the main shrink, he hates Jews too, some of us were positive of that, and he's got a bigger nose than I do, a real beak." He made a noise of disgust. "A dirty bastard, a sick, dirty, pathetic bastard—all of them. Anyway, I'm getting out of here, and I came to ask you a favor."

"What do you mean?"

"I'm getting out. I'm leaving. I'm going up to Canada and lose myself. I'll get a job, I'll forget everything. I'll kill myself maybe— what's the difference? Look, can you lend me some money?"

"Money?"

"Just a little! I have to get to the border, I'm going to take a bus."

"But I don't have any money—"

"No money?" He stared at her. "You mean—you don't have any? Sure you have some!"

She stared at him as if he had asked her to do something obscene. Everything was splotched and uncertain before her eyes.

"You must ... you must go back," she said, "you're making a—"

"I'll pay it back. Look, I'll pay it back, can you go to where you live or something and get it? I'm in a hurry. My friends are sons of bitches: one of them pretended he didn't see me yesterday—I stood right in the middle of the sidewalk and yelled at him, I called him some appropriate names! So he didn't see me, huh? You're the only one who understands me, you understand me like a poet, you—"

"I can't help you, I'm sorry—I . . . "

He looked to one side of her and flashed his gaze back, as if he could control it. He seemed to be trying to clear his vision.

"You have the soul of a poet," he whispered, "you're the only one. Everybody else is rotten! Can't you lend me some money, ten dollars maybe? I have three thousand in the bank, and I can't touch it! They take everything away from me, they make me into an animal. . . . You know I'm not an animal, don't you? Don't you?"

"Of course," Sister Irene whispered.

"You could get money. Help me. Give me your hand or something, touch me, help me—please. . . . " He reached for her hand and she drew back. He stared at her and his face seemed about to crumble, like a child's. "I want something from you, but I don't know what —I want something!" he cried. "Something real! I want you to look at me like I was a human being, is that too much to ask? I have a brain, I'm alive, I'm suffering—what does that mean? Does that mean nothing? I want something real and not this phony Christian love garbage—it's all in the books, it isn't personal—I want something real—look. . . . "

He tried to take her hand again, and this time she jerked away. She got to her feet. "Mr. Weinstein," she said, "please—"

"You! You nun!" he said scornfully, his mouth twisted into a mock grin. "You nun! There's nothing under that ugly outfit, right? And you're not particularly smart even though you think you are; my father has more brains in his foot than you—"

He got to his feet and kicked the chair.

"You bitch!" he cried.

She shrank back against her desk as if she thought he might hit her, but he only ran out of the office.

Weinstein: the name was to become disembodied from the figure, as time went on. The semester passed, the autumn drizzle turned into snow, Sister Irene rode to school in the morning and left in the afternoon, four days a week, anonymous in her black winter cloak, quiet and stunned. University teaching was an anonymous task, each day dissociated from the rest, with no necessary sense of unity among the teachers: they came and went separately and might for a year just miss a colleague who left his office five minutes before they arrived, and it did not matter.

She heard of Weinstein's death, his suicide by drowning, from the English Department secretary, a handsome white-haired woman who kept a transistor radio on her desk. Sister Irene was not surprised; she had been thinking of him as dead for months. "They identified him by some special television way they have now," the secretary said. "They're shipping the body back. It was up in Quebec. ... "

Sister Irene could feel a part of herself drifting off, lured by the plains of white snow to the north, the quiet, the emptiness, the sweep of the Great Lakes up to the silence of Canada. But she called that part of herself back. She could only be one person in her lifetime. That was the ugly truth, she thought, that she could not really regret Weinstein's suffering and death; she had only one life and had already given it to someone else. He had come too late to her. Fifteen years ago, perhaps, but not now.

She was only one person, she thought, walking down the corridor in a dream. Was she safe in this single person, or was she trapped? She had only one identity. She could make only one choice. What she had done or hadn't done was the result of that choice, and how was she guilty? If she could have felt guilt, she thought, she might at least have been able to feel something.

Hal Porter

(b. 1911)

A schoolmaster in his native Australia for over twenty years, Hal Porter has been a full-time writer since 1961. He has written three novels (the most notable being *The Tilted Cross*, 1961), several volumes of short stories, poems, and history, five plays, and two volumes of autobiography. Many critics regard him as the most accomplished modern Australian short-story writer, one whose wit and linguistic precision are brought to bear upon contemporary behavior, and whose analysis of social structures is accurate and keen. "Many of my problems," he has said, "stem from the curious complexities of Australian society, the infinitely subtle class distinctions beneath a façade of egalitarianism, the fine-drawn sensibilities and leeriness underlying the over-all bonhomie, the shrewd ruthlessness below the love-thy-neighbourliness." His characteristic style is observable even within that one sentence. Though asserting a desire to be stylistically "clear," to write "pellucid and author-untainted" sentences, he writes with a deliberate, sophisticated, complex vocabulary in carefully balanced structures, and he takes delight in sequences of words and phrases that cumulatively modify and expand his originally stated idea. The effect of such phrasing (as in "First Love," which appeared in *The Cats of Venice*, 1965) is often to create an ironic distance between the narrator's expression of himself and the reader's perception of him.

The illusion of life that his art strives for is matched in his two-volume autobiography (*The Watcher on the Cast-Iron Balcony*, 1963, and *The Paper Chase*, 1966) where his own life is given the cast of art. Some critics, responding to the vividness with which his memory records details, have even been led to suggest that many of his first-person short stories are autobiographical reminiscences in fact as well as in form. Whatever the case, a story like "First Love" shows how Porter has adapted his style to a conventional initiation narrative. Events in the "real" world take a child out of his naïve, idealistic private universe and expose him to time and experience.

For further reading

John Barnes, "New Tracks to Travel," *Meanjin*, 25 (1966), 154–170.
Mary Lord, "Hal Porter's Comic Mode," *Australian Literary Studies*, 4 (October 1970), 371–382.

First Love

My paternal grandfather was English, military and long-nosed. He married twice, and had seven sons and four daughters. My maternal grandfather, Swiss, agricultural and long-nosed, married once but had six sons and six daughters. As a child, therefore, I was well-provided not only with ancestral aunts and uncles but also with the uncle-husbands and wife-aunts they had married. Since each of these couples were abundantly productive, long-nosed cousins of all ages, from braggart striplings and chatterbox young women to india-rubber babies like tempestuous Queen Victoria with bonnets awry congested my boyhood. It seems to me now that what my grandparents imported to Australia along with fecundity and long noses was largely noise. Noise, in their case, can be enlarged to cover vivacity bordering on uproar, devil-may-care wildness, a febrile intensity about issues of great unimportance. From the most feckless uncle to the most social aunt, from bread-line-treading aunts to rich uncles, all were afflicted by this rowdy insouciance. My mother, essentially provincial, was nevertheless giddy as a porpoise, and lived like a windmill rotating to alternate gusts of temper and charm.

In this uproarious tribal whirlpool I was odd boy out. A throwback inheritance of some less mettlesome blood braked me. I had the same passion for decorous behaviour as they had for fits-and-starts behaviour, for conversations at full pitch, for gambling and gipsying about. This perversity of self-restraint caused me to lag behind, to be a some-time observer rather than a full-time participant. Yet, oddly enough, I also had maximum *esprit de corps.* Nor was I niminy-piminy and stand-offish. Japan-shaped scabs blotched my fruit-stealer's country boy knees; my bare soles were as rind-like as fire-walkers'. I could swim like a toad, swear like a cow-cocky and smoke like a *débutante.* These abilities and simulated ferocities were, however, strictly conventional. In their execution I went just so far. I drew a line. Other members of the family always went farther and further. I would not, for example, kill snakes as Uncle Foster and cousins and brothers did by cracking them like whips. Sticks did me. As well as affecting protective discretions such as this, and making withdrawals from hereditary bravura, I often broke the wrong rules. My brothers and country cousins each had a dog, usually a bossy fox-terrier or a smart-alec mong with lots of heeler in it. I had a cat. I found its relative muteness and disdainful independence preferable to the ostentatious servility and noisily neurasthenic demands of dogs. Need I say that I wore spectacles and spoke in polysyllables?

Not only did I violate the clan code by visible nonconformity but I was mentally and invisibly rebellious. This was harder to swear at. I believed, as all we youngsters did, that broken-backed snakes could not die until the sun set, that warts grew where dogs licked one, that to gash the skin linking thumb with forefinger caused lockjaw which we translated as instant and eternal dumbness. Along with the mob I circumspectly believed in ghosts, the end of the world and Spring-heel Jack. Then I ran off the rails. As logic's advocate I believed, for longer than was deemed orthodox or manly, in Father Christmas: his leavings were evidence. I did not believe in God who had let me down in the matter of prayers for a Meccano set. To the terror of others, I said so piercingly enough for the vast ear in the sky to take in the blasphemy. I became the tree for believers not to stand by when lightning flashed.

More disconcerting and shaming than even blasphemy was my most eccentric trait. I cherished the family caprices and florid behaviour so much that I came out of my comparative silence to exult—in public—over what my kith and kin accepted as one does a birthmark better hidden. I let out, to the dirt-rimmed and contemptuous sons of the washerwoman, that Swiss grandfather's daughters, in order of birth, were named Rosa Bona, Adelina, Sophia, Maria, Meta and Ida. I explained that each name, besides ending in A, had, sequentially, one letter less. My brothers, failing to shut me up or divert interest from my humiliating treason, looked bleakly down their noses. I continued to rattle on, chattily revealing my disappointment that there had not been two more aunts born—a final aunt, a fabulous creature called Aunt A, would have exhilarated me more than my favourite Sago Plum Pudding. The family, boorishly I thought, instead of these cunningly graduated names, used Bon, Addie, Sophie, Ria, Min Min and Doll. It irked my senses of order as much as my sense of possession to hear my mother called not Aunt Ida but Auntie Dolly. As a gesture, although Aunt Rosa Bona and Aunt Adelina were mouthfuls, I prissily insisted on using the full names. I was inflexible in not saying Uncle Whit, Uncle Gat and Uncle Tini to my paternal uncles who had been christened Whitworth, Gatling and Martini-Henry after firearms. My military grandfather's other sons were Lancaster, Enfield, Snider and Mauser.

Though pointing an attitude, my delight in these absurdities of baptism was a little only of the magnetism my flamboyant relatives had for me. Even a porcupine regards its own as soft and sleek. I overdid it: my blood-porcupines were powder-puffs and satin to me.

Each aunt and uncle had at least one dashing foible which still, now, years later, enchants my nostalgic middle age as much as it then enchanted me. I know now, alas, that behind the screen of levity and animal spirits lay concealed human imperfections, guile, improvidence, stupidity, mendacity, anguishes of every variety and even downright tragedy. In those days, however, I gaped at everything I heard or overheard of their vivid and forthright doings. These legends, which they dramatically recounted of themselves and of each other, so magnified them that they swaggered and swept by, heroes and Amazons, along the rim of my mind's horizon, casting miles-long shadows as blinding as searchlight rays. When these nobilities appeared before me in the flesh I could still gape, for I was not yet ready for disillusion. Reality matched imagination. About the family, anyway, I was the Three Wise Monkeys.

I was stimulated by Uncle Martini-Henry's waxed moustache, and malacca,* and watch-chain with its shark-tooth *breloque*† as much as by the saga of his earlier bush-whacking adventures, by Uncle Whitworth's plush-lined pipe-cases, by Aunt Rosa Bona's garden gorged with flowers so large and crisp as to appear edible. I was captivated by their houses which smelt variously of strawberry jam cooking, or furniture polish and Brasso, or cut lemons, or Eau de Cologne, or boiled-over milk, or cats and cigars. Because, indeed, the mind and its shadow senses do preserve a detailed past, I still recall the smell of Uncle Mauser's Turkish cigarettes or Aunt Sophia's glycerine soap, the exact disposition of Mazzawattee tea-canisters and gilt-handled vases long destroyed, still feel the Greek key pattern embossing the rim of Aunt Adelina's fruit-plates, still hear Melba hooting *Home, Sweet Home* through the toffee-coloured, convolvulus-shaped horn of Aunt Meta's gramophone.

I seized every opportunity to stock a granary of impressions. I picked up whole and wonderful sentences thrown carelessly down among cake-crumbs and tea-slopped saucers; tucked away luminous smiles released in happy-go-lucky flights at picnics; carried off, as it were, armloads of cuttings from virile and showy plants in a garden where summer seemed perfect and unending. How cruelly endless now seems a deadlier season.

As children in a spread-out but gregariously inclined sept, my cousins and brothers and sisters and I, during school holidays, were always anywhere but in our own rowdy nests. We were interchanged like home-made tokens of affection. Those of us who were suburban were bundled off to country aunts and uncles; those who were country bumpkins went citywards. Children are pickers-up. Each child returned home bearing objects that, almost valueless otherwise, were sacred mementoes, and doubly sacred as being something for nothing. I remember my sisters bringing back shoe-buckles, wildernesses of embroidery silks, bone crochet needles, Piver's powder boxes, raped-looking dolls, and fans still releasing from their broken wings shadows of a scent long out of fashion and the name of which nobody knew. At one time or another, my brothers

---

Malacca = cane.
†*Breloque* = charm for a watchchain.

brought back wilting lizards in jars of spirits, cigar-boxes of cigar-
bands, a carved emu's egg, tortoise-shell pen-knives with broken
blades, a rectangular tennis-racquet and, on a notable occasion, Uncle
Snider's elderly banjo. These things were rubbish but, like tourist
souvenirs, retained enough glamour just long enough to garnish the
short interval before, coach into pumpkin, holiday turned back to
workaday.

As the one child in this riotous shuffling to and fro who was
family-obsessed and a born archivist, I was a magpie of a different
colour. I wanted more of Uncle Snider's past than an unplayable
banjo. I wanted facts, dates, the how and why and where, all possible
information about the pasts of the living gods and goddesses I paid
homage to. My eyes must have glittered as much as my spectacles
when I was given dated menu cards of P. and O. dinners, Masonic
dinners, mayoral dinners, or old theatre programmes, ball programmes, invitations to exhibitions and weddings. It steadied the
spinning world to fix an eye on the fact that Aunt Adelina had gone
to a wedding on June 24, 1911. It added depth and richness to my
knowledge that she was still going to weddings. Postcards were
special grist to my enthusiastic mill. Since my aunts and uncles had
been young in the late nineteenth century and early twentieth century, that era of postcard-sending and post-card-collecting, I had
many reefs to mine. It was a fascinating find, say, that, in Victoria
Street, North Williamstown, on February 13, 1913, Uncle Gatling
received a certain message on a postcard which showed a ragged
negro Topsy, her head spiked like a battle-mace with plaits, sub-
merging her face in a monster semi-lune of water-melon under the
words AH'S UP TO MAH EARS IN IT. Below her toes which were
splayed out like pianist's fingers, the sentence finished AT ST
KILDA. Written on the back in violet ink was:

Dear Gat,
    Take a gander at the coon on the other side!!!! Just a line to say all
the Jokers will be foregathering at the White Hart next Sat. about 3.
Expecting a hot time!! Don't wear that bokker!!!! Harry.

I begged postcards of all sorts: *Sunset on the Nile, Miss Billie
Burke, Miss Zena Dare,* cards of padded velvet roses, cards garishly
illustrating boarding house and mother-in-law jokes. I was, nevertheless, really hunting photographs—footballer uncles striped like
barbers' poles; Aunt Sophia under a cartwheel hat of ostrich feathers,
and horse-collared by a boa; Uncle Enfield, whom I knew as a well-
tailored sphere with an eye-glass, as a cock-eyed skinamalink in
Little Lord Fauntleroy velvet; Aunt Meta, with unpainted lips, bare

shoulders and a cumulus of hair, emerging glass-eyed as a hairdresser's wax model from a nest of chiffon.

So feverish did I become, repeating my overtures as monotonously as creation, that I exhausted family teasing into recognition of my fervour. I was understood to be some sort of notary. Spring-cleaning aunts sent me packets of photographs; uncles put aside for me dim, henna-coloured snapshots (*Me at Leongatha Woodchop,* 1920) or postcards of magenta-nosed drunks with crayfish semaphoring from their hip-pockets which they had dug out of drawers holding the treasures of a lifetime ... sovereign-cases, insurance policies, opal tie-pins, wives' first love-letters, and the halves of pairs of cuff-links. Proff became my nickname, and my bottom was pinched affectionately. On my behalf, archaeology into their own racy and cluttered pasts became an accepted pastime of my aunts and uncles.

Alas!

At the height of my miniature fame, at the unornamental age of ten, a bee-keeper stung by his own bee, I fell in love with a photograph. I fell deeply, unfalteringly and hauntedly in love.

The photograph came in a packet of postcards from Aunt Meta. Had I not been alone in the house, with nobody peering over my shoulder, I could have been saved a long ecstasy and a savage destruction. Alone I was, however, when the postman came; alone I unwrapped my gift and, among postcards of Gaiety Girls, and snapshots of bowler-hatted uncles in jinkers, and ant-waisted aunts leaning on or being leaned on by bicycles, alone I came upon my fate. Nothing can undo what was done that instant, that day.

I saw the photograph. The door of the one addled world I had known closed softly behind me. I was in the ante-room to Paradise. Its bejewelled throne was mine. I perceived that all loves experienced in the back-room past were imaginary, were delusions, were nothing. I had been wastefully librating above shadows—however spirited; visions—however cock-a-hoop; hollow beings; deceptive shapes; creatures of gauze; dresses empty of women; names without men to them. I had had merely a bowing acquaintance with love.

The photograph was of a girl about my own age. She was dressed in Dolly Varden-ish costume. Since she held a shepherd's crook feminized by a large bow I gathered she was being Bo Peep for a fancy dress party. Or was she Bo Peep herself? There was nothing on the photograph to tell. The tilted oval of hat with its rosebuds and ribbons, the black hatching of the elbow-length mittens, the crisscross-laced bodice, all excited me romantically. What flooded into my being, however, to reveal inner depths and expanses never revealed before, was the illumination from the smile and the eyes. It did not occur to me that what really confronted the smile and the eyes was a camera like half-a-concertina on a tripod which was concealed with a nameless human under a black cloth. No! That faintly scented smile was for me. Those eyes, bottomless, and yet of dark sharpness, were looking into me. A gale of voices whirled through the galleries of my consciousness, aromatizing them, purging them of all former presences, and calling out deliciously, "Thou!"

"Thou!"

I was eavesdropping on eternity.

Eternity is time's victim.

Eternity had scarcely begun when I heard my mother at the front door. With the unflurried movements of a master criminal I put the photograph in an inside pocket. I was aware that the pocket was on the left, and the divine face deliberately turned inwards. The eyes looked directly into my heart which I imagined crimson as a playing-card heart, plump as an artichoke, and composed of a material with the texture of magnolia petals. I extinguished the lights in my face, swept up the other photographs with a gambler's gesture and, as my mother entered, cried out ... oh, perfect imitation of a frank and guileless boy ... "Look what Aunt Meta sent!" Not a word about the divinity staring into my heart, not a word. I said nothing then. I kept the photograph and my love hidden for seven years. I said nothing ever.

Because my pockets and chest-of-drawers were subject to maternal investigation it was necessary to be on guard against discovery. I cannot remember, now, all my love's hiding-places when I could not carry her with me. When I had to desert her under the paper lining a boot-box of silkworms, behind a loose skirting-board or in the never-read bible, heavy as a foundation stone, I believed the subtle smile to dissolve away and those unflinching eyes to be in sleep.

That my idolatry persisted and became more intense was—still is —astounding for, too violently soon, I was, in years, older than she. In all else but my worship I changed. She did not change, although her beauty took on other meanings; her eyes displayed truths that, at one and the same time, vacillated like the opalescence on black oil, and remained steady and mystifying as infinity.

I changed. The family changed. Their lustihood, animation, over-large gesturings and vitality, if one took a quick look, were unabated. Closer examination showed the gilt flaking off, or a hair-fine crackle of flaws. Like plates left too long in the oven some older aunts and uncles illustrated that they had been long enough in the oven of life. As wrinkles darned themselves more closely around eyes, as hair wore away or became margined with white, as figures broadened or became juiceless, curving downwards towards the earth that was their destination, perhaps what I noticed most was an increase of braggadocio and hullabaloo. High spirits were larded with slangy defiance; hilarity was so constant that cause and effect were lost sight of, and no longer had value. No one seemed to dare to ask, "Why are we laughing?" but went on defiantly laughing. All those epic suns that had warmed my earlier boyhood were declining in a sky flushed with stubborn anger.

Most gaudy of these declines was Aunt Maria's. For years the family had called her the Merry Widow: singular title to hold among so many married couples. Maria's husband had been, I endlessly kept on overhearing and was endlessly told, handsome, rich, gifted, charming, and so on. I concluded that the dead were inevitably possessed of all the attributes the living have few or none of. Luxuriance of graces seemed a necessary qualification for death. It was a tragedy, they all said, that he should have died two months after marriage. He and dear Ria, they all said, had been a perfectly matched couple, madly in love. At first, I gathered, Maria had sought consolation in travel; later, in travel and port wine; ultimately, in less travel, more port wine, and—they lowered their voices so that I listened harder and heard more—and young men.

I saw her rarely. She was sensationally made-up. Her sardonicisms were hoarsely outrageous. Scent breezed from her furs wherein glittered the mean eyes of foxy faces chiselling snouts into their own expensive bodies; rings bulged her kid gloves; she smoked baby-blue primrose and lilac cigarettes tipped with gold. She was the clan scandal. She belonged to the family, but she belonged in the manner of some elaborate pet with unusual vices. These were understood to age her. Virtues, nevertheless, aged the virtuous others as inexorably; simplicities aged to idiosyncrasies, habits to affectations, lovable quiddities to boring eccentricities.

As for myself, I reached the stage of rubbing vaseline on a breath of moustache. I started brilliantine which my parents regarded in much the same light as opium-smoking. I whined for adult castemarks such as cuff-links and a wristlet watch. I was, evanescently, of that self-loving, self-pitying, unbearable race which invents loneliness and boredom, and in which all the major evils of humanity are in powerful bud. I was an adolescent of sour seventeen.

From the arrogant, dirty-minded, unaesthetic and altogether unworthy side of my nature, I found absolution only in my photograph. Since I was insufferably older and in my first long trousers, mother no longer, without fair warning, rifled my pockets with cries of "How long have you been using this revolting handkerchief?" The photograph, therefore, was able to stand constantly at my heart in a morocco wallet Uncle Lancaster had given me. The eyes I had looked into so often during seven years still offered me, from the midst of their dark moonlight, a prophetic truth; the smile seemed still that of one whispering "Thou!" and promising all affirmations, all peace, all wisdom, all love.

At this stage, my moustache still unawakened, brilliantine still anathema to my mother, my wrist still watchless, and the days a passion of ennui, Aunt Maria came to the country town we lived in.

One night, while we were at dinner, the telephone rang. Mother left the table and the room to answer it. We heard her squeal ecstatically in the distance. She returned looking younger, and had gone rosy under the eyes. That rosiness said to us children, *"Rattled!"* Father was away. Mother was at our mercy. The six of us stared at her in a certain manner. Mother stared bravely back.

"Aunt Ria's here," she said at last, over-nonchalantly and not sitting down again. "And stop that. Immediately. I'll tell your father. Take that smug expression off your smug faces."

"Sit down, mother *dear,*" we said. "Relaxez-vous. Collect your thoughts. Don't be shy. Speak out. Give us the dirt, mama. Or *we'll* tell papa."

She remained standing, and said, "Stop that. Immediately. Or I'll scream the house down." She looked at the clock with a pretence of vagueness. "She's travelling through to Sydney. She's staying overnight at the Terminus."

"Ah, *ha!*" It was my twelve-year-old sister. "Is she dee-ah-you-en-kay? Is she coming to see her poor relations?"

"No," said mother, and "How dare you, miss?" and sat down as if there were nothing else to do. "She says she's too tired."

"She *is* dee-ah-you ..."

Stop that," cried mother. "How dare you suggest that Ria ... how dare you, miss? She's had a very tragic life." Her eyes hinted tears, but she finger-tipped her just-marcelled shingle with gratification. Her inward eye was riffling through her wardrobe.

"What's the time? Is that clock fast or slow or right? I have to go down and see her."

Have meant, we knew, *am so excited I can hardly wait.*

As eldest son and deputy man-of-the-house, I went with mother.

The Terminus Hotel was a hive of inactivity. The Guests' Drawing-room, to which several palms gave the atmosphere of a down-at-heel Winter Garden, contained only Aunt Maria and a young man. They sat, deep in moquette armchairs, with the air of people who have been sitting for a long time. Between them a Benares-brass-tray table held their drinks, and a whisky-advertising ash-tray fuming like a rubbish-tip with butts bloodstained by lipstick.

"My loves!" cried Maria huskily, hoisting herself upright. Scarcely less loudly, out of the corner of her mouth, she also said, "Get up, you lout, when a lady enters the room."

From under the horizontal single eyebrow which served both eyes the young man spat a glance at her which I recognized for I had ejected just such a glance at my mother when she had publicly revealed that I wrote poetry or bit my fingernails. The young man, handsome in an unlit fashion, brutally stood.

Most of what happened after does not matter.

Aunt Maria was fairly drunk. For a woman of fifty she had kept enough of her figure. Her dress and shoes were in the safely faultless taste that costs money. Her hair, of dead black, was astrakhan-crinkled, and had obviously also cost, colour and design, much money.

We were an unmatched quartette but, whatever lay under the surface of the evening, Aunt Maria and my mother gave no apparent thought to it. My aunt's one rebuke to the young man had vibrated instantly to silence. She introduced him as Ivan Something but, with a kind of marital mockery, addressed him as Ee-fahn. She disregarded him but not pointedly. One felt she might, later in the evening, as she walked much too carefully bedwards, have to stop and say, "My God! My Ee-fahn! I nearly forgot him!" as of an unbrella. She had, so to speak, already walked away leaving a number of umbrellas.

The conversation was overlapping gabble between the two sisters, and was family, family, family. They giggled, they shrieked. Diagonally across their chit-chat Ee-fahn reconnoitred me with monosyllabic information about weight-lifting. It was Urdu to me. I sat egg-faced wishing this eyebrow on my lip. He lowered this eyebrow like a perambulator-hood, and withdrew under it to drink brandies. Aunt Maria drank port after port. Saying "No, *no,* Ria! Not one more drink. I'll be featherstitching!" mother had two, three and then four Drambuies. I was permitted two beer-shandies.

My adoration of family personalities and goings-on having subsided with puberty, I was not merely uninterested in Aunt Maria, but bored, shamed and revolted. Before me, I thought, were the classic lineaments of immorality. Its surface moved as though lined with decayed elastic, it grimaced, it winked, it pleated itself to laugh, and yet was dead. Its lips, from which the lipstick had worn centrally off to reveal a naked mauve, writhed about. The eyes seemed to flash darkly but that was an illusion fostered by restlessness. They dared not tarry moveless under their glistening blue lids.

So, utterly fed-up, attempting to buy escape by startling mother into awareness of me and the late hour, I took out my wallet and opened it in a manly way. This gesture stopped mother in her tracks.

"I should like to buy ..." I could not think of the word for a number of drinks "... to buy some drinks."

"The naughty love!" cried Aunt Maria. "You know, Doll, he's going to be quite a good-looker, even with the gig-lamps. Dear boy, you mustn't waste your substance on filthy-rich aunts."

She reached and took the wallet from me, took it between forefinger and thumb by one corner, and held it up, and waggled it. This was no more than old-fashioned, ex-girlish playfulness, Lily Langtry skittishness, but was earthquake and annihilation to me. From the wallet on to the brass table fell my secret, my silence, my peace, my dreams, my seven years of devotion, the photograph with its undefiled gaze and smile of my first love.

I was too stricken to snatch, to save, to conceal.

"A dark horse, Doll," said Aunt Maria, taking up the photograph. "A Casanova. The girl friend!" Focusing, she held the photograph at arm's length.

"Who? Who is that? Who?" said mother, hand outstretched.

There is a moment when, for the first time, Life is no longer seen in exquisite profile.

Life turns full-face to one, swiftly and savagely, and unshutters her eyes. There is nothing to be seen in their recesses but the evidence of destruction, of negation, perspectives of nullity. Peace, one sees, is perjury. The gods are down-and-out. The jewelled throne one slumbered on is no more than a rock in wasteland. The flowers one thought to have been thrown at one's feet are seen to be not flowers but the rotting wings of shapes that flew ecstatically into emptiness, and circled in emptiness, and starved there, and fell. One is, for the first time, aware of mortality, and learns in a flash that death is the one sure possession.

"Who?" said Aunt Maria, horribly smiling and smiling at the photograph. "Look, Doll. Look at the sweet, quaint little sobersides."

"Where *did* you get this?" said my mother.

"Found it. I found it," I said, my voice thick with lies and hate. "I found it in the drawer. Where the old photographs used to be. This afternoon."

"Remember, Doll?" said Aunt Maria, knocking over her wine. "Lolly Edward's party? My God, I shouldn't care to shout from the rooftop how long ago that was. You were Miss Muffet. Remember, Doll? Show Ee-fahn what a serious duck of a Bo Peep I was."

And the drunken woman with wine-scummed eyes agitated the dying muscles of her loose and painted mouth, and began to laugh hoarsely, and I heard what I heard, and saw what I saw, and my heart broke.

Katherine Anne Porter

(b. 1890)

Born in Texas, Katherine Anne Porter's formal education was limited to girls' schools in the South; but she learned much from her own reading, and early formed the desire to be a writer. Her first collection of short stories, *Flowering Judas* (1930; augmented edition, 1935), won immediate critical praise for her smooth, spare prose, and for the psychological insights of such stories as "He." The success of *Flowering Judas* brought her a Guggenheim Fellowship, which enabled her to travel; and her subsequent voyage to Europe in 1931 provided the material for her longest work, the novel *Ship of Fools* (1962). From among the many awards and distinctions which have been conferred upon her may be singled out the Pulitzer Prize, which she received in 1966.

In her introduction to the 1940 edition of *Flowering Judas,* Porter described how she sought "to understand the logic of this majestic and terrible failure of the life of man in the Western world"; and to a greater or lesser extent, this concern is reflected in all her work. She dramatizes the human struggle for contact and communication in the face of all fears, prejudices, and frustrations which alienate people from each other. Like the protagonist of her long story "The Leaning Tower" (1944), many of her characters are confronted by a society in the process of disintegration, or experience "an infernal desolation of the spirit, the chill and the knowledge of death. . . ." Porter's stories reflect her sense of the confusion that characterizes human life; she investigates "self-betrayal and self-deception—the way that all human beings deceive themselves about the way they operate. . . . Everyone takes his stance, asserts his own rights and feelings, mistaking the motives of others, and his own . . . " (*Paris Review* interview, 1963). In "He," Mrs. Whipple succeeds for a while in shutting away the truth about her feelings for her son; but the author passes no harsh judgment on her self-delusion and insincerity, and portrays with compasssion the dawning horror of her final recognition of failure.

For further reading

George Hendrick, *Katherine Anne Porter* (New York: Twayne, 1965).
M. M. Libermann, *Katherine Anne Porter's Fiction* (Detroit: Wayne State University Press, 1971).
Barbara Thompson, "The Art of Fiction XXIX: Katherine Anne Porter," *Paris Review,* 8 (Winter–Spring 1963), 87–114.

He

Life was very hard for the Whipples. It was hard to feed all the hungry mouths, it was hard to keep the children in flannels during the winter, short as it was. "God knows what would become of us if we lived north," they would say; keeping them decently clean was hard. "It looks like our luck won't never let up on us," said Mr Whipple, but Mrs Whipple was all for taking what was sent and calling it good, anyhow when the neighbours were in earshot. "Don't ever let a soul hear us complain," she kept saying to her husband. She couldn't stand to be pitied. "No, not if it comes to it that we have to live in a wagon and pick cotton around the country," she said, "nobody's going to get a chance to look down on us."

Mrs Whipple loved her second son, the simple-minded one, better than she loved the other two children put together. She was for ever saying so, and when she talked with certain of her neighbours, she would even throw in her husband and her mother for good measure.

"You needn't keep on saying it around," said Mr Whipple, "you'll make people think nobody else has any feelings about Him but you."

"It's natural for a mother," Mrs Whipple would remind him. "You know yourself it's more natural for a mother to be that way. People don't expect so much of fathers, some way."

This didn't keep the neighbours from talking plainly among themselves. "A Lord's pure mercy if He should die," they said. "It's the sins of the fathers," they agreed among themselves. "There's bad blood and bad doings somewhere, you can bet on that." This behind the Whipples' backs. To their faces everybody said, "He's not so bad off. He'll be all right yet. Look how He grows!"

Mrs Whipple hated to talk about it, she tried to keep her mind off it, but every time anybody set foot in the house, the subject always came up, and she had to talk about Him first, before she could get on to anything else. It seemed to ease her mind. "I wouldn't have anything happen to Him for all the world, but it just looks like I can't keep Him out of mischief. He's so strong and active, He's always into everything; He was like that since He could walk. It's actually funny sometimes the way He can do anything; it's laughable to see Him up to His tricks. Emly has more accidents; I'm for ever tying up her bruises, and Adna can't fall a foot without cracking a bone. But He can do anything and not get a scratch. The preacher said such a nice thing once when he was here. He said, and I'll remember it to my dying day, 'The innocent walk with God—that's why He don't get hurt.'" Whenever Mrs Whipple repeated these words, she always felt a warm pool spread in her breast, and the tears would fill her eyes, and then she could talk about something else.

He did grow and He never got hurt. A plank blew off the chicken house and struck Him on the head and He never seemed to know it. He had learned a few words, and after this He forgot them. He didn't whine for food as the other children did, but waited until it was given Him; He ate squatting in the corner, smacking and mumbling.

Rolls of fat covered Him like an overcoat, and He could carry twice as much wood and water as Adna. Emly had a cold in the head most of the time—"she takes that after me," said Mrs Whipple—so in bad weather they gave her the extra blanket off His cot. He never seemed to mind the cold.

Just the same, Mrs Whipple's life was a torment for fear something might happen to Him. He climbed the peach trees much better than Adna and went skittering along the branches like a monkey, just a regular monkey. "Oh, Mrs Whipple, you hadn't ought to let Him do that. He'll lose His balance sometime. He can't rightly know what He's doing."

Mrs Whipple almost screamed out at the neighbour. "He *does* know what He's doing! He's as able as any other child! Come down out of there, you!" When He finally reached the ground she could hardly keep her hands off Him for acting like that before people, a grin all over His face and her worried sick about Him all the time.

"It's the neighbours," said Mrs Whipple to her husband. "Oh, I do mortally wish they would keep out of our business. I can't afford to let Him do anything for fear they'll come nosing around about it. Look at the bees, now. Adna can't handle them, they sting him so. I haven't got time to do everything, and now I don't dare let Him. But if He gets a sting He don't really mind."

"It's just because He ain't got sense enough to be scared of anything," said Mr Whipple.

"You ought to be ashamed of yourself," said Mrs Whipple, "talking that way about your own child. Who's to take up for Him if we don't, I'd like to know? He sees a lot that goes on, He listens to things all the time. And anything I tell Him to do He does it. Don't never let anybody hear you say such things. They'd think you favoured the other children over Him."

"Well, now I don't, and you know it, and what's the use of getting all worked up about it? You always think the worst of everything. Just let Him alone, He'll get along somehow. He gets plenty to eat and wear, don't He?" Mr Whipple suddenly felt tired out. "Anyhow, it can't be helped now."

Mrs Whipple felt tired too; she complained in a tired voice: "What's done can't never be undone, I know that good as anybody; but He's my child, and I'm not going to have people say anything. I get sick of people coming around saying things all the time."

In the early autumn Mrs Whipple got a letter from her brother saying he and his wife and two children were coming over for a little visit next Sunday week. "Put the big pot in the little one," he wrote at the end. Mrs. Whipple read this part out loud twice, she was so pleased. Her brother was a great one for saying funny things. "We'll just show him that's no joke," she said, "we'll just butcher one of the sucking pigs."

"It's a waste and I don't hold with waste the way we are now," said Mr Whipple. "That pig'll be worth money by Christmas."

"It's a shame and a pity we can't have a decent meal's vittles once in a while when my own family comes to see us," said Mrs Whipple. "I'd hate for his wife to go back and say there wasn't a thing in the house to eat. My God, it's better than buying up a great chance of meat in town. There's where you'd spend the money!"

"All right, do it yourself then," said Mr Whipple. "Christamighty, no wonder we can't get ahead!"

The question was how to get the little pig away from his ma, a great fighter, worse than a Jersey cow. Adna wouldn't try it: "That sow'd rip my insides out all over the pen." "All right, old fraidy," said Mrs Whipple, "*He's* not scared. Watch *Him* do it." And she laughed as though it was all a good joke and gave Him a little push towards the pen. He sneaked up and snatched the pig right away from the teat and galloped back and was over the fence with the sow raging at His heels. The little black squirming thing was screeching like a baby in a tantrum, stiffening its back and stretching its mouth to the ears. Mrs Whipple took the pig with her face stiff and sliced its throat with one stroke. When He saw the blood He gave a great jolting breath and ran away. "But He'll forget and eat plenty, just the same," thought Mrs Whipple. Whenever she was thinking, her lips moved, making words. "He'd eat it all if I didn't stop Him. He'd eat up every mouthful from the other two if I'd let Him."

She felt badly about it. He was ten years old now and a third again as large as Adna, who was going on fourteen. "It's a shame, a shame," she kept saying under her breath, "and Adna with so much brains!"

She kept on feeling badly about all sorts of things. In the first place it was the man's work to butcher; the sight of the pig scraped pink and naked made her sick. He was too fat and soft and pitiful-looking. It was simply a shame the way things had to happen. By the time she had finished it up, she almost wished her brother would stay at home.

Early on Sunday morning Mrs Whipple dropped everything to get Him all cleaned up. In an hour He was dirty again, with crawling under fences after an opossum, and straddling along the rafters of the barn looking for eggs in the hayloft. "My lord, look at you now after all my trying! And here's Adna and Emly staying so quiet. I get tired trying to keep you decent. Get off that shirt and put on another; people will say I don't half dress you!" And she boxed Him on the ears, hard. He blinked and blinked and rubbed His head, and His face hurt Mrs Whipple's feelings. Her knees began to tremble, she had to sit down while she buttoned His shirt. "I'm just all gone before the day starts."

The brother came with his plump healthy wife and two great roaring hungry boys. They had a grand dinner, with the pig roasted to a crackling in the middle of the table, full of dressing, a pickled peach in his mouth and plenty of gravy for the sweet potatoes.

"This looks like prosperity all right," said the brother; "you're going to have to roll me home like I was a barrel when I'm done."

Everybody laughed out loud; it was fine to hear them laughing all at once around the table. Mrs Whipple felt warm and good about it. "Oh, we've got six more of these; I say it's as little as we can do when you come to see us so seldom."

He wouldn't come into the dining-room and Mrs Whipple passed it off very well. "He's timider than my other two," she said. "He'll just have to get used to you. There isn't everybody He'll make up with, you know how it is with some children, even cousins." Nobody said anything out of the way.

"Just like my Alfy here," said the brother's wife. "I sometimes got to lick him to make him shake hands with his own grandmammy."

So that was over, and Mrs Whipple loaded up a big plate for Him first, before everybody. "I always say He ain't to be slighted, no matter who else goes without," she said, and carried it to Him herself.

"He can chin Himself on the top of the door," said Emly, helping along.

"That's fine, He's getting along fine," said the brother.

They went away after supper. Mrs Whipple rounded up the dishes, sent the children to bed, and sat down and unlaced her shoes. "You see?" she said to Mr Whipple. "That's the way my whole family is. Nice and considerate about everything. No out-of-the-way remarks—they *have* got refinement. I get awfully sick of people's remarks. Wasn't that pig good?"

Mr Whipple said, "Yes, we're out three hundred pounds of pork, that's all. It's easy to be polite when you come to eat. Who knows what they had in their minds all along?"

"Yes, that's like you," said Mrs Whipple. "I don't expect anything else from you. You'll be telling me next that my own brother will be saying around that we made Him eat in the kitchen! Oh, my God!" She rocked her head in her hands, a hard pain started in the very middle of her forehead. "Now it's all spoiled, and everything was so nice and easy. All right, you don't like them and you never did—all right, they'll not come here again soon, never you mind! But they *can't* say He wasn't dressed every lick as good as Adna—oh, honest, sometimes I wish I was dead!"

"I wish you'd let up," said Mr Whipple. "It's bad enough as it is."

It was a hard winter. It seemed to Mrs Whipple that they hadn't ever known anything but hard times, and now to cap it all a winter like this. The crops were about half of what they had a right to expect; after the cotton was in it didn't do much more than cover the grocery bill. They swapped off one of the plough horses, and got cheated, for the new one died of the heaves. Mrs Whipple kept thinking all the time it was terrible to have a man you couldn't depend on not to get cheated. They cut down on everything, but Mrs Whipple kept saying there are things you can't cut down on, and they cost money. It took a lot of warm clothes for Adna and Emly, who walked four miles to school during the three-months session. "He sets around the fire a lot, He won't need so much," said Mr Whipple. "That's so," said Mrs Whipple, "and when He does the outdoor chores He can wear your tarpaulin coat. I can't do no better, that's all."

In February He was taken sick, and lay curled up under His blanket looking very blue in the face and acting as if He would choke. Mr and Mrs Whipple did everything they could for Him for two days, and then they were scared and sent for the doctor. The doctor told them they must keep Him warm and give Him plenty of milk and eggs. "He isn't as stout as He looks, I'm afraid," said the doctor. "You've got to watch them when they're like that. You must put more cover on Him, too."

"I just took off His big blanket to wash," said Mrs Whipple, ashamed. "I can't stand dirt."

"Well, you'd better put it back on the minute it's dry," said the doctor, "or He'll have pneumonia."

Mr and Mrs Whipple took a blanket off their own bed and put His cot in by the fire. "They can't say we didn't do everything for Him," she said, "even to sleeping cold ourselves on His account."

When the winter broke He seemed to be well again, but He walked as if His feet hurt Him. He was able to run a cotton planter during the season.

"I got it all fixed up with Jim Ferguson about breeding the cow next time," said Mr Whipple. "I'll pasture the bull this summer and give Jim some fodder in the autumn. That's better than paying out money when you haven't got it."

"I hope you didn't say such a thing before Jim Ferguson," said Mrs Whipple. "You oughtn't to let him know we're so down as all that."

"Godamighty, that ain't saying we're down! A man has got to look ahead sometimes. *He* can lead the bull over today. I need Adna on the place."

At first Mrs Whipple felt easy in her mind about sending Him for the bull. Adna was too jumpy and couldn't be trusted. You've got to be steady around animals. After He was gone she started thinking, and after a while she could hardly bear it any longer. She stood in the lane and watched for Him. It was nearly three miles to go and a hot day, but He oughtn't to be so long about it. She shaded her eyes and stared until coloured bubbles floated in her eyeballs. It was just like everything else in life, she must always worry and never know a moment's peace about anything. After a long time she saw Him turn into the side lane, limping. He came on very slowly, leading the big hulk of an animal by a ring in the nose, twirling a little stick in His hand, never looking back or sideways, but coming on like a sleepwalker with His eyes half shut.

Mrs Whipple was scared sick of bulls; she had heard awful stories about how they followed on quietly enough, and then suddenly pitched on with a bellow and pawed and gored a body to pieces. Any second now that black monster would come down on Him. My God, He'd never have sense enough to run.

She mustn't make a sound nor a move; she mustn't get the bull started. The bull heaved his head aside and horned the air at a fly. Her voice burst out of her in a shriek, and she screamed at Him to come on, for God's sake. He didn't seem to hear her clamour, but kept on twirling His switch and limping on, and the bull lumbered along behind him as gently as a calf. Mrs Whipple stopped calling and ran towards the house, praying under her breath: "Lord, don't let anything happen to Him. Lord, you *know* people will say we oughtn't to have sent Him. You *know* they'll say we didn't take care of Him. Oh, get Him home, safe home, safe home, and I'll look out for Him better! Amen."

She watched from the window while He led the beast in and tied him up in the barn. It was no use trying to keep up, Mrs Whipple couldn't bear another thing. She sat down and rocked and cried with her apron over her head.

From year to year the Whipples were growing poorer and poorer. The place just seemed to run down of itself, no matter how hard they worked. "We're losing our hold," said Mrs Whipple. "Why can't we do like other people and watch for our best chances? They'll be calling us poor white trash next."

"When I get to be sixteen I'm going to leave," said Adna. "I'm going to get a job in Powell's grocery store. There's money in that. No more farm for me."

"I'm going to be a school teacher," said Emly. "But I've got to finish the eighth grade, anyhow. Then I can live in town. I don't see any chances here."

"Emly takes after my family," said Mrs Whipple. "Ambitious every last one of them, and they don't take second place for anybody."

When autumn came Emly got a chance to wait at table in the railroad eating-house in the town near by, and it seemed such a shame not to take it when the wages were good and she could get her food too, that Mrs Whipple decided to let her take it, and not bother with school until the next session. "You've got plenty of time," she said. "You're young and smart as a whip."

With Adna gone too, Mr Whipple tried to run the farm with just Him to help. He seemed to get along fine, doing His work and part of Adna's without noticing it. They did well enough until Christmas time, when one morning He slipped on the ice coming up from the barn. Instead of getting up He thrashed round and round, and when Mr Whipple got to Him, He was having some sort of fit.

They brought Him inside and tried to make Him sit up, but He blubbered and rolled, so they put Him to bed and Mr Whipple rode to town for the doctor. All the way there and back he worried about where the money was to come from: it sure did look like he had about all the troubles he could carry.

From then on He stayed in bed. His legs swelled up double their size, and the fits kept coming back. After four months the doctor said, "It's no use, I think you'd better put Him in the County Home for treatment right way. I'll see about it for you. He'll have good care there and be off your hands."

"We don't begrudge Him any care, and I won't let Him out of my sight," said Mrs Whipple. "I won't have it said I sent my sick child off among strangers."

"I know how you feel," said the doctor. "You can't tell me anything about that, Mrs Whipple. I've got a boy of my own. But you'd better listen to me. I can't do anything more for Him, that's the truth."

Mr and Mrs Whipple talked it over a long time that night after they went to bed. "It's just charity," said Mrs Whipple, "that's what we've come to, charity! I certainly never looked for this."

"We pay taxes to help to support the place just like everybody else," said Mr Whipple, "and I don't call that taking charity. I think it would be fine to have Him where He'd get the best of everything ... and besides, I can't keep up with these doctor's bills any longer."

"Maybe that's why the doctor wants us to send Him—he's scared he won't get his money," said Mrs Whipple.

"Don't talk like that," said Mr Whipple, feeling pretty sick, "or we won't be able to send Him."

"Oh, but we won't keep Him there long," said Mrs Whipple. "Soon's He's better we'll bring Him right back home."

"The doctor has told you, and told you time and again, He can't ever get better, and you might as well stop talking," said Mr Whipple.

"Doctors don't know everything," said Mrs Whipple, feeling almost happy. "But anyhow, in the summer Emly can come home for a vacation, and Adna can get down for Sundays: we'll all work together and get on our feet again, and the children will feel they've got a place to come to."

All at once she saw it full summer again, with the garden going fine, and new white roller shades up all over the house, and Adna and Emly home, so full of life; all of them happy together. Oh, it could happen, things would ease up on them.

They didn't talk before Him much, but they never knew just how much He understood. Finally the doctor set the day and a neighbour who owned a double-seated carryall offered to drive them over. The hospital would have sent an ambulance, but Mrs Whipple couldn't stand to see Him going away looking so sick as all that. They wrapped Him in blankets, and the neighbour and Mr. Whipple lifted Him into the back seat of the carryall beside Mrs Whipple, who had on her black shirtwaist. She couldn't stand to go looking like charity.

"You'll be all right, I guess I'll stay behind," said Mr Whipple. "It don't look like everybody ought to leave the place at once."

"Besides, it ain't as if He was going to stay for ever," said Mrs Whipple to the neighbour. "This is only for a little while."

They started away, Mrs Whipple holding to the edges of the blankets to keep Him from sagging sideways. He sat there blinking and blinking. He worked His hands out and began rubbing His nose with His knuckles, and then with the end of the blanket. Mrs Whipple couldn't believe what she saw; He was scrubbing away big tears that rolled out of the corners of His eyes. He snivelled and made a gulping noise. Mrs Whipple kept saying, "Oh, honey, you don't feel so bad, do you? You don't feel so bad, do you?" for He seemed to be accusing her of something. Maybe He remembered that time she boxed His ears; maybe He had been scared that day with the bull; maybe He had slept cold and couldn't tell her about it; maybe He knew they were sending Him away for good and all because they were too poor to keep Him. Whatever it was, Mrs Whipple couldn't bear to think of it. She began to cry, frightfully, and wrapped her arms tightly round Him. His head rolled on her shoulder: she had loved Him as much as she possibly could; there were Adna and Emly who had to be thought of too, there was nothing she could do to make up to Him for His life. Oh, what a mortal pity He was ever born.

They came in sight of the hospital, with the neighbour driving very fast, not daring to look behind him.

Sinclair Ross

(b. 1908)

Born in Shellbrook, Saskatchewan, Sinclair Ross grew up on the Canadian prairies and was a banker there and in Montreal until he retired to live in Barcelona, Spain. The author of three novels, he is particularly known for his first, *As for Me and My House*, which appeared in 1941. Like many of his short stories, most of which were collected in 1968 under the title *The Lamp at Noon and Other Stories*, it deals with the realities of rural prairie life during the drought and depression of the 1930s.

Ross's art displays the chief characteristics of literary regionalism: scrupulous fidelity to the geographical realities of a place and time, sensitivity to the details of speech, habit, and social convention, and concern not only to invoke the relationships between a landscape and its people but also to elicit from the reader an appreciation of the way in which that relationship gives a particular cast to a universal human dilemma. Recurrently Ross dramatizes the tensions between man and nature, integrates them with Calvinist mores, and then qualifies his response to the Protestant ethic by the importance he attaches to artistic freedom. In the world he draws, nature and society exert uncompromising demands; beauty and art are ephemeral things, and against the pressures of day-to-day survival they seem to have peripheral value —to be sentimental, impractical, and (in the language of that culture) "womanish." At the same time, they are extraordinarily important. As "Cornet at Night," suggests, the characters who appreciate artistry will be all the more frustrated by their immediate environment because of their sensitivity. But in recognizing the limitations of their surroundings they also discover resources upon which less fortunate individuals cannot draw.

For further reading

Keath Fraser, "Futility at the Pump: the Short Stories of Sinclair Ross," *Queen's Quarterly*, 77 (Spring 1970), 72–80.

Donald Stephens, ed., *Writers of the Prairies* (Vancouver: University of British Columbia, 1973).

Cornet at Night

The wheat was ripe and it was Sunday. "Can't help it—I've got to cut," my father said at breakfast. "No use talking. There's a wind again and it's shelling fast."

"Not on the Lord's Day," my mother protested. "The horses stay in the stables where they belong. There's church this afternoon and I intend to ask Louise and her husband home for supper."

Ordinarily my father was a pleasant, accommodating little man, but this morning his wheat and the wind had lent him sudden steel. "No, today we cut," he met her evenly. "You and Tom go to church if you want to. Don't bother me."

"If you take the horses out today I'm through—I'll never speak to you again. And this time I mean it."

He nodded. "Good—if I'd known I'd have started cutting wheat on Sundays years ago."

"And that's no way to talk in front of your son. In the years to come he'll remember."

There was silence for a moment and then, as if in its clash with hers his will had suddenly found itself, my father turned to me.

"Tom, I need a man to stook for a few days and I want you to go to town tomorrow and get me one. The way the wheat's coming along so fast and the oats nearly ready too I can't afford the time. Take old Rock. You'll be safe with him."

But ahead of me my mother cried, "That's one thing I'll not stand for. You can cut your wheat or do anything else you like yourself, but you're not interfering with him. He's going to school tomorrow as usual."

My father bunched himself and glared at her. "No, for a change he's going to do what I say. The crop's more important than a day at school."

"But Monday's his music lesson day—and when will we have another teacher like Miss Wiggins who can teach him music too?"

"A dollar for lessons and the wheat shelling! When I was his age I didn't even get to school."

"Exactly," my mother scored, "and look at you today. Is it any wonder I want him to be different?"

He slammed out at that to harness his horses and cut his wheat, and away sailed my mother with me in her wake to spend an austere half-hour in the dark, hot, plushy little parlour. It was a kind of vicarious atonement, I suppose, for we both took straight-backed leather chairs, and for all of the half-hour stared across the room at a big pansy-bordered motto on the opposite wall: *As for Me and My House We Will Serve the Lord.*

At last she rose and said, "Better run along and do your chores now, but hurry back. You've got to take your bath and change your clothes, and maybe help a little getting dinner for your father."

There was a wind this sunny August morning, tanged with freedom and departure, and from his stall my pony Clipper whinnied for a race with it. Sunday or not, I would ordinarily have had my gallop anyway, but today a sudden welling-up of social and religious conscience made me ask myself whether one in the family like my father wasn't bad enough. Returning to the house, I merely said that on such a fine day it seemed a pity to stay inside. My mother heard but didn't answer. Perhaps her conscience too was working. Perhaps after being worsted in the skirmish with my father, she was in no mood for granting dispensations. In any case I had to take my bath as usual, put on a clean white shirt, and change my overalls for knicker corduroys.

They squeaked, those corduroys. For three months now they had been spoiling all my Sundays. A sad, muted, swishing little squeak, but distinctly audible. Every step and there it was, as if I needed to be oiled. I had to wear them to church and Sunday-school; and after service, of course, while the grown-ups stood about gossiping, the other boys discovered my affliction. I sulked and fumed, but there was nothing to be done. Corduroys that had cost four-fifty simply couldn't be thrown away till they were well worn-out. My mother warned me that if I started sliding down the stable roof, she'd patch the seat and make me keep on wearing them.

With my customary little bow-legged sidle I slipped into the kitchen again to ask what there was to do. "Nothing but try to behave like a Christian and a gentleman," my mother answered stiffly. "Put on a tie, and shoes and stockings. Today your father is just about as much as I can bear."

"And then what?" I asked hopefully. I was thinking that I might take a drink to my father, but dared not as yet suggest it.

"Then you can stay quiet and read—and afterwards practise your music lesson. If your Aunt Louise should come she'll find that at least I bring my son up decently."

It was a long day. My mother prepared the midday meal as usual, but, to impress upon my father the enormity of his conduct, withdrew as soon as the food was served. When he was gone, she and I emerged to take our places at the table in an atmosphere of unappetizing righteousness. We didn't eat much. The food was cold, and my mother had no heart to warm it up. For relief at last she said, "Run along and feed the chickens while I change my dress. Since we aren't going to service today we'll read Scripture for a while instead."

And Scripture we did read, Isaiah, verse about, my mother in her black silk dress and rhinestone brooch, I in my corduroys and Sunday shoes that pinched. It was a very august afternoon, exactly like the tone that had persisted in my mother's voice since breakfast time. I think I might have openly rebelled, only for the hope that by compliance I yet might win permission for the trip to town with Rock. I was inordinately proud that my father had suggested it, and for his faith in me forgave him even Isaiah and the plushy afternoon.

Whereas with my mother, I decided, it was a case of downright bigotry.

We went on reading Isaiah, and then for a while I played hymns on the piano. A great many hymns—even the ones with awkward sharps and accidentals that I'd never tried before—for, fearing visitors, my mother was resolved to let them see that she and I were uncontaminated by my father's sacrilege. But among these likely visitors was my Aunt Louise, a portly, condescending lady married to a well-off farmer with a handsome motor-car, and always when she came it was my mother's vanity to have me play for her a waltz or reverie, or *Holy Night* sometimes with variations. A man-child and prodigy might eclipse the motor-car. Presently she roused herself, and pretending mild reproof began, "Now, Tommy, you're going wooden on those hymns. For a change you'd better practise *Sons of Liberty*. Your Aunt Louise will want to hear it, anyway."

There was a fine swing and vigour in this piece, but it was hard. Hard because it was so alive, so full of youth and head-high rhythm. It was a march, and it did march. I couldn't take time to practise at the hard spots slowly till I got them right, for I had to march too. I had to let my fingers sometimes miss a note or strike one wrong. Again and again this afternoon I started carefully, resolving to count right through, the way Miss Wiggins did, and as often I sprang ahead to lead my march a moment or two all dash and fire, and then fall stumbling in the bitter dust of dissonance. My mother didn't know. She thought that speed and perseverance would eventually get me there. She tapped her foot and smiled encouragement, and gradually as the afternoon wore on began to look a little disappointed that there were to be no visitors, after all. "Run along for the cows," she said at last, "while I get supper ready for your father. There'll be nobody here, so you can slip into your overalls again."

I looked at her a moment, and then asked: "What am I going to wear to town tomorrow? I might get grease or something on the corduroys."

For while it was always my way to exploit the future, I liked to do it rationally, within the limits of the sane and probable. On my way for the cows I wanted to live the trip to town tomorrow many times, with variations, but only on the explicit understanding that tomorrow there was to be a trip to town. I have always been tethered to reality, always compelled by an unfortunate kind of probity in my nature to prefer a bare-faced disappointment to the luxury of a future I have no just claims upon.

I went to town the next day, though not till there had been a full hour's argument that paradoxically enough gave all three of us the victory. For my father had his way: I went; I had my way: I went;

and in return for her consent my mother wrung a promise from him of a pair of new plush curtains for the parlour when the crop was threshed, and for me the metronome that Miss Wiggins declared was the only way I'd ever learn to keep in time on marching pieces like the *Sons of Liberty.*

It was my first trip to town alone. That was why they gave me Rock, who was old and reliable and philosophic enough to meet motor-cars and the chance locomotive on an equal and even somewhat supercilious footing.

"Mind you pick somebody big and husky," said my father as he started for the field. "Go to Jenkins' store, and he'll tell you who's in town. Whoever it is, make sure he's stooked before."

"And mind it's somebody who looks like he washes himself," my mother warned, "I'm going to put clean sheets and pillowcases on the bunkhouse bed, but not for any dirty tramp or hobo."

By the time they had both finished with me there were a great many things to mind. Besides repairs for my father's binder, I was to take two crates of eggs each containing twelve dozen eggs to Mr. Jenkins' store and in exchange have a list of groceries filled. And to make it complicated, both quantity and quality of some of the groceries were to be determined by the price of eggs. Thirty cents a dozen, for instance, and I was to ask for coffee at sixty-five cents a pound. Twenty-nine cents a dozen and coffee at fifty cents a pound. Twenty-eight and no oranges. Thirty-one and bigger oranges. It was like decimals with Miss Wiggins, or two notes in the treble against three in the bass. For my father a tin of special blend tobacco, and my mother not to know. For my mother a box of face powder at the drugstore, and my father not to know. Twenty-five cents from my father on the side for ice-cream and licorice. Thirty-five from my mother for my dinner at the Chinese restaurant. And warning, of course, to take good care of Rock, speak politely to Mr. Jenkins, and see that I didn't get machine oil on my corduroys.

It was three hours to town with Rock, but I don't remember them. I remember nothing but a smug satisfaction with myself, an exhilarating conviction of importance and maturity—and that only by contrast with the sudden sag to embarrassed insignificance when finally old Rock and I drove up to Jenkins' store.

For a farm boy is like that. Alone with himself and his horse he cuts a fine figure. He is the measure of the universe. He foresees a great many encounters with life, and in them all acquits himself a little more than creditably. He is fearless, resourceful, a bit of a brag. His horse never contradicts.

But in town it is different. There are eyes here, critical, that pierce with a single glance the little bubble of his self-importance, and leave him dwindled smaller even than his normal size. It always happens that way. They are so superbly poised and sophisticated, these strangers, so completely masters of their situation as they loll in doorways and go sauntering up and down Main Street. Instantly he yields to them his place as measure of the universe, especially if he is a small boy wearing squeaky corduroys, especially if he has a worldly-wise old horse like Rock, one that knows his Main Streets, and will take them in nothing but his own slow philosophic stride.

We arrived all right. Mr. Jenkins was a little man with a freckled bald head, and when I carried in my two crates of eggs, one in each hand, and my legs bowed a bit, he said curtly, "Well, can't you set them down? My boy's delivering, and I can't take time to count them now myself."

"They don't need counting," I said politely. "Each layer holds two dozen, and each crate holds six layers. I was there. I saw my mother put them in."

At this a tall, slick-haired young man in yellow shoes who had been standing by the window turned around and said, "That's telling you, Jenkins—he was there." Nettled and glowering, Jenkins himself came round the counter and repeated, "So you were there, were you? Smart youngster! What did you say was your name?"

Nettled in turn to preciseness I answered, "I haven't yet. It's Thomas Dickson and my father's David Dickson, eight miles north of here. He wants a man to stook and was too busy to come himself."

He nodded, unimpressed, and then putting out his hand said, "Where's your list? Your mother gave you one, I hope?"

I said she had and he glowered again. "Then let's have it and come back in half an hour. Whether you were there or not, I'm going to count your eggs. How do I know that half of them aren't smashed?"

"That's right," agreed the young man, sauntering to the door and looking at Rock. "They've likely been bouncing along at a merry clip. You're quite sure, Buddy, that you didn't have a runaway?"

Ignoring the impertinence I staved off Jenkins. "The list, you see, has to be explained. I'd rather wait and tell you about it later on."

He teetered a moment on his heels and toes, then tried again. "I can read too. I make up orders every day. Just go away for a while —look for your man—anything."

"It wouldn't do," I persisted. "The way this one's written isn't what it really means. You'd need me to explain—"

He teetered rapidly. "Show me just one thing I don't know what it means."

"Oranges," I said, "but that's only oranges if eggs are twenty-nine cents or more—and bigger oranges if they're thirty-one. You see, you'd never understand—"

So I had my way and explained it all right then and there. What with eggs at twenty-nine and a half cents a dozen and my mother out a little in her calculations, it was somewhat confusing for a while; but after arguing a lot and pulling away the paper from each other that they were figuring on, the young man and Mr. Jenkins finally had it all worked out, with mustard and soap omitted altogether, and an extra half-dozen oranges thrown in. "Vitamins," the young man overruled me, "they make you grow"—and then with a nod towards an open biscuit box invited me to help myself.

I took a small one, and started up Rock again. It was nearly one o'clock now, so in anticipation of his noonday quart of oats he trotted off, a little more briskly, for the farmers' hitching-rail beside the lumber-yard. This was the quiet end of town. The air drowsed redolent of pine and tamarack, and resin simmering slowly in the sun. I poured out the oats and waited till he had finished. After the way the town had treated me it was comforting and peaceful to stand with my fingers in his mane, hearing him munch. It brought me a sense of place again in life. It made me feel almost as important as before. But when he finished and there was my own dinner to be thought about I found myself more of an alien in the town than ever, and felt the way to the little Chinese restaurant doubly hard. For Rock was older than I. Older and wiser, with a better understanding of important things. His philosophy included the relishing of oats even within a stone's throw of sophisticated Main Street. Mine was less mature.

I went, however, but I didn't have dinner. Perhaps it was my stomach, all puckered and tense with nervousness. Perhaps it was the restaurant itself, the pyramids of oranges in the window and the dark green rubber plant with the tropical-looking leaves, the indolent little Chinaman behind the counter and the dusky smell of last night's cigarettes that to my prairie nostrils was the orient itself, the exotic atmosphere about it all with which a meal of meat and vegetables and pie would have somehow simply jarred. I climbed onto a stool and ordered an ice-cream soda.

A few stools away there was a young man sitting. I kept watching him and wondering.

He was well-dressed, a nonchalance about his clothes that distinguished him from anyone I had ever seen, and yet at the same time it was a shabby suit, with shiny elbows and threadbare cuffs. His hands were slender, almost a girl's hands, yet vaguely with their shapely quietness they troubled me, because, however slender and smooth, they were yet hands to be reckoned with, strong with a strength that was different from the rugged labour-strength I knew.

He smoked a cigarette, and blew rings towards the window.

Different from the farmer boys I knew, yet different also from the young man with the yellow shoes in Jenkins' store. Staring out at it through the restaurant window he was as far away from Main Street as was I with plodding old Rock and my squeaky corduroys. I presumed for a minute or two an imaginary companionship. I finished my soda, and to be with him a little longer ordered lemonade. It was strangely important to be with him, to prolong a while this companionship. I hadn't the slightest hope of his noticing me, nor the slightest intention of obtruding myself. I just wanted to be there, to be assured by something I had never encountered before, to store it up for the three hours home with old Rock.

Then a big, unshaven man came in, and slouching onto the stool beside me said, "They tell me across the street you're looking for a couple of hands. What's your old man pay this year?"

"My father," I corrected him, "doesn't want a couple of men. He just wants one."

"I've got a pal," he insisted, "and we always go together."

I didn't like him. I couldn't help making contrasts with the cool, trim quietness of the young man sitting farther along. "What do you say?" he said as I sat silent, thrusting his stubby chin out almost over my lemonade. "We're ready any time."

"It's just one man my father wants," I said aloofly, drinking off my lemonade with a flourish to let him see I meant it. "And if you'll excuse me now—I've got to look for somebody else."

"What about this?" he intercepted me, and doubling up his arm displayed a hump of muscle that made me, if not more inclined to him, at least a little more deferential. "My pal's got plenty, too. We'll set up two stooks any day for anybody else's one."

"Not both," I edged away from him. "I'm sorry—you just wouldn't do."

He shook his head contemptuously. "Some farmer—just one man to stook."

"My father's a good farmer," I answered stoutly, rallying to the family honour less for its own sake than for what the young man on the other stool might think of us. "And he doesn't need just one man to stook. He's got three already. That's plenty other years, but this year the crop's so big he needs another. So there!"

"I can just see the place," he said, slouching to his feet and starting towards the door. "An acre or two of potatoes and a couple of dozen hens."

I glared after him a minute, then climbed back onto the stool and ordered another soda. The young man was watching me now in the big mirror behind the counter, and when I glanced up and met his eyes he gave a slow, half-smiling little nod of approval. And out of all proportion to anything it could mean, his nod encouraged me. I didn't flinch or fidget as I would have done had it been the young man with the yellow shoes watching me, and I didn't stammer over the confession that his amusement and appraisal somehow forced from me. "We haven't three men—just my father—but I'm to take one home today. The wheat's ripening fast this year and shelling, so he can't do it all himself."

He nodded again and then after a minute asked quietly, "What about me? Would I do?"

I turned on the stool and stared at him.

"I need a job, and if it's any recommendation there's only one of me."

"You don't understand," I started to explain, afraid to believe that perhaps he really did. "It's to stook. You have to be in the field by seven o'clock and there's only a bunkhouse to sleep in—a granary with a bed in it—"

"I know—that's about what I expect." He drummed his fingers a minute, then twisted his lips into a kind of half-hearted smile and went on, "They tell me a little toughening up is what I need. Outdoors, and plenty of good hard work—so I'll be like the fellow that just went out."

The wrong hands: white slender fingers, I knew they'd never do —but catching the twisted smile again I pushed away my soda and said quickly, "Then we'd better start right away. It's three hours home, and I've still some places to go. But you can get in the buggy now, and we'll drive around together."

We did. I wanted it that way, the two of us, to settle scores with Main Street. I wanted to capture some of old Rock's disdain and unconcern; I wanted to know what it felt like to take young men with yellow shoes in my stride, to be preoccupied, to forget them the moment that we separated. And I did. "My name's Philip," the stranger said as we drove from Jenkins' to the drugstore. "Philip Coleman —usually just Phil," and companionably I responded, "Mine's Tommy Dickson. For the last year, though, my father says I'm getting big and should be called just Tom."

That was what mattered now, the two of us there, and not the town at all. "Do you drive yourself all the time?" he asked, and nonchalant and off-hand I answered, "You don't really have to drive old Rock. He just goes, anyway. Wait till you see my chestnut three-year-old. Clipper I call him. Tonight after supper if you like you can take him for a ride."

But since he'd never learned to ride at all he thought Rock would do better for a start, and then we drove back to the restaurant for his cornet and valise.

"Is it something to play?" I asked as we cleared the town. "Something like a bugle?"

He picked up the black leather case from the floor of the buggy and held it on his knee. "Something like that. Once I played a bugle too. A cornet's better, though."

"And you mean you can play the cornet?"

He nodded. "I play in a band. At least I did play in a band. Perhaps if I get along all right with the stooking I will again some time."

It was later that I pondered this, how stooking for my father could have anything to do with going back to play in a band. At the moment I confided, "I've never heard a cornet—never even seen one. I suppose you still play it sometimes—I mean at night, when you've finished stooking."

Instead of answering directly he said, "That means you've never heard a band either." There was surprise in his voice, almost incredulity, but it was kindly. Somehow I didn't feel ashamed because I had lived all my eleven years on a prairie farm, and knew nothing more than Miss Wiggins and my Aunt Louise's gramophone. He went on, "I was younger than you are now when I started playing in a band. Then I was with an orchestra a while—then with the band again. It's all I've done ever since."

It made me feel lonely for a while, isolated from the things in life that mattered, but, brightening presently, I asked, "Do you know a piece called *Sons of Liberty?* Four flats in four-four time?"

He thought hard a minute, and then shook his head. "I'm afraid I don't—not by name anyway. Could you whistle a bit of it?"

I whistled two pages, but still he shook his head. "A nice tune, though," he conceded. "Where did you learn it?"

"I haven't yet," I explained. "Not properly, I mean. It's been my lesson for the last two weeks, but I can't keep up to it."

He seemed interested, so I went on and told him about my lessons and Miss Wiggins, and how later on they were going to buy me a metronome so that when I played a piece I wouldn't always be running away with it, "Especially a march. It keeps pulling you along the way it really ought to go until you're all mixed up and have to start at the beginning again. I know I'd do better if I didn't feel that way, and could keep slow and steady like Miss Wiggins."

But he said quickly, "No, that's the right way to feel—you've just got to learn to harness it. It's like old Rock here and Clipper. The way you are, you're Clipper. But if you weren't that way, if you didn't get excited and wanted to run sometimes, you'd just be Rock. You see? Rock's easier to handle than Clipper, but at his best he's a sleepy old plow-horse. Clipper's harder to handle—he may even cost you some tumbles. But finally get him broken in and you've got a horse that amounts to something. You wouldn't trade him for a dozen like Rock."

It was a good enough illustration, but it slandered Rock. And he was listening. I know—because even though like me he had never heard a cornet before, he had experience enough to accept it at least with tact and manners.

For we hadn't gone much farther when Philip, noticing the way I kept watching the case that was still on his knee, undid the clasps and took the cornet out. It was a very lovely cornet, shapely and eloquent, gleaming in the August sun like pure and mellow gold. I couldn't restrain myself. I said, "Play it—play it now—just a little bit to let me hear." And in response, smiling at my earnestness, he raised it to his lips.

But there was only one note—only one fragment of a note—and then away went Rock. I'd never have believed he had it in him. With a snort and plunge he was off the road and into the ditch—then out of the ditch again and off at a breakneck gallop across the prairie. There were stones and badger holes, and he spared us none of them. The egg-crates full of groceries bounced out, then the tobacco, then my mother's face powder. "Whoa, Rock!" I cried, "Whoa, Rock!" but in the rattle and whir of wheels I don't suppose he even heard. Philip couldn't help much because he had his cornet to hang on to. I tried to tug on the reins, but at such a rate across the prairie it took me all my time to keep from following the groceries. He was a big horse, Rock, and once under way had to run himself out. Or he may have thought that if he gave us a thorough shaking-up we would be too subdued when it was over to feel like taking him seriously to task. Anyway, that was how it worked out. All I dared to do was run round to pat his sweaty neck and say, "Good Rock, good Rock— nobody's going to hurt you."

Besides there were the groceries to think about, and my mother's box of face powder. And his pride and reputation at stake, Rock had made it a runaway worthy of the horse he really was. We found the powder smashed open and one of the egg-crates cracked. Several of the oranges had rolled down a badger hole, and couldn't be recovered. We spent nearly ten minutes sifting raisins through our fingers, and still they felt a little gritty. "There were extra oranges," I tried to encourage Philip, "and I've seen my mother wash her raisins." He looked at me dubiously, and for a few minutes longer worked away trying to mend the egg-crate.

We were silent for the rest of the way home. We thought a great deal about each other, but asked no questions. Even though it was safely away in its case again I could still feel the cornet's presence as if it were a living thing. Somehow its gold and shapeliness per-

sisted, transfiguring the day, quickening the dusty harvest fields to
a gleam and lustre like its own. And I felt assured, involved. Suddenly there was a force in life, a current, an inevitability, carrying
me along too. The questions they would ask when I reached home
—the difficulties in making them understand that faithful old Rock
had really run away—none of it now seemed to matter. This stranger
with the white, thin hands, this gleaming cornet that as yet I hadn't
even heard, intimately and enduringly now they were my possessions.

When we reached home my mother was civil and no more. "Put
your things in the bunkhouse," she said, "and then wash here. Supper'll be ready in about an hour."

It was an uncomfortable meal. My father and my mother kept
looking at Philip and exchanging glances. I told them about the
cornet and the runaway, and they listened stonily. "We've never had
a harvest-hand before that was a musician too," my mother said in
a somewhat thin voice. "I suppose, though, you do know how to
stook?"

I was watching Philip desperately and for my sake he lied, "Yes,
I stooked last year. I may have a blister or two by this time tomorrow, but my hands will toughen up."

"You don't as a rule do farm work?" my father asked.

And Philip said, "No, not as a rule."

There was an awkward silence, so I tried to champion him. "He
plays his cornet in a band. Ever since he was my age—that's what
he does."

Glances were exchanged again. The silence continued.

I had been half-intending to suggest that Philip bring his cornet
into the house to play it for us, I perhaps playing with him on the
piano, but the parlour with its genteel plushiness was a room from
which all were excluded but the equally genteel—visitors like Miss
Wiggins and the minister—and gradually as the meal progressed I
came to understand that Philip and his cornet, so far as my mother
was concerned, had failed to qualify.

So I said nothing when he finished his supper, and let him go back
to the bunkhouse alone. "Didn't I say to have Jenkins pick him out?"
my father stormed as soon as he had gone. "Didn't I say somebody
big and strong?"

"He's tall," I countered, "and there wasn't anybody else except two
men, and it was the only way they'd come."

"You mean you didn't want anybody else. A cornet player! Fine
stooks he'll set up." And then, turning to my mother, "It's your fault
—you and your nonsense about music lessons. If you'd listen to me
sometimes, and try to make a man of him."

"I do listen to you," she answered quickly. "It's because I've had to listen to you now for thirteen years that I'm trying to make a different man of him. If you'd go to town yourself instead of keeping him out of school—and do your work in six days a week like decent people. I told you yesterday that in the long run it would cost you dear."

I slipped away and left them. The chores at the stable took me nearly an hour; and then, instead of returning to the house, I went over to see Philip. It was dark now, and there was a smoky lantern lit. He sat on the only chair, and in a hospitable silence motioned me to the bed. At once he ignored and accepted me. It was as if we had always known each other and long outgrown the need of conversation. He smoked, and blew rings towards the open door where the warm fall night encroached. I waited, eager, afraid lest they call me to the house, yet knowing that I must wait. Gradually the flame in the lantern smoked the glass till scarcely his face was left visible. I sat tense, expectant, wondering who he was, where he came from, why he should be here to do my father's stooking.

There were no answers, but presently he reached for his cornet. In the dim, soft darkness I could see it glow and quicken. And I remember still what a long and fearful moment it was, crouched and steeling myself, waiting for him to begin.

And I was right: when they came the notes were piercing, golden as the cornet itself, and they gave life expanse that it had never known before. They floated up against the night, and each for a moment hung there clear and visible. Sometimes they mounted poignant and sheer. Sometimes they soared and then, like a bird alighting, fell and brushed earth again.

It was *To the Evening Star.* He finished it and told me. He told me the names of all the other pieces that he played: an *Ave Maria, Song of India,* a serenade—all bright through the dark like slow, suspended lightning, chilled sometimes with a glimpse of the unknown. Only for Philip there I could not have endured it. With my senses I clung hard to him—the acrid smell of his cigarettes, the tilted profile daubed with smoky light.

Then abruptly he stood up, as if understanding, and said, "Now we'd better have a march, Tom—to bring us back where we belong. A cornet can be good fun, too, you know. Listen to this one and tell me."

He stood erect, head thrown back exactly like a picture in my reader of a bugler boy, and the notes came flashing gallant through the night until the two of us went swinging along in step with them a hundred thousand strong. For this was another march that did march. It marched us miles. It made the feet eager and the heart brave. It said that life was worth the living and bright as morning shone ahead to show the way.

When he had finished and put the cornet away I said, "There's a field right behind the house that my father started cutting this afternoon. If you like we'll go over now for a few minutes and I'll show you how to stook. . . . You see, if you set your sheaves on top of the stubble they'll be over again in half an hour. That's how everybody does at first but it's wrong. You've got to push the butts down hard, right to the ground—like this, so they bind with the stubble. At a good slant, see, but not too much. So they'll stand the wind and still shed water if it rains."

It was too dark for him to see much, but he listened hard and finally succeeded in putting up a stook or two that to my touch seemed firm enough. Then my mother called, and I had to slip away fast so that she would think I was coming from the bunkhouse. "I hope he stooks as well as he plays," she said when I went in. "Just the same, you should have done as your father told you, and picked a likelier man to see us through the fall."

My father came in from the stable then, and he, too, had been listening. With a wondering, half-incredulous little movement of his head he made acknowledgment.

"Didn't I tell you he could?" I burst out, encouraged to indulge my pride in Philip. "Didn't I tell you he could play?" But with sudden anger in his voice he answered, "And what if he can! It's a man to stook I want. Just look at the hands on him. I don't think he's ever seen a farm before."

It was helplessness, though, not anger. Helplessness to escape his wheat when wheat was not enough, when something more than wheat had just revealed itself. Long after they were both asleep I remembered, and with a sharp foreboding that we might have to find another man, tried desperately to sleep myself. "Because if I'm up in good time," I rallied all my faith in life, "I'll be able to go to the field with him and at least make sure he's started right. And he'll maybe do. I'll ride down after school and help till supper time. My father's reasonable."

Only in such circumstances, of course, and after such a day, I couldn't sleep till nearly morning, with the result that when at last my mother wakened me there was barely time to dress and ride to school. But of the day I spent there I remember nothing. Nothing except the midriff clutch of dread that made it a long day—nothing, till straddling Clipper at four again, I galloped him straight to the far end of the farm where Philip that morning had started to work.

Only Philip, of course, wasn't there. I think I knew—I think it was what all day I had been expecting. I pulled Clipper up short and sat staring at the stooks. Three or four acres of them—crooked and dejected as if he had never heard about pushing the butts down hard into the stubble. I sat and stared till Clipper himself swung round and started for home. He wanted to run, but because there was nothing left now but the half-mile ahead of us, I held him to a walk. Just to prolong a little the possibility that I had misunderstood things. To wonder within the limits of the sane and probable if tonight he would play his cornet again.

When I reached the house my father was already there, eating an early supper. "I'm taking him back to town," he said quietly. "He tried hard enough—he's just not used to it. The sun was hot today; he lasted till about noon. We're starting in a few minutes, so you'd better go out and see him."

He looked older now, stretched out limp on the bed, his face haggard. I tiptoed close to him anxiously, afraid to speak. He pulled his mouth sidewise in a smile at my concern, then motioned me to sit down. "Sorry I didn't do better," he said. "I'll have to come back another year and have another lesson."

I clenched my hands and clung hard to this promise that I knew he couldn't keep. I wanted to rebel against what was happening, against the clumsiness and crudity of life, but instead I stood quiet a moment, almost passive, then wheeled away and carried out his cornet to the buggy. My mother was already there, with a box of lunch and some ointment for his sunburn. She said she was sorry things had turned out this way, and thanking her politely he said that he was sorry too. My father looked uncomfortable, feeling, no doubt, that we were all unjustly blaming everything on him. It's like that on a farm. You always have to put the harvest first.

And that's all there is to tell. He waved going through the gate; I never saw him again. We watched the buggy down the road to the first turn, then with a quick resentment in her voice my mother said, "Didn't I say that the little he gained would in the long run cost him dear? Next time he'll maybe listen to me—and remember the Sabbath Day."

What exactly she was thinking I never knew. Perhaps of the crop and the whole day's stooking lost. Perhaps of the stranger who had come with his cornet for a day, and then as meaninglessly gone again. For she had been listening, too, and she may have understood. A harvest, however lean, is certain every year; but a cornet at night is golden only once.

Muriel Spark

(b. 1918)

Born and educated in Edinburgh, Scotland, Muriel Spark spent some years in South Africa, then returned to Britain and worked in an intelligence department during World War II. She made her first impact on the British literary scene as secretary of the Poetry Society and editor of *Poetry Review* from 1947 to 1949. Her first novel, *The Comforters,* appeared in 1957; since then she has written eleven more, including *The Prime of Miss Jean Brodie* (1961), filmed in 1968, and *The Hothouse by the East River* (1973). Spark has also written a number of short stories, plays for stage and radio, and works of criticism, including several books concerned with the Brontës. In 1967 she was made a member of the Order of the British Empire.

Spark's critical interest in figures like Mary Shelley, Emily Brontë, and John Henry Newman reflects tendencies and preoccupations in her own writing. Though the surface of her stories is often whimsical or wryly comic, her interests go beyond the satirical depiction of social manners; she selects solitaries and eccentrics as her principal characters, and draws them in such a way as to suggest the influence of inexplicable forces on human life. As an epigraph for the novel *Memento Mori* (1958), a study of old age, Spark chose to quote the Penny Catechism on "the four last things," "Death, Judgment, Hell and Heaven"; and much of her fiction revolves around these concerns. Her work bears the impress of her religious beliefs (she became a Roman Catholic in 1954), but faith has never blunted her satirical edge; she is critical of the vulgarity and hypocrisy spawned by religion, and freely mocks hidebound attitudes, whether displayed by individuals or by institutions. "Come Along, Marjorie," from *The Go-Away Bird with Other Stories* (1958), mocks the self-conscious posturings of a group of pilgrims in retreat at a religious house, and raises questions about the difference between madness and sanity in a world where appearance means more than substance.

For further reading

Muriel Spark, "My Conversion," *Twentieth Century,* 170 (Autumn 1961), 58–63.
Derek Stanford, *Muriel Spark: A biographical and critical study* (Fontwell: Centaur Press, 1963).
Patricia Stubbs, *Muriel Spark* (Harlow, Essex: Longmans, 1973).

Come Along, Marjorie

Not many days had passed since my arrival at Watling Abbey when I realized that most of us were recovering from nerves. The Abbey, a twelfth-century foundation, lies in Worcestershire on the site of an ancient Temple of Mithras. It had recently been acquired and restored by its original religious Order at that time, just after the war, when I went to stay there and found after a few days that most of us were nervous cases.

By "most of us" I mean the lay visitors who resided in the pilgrims' quarters on two sides of the Annexe. We were all known as pilgrims. Apart from us, there was a group of permanent lay residents known as the Cloisters, because they lived in rooms above the cloisters.

Neurotics are awfully quick to notice other people's mentalities, everyone goes into an exaggerated category. I placed four categories at the Abbey. First ourselves, the visiting neurotic pilgrims. Second the Cloisters, they were cranks on the whole. Third the monks; they seemed not to have nerves, but non-individualized, non-neurotic, so I thought then, they billowed about in their white habits under the gold of that October, or swung out from the cloisters in processions on Feast Days. Into the fourth category I placed Miss Marjorie Pettigrew.

Indeed, she did seem sane. I got the instant impression that she alone among the lay people, both pilgrims and Cloisters, understood the purpose of the place. I did get that impression.

Three of us had arrived at Watling together. It was dark when I got off the train, but under the only gas bracket on the platform I saw the two women standing. They looked about them in that silly manner of women unused to arriving at strange railway stations. They heard me asking the ticket man the way to the Abbey and chummed up with me immediately. As we walked along with our suitcases I made note that there was little in common between them and me except Catholicism, and then only in the mystical sense, for their religious apprehensions were different from mine. "Different from" is the form my neurosis takes. I do like the differentiation of things, but it is apt to lead to nerve-racking pursuits. On the other hand, life led on the different-from level is always an adventure.

Those were quite nice women. One was Squackle-wackle, so I called her to myself, for she spoke like that, squackle-wackle, squackle-wackle—it was her neurosis—all about her job as a nurse in a London hospital. She had never managed to pass an exam but was content, squackle-wackle, to remain a subordinate, though thirty-three in December. All this in the first four minutes. The other woman would be nearer forty. She was quieter, but not much. As we approached the Abbey gates she said, "My name's Jennifer, what's yours?"

"Gloria Deplores-you," I answered. It is true my Christian name is Gloria.

"Gloria what?"

"It's a French name," I said, inventing in my mind the spelling "des Pleuresyeux" in case I should be pressed for it.

"We'll call you Gloria," she said. I had stopped in the Abbey gateway, wondering if I should turn back after all. "Come along, Gloria," she said.

It was not till some days later that I found that Jennifer's neurosis took the form of "same as." We are all the same, she would assert, infuriating me because I knew that God had made everyone unique. "We are all the same" was her way of saying we were all equal in the sight of God. Still, the inaccuracy irritated me. And still, like Squackle-wackle, she was quite an interesting person. It was only in my more vibrant moments that I deplored them.

Oh, the trifles, the people, that get on your nerves when you have a neurosis!

Don't I remember the little ginger man with the bottle-green cloak? He was one of the Cloisters, having been resident at Watling for over three years. He was compiling a work call *The Monkish Booke of Brewes.* Once every fortnight he would be absent at the British Museum and I suppose other record houses, from where he would return with a great pad of notes on the methods and subtleties of brewing practised in ancient monasteries, don't I remember? And he, too, was a kindly sort in between his frightful fumes against the management of Watling Abbey. When anything went wrong he blamed the monks, unlike the Irish who blamed the Devil. This sometimes caused friction between the ginger man and the Irish, for which the monks blamed the Devil.

There were ladies from Cork and thereabouts, ladies from Tyrone and Londonderry, all having come for a rest or a Retreat, and most being those neurotic stigmata of South or North accordingly. There were times when bitter bits of meaning would whistle across the space between North and South when they were gathered together outside of their common worship. Though all were Catholics, "Temperament tells," I told myself frequently. I did so often tell myself remarks like that to still my own nerves.

I joined Squackle-wackle and Jennifer each morning to recite the Fifteen Mysteries. After that we went to the town for coffee. Because I rested in the afternoons Jennifer guessed I was recovering from nerves. She asked me outright, "Is it nerves?" I said "Yes," outright.

Squackle-wackle had also been sent away with nervous exhaustion, she made no secret of it, indeed no.

Jennifer was delighted. "I've got the same trouble. Fancy, all three of us. That makes us *all the same.*"

"It makes us," I said, "more different from each other than other people are."

"But, all the same," she said, "we're all *the same.*"

But there was Miss Marjorie Pettigrew. Miss Pettigrew's appearance and bearing attracted me with a kind of consolation. I learned that she had been at Watling for about six months and from various hints and abrupt silences I gathered that she was either feared or disliked. I put this down to the fact that she wasn't a neurotic. Usually, neurotics take against people whose nerves they can't jar upon. So I argued to myself; and that I myself rather approved of Miss Pettigrew was a sign that I was a different sort of neurotic from the others.

Miss Pettigrew was very tall and stick-like, with very high shoulders and a square face. She seemed to have a lot of bones. Her eyes were dark, her hair black; it was coiled in the earphone style but she was not otherwise unfashionable.

I thought at first she must be in Retreat, for she never spoke at mealtimes, though she always smiled faintly when passing anything at table. She never joined the rest of the community except for meals and prayers. She was often in the chapel praying. I envied her resistance, for though I too wanted solitude I often hadn't the courage to refuse to join the company, and so make myself unpopular like Miss Pettigrew. I hoped she would speak to me when she came out of her Retreat.

One day in that first week a grand-looking north-countrywoman said to me at table, nodding over to where Miss Pettigrew sat in her silence,

"There's nothing wrong with *her* at all."

"Wrong with her?"

"It's pretence, she's clever, that's it."

By clever she meant cunning, I realized that much.

"How do you mean, pretence?" I said.

"Her silence. She won't speak to anyone."

"But she's in Retreat, isn't she?"

"Not her," said this smart woman. "She's been living here for over six months and for the past four she hasn't opened her mouth. It isn't mental trouble, it is not."

"Has she taken some religious vow, perhaps?"

"Not her; she's clever. She won't open her mouth. They brought a doctor, but she wouldn't open her mouth to him."

"I'm glad she's quiet, anyhow," I said. "Her room's next door to mine and I like quietness."

Not all the pilgrims regarded Miss Pettigrew as "clever." She was thought to be genuinely touched in the head. And it was strange how she was disapproved of by the Cloisters, for they were kind— only too intrusively kind—towards obvious nervous sufferers like me. Their disapproval of Miss Pettigrew was almost an admission that they believed nothing wrong with her. If she had gone untidy, made grotesque faces, given jerks and starts and twitches, if she had in some way lost their respect I do not think she would have lost their approval.

I began to notice her more closely in the hope of finding out more about her mental aberration; such things are like a magnet to neurotics. I would meet her crossing the courtyard, or come upon her kneeling in the lonely Lady Chapel. Always she inclined her coiled head towards me, ceremonious as an Abbess greeting a nun. Passing her in a corridor I felt the need to stand aside and make way for her confident quiet progress. I could not believe she was insane.

I could not believe she was practising some crude triumphant cunning, enduring from day to day, with her silence and prayers. It was said she had money. Perhaps she was very mystical. I wondered how long she would be able to remain hermitted so within herself. The monks were in a difficult position. It was against their nature to turn her out; maybe it was against their Rule; certainly it would cause a bad impression in the neighbourhood which was not at all Abbey-minded. One after another the monks had approached her, tactful monks, sympathetic, firm, and curious ones.

"Well, Miss Pettigrew, I hope you've benefited from your stay at the Abbey? I suppose you have plans for the winter?"

No answer, only a mild gesture of acknowledgement.

No answer, likewise, to another monk, "Now, Miss Pettigrew, dear child, you simply can't go on like this. It isn't that we don't want to keep you. Glory be to God, we'd never turn you out of doors, nor any soul. But we need the room, d'you see, for another pilgrim."

And again, "Now tell us what's the trouble, open your heart, poor Miss Pettigrew. This isn't the Catholic way at all. You've got to communicate with your fellows."

"Is it a religious vow you've taken all on your own? That's very unwise, it's . . ."

"See, Miss Pettigrew, we've found you a lodging in the town. . . ."

Not a word. She was seen to go weekly to Confession, so evidently she was capable of speech. But she would not talk, even to do her small bits of shopping. Every week or so she would write on a piece of paper,

Please get me a Snowdrop Shampoo, 1s. 6d encl.

or some such errand, handing it to the laundry-girl who was much attached to her, and who showed me these slips of paper as proudly as if they were the relics of a saint.

"Gloria, are you coming for a walk?"

No, I wasn't going for a trudge. It was my third week. Squackle-wackle was becoming most uninteresting.

I sat by my window and thought how happy I would be if I wasn't waiting uncertainly for a telephone call. I still have in mind the blue and green and gold of that October afternoon which was spoiled for me at the time. The small ginger man with his dark-green cloak slipping off his shoulders crossed the grass in the courtyard below. Two lay brothers in blue workmen's overalls were manipulating a tractor away in the distance. From the Lady Chapel came the chant of the monks at their office. There is nothing like plainsong to eternalize a memory, it puts a seal on whatever is happening at the time. I thought it a pity that my appreciation of this fact should be vitiated by an overwhelming need for the telephone call.

I had hoped, in fact, that the ginger man had crossed the courtyard to summon me to the telephone, but he disappeared beneath my window and his footsteps faded out somewhere round the back. Everything's perfect, I told myself, and I can't enjoy it. Brown, white, and purples, I distinguished the pigeons on the grass.

Everyone else seemed to be out of doors. My room was on the attic floor, under the dusty beams of the roof. All along this top floor the rooms were separated by thin partitions which allowed transit to every sound. Even silent Miss Pettigrew, my immediate neighbour, could not lie breathing on her still bed without my knowing it. That afternoon she too was out, probably over in the chapel.

The telephone call was to be from Jonathan, my very best friend. I had returned from my coffee session in the town that morning to find a letter from him which had been delayed in the post. "I'll ring you at 11.30," he had written, referring to that very day. It was then past twelve. At eleven-thirty I had been drinking coffee with unutterable Squackle-wackle and Jennifer.

"Has there been a call for me?" I inquired.

"Not that I know," said the secretary vaguely. "I've been away from the phone all morning, of course, so there may have been, I don't know."

Not that there was anything important to discuss with Jonathan; the idea was only to have a chat. But at that moment I felt imperatively dependent on his voice over the telephone. I stopped everyone, monks and brothers and pilgrims. "Did you take a telephone

message for me? I should have received a very urgent call. It should
have come at eleven-thirty."

"Sorry, I've been out," or "Sorry, I haven't been near the phone."

"Doesn't anyone attend to your telephone?" I demanded.

"Hardly ever, dear. We're too busy."

"I've missed an important telephone call, a vital—"

"Can't you telephone to your friend from here?"

"No," I said. "It's impossible, it's too bad."

Jonathan did not have a telephone in his studio. I wondered
whether I should send him a wire and even drafted one, "Sorry love
your letter arrived too late was out, please ring at once love Gloria."
I tore this up on the grounds that I couldn't afford the expense. And
something about the torment of the affair attracted me, it was better
than boredom. I decided that Jonathan would surely ring again during the afternoon. I prepared, even, to sit in the little office by the
telephone with my sense of suspense and vigilance, all afternoon.
But, "I'll be here till five o'clock," said the secretary; "of course, of
course, I'll send for you if the call comes."

And so there I was by the window waiting for the summons. At
three o'clock I washed and made up my face and changed my frock
as if this were a propitiation to whatever stood between Jonathan's
telephone call and me. I decided to stroll round the green-gold courtyard where I could not fail to miss any messenger. Once round, and
still no one came. Only Miss Pettigrew emerged from the cloisters,
crossing the courtyard towards me.

I was so bemused by my need to talk to Jonathan that I thought,
as she approached, "Perhaps they've sent her to call me." Immediately I remembered, that was absurd, for she carried no messages
ever. But she continued so directly towards me that I thought again,
"She's going to speak." She had her dark eyes on my face.

I made as if to pass her, not wishing to upset her by inviting
approach. But she stopped me. "Excuse me," she said, "I have a
message for you."

I was so relieved that I forgot to be surprised by her speaking.

"Am I wanted on the telephone?" I said, half ready to run across
to the office.

"No, I have a message for you," she said.

"What's the message?"

"The Lord is risen," she said.

It was not until I had got over my disappointment that I felt the
shock of her having spoken, and recalled an odd focus of her eyes
that I had not seen before. "After all," I thought "she has a religious
mania. She *is* different from the neurotics, but not because she is
sane."

"Gloria!"—this was the girl from the repository poking her head round the door. She beckoned to me, and, still disturbed, I idled over to her.

"I say, did I see Miss Pettigrew actually speaking to you, or was I dreaming?"

"You were dreaming." If I had said otherwise the news would have bristled round the monastery. It would have seemed a betrayal to reveal this first crack in Miss Pettigrew's control. The pilgrims would have pitied her more if they had known of it, they would have respected her less. I could not bear to think of their heads shaking sorrowfully over Miss Pettigrew's vital "The Lord is risen."

"But surely," this girl pursued, "she stopped beside you just now."

"You've got Miss Pettigrew on the brain," I said. "Leave her alone, poor soul."

"Poor soul!" said the girl. "I don't know about poor soul. There's nothing wrong with that one. She's got foolish medieval ideas, that's all."

"There's nothing to be done with her," I said.

And yet it was not long before something had to be done with Miss Pettigrew. From the Sunday of the fourth week of my stay she went off food. It was not till suppertime on the Monday that her absence was noticed from the refectory.

"Anyone seen Miss Pettigrew?"

"No, she hasn't been down here for two days."

"Does she eat in the town, perhaps?"

"No, she hasn't left the Abbey."

A deputation with a tray of food was sent to her room. There was no answer. The door was bolted from the inside. But I heard her moving calmly as ever in her room that evening.

Next morning she came in to breakfast after Mass, looking distant and grey, but still very neat. She took up a glass of milk, lifted the crust end of the bread from the board and carried them shakily off to her room. When she did not appear for lunch the cook tried her room again, without success. The door was bolted, there was no answer.

I saw Miss Pettigrew again at Mass next morning, kneeling a little in front of me, resting her head upon her missal as if she could not bear the weight of head on neck. When at last she left the chapel she walked extremely slowly but without halting in her measure. Squackle-wackle ran to help her down the steps. Miss Pettigrew stopped and looked at her, inclining her head in recognition, but clearly rejecting her help.

The doctor was waiting in her room. I heard later that he asked her many questions, used many persuasives, but she simply stared right through him. The Abbot and several of the monks visited her, but by then she had bolted the door again, and though they tempted her with soups and beef broth, Miss Pettigrew would not open.

News went round that her relatives had been sent for. The news went round that she had no relatives to send for. It was said she had been certified insane and was to be taken away.

She did not rise next morning at her usual seven o'clock. It was not till after twelve that I heard her first movement, and the protracted sounds of her slow rising and dressing. A tiny clatter—that would be her shoe falling out of her weak hands; I knew she was bending down, trying again. My pulse was pattering so rapidly that I had to take more of my sedative than usual, as I listened to this slow deliberated performance. Heavy rhythmic rain had started to ping on the roof.

"Neurotics never go mad," my friends had always told me. Now I realized the distinction between neurosis and madness, and in my agitation I half envied the woman beyond my bedroom wall, the sheer cool sanity of her behaviour within the limits of her impracticable mania. Only the very mad, I thought, can come out with the information "The Lord is risen," in the same factual way as one might say, "You are wanted on the telephone," regardless of the time and place.

A knock at my door. I opened it, still shaking with my nerves. It was Jennifer. She whispered, with an eye on the partition dividing me from Miss Pettigrew,

"Come along, Gloria. They say you are to come away for half an hour. The nurses are coming to fetch *her.*"

"What nurses?"

"From the asylum. And there will be men with a stretcher. We haven't to distress ourselves, they say."

I could see that Jennifer was agog. She was more transparent than I was. I could see she was longing to stay and overhear, watch out of the windows, see what would happen. I was overcome with disgust and indignation. Why should Jennifer want to satisfy her curiosity? She believed everyone was "the same," she didn't acknowledge the difference of things, what right had she to possess curiosity? My case was different.

"I shall stay here," I said in a normal voice, signifying that I wasn't going to participate in any whispering. Jennifer disappeared, annoyed.

Insanity was my great sort of enemy at that time. And here, clothed in the innocence and dignity of Miss Pettigrew, was my

next-door enemy being removed by ambulance. I would not miss it.
Afterwards I learned that Jennifer too was lurking around when the
ambulance arrived. So were most of the neurotics.

The ambulance came round the back. My window looked only on
the front but my ears were windows. I heard a woman's voice, then
in reply the voice of one of our priests. Heavy footsteps and something bumping on the stairs and strange men's voices ascending.

"What's her name, did you say?"

"Marjorie Pettigrew."

The hauling and bumping up the stairs continued.

"Ain't no key. Bolt from the inside."

Whenever they paused I could hear Miss Pettigrew's tiny movements. She was continuing to do what she was doing.

They knocked at the door. I pulled like mad at the rosary which
I was telling for Miss Pettigrew. A man's voice said, kindly but
terribly loud,

"Open up the door, dear. Else we shall have to force it, dear."

She opened the door.

"That's a good girl," said the man. "What was the name again?"

The other man replied, "Marjorie Pettigrew."

"Well, come on, Marjorie dear. You just follow me and you won't
go wrong. Come along, Marjorie."

I knew she must have been following, though I could not hear her
footsteps. I heard the heavy men's boots descending the stairs, and
their unnecessary equipment bumping behind them.

"That's right Marjorie. That's a good girl."

Down below the nurse said something, and I heard no more till the
ambulance drove off.

"Oh, I saw her!" This was the laundry-girl who had been fond of
Miss Pettigrew. "She must have been combing her hair," she said,
"when they came for her. It was all loose and long, not at all like Miss
Pettigrew. She was always just so. And that going out in the rain,
I hope she doesn't catch cold. But they'll be good to her."

Everyone was saying, "They will be kind to her." "They will look
after her." "They might cure her."

I never saw them so friendly with each other.

After supper someone said, "I had a respect for Miss Pettigrew."

"So did I," said another.

"They will very be kind. Those men—they sounded all right."

"They meant well enough."

Suddenly the ginger man came out with that one thing which
stood at the core of this circuitous talk.

"Did you hear them," he said, "call her Marjorie?"

"My God, yes!"

"Yes, it made me feel funny."

"Same here. Fancy calling her Marjorie."

After that the incident was little discussed. But the community was sobered and united for a brief time, contemplating with fear and pity the calling of Miss Pettigrew Marjorie.

Audrey Thomas

(b. 1935)

Born Audrey Callahan in Binghamton, New York, Audrey Thomas was educated in the United States, Scotland, and Canada. Interrupting her formal education to spend two years in Ghana, she returned in 1966 to Vancouver, and now lives on Galiano Island, off the west coast of British Columbia. "If One Green Bottle ...," which was her first published short story, appeared in *The Atlantic Monthly* and was then collected in *Ten Green Bottles* (1967). (For the version printed here, the author has made several textual alterations.) Other stories followed, as did novels, novellas, and a radio play. Like "If One Green Bottle ...," her novel *Mrs. Blood* (1970) concerns a woman experiencing a difficult pregnancy; the one ends in miscarriage, the other threatens to, and both stories are told from the woman's own perspective. One of the key tensions in *Mrs. Blood* is that between the woman's two subjective identities: "Mrs. Blood," the visceral woman, unknowable outside herself, and "Mrs. Thing," the apparent "object" whom she and others can variously regard. That internal division mirrors various kinds of external schisms—most particularly those between men and women, in their attractions toward and misunderstandings of each other's nature.

A sense of isolation also pervades "If One Green Bottle...." The rhythm of the story follows the narrator's experience, and the stream-of-consciousness style carries the associations of her mind, the leaps from fragmentary image to fragmentary image that retell part of her life. But nothing can erase the present—not myth, not philosophy, not the knowledge of history and literature, not memories of her own childhood. The pressures of the here-and-now emphasize for her the inadequacy of ideas and systems. The writer's restraint in evoking those pressures makes the realization of solitariness into a painful discovery for narrator and reader alike.

For further reading

H. J. Rosengarten, "Writer and Subject," *Canadian Literature*, 55 (Winter 1973), 111–113.

If One Green Bottle...

When fleeing, one should never look behind. Orpheus, Lot's wife ... penalties grotesque and terrible await us all. It does not pay to doubt ... to turn one's head ... to rely on the confusion ... the smoke ... the fleeing multitudes ... the satisfaction of the tumbling cities ... to distract the attention of the gods. Argus-eyed, they wait, he waits ... the golden chessmen spread upon the table ... the opponent's move already known, accounted for.... Your pawns, so vulnerable

... advancing with such care (if you step on a crack, then you'll break your mother's back). Already the monstrous hand trembles in anticipation ... the thick lips twitch with suppressed laughter ... then pawn, knight, castle, queen scooped up and tossed aside. "Check," and (click click) "check ... mmmate." The game is over, and you ... surprised (but why?) ... petulant ... your nose still raw from the cold ... your galoshes not yet dried ... really, it's indecent ... inhumane (why bother to come? answer: the bother of not coming) ... and not even the offer of a sandwich or a cup of tea ... discouraging ... disgusting. The great mouth opens ... like a whale really ... he strains you, one more bit of plankton, through his teeth. "Next week ... ? At the same time ... ? No, no, not at all. I do not find it boring in the least. ... Each time a great improvement. Why, soon," the huge lips tremble violently, "ha, ha, *you'll* be beating *me.*" Lies ... all lies. Yet, even as you go, echoes of Olympian laughter in your ears, you know you will return, will once more challenge ... and be defeated once again. Even plankton have to make a protest ... a stand ... what else can one do? "Besides, it passes the time ... keeps my hand in ... and you never know. ... One time, perhaps ... a slip ... a flutter of the eyelids. ... Even the gods grow old."

The tropical fan, three-bladed, ominiscient, omnipotent, inexorable, churns up dust and mosquitoes, the damp smell of coming rain, the overripe smell of vegetation, of charcoal fires, of human excrement, of fear ... blown in through the open window, blown up from the walls and the floor. All is caught in the fan's embrace, the efficient arms of the unmoved mover. The deus in the machina, my old chum the chess-player, refuses to descend ... yet watches. Soon they will let down the nets and we will lie in the darkness, in our gauze houses, like so many lumps of cheese ... protected ... revealed. The night-fliers, dirty urchins, will press their noses at my windows and lick their hairy lips in hunger ... in frustration. Can they differentiate, I wonder, between the blood of my neighbor and mine? Are there aesthetes among the insects who will touch only the soft parts ... between the thighs ... under the armpits ... along the inner arm? Are there vintages and connoisseurs? I don't like the nights here: that is why I wanted it over before the night. One of the reasons. If am asleep I do not know who feeds on me, who has found the infinitesimal rip and invited his neighbors in. Besides, he promised it would be over before the night. And one listens, doesn't one? ... one always believes. ... Absurd to rely on verbal consolation ... clichés so worn they feel like old coins ... smooth ... slightly oily to the touch ... faceless.

Pain, the word, I mean, derived (not according to Skeat) from "pay" and "Cain." How can there, then, be an exit ... a way out? The darker the night, the clearer the mark on the forehead ... the brighter the blind man's cane at the crossing ... the louder the sound of footsteps somewhere behind. Darkness heightens the absurd sense of "situation" ... gives the audience its kicks. But tonight ... really ... All Souls' ... it's too ridiculous. ... Somebody goofed. The author has gone too far; the absurdity lies in one banana skin, not two or three. After one, it becomes too painful ... too involved ... too much like home. Somebody will have to pay for this ... the reviews ... tomorrow ... will all be most severe. The actors will sulk over their morning cup of coffee ... the angel will beat his double breast above the empty pocketbook ... the director will shout and stamp his feet. ... The whole thing should have been revised ... rewritten ... we knew it from the first.

(This is the house that Jack built. This is the cat that killed the rat that lived in the house that Jack built. We are the maidens all shaven and shorn, that milked the cow with the crumpled horn ... that loved in the hearse that Joke built. Excuse me, please, was this the Joke that killed the giant or the Jack who tumbled down ... who broke his crown? Crown him with many crowns, the lamb upon his throne. He tumbled too ... it's inevitable. ... It all, in the end, comes back to the nursery. ... Jill, Humpty Dumpty, Rock-a-bye baby ... they-kiss-you, they-kiss-you ... they all fall down. The nurses in the corner playing Ludo ... centurions dicing. We are all betrayed by Cock-a-Doodle-Doo. ... We all fall down. Why, then, should I be exempt? ... presumptuous of me ... please forgive.)

Edges of pain. Watch it, now, the tide is beginning to turn. Like a cautious bather, stick in one toe ... both feet ... "brr" ... the impact of the ocean ... the solidity of the thing, now that you've finally got under ... like swimming in an ice cube really. "Yes, I'm coming. Wait for me." The shock of the total immersion ... the pain breaking over the head. Don't cry out ... hold your breath ... so. "Not so bad, really, when one gets used to it." That's it ... just the right tone ... the brave swimmer. ... Now wave a gay hand toward the shore. Don't let them know ... the indignities ... the chattering teeth ... the blue lips ... the sense of isolation. ... Good.

And Mary, how did she take it, I wonder, the original, the appalling announcement ... the burden thrust upon her? "No, really, some other time ... the spring planting ... my aged mother ... quite impossible. Very good of you to think of me, of course, but I couldn't take it on. Perhaps you'd call in again this time next year." (Dismiss him firmly ... quickly, while there's still time. Don't let him get both feet in the door. Be firm and final. "No, I'm sorry, I never accept free gifts.") And then the growing awareness, the anger showing

quick and hot under the warm brown of the cheeks. The voice . . .
like oil. . . . "I'm afraid I didn't make myself clear." (Like the detective
novels. . . . "Allow me to present my card . . . my credentials." The
shock of recognition . . . the horror. "Oh, I see. . . . Yes . . . well, if it's
like that. . . . Come this way." A gesture of resignation. She allows
herself one sigh . . . the ghost of a smile.) But no, it's all wrong. Mary
. . . peasant girl . . . quite a different reaction implied. Dumbfounded
. . . remember Zachary. A shocked silence . . . the rough fingers
twisting together like snakes . . . awe . . . a certain rough pride ("Wait
until I tell the other girls. The well . . . tomorrow morning. . . . I
won't be proud about it, not really. But it is an honor. What will
Mother say?") *Droit de seigneur* . . . the servant summoned to the
bedchamber . . . honored . . . afraid. Or perhaps like Leda. No prelimi-
naries . . . no thoughts at all. Too stupid . . . too frightened . . . the
thing was, after all, over so quickly. That's it . . . stupidity . . . the
necessary attribute. I can hear him now. "That girl . . . whatzer-
name? . . . Mary. Mary will do. Must be a simple woman. . . . That's
where we made our first mistake. Eve too voluptuous . . . too intelligent . . . this time nothing must go wrong."

And the days were accomplished. Unfair to gloss that over . . . to
make so little of the waiting . . . the months . . . the hours. They make
no mention of the hours; but of course, men wrote it down. How
were they to know? After the immaculate conception, after the long
and dreadful journey, after the refusal at the inn . . . came the macu-
late delivery . . . the manger. And all that noise . . . cattle lowing (and
doing other things besides) . . . angels blaring away . . . the eerie
light. No peace . . . no chance for sleep . . . for rest between the pains
. . . for time to think . . . to gather courage. Yet why should she be
afraid . . . downhearted . . . ? Hadn't she had a sign . . . the voice . . .
the presence of the star? (And notice well, they never told her about
the other thing . . . the third act.) It probably seemed worth it at the
time . . . the stench . . . the noise . . . the pain.

Robert the Bruce . . . Constantine . . . Noah. The spider . . . the
flaming cross . . . the olive branch. . . . With these signs. . . . I would
be content with something far more simple. A breath of wind on the
cheek . . . the almost imperceptible movements of a curtain . . . a
single flash of lightning. Courage consists, perhaps, in the ability to
recognize signs . . . the symbolism of the spider. But for me . . .
tonight . . . what is there? The sound of far-off thunder . . . the smell
of the coming rain which will wet, but not refresh . . . that tropical
fan. The curtain moves . . . yes, I will allow you that. But for me . . .
tonight . . . there is only a rat behind the arras. Jack's rat. This time
there is no exit . . . no way out or up.

(You are not amused by my abstract speculations? Listen . . . I have more. Time. Time is an awareness, either forward or backward, of Then, as opposed to Now ... the stasis. Time is the moment between thunder and lightning ... the interval at the street corner when the light is amber, neither red nor green, but shift gears, look both ways ... the oasis of pleasure between pains ... the space between the darkness and the dawn ... the conversations between courses ... the fear in the final stroke of twelve ... the nervous fumbling with cloth and buttons, before the longed-for contact of the flesh ... the ringing telephone ... the solitary coffee cup ... the oasis of pleasure between pains. Time ... and time again.)

That time when I was eleven and at Scout camp ... marching in a dusty serpentine to the fire tower ... the hearty counselors with sun-streaked hair and muscular thighs ... enjoying themselves, enjoying ourselves ... the long hike almost over. "Ten green bottles standing on the wall. Ten green bottles standing on the wall. If one green bottle ... should accidentally fall, there'd be nine green bottles standing on the wall." And that night ... after pigs in blankets ... cocoa ... campfire songs ... the older girls taught us how to faint ... to hold our breath and count to thirty ... then blow upon our thumbs. Gazing up at the stars ... the sudden sinking back into warmth and darkness ... the recovery ... the fresh attempt ... delicious. In the morning we climbed the fire tower (and I, afraid to look down or up, climbing blindly, relying on my sense of touch), reached the safety of the little room on top. We peered out the windows at the little world below ... and found six baby mice, all dead ... curled up, like dust kitties in the kitchen drawer. "How long d'you suppose they've been there?" "Too long. Ugh." "Throw them away." "Put them back where you found them." Disturbed ... distressed ... the pleasure marred. "Let's toss them down on Rachel. She was too scared to climb the tower. Baby." "Yes, let's toss them down. She ought to be paid back." (Everything all right now ... the day saved. Ararat ... Areopagus. ...) Giggling, invulnerable, we hurled the small bodies out the window at the Lilliputian form below. Were we punished? Curious ... I can't remember. And yet the rest ... so vivid ... as though it were yesterday ... this morning ... five minutes ago. ... We must have been punished. Surely they wouldn't let us get away with that?

Waves of pain now ... positive whitecaps ... breakers. ... Useless to try to remember ... to look behind ... to think. Swim for shore. Ignore the ringing in the ears ... the eyes half blind with water ... the waves breaking over the head. Just keep swimming ... keep moving forward ... rely on instinct ... your sense of direction ... don't look back or forward ... there isn't time for foolish speculation.

... See? Flung up ... at last ... exhausted, but on the shore. Flotsam ... jetsam ... but there, you made it. Lie still

The expected disaster is always the worst. One waits for it ... is obsessed by it ... it nibbles at the consciousness. Jack's rat. Far better the screech of brakes ... the quick embrace of steel and shattered glass ... or the sudden stumble from the wall. One is prepared through being unprepared. A few thumps of the old heart ... like a brief flourish of announcing trumpets ... a roll of drums ... and then nothing. This way ... tonight ... I wait for the crouching darkness like a child waiting for that movement from the shadows in the corner of the bedroom. It's all wrong ... unfair ... there ought to be a law. ... One can keep up only a given number of chins ... one keeps silent only a given number of hours. After that, the final humiliation ... the loss of self-control ... the oozing out upon the pavement. ... Dumpty-like, one refuses (or is unable?) to be reintegrated ... whimpers for morphia and oblivion ... shouts and tears her hair. ... That must not happen. ... Undignified ... déclassé. I shall talk to my friend the fan ... gossip with the night-fliers ... pit my small light against the darkness, a miner descending the shaft. I have seen the opening gambit ... am aware of the game's inevitable conclusion. What does it matter? I shall leap over the net ... extend my hand ... murmur, "Well done," and walk away, stiff-backed and shoulders high. I will drink the hemlock gaily ... I will sing. Ten green bottles standing on the wall. Ten green bottles standing on the wall. If one green bottle should accidentally fall. ... When it is over I will sit up and call for tea ... ignore the covered basin ... the bloody sheets (but what do they do with it afterward ... where will they take it? I have no experience in these matters). They will learn that the death of a part is not the death of the whole. The tables will be turned ... and overturned. The shield of Achilles will compensate for his heel.

And yet, were we as innocent as all that ... as naive ... that we never wondered where the bottles came from? I never wondered. ... I accepted them the way a small child draws the Christmas turkey ... brings the turkey home ... pins it on the playroom wall ... and then sits down to eat. One simply doesn't connect. Yet there they were ... lined up on the laboratory wall ... half-formed, some of them ... the tiny vestigial tails of the smallest ... like corpses of stillborn kittens ... or baby mice. Did we think that they had been like that always ... swimming forever in their little formaldehyde baths ... ships in bottles ... snowstorms in glass paperweights? The professor's voice ... droning like a complacent bee ... tapping his stick against each fragile glass shell ... cross-pollinating facts with facts ... our pencils racing over the paper. We accepted it all without question ... even went up afterward for a closer look ... boldly ... without hesitation. It was all so simple ... so uncomplex ... so scientific. Stupidity, the necessary attribute. And once we dissected a guinea pig, only to discover that she had been pregnant ... tiny little guinea pigs inside. We ... like children presented with one of those Russian dolls ... were delighted ... gratified. We had received a bonus ... a free gift.

Will they do that to part of me? How out of place it will look, bottled with the others ... standing on the laboratory wall. Will the black professor ... the brown-eyed students ... bend their delighted eyes upon this bonus, this free gift? (White. 24 weeks. Female ... or male.) But perhaps black babies are white ... or pink ... to begin. It is an interesting problem ... one which could be pursued ... speculated upon. I must ask someone. If black babies are not black before they are born, at what stage does the dark hand of heredity ... of race ... touch their small bodies? At the moment of birth perhaps? ... like silver exposed to the air. But remember their palms ... the soles of their feet. It's an interesting problem. And remember the beggar outside the central post office ... the terrible burned place on his arm ... the new skin ... translucent ... almost a shell pink. I turned away in disgust ... wincing at the shared memory of scalding liquid ... the pain. But really ... in retrospect ... it was beautiful. That pink skin ... that delicate ... Turneresque tint ... apple blossoms against dark branches.

That's it ... just the right tone. ... Abstract speculation on birth ... on death ... on human suffering in general. Remember only the delicate tint ... sunset against a dark sky ... the pleasure of the Guernica. It's so simple, really ... all a question of organization ... of aesthetics. One can so easily escape the unpleasantness ... the shock of recognition. Cleopatra in her robes ... her crown. ... "I have immortal longings in me." No fear ... the asp suckles peacefully and unreproved. ... She wins ... and Caesar loses. Better than Falstaff "babbling of green fields." One needs the transcendentalism of the tragic hero. Forget the old man ... pathetic ... deserted ... broken. The gray iniquity. It's all a question of organization ... of aesthetics ... of tone. Brooke, for example. "In that rich earth a richer dust concealed. ..." Terrified out of his wits, of course, but still organizing ... still posturing.

(The pain is really quite bad now ... you will excuse me for a moment? I'll be back. I must not think for a moment ... must not struggle ... must let myself be carried over the crest of the wave ... face downward ... buoyant ... a badge of seaweed across the shoulder. It's easier this way ... not to think ... not to struggle. ... It's quicker ... it's more humane.)

Still posturing. See the clown ... advancing slowly across the platform ... dragging the heavy rope ... Grunts ... strains ... the audience shivering with delight. Then the last ... the desperate ... tug. And what revealed? ... a carrot ... a bunch of grapes ... a small dog ... nothing. The audience in tears. ... "Oh, God ... how funny. ... One knows, of course ... all the time. And yet it never fails to amuse ... I never fail to be taken in." Smothered giggles in the darkened taxi ... the deserted streets. ... "Oh, God, how amusing. ... Did you see? The carrot ... the bunch of grapes ... the small dog ... nothing. All a masquerade ... a charade ... the rouge ... the powder ... the false hair of an old woman ... a clown." Babbling of green fields.

Once, when I was ten, I sat on a damp rock and watched my father fishing. Quiet ... on a damp rock ... I watched the flapping gills ... the frenzied tail ... the gasps for air ... the refusal to accept the hook's reality. Rainbow body swinging through the air ... the silver drops ... like tears. Watching quietly from the haven of my damp rock, I saw my father struggle with the fish ... the chased and beaten silver body. "Papa, let it go, Papa ... please!" My father ... annoyed ... astonished ... his communion disrupted ... his chalice overturned ... his paten trampled underfoot. He let it go ... unhooked it carelessly and tossed it lightly toward the center of the pool. After all, what did it matter ... to please the child ... and the damage already done. No recriminations ... only, perhaps (we never spoke of it), a certain loss of faith ... a fall, however imperceptible ... from grace?

The pain is harder now ... more frequent ... more intense. Don't think of it ... ignore it ... let it come. The symphony rises to its climax. No more andante ... no more moderato ... clashing cymbals ... blaring horns. ... Lean forward in your seat ... excited ... intense ... a shiver of fear ... of anticipation. The conductor ... a wild thing ... a clockwork toy gone mad. ... Arms flailing ... body arched ... head swinging loosely ... dum de dum de DUM DUM DUM. The orchestra ... the audience ... all bewitched ... heads nodding ... fingers moving, yes, oh, yes ... the orgasm of sound ... the straining ... letting go. An ecstasy ... a crescendo ... a coda ... it's over. "Whew." "Terrific." (Wiping the sweat from their eyes.) Smiling ... self-conscious ... a bit embarrassed now. ... "Funny how you can get all worked up over a bit of music." Get back to the formalities. ... Get off the slippery sand ... onto the warm, safe planks of conversation. "Would you like a coffee ... a drink ... an ice?" The oasis of pleasure between pains. For me, too, it will soon be over ... and for you.

Noah on Ararat ... high and dry ... sends out the dove to see if it is over. Waiting anxiously ... the dove returning with the sign. Smug now ... self-satisfied ... know-it-all. ... All those drowned neighbors ... all those doubting Thomases ... gone ... washed away ... full fathoms five. ... And he, safe ... the animals pawing restlessly, scenting freedom after their long confinement ... smelling the rich smell of spring ... of tender shoots. Victory ... triumph ... the chosen ones. Start again ... make the world safe for democracy ... cleansing ... purging ... Guernica ... Auschwitz ... God's fine Italian hand. Always the moral ... the little tag ... the cautionary tale. Willie in one of his bright new sashes/fell in the fire and was burnt to ashes. ... Suffering is good for the soul ... the effects on the body are not to be considered. Fire and rain ... cleansing ... purging ... tempering the steel. Not much longer now ... and soon they will let down the nets. (He promised it would be over before the dark. I do not like the dark here. Forgive me if I've mentioned this before.) We will sing to keep our courage up. Ten green bottles standing on the wall. Ten green bottles standing on the wall. If one green bottle. ...

The retreat from Russia ... feet bleeding on the white snow ... tired ... discouraged ... what was it all about anyway? ... we weren't prepared. Yet we go on ... feet bleeding on the white snow ... dreaming of warmth ... smooth arms and golden hair ... a glass of kvass. We'll get there yet. (But will we ever be the same?) A phoenix ... never refusing ... flying true and straight ... into the fire and out. Plunge downward now ... a few more minutes ... spread your wings ... the moment has come ... the fire blazes ... the priest is ready ... the worshipers are waiting. The battle over ... the death within expelled ... cast out ... the long hike done ... Arrat. Sleep now ... and rise again from the dying fire ... the ashes. It's over ... eyes heavy ... body broken but relaxed. All over. We made it, you and I. ... It's all, is it not ... a question of organization ... of tone? Yet one would have been grateful at the last ... for a reason ... an explanation ... a sign. A spider ... a flaming cross ... a carrot ... a bunch of grapes ... a small dog. Not this nothing.

John Updike

(b. 1932)

In a relatively short time John Updike has become one of the most celebrated writers in the United States. A product of the middle America which gives him much of his material, he was born in Shillington, Pennsylvania, and educated at Harvard and the Ruskin School of Drawing and Fine Art in Oxford, England. After a spell on the staff of the *New Yorker* from 1955 to 1957, Updike became a free-lance writer and journalist, developing a professionalism in his craft ("I would write ads for deodorant or labels for catsup bottles if I had to") which has led at times to a greater concern for surface than for substance, and earned him the charge of superficiality from some critics. Author of six novels and four volumes of short stories, as well as many poems and essays, he writes best (and most frequently) about domestic life, drawing the relationship between husbands and wives, parents and children, with a detailed vividness born of close observation; indeed, many of his stories have an autobiographical basis, and his novel *The Centaur* (1963) is centered on a character modeled after his father.

Updike has summarized his major preoccupations as follows: "Domestic fierceness within the middle class, sex and death as riddles for the thinking animal, social existence as sacrifice, unexpected pleasures and rewards, corruption as a kind of evolution. ... " Sex and death undoubtedly occupy the center of his imagination, sometimes to morbid excess; *Couples* (1968) at times runs perilously close to refined pornography in its portrait of boredom and sexual decadence in suburban Massachusetts. But Updike is no pornographer; in his fiction he repeatedly shows the deadness of sex without love, and the frailty of domestic love in a society devoid of faith or purpose. In "Giving Blood" (from *The Music School*, 1966) he depicts the strains of marriage with compassionate irony, and indicates how the selfish sensuality of modern man has blinded him to the ancient mystery of love, a mystery we can now apprehend only fleetingly.

For further reading

Thadius Muradian, "The World of John Updike," *English Journal,* 54 (October 1965), 577–584.

Charles T. Samuels, "The Art of Fiction XLIII: John Updike," *Paris Review,* 45 (1968), 84–117.

Charles T. Samuels, *John Updike* (Minneapolis: University of Minnesota Press, 1969).

Giving Blood

The Maples had been married now nine years, which is almost too long. "Goddammit, goddammit," Richard said to Joan, as they drove into Boston to give blood, "I drive this road five days a week and now I'm driving it again. It's like a nightmare. I'm exhausted. I'm emotionally, mentally, physically exhausted, and she isn't even an aunt of mine. She isn't even an aunt of *yours.*"

"She's a sort of cousin," Joan said.

"Well hell, every goddam body in New England is some sort of cousin of yours; must I spend the rest of my life trying to save them *all?*"

"Hush," Joan said. "She might die. I'm ashamed of you. Really ashamed."

It cut. His voice for the moment took on an apologetic pallor. "Well I'd be my usual goddam saintly self if I'd had any sort of sleep last night. Five days a week I bump out of bed and stagger out the door past the milkman and on the one day of the week when I don't even have to truck the blasphemous little brats to Sunday school you make an appointment to have me drained dry thirty miles away."

"Well it wasn't *me*," Joan said, "who had to stay till two o'clock doing the Twist with Marlene Brossman."

"We weren't doing the Twist. We were gliding around very chastely to 'Hits of the Forties.' And don't think I was so oblivious I didn't see you snoogling behind the piano with Harry Saxon."

"We weren't behind the piano, we were on the bench. And he was just talking to me because he felt sorry for me. Everybody there felt sorry for me; you could have at *least* let somebody else dance *once* with Marlene, if only for show."

"Show, show," Richard said. "That's your mentality exactly."

"Why, the poor Matthews or whatever they are looked absolutely horrified."

"Matthiessons," he said. "And that's another thing. Why are idiots like that being invited these days? If there's anything I hate, it's women who keep putting one hand on their pearls and taking a deep breath. I thought she had something stuck in her throat."

"They're a perfectly pleasant, decent young couple. The thing you resent about their coming is that their being there shows us what we've become."

"If you're so attracted," he said, "to little fat men like Harry Saxon, why didn't you marry one?"

"My," Joan said calmly, and gazed out the window away from him, at the scudding gasoline stations. "You honestly *are* hateful. It's not just a pose."

"Pose, show, my Lord, who are you performing for? If it isn't Harry Saxon, it's Freddie Vetter—all these dwarves. Every time I looked over at you last night it was like some pale Queen of the Dew surrounded by a ring of mushrooms."

"You're too absurd," she said. Her hand, distinctly thirtyish, dry and green-veined and rasped by detergents, stubbed out her cigarette in the dashboard ashtray. "You're not subtle. You think you can match me up with another man so you can swirl off with Marlene with a free conscience."

Her reading his strategy so correctly made his face burn; he felt again the tingle of Mrs. Brossman's hair as he pressed his cheek against hers and in this damp privacy inhaled the perfume behind her ear. "You're right," he said. "But I want to get you a man your own size; I'm very loyal that way."

"Let's not talk," she said.

His hope, of turning the truth into a joke, was rebuked. Any implication of permission was blocked. "It's that *smug*ness," he explained, speaking levelly, as if about a phenomenon of which they were both disinterested students. "It's your smugness that is really intolerable. Your stupidity I don't mind. Your sexlessness I've learned to live with. But that wonderfully smug, New England—I suppose we needed it to get the country founded, but in the Age of Anxiety it really does gall."

He had been looking over at her, and unexpectedly she turned and looked at him, with a startled but uncannily crystalline expression, as if her face had been in an instant rendered in tinted porcelain, even to the eyelashes.

"I asked you not to talk," she said. "Now you've said things that I'll always remember."

Plunged fathoms deep into the wrong, his face suffocated with warmth, he concentrated on the highway and sullenly steered. Though they were moving at sixty in the sparse Saturday traffic, he had travelled this road so often its distances were all translated into time, so that they seemed to him to be moving as slowly as a minute hand from one digit to the next. It would have been strategic and dignified of him to keep the silence; but he could not resist believing that just one more pinch of syllables would restore the fine balance which with each wordless mile slipped increasingly awry. He asked, "How did Bean seem to you?" Bean was their baby. They had left her last night, to go to the party, with a fever of 102.

Joan wrestled with her vow to say nothing, but guilt proved stronger than spite. She said, "Cooler. Her nose is a river."

"Sweetie," Richard blurted, "will they hurt me?" The curious fact was that he had never given blood before. Asthmatic and underweight, he had been 4-F, and at college and now at the office he had, less through his own determination than through the diffidence of the solicitors, evaded pledging blood. It was one of those tests of courage so trivial that no one had ever thought to make him face up to it.

Spring comes carefully to Boston. Speckled crusts of ice lingered around the parking meters, and the air, grayly stalemated between seasons, tinted the buildings along Longwood Avenue with a drab and homogeneous majesty. As they walked up the drive to the hospital entrance, Richard nervously wondered aloud if they would see the King of Arabia.

"He's in a separate wing," Joan said. "With four wives."

"Only four? What an ascetic." And he made bold to tap his wife's shoulder. It was not clear if, under the thickness of her winter coat, she felt it.

At the desk, they were directed down a long corridor floored with cigar-colored linoleum. Up and down, right and left it went, in the secretive, disjointed way peculiar to hospitals that have been built annex by annex. Richard seemed to himself Hansel orphaned with Gretel; birds ate the bread crumbs behind them, and at last they timidly knocked on the witch's door, which said BLOOD DONATION CENTER. A young man in white opened the door a crack. Over his shoulder Richard glimpsed—horrors!—a pair of dismembered female legs stripped of their shoes and laid parallel on a bed. Glints of needles and bottles pricked his eyes. Without widening the crack, the young man passed out to them two long forms. In sitting side by side on the waiting bench, remembering their middle initials and childhood diseases, Mr. and Mrs. Maple were newly defined to themselves. He fought down that urge to giggle and clown and lie that threatened him whenever he was asked—like a lawyer appointed by the court to plead a hopeless case—to present, as it were, his statistics to eternity. It seemed to mitigate his case slightly that a few of these statistics (present address, date of marriage) were shared by the hurt soul scratching beside him, with his own pen. He looked over her shoulder. "I never knew you had whooping cough."

"My mother says. I don't remember it."

A pan crashed to a distant floor. An elevator chuckled remotely. A woman, a middle-aged woman top-heavy with rouge and fur, stepped out of the blood door and wobbled a moment on legs that looked familiar. They had been restored to their shoes. The heels of these shoes clicked firmly as, having raked the Maples with a defiant blue glance, she turned and disappeared around a bend in the corridor. The young man appeared in the doorway holding a pair of surgical tongs. His noticeably recent haircut made him seem an apprentice barber. He clicked his tongs and smiled. "Shall I do you together?"

"Sure." It put Richard on his mettle that this callow fellow, to whom apparently they were to entrust their liquid essence, was so clearly younger than they. But when Richard stood, his indignation melted and his legs felt diluted under him. And the extraction of the blood sample from his middle finger seemed the nastiest and most needlessly prolonged physical involvement with another human being he had ever experienced. There is a touch that good dentists, mechanics, and barbers have, and this intern did not have it; he fumbled and in compensation was too rough. Again and again, an atrociously clumsy vampire, he tugged and twisted the purpling finger in vain. The tiny glass capillary tube remained transparent.

"He doesn't like to bleed, does he?" the intern asked Joan. As relaxed as a nurse, she sat in a chair next to a table of scintillating equipment.

"I don't think his blood moves much," she said, "until after midnight."

This stab at a joke made Richard in his extremity of fright laugh loudly, and the laugh at last seemed to jar the panicked coagulant. Red seeped upward in the thirsty little tube, as in a sudden thermometer.

The intern grunted in relief. As he smeared the samples on the analysis box, he explained idly, "What we ought to have down here is a pan of warm water. You just came in out of the cold. If you put your hand in hot water for a minute, the blood just pops out."

"A pretty thought," Richard said.

But the intern had already written him off as a clowner and continued calmly to Joan, "All we'd need would be a baby hot plate for about six dollars, then we could make our own coffee too. This way, when we get a donor who needs the coffee afterward, we have to send up for it while we keep his head between his knees. Do you think you'll be needing coffee?"

"*No,*" Richard interrupted, jealous of their rapport.

The intern told Joan, "You're O."

"I know," she said.

"And he's A positive."

"Why that's very good, Dick!" she called to him.

"Am I rare?" he asked.

The boy turned and explained, "O positive and A positive are the most common types." Something in the patient tilt of his close-cropped head as its lateral sheen mixed with the lazily bright mid-morning air of the room sharply reminded Richard of the days years ago when he had tended a battery of teletype machines in a room much this size. By now, ten o'clock, the yards of copy that began pouring through the machines at five and that lay in great crimped heaps on the floor when he arrived at seven would have been harvested and sorted and pasted together and turned in, and there was nothing to do but keep up with the staccato appearance of the later news and to think about simple things like coffee. It came back to him, how pleasant and secure those hours had been when, king of his own corner, he was young and newly responsible.

The intern asked, "Who wants to be first?"

"Let me," Joan said. "He's never done it before."

"Her full name is Joan of Arc," Richard explained, angered at this betrayal, so unimpeachably selfless and smug.

The intern, threatened in his element, fixed his puzzled eyes on the floor between them and said, "Take off your shoes and each get on a bed." He added, "Please," and all three laughed, one after the other, the intern last.

The beds were at right angles to one another along two walls. Joan lay down and from her husband's angle of vision was novelly foreshortened. He had never before seen her quite this way, the combed crown of her hair so poignant, her bared arm so silver and long, her stocking feet toed in so childishly and docilely. There were no pillows on the beds, and lying flat made him feel tipped head down; the illusion of floating encouraged his hope that this unreal adventure would soon dissolve in the manner of a dream. "You O.K.?"

"Are you?" Her voice came softly from the tucked-under wealth of her hair. From the straightness of the parting it seemed her mother had brushed it. He watched a long needle sink into the flat of her arm and a piece of moist cotton clumsily swab the spot. He had imagined their blood would be drained into cans or bottles, but the intern, whose breathing was now the only sound within the room, brought to Joan's side what looked like a miniature plastic knapsack, all coiled and tied. His body cloaked his actions. When he stepped away, a plastic cord had been grafted, a transparent vine, to the flattened crook of Joan's extended arm, where the skin was translucent and the veins were faint blue tributaries shallowly buried. It was a tender, vulnerable place where in courting days she had liked being stroked. Now, without visible transition, the pale tendril planted here went dark red. Richard wanted to cry out.

The instant readiness of her blood to leave her body pierced him like a physical pang. Though he had not so much as blinked, its initial leap had been too quick for his eye. He had expected some visible sign of flow, but from the mere appearance of it the tiny looped hose might be pouring blood *into* her body or might be a curved line added, irrelevant as a mustache, to a finished canvas. The fixed position of his head gave what he saw a certain flatness.

And now the intern turned to him, and there was the tiny felt prick of the novocain needle, and then the coarse, half-felt intrusion of something resembling a medium-weight nail. Twice the boy mistakenly probed for the vein and the third time taped the successful graft fast with adhesive tape. All the while, Richard's mind moved aloofly among the constellations of the stained cracked ceiling. What was being done to him did not bear contemplating. When the intern moved away to hum and tinkle among his instruments, Joan craned her neck to show her husband her face and, upside down in his vision, grotesquely smiled.

It was not many minutes that they lay there at right angles together, but the time passed as something beyond the walls, as something mixed with the faraway clatter of pans and the approach and retreat of footsteps and the opening and closing of unseen doors. Here, conscious of a pointed painless pulse in the inner hinge of his arm but incurious as to what it looked like, he floated and imagined how his soul would float free when all his blood was underneath the bed. His blood and Joan's merged on the floor, and together their spirits glided from crack to crack, from star to star on the ceiling. Once she cleared her throat, and the sound made an abrasion like the rasp of a pebble loosened by a cliff-climber's boot.

The door opened. Richard turned his head and saw an old man, bald and sallow, enter and settle in a chair. He was one of those old men who hold within an institution an ill-defined but consecrated place. The young doctor seemed to know him, and the two talked, softly, as if not to disturb the mystical union of the couple sacrificially bedded together. They talked of persons and events that meant nothing—of Iris, of Dr. Greenstein, of Ward D, again of Iris, who had given the old man an undeserved scolding, of the shameful lack of a hot plate to make coffee on, of the rumored black bodyguards who kept watch with scimitars by the bed of the glaucomatous king. Through Richard's tranced ignorance these topics passed as clouds of impression, iridescent, massy—Dr. Greenstein with a pointed nose and almond eyes the color of ivy, Iris eighty feet tall and hurling sterilized thunderbolts of wrath. As in some theologies the proliferant deities are said to exist as ripples upon the featureless ground of Godhead, so these inconstant images lightly overlay his continuous awareness of Joan's blood, like his own, ebbing. Linked to a common loss, they were chastely conjoined; the thesis developed upon him that the hoses attached to them somewhere out of sight met. Testing this belief, he glanced down and saw that indeed the plastic vine taped to the flattened crook of his arm was the same dark red as hers. He stared at the ceiling to disperse a sensation of faintness.

Abruptly the young intern left off his desultory conversation and moved to Joan's side. There was a chirp of clips. When he moved away, she was revealed holding her naked arm upright, pressing a piece of cotton against it with the other hand. Without pausing, the intern came to Richard's side, and the birdsong of the clips repeated, nearer. "Look at that," he said to his elderly friend. "I started him two minutes later than her and he's finished at the same time."

"Was it a race?" Richard asked.

Clumsily firm, the boy fitted Richard's fingers to a pad and lifted his arm for him. "Hold it there for five minutes," he said.

"What'll happen if I don't?"

"You'll mess up your shirt." To the old man he said, "I had a woman in here the other day, she was all set to leave when all of a sudden, pow!—all over the front of this beautiful linen dress. She was going to Symphony."

"Then they try to sue the hospital for the cleaning bill," the old man muttered.

"Why was I slower than him?" Joan asked. Her upright arm wavered, as if vexed or weakened.

"The woman generally is," the boy told her. "Nine times out of ten, the man is faster. Their hearts are so much stronger."

"Is that really so?"

"Sure it's so," Richard told her. "Don't argue with medical science."

"Woman up in Ward C," the old man said, "they saved her life for her out of an auto accident and now I hear she's suing because they didn't find her dental plate."

Under such patter, the five minutes eroded. Richard's upheld arm began to ache. It seemed that he and Joan were caught together in a classroom where they would never be recognized, or in a charade that would never be guessed, the correct answer being Two Silver Birches in a Meadow.

"You can sit up now if you want," the intern told them. "But don't let go of the venipuncture."

They sat up on their beds, legs dangling heavily. Joan asked him, "Do you feel dizzy?"

"With my powerful heart? Don't be presumptuous."

"Do you think he'll need coffee?" the intern asked her. "I'll have to send up for it now."

The old man shifted forward in his chair, preparing to heave to his feet.

"I do *not* want any *cof*fee"—Richard said it so loud he saw himself transposed, another Iris, into the firmament of the old man's aggrieved gossip. *Some dizzy bastard down in the blood room, I get up to get him some coffee and he damn near bit my head off.* To demonstrate simultaneously his essential good humor and his total presence of mind, Richard gestured toward the blood they had given—two square plastic sacks filled solidly fat—and declared, "Back where

I come from in West Virginia sometimes you pick a tick off a dog that looks like that." The men looked at him amazed. Had he not quite said what he meant to say? Or had they never seen anybody from West Virginia before?

Joan pointed at the blood, too. "Is that us? Those little doll pillows?"

"Maybe we should take one home to Bean," Richard suggested.

The intern did not seem convinced that this was a joke. "Your blood will be credited to Mrs. Henryson's account," he stated stiffly.

Joan asked him, "Do you know anything about her? When is she —when is her operation scheduled?"

"I think for tomorrow. The only thing on the tab this after is an open heart at two; that'll take about sixteen pints."

"Oh . . . " Joan was shaken. "Sixteen . . . that's a full person, isn't it?"

"More," the intern answered, with the regal handwave that bestows largess and dismisses compliments.

"Could we visit her?" Richard asked, for Joan's benefit. ("Really ashamed," she had said; it had cut.) He was confident of the refusal.

"Well, you can ask at the desk, but usually before a major one like this it's just the nearest of kin. I guess you're safe now." He meant their punctures. Richard's arm bore a small raised bruise; the intern covered it with one of those ample, salmon, unhesitatingly adhesive bandages that only hospitals have. That was their specialty, Richard thought—packaging. They wrap the human mess for final delivery. Sixteen doll's pillows, uniformly dark and snug, marching into an open heart: the vision momentarily satisfied his hunger for cosmic order.

He rolled down his sleeve and slid off the bed. It startled him to realize, in the instant before his feet touched the floor, that three pairs of eyes were fixed upon him, fascinated and apprehensive and eager for scandal. He stood and towered above them. He hopped on one foot to slip into one loafer, and then on this foot to slip into the other loafer. Then he did the little shuffle-tap, shuffle-tap step that was all that remained to him of dancing lessons he had taken at the age of seven, driving twelve miles each Saturday into Morgantown. He made a small bow toward his wife, smiled at the old man, and said to the intern, "All my life people have been expecting me to faint. I have no idea why. I never faint."

His coat and overcoat felt a shade queer, a bit slithery and light, but as he walked down the length of the corridor, space seemed to adjust snugly around him. At his side, Joan kept an inquisitive and chastened silence. They pushed through the great glass doors. A famished sun was nibbling through the overcast. Above and behind them, the King of Arabia lay in a drugged dream of dunes and Mrs.

Henryson upon her sickbed received like the comatose mother of twins their identical gifts of blood. Richard hugged his wife's padded shoulders and as they walked along leaning on each other whispered, "Hey, I love you. Love love *love* you."

Romance is, simply, the strange, the untried. It was unusual for the Maples to be driving together at eleven in the morning. Almost always it was dark when they shared a car. The oval of her face was bright in the corner of his eye. She was watching him, alert to take the wheel if he suddenly lost consciousness. He felt tender toward her in the eggshell light, and curious toward himself, wondering how far beneath his brain the black pit did lie. He felt no different; but then the quality of consciousness perhaps did not bear introspection. Something certainly had been taken from him; he was less himself by a pint and it was not impossible that like a trapeze artist saved by a net he was sustained in the world of light and reflection by a single layer of interwoven cells. Yet the earth, with its signals and buildings and cars and bricks, continued like a pedal note.

Boston behind them, he asked, "Where should we eat?"

"Should we eat?"

"Please, yes. Let me take you to lunch. Just like a secretary."

"I do feel sort of illicit. As if I've stolen something."

"You too? But what did we steal?"

"I don't know. The morning? Do you think Eve knows enough to feed them?" Eve was their sitter, a little sandy girl from down the street who would, in exactly a year, Richard calculated, be painfully lovely. They lasted three years on the average, sitters; you got them in the tenth grade and escorted them into their bloom and then, with graduation, like commuters who had reached their stop, they dropped out of sight, into nursing school or marriage. And the train went on, and took on other passengers, and itself became older and longer. The Maples had four children: Judith, Richard Jr., poor oversized, angel-faced John, and Bean.

"She'll manage. What would you like? All that talk about coffee has made me frantic for some."

"At the Pancake House beyond 128 they give you coffee before you even ask."

"Pancakes? Now? Aren't you gay? Do you think we'll throw up?"

"Do you feel like throwing up?"

"No, not really. I feel sort of insubstantial and gentle, but it's probably psychosomatic. I don't really understand this business of giving something away and still somehow having it. What is it—the spleen?"

"I don't know. Are the splenetic man and the sanguine man the same?"

"God. I've totally forgotten the humors. What are the others—phlegm and choler?"

"Bile and black bile are in there somewhere."

"One thing about you, Joan. You're educated. New England women are educated."

"Sexless as we are."

"That's right; drain me dry and then put me on the rack." But there was no wrath in his words; indeed, he had reminded her of their earlier conversation so that, in much this way, his words might be revived, diluted, and erased. It seemed to work. The restaurant where they served only pancakes was empty and quiet this early. A bashfulness possessed them both; it had become a date between two people who have little as yet in common but who are nevertheless sufficiently intimate to accept the fact without chatter. Touched by the stain her blueberry pancakes left on her teeth, he held a match to her cigarette and said, "Gee, I loved you back in the blood room."

"I wonder why."

"You were so brave."

"So were you."

"But I'm supposed to be. I'm paid to be. It's the price of having a penis."

"Shh."

"Hey. I didn't mean that about your being sexless."

The waitress refilled their coffee cups and gave them the check.

"And I promise never never to do the Twist, the cha-cha, or the schottische with Marlene Brossman."

"Don't be silly. I don't care."

This amounted to permission, but perversely irritated him. That smugness; why didn't she *fight?* Trying to regain their peace, scrambling uphill, he picked up their check and with an effort of acting, the pretense being that they were out on a date and he was a raw dumb suitor, said handsomely, "I'll pay."

But on looking into his wallet he saw only a single worn dollar there. He didn't know why this should make him so angry, except the fact somehow that it was only *one.* "Goddammit," he said. "Look at that." He waved it in her face. "I work like a bastard all week for you and those insatiable brats and at the end of it what do I have? One goddam crummy wrinkled dollar."

Her hands dropped to the pocketbook beside her on the seat, but her gaze stayed with him, her face having retreated, or advanced, into that porcelain shell of uncanny composure. "We'll both pay," Joan said.

Kurt Vonnegut, Jr.

(b. 1922)

The writings of Kurt Vonnegut are characterized by a Swiftian sense of despair at the extremes of human folly. His books are about the horrors of war, the dehumanization of modern man, the loss of humane values in a society dedicated to technological progress. Though these are now fashionable subjects, Vonnegut's insights derive from personal experience. After serving in the U. S. Infantry during World War II, and witnessing the fire-bombing of Dresden as a prisoner of war, he became a police reporter in Chicago; then he entered the field of public relations, working for the General Electric Company until 1950, when he devoted his full time to writing. Such a background provided him with ample material for his satire.

Gifted with a Kafka-esque sense of the absurd, Vonnegut works through a mixture of fantasy and realism to depict the deep springs of irrationality which govern men's conduct; and he shows how the intellectual genius of modern science has been perverted to base and violent ends by the moral stupidity of the masses and their leaders. A prominent feature of his work is his interest in science fiction, which provides him with images of an automated and impersonal universe, where the individual is of less and less significance. Vonnegut's first novel, *Player Piano* (1952), depicts an America in which government is conducted by computer, and people are of value only as consumers; while the futility of human endeavor is set in an even bleaker perspective in *The Sirens of Titan* (1959), which presents human history as subject to control by the inhabitants of a distant planet. Vonnegut's vision is not totally pessimistic; his stories often include at least one character aware of the madness around him, who seeks to restore a measure of sanity; thus the brilliant professor in "Report on the Barnhouse Effect" (1950, in *Welcome to the Monkey House,* 1968) and his protegé, the narrator, are determined to turn their amazing discovery to good uses, much to the chagrin of their countrymen. But Vonnegut's recently filmed novel, *Slaughterhouse-Five* (1969) is less hopeful, for in his treatment of the Dresden bombing, he suggests that individual effort is powerless to alleviate the misery and suffering of the human condition. His 1973 novel, *Breakfast of Champions,* is mordant even for Vonnegut.

For further reading

D. H. Goldsmith, *Kurt Vonnegut, Fantasist of Fire and Ice* (Bowling Green, Ohio: Bowling Green Popular Press, 1972).

J. Klinkowitz and J. Somer, eds., *The Vonnegut Statement* (New York: Delacorte Press, 1973).

Stanley Schatt, "The World of Kurt Vonnegut, Jr.," *Critique: Studies in Modern Fiction,* 12, iii (1971), 54–69.

Report on the Barnhouse Effect

Let me begin by saying that I don't know any more about where Professor Arthur Barnhouse is hiding than anyone else does. Save for one short, enigmatic message left in my mail box on Christmas Eve, I have not heard from him since his disappearance a year and a half ago.

What's more, readers of this article will be disappointed if they expect to learn how *they* can bring about the so-called "Barnhouse Effect." If I were able and willing to give away that secret, I would certainly be something more important than a psychology instructor.

I have been urged to write this report because I did research under the professor's direction and because I was the first to learn of his astonishing discovery. But while I was his student I was never entrusted with knowledge of how the mental forces could be released and directed. He was unwilling to trust anyone with that information.

I would like to point out that the term "Barnhouse Effect" is a creation of the popular press, and was never used by Professor Barnhouse. The name he chose for the phenomenon was "*dynamopsychism*," or *force of the mind.*

I cannot believe that there is a civilized person yet to be convinced that such a force exists, what with its destructive effects on display in every national capital. I think humanity has always had an inkling that this sort of force does exist. It has been common knowledge that some people are luckier than others with inanimate objects like dice. What Professor Barnhouse did was to show that such "luck" was a measurable force, which in his case could be enormous.

By my calculations, the professor was about fifty-five times more powerful than a Nagasaki-type atomic bomb at the time he went into hiding. He was not bluffing when, on the eve of "Operation Brainstorm," he told General Honus Barker: "Sitting here at the dinner table, I'm pretty sure I can flatten anything on earth—from Joe Louis to the Great Wall of China."

There is an understandable tendency to look upon Professor Barnhouse as a supernatural visitation. The First Church of Barnhouse in Los Angeles has a congregation numbering in the thousands. He is godlike in neither appearance nor intellect. The man who disarms the world is single, shorter than the average American male, stout, and averse to exercise. His I.Q. is 143, which is good but certainly not sensational. He is quite mortal, about to celebrate his fortieth birthday, and in good health. If he is alone now, the isolation won't bother him too much. He was quiet and shy when I knew him, and seemed to find more companionship in books and music than in his associations at the college.

Neither he nor his powers fall outside the sphere of Nature. His dynamopsychic radiations are subject to many known physical laws that apply in the field of radio. Hardly a person has not now heard the snarl of "Barnhouse static" on his home receiver. Contrary to what one might expect, the radiations are affected by sunspots and variations in the ionosphere.

However, his radiations differ from ordinary broadcast waves in several important ways. Their total energy can be brought to bear on any single point the professor chooses, and that energy is undiminished by distance. As a weapon, then, dynamopsychism has an impressive advantage over bacteria and atomic bombs, beyond the fact that it costs nothing to use: it enables the professor to single out critical individuals and objects instead of slaughtering whole populations in the process of maintaining international equilibrium.

As General Honus Barker told the House Military Affairs Committee: "Until someone finds Barnhouse, there is no defense against the Barnhouse Effect." Efforts to "jam" or block the radiations have failed. Premier Slezak could have saved himself the fantastic expense of his "Barnhouseproof" shelter. Despite the shelter's twelve-foot-thick lead armor, the premier has been floored twice while in it.

There is talk of screening the population for men potentially as powerful dynamopsychically as the professor. Senator Warren Foust demanded funds for this purpose last month, with the passionate declaration: "He who rules the Barnhouse Effect rules the world!" Commissar Kropotnik said much the same thing, so another costly armaments race, with a new twist, has begun.

This race at least has its comical aspects. The world's best gamblers are being coddled by governments like so many nuclear physicists. There may be several hundred persons with dynamopsychic talent on earth, myself included, but, without knowledge of the professor's technique, they can never be anything but dice-table despots. With the secret, it would probably take them ten years to become dangerous weapons. It took the professor that long. He who rules the Barnhouse Effect is Barnhouse and will be for some time.

Popularly, the "Age of Barnhouse" is said to have begun a year and a half ago, on the day of Operation Brainstorm. That was when dynamopsychism became significant politically. Actually, the phenomenon was discovered in May, 1942, shortly after the professor turned down a direct commission in the Army and enlisted as an artillery private. Like X-rays and vulcanized rubber, dynamopsychism was discovered by accident.

From time to time Private Barnhouse was invited to take part in games of chance by his barrack mates. He knew nothing about the games, and usually begged off. But one evening, out of social grace, he agreed to shoot craps. It was a terrible or wonderful thing that he played, depending upon whether or not you like the world as it now is.

"Shoot sevens, Pop," someone said.

So "Pop" shot sevens—ten in a row to bankrupt the barracks. He retired to his bunk and, as a mathematical exercise, calculated the odds against his feat on the back of a laundry slip. His chances of doing it, he found, were one in almost ten million! Bewildered, he borrowed a pair of dice from the man in the bunk next to his. He tried to roll sevens again, but got only the usual assortment of numbers. He lay back for a moment, then resumed his toying with the dice. He rolled ten more sevens in a row.

He might have dismissed the phenomenon with a low whistle. But the professor instead mulled over the circumstances surrounding his two lucky streaks. There was one single factor in common: on both occasions, *the same thought train had flashed through his mind just before he threw the dice.* It was that thought train which aligned the professor's brain cells into what has since become the most powerful weapon on earth.

The soldier in the next bunk gave dynamopsychism its first token of respect. In an understatement certain to bring wry smiles to the faces of the world's dejected demagogues, the soldier said, "You're hotter'n a two-dollar pistol, Pop." Professor Barnhouse was all of that. The dice that did his bidding weighed but a few grams, so the forces involved were minute; but the unmistakable fact that there were such forces was earth-shaking.

Professional caution kept him from revealing his discovery immediately. He wanted more facts and a body of theory to go with them. Later, when the atomic bomb was dropped on Hiroshima, it was fear that made him hold his peace. At no time were his experiments, as Premier Slezak called them, "a bourgeois plot to shackle the true democracies of the world." The professor didn't know where they were leading.

In time, he came to recognize another startling feature of dynamopsychism: *its strength increased with use.* Within six months, he was able to govern dice thrown by men the length of a barracks distant. By the time of his discharge in 1945, he could knock bricks loose from chimneys three miles away.

Charges that Professor Barnhouse could have won the last war in a minute, but did not care to do so, are perfectly senseless. When the war ended, he had the range and power of a 37-millimeter cannon, perhaps—certainly no more. His dynamopsychic powers graduated from the small-arms class only after his discharge and return to Wyandotte College.

I enrolled in the Wyandotte Graduate School two years after the professor had rejoined the faculty. By chance, he was assigned as my thesis adviser. I was unhappy about the assignment, for the professor was, in the eyes of both colleagues and students, a somewhat ridiculous figure. He missed classes or had lapses of memory during lectures. When I arrived, in fact, his shortcomings had passed from the ridiculous to the intolerable.

"We're assigning you to Barnhouse as a sort of temporary thing," the dean of social studies told me. He looked apologetic and perplexed. "Brilliant man, Barnhouse, I guess. Difficult to know since his return, perhaps, but his work before the war brought a great deal of credit to our little school."

When I reported to the professor's laboratory for the first time, what I saw was more distressing than the gossip. Every surface in the room was covered with dust; books and apparatus had not been disturbed for months. The professor sat napping at his desk when I entered. The only signs of recent activity were three overflowing ash trays, a pair of scissors, and a morning paper with several items clipped from its front page.

As he raised his head to look at me, I saw that his eyes were clouded with fatigue. "Hi," he said, "just can't seem to get my sleeping done at night." He lighted a cigarette, his hands trembling slightly. "You the young man I'm supposed to help with a thesis?"

"Yes, sir," I said. In minutes he converted my misgivings to alarm.

"You an overseas veteran?" he asked.

"Yes, sir."

"Not much left over there, is there?" He frowned. "Enjoy the last war?

"No, sir."

"Look like another war to you?"

"Kind of, sir."

"What can be done about it?"

I shrugged. "Looks pretty hopeless."

He peered at me intently. "Know anything about international law, the U.N., and all that?"

"Only what I pick up from the papers."

"Same here," he sighed. He showed me a fat scrapbook packed with newspaper clippings. "Never used to pay any attention to international politics. Now I study them the way I used to study rats in mazes. Everybody tells me the same thing—'Looks hopeless.'"

"Nothing short of a miracle—" I began.

"Believe in magic?" he asked sharply. The professor fished two dice from his vest pocket. "I will try to roll twos," he said. He rolled twos three times in a row. "One chance in about 47,000 of that happening. There's a miracle for you." He beamed for an instant, then brought the interview to an end, remarking that he had a class which had begun ten minutes ago.

He was not quick to take me into his confidence, and he said no more about his trick with the dice. I assumed they were loaded, and forgot about them. He set me the task of watching male rats cross electrified metal strips to get to food or female rats—an experiment that had been done to everyone's satisfaction in the 1930s. As though the pointlessness of my work were not bad enough, the professor annoyed me further with irrelevant questions. His favorites were: "Think we should have dropped the atomic bomb on Hiroshima?" and "Think every new piece of scientific information is a good thing for humanity?"

However, I did not feel put upon for long. "Give those poor animals a holiday," he said one morning, after I had been with him only a month. "I wish you'd help me look into a more interesting problem —namely, my sanity."

I returned the rats to their cages.

"What you must do is simple," he said, speaking softly. "Watch the inkwell on my desk. If you see nothing happen to it, say so, and I'll go quietly—relieved, I might add—to the nearest sanitarium."

I nodded uncertainly.

He locked the laboratory door and drew the blinds, so that we were in twilight for a moment. "I'm odd, I know," he said. "It's fear of myself that's made me odd."

"I've found you somewhat eccentric, perhaps, but certainly not—"

"If nothing happens to that inkwell, 'crazy as a bedbug' is the only description of me that will do," he interrupted, turning on the overhead lights. His eyes narrowed. "To give you an idea of how crazy, I'll tell you what's been running through my mind when I should have been sleeping. I think maybe I can save the world. I think maybe I can make every nation a *have* nation, and do away with war for good. I think maybe I can clear roads through jungles, irrigate deserts, build dams overnight."

"Yes, sir."

"Watch the inkwell!"

Dutifully and fearfully I watched. A high-pitched humming seemed to come from the inkwell; then it began to vibrate alarmingly, and finally to bound about the top of the desk, making two noisy circuits. It stopped, hummed again, glowed red, then popped in splinters with a blue-green flash.

Perhaps my hair stood on end. The professor laughed gently. "Magnets?" I managed to say at last.

"Wish to Heaven it were magnets," he murmured. It was then that he told me of dynamopsychism. He knew only that there was such a force; he could not explain it. "It's me and me alone—and it's awful."

"I'd say it was amazing and wonderful!" I cried.

"If all I could do was make inwells dance, I'd be tickled silly with the whole business." He shrugged disconsolately. "But I'm no toy, my boy. If you like, we can drive around the neighborhood, and I'll show you what I mean." He told me about pulverized boulders, shattered oaks and abandoned farm buildings demolished within a fifty-mile radius of the campus. "Did every bit of it sitting right here, just thinking—not even thinking hard."

He scratched his head nervously. "I have never dared to concentrate as hard as I can for fear of the damage I might do. I'm to the point where a mere whim is a blockbuster." There was a depressing pause. "Up until a few days ago, I've thought it best to keep my secret for fear of what use it might be put to," he continued. "Now I realize that I haven't any more right to it than a man has a right to own an atomic bomb."

He fumbled through a heap of papers. "This says about all that needs to be said, I think." He handed me a draft of a letter to the Secretary of State.

Dear Sir:

I have discovered a new force which costs nothing to use, and which is probably more important than atomic energy. I should like to see it used most effectively in the cause of peace, and am, therefore, requesting your advice as to how this might best be done.

Yours truly,
A. Barnhouse.

"I have no idea what will happen next," said the professor.

There followed three months of perpetual nightmare, wherein the nation's political and military great came at all hours to watch the professor's trick with fascination.

We were quartered in an old mansion near Charlottesville, Virginia, to which we had been whisked five days after the letter was mailed. Surrounded by barbed wire and twenty guards, we were labeled "Project Wishing Well," and were classified as Top Secret.

For companionship we had General Honus Barker and the State Department's William K. Cuthrell. For the professor's talk of peace-through-plenty they had indulgent smiles and much discourse on practical measures and realistic thinking. So treated, the professor, who had at first been almost meek, progressed in a matter of weeks toward stubbornness.

He had agreed to reveal the thought train by means of which he aligned his mind into a dynamopsychic transmitter. But, under Cuthrell's and Barker's nagging to do so, he began to hedge. At first he declared that the information could be passed on simply by word of mouth. Later he said that it would have to be written up in a long report. Finally, at dinner one night, just after General Barker had read the secret orders for Operation Brainstorm, the professor announced, "The report may take as long as five years to write." He looked fiercely at the general. "Maybe twenty."

The dismay occasioned by this flat announcement was offset somewhat by the exciting anticipation of Operation Brainstorm. The general was in a holiday mood. "The target ships are on their way to the Caroline Islands at this very moment," he declared ecstatically. "One hundred and twenty of them! At the same time, ten V-2s are being readied for firing in New Mexico, and fifty radio-controlled jet bombers are being equipped for a mock attack on the Aleutians. Just think of it!" Happily he reviewed his orders. "At exactly 1100 hours next Wednesday, I will give you the order to *concentrate;* and you, professor, will think as hard as you can about sinking the target ships, destroying the V-2s before they hit the ground, and knocking down the bombers before they reach the Aleutians! Think you can handle it?"

The professor turned gray and closed his eyes. "As I told you before, my friend, I don't know what I can do." He added bitterly, "As for this Operation Brainstorm, I was never consulted about it, and it strikes me as childish and insanely expensive."

General Barker bridled. "Sir," he said, "your field is psychology, and I wouldn't presume to give you advice in that field. Mine is national defense. I have had thirty years of experience and success, Professor, and I'll ask you not to criticize my judgment."

The professor appealed to Mr. Cuthrell. "Look," he pleaded, "isn't it war and military matters we're all trying to get rid of? Wouldn't it be a whole lot more significant and lots cheaper for me to try moving cloud masses into drought areas, and things like that? I admit I know next to nothing about international politics, but it seems reasonable to suppose that nobody would want to fight wars if there were enough of everything to go around. Mr. Cuthrell, I'd like to try running generators where there isn't any coal or water power, irrigating deserts, and so on. Why, you could figure out what each country needs to make the most of its resources, and I could give it to them without costing American taxpayers a penny."

"Eternal vigilance is the price of freedom," said the general heavily.

Mr. Cuthrell threw the general a look of mild distaste. "Unfortunately, the general is right in his own way," he said. "I wish to Heaven the world were ready for ideals like yours, but it simply isn't. We aren't surrounded by brothers, but by enemies. It isn't a lack of food or resources that has us on the brink of war—it's a struggle for power. Who's going to be in charge of the world, our kind of people or theirs?"

The professor nodded in reluctant agreement and arose from the table. "I beg your pardon, gentlemen. You are, after all, better qualified to judge what is best for the country. I'll do whatever you say." He turned to me. "Don't forget to wind the restricted clock and put the confidential cat out," he said gloomily, and ascended the stairs to his bedroom.

For reasons of national security, Operation Brainstorm was carried on without the knowledge of the American citizenry which was footing the bill. The observers, technicians and military men involved in the activity knew that a test was under way—a test of what, they had no idea. Only thirty-seven key men, myself included, knew what was afoot.

In Virginia, the day for Operation Brainstorm was unseasonably cool. Inside, a log fire crackled in the fireplace, and the flames were reflected in the polished metal cabinets that lined the living room. All that remained of the room's lovely old furniture was a Victorian love seat, set squarely in the center of the floor, facing three television receivers. One long bench had been brought in for the ten of us privileged to watch. The television screens showed, from left to right, the stretch of desert which was the rocket target, the guinea-pig fleet, and a section of the Aleutian sky through which the radio-controlled bomber formation would roar.

Ninety minutes before H hour the radios announced that the rockets were ready, that the observation ships had backed away to what was thought to be a safe distance, and that the bombers were on their way. The small Virginia audience lined up on the bench in order of rank, smoked a great deal, and said little. Professor Barnhouse was in his bedroom. General Barker bustled about the house like a woman preparing Thanksgiving dinner for twenty.

At ten minutes before H hour the general came in, shepherding the professor before him. The professor was comfortably attired in sneakers, gray flannels, a blue sweater and a white shirt open at the neck. The two of them sat side by side on the love seat. The general was rigid and perspiring; the professor was cheerful. He looked at each of the screens, lighted a cigarette and settled back, comfortable and cool.

"Bombers sighted!" cried the Aleutian observers.

"Rockets away!" barked the New Mexico radio operator.

All of us looked quickly at the big electric clock over the mantel, while the professor, a half-smile on his face, continued to watch the television sets. In hollow tones, the general counted away the seconds remaining. "Five ... four ... three ... two ... one ... *Concentrate!*"

Professor Barnhouse closed his eyes, pursed his lips, and stroked his temples. He held the position for a minute. The television images were scrambled, and the radio signals were drowned in the din of Barnhouse static. The professor sighed, opened his eyes and smiled confidently.

"Did you give it everything you had?" asked the general dubiously.

"I was wide open," the professor replied.

The television images pulled themselves together, and mingled cries of amazement came over the radios tuned to the observers. The Aleutian sky was streaked with the smoke trails of bombers screaming down in flames. Simultaneously, there appeared high over the rocket target a cluster of white puffs, followed by faint thunder.

General Barker shook his head happily. "By George!" he crowed. "Well, sir, by George, by George, by George!"

"Look!" shouted the admiral seated next to me. "The fleet—it wasn't touched!"

"The guns seem to be drooping," said Mr. Cuthrell.

We left the bench and clustered about the television sets to examine the damage more closely. What Mr. Cuthrell had said was true. The ships' guns curved downward, their muzzles resting on the steel decks. We in Virginia were making such a hullabaloo that it was impossible to hear the radio reports. We were so engrossed, in fact, that we didn't miss the professor until two short snarls of Barnhouse static shocked us into sudden silence. The radios went dead.

We looked around apprehensively. The professor was gone. A harassed guard threw open the front door from the outside to yell that the professor had escaped. He brandished his pistol in the direction of the gates, which hung open, limp and twisted. In the distance, a speeding government station wagon topped a ridge and dropped from sight into the valley beyond. The air was filled with choking smoke, for every vehicle on the grounds was ablaze. Pursuit was impossible.

"What in God's name got into him?" bellowed the general.

Mr. Cuthrell, who had rushed out onto the front porch, now slouched back into the room, reading a penciled note as he came. He thrust the note into my hands. "The good man left this billet-doux under the door knocker. Perhaps our young friend here will be kind enough to read it to you gentlemen, while I take a restful walk through the woods."

"Gentlemen," I read aloud, *"As the first superweapon with a conscience, I am removing from your national defense stockpile. Setting a new precedent in the behavior of ordnance, I have humane reasons for going off. A. Barnhouse."*

Since that day, of course, the professor has been systematically destroying the world's armaments, until there is now little with which to equip an army other than rocks and sharp sticks. His activities haven't exactly resulted in peace, but have, rather, precipitated a bloodless and entertaining sort of war that might be called the "War of the Tattletales." Every nation is flooded with enemy agents whose sole mission is to locate military equipment, which is promptly wrecked when it is brought to the professor's attention in the press.

Just as every day brings news of more armaments pulverized by dynamopsychism, so has it brought rumors of the professor's whereabouts. During the last week alone, three publications carried articles proving variously that he was hiding in an Inca ruin in the Andes, in the sewers of Paris, and in the unexplored lower chambers of Carlsbad Caverns. Knowing the man, I am inclined to regard such hiding places as unnecessarily romantic and uncomfortable. While there are numerous persons eager to kill him, there must be millions who would care for him and hide him. I like to think that he is in the home of such a person.

One thing is certain: at this writing, Professor Barnhouse is not dead. Barnhouse static jammed broadcasts not ten minutes ago. In the eighteen months since his disappearance, he has been reported dead some half-dozen times. Each report has stemmed from the death of an unidentified man resembling the professor, during a period free of the static. The first three reports were followed at once by renewed talk of rearmament and recourse to war. The saber rattlers have learned how imprudent premature celebrations of the professor's demise can be.

Many a stouthearted patriot has found himself prone in the tangled bunting and timbers of a smashed reviewing stand, seconds after having announced that the archtyranny of Barnhouse was at an end. But those who would make war if they could, in every country in the world, wait in sullen silence for what must come— the passing of Professor Barnhouse.

To ask how much longer the professor will live is to ask how much longer we must wait for the blessings of another world war. He is of short-lived stock: his mother lived to be fifty-three, his father to be forty-nine; and the life-spans of his grandparents on both sides were of the same order. He might be expected to live, then, for perhaps fifteen years more, if he can remain hidden from his enemies. When one considers the number and vigor of these enemies, however, fifteen years seems an extraordinary length of time, which might better be revised to fifteen days, hours or minutes.

The professor knows that he cannot live much longer. I say this because of the message left in my mailbox on Christmas Eve. Unsigned, typewritten on a soiled scrap of paper, the note consisted of ten sentences. The first nine of these, each a bewildering tangle of psychological jargon and references to obscure texts, made no sense to me at first reading. The tenth, unlike the rest, was simply constructed and contained no large words—but its irrational content made it the most puzzling and bizarre sentence of all. I nearly threw the note away, thinking it a colleague's warped notion of a practical joke. For some reason, though, I added it to the clutter on top of my desk, which included, among other mementos, the professor's dice.

It took me several weeks to realize that the message really meant something, that the first nine sentences, when unsnarled, could be taken as instructions. The tenth still told me nothing. It was only last night that I discovered how it fitted in with the rest. The sentence appeared in my thoughts last night, while I was toying absently with the professor's dice.

I promised to have this report on its way to the publishers today. In view of what has happened, I am obliged to break that promise, or release the report incomplete. The delay will not be a long one, for one of the few blessings accorded a bachelor like myself is the ability to move quickly from one abode to another, or from one way of life to another. What property I want to take with me can be packed in a few hours. Fortunately, I am not without substantial private means, which may take as long as a week to realize in liquid and anonymous form. When this is done, I shall mail the report.

I have just returned from a visit to my doctor, who tells me my health is excellent. I am young, and, with any luck at all, I shall live to a ripe old age indeed, for my family on both sides is noted for longevity.

Briefly, I propose to vanish.

Sooner or later, Professor Barnhouse must die. But long before then I shall be ready. So, to the saber rattlers of today—and even, I hope, of tomorrow—I say: Be advised. Barnhouse will die. But not the Barnhouse Effect.

Last night, I tried once more to follow the oblique instructions on the scrap of paper. I took the professor's dice, and then, with the last, nightmarish sentence flitting through my mind, I rolled fifty consecutive sevens.

Good-by.

Eric Walrond

(1898–1966)

Born in what was then British Guiana, and sensitive to the slave history of the Caribbean, Eric Walrond became an exile and wrote grimly impressionistic accounts of social inequities and private torment. Like Claude McKay, his Jamaican contemporary, he became a member of the Harlem Renaissance group in New York in the 1920s, winning in 1925 one of the literary prizes offered by *Opportunity: A Journal of Negro Literature.* Together with his friends Arna Bontemps and Langston Hughes, and the other members of the group, Walrond attempted to give voice to black experience in the Americas and to rid the English language of its biases and stereotypes. Hughes's manifesto uttered their collective desire: "We build our temples for tomorrow, strong as we know how, and we stand on the top of the mountain free from within ourselves."

Walrond's collection, *Tropic Death,* appeared in 1926; it describes something of a literary odyssey, drawing upon the author's observations of life and death in Guiana, Barbados, Honduras, and Panama. Itinerant workers, enduring old women, American servicemen, and British colonials all walk through his pages, sharply realized in a few words. Of particular importance to his creation of character is his authentic use of dialect, which catches at the vitality of the lives he observed. As "Drought" shows, he gives an insider's view of cultural pressures, and absent from his language is any theorizing or moralizing over them. Yet the images, tonal shifts, and fragmentary utterances have an almost incantatory power, absorbing the reader not only into the oppressive surface realities of daily existence but also into the nebulous world of the folk culture which underlies them.

For further reading

Arna Bontemps, ed., *The Harlem Renaissance Remembered* (New York: Dodd, Mead, 1972).

Kenneth Ramchand, *The West Indian Novel and Its Background* (London: Faber & Faber, 1970).

Drought

I

The whistle blew for eleven o'clock. Throats parched, grim, sun-crazed blacks cutting stone on the white burning hillside dropped with a clang the hot, dust-powdered drills and flew up over the rugged edges of the horizon to descend into a dry, waterless gut.*

*Gut = gorge.

394

Hunger—pricks at stomachs inured to brackish coffee and cassava pone* —pressed on folk, joyful as rabbits in a grassy ravine, wrenching themselves free of the lure of the white earth. Helter-skelter dark, brilliant, black faces of West Indian peasants moved along, in pain—the stiff tails of blue denim coats, the hobble of chigger-† cracked heels, the rhythm of a stride ... dissipating into the sun-stuffed void the radiant forces of the incline.

The broad road—a boon to constables moping through the dusk or on hot, bright mornings plowing up the thick, adhesive marl‡ on some seasonal chore, was distinguished by a black, animate dot upon it.

It was Coggins Rum. On the way down he had stopped for a tot —zigaboo‡ word for tin cup—of water by the rock engine. The driver, a buckra johnny—English white—sat on the waste box scooping with a fork handle the meat out of a young water cocoanut. An old straw hat, black, and its rim saggy by virtue of the moisture of sweating sun-fingers, served as a calabash for a ball of "cookoo"— corn meal, okras and butter stewed—roundly poised in its crown. By the buckra's side, a black girl stood, her lips pursed in an indifferent frown, paralyzed in the intense heat.

Passing by them Coggins' bare feet kicked up a cloud of the white marl dust and the girl shouted, "Mistah Rum, you gwine play de guitah tee nite, no?" Visions of Coggins—the sky a vivid crimson or blackly star-gemmed—on the stone step picking the guitar, picking it "with all his hand. ..."

Promptly Coggins answered, "Come down and dance de fango fo' Coggins Rum and he are play for you."

Bajan§ gal don't wash 'ar skin
Till de rain come down. ...

Grumblings. Pitch-black, to the "washed-out" buckra she was more than a bringer of vituals. The buckra's girl. It wasn't Sepia, Georgia, but a backwoods village in Barbadoes. "Didn't you bring me no molasses to pour in the rain-water?" the buckra asked, and the girl, sucking in her mouth, brought an ungovernable eye back to him.

Upon which Coggins, swallowing a hint, kept on his journey— noon-day pilgrimage—through the hot creeping marl.

*Pone = bread.
†Chigger = a mite larva that causes skin itching.
‡Marl = lime soil.
‡Zigaboo = black.
§Bajan = Barbadian.

Scorching—yet Coggins gayly sang:

O! you come with yo' cakes
Wit' yo' cakes an' yo' drinks
Ev'y collection boy ovah death!—
An' we go to wah—
We shall carry de name,
Bajan boys for—evah!

"It are funny," mused Coggins, clearing his throat, "Massa Braffit an' dat chiggah-foot gal. ...."

He stopped and picked up a fern and pressed the back of it to his shiny ebon cheek. It left a white ferny imprint. Grown up, according to the ethics of the gap, Coggins was yet to it a "queer saht o' man," given to the picking of a guitar, and to cogitations, on the step after dark—indulging in an avowed juvenility.

Drunk with the fury of the sun Coggins carelessly swinging along cast an eye behind him—more of the boys from the quarry—over-alled, shoeless, caps whose peaks wiggled on red, sun-red eyes ... the eyes of the black sunburnt folk.

He always cast an eye behind him before he turned off the broad road into the gap.

Flaring up in the sun were the bright new shingles on the Dutch-style cottage of some Antigua folk. Away in a clump of hibiscus was a mansion, the color of bilgy water, owned by two English dowager maidens. In the gap rockstones shot up—obstacles for donkey carts to wrestle over at dusk. Rain-worms and flies gathered in muddy water platoons beside them.

"Yo' dam vagabond yo'!"

Coggins cursed his big toe. His big toe was blind. Helpless thing ... a blind big toe in broad daylight on a West Indian road gap.

He paused, and gathered up the blind member. "Isn't this a hell of a case fo' yo', sah?" A curve of flesh began to peel from it. Pree-pree-pree. As if it were frying. Frying flesh. The nail jerked out of place, hot, bright blood began to stream from it. Around the spot white marl dust clung in grainy cakes. Now, red, new blood squirted —spread over the whole toe—and the dust became crimson.

Gently easing the toe back to the ground, Coggins avoided the grass sticking up in the road and slowly picked his way to the cabin.

"I stump me toe," he announced, "I stump me toe ... woy ... woy."

"Go bring yo' pappy a tot o' water ... Ada ... quick."

Dusky brown Sissie took the gored member in her lap and began to wipe the blood from it.

"Pappy stump he toe."

"Dem rocks in de gap . . ."

"Mine ain't got better yet, needer . . ."

"Hurry up, boy, and bring de lotion."

"Bring me de scissors, an' tek yo' fingers out o' yo' mout' like yo' is starved out! Hey, yo' sah!"

". . . speakin' to you. Big boy lik' yo' suckin' yo' fingers. . . ."

Zip! Onion-colored slip of skin fluttered to the floor. Rattah Grinah, the half-dead dog, cold dribbling from his glassy blue eyes on to his freckled nose, moved inanimately towards it. Fox terrier . . . shaggy . . . bony . . . scarcely able to walk.

"Where is dat Beryl?" Coggins asked, sitting on the floor with one leg over the other, and pouring the salt water over the crimsoning wadding.

"Outside, sah."

"Beryl!"

"Wha' yo' dey?"

"Wha' yo' doin' outside?"

"Answer me, girl!"

". . . Hey, yo' miss, answer yo' pappy!"

"Hard-ears girl! She been eatin' any mo' marl, Sissie?"

"She, Ada?"

"Sho', gal eatin' marl all de haftahnoon. . . ."

Pet, sugar—no more terms of endearment for Beryl. Impatient, Coggins, his big toe stuck up cautiously in the air—inciting Rattah to indolent curiosity—moved past Sissie, past Ada, past Rufus, to the rear of the cabin.

II

Yesterday, at noon . . . a roasting sun smote Coggins. Liquid . . . fluid . . . drought. Solder. Heat and juice of fruit . . . juice of roasting *cashews.*

It whelmed Coggins. The dry season was at its height. Praying to the Lord to send rain, black peons gathered on the rumps of breadfruit or cherry trees in abject supplication.

Crawling along the road to the gap, Coggins gasped at the consequences of the sun's wretched fury. There, where canes spread over with their dark rich foliage into the dust-laden road, the village dogs, hunting for eggs to suck, fowls to kill, paused amidst the yellow stalks of cork-dry canes to pant, or drop, exhausted, sun-smitten.

The sun had robbed the land of its juice, squeezed it dry. Star apples, sugar apples, husks, transparent on the dry sleepy trees. Savagely prowling through the orchards black-birds stopped at nothing. . . . Turtle doves rifled the pods of green peas and purple beans and even the indigestible Brazilian *bonavis.** Potato vines, yellow as the leaves of autumn, severed from their roots by the pressure of the sun, stood on the ground, the wind's eager prey. Undug, stemless—peanuts, carrots—seeking balm, relief, the caress of a passing wind, shot dead unlustered eyes up through sun-etched cracks in the hard, brittle soil. The sugar corn went to the birds. Ripening prematurely, breadfruits fell swiftly on the hard naked earth, half ripe, good only for fritters. . . . Fell in spatters . . . and the hungry dogs, elbowing the children, lapped up the yellow-mellow fruit.

His sight impaired by the livid sun, Coggins turned hungry eyes to the soil. Empty corn stalks . . . blackbirds at work. . . .

Along the water course, bushy palms shading it, frogs gasped for air, their white breasts like fowls, soft and palpitating. The water in the drains sopped up, they sprang at flies, mosquitoes . . . wrangled over a mite.

It was a dizzy spectacle and the black peons were praying to God to send rain. Coggins drew back. . . .

Asking God to send rain . . . why? Where was the rain? Barreled up there in the clouds? Odd! Invariably, when the ponds and drains and rivers dried up they sank on their knees asking God to pour the water out of the sky. . . . Odd . . . water in the sky. . . .

The sun! It wrung toll of the earth. It had its effect on Coggins. It made the black stone cutter's face blacker. Strong tropic suns make black skins blacker. . . .

At the quarry it became whiter and the color of dark things generally grew darker. Similarly, with white ones—it gave them a whiter hue. Coggins and the quarry. Coggins and the marl. Coggins and the marl road.

Beryl in the marl road. Six years old; possessing a one-piece frock, no hat, no shoes.

Brown Beryl . . . the only one of the Rum children who wasn't black as sin. Strange . . . Yellow Beryl. It happens that way sometimes. Both Coggins and Sissie were unrelievably black. Still Beryl came a shade lighter. "Dat am nuttin'," Sissie had replied to Coggins' intimately naïve query, "is yo' drunk dat yo' can't fomembah me sistah-in-law what had a white picknee fo' 'ar naygeh man? Yo' don't fomembah, no?" Light-skinned Beryl. . . .

It happens that way sometimes.

Victim of the sun—a bright spot under its singeing mask—Beryl hesitated at Coggins' approach. Her little brown hands flew behind her back.

---

*Brazilian *bonavis* = bonavist bean, an edible bean, also called the broke-pot pea.

"Eatin' marl again," Coggins admonished, "eatin' marl again, you little vagabon'!"

On the day before he had had to chastise her for sifting the stone dust and eating it.

"You're too hard ears," Coggins shouted, slapping her hands, "you're too hard ears."

Coggins turned into the gap for home, dragging her by the hand. He was too angry to speak ... too agitated.

Avoiding the jagged rocks in the gap, Beryl, her little body lost in the crocus bag frock jutting her skinny shoulders, began to cry. A gulping sensation came to Coggins when he saw Beryl crying. When Beryl cried, he felt like crying, too. ...

But he sternly heaped invective upon her. "Marl'll make yo' sick ... tie up yo' guts, too. Tie up yo' guts like green guavas. Don't eat it, yo' hear, don't eat no mo' marl. ..."

No sooner had they reached home than Sissie began. "Eatin' marl again, like yo' is starved out," she landed a clout on Beryl's uncombed head. "Go under de bed an' lay down befo' I crack yo' cocoanut. ..."

Running a house on a dry-rot herring bone, a pint of stale, yellow-less corn meal, a few spuds, yet proud, thumping the children around for eating scraps, for eating food cooked by hands other than hers ... Sissie. ...

"Don't talk to de child like dat, Sissie."

"Oh, go 'long you, always tryin' to prevent me from beatin' them. When she get sick who gwine tend she? Me or you? Man, go 'bout yo' business."

Beryl crawled meekly under the bed. Ada, a bigger girl—fourteen and "ownwayish"—shot a look of composed neutrality at Rufus—a sulky, cry-cry, suck-finger boy nearing twenty—Big Head Rufus.

"Serve she right," Rufus murmured.

"Nobody ain't gwine beat me with a hairbrush. I know dat." One leg on top of the other, Ada, down on the floor, grew impatient at Sissie's languor in preparing the food. ...

Coggins came in at eleven to dinner. Ada and Rufus did likewise. The rest of the day they spent killing birds with stones fired from slingshots; climbing neighbors' trees in search of birds' nests; going to the old French ruins to dig out, with the puny aid of Rattah Grinah, a stray mongoose or to rob of its prize some canary-catching cat; digging holes in the rocky gap or on the brink of drains and stuffing them with paper and gunpowder stolen from the Rum canister and lighting it with a match. Dynamiting! Picking up hollow pieces of iron pipe, scratching a hole on top of them, towards one end, and ramming them with more gunpowder and stones and brown paper, and with a pyramid of gunpowder moistened with spit for a squib, leveling them at snipes or sparrows. Touch bams.

"Well, Sissie, what yo' got fo' eat today?"

"Cookoo, what yo' think Ah are have?"

"Lawd, mo' o' dat corn mash. Mo' o' dat prison gruel. People would t'ink a man is a horse!" . . . a restless crossing of scaly, marl-white legs in the corner.

"Any salt fish?"

"Wha' Ah is to get if from?"

"Herrin'?"

"You t'ink I must be pick up money. Wha' you expect mah to get it from, wit' butter an' lard so dear, an' sugar four cents a pound. Yo' must be expect me to steal."

"Well, I ain't mean no harm. . . ."

"Hey, this man muss be crazy. You forget I ain't workin' ni, yo' forget dat I can't even get water to drink, much mo' grow onions or green peas. Look outside. Look in the yard. Look at the parsley vines."

Formerly things grew under the window or near the tamarind trees, fed by the used water or the swill, yams, potatoes, lettuce. . . .

Going to the door, Coggins paused. A "forty-leg" was working its way into the craw of the last of the Rum hens. "Lahd 'a' massie. . . ." Leaping to the rescue, Coggins slit the hen's craw—undigested corn spilled out—and ground the surfeited centipede underfoot.

"Now we got to eat this," and he strung the bleeding hen up on a nail by the side of the door, out of poor Rattah Grinah's blinking reach. . . .

Unrestrained rejoicing on the floor.

Coggins ate. It was hot—hot food. It fused life into his body. It rammed the dust which had gathered in his throat at the quarry so far down into his stomach that he was unaware of its presence. And to eat food that had butter on it was a luxury. Coggins sucked up every grain of it.

"Hey, Ada."

"Rufus, tek this."

"Where is dat Miss Beryl?"

"Under de bed, m'm."

"Beryl. . . ."

"Yassum. . . ."

Unweeping, Beryl, barely saving her skull, shot up from underneath the bed. Over Ada's obstreperous toes, over Rufus' by the side of Coggins, she had to pass to get the proffered dish.

"Take it quick!"

Saying not a word, Beryl took it and, sliding down beside it, deposited it upon the floor beside Coggins.

"You mustn't eat any more marl, yo' hear?" he turned to her. "It will make yo' belly hard."

"Yes ... pappy."

Throwing eyes up at him—white, shiny, appealing—Beryl guided the food into her mouth. The hand that did the act was still white with the dust of the marl. All up along the elbow. Even around her little mouth the white, telltale marks remained.

Drying the bowl of the last bit of grease, Coggins was completely absorbed in his task. He could hear Sissie scraping the iron pot and trying to fling from the spoon the stiff, over-cooked corn meal which had stuck to it. Scraping the pan of its very bottom, Ada and Rufus fought like two mad dogs.

"You, Miss Ada, yo' better don't bore a hole in dat pan, gimme heah!"

"But, Mahmie, I ain't finish."

Picking at her food, Beryl, the dainty one, ate sparingly. ...

Once a day the Rums ate. At dusk, curve of crimson gold in the sensuous tropic sky, they had tea. English to a degree, it was a rite absurdly regal. Pauperized native blacks clung to the utmost vestiges of the Crown. Too, it was more than a notion for a black cane hole digger to face the turmoil of a hoe or fork or "bill"—zigaboo word for cutlass—on a bare cup of molasses coffee.

III

"Lahd 'a' massie. ..."

"Wha' a mattah, Coggins?"

"Say something, no!"

"Massie, come hay, an' see de gal picknee."

"... open yo' mout' no, what's a mattah?"

Coggins flew to the rainwater keg. Knocked the swizzle stick—relic of Sissie's pop manufactures—behind it, tilting over the empty keg.

"Get up, Beryl, get up, wha' a mattah, sick?"

"Lif' she up, pappy."

"Yo' move out o' de way, Mistah Rufus, befo'. ..."

"Don't, Sissie, don't lick she!"

"Gal playin' sick! Gal only playin' sick, dat what de mattah wit' she. Gal only playin' sick. Get up, yo' miss!"

"God—don't, Sissie, leave she alone."

"Go back, every dam one o' yo', all yo' gwine get in de way."

Beryl, little naked brown legs apart, was flat upon the hard, bare earth. The dog, perhaps, or the echo of some fugitive wind had blown up her little crocus bag dress. It lay like a cocoanut flapjack on her stomach. . . .

"Bring she inside, Coggins, wait I gwine fix de bed."

Mahogany bed . . . West Indian peasants sporting a mahogany bed; canopied with a dusty grimy slice of cheesecloth. . . .

Coggins stood up by the lamp on the wall, looking on at Sissie prying up Beryl's eyelids.

"Open yo' eyes . . . open yo' eyes . . . betcha the little vagabon' is playin' sick."

Indolently Coggins stirred. A fist shot up—then down. "Move, Sissie, befo' Ah hit yo'." The woman dodged.

"Always wantin' fo' hit me fo' nuttin', like I is any picknee."

". . . anybody hear this woman would think. . . ."

"I ain't gwine stand for it, yes, I ain't gwine. . . ."

"Shut up, yo' old hard-hearted wretch! Shut up befo' I tump yo' down!" . . . Swept aside, one arm in a parrying attitude . . . backing, backing toward the larder over the lamp. . . .

Coggins peered back at the unbreathing child. A shade of compassion stole over Sissie. "Put dis to 'er nose, Coggins, and see what'll happen." Assafetida, bits of red cloth. . . .

Last year Rufus, the sickliest of the lot, had had the measles and the parish doctor had ordered her to tie a red piece of flannel around his neck. . . .

She stuffed the red flannel into Coggins' hand. "Try dat," she said, and stepped back.

Brow wrinkled in cogitation, Coggins—space cleared for action—denuded the child. "How it ah rise! How 'er belly a go up in de year!"

Bright wood; bright mahogany wood, expertly shellacked and laid out in the sun to dry, not unlike it. Beryl's stomach, a light brown tint, grew bit by bit shiny. It rose; round and bright, higher and higher. They had never seen one so none of them thought of wind-filling balloons. Beryl's stomach resembled a wind-filling balloon.

Then—

"She too hard ears," Sissie declared, "she won't lissen to she pappy, she too hard ears."

Dusk came. Country folk, tired, soggy, sleepy, staggering in from "town"—depressed by the market quotations on Bantam cocks—hollowed howdy-do to Coggins, on the stone step, waiting.

Rufus and Ada strangely forgot to go down to the hydrant to bathe their feet. It had been a passion with Coggins. "Nasty feet breed disease," he had said, "you Mistah Rufus, wash yo' foots befo' yo' go to sleep. An' yo', too, Miss Ada, I'm speaking to yo', gal, yo' hear me? Tak' yo' mout' off o' go 'head, befo' Ah box it off. ...."

Inwardly glad of the escape, Ada and Rufus sat, not by Coggins out on the stone step, but down below the cabin, on the edge of a stone overlooking an empty pond, pitching rocks at the frogs and crickets screaming in the early dusk.

The freckled-face old buckra physician paused before the light and held up something to it. ...

"Marl ... marl ... dust. ...."

It came to Coggins in swirls. Autopsy. Noise comes in swirls. Pounding, pounding—dry Indian corn pounding. Ginger. Ginger being pounded in a mortar with a bright, new pestle. Pound, pound. And. Sawing. Butcher shop. Cow foot is sawed that way. Stew—or tough hard steak. Then the drilling—drilling—drilling to a stone cutter's ears! Ox grizzle. Drilling into ox grizzle. ...

"Too bad, Coggins," the doctor said, "too bad, to lose yo' dawtah. ...."

In a haze it came to Coggins. Inertia swept over him. He saw the old duffer climb into his buggy, tug at the reins of his sickly old nag and slowly drive down the rocky gap and disappear into the night.

Inside, Sissie, curious, held things up to the light. "Come," she said to Coggins, "and see what 'im take out a' 'ar. Come an' see de marl. ...."

And Coggins slowly answered, "Sissie—if yo' know what is good fo' yo'self, you bes' leave dem stones alone."

Patrick White

(b. 1912)

Winner of several literary awards including the 1973 Nobel Prize, Patrick White was born in London to Anglophile parents, brought up in Sydney, Australia, and educated at a British public school and Cambridge University. In the late 1940s, after traveling through western Europe and the United States, serving in World War II, and living for a year in Greece, he returned to Australia to write. Dramatist, novelist, and short-story writer, he has produced eleven books, among which *The Tree of Man* (1955), *Voss* (1957), *Riders in the Chariot* (1961), *The Vivisector* (1970), and *The Eye of the Storm* (1973) won enthusiastic reviews, particularly outside Australia. In Australia itself he was something of an exotic, an observer of tragic depths and spiritual heights in a community that discouraged the display of excessive emotion. He rejected what he considered mediocre in much of Australian society and sought for alternate routes to meaning. Resulting from that confrontation were several hard-edged satires of bourgeois life—he created and populated a suburb he called Sarsaparilla, and could wittily orchestrate the events and perceptions that took place around it, as he does in "Willy-Wagtails by Moonlight" (*The Burnt Ones*, 1964). But beneath the brittle dialogues and surface ironies murmur White's more nebulous assertions about the potential of the human spirit.

Deeply influenced by painting and music, he seeks for ways to make language communicate nonverbal understanding, to convey to a reader the insights of eye and ear. In the process he has developed in his novels a mannered and symbolic prose that is flexible enough to accommodate both his imaginative vision and his social criticism.

For further reading

Barry Argyle, *Patrick White* (Edinburgh: Oliver & Boyd, 1967).
J. F. Burrows, "The Short Stories of Patrick White," *Southerly,* 24 (1964), 116–125.
Patrick White, "The Prodigal Son," *Australian Letters,* 1 (April 1958), 37–39.

Willy-Wagtails by Moonlight

The Wheelers drove up to the Mackenzies' punctually at six-thirty. It was the hour for which they had been asked. My God, thought Jum Wheeler. It had been raining a little, and the tyres sounded blander on the wet gravel.

In front of the Mackenzies', which was what is known as a Lovely Old Home—colonial style—amongst some carefully natural-looking gums, there stood a taxi.

"Never knew Arch and Nora ask us with anyone else," Eileen Wheeler said.

"Maybe they didn't. Even now. Maybe it's someone they couldn't get rid of."

"Or an urgent prescription from the chemist's."

Eileen Wheeler yawned. She must remember to show sympathy, because Nora Mackenzie was going through a particularly difficult one.

Anyway, they were there, and the door stood open on the lights inside. Even the lives of the people you know, even the lives of Nora and Arch look interesting for a split second, when you drive up and glimpse them through a lit doorway.

"It's that Miss Cullen," Eileen said.

For there was Miss Cullen, doing something with a brief-case in the hall.

"Ugly bitch," Jum said.

"Plain is the word," corrected Eileen.

"Arch couldn't do without her. Practically runs the business."

Certainly that Miss Cullen looked most methodical, shuffling the immaculate papers, and slipping them into a new pigskin brief-case in Arch and Nora's hall.

"Got a figure," Eileen conceded.

"But not a chin."

"Oh, hello, Miss Cullen. It's stopped raining."

It was too bright stepping suddenly into the hall. The Wheelers brightly blinked. They looked newly made.

"Keeping well, Miss Cullen, I hope?"

"I have nothing to complain about, Mr Wheeler," Miss Cullen replied.

She snapped the catch. Small, rather pointed breasts under the rain-coat. But, definitely, no chin.

Eileen Wheeler was fixing her hair in the reproduction Sheraton mirror.

She had been to the hairdresser's recently, and the do was still set too tight.

"Well, good-bye now," Miss Cullen said.

When she smiled there was a hint of gold, but discreet, no more than a bridge. Then she would draw her lips together, and lick them ever so slightly, as if she had been sucking a not unpleasantly acid sweetie.

Miss Cullen went out the door, closing it firmly but quietly behind her.

"That was Miss Cullen," said Nora Mackenzie coming down. "She's Arch's secretary."

"He couldn't do without her," she added, as though they did not know.

Nora was like that. Eileen wondered how she and Nora had tagged along together, ever since Goulburn, all those years.

"God, she's plain!" Jum said.

Nora did not exactly frown, but pleated her forehead the way she did when other people's virtues were assailed. Such attacks seemed to affect her personally, causing her almost physical pain.

"But Mildred is so kind," she insisted.

Nora Mackenzie made a point of calling her husband's employees by first names, trying to make them part of a family which she alone, perhaps, would have liked to exist.

"She brought me some giblet soup, all the way from Balgowlah, that time I had virus 'flu."

"Was it good, darling?" Eileen asked.

She was going through the routine, rubbing Nora's cheek with her own. Nora was pale. She must remember to be kind.

Nora did not answer, but led the way into the lounge-room.

Nora said:

"I don't think I'll turn on the lights for the present. They hurt my eyes, and it's so restful sitting in the dusk."

Nora *was* pale. She had, in fact, just taken a couple of Disprin.

"Out of sorts, dear?" Eileen asked.

Nora did not answer, but offered some dry martinis.

Very watery, Jum knew from experience, but drink of a kind.

"Arch will be down presently," Nora said. "He had to attend to some business, some letters Miss Cullen brought. Then he went in to have a shower."

Nora's hands were trembling as she offered the dry martinis, but Eileen remembered they always had.

The Wheelers sat down. It was all so familiar, they did not have to be asked, which was fortunate, as Nora Mackenzie always experienced difficulty in settling guests into chairs. Now she sat down herself, far more diffidently than her friends. The cushions were standing on their points.

Eileen sighed. Old friendships and the first scent of gin always made her nostalgic.

"It's stopped raining," she said, and sighed.

"Arch well?" Jum asked.

As if he cared. She had let the ice get into the cocktail, turning it almost to pure water.

"He has his trouble," Nora said. "You know, his back."

Daring them to have forgotten.

Nora loved Arch. It made Eileen feel ashamed.

So fortunate for them to have discovered each other. Nora Lead-beatter and Arch Mackenzie. Two such bores. And with bird-watching in common. Though Eileen Wheeler had never believed Nora did not make herself learn to like watching birds.

At Goulburn, in the early days, Nora would come out to Glen Davie sometimes to be with Eileen at week-ends. Mr Leadbeatter had been manager at the Wales for a while. He always saw that his daughter had the cleanest notes. Nora was shy, but better than nothing, and the two girls would sit about on the veranda those summer evenings, buffing their nails, and listening to the sheep cough in the home paddock. Eileen gave Nora lessons in making-up. Nora had protested, but was pleased.

"Mother well, darling?" Eileen asked, sipping that sad, watery gin.

"Not exactly *well,*" Nora replied, painfully.

Because she had been to Orange, to visit her widowed mother, who suffered from Parkinson's disease.

"You know what I mean, dear," said Eileen.

Jum was dropping his ash on the carpet. It might be better when poor bloody Arch came down.

"I have an idea that woman, that Mrs Galloway, is unkind to her," Nora said.

"Get another," Eileen advised. "It isn't like after the War."

"One can never be sure," Nora debated. "One would hate to hurt the woman's feelings."

Seated in the dusk Nora Mackenzie was of a moth colour. Her face looked as though she had been rubbing it with chalk. Might have, too, in spite of those lessons in make-up. She sat and twisted her hands together.

How very red Nora's hands had been, at Goulburn, at the convent, to which the two girls had gone. Not that they belonged to *those.* It was only convenient. Nora's hands had been red and trembly after practising a tarantella, early, in the frost. So very early all of that. Eileen had learnt about life shortly after puberty. She had tried to tell Nora one or two things, but Nora did not want to hear. Oh, no, no, *please,* Eileen, Nora cried. As though a boy had been twisting her arm. She had those long, entreating, sensitive hands.

And there they were still. Twisting together, making their excuses. For what they had never done.

Arch came in then. He turned on the lights, which made Nora wince, even those lights which barely existed in all the neutrality of Nora's room. Nora did not comment, but smiled, because it was Arch who had committed the crime.

Arch said:

"You two toping hard as usual."

He poured himself the rest of the cocktail.

Eileen laughed her laugh which people found amusing at parties.

Jum said, and bent his leg, if it hadn't been for Arch and the shower, they wouldn't have had the one too many.

"A little alcohol releases the vitality," Nora remarked ever so gently.

She always grew anxious at the point where jokes became personal.

Arch composed his mouth under the handle-bars moustache, and Jum knew what they were in for.

"Miss Cullen came out with one or two letters," Arch was taking pains to explain. "Something she thought should go off tonight. I take a shower most evenings. Summer, at least."

"Such humidity," Nora helped.

Arch looked down into his glass. He might have been composing further remarks, but did not come out with them.

That silly, bloody English-air-force-officer's moustache. It was the only thing Arch had ever dared. War had given him the courage to pinch a detail which did not belong to him.

"That Miss Cullen, useful girl," Jum suggested.

"Runs the office."

"Forty, if a day," Eileen said, whose figure was beginning to slacken off.

Arch said he would not know, and Jum made a joke about Miss Cullen's *cul-de-sac.*

The little pleats had appeared again in Nora Mackenzie's chalky brow. "Well," she cried, jumping up, quite girlish, "I do hope the dinner will be a success."

And laughed.

Nora was half-way through her second course with that woman at the Chanticleer. Eileen suspected there would be avocadoes stuffed with prawns, chicken *Mornay,* and *crêpes Suzette.*

Eileen was right.

Arch seemed to gain in authority sitting at the head of his table. "I'd like you to taste this wine," he said. "It's very light."

"Oh, yes?" said Jum.

The wine was corked, but nobody remarked. The second bottle, later on, was somewhat better. The Mackenzies were spreading themselves tonight.

Arch flipped his napkin once or twice, emphasizing a point. He smoothed the handle-bars moustache, which should have concealed a harelip, only there wasn't one. Jum dated from before the moustache, long, long, very long.

Arch said:

"There was a story Armitage told me at lunch. There was a man who bought a mower. Who suffered from indigestion. Now, how, exactly, did it ... go?"

Jum had begun to make those little pellets out of bread. It always fascinated him how grubby the little pellets turned out. And himself not by any means dirty.

Arch failed to remember the point of the story Armitage had told.

It was difficult to understand how Arch had made a success of his business. Perhaps it was that Miss Cullen, breasts and all, under the rain-coat. For a long time Arch had messed around. Travelled in something. Separator parts. Got the agency for some sort of phoney machine for supplying *ozone* to public buildings. The Mackenzies lived at Burwood then. Arch continued to mess around. The War was quite a godsend. Arch was the real adje type. Did a conscientious job. Careful with his allowances, too.

Then, suddenly, after the War, Arch Mackenzie had launched out, started the import-export business. Funny the way a man will suddenly hit on the idea to which his particular brand of stupidity can respond.

The Mackenzies had moved to the North Shore, to the house which still occasionally embarrassed Nora. She felt as though she ought to apologize for success. But there was the bird-watching. Most week-ends they went off to the bush, to the Mountains or somewhere. She felt happier in humbler circumstances. In time she got used to the tape recorder which they took along. She made herself look upon it as a necessity rather than ostentation.

Eileen was dying for a cigarette.

"May I smoke, Arch?"

"We're amongst friends, aren't we?"

Eileen did not answer that. And Arch fetched the ash-tray they kept handy for those who needed it.

Nora in the kitchen dropped the beans. Everybody heard, but Arch asked Jum for a few tips on investments, as he always did when Nora happened to be out of the room. Nora had some idea that the Stock Exchange was immoral.

Then Nora brought the dish of little, pale tinned peas.

"Ah! *Pet-ty pwah*!" said Jum.

He formed his full, and rather greasy lips into a funnel through which the little rounded syllables poured most impressively.

Nora forgot her embarrassment. She envied Jum his courage in foreign languages. Although there were her lessons in Italian, she would never have dared utter in public.

"Can you bear *crêpes Suzette*?" Nora had to apologize.

"Lovely, darling." Eileen smiled.

She would have swallowed a tiger. But was, *au fond,* at her gloomiest.

What was the betting Nora would drop the *crêpes Suzette*? It was those long, trembly hands, on which the turquoise ring looked too small and innocent. The Mackenzies were still in the semi-precious bracket in the days when they became engaged.

"How's the old bird-watching?"

Jum had to force himself, but after all he had drunk their wine.

Arch Mackenzie sat deeper in his chair, almost completely at his ease.

"Got some new tapes," he said. "We'll play them later. Went up to Kurrajong on Sunday, and got the bell-birds. I'll play you the lyre-bird, too. That was Mount Wilson."

"Didn't we hear the lyre-bird last time?" Eileen asked.

Arch said:

"Yes."

Deliberately.

"But wouldn't you like to hear it again? It's something of a collector's piece."

Nora said they'd be more comfortable drinking their coffee in the lounge.

Then Arch fetched the tape recorder. He set it up on the Queen Anne walnut piecrust. It certainly was an impressive machine.

"I'll play you the lyre-bird."

"The *pièce de résistance?* Don't you think we should keep it?"

"He can never wait for the lyre-bird."

Nora had grown almost complacent. She sat holding her coffee, smiling faintly through the steam. The children she had never had with Arch were about to enter.

"Delicious coffee," Eileen said.

She had finished her filter-tips. She had never felt drearier.

The tape machine had begun to snuffle. There was quite an unusual amount of crackle. Perhaps it was the bush. Yes, that was it. The bush!

"Well, it's really quite remarkable how you people have the patience," Eileen Wheeler had to say.

"Sssh!"

Arch Mackenzie was frowning. He had sat forward in the period chair.

"This is where it comes in."

His face was tragic in the shaded light.

"Get it?" he whispered.

His hand was helping. Or commanding.

"Quite remarkable," Eileen repeated.

Jum was shocked to realize he had only two days left in which to take up the ICI rights for old Thingummy.

Nora sat looking at her empty cup. But lovingly.

Nora could have been beautiful, Eileen saw. And suddenly felt old, she who had stripped once or twice at amusing parties. Nora Mackenzie did not know about that.

Somewhere in the depths of the bush Nora was calling that it had just turned four o'clock, but she had forgotten to pack the thermos.

The machine snuffled.

Arch Mackenzie was listening. He was biting his moustache.

"There's another passage soon." He frowned.

"Darling," Nora whispered, "after the lyre-bird you might slip into the kitchen and change the bulb. It went while I was making the coffee."

Arch Mackenzie's frown deepened. Even Nora was letting him down.

But she did not see. She was so in love.

It might have been funny if it was not also pathetic. People were horribly pathetic, Eileen Wheeler decided, who had her intellectual moments. She was also feeling sick. It was Nora's *crêpes Suzette*, lying like blankets.

"You'll realize there are one or two rough passages," Arch said, coming forward when the tape had ended. "I might cut it."

"It could do with a little trimming," Eileen agreed. "But perhaps it's more natural without."

Am I a what's-this, a masochist, she asked.

"Don't forget the kitchen bulb," Nora prompted.

Very gently. Very dreamy.

Her hair had strayed, in full dowdiness, down along her white cheek.

"I'll give you the bell-birds for while I'm gone."

Jum's throat had begun to rattle. He sat up in time, though, and saved his cup in the same movement.

"I remember the bell-birds," he said.

"Not these ones, you don't. These are new. These are the very latest. The best bell-birds."

Arch had started the tape, and stalked out of the room, as if to let the bell-birds themselves prove his point.

"It is one of our loveliest recordings," Nora promised.

They all listened or appeared to.

When Nora said:

"Oh, dear"—getting up—"I do believe"—panting almost—"the bell-bird tape"—trembling—"is damaged."

Certainly the crackle was more intense.

"Arch will be so terribly upset."

She had switched off the horrifying machine. With surprising skill for one so helpless. For a moment it seemed to Eileen Wheeler that Nora Mackenzie was going to hide the offending tape somewhere in her bosom. But she thought better of it, and put it aside on one of those little superfluous tables.

"Perhaps it's the machine that's broken," suggested Jum.

"Oh, no," said Nora, "it's the tape. I know. We'll have to give you something else."

"I can't understand,"—Eileen grinned—"how you ever got around, Nora, to being mechanical."

"If you're determined," Nora said.

Her head was lowered in concentration.

"If you want a thing enough."

She was fixing a fresh tape.

"And we do love our birds. Our Sundays together in the bush."

The machine had begun its snuffling and shuffling again. Nora Mackenzie raised her head, as if launched on an invocation.

Two or three notes of bird-song fell surprisingly pure and clear, out of the crackle, into the beige and string-coloured room.

"This is one," Nora said, "I don't think I've ever heard before."

She smiled, however, and listened to identify.

"Willy-Wagtails," Nora said.

Willy-Wagtails were suited to tape. The song tumbled and exulted.

"It must be something," Nora said, "that Arch made while I was with Mother. There were a couple of Sundays when he did a little field-work on his own."

Nora might have given way to a gentle melancholy for all she had foregone if circumstances had not heightened the pitch. There was Arch standing in the doorway. Blood streaming.

"Blasted bulb collapsed in my hand!"

"Oh, darling! Oh *dear!*" Nora cried.

The Wheelers were both fascinated. There was the blood dripping on the beige wall-to-wall.

How the willy-wagtails chortled.

Nora Mackenzie literally staggered at her husband, to take upon herself, if possible, the whole ghastly business.

"Come along, Arch," she moaned. "We'll fix. In just a minute," Nora panted.

And simply by closing the door, she succeeded in blotting the situation, all but the drops of blood that were left behind on the carpet.

"Poor old Arch! Bleeding like a pig!" Jum Wheeler said, and laughed.

Eileen added:

"We shall suffer the willy-wags alone."

Perhaps it was better like that. You could relax. Eileen began to pull. Her step-ins had eaten into her.

The willy-wagtails were at it again.

"Am I going crackers?" asked Jum. "Listening to those bloody birds!"

When somebody laughed. Out of the tape. The Wheelers sat. Still.

Three-quarters of the bottle! Snuffle crackle. *Arch Mackenzie, you're a fair trimmer!* Again that rather brassy laughter.

"Well, I'll be blowed!" said Jum Wheeler.

"But it's that Miss Cullen," Eileen said.

The Wheeler spirits soared as surely as plummets dragged the notes of the wagtail down.

But it's far too rocky, and far too late. Besides, it's willy-wagtails we're after. How Miss Cullen laughed. *Willy-wagtails by moonlight!* Arch was less intelligible, as if he had listened to too many birds, and caught the habit. Snuffle crackle went the machine . . . *the buttons are not made to undo* . . . Miss Cullen informed. *Oh, stop it. Arch!* ARCH! *You're* TEARING *me!*

So that the merciless machine took possession of the room. There in the crackle of twigs, the stench of ants, the two Wheelers sat. There was that long, thin Harry Edwards, Eileen remembered, with bony wrists, had got her down behind the barn. She had hated it at first. All mirth had been exorcized from Miss Cullen's recorded laughter. Grinding out. Grinding out. So much of life was recorded by now. Returning late from a country dance, the Wheelers had fallen down amongst the sticks and stones, and made what is called love, and risen in the grey hours, to find themselves numb and bulging.

If only the tape, if you knew the trick with the wretched switch.

Jum Wheeler decided not to look at his wife. Little guilty, pockets were turning themselves out in his mind. That woman at the Locomotive Hotel. Pockets and pockets of putrefying trash. Down along the creek, amongst the tussocks and the sheep pellets, the sun burning his boy's skin, he played his overture to sex. Alone.

This sort of thing's all very well, Miss Cullen decided. *It's time we turned practical. Are you sure we can find our way back to the car?*

Always trundling. Crackling. But there were the blessed wagtails again.

"Wonder if they forgot the machine?"

"Oh, God! Hasn't the tape bobbed up in Pymble?"

A single willy-wagtail sprinkled its grace-notes through the stuffy room.

"Everything's all right," Nora announced. "He's calmer now. I persuaded him to take a drop of brandy."

"That should fix him," Jum said.

But Nora was listening to the lone wagtail. She was standing in the bush. Listening. The notes of bird-song falling like mountain water, when they were not chiselled in moonlight.

"There is nothing purer," Nora said, "than the song of the wagtail. Excepting Schubert," she added, "some of Schubert."

She was so shyly glad it had occurred to her.

But the Wheelers just sat.

And again Nora Mackenzie was standing alone amongst the inexorable moonlit gums. She thought perhaps she had always felt alone, even with Arch, while grateful even for her loneliness.

"Ah, there you are!" Nora said.

It was Arch. He stood holding out his bandaged wound. Rather rigid. He could have been up for court martial.

"I've missed the willy-wagtails," Nora said, raising her face to him, exposing her distress, like a girl. "Some day you'll have to play it to me. When you've the time. And we can concentrate."

The Wheelers might not have existed.

As for the tape it had discovered silence.

Arch mumbled they'd all better have something to drink.

Jum agreed it was a good idea.

"Positively brilliant," Eileen said.

Rudy Wiebe

(b. 1934)

Born to a Mennonite family in Fairholme, in the hilly woodlands of northern Saskatchewan, Rudy Wiebe notes in "Passage by Land" that landscape and cultural
heritage have always been important to him. Though he did not learn English until
he went to school, and did not see a mountain or a plain until he was almost thirteen,
he later found language and landscape indissolubly wedded to each other. Encounter-
ing the world was a "wandering to find"; and paramount in his work is the sense of
wandering that derives from his early experience, expressing itself as a quest for
knowledge about knowledge itself, about ways of knowing.

His Mennonite background features significantly in two of his novels, *Peace Shall
Destroy Many* (1964) and *The Blue Mountains of China* (1970); the latter, a modern
epic, probes the idealistic impulses behind the sect, traces its spiritual and geographic
journeys, and tries to come to terms with the power of the commitment that impelled
so many people to accept its invitation to individual action. His sympathy for human
beings takes a different form in *First and Vital Candle* (1966), *The Temptations of Big
Bear* (1973), about the Riel Rebellion, and "Where Is the Voice Coming From?" (which
appears here slightly modified from its first published form). The Indians, Eskimos,
and Métis who appear in these works are admirably realized characters, and Wiebe
has endeavored with great sensitivity to cross the cultural barriers that lie between
him and his subject. But he is acutely conscious of the difficulty of being anyone but
oneself, of the limitations that one's perspective erects against complete understanding, and of the problems that face the artist and the historian when they try to
convey their perceptions of truth or reality. "Where Is the Voice Coming From?"
resulted, Wiebe writes, from personal encounters with museum displays and historical accounts of Indian and Royal Canadian Mounted Police history, and from reading
in nineteenth-century newspapers and in volume XII (*Reconsiderations*) of Arnold
Toynbee's *A Study of History*. On top of all that is his overpowering urge to "make
story," for as he writes in his introduction to an anthology, *The Story-Makers* (1970),
a good story seduces "both teller and listener out of their world into its own," illuminating "the world in which teller and listener actually are" and often proving "the
more pleasurable as the seduction becomes less immediate: story worth pondering is
story doubly enjoyed."

For further reading

W. H. New, *Articulating West* (Toronto: New Press, 1972).
Rudy Wiebe, "Passage by Land," *Canadian Literature*, 48 (Spring 1971), 25–47; re-
printed in *Writers of the Prairies*, ed. Donald Stephens (Vancouver: University of
British Columbia, 1973), pp. 29–31.

Where is the Voice Coming From?

The problem is to make the story.

A difficulty of this making may have been excellently stated by
Teilhard de Chardin: "We are continually inclined to isolate our-

selves from the things and events which surround us ... as though we were spectators, not elements, in what goes on." Arnold Toynbee does venture, "For all that we know, Reality is the undifferentiated unity of the mystical experience," but that need not here be considered. This story ended long ago; it is one of finite acts, of orders, of elemental feelings and reactions, of obvious legal restrictions and requirements.

Presumably all the parts of the story are themselves available. A difficulty is that they are, as always, available only in bits and pieces. Though the acts themselves seem quite clear, some written reports of the acts contradict each other. As if these acts were, at one time, too well known; as if the original nodule of each particular fact had from somewhere received non-factual accretions; or even more, as if, since the basic facts were so clear perhaps there were a larger number of facts than any one reporter, or several, or even any reporter had ever attempted to record. About facts that are still simply told by this mouth to that ear, of course, even less can be expected.

An affair seventy-five years old should acquire some of the shiny transparency of an old man's skin. It should.

Sometimes it would seem that it would be enough—perhaps more than enough—to hear the names only. The grandfather One Arrow; the mother Spotted Calf; the father Sounding Sky; the wife (wives rather, but only one of them seems to have a name, though their fathers are Napaise, Kapahoo, Old Dust, The Rump)—the one wife named, of all things, Pale Face; the cousin Going-Up-To-Sky; the brother-in-law (again, of all things) Dublin. The names of the police sound very much alike; they all begin with Constable or Corporal or Sergeant, but here and there an Inspector, then a Superintendent and eventually all the resonance of an Assistant Commissioner echoes down. More. Herself: Victoria, by the Grace of God etc. etc. QUEEN, Defender of the Faith, etc. etc.; and witness "Our Right Trusty and Right Well-beloved Cousin and Councillor the Right Honorable Sir John Campbell Hamilton-Gordon, Earl of Aberdeen; Viscount Formartine, Baron Haddo, Methlic, Tarves and Kellie, in the Peerage of Scotland; Viscount Gordon of Aberdeen, County of Aberdeen, in the Peerage of the United Kingdom; Baronet of Nova Scotia, Knight Grand Cross of Our Most Distinguished Order of Saint Michael and Saint George etc. Governor General of Canada." And of course himself: in the award proclamation named "Jean-Baptiste" but otherwise known only as Almighty Voice.

But hearing cannot be enough; not even hearing all the thunder of A Proclamation: "Now Hear Ye that a reward of FIVE HUNDRED DOLLARS will be paid to any person or persons who will give such information as will lead ... (etc. etc.) this Twentieth day of April, in the year of Our Lord one thousand eight hundred and ninety-six, and the Fifty-nineth year of Our Reign ..." etc. and etc.

Such hearing cannot be enough. The first item to be seen is the piece of white bone. It is almost triangular, slightly convex—concave actually as it is positioned at this moment with its corners slightly raised—graduating from perhaps a strong eighth to a weak quarter of an inch in thickness, its scattered pore structure varying between larger and smaller on its perhaps polished, certainly shiny surface. Precision is difficult since the glass showcase is at least thirteen inches deep and therefore an eye cannot be brought as close as the minute inspection of such a small, though certainly quite adequate, sample of skull would normally require. Also, because of the position it cannot be determined whether the several hairs, well over a foot long, are still in some manner attached or not.

The seven-pounder cannon can be seen standing almost shyly between the showcase and the interior wall. Officially it is known as a gun, not a cannon, and clearly its bore is not large enough to admit a large man's fist. Even if it can be believed that this gun was used in the 1885 Rebellion and that on the evening of Saturday May 29, 1897 (while the nine-pounder, now unidentified, was in the process of arriving with the police on the special train from Regina), seven shells (all that were available in Prince Albert at that time) from it were sent shrieking into the poplar bluff as night fell, clearly such shelling could not and would not disembowel the whole earth. Its carriage is now nicely lacquered, the perhaps oak spokes of its petite wheels (little higher than a knee) have been recently scraped, puttied and varnished; the brilliant burnish of its brass breeching testifies with what meticulous care charmen and women have used nationally advertised cleaners and restorers.

Though it can also be seen, even a careless glance reveals that the same concern has not been expended on the one (of two) 44 calibre 1866 model Winchesters apparently found at the last in the pit with Almighty Voice. It also is preserved in a glass case; the number 1536735 is still, though barely, distinguishable on the brass cartridge section just below the brass saddle ring. However, perhaps because the case was imperfectly sealed at one time (though sealed enough not to warrant disturbance now), or because of simple neglect, the rifle is obviously spotted here and there with blotches of rust and the brass itself reveals discolorations almost like mildew. The rifle bore, the three long strands of hair themselves, actually bristle with clots of dust. It may be that this museum cannot afford to be as concerned as the other; conversely, the disfiguration may be something inherent in the items themselves.

The small building which was the police guardroom at Duck Lake, Saskatchewan Territory, in 1895 may also be seen. It had subse-

quently been moved from its original place and used to house small
animals, chickens perhaps, or pigs—such as a woman might be expected to have under her responsibility. It is, of course, now perfectly empty, and clean so that the public may enter with no more
discomfort than a bend under the doorway and a heavy encounter
with disinfectant. The door-jamb has obviously been replaced; the
bar network at one window is, however, said to be original; smooth
still, very smooth. The logs inside have been smeared again and
again with whitewash, perhaps paint, to an insistent point of identi-
ty-defying characterlessness. Within the small rectangular box of
these logs not a sound can be heard from the streets of the probably
dead town.

Hey Injun you'll get hung for stealing that steer
Hey Injun for killing that government cow you'll get
three weeks on the woodpile Hey Injun

The place named Kinistino has disappeared from the map but the
Minnechinass Hills have not. Whether they have ever been on a
map is doubtful but they will, of course, not disappear from the
landscape as long as the grass grows and the rivers run. Contrary to
general report and belief, the Canadian prairies are rarely, if ever,
flat and the Minnechinass (spelled five different ways and translated
sometimes as "The Outside Hill," sometimes as "Beautiful Bare
Hills") are dissimilar from any other of the numberless hills that
everywhere block out the prairie horizon. They are not bare; poplars
lie tattered along their tops, almost black against the straw-pale grass
and sharp green against the grey soil of the plowing laid in half-mile
rectangular blocks upon their western slopes. Poles holding various
wires stick out of the fields, back down the bend of the valley; what
was once a farmhouse is weathering into the cultivated earth. The
poplar bluff where Almighty Voice made his stand has, of course,
disappeared.

The policemen he shot and killed (not the ones he wounded, of
course) are easily located. Six miles east, thirty-nine miles north in
Prince Albert, the English Cemetery. Sergeant Colin Campbell Colebrook, North West Mounted Police Registration Number 605, lies
presumably under a gravestone there. His name is seventeenth in a
very long "list of non-commissioned officers and men who have died
in the service since the inception of the force." The date is October
29, 1895, and the cause of death is anonymous: "Shot by escaping
Indian prisoner near Prince Albert." At the foot of this grave are two
others: Constable John R. Kerr, No. 3040, and Corporal C. H. S. Hoc-
kin, No. 3106. Their cause of death on May 28, 1897 is even more

anonymous, but the place is relatively precise: "Shot by Indians at Min-etch-inass Hills, Prince Albert District."

The gravestone, if he has one, of the fourth man Almighty Voice killed is more difficult to locate. Mr. Ernest Grundy, postmaster at Duck Lake in 1897, apparently shut his window the afternoon of Friday, May 28, armed himself, rode east twenty miles, participated in the second charge into the bluff at about 6:30 P.M., and on the third sweep of that charge was shot dead at the edge of the pit. It would seem that he thereby contributed substantially not only to the Indians' bullet supply, but his clothing warmed them as well.

The burial place of Dublin and Going-Up-To-Sky is unknown, as is the grave of Almighty Voice. It is said that a Metis named Henry Smith lifted the latter's body from the pit in the bluff and gave it to Spotted Calf. The place of burial is not, of course, of ultimate significance. A gravestone is always less evidence than a triangular piece of skull, provided it is large enough.

Whatever further evidence there is to be gathered may rest on pictures. There are, presumably, almost numberless pictures of the policemen in the case, but the only one with direct bearing is one of Sergeant Colebrook who apparently insisted on advancing to complete an arrest after being warned three times that if he took another step he would be shot. The picture must have been taken before he joined the force; it reveals him a large-eared young man, hair brush-cut and ascot tie, his eyelids slightly drooping, almost hooded under thick brows. Unfortunately a picture of Constable R. C. Dickson, into whose charge Almighty Voice was apparently placed in that guard-room and who after Colebrook's death was convicted of negligence, sentenced to two months hard labor and discharged, does not seem to be available.

There are no pictures to be found of either Dublin (killed early by rifle fire) or Going-Up-To-Sky (killed in the pit), the two teenage boys who gave their ultimate fealty to Almighty Voice. There is, however, one said to be of Almighty Voice, Junior. He may have been born to Pale Face during the year, two hundred and twenty-one days that his father was a fugitive. In the picture he is kneeling before what could be a tent, he wears striped denim overalls and displays twin babies whose sex cannot be determined from the double-laced dark bonnets they wear. In the supposed picture of Spotted Calf and Sounding Sky, Sounding Sky stands slightly before his wife; he wears a white shirt and a striped blanket folded over his left shoulder in such a manner that the arm in which he cradles a long rifle cannot be seen. His head is thrown back; the rim of his hat appears as a black half-moon above eyes that are pressed shut in, as it were, profound concentration above a mouth clenched thin in a downward curve. Spotted Calf wears a long dress, a sweater which could also be a man's dress coat, and a large fringed and embroidered shawl which would appear distinctly Doukhobor in origin if the scroll patterns on it were more irregular. Her head is small and turned slightly towards her husband so as to reveal her right ear. There is what can only be called a quizzical expression on her crumpled face; it may be she does not understand what is happening and that she would have asked a question, perhaps of her husband, perhaps of the photographer, perhaps even of anyone, anywhere in the world if such questioning were possible for an Indian lady.

There is one final picture. That is one of Almighty Voice himself. At least it is purported to be of Almighty Voice himself. In the Royal Canadian Mounted Police Museum on the Barracks Grounds just off Dewdney Avenue in Regina, Saskatchewan it lies in the same show-case, as a matter of fact immediately beside, that triangular piece of skull. Both are unequivocally labeled, and it must be assumed that a police force with a world-wide reputation would not label *such* evidence incorrectly. But here emerges an ultimate problem in making the story.

There are two official descriptions of Almighty Voice. The first reads: "Height about five feet, ten inches, slight build, rather good looking, a sharp hooked nose with a remarkably flat point. Has a bullet scar on the left side of his face about 1½ inches long running from near corner of mouth towards ear. The scar cannot be noticed when his face is painted but otherwise is plain. Skin fair for an Indian." The second description is on the Award Proclamation: "About twenty-two years old, five feet ten inches in height, weight about eleven stone, slightly erect, neat small feet and hands; complexion inclined to be fair, wavy dark hair to shoulders, large dark eyes, broad forehead, sharp features and parrot nose with flat tip, scar on left cheek running from mouth towards ear, feminine appearance."

So run the descriptions that were, presumably, to identify a well-known fugitive in so precise a manner that an informant could collect five hundred dollars—a considerable sum when a police constable earned between one and two dollars a day. The nexus of the problems appears when these supposed official descriptions are compared to the supposed official picture. The man in the picture is standing on a small rug. The fingers of his left hand touch a curved Victorian settee, behind him a photographer's backdrop of scrolled patterns merges to vaguely paradisaic trees and perhaps a sky. The moccasins he wears make it impossible to deduce whether his feet are "neat small." He may be five feet, ten inches tall, may weigh eleven stone, he certainly is "rather good looking" and, though it is a frontal view, it may be that the point of his long and flaring nose could be "remarkably flat." The photograph is slightly over-illuminated and so the unpainted complexion could be "inclined to be fair"; however, nothing can be seen of a scar, the hair is not wavy and shoulder-length but hangs almost to the waist in two thick straight braids worked through with beads, fur, ribbons and cords. The right hand that holds the corner of the blanket-like coat in position is large and, even in the high illumination, heavily veined. The neck is concealed under coiled beads and the forehead seems more low than "broad."

Perhaps, somehow, these picture details could be reconciled with the official description if the face as a whole were not so devastating.

On a cloth-backed sheet two feet by two and one-half feet in size, under the Great Seal of the Lion and the Unicorn, dignified by the names of the Deputy of the Minister of Justice, the Secretary of State, the Queen herself and all the heaped detail of her "Right Trusty and Right Well Beloved Cousin," this description concludes: "feminine appearance." But the picture: any face of history, any believed face that the world acknowledges as *man*—Socrates, Jesus, Attila, Genghis Khan, Mahatma Ghandi, Joseph Stalin—no believed face is more *man* than this face. The mouth, the nose, the clenched brows, the eyes—the eyes are large, yes, and dark, but even in this watered-down reproduction of unending reproductions of original, a steady look into those eyes cannot be endured. It is a face like an axe.

It is now evident that the de Chardin statement quoted at the beginning has relevance only as it proves itself inadequate to explain what has happened. At the same time, the inadequacy of Aristotle's much more famous statement becomes evident: "The true difference [between the historian and the poet] is that one relates what *has* happened, the other what *may* happen." These statements cannot explain the storyteller's activity since, despite the most rigid application of impersonal investigation, the elements of the story have now run me aground. If ever I could, I can no longer pretend to objective, omnipotent disinterestedness. I am no longer *spectator* of what *has* happened or what *may* happen: I am become *element* in what is happening at this very moment.

For it is, of course, I myself who cannot endure the shadows on that paper which are those eyes. It is I who stand beside this broken veranda post where two corner shingles have been torn away, where barbed wire tangles the dead weeds on the edge of this field. The bluff that sheltered Almighty Voice and his two friends has not disappeared from the slope of the Minnechinass, no more than the sound of Constable Dickson's voice in that guardhouse is silent. The

sound of his speaking is there even if it has never been recorded in
an official report:

hey injun you'll get
hung
for stealing that steer
hey injun for killing that government
cow you'll get three
weeks on the woodpile hey injun

The unknown contradictory words about an unprovable act that
move a boy to defiance, an implacable Cree warrior long after the
three-hundred-and-fifty-year war is ended, a war already lost the
day the Cree watch Cartier hoist his gun ashore at Hochelaga and
they begin the retreat west; these words of incomprehension, of
threatened incomprehensible law are there to be heard, like the
unmoving tableau of the three-day siege is there to be seen on the
slopes of the Minnechinass. Sounding Sky is somewhere not there,
under arrest, but Spotted Calf stands on a shoulder of the Hills a little
to the left, her arms upraised to the setting sun. Her mouth is open.
A horse rears, riderless, above the scrub willow at the edge of the
bluff, smoke puffs, screams tangle in rifle barrage, there are wounds,
somewhere. The bluff is green this spring, it will not burn and the
ragged line of seven police and two civilians is staggering through,
faces twisted in rage, terror, and rifles sputter. Nothing moves. There
is no sound of frogs in the night; twenty-seven policemen and five
civilians stand in cordon at thirty-yard intervals and a body also lies
in the shelter of a gully. Only a voice rises from the bluff:

We have fought well
You have died like braves
I have worked hard and am hungry
Give me food

but nothing moves. The bluff lies, a bright green island on the grassy
slope surrounded by men hunched forward rigid over their long
rifles, men clumped out of rifle-range, thirty-five men dressed as for
fall hunting on a sharp spring day, a small gun positioned on a ridge
above. A crow is falling out of the sky into the bluff, its feathers
sprayed as by an explosion. The first gun and the second gun are in
position, the beginning and end of the bristling surround of thirty-
five Prince Albert Volunteers, thirteen civilians and fifty-six policemen in position relative to the bluff and relative to the unnumbered
whites astride their horses, standing up in their carts, staring and

pointing across the valley, in position relative to the bluff and the unnumbered Indians squatting silent along the higher ridges of the Hills, motionless mounds, faceless against the Sunday morning sunlight edging between and over them down along the tree tips, down into the shadows of the bluff. Nothing moves. Beside the second gun the red-coated officer has flung a handful of grass into the motionless air, almost to the rim of the red sun.

And there is a voice. It is an incredible voice that rises from among the young poplars ripped of their spring bark, from among the dead somewhere lying there, out of the arm-deep pit shorter than a man; a voice rises over the exploding smoke and thunder of guns that reel back in their positions, worked over, serviced by the grimed motionless men in bright coats and glinting buttons, a voice so high and clear, so unbelievably high and strong in its unending wordless cry.

The voice of "Gitchie-Manitou Wayo"—interpreted as "voice of the Great Spirit"—that is, Almighty Voice. His death chant no less incredible in its beauty than in its incomprehensible happiness.

I say "wordless cry" because that is the way it sounds to me. I could be more accurate if I had a reliable interpreter who would make a reliable interpretation. For I do not, of course, understand the Cree myself.